DEADLY MAGIC

The VC were easy enough to stalk. They'd gone straight down the trail, making as much noise as any American Army FNG, and they were talking now with one another in excited, low-voiced exclamations that pinpointed their position. One of the more blatantly racist myths of the Vietnam War was that the VC and NVA were at home in the jungle. In fact, most had been raised in fair-sized towns or even cities, and for even the most bucolic of countryside peasants, the jungle was a place of superstition and fear, an enemy to be beaten back with fire and ax, not a place of refuge and rest. People died in the jungle or, worse by far, simply vanished.

The two SEALs were about to arrange a jungle vanishing act.

SEALS
THE
WARRIOR BREED

MARKS OF VALOR

H. JAY RIKER

AVON BOOKS ◆ NEW YORK

AVON BOOKS, INC.
1350 Avenue of the Americas
New York, New York 10019

Copyright © 1998 by Bill Fawcett & Associates
Published by arrangement with Bill Fawcett & Associates
Visit our website at http://www.AvonBooks.com
Library of Congress Catalog Card Number: 98-93173
ISBN: 0-380-78557-9

First Avon Books Printing: December 1998

AVON TRADEMARK REG. U.S. PAT. OFF. AND IN OTHER COUNTRIES, MARCA REGISTRADA, HECHO EN U.S.A.

Printed in the U.S.A.

WCD 10 9 8 7 6 5 4 3 2 1

Author's Note

During the conflict in Vietnam, three U.S. Navy SEALs received the Medal of Honor, this nation's highest decoration for valor. This book, a work of fiction, tells the stories of two of those awards. The names, characters, and backgrounds of the people involved have been changed, of course, as have some of the circumstances surrounding the events described as taking place on the Song Mieu Giang River and on the beach north of Cua Viet, but in general the stories told herein are true.

The changes should not be misconstrued as disrespect for the SEALs and other military personnel who took part in these events. As in all novels, even those based closely on real life, some changes must be made for dramatic purposes; for the rest, the families and comrades of the brave men involved would likely prefer that their names not be used in a work of fiction, and I've preferred, where possible, to keep the historical people anonymous.

But, as always, it is to the brave men, living and dead, who actually participated in the events here lightly fictionalized that this book is respectfully dedicated.

—H. Jay Riker
May 1997

Prologue

Saturday, 22 March 1969

GRU Center
Moscow, Union of Soviet Socialist Republics
1645 hours

Snow blew and flurried across the tarmac at Khodinka, Moscow's old Central Airport, beneath a cold and leaden sky. In his office high up in the nine-story office building that served as the central headquarters of the *Glavnoye Razvedyvatelnoye Upravleniye*, Colonel Dimitri Pavlovich Kartashkin looked down at the airfield and tried to imagine what it would be like in Hanoi. Warm, he decided. Warmer than here.

By Western standards it might be the first day of spring, but winter would not relax his inexorable hold on Moscow for some weeks yet. By the time the old city began to thaw, Kartashkin would be in the tropical paradise of Southeast Asia, serving as the GRU's newly promoted advisor to the People's Democratic Republic of Vietnam.

A knock sounded from the door. "Enter."

Major Grigor Alekseivich Obinin walked into the office, a thickly stuffed manila folder under his arm. "Comrade Colonel? I have the file you requested."

"Ah! Excellent, Grigor Alekseivich. Let's have a look!"

Accepting the folder, he seated himself at his desk and began leafing through the pages inside. Most, like the outside of the folder, were stamped *SOVERSHENNO SEKRETNO* in bold, Cyrillic capitals.

Absolutely secret.

"So, Grigor Alekseivich," he said as he studied the papers. "Are you ready for Hanoi?"

1

"Ah, but, Comrade Colonel," the GRU major replied with a broad grin, "the question is whether Hanoi is ready for us!"

Kartashkin smiled. He envied the younger man his enthusiasm. It would serve him well in what promised to be a boring and thankless—if tropically idyllic—assignment. The GRU's Third Directorate, in charge of Asian affairs, had decided that two special advisors were needed to help keep track of the supply pipeline from North Vietnam to the south, the vast and tangled network of roads and trails known to the American enemy as the Ho Chi Minh Trail. The two of them would travel that road, advising their hosts in such matters as security, camouflage, and air defense . . . and, as a matter of course, taking note of innovations that might be of interest here at the center.

The GRU—Soviet Military Intelligence—was interested in everything. It was often noted that, whereas the GRU's better-known political adversary, the KGB, was ultimately responsible for protecting the Soviet empire from collapse from within, the GRU was responsible for protecting the *rodina* from attack from without. The ongoing war between the Americans and Moscow's allies in Hanoi continued to provide invaluable information about the Soviet Union's most likely enemy in any future war.

This information, for instance, he thought, as he continued to page through the file. Just seven years ago, a new American commando unit had appeared on the scene, an organization named for the elements within which it fought: Sea, Air, and Land . . . the U.S. Navy SEALs. From all accounts gathered so far—from Vietnam, from the GRU's offices in Havana, and from agents in places as far flung as Okinawa, San Diego, and Marseilles—the SEALs were among the very best of the world's covert amphibious operatives. In training, in capability, and in daring they paralleled both the Soviet *Spetsnaz* and Russian naval commandos. Most of their combat operations so far had been in South Vietnam, where they'd proven themselves better at guerrilla fighting than the Viet Cong, repeatedly entering VC havens and besting Moscow's allies on their own ground and on their own terms. The VC called them the Men With Green Faces and held them in terrified, superstitious awe. If even half of these reports were to be believed . . .

He wondered if the SEALs were interested in the Ho Chi

Minh Trail. They must be; the Americans sometimes allowed themselves to be hamstrung by foolish rules involving borders and authorized targets, but a unit this good could not survive unless it broke those rules once in a while. Kartashkin decided that his assessment of security along the Ho Chi Minh Trail was going to have to take the American SEALs into account.

And where SEALs were concerned, nothing could be taken for granted.

This would be, he realized, an interesting assignment after all. . . .

Chapter 1

Monday, 30 June 1969

Cai Song Valley
Khanh Hoa Province
0115 hours

It was raining, a wet, heavy drizzle that had been continuing for the better part of a month, ever since the heavy storms that marked the beginning of the monsoon season in May. The Wheel gave the silent signal, and ET3 Greg Halstead slipped noiselessly over the low, portside gunwale of the LSSC, entering the SEAL support craft's wake with scarcely a splash to mark his entry. The water was mud-thick and warm, the night a moonless, overcast darkness so black he could scarcely see the gray hull of the boat as it motored on upstream, leaving him behind. Greg let himself crouch as the wake lapped past him; the river was only about four feet deep here, with a soft and muddy bottom. As the night and rain swallowed the boat upstream, he began to move.

There are many ways to insert a direct action team deep inside enemy territory, and the SEALs had utilized most of them at one time or another during their service in the Republic of Vietnam. So far as Greg knew, none of the SEALs in the Nam had taken advantage of their parachute training yet, but, truth to tell, there simply weren't that many opportunities to use chutes in the tangled, often swampy, sometimes mountainous, occasionally rice paddy–muddy, frequently heavily forested terrain that made up most of the country. He hadn't done a combat insertion by SDV, either, though he'd worked with the SEAL wet-compartment minisubs several times in training. Vietnam's muddy, twisting, and mostly shallow rivers didn't lend themselves to submarine insertions, though rumors abounded about secret ops off the coast of North Vietnam.

Someday, maybe . . .

Halstead had done most of the rest though, from helocasting—a moderately insane leap from a helicopter flying just above the water—to various types of helo and boat deployments, to the relatively new "parakeet op" that was just now beginning to come into widespread use with the Teams. A parakeet op, generally used to kidnap high-ranking members of the local Communist infrastructure, was not his favorite modus operandi, despite the method's success rate so far. There was something so . . . so *public* about inserting by helicopter into the middle of an unsecured village in broad daylight, grabbing your mark, and hauling tail for the jungle while support helos moved in to cover your ass. It didn't seem to go with the SEALs' usual covert mode, slipping silently through water, mud, and darkness.

He preferred boat insertions. Like this one.

The LSSC, or Light SEAL Support Craft, had already made several rather noisy stops along the Cai Song River, diversions, all of them. There was no easy way to hide the boat's presence on this river flowing through the Cai Valley—a region almost totally given over to NVA and VC regional units operating northwest of Nha Trang. The only way to confuse the enemy watchers out there in the forest was to make several fake insertions . . . with the SEALs slipping off the boat quietly while it was moving from one decoy insert to the next.

Carefully, Greg began moving toward the shoreline that had been to starboard of the LSSC as they'd moved upstream, his weapon—a 5.56mm Stoner Commando—held above his head to keep it out of the mud. He couldn't see the shore, but he could smell it, a pungent mix of earth, rot, and fungus stirred by the incessant rain. With each step, his bare feet sank calf-deep into the yielding bottom. He'd slung his shoes—lightweight coral shoes dyed black—around his neck so that the mud wouldn't suck them from his feet.

Once he reached the riverbank, he paused again, crouching in the water while he listened carefully. The raucous *keek-keek-keek* of insects and small amphibians filled the night uninterrupted. The absence of man-made sounds, as well as the presence of the natural ones, was at once reassuring and a source of pride. Nearby, four other men were moving through the water and darkness, but Greg could detect no trace of their presence.

He crawled ashore, dripping and stinking of river mud, careful to keep his Stoner clear of the muck. Checking his weapon was the first thing he did on shore; second was rinsing his feet and slipping his coral shoes on.

Movement parted reeds and palm fronds to his left. Two quick finger snaps sounded, just audible above the pattering rain.

Greg clicked his fingers twice, then twice again. A face—a sheer nightmare in green and black beneath a pirate's olive drab bandanna stretched tight over the skull—appeared among the reeds. The mustache alone, longer than Navy regulations allowed, with the corners drooping past the ends of the paint-smeared mouth, identified the face as that of Richard Rodriguez, "Bandit" to the other SEALs of Delta Platoon. Bandit reached out and lightly grabbed Greg's shoulder, a silent *Hey, man! Good to see you!* Greg returned the gesture. He was very glad to see Bandit's heavily painted face. It would be all too easy to lose half the squad in the darkness.

Delta Platoon, SEAL Team One, had been operating out of Cam Ranh Bay on the South China Sea coast of South Vietnam for five months now, and they were *tight*, tight as only such combat-forged fraternities as the U.S. Navy SEALs could be, tight enough to damn near read each other's thoughts as they assembled in the darkness. One by one, the other SEALs gathered on the riverbank, each announcing his presence with a pair of finger snaps. There were five altogether, a short squad. Communicating entirely by hand gestures, they formed into a line and began moving silently inland.

Normally, they would have spaced themselves out more, but in the near-pitch darkness, each SEAL stayed close enough to the next man ahead that he could still make out his shape, a slightly lighter blob of darkness against the black of the forest. Bandit Rodriguez took point, and Greg followed almost in his footsteps. Just behind Greg was Lieutenant Connolly, the "Wheel." Behind him was MM3 Joe "Slinger" Amadio with the squad's PRC-77 radio, with Doc Tangretti on rear security. The last two regular members of Delta's First Squad were Chief Ramsey and Robert "Boomer" Cain, both still aboard the LSSC on its slow meander up the Cai Song. Had it been daylight, the five men in the jungle would have presented a most unmilitary aspect. Uniforms, such as they were, tended to be mismatched and nonregulation, chosen for comfort and serviceability rather than for their looks on the parade ground. Most of the SEALs, like Greg, wore blue jeans dyed black. Headgear—"covers" in Navyspeak—ranged from Greg's floppy boonie hat to Bandit's bandanna to the olive drab headband favored by Slinger. BDU blouses included several varieties of camouflage pattern, though the "tiger stripes" favored by South Vietnamese special forces predominated. All of the men wore black combat vests and web gear, but their weapons were as varied as their covers. Their faces were painted green and black, a trademark of the SEAL Teams in Vietnam that was as much for psychological effect as for camouflage; from the DMZ to the Ca Mau Peninsula, Navy SEALs were known as the Men With Green Faces, a name of terror for both the VC and their North Vietnamese comrades.

Ahead, Bandit stopped, his fist coming up in the signal to halt. Greg froze in place, repeating the gesture. Carefully, Bandit cupped one ear: *Listen!* Yeah . . . Greg could hear it, too.

Like shadows, the SEALs melted into the drizzle-laden blackness of the forest, unmoving. Several meters ahead, two Vietnamese dashed along a trail that cut directly across the SEALs' line of march, their footgear—the kind, cut down from cast-off truck tires, that Americans called Ho Chi Minh sandals but the Vietnamese knew as *binh tri thien*—slapping loudly on the wet earth. Just visible against the night, the two men wore the black pajamas favored by Vietnamese peasants . . . and the Viet Cong guerrillas. One carried a long, heavy tube over his shoulder, while between them, by rope handles, both men carried a metal case of some kind. They were heading for the river.

Greg felt a hand on his shoulder. Turning, he looked into Lieutenant Connolly's eyes as the OIC pointed first at him, then at Bandit, and finally toward the two running VC. Greg nodded, touched Bandit's shoulder, and repeated the order. Bandit nodded, and the two of them turned off toward the river, silently following the two men.

There was no discussion. Normally, a SEAL squad with a specific mission would have ignored a chance target like this one, but the tactical situation demanded a more flexible approach. That tube they'd glimpsed was probably a B40 rocket launcher, and the two VC soldiers were headed for a spot on the riverbank downstream from the LSSC that had already dropped the SEALs off. The VC, alerted to the boat's passage, were trying to get a rocket team into place to ambush the LSSC when it returned—as it would have to—back downstream. Upstream there was nothing but more jungle and, eventually, the highlands below Dalat; downstream was Cam Ranh Bay and the LSSC's home base. If the SEALs didn't take out that rocket team, they might find themselves walking home.

The VC were easy enough to stalk. They'd gone straight down the trail, making as much noise as any American Army FNG, and they were talking now with one another in excited, low-voiced exclamations that pinpointed their position. One of the more blatantly racist myths of the Vietnam War was that the VC and NVA were at home in the jungle. In fact, most had been raised in fair-sized towns or even cities, and for even the most bucolic of countryside peasants, the jungle was a place of superstition and fear, an enemy to be beaten back with fire and ax, not a place of refuge or rest. People died in the jungle or, worse by far, simply vanished.

The two SEALs were about to arrange for a jungle vanishing act.

The Vietnamese guerrillas were hunkered down side by side on the riverbank beneath an umbrella of nipa palm fronds, loading the B40 launcher. While the river beyond was all but invisible in the night, they would have a clear enough view of the LSSC when it came back this way a few hours from now.

The SEALs had rehearsed this sort of maneuver time after time, and no words were exchanged. Both men secured their weapons over their shoulders and drew steel—Parkerized Mark I diving knives with razor-keen, black steel blades. Gunfire, even the muffled snaps of their Smith & Wesson Hush Puppies, was definitely a bad idea. It would have to be a knife kill. Greg cut to the left, Bandit to the right, silently counting off one minute.

By the time Greg had reached forty, he was crouched in the weeds directly behind the left-hand soldier, so close he could smell *nuoc mam*—the pungent, fermented fish sauce that the Vietnamese ladled onto everything they ate—on the men's breath. *"Ong toi cho do chura?"* the man in front of him was asking the other. Something about whether or not he'd been someplace yet.

The count reached fifty. Greg tensed, balancing himself on the balls of his feet.

"Nha Trang?" the other Vietnamese replied. *"At la! Toi toi do roi."*

So you've been to Nha Trang, you son of a bitch? Greg thought. After five months in-country, his Vietnamese was getting pretty good, good enough, at any rate, to follow the gist of the conversation.

And good enough to pick up something unusual about these two. He wondered if he should abort the kill, but . . . no. Too much chance of a screwup. *Fifty-eight . . . fifty-nine . . . sixty!*

Smoothly and silently, Greg reached around the man's head, left hand clamping down across the target's mouth, snapping back, right hand bringing the razor-edged blade across the soldier's windpipe and slicing it open. His right forearm then clamped down across the gaping wound, muffling the dying man's gurgles. Bandit was a second or two behind on his count, but close enough that it made no difference. A pair of black-clad arms enfolded the other target's head, the knife slicing once with the clean precision of a surgeon's scalpel. Bandit and Greg clung to their victims a moment more until the death thrashings ceased. Silently, they lowered them to the ground.

While Bandit searched the bodies for papers or other useful intelligence, Greg dragged the launcher tube out into the river and planted it deep in the mud, where the enemy would not find it. He repeated the operation with the wooden box, which contained four rockets. If he'd had more time, if they'd not had another, more important mission to complete, he would have left the box in place, booby-trapped to catch a few more of the enemy.

Dripping wet, he rejoined Bandit on the shore. "Anything?" The word was a harsh whisper, almost lost in the drizzling rain.

"Negative."

He nudged one of the bodies. "You heard the accent?"

"Yeah. Looks like we caught a couple of Uncle Ho's finest in black PJs."

Greg's ear was good enough now to detect the difference in dialects between the Vietnamese spoken in the south, and that of the north. The Hanoi dialect had six tones, but the Saigon dialect blurred the high-rising tone with the mid-low tone, a small but distinct difference. There were differences in vocabulary, too. *At la* was how they said "surely" in North Vietnam. In the south, the phrase was *ak la.*

These two might be dressed as Viet Cong, members of the People's Liberation Front of South Vietnam . . . but they were almost certainly from the north. That squared with the intel the Teams had been gathering lately. The Viet Cong had been badly mauled during the Tet Offensive, in early 1968, their ranks so badly thinned that many VC units had been filled out by North Vietnamese volunteers.

After checking the bodies thoroughly, Greg and Bandit dragged them into the river after the rockets and launcher, weighing them down beneath a water-heavy log. After policing the area carefully, making sure they'd left nothing to betray their presence, the two SEALs made their way back through the woods to the waiting squad.

Lieutenant Victor E. Connolly
0248 hours

Lieutenant Connolly crouched in the brush, trying to reach out with all of his senses and embrace the waiting darkness.

If something went wrong, if Bandit or Twidge screwed up and found themselves in a firefight, Connolly and the two SEALs with him were braced to hit any VC reinforcements that came down that trail and to support the kill team, if necessary. Each move the squad might have to make had been discussed and rehearsed time and time again. Each man knew what to do, and how to do it.

Even that knowing, however, couldn't settle the churning in Connolly's gut. With less than three weeks to go, they were all getting short . . . short enough to skydive off a dime, as Chief Ramsey had put it the other day, and that could translate as trouble even in an elite unit like the SEALs. Men got careless . . . or, worse, they became *too* cautious, knowing that a universe that delighted in playing practical jokes on its inhabitants was certain to drop a surprise in their laps just before they were due to rotate home. In this game, excessive caution could kill you as dead as carelessness could.

A low, two-tone whistle, warbled like the call of some night bird, sounded from close by, to Connolly's left. He pivoted to bring his Swedish K submachine gun into line with the sound. Too far for finger snaps to be heard. "Alaska," he challenged, his voice pitched just loud enough to carry to the black wall of vegetation in front of him.

"Juneau" was the response, and, a few seconds later, two black shapes separated from the night and joined the rest of the squad by the VC trail. There were dark stains on the sleeves of both SEALs' tiger-stripe BDUs, and Connolly caught the coppery stink of blood.

"Everything go okay?"

Twidge Halstead gave a thumbs-up, the gesture all but invisible in the night.

"We had us a couple of NVAs, Lieutenant," Bandit whispered. He handed over two small folding wallets and what looked like some ID papers. "Not much on 'em."

"Just so our way home isn't blocked, Bandit," Connolly replied. The papers and wallets went into a waterproof pouch, for delivery to the platoon's NILO back at Cam Ranh. The Wheel signaled, then, and the other SEALs, crouched watchfully in the darkness, rose to their feet. "Move out."

Their trek through the jungle took over an hour, with frequent stops while Bandit consulted his compass or made brief forays to left or right to find a way through some particularly thick and impenetrable wall of vegetation. Progress was agonizingly slow at times. Patrolling the forest at night was always risky, and each SEAL moved with precise and careful steps, alert to the possibility of booby traps. Bandit was using a stick to probe the ground and brush ahead, investigating anything that offered resistance . . . like a trip wire. Twice in that hour, they stopped to listen carefully to the jungle, alert to the sounds of anyone else sharing the forest with them, following on their trail. Once they circled around toward the right, coming back on their own trail well behind where they'd been, checking for trackers.

So far, at least, and except for the now-deceased NVA rocket team, they had the forest to themselves.

Their first goal was a hill two kilometers inland from the river. Bandit vanished again, slithering up the rocks and exposed tree roots to reconnoiter and to make contact with the people they'd come here to meet. A small eternity later, he reappeared, signaling for the team to come ahead. Their two LDNN contacts were waiting for them at the top of the hill.

The *Lien Doc Nguoi Nhia*—the name literally meant "Soldiers Who Fight Beneath the Sea"—were the South Vietnamese equivalents of the U.S. Navy SEALs. The two LDNNs, small but with bodybuilder physiques, powerfully muscled, might have been cast from an identical mold. The South Vietnamese SEAL program had been carried out under American SEAL supervision at the LDNN center back at Cam Ranh Bay; Navy SEAL advisors had seen to it that the course was similar in most respects to BUD/S—Basic Underwater Demolition/SEAL training back Stateside. Many of the Vietnamese in the regular army, the ARVN, were so small they had trouble shouldering any weapon larger than an obsolete U.S. M1 carbine; LDNN frogmen could carry any weapon their SEAL advisors carried and without complaint or fatigue. Some seemed to keep going forever, even when exhaustion slowed their American counterparts.

"The area is clear," Tien Pham Vinh told Connolly. "We are three klicks from the objective." White teeth flashed in the darkness. "I do not think we are expected."

Vinh and the second LDNN, Nghiep Van Dong, both held ranks in the RVN Navy equivalent to the U.S. Navy's petty officer first class, and both had been working with Delta Platoon almost since the SEALs had deployed to Cam Ranh Bay in January. Vinh, especially, was much in demand as a local operator with the American teams. He'd been with Delta Platoon back in March, when Lieutenant Casey had lost his leg in an op on an island near Nha Trang.

After that op, Connolly had been flown in to take over command of Delta Platoon, the sort of situation that's always a nightmare for an incoming CO. It's impossible, always, for a new commanding officer to fill the shoes of a larger-than-life predecessor; with everything he does seen in comparison with the other officer, it's twice as hard for the newcomer to earn the respect of the men. Several of these men had been classmates of Casey's, in BUD/S Class 42, and that had made them exceptionally tight. Even after three and a half months working with this platoon, Connolly still felt like the outsider.

Hell, Vinh was more a member of Delta Platoon than he was, it seemed. He had an extensive network of contacts throughout Khanh Hoa Province, and his sources rarely came up dry. Assigned to the platoon originally as an LDNN liaison "officer," he possessed a correct, almost fastidious manner, so the enlisted SEALs had taken to calling him "Mr. Vinh" as though he were a commissioned officer.

It was, in fact, a kind of in-joke among the SEALs, a covert declaration that they trusted some of the Vietnamese LDNNs more than they trusted most regular Navy officers. Morale in Delta Platoon had not been good, lately. Not since Nha Trang.

And idiot missions like this one didn't help matters.

Dawn was approaching fast, lighting the eastern sky. The rain was easing too, bringing some detail to the blackness of the forest as the squad finally reached their objective, a cluster of hooches raised in a small clearing. Most of the hooches were little more than huts or lean-tos, but the one at the center of the compound was as large as a good-sized barn, if not as tall. Connolly reached into a canvas bag attached to his belt and slowly removed an AN/PVS1 nightscope. Switching it on, he raised the eyepiece to his left eye, taking care not to let the green glow show toward the target or to reach his right eye. It took thirty minutes or more for dark-adjusted eyes to recover from a single flash of light.

Two guards were in sight, both wearing the light khaki

uniforms of the People's Army of North Vietnam and the stiff, broad-beamed sun hats that Americans mistakenly called "pith helmets." Both carried AK-47s slung over their backs as they paced off their rounds. Likely, there were other sentries in the forest, but Connolly saw only the two.

He signaled, dispersing his men left and right. They knew what to do, even if some of them were less than happy with the assignment.

He smiled mirthlessly in the dark. *Shit detail . . .*

Chapter 2

Monday, 30 June 1969

Cai Song Valley
Khanh Hoa Province
0435 hours

HM3 Bill Tangretti was not quite as wet, cold, muddy, and generally gut-shot miserable as he'd been during Hell Week at BUD/S, which, he supposed, was a comforting thought. In fact, no matter what SEALs were forced to endure in the field, they could always say that it wasn't as bad as Hell Week . . . the best recommendation Bill knew for continuing that venerable institution.

That didn't make his current situation comfortable, of course, but it helped make the mud and endless drizzling endurable as he eased himself forward, sliding across mud and rain-soaked moss and ferns until he was less than fifteen meters from the nearest sentry. The rain had eased to little more than a heavy mist now, and the eastern sky was markedly brighter. Full daylight was less than an hour away, given the speed of the tropical summer dawn, and the SEALs were soon going to lose the darkness that was their chief ally on this op.

The sentry was too far away for a knife kill. They were going to have to go with Hush Puppies.

The Hush Puppy was a Smith & Wesson 9mm automatic pistol specially designed for the Navy SEALs, with a long, heavy suppressor attached to the muzzle, which reduced the sound of the gunshot to a sharp hiss. Subsonic ammunition eliminated the sound-barrier crack as well, making the weapon perfect for covert SEAL ops and silent kills. Originally intended as a weapon for silently taking out guard dogs and—unique to the war in Southeast Asia—guard *geese,* the Hush Puppy was routinely used by the SEALs for silent kills on human targets as well.

Bill was facing two serious problems, however. Despite the best efforts of generations of Hollywood shoot-em-ups, pistols remained notoriously inaccurate at ranges much above point blank, even for an expert marksman. He had practiced long hours at the Cam Ranh pistol range and, like all of the other SEALs in Delta Platoon, was a good shot. But fifteen meters, with a moving target in bad light from a difficult prone position, was a *long* way. . . .

And the second problem was worse. There was another guard, and he was on the other side of the perimeter, a good fifty meters away. Without personal transceivers—SEALs in the Nam rarely used them on routine ops because of the dangers imposed by a sudden burst of static over an open channel—there was no way to coordinate a fire attack between separate groups of SEALs. They had to rely on practice and on an almost sixth-sense understanding of what their comrades were doing at that moment.

Bill and Mr. Vinh were stalking one sentry, while Bandit and Nghiep, unseen in the darkness perhaps a hundred meters away now, took the other, with the rest of the SEALs covering them from the woods. Bill had worked himself into a position where he could brace the suppressor of his Hush Puppy across the slick, mossy surface of a fallen log, carefully sighting over the muzzle at the center of the sentry's chest. He sensed Vinh several yards to his left, also taking aim. In the distance, the other sentry suddenly doubled over, though there was no sound. . . .

Gently, Bill stroked the Smith & Wesson's trigger, and the weapon gave a short, hard chuff of sound, bucking in his hand. As a second suppressed shot hissed from Vinh's position, the NVA soldier spun sharply, then collapsed in the mud with a wet thud.

The two SEALs crawled ahead, alert to any alarm from other parts of the camp, but there was nothing to be heard other than the drizzling rain. Bill signaled to Vinh to take care of the body, then eased forward, flat on his belly, as the rain pattered and hissed through the leaves overhead. His destination was clearly in view now, just where Intelligence had located it for him on the aerial reconnaissance photos he'd studied before the mission. The target was a low, thatched, partly open building at the far west side of the compound, a structure like a chicken coop with the lower foot or two of the walls left open all the way around, built above a reeking, open trench that connected with a stream flowing nearby. He could smell the damned thing from twenty yards off.

The officers' latrine.

This, Bill told himself as the stink spilled over the rim of the trench and washed across him like a palpable fog, was the shit detail to end all shit details. He'd had to do some damned silly things since he'd joined the Navy . . . most of them back in BUD/S when nine out of ten of the orders bellowed at you didn't make any sense at all. This one, though, really took the cake. Someone in Intelligence—probably a Christians in Action man, if Bill Tangretti was any judge—had decided that he really, *really* had to know whether or not the VC and NVA officers in this district were eating good, balanced, nutritious meals. And the best way to do that, of course, was to obtain a sample of genuine NVA officer's shit.

Bill still wasn't sure he believed this nutcase scenario. The platoon's NILO—that was their Navy Intelligence Liaison Officer, Lieutenant Commander Handley—had explained that this was part of the new and scientific means of waging war, that a part of knowing your enemy was being able to rate his physical endurance and health in the field. Bill, and most of the rest of Delta's SEALs, had pegged the notion as pure and unadulterated bullshit. The SEALs knew their enemy, all right . . . but as a *person*, not as a collection of statistics or a sheaf of health records. They knew him because they hunted him, and sending a SEAL team out to collect shit instead of killing the enemy was about as idiotic a misuse of assets, firepower, and elite personnel as Bill could imagine.

SEALs had been asked to do this kind of thing before, of course . . . but as part of a larger mission. A SEAL team might enter a Vietnamese village in order to question the local civilians or raid a known enemy ville to capture weapons and documents and burn VC rice stores . . . and while they were at it, they would collect some samples from the latrine pits to satisfy the scatological curiosity of someone in Intelligence, but this was the first time Bill could remember when the primary purpose of the mission had been to get a fecal sample. The only thing that made the op worthwhile, so far as Bill was concerned, was the fact that Delta had decided to add a little twist of their own to it; while he was collecting the specimen, Nghiep and Bandit were planting explosives at the base of the big hooch, which was almost certainly an enlisted barracks. The original idea had been to sneak in, grab the sample, and get away clean. Eliminating the two sentries had made that impossible, so the squad was preparing a surprise ending to the night's festivities, one that would discourage the NVA from pursuing the SEALs if things turned hot, and that took some of the sting out of a literal shit detail.

Bill took his time covering that last twenty yards. The latrine was at the edge of the encampment, but it was in full view of every one of the hooches, and there was already enough light that he could be seen, if someone happened to look in the right direction at the wrong time.

Finally, he lay on the ground directly behind the latrine and next to the reeking trench. Most VC and NVA latrines were nothing but a hole or a slit trench in the woods; the fact that this one had been put up with at least a nod to privacy, convenience, and comfort suggested that it had been built for the officers. Intelligence thought that the base supported a company or two of troops—perhaps a hundred men, altogether—but no one was willing to go on record with a guess involving hard numbers.

Reaching up to the scabbard on his combat vest, he unhooked his diving knife and drew it with a soft *snick*. Then he fished into one of his vest pockets and pulled out the small, hard-plastic specimen container Handley had given him. All he had to do was reach in underneath the lower rim of the latrine's back wall with his knife and scoop up a sample from the bottom of the trench.

Only then did he realize that someone back in Cam Ranh Bay hadn't thought this thing through quite far enough. It was raining, had been raining for days because this was the monsoon season, and the trench was full of tar-black water and muck. The samples he'd been sent to collect had been either washed away or so thoroughly homogenized with mud and rainwater that they would be useless for analysis.

Fuck it, Bill thought viciously. Right now, he'd had just about all he was willing to take from the Intel people. *I'll fill the damned specimen bottle with mud, motor oil, and a little blob of napalm. Let's see what the spooks make of* that! . . .

A door banged somewhere close by, and Bill froze. From his vantage point flat on the ground, he could see through the space beneath the latrine building, across the compound to one of the smaller hooches. A Vietnamese had just appeared inside the doorway, wearing only trousers and staring out into the early morning half-light. Since he hadn't come from the large building, which was almost certainly an enlisted barracks, he was probably an officer. He stretched, looked about, scratched himself contentedly, then ducked out into the rain and trotted toward the latrine, his bare feet splashing in the mud as he ran. A moment later, the swinging door to the latrine squeaked and banged; the Vietnamese officer dropped his trousers and settled down on the board that ran from one end of the small building to the other, just above the trench.

The man was happily seated less than four feet away from the spot where Bill was lying.

The SEAL held his position, not moving, scarcely breathing, as the morning light grew steadily stronger. How long was this guy going to stay there? At any moment, either more NVA soldiers would emerge from the barracks, or the guy in the latrine was going to wake up enough to notice that the compound sentries were no longer around.

Either way, the alarm would be given, the mission compromised.

The man on the board gave a heartfelt grunt, and the sample Bill was waiting for splashed into the trench in a half-liquid stream.

Shit, Bill thought, with considerable feeling. *The guy's got diarrhea.* Well, the analysts back at Cam Ranh Bay could make what they wanted of that. It did make the SEAL's job a bit easier, since the stuff was now floating on top of the water-filled trench. Careful not to make any noise, he reached out with the knife blade and scooped up a tablespoon's worth of the noisomely steaming stuff as it drifted past. *Nah ... make it two spoonfuls, and* really *give the spooks their money's worth. . . .*

With the specimen safely capped off and returned to his combat vest pocket, Bill considered again how best to extricate himself. The Vietnamese sitting above him showed no indications of moving. Hell, from the look of things, the guy'd nodded off and gone to sleep. Maybe . . .

He considered taking the man out with his knife as he sat there; there was something appealing about the thought of leaving him there on the two-holer, his throat slit ear to ear. The SEALs played a continuing mind game with their opponents in Nam, and leaving the officer dead in his latrine would certainly deliver one hell of a psychological message. *We can get you anywhere, any time. . . .*

But . . . no. It was too damned risky. He would have to work his way inside the latrine to take the man out, and if the guy managed to get off a single scream—

He would have to stay where he was, until the next part of the op went down. *Damn it, Lieutenant,* he thought. *Let's get the show on the road! . . .*

ET3 Halstead
0440 hours

Greg Halstead waited at the edge of the forest with Slinger and the Wheel, watching Bill get his sample. To his right, Nghiep and Bandit were almost invisible as they crawled about the base of the barn-sized hooch, planting explosives at each of the four corners and connecting them with a single length of detcord connected to a pull-ring igniter. Greg kept his Stoner at his shoulder, the muzzle aimed at the building. A firefight now meant that the four SEALs inside the village compound would be caught under a hail of friendly fire, but the squad was ready to deliver that fire if a bailout was necessary.

The entire philosophy of SEAL combat tactics was predicated on the notion of overwhelming firepower. SEALs operating in the field were always heavily outnumbered, but they carried more heavy weapons, more ammo, more explosive ordnance of various types than any other combat unit of a similar size, and they'd been trained to use those weapons suddenly and with demoralizing effect. That was the reason Greg felt vulnerable at moments like these, when the squad was split up. With Bill and Vinh off playing in the latrine trench, and Bandit and Nghiep planting explosives, there were only the three of them—Slinger, the Wheel, and himself—to lay down that demoralizing blanket of fire if things turned sour.

And in Greg's short experience with combat so far, things *always* turned sour, one way or another. Every SEAL learned quickly that the real god of battles was the notorious and omnipresent Murphy.

He could feel the tension rising from his two SEAL teammates nearby. The appearance of that lone NVA officer could mean trouble. If others in the camp were beginning to stir, the missing sentries might be discovered at any moment.

A burst of noise from the big hooch signaled Murphy's arrival at the festivities. The door banged open, and, one after another, four North Vietnamese soldiers stepped out into the predawn light, their voices carrying across the compound in a singsong chorus. They were all dressed in khaki uniforms and sun hats, gear that clearly identified them as North Vietnamese regulars. Two carried AK-47 assault rifles, while the others had SKS carbines slung from their shoulders. They stood together, talking for a moment, until two more Vietnamese appeared, exchanged greetings, and started crossing the compound toward another hooch.

Greg felt Connolly tensing as he swung the muzzle of his Swedish K to cover the group. No! Not yet! The guys in the compound still had a few moments to get clear. With the noise and chatter, Bill ought to be able to slip away from his hiding place and . . .

Connolly clamped down on his submachine gun's trigger, loosing a short, sharp burst on full-auto. Greg opened up with his Stoner an instant later, as Slinger's M203 vented a hollow *thump*, hurling a 40mm HE grenade into the clearing between the big hooch and the outhouse.

Yeah. Old Murphy had just arrived with a vengeance. . . .

HM3 Tangretti
0444 hours

For Bill, it was as though Armageddon had just made a crashing entrance, all four horsemen at a dead run, with lightning and thunder in attendance. He'd been backing away from the latrine, moving slowly, a few inches at a time, when the four NVA troops had appeared. Then full-auto gunfire erupted from the edge of the forest, followed a second later by the *thump-crash* of a 40mm grenade.

The man in the latrine leaped to his feet, scrambling to pull up his trousers. Bill pulled his Hush Puppy, chambered a round, and fired once directly through the thin wooden wall of the stall, aiming at a point about three feet above the man's bare knees. The scream indicated that he'd hit the target . . . but also that it hadn't been a clean kill. He chambered a second round—the Smith & Wesson had been retooled to require a manual chambering with each shot, to further reduce noise—and fired again, chopping the scream short.

Bill began working his way toward the edge of the forest, when the distinctive snap of bullets passing close by told him he'd been spotted. Rolling onto his side, he swung his M-16 off his shoulder and brought it around to return fire.

The situation had just dissolved into a class-one SEAL nightmare. Three of the armed NVA troops were down, but a fourth was still on his feet, spraying the woods blindly with his AK-47 and screaming at the top of his lungs. More Vietnamese were spilling out of the hooch, and the shouts and gunfire from other directions suggested that the entire camp was up and on the move. Bill fired at the standing soldier and watched him go down. Then he was on his feet and running, doubled over so low that he was almost on all fours.

Ahead, Vinh—who'd moved back to the treeline to dispose of the sentry's body—rose from the vegetation like an avenging green ghost, firing his M-16 past Bill in short, carefully controlled bursts. It looked like Vinh was firing *at* him, but

Bill kept running, feeling the snap of rounds as they flicked past a few yards to his left.

Vinh kept blazing away, laying down cover fire as Bill ran. Muzzle flashes from the edge of the woods to the left showed where Slinger, Twidge, and the Wheel were adding their firepower to the fight. Shouts from behind told him more troops were coming into the open, that he'd been seen, and the *snick-snap* of bullets cracking past his head gave him an adrenaline kick that shoved him ahead with renewed strength and speed.

Bill saw the grenade a second or two before it exploded, a crudely made stick grenade reminiscent of the German potato mashers of World War II, bouncing along the ground just in front of him. He tried to turn away, digging in his heels, bringing his hands up to shield his face . . . and then he was flying through the air.

He landed hard, on his back, the air whooshing from his lungs as though driven out by a hard-rammed fist to the gut. Dazed, he tried to gulp down a breath . . . failed . . . tried again, rolling over onto knees and forearms that nearly refused to support him. The sounds of gunfire had ceased, replaced instead by a dull, hollow rushing sound that surged and ebbed with the pounding of his heart. Only when the gunfire started to return, dim and muffled, did he realize that the blast—which he did not remember hearing at all—had momentarily deafened him. *Damn!* He still couldn't get his breath. . . .

He felt a strong hand underneath his arm, lifting him. It was Vinh, snatching up his M-16 with one hand and dragging Bill with the other; he'd charged back into that fire-swept clearing to pick him up. The Vietnamese frogman was shorter than the American SEAL but so powerfully muscled that he nearly lifted him from the ground as he hauled him bodily toward the trees.

Bill tried to get his feet under him as he dragged at another breath. Then, at last, air rushed in to fill his aching chest, and he gulped in a cool and blessed lungful. His hearing was coming back, too; the flat, staccato crack of gunfire crowded in above the rushing-wave sound hissing in his ears as he crashed through a wall of ferns and into the sheltering shadows of the forest's edge.

Still gasping, Bill took his M-16 back from Vinh, shoul-

dered it, and began loosing short, controlled bursts, aiming at
the muzzle flashes sparkling along the treeline on the other
side of the clearing. An instant later, the big hooch blew, as
the fuses set by Nghiep and Bandit burned down. Packs of
C4 set at each corner of the flimsy wooden structure lifted
the building high into the air, then dissolved it in a whirl of
smoke and flame and splinters.

"We *di di mau,* Doc!" Vinh yelled as the debris rained
across the clearing and the thunder of gunfire was momentarily shocked to silence by the blast.

"I'm with you!" Bill's ears were ringing now, and he was
aware of a hot, wet smear of blood on his cheek. That grenade
had been *entirely* too close. "Time to get the hell out of
Dodge!"

Vinh leaned against the mossy, upright pillar of a tree trunk
and snapped off another burst at the enemy compound. "You
go first!"

Bill didn't stop to argue. As Vinh continued laying down
fire, Bill turned and rushed deeper into the woods, moving
about thirty yards before finding a large and comfortably massive tree, settling down behind the roots, and taking aim. Seconds later, Vinh appeared, bounding through the tangled
brush as Bill opened fire, hosing down the leaves and fronds
at the LDNN's back.

They leapfrogged through the woods, one covering the
other while the other dashed past to take up a new firing
position further back, then swapping roles. After several
moves, they reached the top of a thickly wooded ridge, where
they waited together, listening and watching.

They could hear shouts in the distance and occasional, sporadic gunfire. There appeared to be no immediate pursuit, so
Bill took one of the four M18A1 Claymore mines he was
carrying in his rucksack and set it up facing back the way
they'd come, with a fishing-line trip wire strung across their
trail. *That* ought to discourage anyone who started dogging
them a little too closely.

"The others will be waiting for us at Bravo-Two," Vinh
said.

"That's affirmative," Bill replied. Bravo-Two was a prearranged emergency rendezvous site, another hill about a mile

to the southeast of the NVA encampment. "The faster we get away from here, the better."

The rain was falling harder again, hissing among the broad leaves of the forest canopy. Bill was grateful—one small thing, at least, that was going right. Rain would mask the sounds of their withdrawal from the area and make it harder to follow the retreating SEALs. Pausing only long enough for Vinh to bandage Bill's scalp wound with a gauze pad and a length of olive green roller bandage from his first-aid kit, they started down the east side of the ridge, angling through the forest in the general direction of their rendezvous.

Half an hour later, they reached the hill code-named Bravo-Two on their maps. The others, all of them, were already there waiting for them.

"Bill!" Greg exclaimed. "Are you okay, buddy?"

"Just a scratch," Bill replied, grinning. "But old Mr. Vinh here saved my green SEAL ass."

"You get it?" Connolly asked.

"Right here, Boss," Bill replied. But when he reached for the canvas pouch slung from his web belt, he felt a sickening jolt. The flap was open, the plastic container was still inside, but the pop-on lid was missing . . . and the semiliquid contents had spilled. The grenade blast must have smashed the cup beneath his hip when it had knocked him down.

The mission was a failure, the hard-won sample lost.

Connolly barked a single, foul expletive. "So . . . this whole thing was all for nothing."

"No shit," Bandit said.

"Exactly," Greg added. "Unless you guys want to go back for some more."

"Let's get the fuck out of here," Slinger said, eyeing the surrounding forest, his M203 probing left and right as though he was waiting for something nasty to pop out at any moment.

After a brief, silent check of the area to make sure they'd left nothing behind to betray their movement to the enemy, they started moving through the forest, hiking due west, toward the river.

Chapter 3

Monday, 30 June 1969

Cai Song Valley
Khanh Hoa Province
0625 hours

The sounds of pursuit were all around them . . . shouts and thrashings about and occasional bursts of full-auto gunfire or single shots. *Recon by fire,* Greg thought, moving quickly through the brush. It was a favorite Communist tactic, firing at random into areas where U.S. forces might be hiding, in an attempt to coax a response. SEAL training emphasized the importance of controlled fire and the strength to wait out the enemy's probes without a response. After all, if the bastards were still looking for you, it stood to reason that they hadn't found you yet. . . .

He had drag, meaning that he was at the end of the SEAL line, responsible for covering the area to their rear. Just ahead, Doc and Vinh were moving together, the LDNN helping the corpsman through the forest. Bill Tangretti's scalp wound didn't appear to be too serious, thank God. Bill had taken a grazing hit at almost the same spot a few months ago, during the Ham Tam op with Lieutenant Casey, and he'd been in a pretty bad way when they'd evacked. This time, though, it looked like a fragment of shrapnel had just scratched the skin as it whistled by, leaving a lot of blood but not much damage.

Of course, Bill Tangretti would be dead or a POW right now if it hadn't been for Vinh. Greg had watched as the powerfully built little Vietnamese SEAL had raced out into that firestorm to gather Bill up and drag him to cover. It was a damned good thing that Bill was as short as he was, or Vinh wouldn't have been able to manage the rescue on his own . . . and there'd been no one else near enough to lend a hand.

When Vinh and Bill had emerged from the woods at Bravo-Two, bloody, bedraggled, and muddy, it had been all Greg could do to restrain a wild and position-revealing whoop of joy. He and Bill had become close over the past year . . . and closer still since Bill had gotten serious about Greg's sister. He'd promised Pat that he would do everything he could to see that Bill got back to the World alive—not that he wouldn't have done as much for any teammate. But a part of him had died inside when that grenade had gone off and knocked Bill down. *What am I going to tell Pat? . . .*

The trouble was, there were no guarantees in the Nam. So far, in this vicious little war, some thirty Navy SEALs had been listed as KIA. Last month alone, three SEALs from Team One's Charlie Platoon had been killed in one incident down at Rach Gia, on South Vietnam's west coast, when the 82mm mortar round they'd been trying to disarm had gone off, and a fourth member of Charlie, a corpsman like Bill, had died a week later from his wounds. So far, no SEAL had been captured in Nam, a statistic in which the Teams took enormous pride. SEALs *never* left one of their own behind, no matter what the circumstances.

But Bill Tangretti had been that close to becoming a statistic—KIA or POW—and there wouldn't have been a damned thing Greg could have done about it.

Cai Song Valley
Khanh Hoa Province
0732 hours

They neared the river almost an hour later, the sounds of search and pursuit still cracking and snapping in the distance behind them. Bill Tangretti set his last Claymore on their trail, the trip wire strung between two trees and the convex, FRONT TOWARD ENEMY side aimed back the way they'd come. Vinh and Greg covered him, then dropped back after he pulled the safety and armed it.

The other SEALs were already in the water by the time Bill and Vinh reached the bank and slid down into the cold but welcoming muck. He could hear the Wheel calling on the radio. "Fat Cat, this is Green Arrow. We're ready to extract, over."

"Green Arrow, Fat Cat," a voice, just audible above the hiss of static and the rain, replied. "On the way."

"Make it fast, Fat Cat. We've got unfriendlies on our trail."

"Roger that, Greenie. We're coming in loaded for bear."

Bill smiled. That last had sounded like Boomer Cain, who by now would be having fits because he'd had to stay on the boat and miss all the fun.

The SEALs crouched unmoving in the water, listening intently to the sounds around them. The NVA troops were crashing about in the forest some distance to the northeast, at their backs, loosing occasional bursts of gunfire. His weapon held carefully above the water lapping quietly at his chin, Bill tried to clear the grogginess from his brain. Damn . . . he'd been more shaken by that blast than he'd realized. . . .

He found himself thinking about Pat.

It was disconcerting. SEALs were always aware of the need to stay focused during an op, when one slip, a bit of drowsiness, a single careless act could kill not only the SEAL in question but every man on the squad as well. Standing in an uncomfortable crouch, in cold, muddy water up to his chin, was *not* the time to think of Twidge Halstead's sister. He'd just met her six months ago, before his deployment to Cam Ranh Bay, and he was pretty certain that it was love.

Damn it, Tangretti, he thought bitterly, shaking his head. *Snap out of it, man!* He tried flexing the muscles of his thighs, deliberately making his posture more uncomfortable. That was standard SEAL technique, used by men who had to stay awake for long hours while playing cat-at-the-mouse-hole on an ambush or prisoner snatch. He felt like he was starting to nod off, losing all focus and self-control. It was a scary feeling.

Pat . . .

He wondered what she was doing now. He'd been writing her regularly, ever since he'd met her, and her letters in reply had been growing increasingly . . . warm.

Gunfire crackled in the forest, dragging his mind back to where it belonged. Sunlight was touching the tops of the trees, now. The river itself was still in shadow, but the sky was full light. A careful search by the NVA would eventually find the SEALs at their pickup point. They would have to move out pretty soon, if their ride didn't show up damned quickly now.

A soft purr of engines sounded from upriver, and a few seconds later, the low-slung bow of the SEAL LSSC pushed into view. Twenty-six feet long, with a draft of just eighteen inches and powered by twin 300 horsepower engines, the Light SEAL Support Craft was one of the most heavily used of the various boats and small craft used for infiltration and extraction by the Teams. Two men manned the controls; two more stood at the .50-caliber machine guns, mounted fore and aft. The SEALs in the water watched as the LSSC cruised slowly toward them on muffled water jets . . . then edged away from the shore and kept traveling downstream.

"Fat Cat!" Lieutenant Connolly called over the radio. "Fat Cat! Turn around, damn it! You're missing us!"

"Where the hell are you, Greenie?" a voice crackled back. The LSSC continued receding downstream. "We don't see you!"

Connolly reached up and waved, but the LSSC was already too far away. Popping smoke was out of the question; the enemy was close and would vector in on a smoke cloud in seconds.

"Ah . . . Fat Cat," Connolly said, "we'll talk you in. Come about hard to port and head back upstream."

In reply, the LSSC made a sharp turn to the left and accelerated slightly, traveling back up the river toward the SEAL position.

"That's good, Fat Cat," Connolly said. "Come right about ten degrees . . . yeah, that's it. You're pointed dead-on at us now. Come on in!"

The SEAL craft throttled back as it drew to within eight or ten yards of the riverbank. It was clear from the expression of the crew and the two SEALs aboard that they still hadn't seen the men crouching in the water. As the boat drew closer still, Connolly waved again, and, at last, less than five yards away, the eyes of the boat's coxswain widened, and Chief Ramsey's face split into an enormous grin.

The SEALs in the water moved apart as the LSSC nudged up all the way to the bank, riding up a little as the bottom hit mud and the coxswain throttled full back. Quickly, they started scrambling aboard, helped over the gunwale by the others. Boomer Cain reached down and hauled Bill out of the water bodily. "Son of a *bitch!*" he exclaimed, shaking his head. "You guys are hard to see!"

Bill turned to help pull Greg aboard, and then the two of them helped Nghiep. All of the SEALs on the op were so thickly coated with river mud that it obscured even their green and black facepaint.

"Well, they say in training to become one with the forest," Greg said as he scrambled aboard, dripping. "I'd say—"

He was interrupted by a sharp, savage *boom* from the woods, just beyond the wall of trees and vegetation, and a chorus of shrill, agonized screams. Gunfire opened up an instant later, sprayed randomly, snipping leaves and branches and scattering them above the riverbank.

"Claymore!" Boomer said, identifying the explosion by its weight and timbre.

"Let's get this bucket moving!" Slinger yelled. He raised his M203 to his shoulder, aiming at the woods but withholding fire until he had a target.

"Belay that!" Chief Ramsey shouted. Connolly, Bandit, and Vinh were still in the water. "Get those men on board!"

Then a pair of North Vietnamese soldiers broke from the forest, AK-47s blazing. "Commence firing!" Connolly called from the water, but every SEAL on the LSSC was already hammering away at the woods, pouring a devastating fusillade into the shivering, thrashing wall of vegetation. One of the Vietnamese troops pitched forward into the water, as the other threw his hands high and toppled backward into the brush. Boomer, manning the aft fifty, swung the heavy weapon about and brought it into action, its deep-throated yammer mingling with the volleying auto-fire from the SEALs' individual weapons. Saplings on the riverbank were shredded, and one small tree slowly dipped toward the water, its trunk sawn almost all of the way through.

The sheer volume of gunfire had served as a kind of rocket, nudging the LSSC back off the riverbank, but the engines, rather than roaring to full life, were giving an unpleasant grinding sound. Together, Greg and Bill hauled Connolly out of the water, as Bandit scrambled over the stern. Vinh, the last man in the water, splashed up to the hull, reaching high to grab the railing.

An explosion erupted from the river between the LSSC and the bank, throwing a white geyser of spray high into the air. Something metallic clanged sharply off the hull just below the spot where Greg was standing. Vinh staggered, then slumped backward, sinking into the water.

"Man down!" Greg screamed. "Man down!" Dropping his Stoner, he vaulted the LSSC's railing and hit the water with a splash. More Vietnamese troops were emerging from the forest just a few yards away, pouring fire into the LSSC's thin hull; the SEALs fired back in a point-blank, toe-to-toe slugging match, the big Ma Deuce in the stern drowning out the clatter of assault rifles.

Greg reached Vinh as the LDNN started to go under. He slipped one arm around the wounded man's shoulders and hauled him back toward the SEAL boat. Bullets clipped above his head and smacked the water a few feet away, sending up spurts with each impact. Slinger's M203 voiced its hollow thump, and the concussion of the blast a moment later made the river's surface dance.

Nghiep dropped into the water and helped Greg keep Vinh's head above water as they shoved him up alongside the boat. Bill and Ramsey reached down to haul him out of the water, then helped the other two SEALs aboard. Vinh sprawled limply on the deck, blood rapidly staining the front of his sodden, tiger-stripe BDUs. Bill dropped to his knees alongside the Vietnamese SEAL, tearing open combat web gear and camo shirt. A thumb-sized hole bubbled and bled in the man's chest, just left and below center. Vinh's mouth was open, and blood and pink froth were spilling from his throat. His eyes were wide open, startlingly white against his dark, paint-smeared face.

Sucking chest wound. Vinh's left lung had been pierced and was collapsing. The shrapnel that had felled him might have hit the heart, too, or possibly the aorta, but there was nothing Bill could do about that, not now, not here. He fumbled inside his medical kit for one of the wads of cellophane he always carried there, slapping it over the wound to stop the relentless seepage of air into Vinh's pleural cavity.

He couldn't find a heartbeat.

"Damn it, don't you die on me, Vinh!" Bill screamed. He used his forefinger to hook blood and mucus from the man's mouth and throat, then braced one hand over the other and leaned down sharp and hard on the bottom of Vinh's sternum. An hour ago, the Vietnamese SEAL had saved him from death or capture. He *couldn't* die. . . .

The LSSC was drifting into the middle of the river now, its bow slowly swinging about. The engine gave a harsh cough and a sputter but refused to catch. Bullets slammed into the hull in high-pitched, staccato thunks.

"*Goose* it, damn it!" Connolly yelled. "Let's get the hell out of here!"

"We're clogged, man!" the coxswain shouted back. "We're fucking clogged!"

The LSSC was a good craft for shallow-draft operations, but it had one devastating weakness. Powered by Jacuzzi-style water jets, the craft was susceptible to clogged pumps and intakes, a fault that had crippled it more than once on previous SEAL ops. As the boat drifted with the current, momentarily out of control, it began to turn. The men manning the machine guns pivoted their weapons on their mounts, keeping up a furious ongoing barrage at the woods, while the other SEALs shifted from port to starboard, firing into the east bank.

All except Connolly. As he worked on the badly wounded Vinh, Bill noticed that the SEAL squad leader was firing wildly across the starboard gunwale, spraying the woods on the *west* bank. "Sir!" Bill yelled above the thunderous racket. "What the hell are you shooting at?"

Connolly blinked stupidly at him through layers of green and black paint, the whites of his eyes startlingly visible, betraying . . . what? Bill couldn't tell if it was fear, shock, confusion, or battle lust. He only knew that, whatever it was, he didn't like it.

With a roar, the engines gunned to life as the coxswain succeeded in backflushing the intakes. Circling on a tight O of a wake, the LSSC swung about until its nose was again pointing downriver, toward distant Cam Ranh Bay. More Vietnamese troops spilled out of the woods just ahead, then faltered as the SEAL squad took them under fire. They backed off quickly then, leaving several of their number floating facedown in the water. "Hit 'em!" Slinger was shouting as loud as he could. He triggered the grenade launcher and sent a 40mm high-explosive round tumbling into the woods. The explosion scattered leaves and knocked down another tree. Boomer was yelling a wordless keen of battle lust and adrenaline as he depressed the butterfly trigger of his Ma Deuce, slashing away at the woods. Even Lieutenant Connolly was back in action, dropping a spent mag to the deck and snapping a fresh one home, then adding his Swedish K's firepower to the rest, hosing down the east bank woods.

The engine roar keened louder, and the LSSC went up on a step, spray roostertailing astern as the coxswain pushed the throttle full forward. At twenty-six knots, the SEAL support craft raced down the river, leaving the sounds of pursuit behind.

"He's gone, man," Bandit said, laying a hand on Bill's shoulder.

Bill kept pumping for minutes more, pausing every ten beats so that Nghiep could blow a few quick breaths into the wounded LDNN's mouth, but Vinh was not responding. There was no pulse, no breathing. At last, as a wave of dizziness nearly overcame him, Bill leaned back on his heels, tears flowing down his cheeks. *He couldn't be dead. Not Vinh . . .*

"C'mon, Doc," Greg said, helping him sit down against a bulwark. "You don't look so good yourself."

Clear of the fire zone, the coxswain throttled back, and the LSSC proceeded downriver at a more sedate pace. Bill stared at the passing green wall of vegetation. He remembered the rocket team that had been setting up its ambush not far downriver from here and was glad they'd decided to take that roadblock out. He felt . . . tired, as weak and as boneless as he'd ever felt in his life.

"Doc, y'okay?" Boomer asked. "You hurtin', man?"

"Nah," he mumbled. He reached up and felt the trickle of warm blood on his face. A scratch. Scalp wounds always bled like hell. And losing a patient always took a lot out of him. Damn it, though, why did it have to be Vinh? "M'all right. . . ."

He remembered little of the trip back to the SEAL base on the coast.

Chapter 4

SEAL Facility, Cam Ranh Bay
Republic of Vietnam
0920 hours

Bill Tangretti and Twidge Halstead walked into the cube they shared in the SEAL barracks, filthy, tired, and angry. The op had been for nothing, and a friend and fellow SEAL was dead.

"I'll tell you what," Bill said as he began stripping off his mud-soaked BDUs. "When it comes to support from the top, we're not getting shit . . . and that starts right here in this platoon."

"You mean the Wheel?" Greg replied.

"I don't mean Admiral Zumwalt."

Their BDUs fell into a stinking pile on the linoleum deck, and they began peeling off the panty hose they wore underneath. Few SEALs wore underwear. That was a lesson learned the hard way by every trainee in BUD/S, where sadistic instructors delighted in having their men sit in the incoming surf at the ocean's edge until their underwear was filled with sand . . . then leading them through hours of grueling PT and ten-mile runs. There was method to the madness, as there was to most BUD/S evolutions; in the tropics, damp underwear was a guaranteed prescription for any of a dozen different varieties of crotch rot.

Some unsung SEAL in the Nam, however, had discovered that a pair of women's panty hose provided excellent protection from the thumb-sized leeches that swarmed in South Vietnam's waterways . . . and that seemed to delight in find-

32

ing delicate and tender places beneath a SEAL's trousers to latch on and chow down. Though there was plenty of kidding about it back and forth within the Teams, the incongruity of SEALs—the last word in testosterone-drenched military machismo—wearing women's undergarments was never an issue. SEALs were infamous for their ingenuity and adaptability, a trait that went back to their UDT forebears and such tricks of the trade as rubber condoms used to keep fuse igniters dry and ready.

"Griping's not gonna do anything about it," Greg said, fishing about in his locker for a towel, soap, and plastic clogs. "Anyway, you know as well as I do that an officer coming into a unit to replace someone else is at a hell of a disadvantage. The men are always comparing him against the other guy, you know?"

"That doesn't have anything to do with it. We never should've been sent out on that op. Some desk jockey at G-2 got delusions of grandeur again, and we get sent out to collect shit. And poor Mr. Vinh paid the price."

They walked down the passageway to the platoon's shower head, where most of the other SEALs of First Squad were already scraping off the night's accumulation of mud, blood, and sweat in a swirling cloud of steam. "Can't argue with you there," Greg told him. "But Mr. Connolly might not have had any choice in the matter. Lieutenants don't usually have the luxury of turning down assignments, you know. Even if they *are* stupid."

"What? The assignments? Or the lieutenants?"

"Asshole."

Clean once more, they padded back to their cube wearing nothing but their plastic shower clogs. "So how's the head?" Greg asked. "You ought to stop by sick bay and get that tended to."

Bill touched the scalp wound gingerly. He'd removed the field dressing along with his clothes. The bleeding had stopped, but it was still tender. "Ah, it'll keep. I've cut myself worse shaving."

"Shit."

A young Vietnamese girl was in their cube, holding a pair of mud-caked panty hose between thumb and forefinger. Her name was Thai Li, and she was one of the hooch maids assigned to their barracks. "You want wash?" she asked, holding up the offending garment for a closer inspection. Her face was puckered up with unspoken questions.

"Uh, no, Thai Li," Bill said, embarrassed. "No wash." He wished he hadn't left his towel in the shower room.

"Those things don't last more than one op, Thai Li," Greg said. He didn't seem as disturbed by his nakedness in front of the young woman as Bill was.

"You say . . . what?" The woman was having a little trouble with English.

"Khong giat," Bill said in thickly accented Vietnamese. "No wash." He pointed to the BDUs on the deck. "Just those."

"Okay," she said. She smiled shyly at the men. "You two look pretty. You come my place later, yes? Number one boom-boom. Good time. Good price."

"You'd better get out of here, honey," Greg said, rummaging in his locker for a clean set of BDUs. "You could ruin your reputation for life."

Bill followed her with his eyes as she left the cubicle.

"What's the matter, son?" Greg asked. "You thinking of having some?"

"Hell, no."

"That's good. As your SEAL teammate, I'd tell you to go for it, but as Pat's brother—"

"Nah, I was just thinking how we've managed to fuck over the Vietnamese culture. Americans, I mean. I never thought of Thai Li as a whore, but, well, I guess that must be a pretty decent way to pick up some extra money for these folks, huh?"

"Life's pretty hard for them, with the war and everything. For the ordinary people, anyway. Some of 'em'll do anything to survive."

"Yeah. But before we came along, Thai Li would never have dreamed of making money that way. Or of talking to a couple of strange men that way."

A small refrigerator in the cube was just large enough for a couple of six-packs. "Ah," Greg said, tossing one can to Bill and popping the top on another. "All the comforts." He took a long sip. "So what are we supposed to do?" he asked at last. "Chuck it all and pull out? How do you think Thai

Li and her little handwash laundry would do under the Communists?''

"Even Communists need to wash their shirts once in a while."

Greg eyed Bill uncertainly. "You're not going peacenik on me, are you, Doc?"

"Shit, you know better than that, Twidge. But it'd be nice to save these people without destroying them, you know?"

"Now you sound like Dr. Spock."

Bill chuckled. A year ago, the famous pediatrician-turned-activist had said that to win in South Vietnam, it would be necessary to destroy the nation. Not long after, a U.S. Army officer had made the memorable statement "In order to save the village, we had to destroy it." The American press had had a field day with that one.

It was a hell of a way to fight a war.

Bill was feeling more and more ambivalent about the war. During his first tour in Nam, he'd been about as gung-ho as they got. He'd been wounded, however, almost as soon as he'd gotten off the plane, during the prelude to the Tet Offensive of early 1968. He'd done a lot of thinking about the war while lying in a hospital ward at the naval hospital at Bethesda, Maryland. Later, he'd been accepted in Hospital Corps School and become the Navy's equivalent of a medic . . . and that had raised a whole new raft of moral issues once he went back to the Teams. When he went on patrols with his fellow SEALs, he went as both warrior and healer, carrying both weapons and first-aid kits. That fact, not understood by American reporters steeped in old-fashioned notions of the Geneva Accords and big red crosses on medics' helmets, had nearly gotten him into trouble one time, when a reporter had braced him about his weapon. Only the timely intervention of Admiral Zumwalt himself, the chief of Naval Operations and a powerful ally of Navy Special Warfare, had kept Bill from swallowing the foot he'd so neatly placed in his own mouth.

But the problems he'd had reconciling his medical training with his SEAL status were a small picture of the larger moral issue of the war. Bill had come to believe that America had no business being in this country, that the original decision to support the corrupt Saigon regime had been a mistake.

At the same time, though, he'd gotten to know some South Vietnamese . . . men like Vinh. Once, several weeks before, Bill remembered, he and Greg and some other SEALs had been drinking with Vinh in a bar outside the base at Cam Ranh Bay. "You Americans," Vinh had said, raising a glass of watery 33 beer, "you fight well, but you will not stay here. You fight today, go home tomorrow. But me and other LDNN, we stay, we fight forever. That is difference between you and us."

It was one hell of a difference. Vinh had died defending his country. Bill and Greg and the other SEALs were fighting . . . why? Because the U.S. government was supporting a tottering ally against the Communist threat. Because he was a SEAL, and SEALs were trained to fight, were expected to fight.

Because he was fighting alongside his teammates.

"So what did you think about the Wheel out there today?" Bill asked, abruptly changing the subject.

"How d'you mean?" Greg knocked back a long chug of beer. "You mean his timing on that ambush?"

"Partly. It'd have been nice if he'd held fire a little longer, given us a chance to get clear. But did you see him on the boat, though?"

"I was kind of busy." Greg's voice was flat, almost disinterested.

"No shit. When we came about with the current, he was firing away at the wrong side of the river. Shooting at nothing."

A shrug. "It happens. Things can get hairy in a firefight. You don't always know what you're doing."

"Aw, can it, Twidge! SEALs are supposed to know. There was, I don't know . . . something about his eyes. Scared the hell out of me. And, well, I think he screwed the pooch at the NVA camp."

"That's a damned serious charge, Doc."

Bill drained the last of the beer, then crushed the empty can in his fist. "I know."

"You prepared to take it somewhere? Over the Boss's head?"

"Shit, I don't know, Twidge. I just wanted to know if you'd seen the same stuff I had."

"Doesn't really matter, does it? I mean, we've got . . . what? Three more weeks on this deployment? And then we go home. Won't matter then, right?"

"Yeah, we're double-digit midgets, man. I guess it's getting through these last few weeks that's worrying me."

"Well, you'd damned well better get over that nonsense, and like right now. I don't know a better way to engineer a self-fulfilling prophecy."

"He doesn't act like he's one of us, Twidge."

"He's a SEAL, Doc. He's been through BUD/S. Diving school. Jump training. The whole nine yards. What more do you want . . . for him to tuck you into your rack at night? Cut the guy some slack."

"I know, I know. Somehow, he never quite fit in with the platoon, though."

"Don't see why the hell not. I mean, it's his platoon."

"Damn it, Twidge, you know what I mean."

"Yeah. Yeah, I guess I do." Greg hesitated, as though choosing his words carefully. "Just remember though, Doc. The thing that puts the Teams a cut above the rest isn't just the training, though that's a big part of it. It's because we're tight. We trust each other, and that means we trust our officers and they trust us. That's why they have to go through the same shit we do at BUD/S, right? If Mr. Connolly says to me, 'C'mon, we're gonna go pull a snatch on Ho Chi Minh tonight,' well, I'm gonna go, right? It's not like he's some upper-class snot from West Point or the Academy giving orders without knowing the score. He's been there, knows what's what. One of *us.*"

"Well, that's the theory, anyway."

Most SEALs had a near fanatical devotion to the principles of Basic Underwater Demolition/SEAL training. Sure it was tough. Every SEAL, officers and enlisted men alike, went through that rigorous program designed to weed out the unfit, the unsuitable, and the ones who might fold in a tight situation. You could trust your swim buddy because he'd been through the same hellfire as you. Thanks to BUD/S, the guy running the platoon with the lieutenant's railroad tracks on his collar wasn't just an officer. He was another SEAL, and that meant a hell of a lot.

For that reason, Bill had been feeling guilty about his

doubts. Connolly *was* a SEAL. But, damn it, he wasn't *Casey.* . . .

There'd never been a question that Lieutenant Frank Casey was a part of the Teams. Hell, he'd been through Class 42, Greg's BUD/S class. Sharing that sort of experience made men *tight.*

Even then, however, everyone in the Teams knew that just because you'd completed all of the required training, that alone didn't make you a SEAL. There was a kind of probationary period that followed the training, when a newbie was evaluated by both his superiors and his teammates.

Connolly had been on combat ops with the platoon for three months now. He didn't go out on every mission, but he seemed to be a decent enough operator.

The problem, Bill was beginning to suspect, was the fact that he didn't always stand up for his men against the powers-that-be . . . not the way SEAL officers were supposed to. Over the past years, a kind of unwritten law had evolved within the Teams, a law that said a SEAL was a SEAL first, and he looked after his teammates, no matter what his rank.

Bill had heard of one lieutenant bossing a platoon over in the Delta, a young fire-eater who'd told a Navy captain precisely and with considerable and colorful anatomical detail exactly where he could place his orders for what amounted to a suicide mission. SEALs, that officer had contended, were too valuable, too highly trained, to throw away in frontal charges against prepared enemy positions.

SEALs weren't supposed to be used up on shit details, either. Bill could think of half a dozen ways that the Company could have gotten that fecal sample without risking an entire SEAL squad. The war, he was becoming increasingly convinced with each passing day, was being prosecuted by complete and total idiots.

And so far as he'd been able to tell, Connolly had accepted the assignment for Delta Platoon without protest.

"I'm gonna go see the Wheel this afternoon," Bill said.

Greg looked at him with interest. "Why? Thinking of telling him off?"

"No. But I am going to ask for a couple of days off."

"How come?"

"Somebody's got to take Mr. Vinh back to his people,

Twidge. He's got a wife and family in Saigon, someplace. I thought I'd see if I could get back there and attend the funeral.''

Greg considered this a moment. "Nice thought."

"You want to come?"

Greg considered the question a moment more. "Yeah. Yeah, I do. But we might have some trouble getting clearance. Mr. Connolly's kind of a stickler for the regs.''

"Tell me about it. But, well, I had this idea, see?"

Greg closed his eyes. "You and your ideas." He sighed. "Okay. What's the scam?"

"Oh, not a scam, exactly. You know how we're always running short of belt-feed clips for the Stoner, don't you?''

"Do I ever!" The Stoner was one of the finest weapons systems in American service, despite a nasty tendency to jam when it got dirty. SEALs kept their Stoners working by keeping them meticulously clean. The weapon's second shortcoming, though, was largely outside the SEALs' control. The 5.56mm rounds were individually linked together into 100-round belts, but the links were always in short supply . . . so much so that the SEALs had taken to policing their positions and picking up all expended links even in the middle of a firefight. In the Nam, belt links for the Stoner were worth their weight in gold.

"Well, let's just say I know this guy in supply, over in Saigon," Bill said. "He might be able to get us a case or two of links, hot off the plane from the World.''

"Doc . . . is that straight, or are you making it up?''

"What's it matter? We tell the Boss we need to go try to pick up those links before some Army puke deep-sixes 'em or uses 'em for paperweights, and say that we could escort Mr. Vinh back, too. I think he'd go along with that, don't you?''

Greg laughed. "It's worth a try, Doc. But damn, you're sneaky!''

"Just be glad I'm on *your* side, Twidge!''

"My friend, not a day goes by without my thinking those very words.''

Connolly gave them permission to escort Vinh's body to Saigon, and he wrote out the necessary passes and clearances. He also found space for them aboard a C-130 Hercules that

would be flying from Cam Ranh Bay to Saigon's Tan Son
Nhut airport the following afternoon. Bill had the impression,
as they stood in Connolly's office, that the lieutenant hadn't
been fooled by the suggestion that they were going to Saigon
to find Stoner belt links. He merely nodded and offered to
call the LDNN base in Saigon to arrange for someone to pick
up the body at the morgue there.

Maybe he's not such a son of a bitch after all, Bill thought.
Still, the guy was going to have to learn how to stand up for
his people against the REMFs and desk jockeys who were
running this damned war.

A joke had been circulating among the Americans at Cam
Ranh Bay lately: *What is the difference between the U.S. military and a pack of Boy Scouts?* The answer: *Boy Scouts are
led by adults.* Bill had heard the story told in different ways
and in different contexts. Most popular was the version told
among Marines, which emphasized the fact that too many
Marine platoons were led by fresh-faced kids barely out of
diapers. Told with a slightly different emphasis, though, it
brought to mind images of ten-year-old generals, admirals,
and politicians pushing toy ships and soldiers about on a map
and arguing over who had won. Somehow, the leaders tasked
with fighting and winning the war in Southeast Asia had lost
all touch with the men who were doing the real fighting, and
with whatever it was those men were supposed to be doing
there. With a few all-too-rare exceptions like Admiral Zumwalt, the senior command in Vietnam appeared to have lost
all sense of purpose, and their strategy and long-term goals
had little or nothing to do with reality.

Mama San's
Cam Ranh
2030 hours

That night, the SEALs of Delta Platoon gathered at Mama
San's, a bar just outside the main gate of the sprawling Cam
Ranh compound that the SEALs—both American and Vietnamese—had appropriated as their own. "Mama San" was
actually Thu Ha Dinh, an enormously fat Vietnamese woman
who sat on a stool by the door, greeting each SEAL who
entered with a hug and a wet kiss. Her son, it was said, had

been an LDNN killed early in the program, during a raid into North Vietnam; she'd adopted the SEALs as her own, as if to replace her boy.

Tonight was Mr. Vinh's wake, and the first round of drinks was on the house. The bar's interior, an eclectic mix of Vietnamese and faux Japanese decor, was thick with blue cigarette smoke and the mellow tones of Simon and Garfunkle's "Mrs. Robinson." The party had been going for some time by the time Greg and Bill walked in and sat down at the big table in the back.

For some years now, SEALs had maintained a fraternal tradition, beginning with the several-month period of advanced training immediately after BUD/S: Each SEAL put aside some money—usually the platoon commander held it—with instructions that it was to be spent on a party in the event of his death. The Americans had started the custom, but it had swiftly taken hold among the Vietnamese, as well. Vinh, it turned out, had saved several thousand piasters against his wake, enough to throw quite a nice little bash.

As usual, one chair at the big table was left empty for the missing man, and a glass in front of the chair was filled—and surreptitiously emptied—with each fresh round. Sometimes, talk centered on memories of the dead man; more often the conversation revolved around other things of import to the SEALs—weapons and war stories, women and sex, the latest events back in the World and what the frigging politicians in Washington might be up to . . . and women and sex again. Some of the men were well on their way to a serious drunk.

And if the party was less than dignified, well . . . SEALs rarely appreciated formal occasions.

"Old Vinh sure saved your tail today," Slinger told Bill, nursing his drink. "When that NVA compound started to wake up, man, I could've shit."

"It was amusing," Bill agreed. He looked around the table. "Is the Wheel here yet?"

Greg followed Doc's glance. Mama San's believed in equal opportunity, catering to enlisted men and officers alike, accepting money from either without preference. "Doesn't look like it, Doc." He wondered if Connolly was going to put in an appearance tonight. Sometimes the lieutenant seemed

downright standoffish . . . at least for a SEAL. Lieutenant j.g.
Charles Dubois, the assistant platoon leader and the boss of
Second Squad, was there. And Lieutenant *Casey* sure as hell-
fire would've been there.

"How about you, Greg?" Boomer Cain said. "You were
pretty close to Mr. Vinh. What'd you think of the guy?"

Greg hesitated for a moment, staring into his drink as
though to find an answer there. "I was just thinking," he said
after a moment, "of something he told me a few weeks ago.
We were here in Mama San's, in fact, at that table right over
there in the corner. He said the difference between him and
his LDNNs and us was the fact that we were going home
someday, but that he would stay here and fight forever." He
looked up and met Nghiep's eyes. "I've been trying to imagine what that must be like. If Americans were fighting Americans in the streets of Los Angeles or Chicago—"

"Shit, Twidge," Chief Ramsey said with a harsh laugh.
"Don't you read the news, man? The Democrat convention
in Chicago last year turned into a street battle. Mayor Daley
gave the cops shoot-to-kill orders!"

"If that ain't a war, what is?" Boomer added.

"Ha! You walked into that one, Twidge," Bill told him.

Greg flushed, then hid his embarrassment in a quick, hard
down-the-hatch of whiskey. For a long time now he'd been
compartmentalizing any news or thoughts of the problems
back in the States under the general mental heading of "unrest" or "student protest." He tried not to think of the number of times when peaceful demonstrations had escalated into
rock-throwing and club-swinging mayhem. He'd been going
with a girl, Marci Cochran, back in college, but she'd dumped
him hard and fast when he announced his intention of dropping out of school to join the Navy. She'd been an activist—
attending rallies, organizing marches and demonstrations,
arguing passionately that America had no business in Vietnam—and the memory of their parting still burned a little.
Greg thought of himself as a patriot, and he had trouble understanding the mind-set of people, of *Americans,* who fled
to Canada or Sweden to avoid the draft . . . or who called for
the active overthrow of the government.

"You guys know what I mean," he said stubbornly. "That
shit going on back home, that's not a *war.* . . ."

BM1 Sam Thayer brought his empty glass down on the tabletop with a sharp bang. "I heard that some Negro professors at Berkeley were telling their Negro students to start bringing guns to class, when things were getting bad last year," he said. "It's a war, Twidge, believe me. Or it's gonna be, damned soon."

That brought conversation at the table to a dead stop. Sam was the 60-gunner for Second Squad, a big, lanky, likable guy from Cleveland who also happened to be black. Soft-spoken, well-educated, he didn't believe in what he called "that damned black-power nonsense back home." He even used the word *Negro,* rather than the more recent and socially correct *black.*

For a moment, Greg wondered what Thayer thought, what he *really* thought, about the rising tide of black revolution back in the States. Did he compartmentalize things, shut them away, the way Greg shut away thoughts of antiwar protests turned violent? The two movements were closely linked; they couldn't help but be, when it was undeniable that blacks—usually less educated than most whites, usually unable to win college deferments from the draft—made up a disproportionate percentage of the young Americans fighting and dying in Southeast Asia.

The SEALs were as color blind as any military unit Greg knew, and a hell of a lot more color blind than most. SEALs tended to be closer than most families; you respected a teammate because he knew his craft and had been through the same training as you and would put his life on the line for you the way you would risk your life for him . . . and skin color never even entered the equation.

"Aw, cut Twidge some slack," Bandit said in the uncomfortable silence. GMG1 Richard Rodriguez was Hispanic, with skin as dark as Sam's. "It's not as bad back in the World as it is in Saigon. Not by a hell of a long shot."

"No," Chief Ramsey agreed. "It isn't. Not *yet* . . ."

It took a while for the party to regain its earlier air of cheerfully rambunctious camaraderie.

And, for a time, Greg tried picturing himself in a SEAL team forced to hunt down and kill Americans in a civil war as vicious as the one in Vietnam.

He wondered, if it ever came to that, if he would feel as strongly, as *righteously* about what he was doing as Vinh had.

Chapter 5

Wednesday, 2 July 1969

C-130 en route to Tan Son Nhut Airport
Saigon
1620 hours

Greg Halstead leaned back against the heavy, black rubber case and eyed the Air Force sergeant with lethal appraisal. He wasn't certain how much more of this he was going to be able to take.

To his right, Bill Tangretti was also stretched out on the C-130 Hercules's deck, his back propped up against the bulky, black carrying case for a SEAL IBS—an Inflatable Boat, Small. Both men wore their dress whites, their left chests heavy with colored ribbons, and they were sitting on a sheet of plastic put down on the deck to keep their trousers presentable. The droning of the Herky Bird's four powerful engines made conversation a challenge.

"See, I heard all about you SEAL guys," the sergeant was saying, shouting to be heard above the thundering engines. "I got a friend in Personnel, back at Cam Ranh. Frogmen and secret commandos, all rolled into one. Real James Bond stuff, am I right?"

Greg glanced at Bill, then rolled his eyes toward the aircraft's overhead. Bill grinned and shook his head. The sergeant, a sandy-haired kid in his early twenties, was aboard as assistant crew chief on the flight, which was flying from Cam Ranh Bay to the international airport just north of Saigon with a mixed cargo of everything from machine parts to a couple of lashed-down jeeps to the two SEALs and the dead LDNN they were escorting.

The sergeant's glossy black name tag on his light blue uniform blouse read KIRKPATRICK, and he'd apparently picked up on the fact that his two passengers were SEALs from scuttlebutt back at the Cam Ranh airstrip. That was bad enough. SEALs preferred to preserve their anonymity, and when an outsider asked them about their work, they generally changed the subject. Worse, though, he had all the enthusiasm of a bright and eager puppy and had been pressing them for details about their assignment at Cam Ranh, their recent ops, and how many VC they'd capped so far.

The two SEALs had tolerated the onslaught so far. Kirkpatrick had earned points at the outset of the flight by providing them with chicken salad sandwiches and some most welcome hot coffee from the plane's small mess, a measure of hospitality that had helped both Greg and Bill overcome their normal reticence at opening up with people outside the Teams.

The sergeant was fascinated by SEALs and what they did, though, refusing to be put off by gentle hints or attempts to redirect the conversation, and his inane prattle was beginning to wear at Greg.

Kirkpatrick was seated on a crate opposite the two SEALs. He paused long enough to take a bite from his own sandwich. "So, like," he continued, "I was wonderin' if you guys collected gomer ears, like I heard about, see?"

Greg paused in his chewing, swallowed, then shook his head. The prattle had just taken a rather unpleasant turn. "No," Greg said, his voice cold.

"Well, now, that ain't the way I heard it," the talkative sergeant went on. "See, I have this friend stationed down in Saigon, and he said all you Sneaky Pete guys collect VC ears, you know, string 'em up like a necklace. Man, that'd be one cool souvenir."

"You think so?" Bill said. He drained the last of his coffee from his Styrofoam cup. He sounded angry, the anger kept under a thin but rigid control.

Oblivious, the sergeant winked. "Hey, I got connections. My staff sergeant, down at Tan Son Nhut, he's got a deal goin' where he pays top dollar for genu-wine war souvenirs, and I'm thinkin' he'd pay great for a boss trophy like that, y'know? I mean, anyone can get AKs and SKS carbines and

VC flags and shit. But a necklace of gook ears, man, that'd take the cake!''

Greg felt cold inside. There were some units in the Nam that boasted of collecting the ears from the VC and NVA they killed. Hell, he'd seen an Army guy once in a bar with about ten of the grisly trophies strung like beads on a wire, all shriveled and blackened. He'd ended up provoking a fight with the guy and pounding the shit out of him. The soldier had been a swaggering braggart anyway, begging to be taken down a couple of pegs, and Greg had been only too willing to oblige.

SEALs weren't above playing mind games with their enemies. In fact, they excelled at it and had come up with myriad ways of confusing, demoralizing, and downright terrifying their foe. Some members of the Teams liked to leave a single playing card, the ace of spades, on their kills, because the card represented death to superstitious Vietnamese. Others daubed the faces of their victims with green paint. The enemy knew well what that meant: the dreaded Men With Green Faces had paid a call, creatures that some Vietnamese were convinced were part ghost and part jungle monster . . . and the green paint hinted that those creatures had taken the victim's soul as well as his life.

Often, the best mind-fuck possible lay in the sheer, simple stealth of the Teams, their ability to sneak into an encampment, snatch one particular man, and vanish again with their victim, unseen and unheard. Once on a recent parakeet op, Greg had left a rather original calling card. The man they'd come to capture had been eating rice when the SEALs had burst in; Greg had left the half-full bowl on the mud floor with two chopsticks embedded, straight up, in the rice. That symbol—a bad-luck sign in East Asia mirroring the incense sticks burned for the dead in a Buddhist temple—held special and chilling meaning for the VC who'd come looking for the missing man later.

But collecting ears? For starters, mutilating the dead was a violation of a dozen different regs and a court-martial offense. While SEALs weren't known for their law-abiding and regulation-observing natures, that was one rule they followed. Ear necklaces were for amateurs . . . and *sick* amateurs at that.

Kirkpatrick seemed unaware of the fast-growing chill in the

aircraft's cargo bay. "So, if you like, I could set you guys up, y'know? I mean, I hear you guys kill gooks just about every time you go out, and it wouldn't be a big thing to bring back some trophies, right?"

"How much?" Greg wanted to know.

Kirkpatrick's eyes betrayed a sudden eagerness, an unpleasant craftiness. He preened. "Well, now, that depends on a lot of things, y'know? And I'd have t'talk to my contact in Saigon. But, like I said, man, top dollar for gook ears—"

"You know," Greg said abruptly, interrupting the airman, "that's the third time you've called them 'gooks.' Our friend here wouldn't like that, you know."

"Your . . . friend?"

"That's right," Bill said. Turning, he grabbed the top of the rubber case behind him and popped it open. Greg reached in and grabbed the back of Vinh's neck, levering him into an upright position out of a small avalanche of crushed ice.

The morgue back at Cam Ranh had been running short of body bags that week, and, in any case, none had been requisitioned for the SEAL platoon there. Vinh was making his last flight home inside an ice-filled IBS case.

There was a fitting symbolism in that; Greg remembered watching a military parade at Cam Ranh a few months before that had featured the LDNNs. Vinh and two other Vietnamese SEALs had ridden in an IBS carried on the shoulders of four of their teammates, posing with their paddles as though battling the waves. The rugged little IBS was as much a part of the LDNN mystique as it was for American SEALs, and it seemed appropriate that his body go home this way.

Now, though, as Greg held Vinh's corpse in a sitting position, he looked as if he were about ready to climb out of the case and have some rather particular words with the Air Force sergeant. Bill had carefully washed the body and dressed the wound before packing it in ice. Except for the pallor, he looked quite natural.

"Who . . . what . . ." Kirkpatrick's mouth gaped and flopped in a perfect imitation of a large fish. His eyes grew huge.

Greg took another bite out of the sandwich in his left hand, while bracing Vinh's corpse with his right. "This is our friend, Tien Pham Vinh. Mr. Vinh, say hello to the nice sergeant.''

"Ah . . . wha . . ."

"Mr. Vinh is a Vietnamese SEAL," Bill added. "He's one of the bravest *men* I've had the privilege of knowing. The other day, just before he was killed, he ran out into a clearing under heavy fire to save my ass."

"Believe me," Greg said, "he would not like to hear you talking about 'gooks' or 'gomers' . . ."

"Or 'slants' or 'slopes.' "

". . . and he *really* wouldn't like to hear you talking about collecting gook ears."

"You see, the war's a very personal thing for him."

"He probably has relatives fighting with the VC."

"But he's not a 'gook' and he's not a 'gomer.' He's a *man* . . ."

". . . and he's a SEAL, and SEALs always look after their own."

"Ah . . . I . . . uh . . ." The sergeant gaped and stammered for an unpleasant moment, the color draining from his face as though someone had just pulled a plug. Somehow he staggered to his feet and held himself upright, one hand gripping one of the green canvas straps that festooned the interior of the Herky Bird's cargo compartment. He looked like he was about to say something more, but then Greg took another bite from his sandwich, chewing with leisurely deliberation. Kirkpatrick's color went from pallid to green; cupping his hand over his mouth, he ran forward, vanishing behind some cargo stacks. For several long minutes after that, the SEALs were entertained by the muffled sounds of his retching.

Carefully, they lowered Vinh's cold body back into the ice and sealed him up once more. "Well," Bill said pleasantly, "that was successful."

"Mr. Vinh would have enjoyed it."

"I think he would have approved."

They saw nothing more of the airman for the rest of their short flight.

Half an hour later, the C-130 began its descent toward at Tan Son Nhut, the immense airfield just north of Saigon that was the hub of most flights coming into or leaving South Vietnam. As they stepped out onto the tarmac, the muggy heat of the monsoon season struck them full force, wilting their dress whites. Thunder rolled . . . but not from the monsoons. Air Force jets were constantly lifting off from the runway or gentling in after carrying out missions elsewhere in-country, and their roars drowned even the incessant clatter of a flight of Huey helicopters landing nearby.

It took another half hour to requisition a jeep and driver, load Vinh's body onto the back, and ride across the airfield to the U.S. morgue at the far end of the sprawling complex.

Away from combat areas, most military facilities operated on an eight-to-five schedule, just like real jobs back in the World, and it was after working hours when they arrived at the morgue. Bill remained outside with the IBS case, while Greg went inside to talk to the watch officer on duty. He turned out to be an Army staff sergeant, the equivalent of a Navy first class. His feet were up on his desk, a radio tuned to the Armed Forces Radio station was crooning the sad strains of "Galveston," and he had a copy of *Playboy* open to the June centerfold. He gave Greg a cursory once-over. "Yeah?" His voice was sour, and he didn't sound pleased at being disturbed.

"We got one to check in," Greg said. He handed a string-tied manila envelope across the desk. "Here's the paperwork."

"Let's have a look." Tossing the *Playboy* on the desk, the man opened the envelope and studied the top sheet of typewritten forms for a moment. "Whoa, there," he said, and he sounded almost relieved, as though some difficulty had just been unexpectedly resolved. "This stiff's a gook. Can't take him."

Greg was around the desk and reaching for the staff sergeant's collar before the paperwork hit the desk. In one clean motion, he'd lifted the man from his chair and jerked his face to within an inch of his own. "I have had just about enough," Greg said, his voice a low growl, "of people calling our friend a *gook*."

The man's face flushed. Navy third-class petty officers did not get away with manhandling Army staff sergeants. "You are *way* out of line, mister!"

"I don't think I am. The man's name is Tien Pham Vinh. He's LDNN . . . a *SEAL*, and that makes him a better man than any fat-assed knuckle-dragging pencil-dicked REMF of a bureaucrat in this whole damned stinking war.''

The door to the morgue office banged open, and Bill Tangretti stepped inside. ''Is there a problem here, Twidge? I heard some shouting.''

''No,'' Greg said, his eyes not leaving the staff sergeant's face. ''No problem. *Is* there . . .'' He stopped long enough to look down and read the man's name tag. ''. . . Staff Sergeant Westible?''

Westible's eyes dropped to the ribbons on Greg's dress whites. SEALs did not as yet have a specific badge or emblem to distinguish them from other Navy personnel; quite possibly, he wouldn't even have known what a SEAL was, since the unit didn't have a very high profile. Still, the jump wings, the expert rifleman's badge, and a Presidential Unit Citation said something about Greg's abilities . . . and his will.

''Look, I'd like to help you, sailor,'' the staff sergeant said. As his tone changed, Greg released his collar but remained where he was, crowding Westible's personal space. With his chair and the wall blocking his escape, Westible had no choice but to stand where he was, face to face with an angry and aggressive SEAL. ''But it's against regs, see? The morgue's full up right now, and it wouldn't be right to dump one of our guys for a goo—for a Vietnamese.''

''I'm sure you have *some* procedure to follow when you run out of space.''

''Uh . . . well . . . there's the overflow reefer shed out back . . .''

''That sounds adequate. Mr. Vinh's people will be picking him up tomorrow. We only need someplace to put him for the night.''

''I'll . . . I'll put him in the overflow shed, then. Out back.''

''Good. Do that.'' He turned to leave.

''I could have you up on charges, you know,'' the man said, trying to recover some few shreds of his routed dignity. ''Assaulting a senior enlisted—''

''Stow it, Mac,'' Greg snapped. ''You want to write me up, then do it. But shit-can the threats and bluster because I've just about had it up to here with bigots and mindless bureaucratic crap. You hear me?''

''Uh . . . yeah. Yeah, I hear you.''

"Good." He drew the word out, smiling sweetly. "And if you want to write me up, I damn sure hope you don't suffer from writer's cramp, because I know a few dozen SEALs and LDNNs who feel exactly the same way I do, and they're just liable to pay you a visit. You'd have to write every one of them up, probably with both of your arms in casts and your pencil stuffed up your ass, and that wouldn't be very comfortable, would it? Do we understand each other?" Westible nodded, a bit reluctantly. "Good. Now, can we help you put our *friend* in that shed out back?"

The overflow shed turned out to be a refrigerated structure next to a noisily *putt-putting* diesel generator. Inside were stretcher racks, rows and rows of them, and already most were filled. The sight put Greg in a somber mood as he and Bill removed Vinh from his rubber IBS shroud, placed him on a stretcher, and carried him into the building, which was dimly lit by a single sixty-watt bulb and stank of death and coppery blood despite the chill. Each year, American casualties in Vietnam had been climbing; last year, in 1968, he'd heard, the war in Southeast Asia had become the longest war in United States history . . . and the total number of casualties had exceeded the thirty-some thousand of the Korean War. This year, with Vietnamization fully underway and the first troop withdrawals already begun, combat losses had been considerably fewer than the year before . . . the year of Tet.

Those facts, though, could hardly be of comfort to the still, cold, body-bagged forms on those ranks of stretchers . . . or to the families being notified now, back in the World.

"Thank you, Staff Sergeant," Greg told Westible when they stepped back into the warm, humid, and deliciously clean air outside the shed. "We appreciate your help."

Westible gave the SEALs a sour look, and he seemed to be about to say something, but then he clamped his mouth shut, locked the shed door, and stalked back to the morgue without another word.

"Friendly sort," Bill observed.

"It's the people he works with," Greg said. "I doubt that he sees much in the way of job satisfaction. C'mon. Let's find out where we rack out for tonight."

He was tired. Sometimes, the daily war with the bureaucrats and the REMFs was more wearing than the real war with the enemy. At least you could track and kill the Viet Cong.

The thought of killing a few rear-echelon paper shufflers for God and country was a pleasant one. Even if it was nothing more than a daydream.

Chapter 6

Thursday, 3 July 1969

Saigon
1620 hours

Early the next morning, after spending the night in the enlisted transients' barracks at Tan Son Nhut, Bill and Greg met Lieutenant Truong Van Nhuong at the morgue, finished up with their paperwork, and formally turned Vinh's body over to his own people. As a couple of brawny LDNNs were loading Vinh onto the back of the truck, the Vietnamese naval officer turned to the American SEALs.

"Thanks again," he said. He was a precise, almost fussy, man, small but heavily muscled, like the LDNNs in his command. "We appreciate what you've done."

"Mr. Vinh would have done the same for us, sir," Bill said. It was nothing less than the truth.

"I know Vinh's family," Truong said. "It's going to be hard on them. The funeral is being held later this morning."

"Speaking of that, sir," Greg said, glancing at Bill for confirmation, "we were wondering if it would be possible for us to attend the service."

Truong looked surprised. "Does either of you speak French?"

"No, sir."

"Vinh was a Vietnamese Catholic," Truong explained.

"The service will be in French. I don't know if you would care—"

"The language doesn't matter, sir," Bill said. "Vinh was a good man and, well, we'd like to see him off."

Truong nodded. "I understand. Very well. Of course you may attend. Do you have your own transportation?"

"Negative, sir," Greg said.

"No matter. You can ride with me in my jeep."

They drove first to Saigon's LDNN headquarters, a modern, concrete block structure near the Sai Gon River, where they spent some time with a dozen or so other enlisted LDNNs, Vinh's former teammates. As with the American SEALs during the party two nights before, they didn't talk that much about their fallen comrade. Instead, they talked about *Sat Cong,* killing Communists. The two Americans had trouble following much of the conversation, but the sense of belonging, of camaraderie among warriors who shared a common heritage and a common cause, was unmistakably the same as that among U.S. SEALs, both in Nam and back in the States.

Nearly an hour later, another LDNN arrived, one both American SEALs immediately recognized. "Dong!" Bill exclaimed. "What the hell are you doing here?"

Nghiep Van Dong seemed embarrassed by Bill's exuberance. "Hello, Doc, Twidge. I fly in this morning. Got two-day pass, attend funeral, as friend of family, you know?"

"Outstanding," Greg said. "I think we're already getting in pretty deep, here. Not everyone speaks English, and our Vietnamese is only so-so."

"Yeah," Bill added. "I know just about enough to order dinner, and to order a VC to come out with his hands up. Look, we need you to give us a fast course in Vietnamese customs. We heard somewhere that it's customary to give money to a man's widow at his funeral, is that right?"

Nghiep's eyes widened. "That is custom," he said. He shook his head. "But not necessary for you two take part."

"Hey, we want to," Bill said. "We don't want to offend your teammates or upset Mrs. Vinh or anything like that, but we want to be a part of this."

"We'd really appreciate it if you'd fill us in," Greg added.

"How much do we give, who do we give it to, you know, stuff like that. So we don't cause a scene."

"Yeah. We wouldn't want to make the gift too big, and embarrass somebody. Or too little and, well, you know. . . ."

Nghiep nodded slowly. "I understand. Number one. Viet people think much about appearance, by what you call 'face.' Inappropriate gift is worse than no gift at all." He considered a moment. "Three thousand piaster about okay for you. You stay with other LDNNs. Do what we do, you be okay."

"Thanks, Nghiep," Bill said. "We won't forget this."

Nghiep broke into a rare smile. "We not forget also."

The service was held at noon, at Notre Dame Cathedral, on Dong Khoi Street in the heart of Saigon's government district. A neo-Romanesque church completed in 1883, Notre Dame was one of the more familiar landmarks of Saigon, with its two square, forty-meter towers that dominated the city's skyline. The place was enormous . . . and packed.

"I didn't know there were so many Catholics in South Vietnam," Greg said, as they stood in line beside the big statue of the Virgin Mary outside the main door.

"Shows what you know, Twidge," Bill replied lightly. "South Vietnam has more Catholics than any other country in Asia, after the Philippines. A lot of Catholics fled the north, after the country was partitioned, in '54."

"Yeah? What makes you such an expert, Doc? Oh, hell. What am I thinking of. With a name like Tangretti, you must be Catholic."

Bill grinned back at him. "Actually, no. My dad's family was, I think, but he was adopted, and I guess religion didn't take with him. I do read occasionally, though."

"I wonder," Greg said, taking a tourist's rubbernecked gawk at the iron-spired towers high overhead. "If the Communists win . . . I mean, if they take over South Vietnam, what happens to all these people?"

Bill arched one eyebrow. "Man, you're in a fucking cheerful mood this morning."

"I was just wondering. If so many Catholics fled North Vietnam . . . where will they go if South Vietnam gets overrun?"

"Nowhere," Bill replied bluntly. "Because the South's not gonna fall."

"You seem damned sure of that."

"*We're* here, aren't we? And people like Nghiep and Truong. And others like Vinh. They'll be here, even if we leave."

"Yeah. I guess you're right."

" 'Course I'm right. Now knock off with that defeatist talk. You want someone to overhear you? You'll start a riot with this bunch."

"Not a good thing to do in church," Greg agreed.

As they'd been warned, they understood little of the service, which appeared to be conducted partly in Vietnamese, and partly in French. The Americans found seats near the back and spent most of their time standing when others stood, kneeling when others knelt, and sitting during the times between. Vinh's coffin rested in front of the altar, with a Vietnamese flag draped across the top. At the end of the service, six LDNNs in dress white uniforms, Nghiep among them, solemnly carried the coffin out of the church on their shoulders, flag and all; a framed photograph of Vinh, smiling and wearing a white, black-billed chief's hat, rested atop the coffin.

"I thought he was only a first class," Bill whispered as the procession moved past. "What's with the chief's hat?"

"Vietnamese Navy custom," Greg whispered back. "Didn't you know? You get killed in the line of duty, you automatically get bumped to the next rank."

"Hell of a tough way to win your rockers," Bill said, using Navy slang for a chief's insignia.

"I just wonder about that photo," Greg said as they filed out of their pews and followed the crowd outside. "Was it airbrushed on, or did he have to go get a photo taken that he *knew* wouldn't be used unless he got killed?"

"Didn't look faked to me. Maybe they all get their pictures taken like that, just in case they buy the farm."

"Man, no thanks," Greg said, shaking his head. "That'd put a jinx on me for sure!"

The drive to the cemetery was a long one, slowed first by the snail's pace congestion in the center of Saigon, then by the speed of the funeral procession, which was limited to the velocity of its slowest, most ramshackle members. The American SEALs were just beginning to get nervous about being so far out in the country without weapons when they turned off the main four-lane highway, proceeded a short distance, and finally entered a Vietnamese cemetery.

The events that followed were blurred, somewhat, by emotion and by strangeness. There was much that was identical to an American military funeral; the cemetery was so large that Bill was forcibly reminded of Arlington, across the Potomac from Washington, D.C., with its unending row upon row upon melancholy row of grave markers. How many of these graves, he wondered, had only recently been filled by the fallen sons of South Vietnam?

They stood at attention with Vinh's teammates, in ranks, while the civilians gathered in a large and untidy mass in front of the grave. Lieutenant Truong addressed the crowd in Vietnamese; the casket was lowered into the ground; the pallbearers folded the flag, and Nghiep handed it over to Truong, who formally presented it to Vinh's widow, a tiny wisp of a china-doll woman in traditional Vietnamese dress—black slacks, with a white top slit almost to her waist. She looked far too young to be anyone's wife, much less to be the mother of the three children at her side, two boys and a girl. An older woman in the party was probably Vinh's mother, while a younger woman, Bill guessed from the similarity of features, was the widow's sister. All of the women looked so small and vulnerable and hurting . . . but he didn't know what he could say to make things better. There was nothing *to* say, not in a tragedy like this.

Afterward, the LDNNs filed past, each dropping an envelope into a basket held by the sister, taking Mrs. Vinh's hands, and murmuring something to her. The Americans took their place in line. When Greg reached her, he dropped his envelope in the basket with the others, and said in thickly accented Vietnamese, *"Toi rat tiec, Ba Vinh.* I am very sorry."

Bill slipped the envelope in the basket, careful not to look at it. *"Toi rat tiec,"* he said, grasping the widow's tiny hands, bowing slightly over them, as he'd seen the others do.

She looked up at them, a bit shyly, perhaps. "He spoke of you often," she said in singsong-accented English. "Thank you for coming."

"He saved my life, ma'am," Bill told her simply. "Wouldn't have been right not to come."

That afternoon, as was the custom, a number of Vinh's friends, LDNNs and the two American SEALs, were invited to a meal at Vinh's house—*pho*, a kind of noodle soup, followed by bowls of rice mixed with several kinds of vegetable and chunks of fish and pungent *nuoc mam*, the notorious fermented fish sauce that no Vietnamese meal was without. Bill was astonished that Mrs. Vinh served the men, then retired with the other women to eat separately in another room, not to be seen again. He was disturbed at this but managed to rein in his feelings. In America, he thought, the widow's friends and neighbors would be serving *her*, not the other way around. Never before had Vietnam seemed so alien in its customs . . . even when so much was familiar. They ate with the LDNNs in an uncomfortable silence; when they rose, they left several hundred piasters apiece beneath their bowls.

Later, they returned to the LDNN base, where Lieutenant Truong had arranged for quarters for them for the night. They managed to line up a flight for themselves back to Cam Ranh Bay that would leave Tan Son Nhut early the next morning, though it took some doing. Seats on military aircraft were on a space-available basis only, and the officer they spoke to on the phone was unwilling to promise that there would be room. After that, they put a call through to the SEAL barracks at Cam Ranh Bay to let Lieutenant Connolly know when they would be arriving. Phone connections were uncertain between Saigon and Cam Ranh, however, and it took longer than expected to get their call put through.

At last, though, their administrative chores were done, and they were ready for a night on the town with their LDNN hosts. Nghiep told them that there was a combination bar and restaurant on Le Duon Boulevard, a high-class place not far down the street from the brand-new American Embassy, that was favored by the Vietnamese SEAL community.

Saigon bustled and swarmed around them, the streets a tangle of pedestrians, buses, private cars, military vehicles, trucks, bicycles, and cyclos. It had been raining earlier, and the streets were wet, the pools of water capturing the light and life above and reflecting it in smears of gorgeous color. Though it was not yet fully dark, the city was brilliantly lit with neon and looked as modern and as unconcerned as any peaceful Western city. Some buildings showed evidence of the war—a shell hole here, the pockmarks of bullets there, a crumbled plaster facade revealing bricks behind—scars still unrepaired since the enemy's Tet Offensive a year and a half before. Still, the people showed no outward sign that they were a people at war. Across the street, a group of schoolgirls in proper blue-and-white uniform dresses followed their teacher along the sidewalk on an outing. A cyclo driver engaged in heated debate with a taxi driver. A uniformed traffic cop directed traffic with stolid aplomb. Soldiers and sailors, American and Vietnamese, threaded their way through the teeming crowds, searching out the local hot spots and watering holes. For the most part, the LDNNs and two SEALs were treated with complete indifference.

Bill always found crowds in Vietnam to be unnerving, though. The unique character of the war in Southeast Asia guaranteed that the smiling shopkeeper or shoeshine boy or vegetable vendor you met in the street by day might be trying to kill you at night . . . and, if not him, then his son or his nephew or his sister, and he might well be passing information to them. Information that could lead to more Americans lying in Staff Sergeant Westible's morgue, awaiting their final plane trip home.

"You know," Bill told Nghiep as they waited at a crosswalk for the signal, "Mr. Vinh said once . . ." He stopped himself. "*Chief* Vinh said once that someday, after the Americans were gone, he would still be here, still fighting."

"This is something we all believe," Nghiep said, his dark eyes solemn.

"Yeah, but don't you guys think there will ever be peace?" Greg asked. "I mean, after you win the war?"

Nghiep sighed. "It hard to think about peace. For most of us, war all we know. Before Americans come, we fight French for independence."

That jolted Bill. It was too easy for Americans to assume that the modern Viet Cong were simply the older Viet Minh in another guise . . . and, indeed, most of North Vietnam's present military leaders had started as Communist revolutionaries fighting the French. The thought that anti-Communists could have also been anti-colonial was a new and slightly uncomfortable one, a thought that confused the American tendency to put people in neat little pigeonholes labeled "loy-alist" or "revolutionary" or "Communist."

"Before French," Nghiep went on, "we fight Japanese. Before Japanese, we fight more French. This country not know what you call 'peace' in very long time. You Americans occupiers too. Many occupiers, some good, some bad. And war go on forever."

What would it be like, Bill wondered, to live with that kind of background, that kind of philosophy, born to unending war, never knowing anything else? The SEALs prided themselves at being warriors, and they were very, very good at what they did. But even SEALs could look forward to leaving Navy Special Warfare one day, settling down with a wife and family in a neat little home in some suburb, someplace . . . and not have to think about booby traps or exfiltration routes or how best to silently take out a sentry. No matter what the other SEALs said back at Mama San's, America, even with its political fragmentation and racial hatreds and mass demonstrations, was a nation at peace.

Hell, that was half the trouble. American boys were dying in Vietnam, fighting one hell of a long and viciously bloody war, and half of the people back home who'd sent them here to fight and die didn't even know their country was at war. And half of the ones who did were against the war and everything Americans were trying to do here.

They could see their destination up ahead and across the street, the My Canh, which Nghiep told them had formerly been called *Le Petite Paris*. To one side of the ornate, colonial architecture of the two-story structure was an outdoor café that would not have been out of place on a street in Paris, complete with neat, white, round tables, each with its own red-and-white striped umbrella. The café was fenced in by a low hedge and surrounded by large, spreading trees growing from planters opened in the sidewalk pavement. About half of the café tables were occupied; the street outside was, as usual in this part of Saigon, congested with both people and cars.

One of Saigon's ubiquitous motorbikes was tooling up the street, weaving in and out to avoid pedestrians and larger vehicles. Two young Vietnamese men rode the bike; the one in front wore a Western-style plaid shirt and blue jeans, the one behind, a white shirt and leather jacket. They looked like any of the hundreds of other Saigonese men in the streets, but something about them, about their manner, perhaps, about their carefully controlled facial expressions, *something* triggered a warning in Bill's mind. He held up his hand, stopping the others. "Hold it, guys," he said. "I don't like the look of—"

And at that moment, the man riding behind the motorbike's driver pulled something from beneath his jacket, a long bundle of slender tubes that he tossed into the My Canh's café area in a high, spinning arc. The motorbike's driver gunned his machine before the object struck the pavement, roaring off down the boulevard, weaving madly through the traffic.

"Down!" Bill yelled, and the SEALs went to ground, hitting the street just as the object hit the concrete in the middle of the café, bounced once, and exploded in a deafening roar.

Pipe bomb. Or, rather, a bundle of lead pipes taped together, each packed with explosives and connected by blasting caps to a detonator—probably the three-second fuse removed from a hand grenade and armed by the pulling of a cotter pin. The detonation—confined, then amplified, by the pipes—was unimaginably violent, ripping through the café and its tables and colored umbrellas and chatting people like a lightning bolt. Windows on all sides of the street shattered as though punched by giant fists; trees shuddered, the leaves stripped from their branches as though by a storm. Thunder rolled from the faces of distant buildings and continued echoing for seconds after.

Bill looked up as bits and pieces of debris continued to clink and clatter across the pavement. The café had been wiped away as though it had never been; the facade of the My Canh itself had been smashed open, the rubble scattered everywhere, and a half dozen fires were burning in the ruin that was left.

In the street and on the sidewalks, people were slowly getting to their feet, cars were beginning to move again, voices were rising in fear or anger or confusion. Mingled with the growing commotion were other, more piercing sounds, the shrieks and wails of the wounded.

"C'mon!" Bill said, rising to his feet. "Let's see if we can help."

But there was pathetically little that could be done, save the barest rudiments of first aid for the injured. A crater a foot deep and six across had been gouged into the middle of the café grounds, the white tables overturned, the umbrellas scattered across the street. A dozen people at least lay still and bloodied; three times that number were wounded, some so badly that it was clear they wouldn't last for long.

The SEALs did what they could, concentrating their efforts on people who were bleeding so badly that they might die in minutes if they weren't treated, and ignoring those who, from experience, they knew wouldn't make it, as well as those who seemed only superficially cut by flying glass or stunned by the blast.

Bill finished tying a tourniquet around the leg of one man who'd been bleeding badly from a savage, to-the-bone gash on the inside of his thigh, telling him as best as he could to lie still. Sirens were nearing the disaster, and the flash of red lights down the street showed that emergency vehicles were trying to work their way through the traffic. He turned, looked up, and suppressed a startled jump. A young girl, perhaps nine or ten years old and wearing a schoolgirl's uniform, was looking down at him from the crotch of one of the trees on the sidewalk. She seemed quite calm and was watching him from her perch seven feet up without emotion. He wondered how she'd gotten into the tree, and why. Was she hurt? He started toward her, holding out his arms. "C'mon, honey," he called. "*Di den duoi.* Come on down. . . ."

Only when he got close did he see that the lower half of her body was missing, and her steadfast stare, now accusing, somehow, was that of death. It was a stare that he knew would be burned indelibly into his memory for the rest of his life.

Late that night, neither Bill nor Greg could sleep. They stood on a narrow porch outside the door to the LDNN barracks. The air was thick and humid, promising more rain before the dawn.

"What do you think, Greg?" Bill said. "Were we being set up?"

"The bombing, you mean? Could've been coincidence."

"I keep wondering if one of the LDNNs called ahead and made reservations. We were supposed to be there at seven, I know. The attack was at seven-thirty."

"Yeah. Good thing it took us so long to get that call to Cam Ranh through, or we might've been there in the café."

"That's what I mean." Bill felt the twistings of nausea once more and ruthlessly suppressed them. "I'm wondering if that bomb was meant for us."

"Hell, these people've been throwing bombs at each other since long before we got here. We can't second-guess what happened today, Doc. You know that."

"I'd hate to think . . . well, that we were the targets this evening. That all those people died because of us."

"They would have died whether we were in the café or not."

"Not if we hadn't been there as targets in the first place. I keep thinking that someone knew we were going to be there at seven and arranged for that package to be delivered."

"You say anything to Nghiep or the others?" Greg asked.

"Nah. If I did, it would be like an accusation. They'd lose face. And it might, I don't know. Hurt our relationship with the Viet SEALs. That's too valuable to lose over something . . . like this."

"I just can't believe they'd be stupid enough to reserve a table," Greg said. "Nghiep and the others, they're too smart for that." He looked up at the overcast sky. "Maybe it wasn't us. Maybe the enemy knew the LDNNs liked to hang out at that place, and they were the targets."

"Maybe. Still pretty stupid, letting yourself fall into a rut. An identifiable pattern." Realization quickened his heartbeat a little. "Maybe we should kind of spread the word back at Cam Ranh, Twidge. Tell 'em not to hang out at Mama San's so much."

"Now you're sounding paranoid."

"I'd like to survive this war." He sighed. "Damn. I feel awful about this."

"Put it behind you, Doc. If you let it gnaw at you, it'll kill you."

Suddenly, Bill felt a strong and uncontrollable longing to be . . . home. Back in a sane world of neat lawns and American values and sitcoms on television and neighborhood schoolyards where little girls didn't get torn in half by a terrorist's bomb.

He had never been so homesick in his life.

Chapter 7

San Diego Airport
1815 hours

"Oops!" Pat Halstead said, "we just missed that one!"

"Damn!" Wendy Frasier tossed her red hair in disgust as she scowled at her rearview mirror. "Why couldn't that guy've pulled out fifteen seconds ago?"

"Take it easy, Wen," Pat said. "Look. There's a spot up ahead."

"Yeah, and a lot farther away from the terminal, too." Still grumbling, Wendy pulled her dark green Chevy into the vacant parking place. "What time's their flight due in?"

"Not till almost seven. We've got loads of time." Pat grinned at her friend. "You'd think *you* were the one who was anxious to meet this plane."

"I'm only anxious on your behalf, Pat. After you dragooned me into driving you down here, it'd be a lousy deal if I ended getting you here late!"

"Well, we're not late, in spite of the traffic, and in spite of the parking. C'mon!" The two women got out of the car and walked to the terminal. Inside, a confusion of people—servicemen, families, businessmen, wives, porters, attendants—swarmed through the lobby in every direction or patiently queued up in lines at the ticket counters. It took the women ten minutes and a wait at an information kiosk to find out where they were supposed to go. The plane they were meeting was a military charter, and instead of pulling up to one of the main gates, it was apparently going to be stopping further out, letting its passengers off at a side gate normally

63

reserved for mail flights and charters to Mexico. The woman in the information booth was able to direct them to the terminal's west wing, and a door where family and friends of the returning servicemen were being ushered outside. "Looks like our boys don't get to use those fancy accordion walkways that go straight from the plane to the terminal," Pat said, joking. "They have to use the servants' entrance, around to the side."

"So, Pat. Tell me," Wendy said as they walked down the long, long hallway past waiting lounges and snack shops. "Are you going to go through with it?"

They walked in silence for quite a while before Pat answered. "I think so," she finally said. "I mean, I know I *want* to, but as it's getting closer and closer, I find myself getting more and more nervous. I mean, well, his letters have been great. But how much of that is real, and how much is just, oh, I don't know. Lonesome sailor disease. Wanting to be connected with somebody from, from 'Back in the World,' as they call it."

" 'Back in the World'?" Wendy laughed. "You make them sound like the astronauts going to the Moon!"

Pat grew thoughtful as they walked. Outside, the roar of a jet's engines revving up for takeoff competed with the sounds of wind, baggage carts, and people, momentarily drowning them out. The Moon? Only two days ago, that skyscraper of a Saturn V rocket had thundered skyward from Cape Kennedy, with three astronauts, Armstrong, Aldrin, and Collins, sardined into the tiny capsule at its tip. According to Walter Cronkite, who'd been following the Apollo story from the beginning, they were due to go into orbit around the Moon sometime tomorrow. And a day or two after that . . .

The whole idea of a man walking on the Moon still seemed so unreal, so much a fantasy spun by some crazy science fiction writer . . . and not a nuts-and-bolts piece of American engineering, hardware, and know-how. For as long as Pat had been alive, reaching for the Moon had been a metaphor for trying to accomplish the impossible.

Wendy's comment, though, brought home another aspect of the Man-to-the-Moon project. Those three guys up there were cut off from the rest of humanity like no three men in history.

But maybe, just maybe, she could begin to understand how cut off from civilization, friends, family, and home the boys in Vietnam felt.

The similarities were a little startling, now that she thought about them. The astronauts were flying into terrible danger; they might not come back. That was the day-to-day reality of Americans in Vietnam . . . and more so for some of them, like combat Marines or Navy SEALs. The astronauts were thousands of miles away from their homes and families. So were the boys in Nam. The astronauts were forced to live in a strange and unfamiliar environment; same for the Americans in Nam . . . and the alien environments were similar, too, when you realized that both could kill you for making a single mistake.

"Here we are!" Wendy said suddenly, breaking into her thoughts.

"Military Charter one-twelve?" a smiling male attendant asked them, then pointed. "Right down those stairs and to your left. Please stay behind the fence."

Down the stairs and to the left took them through another door, this one leading outside onto black pavement painted with yellow lines. It had been cool inside the terminal. The southern California heat of the early evening hit them full force as they pushed through the door and began walking toward the gate.

Pat glanced up toward the eastern sky, where a nearly full moon hung pale and ghostlike above the horizon. She thought again of astronauts . . . and the boys in Vietnam.

It was a short stroll to the tall, wide, chain-link fence that separated the area near the terminal from the aircraft taxi bays and runways. Other people, mostly women, several with kids in tow, were already gathering along the fence. A little girl in a pink dress pointed excitedly at a huge TWA jet cruising slowly past on the taxiway, on its way to the main terminal building.

"So," Wendy said, obviously trying to continue the earlier conversation, prompting with voice and expression, "don't go all quiet on me. C'mon, talk to me! You're nervous, you said. So . . . what? You think he doesn't really care for you? He's looking for a one-night stand? It's just . . . what did you call it? 'Lonesome sailor disease'? I like that."

"Well, sometimes I wonder how real it all is. I mean, I've really only spent two weeks with him."

"So you're chickening out, is that it?"

"No. Let's just say I'm not going to blurt it out right here in front of God and everybody. I'm going to wait and . . . and see. How he acts, what he says. Is he as anxious to see me again as, as I am to see him. That kind of thing."

"And if he is?"

"Come on, Wen. Don't press me. I just want to wait and see, okay?"

Wendy snorted. "Don't know what you have to wait for. You probably know Bill better from his letters than I knew Roger after going out with him for almost three years. And anyway, he's Greg's best buddy, isn't he? He's *got* to be a great guy if Greg likes him, right?"

"I know he's a great guy. *That's* not the question."

She laughed. "So snag him, already."

Pat punched her in the arm, and they both grinned.

"You know, it's funny," Wendy said, "in all the time we've known each other, I've never actually met this marvelous, wonderful, stupendous brother of yours."

"Wendy! I haven't bragged about Greg *that* much, have I?"

"Only told me about every little thing he did in SEAL training, from the time he almost got picked up by the Border Patrol to the day he made his first parachute jump." She began stroking her chin, mimicking extreme thoughtfulness. "Strange, though. After Christmas break I didn't hear so much about Greg any more. All of a sudden I began hearing an awful lot about a certain *other* sailor."

Pat felt herself redden, but Wendy ignored her embarrassment and pushed ahead. "You know, it's a real shame I had to work through the break. If I hadn't, I could've taken you up on your invitation and I would've gotten to meet those peripatetic pinnipeds of yours seven months ago!"

"I wish you had! I just know you'll like Greg a lot. And Bill is, well . . ."

"Yours. I know. But don't be so eager to match me up with your brother. Me, I've sworn off men for a while."

"Come on, Wendy," Pat said, resting a hand on her arm. "Not all guys are assholes like Roger."

"Yeah, yeah, right." Wendy pulled away from Pat and walked along the chain-link fence, moving closer to the gate, abruptly terminating the conversation.

Oh, damn, Pat thought fiercely, watching her friend walk away. *You and your big mouth . . . had to go and remind her. Why don't you just take your size five pumps and cram them both in your mouth, Patricia?*

Out above the runway, a jet was descending, wheels down, and she wondered if that was the one.

Aboard Military Charter 112
1852 hours

The Boeing 707's wheels touched down on the runway with a thump, and the whine of the turbojets spooled to a higher pitch as the pilot put the engines into reverse, slowing them fast and hard.

"And about fucking time!" Bill Tangretti said with considerable feeling.

Greg Halstead turned and grinned at him. "You seem awfully eager to get down, Doc," he said. "Hell, you've been antsy ever since we climbed on this here big silver bird back at Tan Son Nhut."

Bill looked at his buddy with an evil, don't-mess-with-me glare. "You've got to be kidding, Twidge. After a goddamned fifteen-hour flight?"

"What's the hurry? You'll get to see her in a day or two. You've waited six months, what's another coupla days?"

"Coupla days, nothing. It's fifteen hours in this flying box, with nothing to look at but ocean. We might as well be inside the moon ship."

"Nah, I'll stick with Earth, thanks," Greg replied. He peered out the tiny window as though looking for someone.

"Fuckin' A," Boomer Cain called from the other side of the aisle. "The food's better, the women are prettier. And you can usually breathe the air."

Bill grunted. He wasn't really in any mood to spar with either Halstead or the other SEALs of Delta Platoon, not now. He was tired from the long flight, yes, but more than that he was eager to see Pat, and Twidge's barbs and ribbings could get just a little bit too close to the mark sometimes.

Also, he kept wondering if this relationship could be right. *I mean, it's not like you've really known her all that long, is it?* he asked himself. *You've spent . . . what? Two weeks with her?*

Yeah, but they were really wonderful *weeks. . . .*

He just wondered if she felt the same way about him that he felt about her. Pat wasn't just a quick date or a one-night stand or even entertainment for a weekend liberty. The attraction had started out physical, sure, back when he'd met her at Greg's place up in Jenner over Christmas. She was beautiful, so small she hardly made a double armful, with long blond hair a guy could get lost in.

But even before he'd started exchanging letters with her, he'd begun to know her as a person, to appreciate her intelligence, her poise and confidence . . . and her dry, sometimes biting, wit.

He'd never felt like this about anyone before. But was it *real? . . .*

He glanced again at Greg, who was watching him with that mischievous, I-know-something-you-don't grin of his that could be positively maddening. The hell with it. Two more days. *One,* if Bill Tangretti had even one ounce of the cumshaw-and-scrounging skills of his near-legendary father.

Flight 112 had originated in Saigon, a military charter to fly a planeload of veterans back to the World, with stops at Subic Bay, Guam, and Hawaii. The problem was that *this* flight, unlike most of the Vietnam-to-Stateside flights, ended in San Diego instead of San Francisco.

The SEALs of Delta Platoon *could* have waited, of course, for a San Francisco–bound flight, but that would have left them hanging around a transients' barracks in Saigon for a week or possibly more while they waited for a flight with available seats . . . or they could have tried to get back by grabbing space on a military transport, and risk sitting in Guam for a week or more, waiting for the next space-available out.

But Lieutenant Connolly had come through for them, pushing the bureaucrats until they fell into place and found space aboard the first flight out. Funny. Bill had had his doubts about the new Wheel at first, but Connolly had damn well gotten all his shit together in one seabag and become part of the *team*.

Hell, it made better sense to be going to San Diego anyway. Delta Platoon would be breaking up soon, its members scattering to other billets in the SEAL Team One community . . . but most of those billets would be in or near San Diego, and Team One's headquarters were across the bay at Coronado. Tangretti and Halstead both already had orders in their carry-on bags assigning them to the Team's BUD/S training command. Bill was going to be working at the BUD/S sick bay again, while Greg was going to be an instructor.

The rest of the men on Charter Flight 112 were Marines coming home after a year in Danang, and most of them were probably headed for new assignments in southern California as well.

All of them, though, would first be enjoying anywhere from two weeks to a whole beautiful month of leave. Tangretti and Halstead were going to spend their two weeks together, staying with Greg's folks north of San Francisco.

"It just would have been *so* much more convenient if this flight could've dropped us off in San Francisco," Bill said abruptly, picking up on a conversation begun much earlier. "I mean, we would've been just a stone's throw from Jenner!"

"Whoa, there, Doc," Greg said, laughing. "I thought Jenner was *my* hometown, not yours!"

"Screw you, Twidge. Place a flat-bladed screwdriver into the slot across that flat head of yours and *screw* you."

"Okay, man! Okay!" He raised his hands. "Just making conversation!"

"It's just gonna be tough getting transport five hundred miles, up to Jenner," Bill continued, thinking out loud. "Of course, we'll need transport around here. I just hate having to buy a used car in a hurry, y'know?"

"There's always the bus," Greg said, still grinning.

"Yeah. The bus." The two of them had done the San Diego to San Francisco round trip on Greyhound once six months ago, just before their last deployment overseas. Once had been enough.

"Cheer up, swim buddy," Greg said, looking out the window. "Maybe something'll turn up unexpected like."

Gate 27C, San Diego Airport
1857 hours

Damn it all! Wendy knew she was being irrational, but knowing that didn't help matters. She was sorry now that she'd agreed to drive down here. It was good to spend time with her old roommate, but Pat seemed bent on matchmaking, and that was going to be *damned* uncomfortable. She was fully prepared to admire Greg Halstead, but she sure as hell wasn't going to get involved with him.

She just hoped that Bill Tangretti was as much of a paragon as Pat seemed to think he was. From what she'd heard, he was a definite improvement on Andy, Pat's boyfriend back before she'd gotten involved with Bill . . . but then that wasn't saying very much. Andy had always struck her as one of those accidental activists, someone who said the right words to belong to the right crowd without actually *believing* anything, the sort of person she'd always felt a great deal of scorn for. The sort of person, in fact, that she'd thought Pat was when she first met her.

They'd been lab partners their junior year at San Francisco State, and it had taken her months to realize that Pat was in the process of moving away from the activism that had engrossed her the previous two years. When Wendy finally began talking to her seriously, instead of judging her by the company she'd been keeping, she discovered that Pat had been struggling with her beliefs. The fact that Greg was now in the Navy certainly had something to do with that struggle, and Greg's ex-girlfriend, Marci, who'd been a close friend of Pat's, had apparently had something to do with it, too, but Pat had never volunteered details. All she'd ever told Wendy was that there'd been a nasty scene when Greg had announced that he was dropping out of college to join the service, and that after that, she and Marci had just "drifted apart," to use her words.

Wendy Frasier had never had to face that particular struggle. A bad knee had kept her father out of the service during World War II, but he'd been a patriot and had raised Wendy to honor her flag and her country. Before he died, he'd taught her to distinguish between the nation and the men who ran her, between the Office of the President and the man who happened to fill that office at any given time. He'd also taught her enough about history to realize that, if America wasn't perfect, well, living here sure beat the hell out of living in most other places in the world.

Shit, shit, *shit!*

"Thinking about Roger again?"

Wendy jumped. She turned to see Pat looking at her with a mixture of amusement and concern. "Sorry," she said, turning away again. "Didn't realize I was thinking out loud."

"You weren't. But when your shoulders get that tight and your fists clench up and you look like you want to punch somebody out, it's usually about Roger."

Wendy laughed, a mirthless sound. "You'd think I'd be over the bastard by now."

Pat didn't answer right away, for which Wendy was grateful. When she did speak again, her voice was low and thoughtful. "It can take a long time to get over feeling betrayed."

Wendy turned to look at her friend. "Are you thinking about Greg and Marci . . . or about yourself?"

Pat shrugged. "I guess both, really. Greg doesn't talk about it, but I think he and Marci were pretty serious. When she turned on him the way she did, it really hurt."

"Hurt both of you."

She nodded. "Marci'd been my best friend. And I'm the one who introduced her to Greg."

"That's not much of a recommendation for your matchmaking skills." When Pat didn't respond, Wendy reached out a hand to her friend's arm. "Hey. Joke, okay?"

Pat smiled weakly. "Sure. You're right, though. I haven't had much success in that field." Then her mouth quirked, she sighed, and the smile turned mischievous. "I promise I won't say another word about Greg or about how well you two would get along."

Wendy was instantly suspicious. "What gives? Why the sudden onset of virtue?"

"Because you'll find out for yourself in a few minutes. Look."

A jet, a huge, sleek 707, was taxiing away from the runway, but instead of turning left and heading for the main gates, this one turned right, aiming straight for the crowd waiting behind the fence.

The crowd had swollen rapidly during the past few minutes. Wendy hadn't really been aware of just how many people there were waiting with them, but now others noticed the oncoming plane, and there was a growing swell of noise. Lots of the people waiting there looked like teenagers ... sons and daughters of the older returning servicemen, she decided. It was a fairly cool day for July, but still it was warm enough that she was surprised by how many people were bundled up in raincoats.

"Is it supposed to rain today?" she asked Pat.

"Hmm?" She glanced up at the clear, evening sky. "I don't think so. Why?"

"I was just wondering what they know that we don't," she said, nodding toward a long-haired, raincoated teenager in the crowd.

"Who cares? Let's get a place close to the gate."

A man in an airport uniform got to the gate just ahead of them. As he opened the gate, he began announcing in an official-sounding voice that everyone should make two lines on either side of the gate, stand back, give them room. The crowd obediently parted, and everyone watched as the plane came to a stop thirty feet away.

"Bill knows you're going to be here, doesn't he?" Wendy had to raise her voice above the noise of the plane's engine.

"No. I wrote Greg about it and asked him not to tell Bill."

"No! Really? Why the secrecy?"

"It's like I said before. I want to see how he reacts. I don't want to ... I don't know. Throw myself at him."

"Aw, the light dawns. You want *him* to be the one to throw himself at *you*."

"You got a problem with that, Wendy?"

"Not a one, my dear Patricia. Not a one."

Flight 112, Gate 27C
San Diego Airport
1901 hours

Even before the plane came to a complete stop, dozens of Marines and Navy personnel were already standing and forming a line to the exit, but Greg Halstead remained in his seat, staring out the window at the people crowding behind a chain-link fence, waiting for their arrival. He couldn't see Pat, but then she was such a pipsqueak, it'd be hard to spot her. A lot of people were wearing what looked like raincoats, even though the sky was clear. Maybe they'd thought it'd be windy out there.

"Hey, Twidge, c'mon. Let's get out of here."

"Man, you *are* anxious!" He wondered what Bill would think if he knew that Pat was here at the San Diego Airport waiting for him, instead of five hundred miles north.

They slung their carry-ons over their shoulders and crowded into the line of men standing in the aisle. Most of the passengers were in uniform, and most were either Marines in khaki or sailors in dress whites. Both of the SEALs were wearing tropical white longs—which meant short-sleeved white shirts instead of the traditional white cotton jumpers with the ridiculous flap in the back.

"Hey, squid!" a Marine growled as Bill pushed in front of him. "Watch it, there, or your faggot ass is grass!"

The SEALs had sat more or less together on the flight and hadn't fraternized much with the other men on board. Greg had seen this particular Marine—a sergeant—talking with his buddies, but he'd never spoken with him. The guy looked mean.

Bill turned, looking up into the Marine's face. "And you've got the lawnmower, I suppose," he said. "You anxious to kiss it now, or do you want to wait until you've finished up trimming?"

The Marine's eyes dropped—briefly—to the rack of medals on Tangretti's chest, then widened. The long-standing rivalry between the Navy and the Marine Corps frequently led to physical exchanges of opinion and belief, but one combat veteran always respected another, no matter what the uniform.

Most SEALs carried medals enough to impress the most jaded of combat vets. Tangretti's ribbons started with the maroon of the Bronze Star, with its narrow, white-bordered blue stripe down the middle, and went on to include the Purple Heart, the Vietnam Service Medal, the Republic of Vietnam Service Medal, and several lesser awards, as well as the gold-bordered blue of a Presidential Unit Citation. The Marine's eyes also rested momentarily on Tangretti's expert pistol marksmanship badge and the expert rifle marksmanship badge next to it, awards not usually seen on a sailor's chest, but identical to the marksmanship awards on the sergeant's khakis.

The Marine, too, wore a Bronze Star, a Purple Heart, and the various Vietnam service ribbons. In fact, except for the PUC, the two men's fruit salad racks were nearly identical.

"You were saying, Marine?" Greg said, crowding a little closer. His own fruit salad didn't match Bill's, yet. This had been Bill Tangretti's second tour in Nam, and Greg's first. There were rumors that everyone on the Ham Tam Island raid was going to pick up at least a Bronze Star, but those awards were still making their way through official channels. Nor had Greg been wounded, qualifying him for the Purple Heart, though Bill had been wounded three times so far, once badly in his first tour, again at Ham Tam, and a third time, lightly, on the op that had killed Mr. Vinh.

Perhaps it was the medals on Tangretti's chest. Or maybe it was the fact that the other SEALs of Delta Platoon were crowding a little closer to the confrontation in the 707's aisle. Either way, the Marine apparently decided that this was neither the time nor the place to pick a fight with the Navy.

"Ah . . . fergit it," the sergeant growled. "After you, sailor." He looked at Halstead. "You, too."

"Why, thank you, Sergeant," Greg said, moving ahead. "You're too kind."

Just then the door at the front of the aircraft opened up, and the servicemen began filing ahead, smiling and nodding their thanks at the pretty stewardess waiting beside the cockpit entrance or, in several cases, holding things up to ask her for a date. By the time Greg reached her, she was looking a little worn about the eyes, so he grinned and said, "What is a nice girl like you doing in a place like this?"

She laughed and rolled her eyes. "Baby-sitting," she said.

"Well, thanks for a nice flight."

"You're welcome, sailor. Good luck!"

They emerged into the California early evening at the top of a mobile stairway and clattered their way down to the tarmac. The crowd waiting a few feet away on the other side of a chain-link fence stirred and rippled. The gate was open, and an airport employee in a blue jacket was trying to open a way for the oncoming column of military personnel.

"Charlie!" a woman called out. "Charlie! Over here!"

Other women called to their men. One with tears streaming down her face held a cute little girl in a pink dress up high so that she could see over the heads of the crowd. "There's Daddy!" the woman cried. "Wave to Daddy! Oh, *God*, wave to Daddy!"

One Marine up ahead swung to the left, dropped to all fours, and kissed the tarmac. Several in the crowd cheered and applauded. Greg turned to look at the big sergeant who'd followed them off the plane, and saw just a slight glisten of tears in the eyes. "Good to be home, isn't it, Sarge?" he said.

"You can goddamn fuckin' roger *that*," the Marine replied.

It hardly seemed possible. *Home.* . . .

He saw Pat standing with a pretty redheaded woman off to the left and grinned. Bill was in for one hell of a surprise when he saw them in another moment or two.

Greg was just walking through the gate when a lanky young man with a threadbare beard, wearing a dark raincoat, leaned toward him. "Hey, man," the kid said. He wore a bright red headband to keep his long hair back out of his eyes and . . . God, he *stank*. A peace symbol gleamed on the end of a chain, just visible through the open top of his coat. His eyes had a glassy, big-pupiled look to them, and Greg wondered if the guy was stoned.

"Hey, man," the kid said again. "How many *babies* y'kill, huh?"

Greg was so taken aback by the question that he didn't have an immediate reply. What the *hell?* . . .

The kid's raincoat fell open, and a handmade sign slipped out from beneath, a white sheet of cardboard stapled to a length of plywood. PIGS OUT OF VIETNAM! was painted on it with bright red marker.

"Yah, pig! *Pig!*" another kid shouted nearby. He screwed up his face, then spat at Bill. The gobbet of mucus fell short, hitting the tarmac with a wet splat; a woman nearby waved a sign wildly back and forth. STOP THE MURDER OF CHILDREN! it said.

"Aw, shit!" Chief Ramsey said. "A fucking demonstration!"

"Make way, there!" Lieutenant Connolly bellowed up near the head of the line. "Make a hole!"

"Hey, babykiller!" the first bearded man bellowed again, leaning into Halstead's face.

"Get the fuck out of my way, asshole," Greg shouted back.

"Oh, tough pig!" the kid replied. "Hey, we got us a tough pig in a white suit, here!"

"Fuck the pigs!"

Signs danced and waved on every side. END THE WAR! STOP THE KILLING! G.I.S BUTCHER BABIES!

"Ho! Ho! Ho Chi Minh!" a girl who couldn't have been more than fifteen shouted, her voice nearly pitched to a squeak. "North Vietnam is gonna *win!*"

The chant was taken up by the rest of the demonstrators. *"Ho! Ho! Ho Chi Minh! North Vietnam is gonna win!"*

Greg could see the airport employee a few yards away, frantically talking to someone on a walkie-talkie. The demonstrators had closed in on every side, jostling the military men who'd already passed through the chain-link fence and making it impossible for the men still outside the gate, like Greg and Bill, to get through. He looked off to the left, trying to spot Pat and her redheaded friend, but he couldn't see either of them.

"Ho! Ho! Ho Chi Minh! North Vietnam is gonna win!"

Greg did see the little girl in the pink dress, however, standing in the crowd, finger in her mouth, crying. Her mother was several feet away, trying to reach her through the press of the crowd.

He pushed his way forward, squeezing through the gate. The shouting and noise were rising in both pitch and ferocity, and over it all, the demonstrators' chant continued like a political mantra.

"Ho! Ho! Ho Chi Minh! North Vietnam is gonna win!"

A tall, brawny demonstrator, a bearded man with a sign reading MAKE LOVE, NOT WAR, blocked his way. "Excuse me," Greg told him, reaching out with his left hand and gently cradling the demonstrator's right elbow. A very slight pressure, just so . . . and the man went to his knees, eyes bulging behind his wire-frame granny glasses. It wasn't quite a Star Trek nerve pinch, but it was damned near as effective. Greg shoved past the kneeling man before the guy could scream, scooped up the little girl, then shouldered his way through to the crying, desperate woman.

The Ho Chi Minh chant dissolved into random crowd noise, then reformed into something new. "*Baby* killers! *Baby* killers! *Baby* killers! . . ."

He handed the child to the mother, then turned to try to find Pat again. She'd been over here, somewhere. . . .

A line of police officers appeared out of the terminal building, some of them San Diego Police, others wearing the arm patches that identified them as airport security. They carried nightsticks but didn't seem ready to use them aggressively. For one thing, they were badly outnumbered by the demonstrators, and while there'd been no overt violence as yet, it could still erupt at any moment.

"Greg! Greg! Over here! Greg!"

He turned and spotted her, jumping up and down to make herself seen behind a throng of protesters and bewildered-looking civilians. "Pat!" He looked over his shoulder and saw Bill plowing toward him through the mob. He waited until Bill reached him, then started bulldozing his way toward Pat.

The police were wedging themselves into the mob, forming a double line, then pushing out to clear a corridor from the fence to the terminal for the homecoming vets. Lunging ahead, Greg caught Pat's hand and pulled her to him.

"Good to see you!" he shouted. "C'mon!"

"Wait!" Pat cried, turning away. "Wendy! Wendy! *This* way!"

A pretty, slender woman in a green dress, the redhead he'd glimpsed earlier, grabbed Pat's hand. Greg turned, grabbed Bill's hand, and nodded back the way they'd come, and the four of them, a human chain now with Bill in the lead, fought their way back toward the corridor cleared by the police. Shoving between two cops, they broke into the open once more.

"Extraction complete!" Bill yelled.

"I'd say it's time for a little E & E, Doc," Greg replied. "Let's get the hell out of Dodge!"

The protesters' chant had changed once again, orchestrated now by a skinny guy in an army jacket wielding a bullhorn. *"One! Two! Three! Four! We don't want your fucking war!"*

Ahead, a Marine scuffled with a protester as a cop tried to separate them. Chief Ramsey and Boomer Cain appeared to be stuffing a wildly thrashing demonstrator, head first, into a garbage dumpster on the far side of the mob, but it was a little hard to see. Something hurtled through the air and struck Greg hard in the left shoulder, then bounced to the street, shattering in tinkling brown shards. He whirled and saw the thrower cocking his arm to hurl another bottle from just the other side of the police line. He lunged forward.

"Easy, there, fella!" a San Diego police officer shouted as he tried to bull his way back into the crowd. "Just get the hell out of here, okay?"

"That son of a bitch threw a bottle at me!"

"Look, get the fuck out of here or I'll run you in!" the cop yelled back.

Greg blinked, and for one blind moment he nearly went for the cop's throat. Who was breaking the law here? He felt a hand on his shoulder. "C'mon, Twidge," Bill told him. "It's not worth it."

The bottle thrower had caught the look in Greg's eyes and was fading further back into the crowd. Hell, this was worse than fighting VC. Greg stepped back, then let Bill tug his arm and redirect him toward the terminal. Sirens wailed in the distance.

"One! Two! Three! Four! We don't want your fucking war! . . ."

Through the door and to the right, then up the stairs to the main terminal concourse, away from the press of the crowd. The four of them found a free spot tucked away just beyond a line of public telephones, near a broad window overlooking the near-riot outside. More police were arriving, and some of the demonstrators were scattering now, leaving homemade signs and flowers and Viet Cong flags trampled on the pavement.

Greg turned to say hello to his sister and was confronted by the spectacle of Pat and Bill Tangretti in a very close embrace. Awkwardly, he found himself facing Pat's friend.

"Uh . . . hello," he said. He stuck out his hand. "Greg Halstead."

"Wendy Frasier," she replied. She had very light skin with a dusting of freckles across her cheeks, and the deepest green eyes Greg had ever seen. "Pat's told me a lot about you. Welcome home."

"Thanks." He looked away, gazing down at the demonstration outside. A van with the logo for KSDL News had pulled up not far from the dumpster, where a protester was emerging from the garbage, and a man in a flak vest was filming the scene with a camera balanced on his shoulder. No doubt the airport riot would be on the evening news that night, billed as "a peaceful spontaneous demonstration," and never mind that homemade signs, raincoats, and bullhorns suggested something other than spontaneous . . . and that thrown bottles suggested something other than peaceful.

Yeah, he thought, bitterly. *Welcome home! . . .*

Chapter 8

Friday, 18 July 1969

San Diego Airport
1916 hours

"What are you doing here?" Bill Tangretti whispered, his hands cradling Pat's face.

She grinned mischievously, and her eyes were shining. "Are you sorry I came?"

"Hell, no! It's just . . . well, I mean, I know I . . . but I didn't know if you . . ." Damn it, why couldn't he say what he wanted to say? "How did you get here?"

"You remember me telling you about my roommate Wendy?"

He nodded, reveling in the feel of her arms around his neck. "Wendy, yeah. Your lab partner. You moved in with her after you ditched your activist friends." He ran a finger down the curve of her cheek. "Didn't you say she was working in San Francisco?"

"Mmm-hmm. Well, I managed to hornswoggle her into taking a day off and driving me down here to meet your plane."

"She drove you, huh?" *Transport! All right!* "So where is this angel of mercy? I've got to thank her."

Pat nodded, and Bill turned to see a tall redhead standing next to Greg. Not bad-looking, he supposed, if you liked that sort of coloring. He strode over and give her a big kiss full on the lips, then stepped back and bowed. "Madam, I am forever in your debt." Greg had a knowing grin on his face, and a sudden suspicion of Bill's was confirmed. "Twidge, you bastard, you knew all along, didn't you?"

"Well, I hardly think it strange that my own sister would confide in me, Doc," Greg said, putting a protective arm around Pat. "We're very close, you see."

"But you knew! And you didn't tell me? What kinda buddy are you?"

"Hey, man! She asked me not to."

"Enough, you guys!" Pat interrupted. "Let's go pick up your bags and get out of here. I imagine you two sailor boys wouldn't mind some genu-wine American food tonight?"

"Would we?" Greg said. "Visions are dancing in my head: steak, the biggest, thickest, rarest steak you can find, covered with mushrooms. Baked potato dripping with butter—"

"No, no, no, no, no," Bill said. "You got it all wrong, Twidge. It's chicken. Fried chicken. Deep batter fried chicken. A mountain of mashed potatoes and gravy."

"Come on, Wendy," Pat said. "Maybe if we head for baggage claim, they'll get the hint." The two women started down the corridor, and the men quickly followed.

Bill still couldn't get over his amazement at seeing Pat here, actually getting to look at her beautiful face, to *touch* her, after all these months of writing to her and dreaming about her. Oh, God, it felt so good to kiss her, to hold her.

It was a new feeling for Bill Tangretti. Unlike his older

brother—well, half brother, really . . . or stepbrother—Hank Richardson, Bill had never had much experience with girls. He hadn't gone on dates in high school, and despite three years in the Navy, he'd never gone farther than having a Vietnamese B-girl sit on his lap.

A strangled sound to his left brought his head around. It was Greg, sniggering. "All right, Twidge. What's so hysterical?" He tried to put an edge into his voice, but he was too damned happy to be really successful at it.

The other SEAL shrugged. "Just the sight of you floating down the corridor about three feet off the ground, that's all." He grinned. "Almost brings you up to my level, shrimp."

"Lucky for you I'm feeling so good right now, or I'd bust your arm off for that crack. You may outmass me, brother, but mass ain't everything."

"Brother, huh? Mmm. That sounds pretty good. Yup, I could go for you being my brother, all right. So when're you going to ask her?"

Bill suddenly felt uneasy. He was still dealing with the amazing realization that, well, that Pat seemed to really care for him, that the love he'd hoped he'd been reading in her letters was real. To go from there to a proposal, though, was a big leap. He watched her strolling ahead with her friend. *God,* she was beautiful from any direction.

Greg must have sensed his uncertainty. "Hey, what gives, Doc? You do still love her, don't you?"

"Hell, yes! Of course I love her. That hasn't changed."

"So what's the problem? If it's reciprocation you're worried about, forget it."

"What? She's been talking to you about it?"

"Well, I'll tell you, Doc. I'm very close to my sister. Her letters really helped me through some rough spots the last couple of years, especially during my first sea duty. But then the past six months I haven't been getting as many letters from her. And what letters I did get were all full of questions about this guy she met back over Christmas. And as for this stunt she pulled, getting down here to meet us? Well, that took some doing. She sure as hell wouldn't have driven five hundred miles just to see her brother a day or two early!"

Bill watched Pat laughing at something her friend said to her. She must have sensed him looking at her, because she turned and flashed a dazzling smile at him. Even at that distance, he could see the love in her eyes. "So, um, so you think she'd say yes?"

"Bill, my good man, I guarantee it. Hell, you're already part of the family. My mom writes to you as often as she writes to me. You might as well make it official."

Official. "Um, Twidge?"

"Yeah?"

"Is there a good jeweler in Jenner?"

Greg erupted in laughter, startling several passersby and stopping the girls in their tracks. Wendy turned to Pat. "Nice to see your sailor boys being so happy, isn't it, Pat?" she said.

"Care to let us in on the cause of your merriment, Greg?" Pat asked.

"Never you mind, sister dear," Greg said, grinning at Bill. "You'll find out soon enough. Right, Bill?"

"Right!"

The only thing Bill was worried about now was whether he could wait till they got to Jenner to pop the question.

Interstate 5 north
2337 hours

After dinner at an all-you-can-eat steakhouse, the four of them piled into the Chevy for the trip north. Pat had insisted on taking the first shift, since Wendy had had the last shift on the drive down from San Francisco, but after a couple of hours she'd been more than happy to hand the wheel over to her brother. Now she was happily snuggled with Bill in the backseat. Suddenly she giggled.

"What's so funny, sweetie?" Bill asked, lifting her chin with his hand. He ran a finger across her lips, and a shiver coursed through her body.

"I was just remembering the look on your face when you first saw me at the airport. Your eyes got *so* big."

Bill shrugged. "Well, I guess I was . . . a bit surprised."

"What's the matter? Don't you like surprises?"

The look in his eyes turned her bones to jelly. "This kind of surprise I like very much."

Something halfway between a snort and a cough brought

her head up. "Did you say something, Greg, or were you quietly strangling?"

"Sorry. I just . . . well, you were talking about surprises," Greg said in a harsh voice, "and I guess I was thinking about our 'surprise' reception back there at the airport."

Pat reached up and rested a hand on her brother's shoulder. "I'm sorry, Greg. Not a very nice welcome home, was it?"

"You're not kidding. You know, back when Dad was in, everyone agreed on who the enemy was. But now . . ." Greg shook his head.

"I know what you mean," Wendy said. "Nowadays it seems like it's the jerks who run off to Canada who are the heroes."

Pat heard the bitterness in her voice and knew she was thinking about Roger. In the rearview mirror, she also noticed Greg's startled glance over at Wendy. *Those two have a lot in common,* she thought. *Now if only I can get* them *to see it.*

"I believe that people have a right to disagree with our government's policy," Bill said. "But those idiots've got their stories all wrong. Hell, I don't know what the TV news has been showing back here, but *we're* not the ones who've been murdering babies!"

Bill's muscles tensed under Pat's fingers. "Did you see anything . . . like that when you were over there?" she asked.

There was a hardness on Bill's face that she had never seen before. "Yeah. I saw something."

"You don't want to know, Pat," Greg added. "Believe me."

From the tone of his voice, she knew Greg had seen the same thing, whatever it was. What horrors these men must have witnessed over there!

"What you did back there, Greg, picking up that little girl and getting her back to her mommy?" Wendy said. "That was great."

"Yeah. She's sure gonna have a great memory of the day her daddy came home!" Greg said.

"From this day forward, she's going to know that there are two kinds of people in the world. People like her daddy and that brave sailor who rescued her . . . and people like those assholes back there." Wendy laughed, but there was no humor in it. "That's a lesson some of us take years to learn."

"What worries me," Pat put in, "is the third kind of people. The ones who refuse to get involved, the ones who just don't care. They're the ones that scare me."

"You thinking about anybody in particular, Pat?" her brother asked.

She stopped and thought for a moment. "Yeah, I guess I am. I guess I was thinking about Andy."

Greg snorted. "Huh. That jerk you went with back at State?"

Pat could sense Bill looking at her. She hadn't told him about Andy, not because she was keeping secrets from him, but just because it hadn't been important. Andy was such a *child* compared to Bill. "Yeah. I think after you left for the Navy, I began looking for friends who weren't so . . . so *strident* as some of the people I'd been hanging out with before. Andy seemed like a refreshing change, more open-minded, more tolerant."

"But then something happened to change your mind about him?" Bill asked.

She reached up and stroked the line of his jaw. "I guess it started after Tet. Last year I mean. A bunch of us were watching Walter Cronkite's special on Vietnam, and it seemed like Andy would refuse to venture an opinion until he knew what everyone else thought. Kept asking everybody questions but never committing himself, you know what I mean?"

"He was a psych major, wasn't he?" Wendy put in.

"Yeah. It was like he was more interested in *why* I thought what I did than in what I actually thought. I guess I felt like he was trying to psychoanalyze me." She looked up at Bill and smiled. "Somehow I don't imagine you're all that thrilled to hear me talk about an old boyfriend."

"Just as long as he is an *old* boyfriend," Bill said in a low growl. " 'Cause otherwise I'd just have to beat the shit out of him."

Pat burst out laughing. One thing was for certain. *Apathetic* was a word she'd never have to apply to Bill! "Don't worry, darling. I stopped caring for him a long time ago."

Bill's voice was still low, but much softer, much gentler. "Darling. I like the sound of that."

"Do you?"

"Mmm-hmm. Darling. My darling Pat."

He ran his hand down her arm, carefully avoiding her breast, so she shifted her position slightly, making it clear that she welcomed his touch. She shivered as he caressed her breast through the thin fabric of her blouse. "Oh, Bill."

"Well, Wendy," Greg said in a loud voice. "With those two lovebirds billing and cooing back there in the backseat, it looks like it's up to us to keep the conversation rolling."

"Gee, Greg!" Wendy copied his tone. "I guess you're right. So what shall we talk about?"

"Pipe down up there, will ya!" Bill said. "You're disturbing the passengers."

Pat could see Greg's grin in the rearview mirror. She punched him in the shoulder. "Mind your own business, brother."

"Hey, no beating up on the driver!"

Wendy turned around and gave her a quizzical look with one eyebrow raised. Pat shook her head. "Wendy, just talk to Greg, okay? But quietly." Wendy cocked her head, but then she turned back to the front and started speaking to Greg in a low voice.

All through dinner Wendy had been giving her that same look, with the same eyebrow. It was good to know that her friend approved of Bill, but she wasn't going to let anybody pressure her. Besides, she wasn't about to make a pronouncement in the middle of a crowded restaurant. She wanted the timing to be perfect.

"I missed you so much, Pat," Bill whispered. "I thought about you a lot over there. Read your letters over and over again. And then it seemed like that damned plane ride would never end. I wanted to get out on the wings and push. And then I thought I was looking at another day or two before I could find transportation up to Jenner to see you. I was about going crazy. Wanting you so much."

"Well, now we have two whole weeks together. I may have to work at the store some, but Dad'll be good about giving me time off."

"Two weeks. Just two short weeks, and then it's back to Coronado, and five hundred miles away from you. I'm not sure how much of that I can take."

Suddenly the timing seemed perfect. And what better witnesses than her brother and her best friend? Pat cleared her throat noisily.

"Hey, pipe down back there, will ya? You're disturbing the driver!"

"Ladies and gentlemen, may I have your attention please?" Pat cried in a master of ceremonies voice.

"Don't you mean 'lady and gentlemen'?" Wendy asked. "Last time I looked, I was the only female type here except for you."

"Very well, then. Lady and gentlemen, may I have your attention please?"

Greg made a drum roll on the steering wheel. "Ta-dah! We're all ears, sis."

Pat pulled away from Bill and turned so she could hold his hands. "William Wallace Tangretti, will you marry me?"

Bill's jaw dropped, and his eyes grew wide. Greg burst out laughing. "Hey, sis, way to go! Looks like she one-upped you, Doc!"

Wendy turned around and grinned. "It's about time, Pat. What took you so long? Well, Bill? What's your answer? Come on, we haven't heard your answer yet."

"Hey, give me a moment to get my heart back where it belongs, okay? Yes, yes, *yes*, of *course*, yes. Pat, you wild, crazy woman, I was going to ask you! Just as soon as we got to Jenner and I could find a ring!"

"Well, you know these modern women, Bill," Wendy said. "Taking charge of their own lives."

"I like it. I definitely like it." Then he pulled Pat back into his arms. "In fact," he said in a softer voice, "I love it. I love you."

Gently he touched his lips to her neck, then worked his way around to the line of her jaw, her cheek, her mouth, lighting a fire deep within her. One hand pushed her skirt aside, caressing her thigh, and she felt a sudden desperate longing to be alone with him. She moved a hand down to test his readiness and felt him quiver. Moving her lips next to his ear, she whispered, "Don't you think it's time we found a motel?"

Startled, he pulled away and stared into her eyes, as if searching her heart. "Are you sure? 'Cause we can wait, if that's what you want. Are you really sure you want to do this?''

She nodded. "I love you, Bill, with all my heart. I want to love you with my body, too.''

He enfolded her in his arms again, and she could feel the beating of his heart. "Um, Twidge?" he said after a while. "I think you'd better find a motel real soon.''

The only response from the front seat was a long, low whistle.

Easy Rest Motel
2352 hours

Bill was still a bit dazed by all that had happened. Just five hours ago he'd been sitting on that charter, looking at at least a day before he could even see Pat, and probably two. Now here he was engaged to be married, and about to spend the night with the girl of his dreams.

"I must be dreaming," he said as he unlocked the door to 211.

Pat took his arm, and they walked into the room together. "If you are, then I'm dreaming the same dream.''

"Really, Pat? I mean, are you really sure you want to do this?''

Her face crinkled up in an amused grin. "You're not chickening out on me, are you, Bill? I thought SEALs were supposed to be brave.''

He dropped his duffel next to Pat's overnight and wrapped his arms around her. "Brave, huh? Well, I guess when it comes to jumping out of airplanes at thirty thousand feet or swimming ten miles in shark-infested waters or shooting it out in a firefight with a whole regiment of pissed-off VC, then, yeah, I guess we're brave.'' Pat began unbuttoning his shirt and running her fingers along his chest. "B-but when it comes to ensuring the happiness of the woman I love more than anything in the world, then I . . . I'm a real coward.''

She reached up and pulled his face down to hers. "Did anyone ever tell you you talk too much?''

His lips melted against hers, and he groaned with wanting her. As he moved his hands along her back, he found he'd pulled her blouse out of her skirt and was stroking her bare skin. Sliding up, he undid the clasp of her bra, then followed the curve of her body around to the soft, warm mound of her breast, feeling the nipple stiffen under his touch. "Oh, Pat, I love you so much," he murmured. "How can one guy be so lucky?"

"Pure, raw, natural talent, I guess," she said, unzipping his pants and sliding them off his hips, letting them fall to the floor. "Have you noticed, by the way, that I seem to have a lot more clothes on than you do?" Her hand stroked his remaining article of clothing, causing a sudden and violent response.

"Ah, yes. I . . . noticed."

"So what are you going to do about it?" She stopped stroking and stretched her arms out in a pose. "Take me, I'm yours."

"Pat." He took both her hands in his and kissed them. "Um, darling. I . . . I've never done this before."

Her eyes grew wide. "Come on, Bill, I know something about the reputation you SEALs have. Are you telling me you've never been with a woman before?"

"Hell, I never even had a girlfriend before!" His pants wrapped around his ankles, he shuffled over to the bed, so he could sit down and take his shoes off. "Girls wouldn't even look at me in high school. I was little and scrawny and always buried in my books."

She laughed. "You! Scrawny?" Kicking her shoes off, she walked over to the bed and began stroking his arms, his chest. "You call this scrawny?"

"I was before BUD/S." He undid her blouse and slid her bra straps off her shoulders. *God*, she was beautiful! "I almost didn't make it through SEAL training." He reached up to cup her breasts in his hands and gently massage them. "I guess by the time I got used to the idea that women didn't run screaming at the sight of me anymore, my platoon went overseas and I was medevacked out almost immediately." He eased the zipper on her skirt down and slid the skirt off her hips, caressing them lingeringly. "And then I went straight to Corps School, and, man, there ain't *nothing* a hospital corpsman doesn't know about venereal disease. After that bar girls couldn't tempt me." He pulled her close and took one nipple in his mouth, suckling it gently.

"You sure you've never done this before, Bill?" she asked, breathily. "You do it very . . . well."

He knelt down in front of her, stripping her panties off to reveal a triangular mound of curly blond hair. "You bring out the best in me, sweetheart." It was amazing, but all of a sudden he felt supremely confident.

"Mmm. I guess that means . . . I'm talented, too, huh?" She ran her fingers through his hair.

"It takes a lot of talent to bring a SEAL to his knees." He pulled back to look at her, standing fully naked in front of him. "You are so beautiful, Pat. You know, I dreamed about this, you and me together."

She smiled as she lay down on the bed. "Me too." She reached out her hands and drew him down on top of her. "Bill?" she murmured, her eyes closed.

"Hmm?"

"You talk too much."

And then neither of them said anything for a long time.

Chapter 9

Saturday, 20 September 1969

Jenner, California
1535 hours

"Will I do?"

Wendy Frasier put a hand to her chin and nodded thoughtfully. "Hmm. Let me see." She walked slowly around her friend, examining the long, white, satin gown from every angle. When she got around to the front again, she stopped and spread her hands wide. "Patricia Eleanor Halstead," she said, "you are magnificent!"

Pat flushed. "You think Bill will like it?"

"Pat, Bill wouldn't care if you wore faded blue jeans and a tie-dyed shirt to your wedding. I have never *seen* a man so lovestruck."

"Well, it's mutual."

Wendy sat down at the vanity and checked her hair. "You're very sure, aren't you?" she asked.

"About what?"

"That you're doing the right thing."

"Marrying Bill? Of course." Pat sounded puzzled.

Wendy turned around on the vanity bench and smiled. "Don't worry, Pat, I'm not suggesting that you shouldn't marry him or that the two of you won't be the happiest couple that ever lived. I guess what I mean is, well, I guess I'm envious in a way."

"Oh, yeah? Ya wanna fight me for him?" Pat dropped into a dangerous-looking stance, extending her hands menacingly out in front of her.

Wendy burst out laughing. The sight of her diminutive friend in a bridal gown assuming a martial arts position had her in hysterics. "What in the world is *that?*"

"*Hwrang-do,*" Pat said, relaxing her pose. "Bill's been teaching me. He says he can get me into a class when we get down to Coronado."

"You're going to learn rang—whatever you said?"

"Actually, it'll probably be Tae Kwon Do. There are more schools available. You know I've wanted to learn some kind of self-defense for a long time."

"Yeah. Especially since that time in San Francisco last Christmas when those punks jumped you." Bill had visited Greg's family over Christmas; that was when he and Pat had met. When Wendy got back to college after the Christmas break, Pat had told her what had happened.

The three of them had spent a night on the town before the guys had to take a bus back to San Diego, and they'd been walking along the street looking for a cab when five punks had emerged from an alley and had begun taunting them. Greg and Bill had tried to avoid trouble, but when the thugs approached with knives and broken bottles, threatening to kill the men and rape Pat, the two SEALs had gone into action. In three seconds it was all over, and two of the attackers were dead.

"How does it feel to be marrying someone who's so good at killing?" Wendy asked, then mentally kicked herself. "I'm sorry. I didn't—"

"No, it's a valid question, Wen." Pat pulled the chair out from her desk and sat down. "Dad and Grandpap were both in the service, but they were pharmacist's mates—that's what they called hospital corpsmen back then—so the question never came up for them. Bill and Greg are, quite frankly, trained killers, but killing isn't something they enjoy doing. It's a job. They do it when they have to." She smiled. "In any case, it's certainly nice to know that I never have to be afraid walking the streets at night with either of them."

Wendy grew thoughtful, wondering what it would be like to be involved with someone who confronted danger rather than running from it.

"So anyway, what's this about your wanting to take Bill away from me?" Pat said, with a twinkle in her eye.

"Nah. He's not my type. Too short."

Pat stuck out her tongue, and Wendy grinned.

"Seriously, though, I can't help being a little envious of what you two have together. You guys obviously love each other a lot, and you don't seem to have any doubts about each other. I guess it would just be nice to be so sure of . . . someone."

The thought of Roger didn't hurt quite as much as it used to, but Wendy was still fighting a sense that she was an idiot to have fallen for him in the first place, that she should have figured out earlier on what he was like.

"I wish you'd think about my idea of moving down to San Diego with us, Wen."

"Right. Leave my first job out of college after only three months? That would look just fine on my résumé, wouldn't it?"

"I'm really going to miss you."

"Well, damn it, I'm going to miss you, too. But I don't have parents or a husband to take care of me, Pat. I've got to do it myself." She saw a familiar look of pity creep onto Pat's face and hurried to redirect the conversation. "And don't you dare start in on Greg again."

"I didn't say a thing!"

"You were thinking it. I could hear you."

"I was not. But now that you mention it, what's wrong with Greg?"

"Not one damned thing, and you know it. He's devastatingly attractive, he's mature, responsible, funny, caring . . ." She broke off with a wry smile. "Not only that, he's actually tall enough for me."

"Hey, he sounds perfect for you."

Wendy nodded. "Well, maybe he is. But I'm not going to be able to find out, am I? Not with him down the other end of the state . . . when he's even *in* the States at all."

She suddenly realized that she was going to feel that five-hundred-mile separation more keenly for Greg than she was for his sister, and it shocked her. Ever since Bill and Greg had come back from Vietnam two months ago, Pat had been trying to maneuver Greg and her friend into a relationship together. Wendy had insisted that it was too soon after the Roger mess-up for her to even think about anybody else, but apparently her feelings weren't paying any attention to what she thought about the matter.

Pat had just walked over and put her hand on Wendy's shoulder when Ellie Halstead walked in. "Oh, Pat, dear," she said, "you look so lovely! And Wendy, that green sets off your complexion so nicely. You both are stunning."

"Thanks, Mom. Is it time?"

"Yes. Your father has the car warmed up and waiting. Oh, he's just so excited and nervous."

Pat laughed. "And you're not, of course."

Ellie gave her daughter a fond look. "I'm not the one who has to walk down the aisle with you. Now where's your bouquet?"

"I've got it, Mrs. Halstead." Wendy picked up the florist's box. "Come on, Pat. It's show time!"

The conversation had been taking an unexpected and not entirely welcome turn. Wendy was just as glad to move on to concerns about flowers and processionals and keeping time to the music as she walked down the aisle of Grace United Methodist. She barely noticed the details of the wedding service, she was so aware of Bill's best man, across the aisle from her.

The two SEALs were resplendent in their white dress uniforms, both wearing their brand-new second-class rank insignia on their left arms, both with their new Bronze Stars at the tops of their ribbon racks. Their promotions had come through at the same time, part of the fall promotion list, and both SEALs had received their Bronze Stars for the Ham Tam op at the same small ceremony in the office of the CO of SEAL One the week before. It was a nice touch, Wendy thought, coming just in time for the wedding.

Greg looked thoughtful and serious as he listened to the ceremony. Suddenly he turned his head and grinned at her, turning her knees unaccountably wobbly. Yes, she definitely could go for him in a big way . . . if only . . .

She thought back to the night Pat asked Bill to marry her. After the two lovebirds were ensconced in their motel room, Greg asked Wendy if she wanted to join him for a drink in the motel lounge. They'd talked for hours, which was idiotic, since she'd been up since 5:00, but Greg was a fascinating guy. He told her about leaving San Francisco State to join the Navy, though he didn't mention Marci. He told her about the humiliation of getting seasick on his first sea duty and the excitement he felt when he was accepted into the SEAL program. He told her about BUD/S training and about long ocean swims and about diving out of airplanes and about sneaking barefoot through the jungle. He told her how he'd met Bill and the scam Bill had pulled with the aspirin. He told her how much Pat's letters had meant to him when he was overseas and how glad he was that his sister and his best friend had hit it off.

And somewhere in there she'd begun telling him about herself. About her wonderful father and how much she'd adored him. About her lovely but weak mother who'd had a nervous breakdown when Dad had died. About the . . . man her mother had married when she was twelve. She didn't tell Greg why she hated her stepfather, just that she no longer had anything to do with that branch of the family. That was why she'd picked SFSU, instead of a college back East, to be as far away from them as possible.

She told him about how lonely it had been at college, not knowing anyone and not having any time for parties. She'd worked two jobs during the school year to help pay for tuition, plus full-time summers, but even so she was looking at several years before she could pay off her student loans. She

talked about meeting Pat and how much her friendship meant.
Pat was probably the first person she'd opened up to since
junior high.

By the time she'd realized that she was going to fall asleep
at the table if she didn't get out of that lounge and into a bed,
she'd been well on her way to being hooked. She'd considered inviting him to her room but finally decided that she was
too tired to think straight. After a good night's sleep, she'd
congratulated herself for her restraint. It just didn't make any
sense to get involved in a relationship that didn't have a
chance of going anywhere.

As long as she kept telling herself that, she'd be okay.

A sudden flourish on the organ jolted her out of her reverie.
It was over. Pat and Bill were marching down the aisle, and
Greg was holding out his arm for her. By the time they'd
followed the newlyweds out of the church and into the fellowship hall for the reception, she'd managed to get her knees
under control again.

Stupid, stupid, stupid, she thought. After today she probably wouldn't ever see the man again. *Just relax and enjoy the
party, girl,* she told herself firmly. Suddenly she burst out
laughing.

"What's so funny?" Greg asked, looking down at her with
those gorgeous blue-gray eyes.

She shook her head. "Nothing. Just a . . . private joke."
She couldn't tell him what she'd just realized, that in falling
so hard for Greg, she'd managed to completely forget about
Roger.

She wondered if Greg still thought about Marci.

Greg Halstead looked down at the girl at his side and wondered what she was thinking about . . . or who. That night
back in July when they'd stayed up talking for hours in the
motel lounge, he'd thought they'd had something going between them, but then she'd seemed to cool toward him over
the weekend. While obviously not telling everything she
knew, Pat let slip that Wendy had been involved with a guy
who'd dumped her, implying that she was still kind of broken
up about it. Greg's muscles tensed, thinking about it. He'd
like to find that guy, whoever he was, and push his face in.

He laughed. That was a pretty strong reaction. Was he really that far gone over Wendy? He hardly knew her, and she certainly hadn't been encouraging him, at least, not since that first night. He did know he'd like to know her better.

"Now you've got one, too." Wendy's eyes crinkled delightfully when she grinned.

"One what?"

"Private joke."

"Ah. Yes, well, maybe I'll tell you about it once we're done with this receiving line."

They spent the next ten or twenty minutes standing in line next to the bride and groom, shaking hands with all the guests and enduring all the well-meant comments from his parents' friends about what a lovely couple the two of them made and whether wedding bells would be ringing again soon. The Whitmans were especially bad, with Mrs. Whitman making pointed references to the fact that he used to go out with her daughter Kathy. Kathy's expression was a cross between wistful and jealous. He wondered what Wendy was making of all this.

Eventually the last of the guests had funneled through. The band started playing, and Doc and Pat took the floor for the first dance, followed shortly by his parents. Then the two couples exchanged partners, and after that the dance floor began to fill up.

"Look, Wendy, I'm really sorry about all the comments . . ."

"Well, what did you expect? Best man, maid of honor . . . it's inevitable."

"Inevitable, huh?"

She looked at him sternly. "The talk, I mean."

"Ah. Okay, so what would you like now? Champagne? Food? Dance? Fresh air?"

"Well, I always wondered what a dancing SEAL looked like," she said, "but how about some champagne first. I've decided I'm going to enjoy this party."

"Great." He wished he could tell what she was thinking. That last comment of hers had sounded almost desperate.

They found a table off in a corner. Wendy took the glass he offered her and took several large sips. He didn't like champagne much, but he drank a little.

"Nothing like champagne to make a party, right?" She

raised her glass and smiled. "Now what about that private joke of yours?"

Maybe another sip or two. "Okay. Well, I was just . . . Pat told me, she said that you'd been going with a guy and she didn't say much about it, just that he'd dumped you and—"

"And you think that's funny, huh?" Her mouth tightened and her eyes grew cold.

"Shit, no." Damn it, he was saying this all wrong. He rested his hand on hers. She twitched, but she didn't move away. "No, what was funny was my reaction. Every time I think about that guy and how he must've hurt you, I just want to find him and punch his lights out."

You've got to be kidding, was what her expression said.

"Honest. I hardly know you, but I know I couldn't stand the thought of you hurting."

"That's . . . kind of you."

"Kind? Kind is what I am to my mother or to Pat or to Mrs. Whitman or to little old ladies crossing the street. Not to you."

"Just what are you saying, Greg?"

He let out a deep breath. He wasn't exactly sure. Maybe he'd find out as the words came out.

"I'm saying that I think you're a very special person and I'd like to get to know you better. I thought at first that you felt the same way about me, but then you seemed to change your mind. I figured it was probably because of that guy . . ." Something in her expression made him stop. "What?"

"I think it's time for me to share my private joke," she said.

"If you want to."

"A little more bottled courage first." She finished off the glass of champagne. "What I was laughing about earlier was, I realized that since I met you, I've almost forgotten about Roger."

Suddenly he was determined to turn that "almost" into a "completely." He got up and took Wendy's hand. "I think it's time for that dance now."

Just as they reached the dance floor, the band switched to a slow dance. *Perfect!* He held her close, and she rested her head on his shoulder. He reveled in the feel of her in his arms, the scent of her hair. After a while she lifted her head and smiled at him. *God, those eyes!*

"This is nice," she said.

"Nice. Nice? This is a hell of a lot better than nice." He suddenly had a feeling he was going to be riding the bus between San Diego and San Francisco a lot this winter. Then he felt a hand on his shoulder.

"You can't hog all the pretty girls for yourself, son. Let your old man have a turn."

"You're not old, Mr. Halstead. Anyway, I like mature men."

David Halstead laughed as he swept Wendy into an expert fox trot. Greg watched the two of them from the edge of the dance floor, occasionally catching Wendy's eye.

"You're looking somewhat forlorn, brother mine. Aren't you going to dance with the bride?"

He turned and grinned at his kid sister. "Aye-aye, ma'am. Duty calls, and I obey."

Pat punched him playfully on the shoulder. "Think you can bear up under the strain?"

"I'll manage," he said, swinging her onto the floor. "Hey, sis?"

"Yeah?"

"You have any idea what Wendy thinks of me?"

"I noticed you two seemed to be, ah, having a good time this afternoon." Her eyes twinkled. "Well, let me see what it was she said about you. We were talking about you back at the house."

"I always wondered what it was girls talked about when they got together."

"You'll never really know the gruesome details, brother dear. Just the few snippets we deign to let you in on. So where was I? Ah, yes. Wendy. Well, I believe 'devastatingly attractive' was one phrase she used."

Greg looked at Pat sharply to see if she was kidding him. He'd never thought of himself as particularly good-looking.

"Oh, and she likes your being tall enough for her."

"Well, I'm glad to know I don't have to go buy elevator shoes." He tried to make it a joke, but it came out sounding bitter.

"What's the problem, Greg?"

"It's . . . I guess it's just that I can't tell where I stand with her. That first night we hit it off great. But then she got all frosty on me. And now today she's warming up again. I suppose I'm afraid she'll get turned off again, and I don't know what I can do to make sure she doesn't."

Pat was silent for a moment. "Wendy's had a rough time, Greg."

"You told me about Roger."

Pat's eyes showed surprise. "So she told you his name. That's progress. But no, I meant more than that. Going way back. She's always been a bit prickly. Like she doesn't dare trust people. But when she falls, she falls hard."

"So she's scared of falling for me and getting betrayed again, is that it?"

"Bingo. I think if you weren't stationed five hundred miles away, you'd have a better chance."

"Hey, I'm not afraid of an all-night bus ride."

"Just make sure she knows that, okay? I've been trying to persuade her to move down to San Diego, but so far no go. Maybe you'll have better luck. I'm rooting for you, bro."

"Thanks, sis."

When the music stopped, he went looking for Wendy. He spotted her dancing with Grandpap and was about to go cut in when he was waylaid by his mother, who had about a dozen people she wanted to introduce him to. He smiled and made polite chitchat, but he kept his eyes out for a flash of red hair above a green dress. Finally he was able to make good his escape, and then it was time to cut the cake. He grabbed two plates and heard her voice behind him.

"Hungry, sailor?"

He whirled, almost dumping the cake on the ground. "Not really, but I thought you might be. You want to get us something to drink?"

She nodded. "I'll make it Cokes this time, though. I think I've had enough champagne."

They wound their way between the tables, aiming for one in the corner. People kept stopping them, telling Greg what a beautiful bride his sister made, how handsome he and Bill looked in their uniforms, how proud the town was of him, not like that awful Robbie Andrews.

"Phew!" he said as they finally sat down. "I'd sooner face

a company of VC than run that gauntlet again.''

"I think it's wonderful that so many people here know you and wish you well.''

"It's because of Dad, really, and Grandpap. Halstead Drugs is an institution in this town.''

Wendy picked at her cake, taking small bites and chewing thoughtfully. "Who was Robbie Andrews?''

Greg looked around carefully, making sure Robbie's parents weren't within earshot. He kept his voice low. "He was . . . it wasn't Pat's class he was in at Jenner High, must have been a class below, maybe two. Seemed like a nice, ordinary kid. Then he went to college, flunked out, and ran off to Canada. Wrote his folks a nasty letter, in effect disowning them because they supported the war.'' He stopped at the stricken look on Wendy's face. "Wendy, what is it?''

"Roger,'' she whispered. "That's what Roger did. The day after we graduated, he told me he was going to Canada. Asked me to join him. We had a horrible fight. He said some . . . some awful things.'' Her voice cracked.

Greg quickly moved his chair around next to hers, and when he reached out to touch her, she leaned over into his arms and began sobbing. He held her gently, stroking her hair. All too quickly she pulled away, mopping her face with a napkin.

"I'm sorry.'' Her voice was muffled behind the napkin.

"I'm not,'' he said. "I'm glad you told me.''

"I'm so embarrassed.''

"Hey, what's to be embarrassed about? All maids of honor cry at their best friends' weddings. It's part of the job description.''

"You're very kind.''

"Oh, no, not that word again. Listen, Wendy, what do I have to do to convince you that I'm not being 'kind' when I say that I enjoy being with you, that I want to spend more time with you, that I want to see you happy?'' With one finger he traced the path of a tear along her cheek, then moved his hand along the line of her jaw and around to the back of her neck. Lowering his head, he pulled her to him for a long, gentle kiss.

"How about let's go for a walk?'' he asked when they finally broke apart.

She nodded.

They walked down Church Street all the way to the river, holding hands and talking. Something seemed to have broken loose in Wendy, and she talked nonstop about Roger. Greg didn't particularly enjoy hearing about the guy, but he sensed she needed to get it out. When she finished, he told her about Marci.

"So when I first told her I was dropping out of college, she assumed that I was running off to Canada. Then when she realized I was planning to enlist, planning to—what was it she said?—join the military-industrial complex, she turned vicious."

"Like Roger."

He looked down at her walking next to him. The edge that had always been in her voice before whenever she'd mentioned his name wasn't there anymore. "Yeah. Like Roger."

What Pat had said, about Wendy being prickly and not trusting people, resurfaced in his mind. He would have to move slowly and carefully, he knew that, but she seemed to be cautiously letting him inside her fence. Stopping, he raised a hand to stroke her hair. She was so exciting, so *alive*. He was already halfway to being in love with her. He chuckled.

"What?" Wendy looked up at him curiously.

"Oh, I was just thinking about how much time I'm going to be spending on Greyhound buses from now on. Probably every weekend I have off, I'll be riding up to San Francisco."

"You will, huh?"

"Mmm-hmm. If you don't object, that is." He bent down to take her mouth in his.

"I don't object," she murmured against his lips. She slid her arms up his chest and around his neck, holding him tight.

The only thing he was wondering now was how many bus trips it would take before he could convince her to move down to San Diego.

Chapter 10

Thursday, 12 March 1970

Off Sihanoukville, Cambodia
0120 hours

Lieutenant j.g. David R. Nolan didn't look like a SEAL, and he was not wearing panty hose beneath his trousers. For this night's op, he was wearing peasant's garb, the traditional "black pajamas" worn by most rural Vietnamese . . . and by the Viet Cong. He wore a black, floppy boonie hat on his head, and slung from his right shoulder was a ChiCom-manufactured AK-47. His face was blackened with grease paint to cut down reflective shine off his face, but from a distance, especially given the fact that Nolan was fairly short, he looked exactly like Charlie himself.

He was crouched in the stern of a low-slung native-built sampan, steering with gentle pressure to the tiller of an ancient, Evenrude outboard motor salvaged in ages past from God-knew-where. In the sampan's bow, fellow SEAL QM1 Mark Ringold was also wearing black pajamas with an AK-47 as matching accessory and a flat, conical "coolie hat" covering his yellow hair. Between them, in the middle of the boat, two LDNNs in black garb completed the picture of four Viet Cong slipping back north past the border after an infiltration run into the south. With the exception of the "deep-six locker" amidships, all four were traveling sterile. There was nothing on any of them, not even a dog tag, that would connect them with either the United States or the government of South Vietnam. Clothing and weapons had been liberated from captured VC who would no longer be needing them. Special equipment that ordinary Vietnamese would not be expected to carry was stowed inside the locker; if capture seemed likely, specially placed scuttle charges would send the sampan to the bottom in seconds.

They were now well inside Cambodia's territorial waters. They'd not made the entire voyage from the waters of South Vietnam in the sampan, of course. That would have invited interception by anyone from Cambodian patrol boats to Viet Cong to pirates, and the sampan, with only inches of freeboard, was not exactly a seaworthy craft.

Instead, they'd come north in a junk belonging to the South Vietnamese Navy. The skipper had brought them as far inside the twelve-mile territorial limit imposed by the Cambodian government as he dared; then, shortly before midnight, they'd lowered the sampan and their equipment over the side, clambered aboard, and continued the rest of the voyage on their own. The sampan, identical to thousands of similar craft plying this coast, was too low to the water to be detected by even the best radar, and it was a near-certainty that the Cambodians were turning a blind eye to illicit traffic in this region.

That, after all, was one of the things Nolan and his three piratical teammates were here to check.

In recent months, America's attention had been drawn more and more to Cambodia, that ancient kingdom lying directly north of South Vietnam's vital and vulnerable Mekong Delta, as well as Saigon itself. Everyone knew that the North Vietnamese had been funneling supplies south to the Viet Cong through Laos and Cambodia; the Ho Chi Minh Trail—in reality a vast complex of intertwining roads and trails—followed the Vietnamese border all the way from well above the Demilitarized Zone to the rice paddies and forests west of the Mekong River, and uncounted thousands of tons of supplies flowed south along that highway each month. For too long, political considerations—in particular, Washington's fear of the growing antiwar protest movement at home—had prohibited the military forces of America and her allies from crossing the border into Cambodia, where the NVA had set up hundreds of way stations, rest camps, training centers, and supply dumps and caches, and where the almost mythical COSVN, the Central Office for South Vietnam—a kind of Communist Pentagon hidden somewhere in the jungle and thought to be directing all NVA and VC activity inside South Vietnam—was believed to reside.

Nolan reflected on the new turn the war in Southeast Asia had been taking of late. By the end of 1969, President Nixon had made good on his campaign promise to begin troop withdrawals from South Vietnam; some 115,000 troops had been pulled out, down from the over half a million men in-country the previous January. Covert bombing of Cambodia, under the code name Operation Menu, had been resumed in March of 1969. There were rumors of secret air attacks in Laos, as well. The on-again, off-again bombing of North Vietnam had been resumed as well, and Nixon had recently predicted peace within three years.

This, despite the fact that the Paris Peace Talks had so far accomplished little beyond agreeing on a shape for the meeting table.

But while Operation Menu was a step in the right direction so far as Nolan and most SEALs he knew were concerned, ground forces were strictly forbidden from crossing the line. It was like Korea all over again.

David Nolan had been just five when the Korean War had begun, but his father, a colonel in the U.S. Marine Corps, had told him plenty of stories. During that bloody little "police action," as it had been euphemistically known, American aircraft had been forbidden to cross the Yalu River—North Korea's border with Communist China—even when in hot pursuit of enemy aircraft, and even after massive numbers of Chinese "volunteers" had begun flooding south, bringing China into the war against the UN forces in Korea. Airfields, supply depots, and sanctuaries used by Chinese and North Korean forces north of the river were off-limits; at the height of this silliness, American aviators were ordered to bomb only the *south* half of the bridges across the Yalu, and only by flying *along* the river rather than across it—a tactic guaranteed to take the aviators through the heaviest concentrations of antiaircraft fire.

The Cambodian border was nothing but a replay of the Yalu River, or so it seemed to the American troops who could do nothing to halt the incoming tide of fresh troops, ammo, and supplies from the north. More and more frequently, the protest was heard from the ranks: "They're not letting us *win* this damned war. . . ."

That wasn't to say that SEALs hadn't been across the line. The first excursion that Nolan knew of personally had been made in 1968 by a couple of SEALs in Team Two. Lieutenant Daniel Mariacher, whom Nolan had met, and a TM2 Hank Richardson, whom he had not, had been working out of Chau Doc just south of the line, during the Tet Offensive. In mid-February, they'd slipped across the border far enough to observe traffic coming down the highway on the way to Sihanoukville and raided an enemy support base for hard intel. The intelligence they'd secured indicated that some, at least, of the supplies coming down from the north were not coming straight across the border but were being loaded onto ships at Cambodia's main port on the Gulf of Thailand, then dropped off at various points along the Vietnamese coast.

In a way, Mariacher's impromptu two-man invasion of Cambodia had prompted tonight's op, and probably a number of others of which, for reasons of security, Nolan was unaware. American interest in Cambodia had reached a fevered pitch during the past few weeks, and there were numerous ongoing rumors of a U.S.–South Vietnamese invasion sometime in the near future.

It would be about fucking time, Nolan thought. It was possible—he didn't know, since he didn't have a need to know—that this mission tonight, which Navy Special Warfare Group–Vietnam had given top priority, was a part of the prelude to the invasion. He hoped so.

Whatever the mission's importance, it was a welcome break indeed from routine. Nolan had arrived in Vietnam five months ago, as part of SEAL Team Two's operational deployment in-country. His platoon was operating as part of SEALORDS out of the Ca Mau Peninsula and in the adjacent U Minh Forest. Earlier in the war, SEALs had been assigned to the Rung Sat Special Zone, just south of Saigon and embracing the waterways leading to that city from the South China Sea. The U Minh Forest was similar in many respects to the Rung Sat "Forest of Assassins," a tangled, inhospitable area in which Charlie had entrenched himself and in which conventional forces were all but helpless. Before the VC, the area had been a stronghold of the Viet Minh. SEALs liked to circulate the story of a crack French paratrooper regiment that had entered the U Minh back in the early fifties. After a few confused radio calls for help, there'd been no further word . . . and none of those men had been seen again.

Since SEAL Two had started operating in the region, however, the tables were finally being turned against the U Minh's inhabitants. The VC hidden there were finding that the Men With Green Faces were even more adept at jungle fighting, ambushes, and silent night ops than they, and more and more were coming out of the forest to take advantage of Saigon's *Chieu Hoi* amnesty program.

Still, operations in the U Minh had become a wearing and deadly routine of insertion, patrol, ambush, and extraction, and Nolan was delighted when the head Navy Intelligence Liaison Officer with SEALORDS had come to him with the offer of a special assignment, one that would take him out of South Vietnam, one that might, the NILO had said, make a tremendous difference in the war.

Not until he'd agreed to volunteer for the mission was he told that his objective was Sihanoukville, in Cambodia.

This was Nolan's second attempt at the infiltration. Two weeks ago, he'd led an entire squad of SEALs and LDNNs ashore near Kâmpôt, a nothing of a village seventy-five miles down the coast from Sihanoukville. The idea had been to move overland down the peninsula to the hills overlooking the port area, but there'd been such heavy traffic on the road that Nolan had been forced to abort the mission and order a withdrawal. During the following week, plans had been drawn up to move the USS *Marshall* into the area, together with a couple of SDVs carried in shelters on the *Marshall*'s afterdeck. The idea was for the *Marshall* to carry them in close to the mouth of the Sihanoukville Harbor, so that the SCUBA-equipped SEALs could lock out underwater, board the SEAL Delivery Vehicles, and ride them the final few miles to their destination.

That plan, though, had been called off when someone higher up the chain of command had gotten cold feet. The gulf waters in that area were shallow, and Washington distinctly did not need a U.S. submarine on an obviously clandestine mission going aground inside Cambodian waters now.

Finally, though, Nolan had submitted his own plan. Two

SEALs and a couple of LDNNs, he contended, were all that were necessary—or desirable—to slip into Sihanoukville. More men would just attract unwanted attention.

The plan did not at first win complete acceptance from his superiors at NAVSPECWARGRU-SV headquarters, in Saigon. The Navy Special Warfare people didn't want to deploy only four men. "You're always taking unacceptable risks, Lieutenant," Commander Vince Hawkings, the current SEAL Team CO in Vietnam, had told him. "Suppose you run into something out there that you can't handle?"

"I don't intend to do that, sir," Nolan had replied with a grin. "That would be stupid."

"Mmm. That it would be," Hawkings had replied, looking the younger officer up and down. "You have quite a history of this sort of thing, don't you?"

"I get the job done. Sir."

Nolan had been called on the carpet more than once thus far in his first Vietnam deployment. One of his personal fitness reports described him as a lone wolf, with a tendency to go it alone. Entries like that did not do a naval officer's career any good.

But, damn it, there were times when a few men—or one man, well equipped and well prepared—could do what an entire squad or platoon could not. He'd proved that already, by slipping into places and carrying out missions that had been too much for a traditional SEAL squad.

Perhaps it was the success he'd had already that finally brought official approval to his version of the operations plan, with only a few last-minute touches from Navy Intelligence.

And tonight, finally, they were carrying it out.

Ahead, Nolan could see the sky glow from the lights of the port. Indeed, the glow had been faintly visible far out at sea, when the Vietnamese trawler had put them over the side. Now, though, it was possible to see the black loom of the harbor's southern headland just ahead, backlit by the glow of the harbor lights. Pulling slightly on the tiller, he adjusted their course, angling toward the headland. He'd carefully memorized maps and high-altitude reconnaissance photos of these waters during the past few days and, from the outline of the hill, knew precisely where he was. There was no sign of patrol boats or of sentries on the coast. If there were any, they would probably turn a deliberately blind eye to the activities of a lone sampan occupied by four Viet Cong. That was the reason for the disguises.

Technically, of course, Cambodia was neutral in the war in Southeast Asia. The country was ruled by Prince Norodom Sihanouk, a remarkable man who, in 1945 at the age of nineteen, had been placed on the throne by the French, who'd expected him to be an easily handled puppet. In 1953, the puppet had cut the strings, however, when he'd ordered the French out, then stepped down as ruler in order to run in public elections.

Winning easily, Sihanouk had since then steered Cambodia through the gathering storm by proclaiming his neutrality and favoring everybody; he was as likely to accept aid and advisors from the People's Republic of China or the Soviet Union as he was from France or the United States. He did not seem able, however, to keep the North Vietnamese from using the eastern and southern frontiers of his country as a highway south; infiltration continued despite the bombing, and most military experts felt the only way to shut off the pipeline was to go in on the ground and take it by force.

There were some, within the U.S. intelligence community in South Vietnam, who hinted darkly that Sihanouk might not be able to hold onto his throne for very much longer. A pro-American government in Phnom Penh might give Washington the leverage it needed to smash the NVA pipeline once and for all.

None of that was of immediate concern to Nolan and his small team, though he'd been studying the political background of the area while working out an operational plan. He just needed to know what he was likely to face in the way of guard boats or hostile patrols.

Of course, there were no guarantees. There never were.

There was little surf off the Gulf of Thailand; the water was warm and clear. When they were fifty yards off the shore, he throttled the engine down to a soft mutter, and Ringold, after giving a thumbs-up, silently rolled over the side and into the water with scarcely a ripple to mark his passage. For the next thirty minutes, Nolan waited in the sampan with the two LDNNs, Phan Chi Binh and Hyunh Van Thanh, bobbing uncomfortably in the gentle swell.

At last, a red light winked against the black of the headland, once . . . twice, then three times in rapid succession. Nolan throttled up the outboard, swung the sampan's prow toward the coastline, and took them in the rest of the way.

He ran the sampan into a shallow and well-sheltered inlet, dragging it ashore once the bottom hit sand. Ringold emerged from the dense vegetation, AK-47 in hand, and helped haul the boat from the water. Breaking open the deep-six locker, Nolan extracted a waterproof case, which he slung over his shoulder, and then the four SEALs hid the sampan under a pile of palm fronds and dead vegetation.

Using hand signals, Nolan told Ringold and Phan to stay put, guarding the sampan. He would make the initial sneak-and-peak with Hyunh.

Silently, they moved up away from the beach and into the forest, climbing ground that grew rapidly steeper. The last twenty feet were almost vertical up a sheer rock face, but there were plenty of crevices and easy hand- and footholds for the ascent. Hyunh rolled over the top first, checked the area out, then waved Nolan up. The top of the headland was bare of trees, but there were plenty of large boulders scattered about to provide excellent cover.

From here, some fifty feet above the water, they had an excellent view north into Sihanoukville.

Carefully, Nolan opened the large, watertight case and pulled out his camera, a specially made Hasselblad with a telescopic lens extension as big as a man's head—in fact, a small telescope. Screwing the scope on the short tripod mounting and setting it upright, he attached the camera to the objective lens receiver, then sighted through the finder at the dockside perhaps a mile away.

A number of ships were in the harbor, but Nolan was most interested in a small and decrepit rustbucket somewhat apart from the others, on the south side of the waterfront. The name painted across her transom in both English and Chinese characters was *Danlin*, and the home port was listed as Shanghai. She was a small vessel, sixty meters long overall, with a total displacement of perhaps 1,200 tons. She had a single deckhouse, far aft, and a thick mast and cargo boom mounted amidships. Two 37mm antiaircraft guns were mounted on her decks, one forward, one aft. She would have, Nolan knew from his research, a 600-horsepower diesel engine with a single screw, a cargo capacity of 600 tons, and a top speed of perhaps nine knots. The red banner of the People's Republic of China hung from her taffrail flagstaff.

The *Danlin* was pulled up snug against the dock, port side to. The harbor area was ablaze with light, both from streetlights ashore and from spotlights mounted on the ships. In the glare, he could easily make out men's faces on the waterfront. Rapidly, he began taking pictures, shooting cargo stacked on the wharf, men working on the dockside, and the ship itself.

Interesting. A number of the people on the dock were clearly Cambodian military officers, judging by their khaki uniforms, including one high-ranking officer. But there were others in North Vietnamese Army uniforms, and the deckhands aboard the Chinese ship had the carriage, the discipline of movement, the *look* of military men.

No surprises there.

The dockside was piled high with cargo; Russian Zil trucks were lined up in the shadows between the warehouses beyond the waterfront, suggesting a considerable stockpile of supplies. It looked like several ships had off-loaded their wares here before the *Danlin*.

And they were doing it almost openly, apparently under the protection of Cambodian troops. They were swaying a stack of crates—they looked like ammunition crates—out of the freighter now, hauling them up in a cargo net suspended from the ship's boom.

He wondered if Prince Sihanouk knew what was going on here. Probably not, he decided. The Khmer Rouge Communist rebels fighting against the Phnom Penh regime were being secretly supplied by the North Vietnamese and probably the Chinese as well; he doubted that Sihanouk had knowingly entered into an alliance with Hanoi.

Nolan kept taking pictures, zooming in on faces where possible, documenting the activities on the wharf. Likely, what he was seeing had nothing to do with official government policy. Sihanouk's government was as corrupt as the Saigon regime, perhaps more so, if that were possible, and there were certainly antigovernment factions within both the military and within the civilian government structure. It was not at all un-

likely that the North Vietnamese had found some willing ac-
complices in the Cambodian Army: that general, there, for
instance, strutting around in his gold braid, peaked cap, and—
despite the fact that it was the middle of the night—aviator's
sunglasses. Possibly the local civil authorities had been in-
duced through bribes or intimidation to ignore what was happening here. Perhaps that general commanded this military
district. Either way, he'd apparently managed to control this
end of the Sihanoukville waterfront at least and was allowing
military supplies to be off-loaded from a Chinese ship in the
middle of the night. From here, no doubt, those supplies
would make their way east and then south, passing the border
into South Vietnam at dozens of different points. There were
some in Navy Intelligence, Nolan knew, who'd long been
arguing that more arms and military supplies reached the
Communists in the south this way than overland.

Finally, the SEALs had all of the pictures they could use.
After removing the film and sealing it in a separate waterproof
canister, Nolan repacked the camera, signaled Hyunh, and the
two started back down the hillside to the inlet where they'd
left Ringold and Phan.

The dockside at Sihanoukville
0235 hours

Colonel Dimitri Pavlovich Kartashkin stood on the dock,
smoking a cigarette and studying the harbor of Sihanoukville.
For so vital a seaport, the Cambodians had little in the way
of serious defenses; the city could be overrun easily, by attack
from either sea or land. Until recently he'd doubted that the
Americans would risk such an adventurist gamble. They had
the military might, yes, but they simply did not have the political will to act. The latest intelligence reports, however,
suggested that the political situation might well be changing.

"When the attack comes," he said to his companion,
speaking Vietnamese, "you will have to suspend your activities here. At least for a time."

General Hong Chu Minh gave the Russian a surprised look.
"The Americans would not dare attack Cambodia's largest
port!" he said, echoing Kartashkin's own thoughts on the
matter.

"Overtly, no," Kartashkin said. He drew hard on his cigarette, one of the hoarded last of the acrid Turkish brand that was his favorite. "They would not risk upsetting world opinion. But you can be sure that this port will be flooded with their agents . . . possibly even with commandos, operating in secret. They could arrive openly by plane or ship." He pointed into the darkness toward the southwest, where the headland sheltering that arm of the harbor could just be made out against the starlit night. "Or they could come as swimmers or in small boats."

"Commandos," Hong said, spitting the word. "Their Army Special Forces? Green Berets? We can handle *them*. The Americans are bungling children, chasing our forces from ambush to ambush and never finding them."

"Do not underestimate the American Special Forces, comrade, and never confuse them with regular army units made up of unwilling draftees. Training standards and qualifications for their Green Berets have slipped some in recent years, it is true, but they are still a dangerous force. And . . . there are other groups, more secret, and perhaps more skilled in the arts of covert warfare."

"What units?"

Kartashkin regarded the sea a moment longer before answering. "I was thinking of their Men With Green Faces."

Briefly, the color drained from Hong's face, giving him an unhealthy pallor beneath the dockside lights. "What . . . them? Stories invented by frightened cowards. Or by counterrevolutionaries hoping to shake the Marxist fervor of our men."

"Not true, General," Kartashkin replied. "I have studied the American naval commandos closely. I have read reports . . . and seen photographs." There had also been that article in *Male* magazine, though it was maddening how little of substance it had managed to convey. "They are secretive, and it is difficult to learn much of use about them, but they *do* exist. They fight the National Liberation Front with the Front's own tactics, striking at night, spreading terror and confusion wherever they operate. You have seen too many reports of their activities, General, many of them from my department, to believe that they are fabrications."

"No," Hong said. He exhaled softly. "No. They are not
... *total* fabrications."

Kartashkin allowed Hong his small, face-saving reserva-
tion. He smiled. "My sources are excellent and well-
confirmed, General. Within a few weeks, the Americans will
invade Cambodia in an effort to shut down what they call the
Ho Chi Minh Trail."

Chapter 11

Thursday, 12 March 1970

Southwest of Sihanoukville
0240 hours

The film went into Hyunh's keeping. It was time for phase
two of the mission.

With the two Vietnamese mounting guard invisibly in the
night, Nolan and Ringold broke the rest of the gear out of the
big deep-six locker, complete rebreather rigs, plus standard
diving gear, for two men. Nolan had considered bringing rigs
for four, but that would have made their load too bulky to be
easily carried or hidden, and, in any case, it was important to
have someone left behind with the boat to report back home,
just in case something went wrong on the dive. Because they
were the most familiar with the Emerson units, Nolan and
Ringold would make the dive, leaving the two LDNNs behind
with the boat. Hyunh and Phan had both protested that decision; it wasn't often that the *Lien Doc Nguoi Nhia* got to
live up to their name Soldiers Who Fight Beneath the Sea . . .

But then, the same could be said for the SEALs, who'd
trained endlessly with all types of diving rigs and equipment
back in the States, trained to operate as commandos who
could strike silently from the sea . . . and who then spent most

of their time in Vietnam ashore, setting ambushes, capturing VC officials and intel, even running spy nets for the CIA. Well, Sea, Air, *and* Land . . . but the SEALs weren't going to let an opportunity like this pass them by. Nolan had grinned, cheerfully pulled rank, and told the LDNNs to stow it.

It only took a few minutes for the two men to get ready. Stripping down to swim trunks, they donned their Emersons, strap-on knives, compasses and depth gauges, weight belts, and satchels.

The Emerson closed-circuit oxygen breathing apparatus had been accepted by the SEALs in 1963, a welcome replacement for the older and more hazardous German-made Draeger Lt Lund II rebreathers. The unit consisted of a zippered vest with two breathing bags, an oxygen cylinder in a turtleback assembly charged to 2000 psi, regulator and cutoff valves, a full-face mask with hose connections to both breathing bags, and a cylindrical canister charged with six pounds of baralyme. The complete rig, with baralyme, weighed thirty-five pounds out of water and was neutrally buoyant underwater. The diver breathed in from the right bag; when he exhaled, a one-way valve sent the air to the left bag, from which it was forced into the baralyme canister, where the carbon dioxide was removed. The gas was then forced into the right bag again, where it was mixed with a constant inflow of oxygen from the turtleback, and breathed again.

By recirculating the breathing gases—the O_2 tank had a useful duration of 160 minutes—the Emerson rig had the supreme advantage of being undetectable. There were no telltale bubbles rising to the surface to give away the diver's position, as there were with open-circuit SCUBA gear.

Standing in shallow water, the two men checked one another's rigs, making certain that all valves were properly positioned and the units were operating according to the manual. Then they donned their swim fins and, with a final wave to their South Vietnamese teammates, flip-flopped their way into deeper water. In moments, they were submerged in the silky warm, clear waters of the Gulf of Thailand.

It was almost pitch black beneath the surface, with just enough light filtering down from the sky for the two men to be aware of one another's positions. They would have to constantly check the luminous dials of their compasses to stay on course.

No problem. SEAL Team Two had done plenty of practice dives tougher than this, in the dark and in water so murky you could scarcely see three feet ahead of yourself. The main things to watch were your pacing and your depth. Push too hard, and you started using oxygen too fast. A nice, slow, steady beat-beat-beat with gently scissoring legs kept the SEALs moving steadily, without tiring them. Depth was critical. Oxygen became toxic at two atmospheres—the pressure at just thirty-three feet beneath the surface. Allowing for a safety margin, the dive limit with an Emerson rig was twenty-five feet . . . and ten to fifteen feet was preferred, since the diver used gas more quickly at greater depths.

Fifteen minutes carried them far enough northwest that they should be past the point and well into the mouth of Sihanoukville Harbor. Turning right then, they began swimming toward the harbor area.

So far, everything was going perfectly and according to plan.

The dockside at Sihanoukville
0255 hours

"What is all the excitement?" Colonel Kartashkin wanted to know. Moments before, a Cambodian naval officer had appeared on the dock and whispered something to General Son Lop. The elegantly clad little Cambodian general had begun issuing orders in response, causing a stir of activity across the entire waterfront. Xiang, the Chinese naval liaison officer, had hurried back aboard the *Danlin*.

"A report of a South Vietnamese vessel offshore, Colonel, at just about the twelve-mile limit," General Dong said. "My own people just informed me."

"What kind of vessel?"

"One of their naval junks. A coastal defense vessel, most likely, probably out of Phu Quôc."

"Ah. That seems a bit far from their home waters to constitute coastal defense. Is any action to be taken?"

"That, I would say, depends on our friend General Lop."

Kartashkin scowled. He reached for the pack of cigarettes

in his shirt pocket, then reconsidered. He only had four left, and it would be a while yet before he could get more of that brand. The political situation in Cambodia was extraordinarily delicate just now, with faction balanced against faction like a house of cards.

To begin with, the Cambodians hated the Vietnamese—a feeling that had very little to do with whether the Vietnamese in question were Communists from the north or fighters with the National Liberation Front in the south, or American puppets with the Saigon regime. Most Cambodians still dreamed of the glory days of the Khmer Empire, when they had ruled most of Southeast Asia. Over the intervening centuries, the country's territory had been steadily whittled away by both Vietnam and Thailand, leaving it with a fraction of the land and with deep-rooted animosity toward its neighbors.

To make matters worse, Cambodia, though officially neutral in the Vietnam conflict, had been relying more and more on help from the People's Republic of China, while North Vietnam supported the guerrillas known as the Khmer Rouge, who were fighting to topple the Phnom Penh government. North Vietnam, in turn, was supported by advisors, such as Kartashkin and his associates, from the Soviet Union . . . which had been opposed to the revisionist philosophies of China for a number of years now.

The political tangle made for interesting negotiations at times. Kartashkin had accompanied General Dong south on the Ho Chi Minh Trail, observing how the North Vietnamese managed to keep supplies and troops flowing south despite incessant air strikes by American war planes. His host had brought him all the way here, to Sihanoukville, to see the seaborne leg of the journey that at least some of the supplies made, but his tour would end without his setting foot on a Chinese merchant ship. He remained now in the shadows, out of sight of the Chinese sailors, some of whom were almost certainly members of Chinese Intelligence.

This covert meeting on the Sihanoukville waterfront, then, was a fascinating exercise in political expediency and mutual dislike. General Lop, while officially loyal to the current Sihanouk government, was in fact maneuvering for power and quite possibly involved in a planned antigovernment coup. He was probably working with Heng Samrin, a pro–Khmer

Rouge dissident, and was helping the North Vietnamese by providing security for this out-of-the-way corner of Sihanoukville Harbor. As for the Chinese . . . why did they ever do anything? Possibly, even probably, they were going to become more influential in the politics of the Cambodian people's revolution. Or perhaps they were just hedging their bets, supporting both the current Phnom Penh regime and the Khmer Rouge, just in case.

In any case, it would be best, Kartashkin thought, if he stayed out of sight. The Chinese comrades would become nervous if they knew any Occidentals were about, Russian or American.

"See if you can find out just how close this visitor is to the twelve-mile limit," Kartashkin told Dong. "I am concerned about the possibility of naval commandos."

Dong smiled. "Those American green-faces, you worry about?"

Kartashkin couldn't tell if his host was covering his earlier fear with light spirits, or if he'd simply decided not to take the threat seriously. *Idiot.*

"Possibly. Or their Vietnamese protégés. We should be on the alert, just in case."

"I will pass the word to my people to redouble their vigilance, Colonel."

"See that you do."

Not that vigilance by itself would be of particular help if the harbor was about to be visited by American SEALs. He began giving thought to other means of deterrence.

Southwest of Sihanoukville
0323 hours

Thirty minutes more, on a compass bearing of zero-four-zero degrees, had brought the two SEALs to the immediate vicinity of their target. The surface above them was aglow now with light from the dock. Nolan signaled Ringold to stay put, then carefully, carefully, let himself rise through the water until just the upper half of his face mask broke into the night air.

He needed only a second or two to establish their exact

position. The *Danlin* was about fifty yards away and almost directly ahead. The dockside swarmed with armed men—Vietnamese or Cambodian, he couldn't tell—but Nolan was confident that he would not be seen; a black speck adrift on the black surface of the harbor would be invisible to men whose eyes were night-blinded by the glare of lights on the dock.

Submerging again, he rejoined Ringold ten feet down, pointed, and the two resumed their journey.

Despite the clarity of the water, which near the dockside seemed to take on an illumination all its own with the reflected light from myriad dancing particles of debris suspended beneath the surface, the appearance of the *Danlin*'s hull was abrupt, almost unexpected. One moment, the two SEALs were swimming along side by side through the misty, empty glow; the next, a vast, shadowy bulk materialized out of the glow in front of them, a rounded shape turned soft and fuzzy by the algae growing on the bottom. It had been a while since this old vessel had seen a dry dock or had its bottom scraped and painted. Ringold surfaced briefly, to verify that they did, indeed, have the right ship. When he returned, signaling okay, they swam together beneath the vessel's stern and into the forest of dock pilings beyond.

The two SEALs surfaced, looked around, then crawled up onto a mudflat in the shadows of the pier. Timing their moves to the movements of the dockworkers, they slipped from shadow to shadow until they were hidden behind one of the piles of crates.

Nolan used his diving knife to check inside several of the long, heavy boxes stamped with Chinese ideographs. Rocket grenades . . . 7.62mm ammunition . . . hand grenades . . . 105mm artillery shells . . .

Jackpot.

Working quickly but with careful precision, they began deploying the explosives. Each man carried two blocks of C4 plastique in a belt satchel, along with detonators, explosive detcord, and electric timers. They selected different crates at different points within the stockpile and began placing the explosives inside.

Sihanoukville waterfront
0348 hours

"Honored Colonel?"

Kartashkin turned, startled. He'd been standing at the end of the dock, staring down into the water . . . wondering. Though relatively clear, the water was opaque when viewed under the lights of the waterfront. An army could be moving around down there, and there'd be no way to tell.

"Yes?"

A young Vietnamese captain, a member of Dong's personal staff, saluted him. "Sir, General Dong says that General Lop has decided against your precautionary request. It would, he says, attract unwanted attention to the operation here."

The Russian chuckled. Yes, dropping armed grenades alongside the ship and nearby docks every few minutes would make some noise, certainly . . . though it would be easy enough for Lop to explain the activity as exercises, or precautions, or a little unauthorized fishing, if it came to that. The fool was more afraid of alarming his Chinese clients than he was of the possibility of enemy commandos.

"Is there any word on that Vietnamese naval junk?"

"A patrol boat has been dispatched to investigate, sir. There is no report as yet."

"I see. Very well."

The captain saluted again and left Kartashkin with his thoughts.

He studied the waters below the dock again. It looked quiet enough, and there were no telltale bubbles from open-circuit SCUBA gear. Not that *that* meant anything, of itself. Russian Spetsnaz had been using various types of oxygen rebreathers for years to penetrate foreign naval bases and installations, including some that would have given some senior American naval officers heart failure had they known. And some Spetsnaz units routinely trained along portions of the Alaskan coastline. . . .

It was too bad there weren't some Spetsnaz here, with diving gear. Or even some decent sonar equipment. Kartashkin would have felt better if he could have established an underwater security patrol.

Ah, well. Perhaps the Vietnamese ship was conducting an

electronics survey or was on its way to Sihanoukville on a courtesy call . . . or was legitimately off-course. There were numerous innocent explanations available. Besides, the security of this port was not his responsibility.

But as both a professional military man and one with a special interest in covert operations, he would have liked to have been sure. . . .

Sihanoukville waterfront
0350 hours

The charges were placed where they would do the most good, deep among stores of high explosive shells. Detonators were inserted in the C4 blocks and interconnected with detcord. Two timers were attached, one serving as a backup for the other. Both were set for two hours from . . . *now,* at zero-five-fifty hours, which gave the two SEALs plenty of time to get clear.

That done, Nolan and Ringold gave one another a silent high five, and then they slipped silently back into the water, using the shadows of the pier for cover. Underwater, they began swimming once more, following a reciprocal course of two-two-zero to take them out past the point before turning southeast to return to the sampan. It had been tempting, back when Nolan was working out the details for this op, to arrange things so that they could watch the explosion from the hilltop and document the attack's damage assessment on the spot. The risks were too great, however. Once those charges went off, the entire harbor area would be swarming with troops ashore and patrol boats on the water, all searching for the attackers.

They emerged from the water southwest of the headland, and Ringold used a red-lensed light to flash a signal toward the black shore. The answer came back almost at once, and the two swimmers changed course to rejoin their LDNN comrades. Twenty minutes later, again wearing black pajamas and with their gear stowed safely in the deep-six locker, the four men were motoring back toward the boundary line marking the edge of Cambodian waters. The Vietnamese naval junk was supposed to be waiting for them, anchored in the shallow waters south of the Cambodian island called Kaoh Rung Sanloem on their maps, twelve miles southwest of the harbor.

The only problem was that the junk was not there. The sky was brightening now, as the time approached zero-five-thirty hours, with light enough that they could see the headland behind them, the island to the north, and enough of the horizon round about to be very sure the junk was nowhere nearby. Several possibilities flashed through Nolan's mind, none of them pleasant. The junk's skipper could have panicked and left, or his vessel could have been boarded by the Cambodians' equivalent of the Coast Guard. He could also have sold the SEALs out, though if that had happened, Nolan was pretty sure there would have been a boat waiting for them at the rendezvous. It just wouldn't have been the boat the SEALs were expecting.

The operation had just taken a very nasty turn.

Sihanoukville waterfront
0550 hours

Kartashkin had just decided that it was time for him to return with Dong to the Vietnamese rest camp at Kâmpôt. The off-loading of the Chinese ship was nearly complete, and, though the sun was not yet risen, the sky was fully light. According to Lop, the ship was due to leave Sihanoukville Harbor later that morning. There was nothing more to be seen here that would be of any use in his reports either to the Central Committee or to GRU headquarters. He did intend to suggest that the Soviet Union might want to involve itself in this kind of transshipment of military material, but only if the ships were able to provide better local security than he'd seen here today. The USSR could not afford to be caught *directly* supporting the Communist effort in Southeast Asia, even if all parties concerned took such involvement for granted. It was necessary politically that Moscow maintain some leverage as a peacebroker in the region, and that would be possible only if his government could appear to be an innocent, helpful, and peace-loving bystander.

He was walking past one of the waterfront warehouses when a dull, leaden *whump* transmitted itself through the concrete beneath his boots, followed at once by a crashing blast of thunder that clawed at his ears and face as an orange-shot black pall of smoke the size of a small mountain unfolded into the morning sky. *An accident . . . was his first thought. Someone smoking, and a stray spark . . .*

That thought was crowded out by another. *Suppose it wasn't an accident?*

More explosions went off, making him duck and sending projectiles trailing long streams of white smoke into the air like fireworks. He dropped to the ground again as more secondary explosions ripped through one of the warehouses. Flames boiled from the shattered wreckage of a waterfront building. Ammunition was cooking off with a curiously soft *pop-pop-pop* sound.

Staggering, he made his way back toward the waterfront, painfully aware that if he'd stayed on the dock a few moments longer, he might well be dead now. Dozens of Cambodian and Vietnamese soldiers lay on the ground, some motionless, others writhing in pain. Others ran back and forth, some fighting the fire raging on the docks and in a collapsed warehouse nearby, others simply scattering in panic-stricken confusion. A long, staccato burst of automatic fire churned the surface of the harbor, no doubt making the firer feel better but doing absolutely nothing else beyond contributing to the confusion.

The *Danlin*, he saw, was listing slightly away from the dock and settling a bit by the stern as well, and men aboard were fighting fires with hand extinguishers. As he hurried back to the wharf, he could hear the high-pitched shrilling of tortured metal and inrushing water. Had someone planted explosives aboard her? As he stood on the wharf looking at the devastation, he decided that the likeliest explanation was a sympathetic detonation; the explosions on the dock had triggered the detonation of the explosives and ammunition still aboard the freighter.

And the explosion on the dock had been caused by . . .

He caught General Dong rushing away from the dockside. "General! What is it?"

"An attack! All of the stores, all of them . . . including those aboard the *Danlin*!" His eyes widened. "You! You knew this was going to happen! You told me so, only a few hours ago!"

"Don't be—" He stopped himself. Though Dong, as a general officer, outranked him, Kartashkin's position both

with the Soviet military aid program and with the GRU gave
him virtual immunity. Proper protocol and the need for these
people to maintain face, though, required a softer answer than
the one he'd been about to give. "Of course not, General,"
he said. "I was simply expressing concern for the possibility.
You think it was a naval commando assault?"

"Without a doubt. There was no one close to the explosives, no one closer than the guards, and they were under
strict orders not to smoke."

Kartashkin suppressed a smile. Dong, obviously, had more
faith in the willingness of enlisted personnel to follow explicit
orders when no one was watching than he did.

Still, an attack was the most probable explanation. Modern
explosives, like those inside shells and ammunition, were actually notoriously hard to detonate. You could *burn* plastic
explosive like firewood, and artillery rounds and grenades
needed detonators or a savagely powerful explosion to set
them off.

He didn't think that what had happened here was an accident, not for a moment.

"And I suppose the possibility of sabotage by our Khmer
Rouge or Vietnamese hosts can be ruled out."

Dong looked as shocked as his normally expressionless
face could manage. "Comrade Colonel!"

Dong, evidently, was not as conversant with the ideological
and cultural differences that divided the Communist international in this part of the world; either that, or he was better
at ignoring them than was Kartashkin. He wondered what
Dong would have thought if he knew that the GRU had given
some thought to the possibility of mining a Chinese ship or
destroying cargo in this very harbor, in order to send an unmistakable message to Beijing that their adventurism in this
region would not be tolerated.

The Americans, evidently, had just done the same thing.
He gave a grim smile. Perhaps the two governments had more
in common in the region than he'd realized.

Dong turned and stared at the ruin of the waterfront, his
face warmly lit by the flames. "What should we do, Colonel?"

He gave a bitter, Slavic shrug. "Fight the fires, of course.
I doubt that you will find the perpetrators, though you might

suggest to Lop that he use his patrol boats to search the waters
beyond the harbor.''

"Yes! Yes, you are right, of course."

"You should also give some thought to the possibility that
the damage was caused by Cambodians working against General Lop to discredit him.''

"Ah. This is a possibility I'd not considered."

"The political situation within Cambodia is . . . interesting,
just now. Anything is possible.'' But, no. This didn't feel like
political infighting or maneuvering. The American commandos had been *here,* perhaps within an arm's reach . . .

"If Xiang or Lop claim you're at fault for not providing
adequate security, give them those possibilities. You might
also remind Lop that we suggested fishing for enemy commandos with grenades.''

Dong brightened. "Yes. We . . . we *did* warn them."

Perhaps the Vietnamese general was more concerned about
how this would look on his record than whether or not the
supplies could be salvaged. At the dockside, the *Danlin* was
settling now onto her keel, the water lapping just below the
level of her well deck. Her cargo hold must be almost completely flooded.

Fortunately, the water was not deep . . . and the damaged
ship had remained more or less upright. It would not be difficult to salvage the *Danlin* . . . but Beijing might think twice
before participating in the distribution of materiel in the south
again anytime soon. All of which left Kartashkin with just
one question.

Was this attack the prelude to the American invasion of
Cambodia?

He would have to take up that possibility with his superiors
at once.

At the Cambodian twelve-mile limit
0550 hours

They bobbed in open ocean, alone. Their sampan was
larger and more seaworthy than the tiny things that plied Vietnam's internal waterways, but it was still not a craft designed
for long journeys at sea. Fortunately, this part of the Gulf of
Thailand was sheltered, and the weather was calm. There was

little more than a gentle swell to the moving water.

Northeast, the crisp blue of the morning sky was stained by a looming black cloud, huge and tattered and vaguely mushroom-shaped. A siren wailed in the distance, from the direction of the port. Nolan looked at his watch. "Right on time," he said.

"So. What now, Lieutenant?" Ringold asked.

Nolan didn't have to think long about that one. SEALs never surrendered, and they never gave up. "We make a run for it," he said. He pointed east. "That-a-way."

It was fifty miles from the rendezvous to the nearest piece of South Vietnamese territory, the large island called Phu Quôc. Just fifteen kilometers south of the Cambodian coast, the mountainous island had long been claimed by Cambodia, and the dispute showed no signs of being settled anytime soon. For that reason, there was a fair-sized ARVN garrison there stationed near the Duong Dong airfield.

"Fifty miles?" Ringold said.

"We have gas to get that far?" Hyunh asked.

"Nope. But when we run dry, we've got paddles."

"That's a hell of a long IBS exercise." Ringold was referring to the long ocean excursions made by BUD/S recruits in SEAL inflatable boats. The longest were on the order of fifteen or twenty miles at a time.

"No sweat," Nolan replied, letting confidence put an edge in his voice. "We dump the deep-six locker here, with all of our gear except for the film. The Navy can send a recovery team if they feel they need to, and that'll make it easier for us to paddle. We'll also be a little less suspicious looking, if someone stops us. Then we head due east, along the Cambode coast. If we have to pull over and lay low, we'll do it there. Once we're opposite Phu Quôc, we turn south and make a dash for it. Piece of cake."

That particular piece of cake took nearly three days. They were stopped only once, by a Cambodian navy patrol boat, but Hyunh and Phan answered the questions barked at them through a loud hailer in Vietnamese, and they were allowed to proceed on their way. By that time, they were so close to the shore that they could have swum for it if they'd had to. Nolan was more concerned about four "Viet Cong" in black pajamas carrying AK-47s getting shot by ARVN sentries as they came ashore at Phu Quôc.

He needn't have worried. Security on Phu Quôc, it turned out, was even more pathetic than it had been at Sihanoukville.

Three days after their return to South Vietnam, Prince Norodom Sihanouk was deposed by a military coup while he was out of the country. The new ruler, General Lom Nol, a passionate anti-Communist, lost no time requesting U.S. and South Vietnamese help against the North Vietnamese forces using his country as sanctuary.

Chapter 12

Wednesday, 15 April 1970

BUD/S Training Center
Coronado, California
1045 hours

"The water," ET3 Greg Halstead said with an evil grin on his face, "is your *friend*. If and when you tadpoles ever become honest-to-God frogmen, you'll learn the truth of what I'm saying. I've *been* there. I *know*."

He paced the tile deck of the big indoor swimming pool at Coronado's BUD/S training center as he spoke, walking past the long line of shivering, half-dazed kids. He was wearing his SEAL instructor's blue-and-gold shirt and shorts; the trainees were wearing swim trunks. This far into the BUD/S program, they were on the go pretty much every waking moment . . . and there weren't all that many moments when they *weren't* awake. Most had taken on that characteristic thousand-yard-stare that looked so much like the eyes of a deer caught in an oncoming car's headlights.

Well, if they thought this was tough, wait until they hit Hell Week!

"The enemy," Halstead continued, "is not a frogman. He is not a United States Navy SEAL. When you've got your backs to the sea, head for the water where the enemy can't follow you. Any time you find yourself in a tight spot, just make sure you've got an escape route toward the sea or a river or a canal, and you'll be okay.

"You, however, must overcome your natural fear of the water. You must become, as we say, *drownproofed*. And that is why you gentlemen are here with us today."

As he spoke, two of his assistants made their way down the line of shivering recruits, using a length of white nylon cord to tie each man's hands firmly behind his back.

"Hey!" one man shouted, a sharp bark of protest that echoed among the steel rafters high above the blue water in the pool.

"You have a problem over there, Mr. Morgan?" Halstead snapped.

The recruit turned his head, looking up at Greg as RM3 Jarwalsiac finished tying off his wrists. "Uh . . . no, Petty Officer Halstead."

Greg walked up to the man and studied him for a moment. "That line too tight? If you want, we can have it right off of you. You'll need your hands free to ring the bell."

"I don't need to ring the bell, Instructor." The man sounded grim . . . and cold.

"That's good," Greg said. He turned, walked to a table nearby, and picked up a face mask from among the diving gear laid out on the top. "That's very good," he continued, dropping back into what he thought of as lecture mode. "A Navy SEAL *lives* in the water. The water protects him, shelters him, and is his most valuable ally when he is on an op. You gentlemen *will* lose your instinctive fear of the water . . . or you will ring the bell."

The bell was a small brass ship's bell mounted on a pole outside on the grinder—the parade field—just behind the SEAL recruits' barracks. Any BUD/S recruit, at any time during his training, could walk up to the bell, throw his colored, white-numbered helmet liner down at the foot of the pole with the helmet liners of all the other men in his class who'd already DORed—Dropped On Request—and give the bell three sharp rings. It was his official announcement that he was through with being cold, wet, muddy, sandy, tired, and abused by sadistic instructors, that he wanted a full night's sleep and some dry clothes and no beach sand in his underwear, that he knew that he simply did not have what it took to be a Navy SEAL. The SEAL training program actually prided itself in the fact that fewer than half, usually fewer than a quarter, of the men who joined the program actually made it all the way through, despite increasing pressure from on high to turn out more graduates.

One memorable class had vanished completely, with no graduates at all.

"Today's exercise is quite simple, gentlemen," Halstead continued, walking up to the edge of the pool. "The only thing you need to remember is *don't panic*. The human body is naturally buoyant. You will not drown unless you, yourselves, allow that to happen." He tossed the face mask into the pool and waited for a moment as it filled with water, then sank to the bottom. "Mr. Morgan! Suppose you demonstrate for the rest of the class!"

"I . . . huh?"

Greg grinned mirthlessly and pointed. "Go get it, tadpole."

Morgan hesitated only a moment before standing, taking a deep breath, and jumping feet-first into the pool. With his hands tied, he couldn't swim.

And he soon learned that with his lungs filled with air, he couldn't sink, either. The face mask was lying on the bottom in about fifteen feet of water. His first attempt to reach it failed, and he surfaced with a splash, kicking hard to keep his head above water as he gulped down another breath.

Greg leaned over, his hands braced on his thighs. "You okay, Mr. Morgan?"

The man nodded convulsively, struggling to stay afloat.

"Okay. Stay calm, and don't panic. You will have to exhale, get rid of the air in your lungs, in order to let your body sink to the bottom. Pick up the face mask with your teeth, then kick off, hard. Got it?"

Morgan nodded, kicked for a few seconds more, then blew out, hard. Feet straight and toes pointed, he sank quickly to the bottom. From the poolside, it was hard to see anything of the SEAL recruit save a shimmering blur; Halstead's two assistants stood by, one with a long pole, the other ready to dive in, should either be necessary. The seconds passed with Greg silently counting them off . . . eight . . . ten . . . fifteen.

Suddenly, Morgan rocketed to the surface, emerging in a white flower of spray, the mask's strap firmly clenched between his teeth. He tried to gulp down another breath before he sank again, and managed to let go of the strap.

"Ah!" Halstead warned. Stooping, he slapped the side of the pool. "Don't you *dare* drop that! Bring it here!"

Morgan plunged his head once more, snagging the strap once again in his teeth, before surfacing, then clumsily kicking his way over to the side of the pool. Greg reached down and retrieved the mask. "Good boy!" he said, grinning mischievously. He hefted the mask once, then tossed it back into the pool. He nodded to Jarwalsiac, and the other SEAL instructors began tossing more masks into the pool, one for every one of the thirty-seven other men remaining so far in the class.

He called to Chief Whittaker, who was standing nearby, arms folded. "Take over here, Chief, will ya? I want to watch this from below."

"Below" was a room one level down with a large underwater window looking out into the pool. Here, the BUD/S instructors could watch the men as they performed their various exercises underwater. A corpsman was assigned here to keep an eye on the recruits; an intercom on the wall put him in immediate touch with the instructors topside, by the pool.

"Hey, Doc. How's it going?"

"Twidge!" HM3 Bill Tangretti turned and smiled. "Pretty good group, this time."

"They'll do. So! How's the new father holding up?"

Bill gave a rueful laugh. "Shit, *combat* wasn't this bad!"

Greg chuckled. His sister was now seven months pregnant, with the baby expected sometime late in June. Bill certainly hadn't wasted any time getting a family started. Greg had been talking with Pat almost every evening for the last few weeks, and knew that she was coming along fine. His brother-in-law, though, was fast becoming a nervous wreck.

"Women have been having babies for a good many years, now," Greg said with a grin, "and the guy's worrying doesn't seem to help one damned bit!"

"I suppose that's supposed to be encouraging."

"The only easy day . . ." Greg began.

"... was yesterday," Bill said, finishing the SEAL training motto for him. "Yeah, yeah. I know that. You know, Pat says it's all in my head. She says that, being a Navy corpsman, I know just enough about what *could* go wrong to lather myself up into a class-one worry."

"She's right," Greg said with matter-of-fact confidence. Pat had always been the one with the solid, well-grounded common sense. He walked over to the window and leaned against the glass. Recruits in swim trunks, their hands tied behind their backs, dropped to the bottom in uneven formation, crouching as they looked about for a mask, nuzzling their faces against them until they could grab strap or rubber face seal in their mouth, position their legs on the bottom, and kick off toward the surface with their prize. "The first one down, a moment ago. What the hell was he doing?"

Bill checked a list on a clipboard. "Lieutenant Morgan?" he shrugged. "He had some trouble finding the mask, but he didn't seem to be in any difficulty."

"He wasn't hotdogging it?"

"Not that I could see. Why?"

"I don't know. Just a funny feeling about the guy, is all. I thought maybe he was deliberately dragging things out, just to get a rise out of me." He watched the trainees a moment more. The next part of the evolution was harder. The men had to position the masks in the bottom with their mouths, press their faces into them, and clear them ... then rise to the surface wearing them. Normally, a diver cleared his mask by pressing one side hard against his face to seal it, tilting his head, and exhaling through his nose to expel the water. Without hands, the task was a lot tougher ... and it was impossible to get all of the water out. The students had to have presence of mind enough, though, to work the problem through without panicking, and to clear them at least enough that water pressure would hold them on their faces until they surfaced.

And things would only get tougher. By tomorrow, drownproofing would involve having the men perform the same exercise tied hand *and* foot. Before the week was out, they would be dolphin-swimming the entire length of the fifty-meter pool, hands tied behind their backs, ankles tied tightly together. *That* was a real confidence builder.

"Uh-oh," Bill said. One of the men had gotten all the way

to the bottom but had started to thrash around, unable to get his feet under him. Bill hit the intercom. "Pool! It's Doc. Number twelve's in trouble!"

Shaking his head wildly, the recruit finally started for the surface, without his mask. Two instructors were with him in the water an instant later, but he no longer seemed to need help. They watched him struggling for the poolside, legs flailing, until someone pulled him up and out.

"Walker," Greg said. "Damn. I thought he'd stick."

"He still might."

"I don't know. The way he went for the surface, I have a feeling he was telling himself he'd had enough of this shit." He looked at Morgan, who by now had donned his mask, cleared more than half the water from it, and was positioning his legs for the push-off to the surface. He looked directly at Halstead and made a kissing pucker with his lips . . . or was he trying to imitate a fish? In either case, Greg knew that Morgan could see him, with his mask on and clear.

"Smart-ass," Greg said.

"You trying to run him out, Twidge? Make him DOR?"

Greg arched one eyebrow at his friend. "Hell, I don't think I'd dare. He's got some high-powered friends behind him somewhere, even if I can't see his service record. But I sure as hell can make life interesting for the son of a bitch."

Bill pretended to be shocked. "You're not allowing outside pressure to influence your judgment with a BUD/S trainee now, are you?"

"Screw you, Doc. I wouldn't be doing my job if I treated him any differently . . . and maybe the fact that he's got those friends makes me bear down just a little bit harder. Got to see that he gets his money's worth, you know. But run him out? No."

"Then what is it with you and him, anyway?"

"I'm not sure. I just can't get the measure of him, y'know? He doesn't have that same do-or-die attitude most of the tadpoles have by now. I keep pushing, looking for limits, and I haven't found any yet."

"Is he that good?"

"He thinks he is. That's what worries me."

Morgan was definitely an unusual exception to the run-of-the-mill BUD/S recruits in this class. Most SEAL trainees came to Coronado right out of A-school, one of the trade schools that determined a seaman's rate, like boatswain's mate or signalman. Usually, each class would have one or more officers as well, men who'd been through OCS and received their commissions and now, as ensigns or lieutenant j.g.s, were going through the same training that the enlisted men were forced to endure, with the goal of becoming SEALs.

All of them, though, were relatively new to the Navy, with no more than a year or eighteen months in service. Lieutenant Morgan, according to his records, had been in for four years already. The unusual aspect, though, was that much of his service record was classified. Halstead's own security clearance wasn't high enough for him to even find out where Morgan had been stationed, or what he'd been doing.

And there was that "civilian" who kept such close tabs on Morgan, the guy whose papers said he was an FBI special agent named Hunter, but who had *company man* written all over his bland and expressionless face.

"The guy's got to be with the Christians in Action," Bill said, echoing Greg's thoughts.

"That's what I figured," he replied, "after I met 'Mr. Hunter.' But what the hell does the CIA want with Morgan . . . and why are they putting him through SEAL training?"

"Special ops," Bill said with a sour expression. "They must need them more than ever, y'know?"

"Maybe. Though I don't know why they don't want to use the regular covert groups for that stuff. Us, Army Rangers and Green Berets, Marine Recon."

"Maybe it's stuff too secret for the likes of us to know about. This wouldn't be the first time."

Greg chuckled, a dry sound. Though no one knew anything, there were plenty of rumors and stories circulating through the SEAL community about highly secret, "deep black" special operations groups. During the mid-sixties, the CIA had organized one in Vietnam called "FRAM-16" that was supposed to have involved SEAL training for some of its members. Scuttlebutt within the Teams had it that most of the FRAM people hadn't made it back.

Nearly all of the deep spooky stuff in Southeast Asia was run under the general heading of SOG, an acronym which, depending on who you talked to, meant either Studies and

Observations Group or Studies and Operations Group. Either way, it was a highly secret department organized by the CIA for the purpose of gathering intelligence and, occasionally, running special direct action missions against the enemy. SOG used a variety of assets—mostly the Army Special Forces, but it tapped the SEALs too, from time to time, as well as using its own groups. Many SEAL missions, Halstead knew, were actually originated by SOG, but the orders always came down the ladder through MACV, the Military Assistance Command–Vietnam, and on any given op the Teams rarely knew whether they were working for the CIA or Navy Special Warfare.

Another rumor, current in the Teams just now, was that SOG had arranged for several American and Vietnamese SEALs to slip into Sihanoukville—or Kâmpong Saôm, as they were calling it these days—to mine a ship, Chinese in some versions of the story, Russian in others.

"With everything happening in Cambodia these days," Greg said softly, "maybe SOG is having a special recruiting drive."

Although Halstead held the veteran's wariness for scuttlebutt and rumor, he would not have been at all surprised to learn that SEALs had, in fact, raided the Cambodian port, either to gain intel about that end of the supply line coming down from North Vietnam, or to send a powerfully expressed message to North Vietnam's Chinese or Russian friends, or both. Events in Cambodia had been proceeding in a headlong tumble; hardly a day went by without some new revelation or other. Prince Sihanouk had been deposed on March 18, while he was visiting China. The word was that he'd been in search of leverage against the North Vietnamese forces infiltrating the southern and eastern third of his tiny nation, but some factions within his government, evidently, had felt that putting pressure on Hanoi by way of Beijing and Moscow simply wasn't enough.

By March 20, Cambodia's new leader, General Lom Nol, had requested direct South Vietnamese and American assistance against the NVA. So far, American ground forces hadn't been involved, but most people in a position to know felt that that step was not far off. U.S. air strikes were now openly—rather than covertly—assisting Cambodian ground forces, especially in interdiction strikes against the infamous Ho Chi Minh Trail, and South Vietnamese and American artillery south of the border had begun shelling NVA positions on Cambodian soil. On March 27, South Vietnamese ground forces had crossed the border and begun moving against known enemy bases and encampments. Everyone knew that U.S. advisors were with them, though the fact wasn't being advertised. Sooner or later, U.S. ground forces would move north as well.

And it was about damned time, so far as Greg was concerned. He was less worried about the spread of war in Southeast Asia than he was about the difficulty, no, the *impossibility* of prosecuting a war against a stubborn, resourceful, and determined enemy with one hand tied behind America's figurative back. What the hell was the point of ambushing Communist patrols or raiding their supply caches of rice, arms, and ammunition in South Vietnam, when the NVA maintained enormous supply dumps right across the border, where U.S. forces and their allies were not permitted to operate? For every VC or NVA killed in the South, it seemed, two or three more came down the Ho Chi Minh Trail to take his place.

Escalate the war? Hell, yeah, if it meant ending the damned thing, once and for all, or forcing Hanoi to quit turning the peace talks into a circus, or even saving a few American lives. It would be worth it, would be worth the risk of a bigger war.

SEALs knew well that no military action came without risk and that trying to ensure *no* risk in an operation was a great way to lose.

In the pool, the men were beginning another evolution, trying to don and clear their face masks, no hands. Two more men had been pulled out, but the others seemed to be getting the hang of it, learning not to fight against the water or the bonds, but to function smoothly, and without panic. *The water is your friend.*

Lieutenant Morgan was having no trouble at all.

"We're going to have to find some way to challenge him," Greg said, more to himself than to Bill.

"And the hell with the Company, huh?"

"The Company has nothing to do with it, Doc. But if that guy's going to be a SEAL, by God he's going to get pushed to his limits, and then we're going to push him beyond."

Chapter 13

The Pit
BUD/S Training Center
1530 hours

"All right, tadpoles! It's everybody's favorite ... log PT! Take your positions!"

Lieutenant Thomas Morgan stumbled down onto the stinking mud flat and took his place with the rest of his boat crew, down now to six men since Pete Walker had rung the bell that morning. He took his place next to Boat Crew Three's log, a massive, creosote-soaked telephone pole weighing several hundred pounds, lying in the mud with a dozen others. Some wag had stenciled the words MISERY LOVES COMPANY onto the wood.

ET3 Halstead stood on top of the hill, overlooking the flats, a bullhorn in his hand. "Okay, tads!" he boomed. "By the numbers. *One!*"

All six members of the boat crew bent at the waist, grasping the log. The men were wearing olive drab utilities and bright orange life jackets, but they were so covered with mud after the afternoon's fun and games in and around the mud pit that they looked very much as though each man had been rather crudely molded from wet clay.

"Two!" Halstead thundered, and with one swift, smooth movement, each boat crew hoisted its telephone pole to waist level, standing there with their arms braced beneath its slippery weight.

"Three!" The poles went to shoulder level, each man

134

struggling now to stay beneath his boat crew's log and still maintain his footing in the black muck beneath his boon-dockers.

"Four!" With a heave, the telephone poles went high over-head, supported on forests of trembling, muddy arms.

"Three!" The poles went back to shoulder position.

"Two!" Back to the waist.

"Three!" Back to the shoulders.

"Two! . . . Three! . . . Four! . . . Three! . . . Four! . . . Three! . . . Two! . . ."

Morgan strained and sweated with the other men, concen-trating furiously on the barked numbers, because all it took was one man to get it wrong and push the log up when he was supposed to lower it, and the whole line would go down. You had to learn to feel the other men on your team, to know exactly what they were doing and match your own efforts to theirs. Morgan was tall, with long, lanky arms and legs, which put him at a disadvantage in this drill. When the log went up to the Four position, it could only go as high as the shortest man on the boat crew could reach, which meant that the tallest men, like Morgan, couldn't straighten out their arms.

After a time, the ache in his shoulders, back, and elbows began to grow and throb, embracing him like a living thing, but he pushed awareness of the pain aside, walling it off in a part of his mind kept carefully under lock and key. Morgan had already been in excellent shape when he'd arrived at Cor-onado to start BUD/S training, and he knew he could last out the purely *physical* torment of the program.

The mental torture, on the other hand . . .

"Three! . . . Four! . . . Three! . . . Four! . . ." The amplified voice fell suddenly silent. Morgan stood there, arms trem-bling, braced against the weight of the log above his head. Was this some kind of new torture? How long were they going to have to hold this position? Carefully, not wanting to call attention to himself or his team, Morgan turned his head until he could just see Halstead out of the corner of his eye. A sailor in dungarees and white hat—one of the messenger runners assigned to the Amphib Command—was talking with the instructor. *Now* what? . . .

"Morgan!" Halstead barked through the bullhorn. "Get your ass up here!"

Trying not to unbalance his team, he eased out from under the log, then double-timed up the slippery mud slope.

"Trainee Morgan reporting as ordered, Petty Officer Halstead!" This was one place where rank meant nothing. Officers assigned to BUD/S were trainees, and the chiefs and petty officers who ran the program wielded an authority just short of that of God Himself. A trainee who happened to be an officer might be addressed as *mister*, but often there was a sarcastic edge to the word, an unspoken sneer reminding the trainee that all BUD/S recruits were definitely at the bottom of the heap and would stay there until they'd proven themselves.

"You've got a visitor," Halstead told him. He didn't sound exactly pleased. "Go with the runner."

"Aye, aye, Petty Officer Halstead."

"And . . . Mr. Morgan?"

"Yeah?"

"Hurry back. Your boat crew's gonna miss you pulling your weight."

He hurried. As he expected, Hunter was waiting for him just over the sandy rise.

The man was in civilian clothes, a nondescript gray suit. He might have been a sales rep for some moderately successful company. Puffing at a cigarette, he watched Morgan's approach emotionlessly, through impenetrable sunglasses.

"How's it going, Tom?" the man asked.

Morgan felt faintly ludicrous, standing on a sandy beach talking with this . . . this suit, while covered from boondockers to helmet with slimy, gray-green mud. He wondered if he smelled as bad as he looked—the mud pit, rumor had it, was an old septic field—but shook the thought off. Hunter had called for this meeting, not him.

"Well enough." He tried to stop his teeth from chattering. There was a stiff breeze blowing in from offshore, unfelt in the pit. "I'm getting damned sick and tired of this Mickey Mouse shit."

"Ah, I know how you feel, kid," Hunter said. He dragged a final puff from the cigarette, then flicked the stub into the sand. "Like Basic all over again, but worse. I just want to know you're hanging in there."

Morgan realized he'd been misunderstood. The Mickey

Mouse he'd been referring to was the cloak-and-dagger non-sense . . . especially the occasional meets with his handler, like this one. He couldn't think of a better way to paint the words SPECIAL COVERT OPERATIVE all over his body in screaming neon letters. He decided not to try correcting Hunter's impression, however. The man never really *listened* and had an appalling tendency to believe what he wanted to believe in the first place. From what Morgan had heard so far, that kind of attitude in American intelligence was a large part of what was going wrong in Southeast Asia.

"So you gonna stick it?" Hunter asked.

"Two more weeks of Phase One. Yeah, I'll stick." The first phase of BUD/S was the purely physical and mental conditioning of would-be SEALs, the thresher that separated the few kernels of wheat from the far more common chaff. The second phase was where he'd begin the demolition and land warfare portion of his training. Of course, he was already well versed in most of what the Navy would be teaching him there. The third phase, nine weeks after that, was where he'd hit the underwater portion of his training, and that ought to get more interesting.

"That's what I like to hear! Yeah, you can put up with two weeks of anything, right?"

Except, possibly, you, Morgan thought. "Yes, sir. Piece of c-c-c-cake." He clamped down on his jaw, hard, trying to stop the chatter. His physical exhaustion was betraying him, and that angered the mud-caked trainee. In the distance, he could hear Halstead on the bullhorn, counting off the cadence. *"Three! . . . Four! . . . Three! . . . Two! . . .* Get it together, tadpoles! *Three! . . ."*

"That's what I like to hear! You know, the war over there is changing, and it's changing fast. We're going to need specialists like you more than ever. Good men, with good training. Especially as Bright Light starts coming on-line."

Morgan stood shivering as the pep talk rolled over him. He'd heard versions of it before.

Technically, Morgan hadn't begun as a Naval officer, and, even now, most of his official service record was fictitious. He'd started off as a recruit for the CIA. His original basic training had been not in Navy boot camp but in the Agency's training center at Camp Peary, just outside of Williamsburg,

Virginia, a highly secret facility better known to insiders as "the Farm." The place was officially a Pentagon research-and-testing facility, but hidden away on its 480 wooded acres were barracks, classrooms, weapons ranges, jump towers, obstacle courses, an airfield, and even a detailed mock-up of a fictitious Eastern European town, complete with border station and sentries. Nearby was "the Zone," a special combat range in which "CTs," or "Career Trainees," learned what was euphemistically called "crisis orienteering," as well as infiltration and exfiltration techniques, field survival, and armed combat against both dummies and live opponents.

He'd also had one assignment in Cambodia already, which was better training by far than anything they could come up with at the Farm. He'd volunteered for a new program, however, one that required additional training, *SEAL* training, which was why he'd been transferred to the Navy, granted a commission, and placed in BUD/S.

"As soon as you graduate here, Tom," Hunter was saying, "we'll arrange for you to—"

"Ah, listen," Morgan said, interrupting. "With all due respect, *sir,* I don't think it's a good idea to discuss this out here . . . and I don't think it's a good idea for you to always be interrupting my training to give me these pep talks. I won't let you down, I promise that. But this . . . well, it's making me stand out." *That* had been one lesson he'd learned, and learned very well, when he'd been a CT.

He could feel Hunter measuring him through those black sunglasses. "I understand how you feel, son. This ought to be safe enough, though."

Morgan pointed. A hundred yards up the beach, civilians were lounging out on blankets. The BUD/S recruits often found themselves sharing pieces of the beach, along Coronado's Golden Strand, with tourists and sunbathers. Sometimes, it seemed like a glimpse of some bikini-clad California girls was all that kept a man going, especially when he was slogging along on a fourteen-mile run through loose sand, with an IBS or a telephone pole on his shoulder.

Hunter chuckled. "I scarcely think we have to worry about *them.*"

Where the hell had this jerk learned his tradecraft? *"Sir."*

The word carried a measure of scorn with it, and of disgust. "In case you hadn't noticed, we're at war."

"I don't see any gooks on this beach, Mr. Morgan."

"No. But those kids on the beach could be radicals. SDS, Weathermen, or worse. This war, for your information, is turning into a *civil* war. And sometimes it's as hard to know who the enemy is right here, in America, as it is in Vietnam."

He said the words quietly, almost in a growl. Morgan considered himself to be a patriot; his love of country had led him to that CIA recruiter, in college. He detested the people he considered to be traitors, who gave aid and comfort to the enemy by attacking America, by demonstrating against government policy, by taking over student union buildings, administrative offices, and whole college campuses in order to call attention, as they claimed, to the evils of the Vietnam War . . . when all most of them wanted was to avoid being drafted.

If Morgan had his way, traitors, draft dodgers, and Communist sympathizers would be given a choice: shut up . . . or get out. America didn't need them, and if they thought Moscow or Hanoi were so great, they could go live *there*.

Unfortunately, though, they were here, and probably with a very great deal of direct support from Moscow, the Weathermen especially—that ultraviolent offshoot of the Students for a Democratic Society. Last October, they'd gone on a two-day rioting spree in Chicago, their so-called Days of Rage, smashing windows, fighting with police, and ending with the arrest of three hundred. The Weathermen seemed to have gone underground since then, but that made them even more dangerous. Just this past March, an accidental explosion had demolished their bomb-making shop in New York City. Morgan had been delighted at *that* piece of news . . . but the Weathermen were still dangerous. They could be up to anything, and they had to be stopped.

Morgan often wondered if it wouldn't be wise for the government to organize some sort of counter-guerrilla force right here in the States.

Hell, maybe they already had. He could hope . . . and maybe after his Bright Light tour, he'd be given a chance to take part. Though Thomas Morgan hated Communism, he didn't really care if South Vietnam survived or not. What worried him was the obvious presence of Communist agents and sympathizers right here in the United States.

"Well, perhaps you're right, m'boy," Hunter said, turning to look at the kids on the beach. "It's always good to play it paranoid, anyway. Good tradecraft."

"Right. If you'll excuse me, sir? I ought to get back to my boat crew."

"I'll still be checking up on you from time to time, Tom. My bosses are most interested in this experiment. I just want to encourage you—"

"As I said, Mr. Hunter, I don't need the pep talk. Goodbye."

He turned and double-timed back up the sand dune, without waiting to be dismissed. That was not, perhaps, the wisest thing to do. Hunter was an idiot, but he was a powerful idiot, with a lot of influence in the Agency, and Morgan was still a very junior officer indeed. It wouldn't do to make the man an enemy. But, God in heaven! If other officers were as careful about their work as he was, no *wonder* the war was going badly!

"Glad you could join us, Mr. Morgan," Halstead barked through the loud hailer. "Join your crew. You're just in time to join us on a little run!"

Good. Maybe a "little run" would let him work off some of his frustration.

Friday, 1 May, through Monday, 4 May 1970

Tom Morgan's concerns about Communist influences inside the United States of America were not entirely inaccurate. It would be decades yet before the opening of long-secret files in Moscow and East Germany proved, once and for all, that money, encouragement, and even some training and equipment had, indeed, been passed from the agents of various Communist regimes to activist groups in the U.S., including the American Communist Party, the SDS, and others.

What he'd missed, however, was the fact that the war was not being won or lost according to the failures or successes of America's native revolutionaries or radical factions. The war was being lost on the home front . . . and that meant in the living rooms of ordinary Americans each time they sat down to listen to the evening news. The hard-line radicals had no real chance of inciting widespread revolt in America; by and large, most people were simply too comfortable for that to happen. But their campaign had focused widespread attention on the war, enough so that more and more of those comfortable Americans were wondering what business the United States had being in Vietnam in the first place. Since the Tet Offensive, in particular, in early 1968, more and more of the *real* America—as opposed to the strident but tiny minority of students and radicals—had been turning against the war. Johnson's War, as many now called it, had become so unpopular that Lyndon Johnson himself had decided shortly after Tet not to run for re-election, and Nixon, by his promise to end the war, had handily defeated Hubert Humphrey, Johnson's chosen successor.

And Nixon *was* ending the war. Vietnamization was proceeding rapidly . . . if with indifferent or often unfortunate consequences on the battlefield. Troops had been steadily withdrawn throughout the past year, and the weekly U.S. casualty figures were dropping quickly. The de-escalation wasn't fast enough for the hard-line radicals, perhaps, who continued their campaign of bombings and campus violence, but when Nixon announced, in December of 1969, that the war would be over within three years, most Americans believed him.

Nevertheless, the radicals continued their campaign aimed at forcing a total withdrawal from Southeast Asia. And, in late April and early May of 1970, events gave them precisely the incident they needed to rally huge numbers of Americans to their cause.

The explosion began on April 30, when Nixon announced that American ground troops were now committed in Cambodia, that they had moved into the regions known as the Parrot's Beak and Fish Hook on April 29, searching for North Vietnamese weapons caches and bases. It didn't seem to make much difference that U.S. pilots had been flying missions over Cambodia for some time now, or that South Vietnamese troops had crossed the border a month before. U.S. troops invading "neutral" Cambodia touched off a firestorm of protest across the country.

On Friday, May 1, at Kent State University in Ohio, a small group of history graduate students calling themselves World Historians Opposed to Racists and Exploitation—a somewhat contrived name, but the acronym WHORE had simply been too good for its organizers to pass up—put together an antiwar rally at the Victory Bell on the campus's grassy Commons. In front of five hundred spectators, they publicly buried a copy of the U.S. Constitution to symbolize its murder by Nixon, and a student who'd won the Silver Star while serving with the 101st Airborne in Vietnam burned his discharge papers. Buoyed by their modest success, the organizers called for another, bigger demonstration on Monday, May 4, to protest the war and the invasion of Cambodia, and to push for the closure of the Reserve Officers Training Corps facilities at the campus.

The demonstration had started peacefully, but Friday night it began turning ugly. Bands of students roamed the streets of the college town. A human chain blocked traffic on Water Street, and drivers were confronted with demands to know their views of the war and its escalation. An angry crowd hurled beer glasses at police cars, and a bonfire was set in the middle of the street. Cars were smashed and windows were broken as the mob moved through the town, causing some ten thousand dollars of property damage.

The town's mayor, Leroy Statrum, declared a state of emergency and ordered a curfew. He also ordered the bars shut down, which curbed the drinking but forced even more angry students into the streets, where they were met by police and eventually dispersed with tear gas.

On Saturday, city officials conferred with officers of the Ohio National Guard, who told them that if the guard was called in, it would assume total control of the university. They dithered at first, but as rumors circulated that the Weathermen were behind the rioting, the decision was made to bring in the National Guard. Curfews were set: 10:00 P.M. for the town, 1:00 A.M. for the campus. That evening, another mass demonstration developed, as some fifteen hundred students took to the streets chanting "One-two-three-four, we don't want your fucking war" and similar pleasantries. Some called for armed revolution. Others displayed North Vietnamese flags. Still others hurled rocks, beer cans, or trash at police. Kent State was fast becoming a town under siege.

The mob's attention was focused on one building in particular, the aging, wooden campus barracks of the university's ROTC. The windows were smashed, garbage was hurled through ground-floor windows, and before long the structure was ablaze. When fire department vehicles arrived to fight the fire, their hoses were cut, firemen found their movement blocked by chanting mobs, and the building swiftly burned to the ground. By ten o'clock Saturday evening, Ohio National Guard troops were moving in behind fixed bayonets and clouds of tear gas, clearing the campus. A huge crowd of students gathered in the town, singing "Give Peace a Chance," as a government helicopter circled ominously overhead, bathing them in the beam from its searchlight.

By Monday, the battlelines had been drawn in a pattern set for tragedy.

Ohio governor Jim Rhodes had already declared that the weekend's violence was the most vicious yet perpetrated in the United States, that the troublemakers were worse than brownshirts or Communists, worse than night riders or vigilantes, that they were, in fact, "the worst type of people we harbor in America." He now suspended the right to assembly, banning all demonstrations, even peaceful ones . . . an unlawful order by any standards, and one in direct violation of the Constitution of the United States.

Many on campus had already decided that the burial of the Constitution on Friday had been more than simply symbolic.

Despite the order, two to three thousand students gathered at the Victory Bell on Monday morning for the promised antiwar rally. At just before noon, guardsmen ordered the crowd to disperse and were met with jeers, hoots, and cries of "Sieg Heil." Several students began ringing the Victory Bell, usually rung after football games.

General Canterbury, the National Guard commander, ordered his men to load with live ammo and don their gas masks. One hundred men advanced in a single line toward the grassy knoll known locally as "Blanket Hill," a place where lovers met on campus. Tear gas canisters were fired into the crowd, but students threw them back, screaming obscenities. When they ran out of tear gas, the students used rocks and chunks of concrete pulled from walls and walks.

Forty of the guardsmen advanced to confront the crowd with fixed bayonets, assuming firing stances to threaten the mob, but forty against two thousand was not exactly comfortable odds, and they began to retreat.

A shot was fired.

As at the Battle of Lexington, 195 years before, no one ever learned where that first shot came from, or even which side fired it. Possibly it was an accidental discharge, a guardsman rattled by the crowd, fearful of its advance, his finger too tight on the trigger. In the next three seconds, sixty-one shots volleyed across the knoll.

And in three seconds, the one-sided battle was over.

"They're firing blanks!" one student yelled. No one could believe that Americans would fire deliberately into a crowd of Americans . . . but screams and shrieks clawed at the sky above Blanket Hill, and blood splashed the pavement of a walkway. Ten students were wounded—one paralyzed for life with a bullet in his spine; the guardsmen ignored him as they marched past.

Four were dead. Jeffrey Miller. Allison Krause. William Schroeder, a member of the ROTC. Sandra Lee Sheuer, who'd not even been a part of the demonstration; she'd been passing by on her way to class, tragically in the line of fire during those terrible three seconds.

And in those three seconds, the horror of Vietnam had been made real to ordinary Americans in a way that even body bags and the nightly news had been unable to manage. Those four dead were not blacks rioting in a burning Detroit ghetto. They were not helmeted, club-wielding Weathermen smashing windshields in Chicago. They were not hippie freaks or dropouts or acid-heads or pot-smoking flower children or any of the other categories assigned to America's counterculture.

They were white, middle-class, suburban kids, attending an ordinary college in an ordinary town, caught up in events far larger than themselves.

And with their deaths, the peace movement was torn from the hands of the activists by Americans who, until then, had supported or simply tolerated the war. It was now in the hands of union members, the news media, veterans groups, and others.

The war had just come home to middle America.

Chapter 14

Monday, 4 May 1970

**Bill and Pat's apartment
El Cajon, California
1230 hours**

Wendy rolled over on the sofa, pried her eyes open, and tried to find something to focus on. It had been a long drive, a very long drive, down from San Francisco, especially alone. She'd had to stop every few hours to get the kinks out and stoke up on coffee, but she'd finally made it, pulling in to El Cajon shortly after ten o'clock last night. After talking to Greg briefly on the phone, she'd crashed on the sofa. Bill had laid out sheets and blankets and a pillow for her, but she wouldn't have cared if it had been a straw mattress on the floor.

She rolled over once more and fell off the sofa.

"Well, good morning," a far too cheery voice called out. "Or rather good afternoon."

"No more wisecracks out of you, fat lady," Wendy said, hauling herself upright.

"Fat lady indeed," a very pregnant Pat said, hands on her hips. "Dr. Hamilton said I've gained just the right amount of weight, thank you very much. He said he's rarely seen an expectant mother in such good shape."

"Shape?"

"Well, such good condition, then. Are you sure you're going to be up for the party tonight, Wen? Maybe I was silly, setting it for so soon after you got here."

Wendy yawned and stretched. "Don't worry. I'll be fine after a shower and some coffee."

"Then go soak your head. I'll make up a fresh pot."

Wendy gave her friend a gentle hug. "You're a doll, fat lady. I'll be out in ten."

"I'm so glad you came, Wendy."

She nodded and then yawned again. "Me, too, Pat," she said through the yawn. "Me, too."

After a few minutes of standing under the shower, just letting the hot water blast her, Wendy began to feel human again. As she lathered up the washcloth, she thought about Greg and smiled. He'd wanted to come over last night, but she'd insisted she'd rather see him when she was awake. Tonight would be the first time they'd seen each other in, let's see, five weeks. Between their two work schedules it had been hard to find a lot of weekends when they were both free; they'd only managed nine weekends together over the past eight months. But frequent letters and occasional phone calls had helped.

And now finally she was here. Ever since Pat and Bill's wedding last September, she'd become more and more tempted by Pat's idea of moving down to San Diego. To be honest, Greg was even more of a draw than his sister, but Pat's pregnancy had provided a useful excuse. And the timing was great, too. Pat had really wanted her here for her last month, and it was now just a year since she'd started working at California Pacific. A solid year of employment at one hospital looked much better on a résumé than six or even nine months.

And as soon as she got a job here, she could find herself an apartment. She was already looking forward to inviting Greg over to her new place. Maybe on a weekend when he didn't have to be at work the next day.

Assuming, of course, that he was still as interested in her as she was in him.

1725 hours

"God!" Pat Tangretti said, placing her hands squarely over her kidneys and leaning back against the ponderous weight of her distended stomach. "If this kid doesn't come soon . . ."

"Why don't you go into the living room and put your feet up, Pat?" Wendy said, turning from the kitchen sink with a dish towel in her hand. "I can finish up out here."

"*That's* hardly fair," Pat told her, "making you do all the work for your own party!"

"Hey, we're almost done. Just let me finish drying the glasses, and I'll come join you. Where do you think the men folk are, anyway?"

"Oh, Bill told me this morning that he'd be taking Greg back to the barracks so he could change. They should be home in about fifteen, twenty minutes."

"Good. When they get here, we can put *them* to work!"

"Sounds like a plan." Pat fished several slices of cheese from the arrangement already laid out on the lazy Susan.

"Out," Wendy said. "This kitchen ain't big enough for the three of us."

"Aye, aye, ma'am. Boss. Slave driver." Pat turned and made her belly-heavy way out to the living room. It was nearly time for the local news on TV, and she thought she would catch a bit of it with her feet up.

She was not sure what she would have done without Wendy. For months she'd been urging her to move down to San Diego, mostly because she missed her, missed the close relationship they'd had as college roommates and best friends. But now, during the last and most difficult month of her pregnancy, she needed her as well. The doctor and Bill both said that the baby was fine, and most of the health problems she'd heard about ahead of time—morning sickness and backaches and all the rest—hadn't been as bad as she'd feared. So far, the worst part of being pregnant was simply how damned awkward it was, like trying to move around with a heavy, water-filled backpack strapped to her abdomen.

It was going to be so nice having Wendy around to help her out, even though it was going to be cramped with the three of them in this tiny apartment. She knew Wendy wanted to get an apartment of her own, just as soon as she got a job. Well, that shouldn't be a problem. Wendy's medical technologist's credentials pretty much guaranteed her a spot at San Diego General or almost any other hospital in the area she wanted to try for; she already had an interview lined up for a civilian job at the Navy Hospital at Camp Pendleton.

Pat switched on the TV, then sank gratefully into the big stuffed chair and put her feet on the ottoman. It was pretty loopy, she decided, trying to throw a welcome to San Diego party for Wendy now, tonight, but she'd been looking forward to her moving down here for a long time. Of course Greg would probably have preferred to have Wendy all to himself tonight, but tough—Wendy was her friend first. And as long as she didn't mind helping out with her own party . . .

Chet Huntley was on the screen, and she had to look at her watch to make sure it wasn't later than she'd thought. This wasn't the local news. The headline on a black-and-white photograph of people running in what looked like a park of some sort read ''Kent State Shootings.''

Pat listened with dawning horror as an on-site reporter told of a confrontation at Kent State University between National Guard troops and student demonstrators, of gunfire that had left at least four kids dead and others wounded. *How could something like this happen? How could it happen here?* She slipped one hand protectively over her stomach, as if to shelter the baby inside, and a moment later felt a strong kick. *What kind of a world are you going to inherit?*

She wondered how this was going to affect Bill and Greg. Bill generally seemed pretty laid back about the campus protests and student riots and all, but Greg felt a lot more deeply about these things.

Wendy walked in and handed her a large glass of milk. ''Here. You've got a baby SEAL in the oven. Feed him.'' She glanced at the screen. ''What's that all about?''

''Special report,'' Pat replied. ''National Guard troops opened fire on some demonstrators.''

''Oh, God. Where?''

''Ohio. Place called Kent State.''

''Never heard of it.''

''The whole country's going to hear about it now. Oh, Wendy! It's like . . . it's like the war's starting to spread over here! Just like Greg always said it might!''

Wendy shrugged. ''I don't think it's as bad as all that. The student protesters, well, there aren't that many of them. They're *loud,* maybe, but still a definite minority.''

''I wish I could be sure.''

''You know, maybe you shouldn't watch stuff like this. . . .''

''Touch that dial and you're a dead woman.''

They watched for some time more, though it quickly became clear that NBC didn't know much more than they'd already revealed, and when Wendy switched channels to CBS and Walter Cronkite, the story was the same over there. Kent State was under martial law, no one could more than speculate about who had fired the fateful shots or why, no one knew what legal problems the guard or its leaders might face.

And four students were dead.

Wendy heard them outside even before the door opened and Greg and Bill walked in, Bill still in his green fatigues, Greg in a plaid shirt and jeans. The look in Greg's eyes set her pulse racing. He *did* still care.

"Hey, girls," Bill said, coming over to Pat's chair and leaning down to greet his wife.

"Hey yourself," Pat said. "You hear the news?"

"Yeah," Greg said. "It was all over at the base today. We almost canceled class."

"They put the whole base on alert," Bill added. "You know, just in case the antiwar people get pissed and try storming the gates of Coronado. There was a rumor going around that the SDS was going to call for an all-out rising all across the country."

"Bill, I don't think Pat needs to hear—"

"Nonsense, Wendy. I'd rather know than just sit here stewing. Or have it catch me by surprise." Pat looked at Bill. "Do you think there's going to be trouble here?"

Bill shook his head. "I really doubt it. Everything seems pretty quiet in the streets. I imagine there'll be more demonstrations throughout the week. You know, at some of the campuses, Berkeley, and places like that." He looked down at his uniform. "I'm gonna go shower and get some clean clothes."

"Can I get you anything, Greg?" Wendy asked casually as Bill walked off down the hall toward the bedroom.

"Sure, a beer would go down great." He followed her into the kitchen.

She reached for the refrigerator handle, but Greg stopped her. "Forget the beer, Wendy. I just saw something I like even better." He put his hands on her waist and drew her close.

"Oh? And what might that be, Petty Officer Halstead?"

"You, you silly goose." He bent his head and kissed her, a long, lingering kiss as if to make up for lost time. "God, I've missed you so much, Wendy," he said when they finally came up for air.

"I've missed you, too," she murmured into his shoulder. It felt so good to be in his arms again.

He pulled away to look at her, giving her that smile that always made her wobbly in the knees. "I'd like to say, 'Can I take you home from the party?' but since you're staying here and I don't have a car, I guess I'll have to say, 'Will you take me home from the party?' "

"Be glad to," she said in a masterful understatement. "Now let's get out there and keep your sister company."

Greg pulled a couple of beers out of the refrigerator, and the two of them walked back into the living room, arm in arm.

"So what do you think of this mess, Greg?" Pat asked. She gave Wendy a raised eyebrow but said nothing.

"I think the bad guys just escalated, sis. The homefront war has just gone from being a handful of agitators to something much bigger." He quirked a small, brief smile. "The Boston Massacre."

"The Boston what?" Wendy asked as he sat down on the sofa and popped his beer open.

"Greg's always pulling obscure bits of history out that everyone else has long forgotten," Pat explained. "He should have been a history teacher, not a SEAL."

"On the contrary, sis," Greg said, pulling Wendy down onto his lap. "Knowing history can be a real asset in my line of work. You can tell if some goddamn idiot is about to make the same mistake that some other goddamn idiot made two hundred years ago, and maybe take a fair guess at what might happen as a result."

"So what was with Boston?" Wendy wanted to know.

"Just before the Revolutionary War," Greg explained, "the city of Boston was a hotbed of radical activity."

"Sort of like Berkeley today," Wendy suggested.

"I find it hard to compare Sam Adams with Abbie Hoffman, but I guess, yeah. Anyway, a group that called itself the Sons of Liberty was always trying to stir up trouble with the

British authorities, hoping to spark an incident that would get more Americans to side with the independence faction. A snowball and name-calling fight, late one March night in 1770, escalated into a riot, and some British troops panicked and opened fire on the mob. Five Americans were killed. The Sons of Liberty managed to blow the incident into a 'massacre' and used it to inflame the entire population.''

"So what are you saying?" Wendy asked. "That the campus radicals are starting a revolution?"

"That they're using some of the same tactics." He shook his head. "I can't believe that most Americans hate the government today as much as the colonists who revolted against King George, but it'll be damned interesting to see how this Kent State thing plays in the media."

"Well, what do you think, Greg?" Pat asked him. "Are the protesters right? Or wrong? Traitors? Or patriots?"

"In my book," Greg said, "traitors. Or, if that's too harsh a word, cowards. I haven't seen anything in the peace movement yet that suggests that their desire for peace is more than self-interest. They march and burn their draft cards and run away to Canada because they're afraid of being drafted, not because of any high ideals."

"I'm not sure that's fair. Some of them, certainly . . . maybe even most of them . . . run away because they're afraid, but lots of them believe in what they're doing, maybe more than most of the kids in Vietnam do."

Greg looked as though he was about to give a quick reply, but he stopped, his gaze going to the television. Images flashed across the screen in quick succession: students running; Guardsmen in gas masks and carrying rifles with bayonets; more students running, as tear gas canisters bounced across the grass, trailing white smoke.

When he finally spoke, it was with a small shrug. "You may be right."

There was a knock at the door, and Pat began to struggle out of her chair. Wendy leaped out of Greg's lap. "I'll get it, Pat. You stay put."

"No, no, I've got to get up or that chair will eat me alive." She waddled over to answer the door. It was a pretty young woman in an ankle-length print dress followed by a tall, brawny, and rugged-looking man with a used car salesman's smile.

"Praise the Lord!" the woman said, hugging Pat.

"Thanks for coming, Melissa!" Pat said.

"Oh, thank you for asking us. And how's the little one?"

"Kicking up a storm. Sometimes it feels like he's running an obstacle course in there."

The man advanced on Greg and Wendy with hand outstretched. "Hey, good to see you, Greg." He nodded at Wendy.

"Hi, Jerry. This is Wendy Frasier, just moved down here from San Francisco. Wendy, Jerry Logan. He lives in the apartment next door."

"I'm real pleased to meet you, Wendy. That's my wife, Melissa, over there."

"Nice to meet you, Jerry. Are you a SEAL too?" Wendy asked.

Jerry laughed and shook his head. "No, ma'am, I'm black-shoe Navy. Aviation machinist's mate. Just made first class, praise the Lord! I work at the naval air station at North Island."

Just then Pat and Melissa came over. "Wendy," Melissa gushed. "I'm so delighted to meet you. We've heard so much about you from Pat and Bill. It's such a blessing that you're able to be here to help Pat in her time of need."

Wendy was a bit overwhelmed. As soon as she could, she excused herself to go check on the food in the kitchen. Greg followed her.

"Greg, what gives with these people?"

"Damned if I know. They're both rather . . . enthusiastic Christians. Charismatics, they call themselves. The sort who don't mind spending an entire evening telling anyone who will listen how Jesus has changed their lives."

"They come on a little strong. Do Pat and Bill really like them?"

"I think Pat does. At least she likes Melissa. I'm not sure about Bill."

"I'm not sure I'm up to an entire evening of their brand of cheerfulness, Greg."

"Hmm. You know, I probably need to get back to the base

kind of early tonight. Like right after dinner? That okay with you?''

"Wonderful!''

By the time they emerged from the kitchen, Bill had reappeared in civilian clothes, and the festivities began.

Still, Kent State had cast a pall over the evening that could not be lifted.

2150 hours

"Thanks again for rescuing me," Greg said, settling in on the passenger side of Wendy's Chevy.

"You're the one who rescued me, by giving me an excuse to get out of there," she told him, pulling out of the apartment parking lot. "I swear, if I heard that cheerful 'praise the Lord' of theirs just one more time . . .''

He shook his head. "I know what you mean. They were getting to be a bit much." He made a face. "I mean, they're so *wholesome!*''

She laughed, a delightful sound. He still hadn't quite taken in the fact that she was really *here,* that he wasn't going to have to say good-bye tomorrow and get on a bus heading south. "So where do you want to go? Or do you want to just take me back to the base? I know you must be tired.''

"I am, I must admit. How about if we go to the base and then just sit and talk for a while?''

"Sounds good. Take a left at the next light.''

Except for Greg's occasional directions, they rode in silence for a while. He was enjoying looking at her.

"What are you looking at, sailor?''

"You.''

"God, whatever for?''

"I like looking at you, Wendy, in case you hadn't figured that out by now. You're a very look-at-able person.''

She shook her head. "You're nuts. Definitely nuts. Certifiable, in fact.''

"Not me, lady. You're the one who upped anchor and moved five hundred miles south just to be with me.''

"I moved here to be with Pat.''

"That's right. In her . . . what did Melissa call it? . . . her time of need. And the fact that I was down here didn't have anything to do with your decision?''

''Not a thing,'' she said, with a quirk to her smile that said she was lying.

''Well, I'll just have to be grateful to Pat for getting pregnant and luring you down here then.''

He didn't know where this relationship was going—he sure as hell wasn't ready to think about getting married or anything like that—but he just knew that he felt great, really *alive,* whenever he was with her. Wendy seemed just as happy as he was to take things slow and not talk about long-term commitments.

He wondered how quickly she'd be able to get an apartment so they'd have a place to spend some time alone.

''Oh, look!'' she said, as she drove up the highway toward the amphib base's main gate. The lights of San Diego dazzled off the waters of the bay to their right. To the left and ahead, the bright, steady sweep of the beam from the Point Loma Lighthouse periodically illuminated the black waters of the Pacific.

''Beautiful, isn't it?''

Wendy shuddered.

''Are you cold?''

She shook her head. ''No. It's just . . . I was just thinking about what happened today at Kent State. It's horrible to think that something like that could happen here.''

''Yeah, I know.''

''What do you think about what happened? I mean, really?''

He turned his head, watching the lights of San Diego. It all looked so peaceful from here. ''Damfino. Hard to know what to think, really. I do know that I can understand what happened, from the Guardsmen's point of view.''

''You think they were right to open fire?''

''I think they probably felt they were outnumbered and in serious trouble. I doubt that they had all that much training with that kind of situation, and when you see a mob coming toward you, well, it's easy to lose your head, y'know?''

''Like that story about the Boston Massacre you were telling us about.''

Greg chuckled. ''You know, the British soldiers charged

with perpetrating the massacre went to trial a year later. They were defended by no less a Boston attorney than John Adams."

"The John Adams? The Declaration of Independence John Adams?"

"None other. He actually got those soldiers acquitted of murder . . . though two, I think, were convicted of manslaughter, a lesser offense. His chief argument was that the soldiers felt threatened by the angry mob that had gathered around them. The mob's leader was a guy named Crispus Attuks, a big, muscular mulatto who apparently had a rather, um, threatening demeanor. Adams argued, in effect, that one look at Crispus Attuks would've scared the shit out of anybody, and the soldiers couldn't be blamed for firing at the crowd."

"It didn't sound to me like there was any Crispus Attuks at Kent State today."

"No. But from what I heard, the crowd had already burned a building down and were defying the local civil authorities."

"You're not saying," Wendy said, "that you think what the Guardsmen did was right, are you?"

"No, not at all. I'm just saying you can't blame *them* for being thrust into a situation they weren't trained to handle. You know, the National Guardsmen behind those rifles today probably weren't any older than the kids they shot."

"And probably more scared than the demonstrators."

"That would be my guess."

They reached the front gate, and Wendy pulled the car over to the side of the road. "Well, here we are." She switched the ignition off but left the key in the lock.

"Get over here, woman."

"Oh?" Wendy slid over to the middle of the seat and moved her purse to the other side. "Now why would I want to do that, sailor?"

"This is why," he said, wrapping his arms around her and slowly reaching down to take her mouth with his. Her response was immediate and eager as she caressed the back of his neck, pressing herself into him.

Well, maybe he wasn't in love with her exactly, but it sure felt good knowing she wasn't five hundred miles away anymore.

He was whistling as he showed his ID to the Marine sentry and walked back to his barracks.

Chapter 15

C-130 Hercules
Above Twentynine Palms
Marine Corps Base, California
2240 hours

Christ, it was cold. . . .

It was also dark outside, making the red illumination of the C-130 Hercules cargo bay seem warm and homey by comparison with the blackness visible through the ports. Bill Tangretti looked across the aisle and caught Greg's eye. Greg mimed slapping his arms across his body, as though to say, *It's cold.* Bill gave him a thumbs-up. The other six men in the compartment sat impassively, their expressions all but blocked by the helmets, goggles, and black oxygen masks they wore. One was the Marine gunnery sergeant serving as jumpmaster for this training exercise.

The others were SEALs: Lieutenant Tom Morgan was in command of the ad hoc SEAL squad, while MM1 Chris Hochstader, RM3 Gary Panopolis, QM1 Mark Ringold, and Lieutenant David Nolan made up the rest of the team. Having two lieutenants in one squad was a bit unusual, of course, but sometimes the demands of training schedules and rotations made the organization of these exercises a bit of a catch-as-catch-can. Nolan and Ringold had just returned from Nam a few weeks before and, like Tangretti and Halstead, they needed to catch up on their jump quals.

Every SEAL was expected to pull a certain number of jumps during each qualifying period, to keep his training current. Bill and Greg had gotten in a couple of jumps apiece while they were assigned to BUD/S training command, but they hadn't done any HALO work for some time.

Morgan, Hochstader, and Panopolis, on the other hand, were all BUD/S classmates. They'd only recently completed the jump portion of their SEAL training, spending several weeks at Fort Bragg jumping out of airplanes with the 101st Airborne, and were now back in California, polishing up the skills they'd learned, and adding that special SEAL twist. Tangretti gathered that all three still needed to work in some night HALO jumps to complete their training quals; Lieutenant Morgan also needed some time in leading a live exercise—hence his presence aboard the Herky Bird tonight as squad leader. Nolan, when told that afternoon that Morgan would be leading the squad on their night exercise, had grinned and said, ''S'okay. I kind of like the idea of being a low-life third class for a change.''

Tangretti still didn't know what to make of Morgan, who seemed standoffish, a loner who was just going through the motions of becoming a SEAL, something Tangretti didn't care much for at all. The point of putting SEAL officers and men through the same training was to make sure they trusted one another when they were in the field. That made for a more closely knit unity between the leaders and the led than was possible in almost any other branch of military service Tangretti had heard of. Somehow, though, Morgan just wasn't clicking with the rest of the men.

He liked Nolan, though, an easygoing man with a relaxed sense of humor and a store of tales about his work with SEAL Team Two in the U Minh Forest. Scuttlebutt had it that he and Mark Ringold had pulled a deep spooky across the line in Cambodia before the invasion, but exactly what they'd been doing was secret, and Tangretti knew better than to discuss classified ops, even with another SEAL.

Mark Ringold had been a hell of a surprise. They said that in a community as small as the Navy, you met everybody sooner or later, but Mark's identity had been a startling coincidence. It turned out that Mark Ringold was the son of an old friend of Greg Halstead's father. Greg hadn't picked up on that fact until just the other day, but then it had been like old home week, with Greg and Mark becoming good friends, and with Bill drawn into the circle because of his friendship with Greg.

Ringold's father had been a war buddy of Greg's dad, and the coincidence didn't end there. Both men had served together aboard the USS *Blessman* during World War II, a ship that had figured large in the history of the Navy's Underwater Demolition Teams, the UDT, precursors of the SEALs. The *Blessman* had been struck by a Japanese bomb just before Iwo Jima, and a detachment of frogmen aboard her had helped fight the fire and save the ship. The elder Halstead had mentioned several times in Greg's hearing that his old friend's son was now a SEAL.

And Mark was that son.

It was a small Navy.

And the hell of it was that, in the normal unfolding of events, they never would have met Mark. Both Nolan and Ringold were Team Two—East Coast SEALs operating out of Little Creek, Virginia. They were in California, Team One's turf, on Temporary Attached Duty. Again, Tangretti didn't know the details, but he'd heard plenty of scuttlebutt around the base. The word was that Team Two would be packing up and pulling out of Vietnam soon, possibly within a year, but that some sort of new initiative was being planned in Nam that would employ SEALs from both Teams in a new role. Tangretti had no idea what that new role might be, but the standard operating procedure almost since the SEALs had arrived in Vietnam had been to conduct raids and ambushes, reconnaissance patrols, and prisoner snatches, all types of operations that would have to be taken over exclusively by the South Vietnamese military if *Vietnamization* was ever going to be more than a word.

The aircraft gave an uncomfortable lurch, but the engines continued their deep-throated rumble, making casual conversation in the back difficult. They were currently flying at an altitude of 30,000 feet in an unheated, unpressurized aircraft, which explained the chill in the air and the masks on their faces. SEALs tried to make as many HALO training jumps at night as they could manage, which explained the darkness.

The Marine jumpmaster was standing next to the cargo bay's forward bulkhead. The coiled black rubber-coated line of an intercom jack plugged into his helmet so he could relay information from the C-130's crew forward.

"So, Gunny!" Tangretti called out, shouting to make himself heard above the roar of the engines. "How come it's called Twentynine Palms?"

The Marine barked laughter, muffled behind his face mask. "Damned place is in the middle of a desert!" he called back. "There was this oasis, see? Twenty-nine palm trees. Only trouble was, when they did a survey of the place, back in 1885, they could only find twenty-six of the things."

"Sloppy. Losing trees like that."

"Ah, somebody probably snuck in an' hijacked 'em for cumshaw." He shook his head. "You squids watch yourselves down there, okay? Ain't an ocean for miles and miles. What you got is your basic Mark I scorpions, rattlesnakes, and gila monsters, so watch where you put your feet."

"Roger that!"

"What kinda sailors jump out of airplanes over the middle of the desert, anyway?"

Tangretti chuckled. "*Mean* ones, Gunny. So watch it!"

"Yeah, I'm shaking with fear, all right. I just want to know where you guys are gonna find a boat, down there in all that sand!"

SEALs used the Marine range at Twentynine Palms occasionally for exercises like this one, but even so, SEALs were not yet that well known outside of the Navy Special Warfare community. It was possible the gunny sergeant had never heard of them . . . or that he'd simply not made the connection. SEALs might operate in sea, land, and air, but most people who'd heard of them still thought of SCUBA-clad frogmen slipping into enemy harbors underwater.

"Don't need to find one, Gunny," Greg called out. "We're gonna *build* it."

"Yeah!" Ringold added. "Out of rocks, sand, and spit! And three palm trees we got stashed away in a secret hiding place. And then we're going to pick it up and march it right down to the sea!"

"You guys are friggin' crazy." The sergeant paused, holding one gloved hand against the side of his helmet, listening a moment. Then he held up his hand, fingers spread. "Okay, everybody," he bellowed. "Five minutes to jump!"

Bill stood up, a bit clumsy in his HALO rig. Altogether, he was carrying over one hundred pounds of equipment, including O_2 bottle, full combat gear, ammunition, and M-16, and he had to move carefully to avoid bumping either bulkhead or teammate with part of his load. The rifle was strapped to his left side, muzzle down, with the butt behind his shoulder and the barrel pressed against his thigh. His altimeter was mounted on his reserve chute, which was strapped to his belly; a heavily loaded rucksack was slung beneath his main chute, hanging down behind his butt. He faced Greg Halstead, his jumpbuddy for this exercise, and carefully inspected each harness snap, each buckle, each piece of equipment, tugging at them to make sure that all were securely fastened. After Greg had about-faced so that Bill could complete the inspection from the rear, it was Bill's turn to be inspected. For good measure, Morgan came down the line, checking each of the men in his squad. Nothing could be left to chance.

"Okay!" the jumpmaster called, shouting to be heard through his mask and above the steady droning of the Herky Bird's engines. "Altitude is thirty thousand. Winds at the ground are light, four to six knots, from the west. The pilot has your DZ in sight, bearing two-five-zero. Two-minute warning! We're opening up!"

With a grinding hum, the C-130's tail door began slowly opening, until the aft end of the cargo bay gaped out into night and emptiness, and the roar of the aircraft's engines was mingled with the wind-rushing thunder of the slipstream. The seven SEALs trudged aft until they stood just forward of the ramp, supporting themselves by leaning against one another, or hanging from the canvas straps that lined the cargo bay's interior. As the hatch lowered far enough for Tangretti to see, he found himself looking out across the southern California night. The sky was clear, the stars hard and cold and bright as they can only be six miles up, where the air was so thin it seemed almost like he was standing one rung below space itself.

Below, the desert was lost in darkness, though a haze of light toward the west marked San Bernardino and other eastern suburbs of Los Angeles. The black bulk of the San Bernardino Mountains sawtoothed their way across the light haze like some huge, black, humpbacked beast.

"Long way down," Panopolis said, craning his neck.

"That's the short way home, son," Nolan said. "You don't want to go back with these Marines. They're *crazy!*"

"That's ay-firmative," Ringold added. "I don't think some of these jarhead flyboys know what the hell they're doing."

"So how 'bout it, Doc," Greg called. "You sorry yet that you re-upped?"

Bill laughed. Just a few weeks earlier he'd signed the papers to extend his enlistment—"shipping for six," as it was called. "Man, it's the only way to fly!"

"Knock it off, people," Morgan shouted. "Get ready to exit the aircraft! Stand in the door!"

Bill exchanged glances with Greg. Morgan seemed a bit uptight, with a fast-rising pucker factor. Well, that was one of the reasons for exercises like this one. Shake the men out, officers and enlisted both, and get them used to doing the impossible.

Their mission plan called for a HALO from 30,000 feet and an assembly at the DZ, followed by a ten-mile overland hike to a featureless patch of desert called Waypoint Bravo, then a three-mile hike to an encampment manned by an unknown number of U.S. Marines. The SEALs' objective was to find some way—any way—to disable a number of armored vehicles parked at the camp. To that end, all of the SEALs were carrying dummy munitions, though Tangretti still favored the simple but direct expedient of sand in their transmissions. The exercise was made more fun by the knowledge that the Marines *knew* the SEALs were coming and were ready for them.

This sort of war-gaming was done all the time, with SEALs and UDT taking on armed and alert Marines. Tangretti had participated in a number of amphibious exercises at Coronado, or offshore at the Navy test range on Catalina Island, sneaking onto a Marine base, taking out the sentries and leaving them tightly tied and gagged, then going on to leave a message in some impenetrable site, like the office of the base CO. Usually, the message was something simple and cheerful, like a sign reading SEAL ONE WAS HERE. The only rules were not to kill or maim anyone permanently. *Anything* else was allowed, anything at all. It was good training for the Teams, of course. It had the added benefit of teaching the

Marine sentries to stay on their toes. The guys they might be facing overseas one day wouldn't be *nearly* as gentle as the SEALs.

"Ready!" Morgan called out, shouting to be heard. "One! Two! Three! *Go!*"

"Hooyah!" Greg yelled, giving the SEAL battle cry, and Bill and the rest echoed the shout.

"Hooyah!"

Together, moving in a tightly clumped rush of arms, legs, chute packs, and gear, the seven men raced down the lowered ramp and launched themselves into space, spilling off the end of the ramp like dominos falling in a line.

Instantly, the air hit Bill like a living thing, setting the material of his pants crackling and snapping against his legs, buoying him up as he arched his back and assumed the starfish position for free fall. It was also cold, colder by far than it had been inside the Herky Bird. Despite mask, goggles, and helmet, enough of the skin above his collar was exposed to really feel the chill, as was some of the skin between his black thermal gloves and the ends of his sleeves. A man could easily get a nasty case of frostbite jumping at this altitude, where the temperature routinely was forty below or worse, and where the speed of his descent created a wind chill effect that made even a Minnesota winter tame by comparison.

Dimly, he sensed the other members of the team all around him, black shapes against the blacker night, obscuring the stars as they fell. Gradually, they began drifting apart, receding into the wind-howling darkness; each man needed a clear safety zone about him when he deployed his chute, and even during the free fall portion of the descent it was possible for someone to be knocked unconscious if one HALO jumper or another accidentally zoomed into a buddy.

They wouldn't let themselves drift too far, though. The idea of the clustered run-and-jump was for all members of the team to exit the rear of the aircraft within the space of a few seconds, guaranteeing that they would come down more or less in the same place. On a real combat jump, the parachutists wouldn't have the time to conduct an extensive search for scattered teammates, or to rally the party at a specific rendezvous. It was all too easy to get completely lost on a jump, *especially* a free fall jump from 30,000 feet in the middle of the night; once the SEALs hit the ground, they had to be ready to form up and move out without taking time for anything else. Part of the success of tonight's exercise would be measured by how close they all came down to the target drop zone.

Carefully, Tangretti dropped one shoulder, turning in space, searching for the ground target below. There! A tiny, glowing red cross, five ruby pinpoints, shone in the black desert below and to the right, where a Marine pathfinder team had already marked their target in flares.

He checked the luminous dial of his watch. Forty seconds had passed, and by now he would be approaching terminal velocity for a free fall jump, about 120 miles per hour. He'd fallen the better part of a mile already, with five more to go. He oriented himself in space to keep the drop zone in sight. It was possible to steer in free fall. By moving his arms in and dropping the forward half of his body, he could move ahead like a rocket, giving him considerable mobility . . . albeit by significantly increasing the vertical component of his drop velocity. He reined in the temptation, however. Success on this jump depended on perfectly disciplined coordination. It wouldn't do to have the team members maneuvering separately, and possibly getting in one another's way when it was time to deploy.

HALO techniques had been used by special forces for some time now, not only in the United States but by foreign elite units as well, including the British SAS and the Soviet Spetsnaz. The HALO acronym stood for High Altitude Low Opening, and the idea was deceptively simple. A lone aircraft flying above twenty or thirty thousand feet didn't attract the same attention as one passing at an altitude of a few thousand feet, and enemy soldiers on the ground would neither see nor hear it. Rather than using static lines to open their chutes as soon as they left the aircraft—the technique used in all of the airborne assaults of World War II, for instance—HALO jumpers rode the winds down in free fall, deploying their chutes when they reached low altitude. Normal chute deployment took place at four thousand feet, high enough to allow a margin of safety for the jumpers while ensuring that the crack of their canopies opening would not be heard on the ground. A team of jumpers could be on the ground and taking out the sentries before the bad guys even knew there was a threat.

SEALs trained initially with at least forty HALO jumps over a six-week period, starting at 12,000 feet, and working their way up to 25,000 feet and higher, and qualifying jumps were made periodically thereafter. As Tangretti floated through the roaring night, the wind blasting at his chest and goggles, he wondered about the fact that HALO wasn't used by the Teams in Vietnam.

Well, there was no major mystery there. Opportunities for parachute insertions were sharply limited in a country where the vast majority of the land was cloaked in jungle, forested mountain, or rice paddies with mud so deep that a man in full combat gear coming down by parachute would vanish completely in the mud, never to be seen again. He'd heard a number of horror stories already about Air Force pilots forced to eject over the jungle.

Tree jumping, as that kind of landing was known, had been briefly in vogue with the British Special Air Service during their involvement in jungle-clad Malaysia in the fifties. SAS parachutists carried several hundred feet of rope carefully looped and tied above their abdomens. Theoretically, the jumper's chute would snag in the jungle canopy; the jumper could then deploy the rope, unhook his harness, and lower himself to the ground. So many men had been killed or badly injured performing this maneuver, however, which was a *lot* chancier than the simple description of the thing made it sound, that tree jumping had eventually been abandoned.

Driving the pointy end of a tree trunk up your ass could ruin your whole day.

HALO jumps were dangerous enough. Oxygen was required for any jump over about 17,000 feet, and all too many things could go wrong there, from valves or feed lines icing up and cutting off your air, to forgetting to turn on the valve in the first place. Tangretti had no visual referents at all to the ground, since the distant glimmer of the DZ lights couldn't give him a feeling for depth. Instead, he had to rely on his altimeter ... which could freeze, malfunction, or be misread because of a fault in his oxygen system. He was coming down past 22,500 feet now. He was having a little trouble seeing, and it took him a moment to realize that he was growing a thin layer of ice over his goggles. He tried clearing them with a gloved finger but only managed to smear the frost around. Well, it would melt when he got lower.

Damn, but his wrists were burning, though.

One minute of free fall . . . and he was almost down to 20,000 feet. Looking up, he saw stars being occulted by something black—one of his teammates. Good, he should still be with the pack. The buffeting he was taking from the wind seemed to be growing stiffer; at the same time, the whole front of his body was starting to feel a bit numb, just from the force of the wind. He also felt the characteristic exhilaration of free fall, though, the part he loved the most about HALO jumps. This must be something like what the astronauts felt on their way to the Moon. He didn't really feel like he was falling at all, and, for all he could see, he might as easily have been hanging suspended in a great, black room, completely weightless.

The roar increased as he floated on the wind.

Two minutes, and 10,000 feet. He would have to start paying close attention to his altimeter now, its round, luminous dial easily visible extending from his reserve chute when he ducked his head down a bit. The air felt a bit warmer, and his wrists were no longer burning. Either it was actually warmer here, four miles beneath where he'd stepped out of the airplane, or his skin had stopped registering the sharp sensations of incipient frostbite. He watched the altimeter closely, willing himself to see through the thin rime of frost on his goggles. His heart hammered beneath his coveralls. *God, I love this* was his adrenaline-charged thought.

Five thousand feet.

Forty-five hundred.

His goggles were clear now, the ground, still invisible in the darkness, close enough to sense as a vast, onrushing presence. There was a terrible danger now that even an experienced jumper would fall right through his safety envelope, riding the wind until it was too late to deploy.

Four thousand.

Thirty-five hundred. His gloved hand reached across and took hold of the reassuringly solid heft of the rip cord's D-ring. *No, that's just a loose string,* the angel at the gates of heaven said to the parachutist in the old joke. *There.* That's *your rip cord.*

The exercise schedule called for chute deployment at 3,000 feet. As the altimeter's luminous hand swept past the 3, he yanked the rip cord, felt the lazy unfolding of his chute at his back . . . and then the savage yank of deployment and the momentarily disconcerting sensation that he was now rising, going back the other way, as his harness straps bit hard at shoulders, chest, and groin. He heard the solid crack of his chute grabbing air. Nearby, from the darkness, he heard another, answering crack . . . and a third . . . and a fourth. The other SEALs' chutes were deploying as well, three thousand feet above the ground.

Tangretti looked up but could barely see his own chute, a black nylon rectangle blotting out the stars. Still, he would have been able to tell if it had twisted in the middle, a dangerous fouling of the lines known as a "bow tie" or, more picturesquely, as a "Mae West" because it resembled an enormous brassiere. His ram-air chute had deployed perfectly, and he was drifting down now at a saner velocity of a handful of feet per second.

He could see the DZ clearly now, easily within reach. Reaching up, he grabbed his steering risers and spilled a little air from the left, turning in that direction. SEALs preferred the relatively new ram-air chutes to the old World War II–era canopies. More like aircraft wings than traditional chutes, they possessed remarkable maneuverability, allowing the jumper to fly into a pinpoint landing on-target.

In the last few moments of his descent, he could see the ground by starlight and the red gleam of the guttering flares, a smooth expanse of uncluttered desert gravel. He held his legs together, knees slightly bent, his head up and his eyes on the horizon. At the last moment, he brought the controls down, spilling more air from his chute and going into a deliberate stall. The front of the chute came up, the balls of his feet touched the ground, and he stepped into a perfect landing, so light that he didn't even need to drop in a shock-absorbing fall. He took a couple of steps, already beginning to gather in his chute. He was pleased with himself. The nearest of the flares was less than fifteen feet away.

As he wadded up the lightweight nylon, he heard a whoosh

to his right, followed by the crunch of gravel. A moment later, Lieutenant Nolan stepped out of the darkness, his chute wadded up in front of him.

"Four!" Tangretti said, even though he could see who it was. The agreed-upon password was a number, with the reply a second number that would bring the total to ten.

"Six! Tangretti?"

"Yes, sir." The SEALs quickly unbuckled their rigs, unsnapped their weapons, and dropped into a crouch. This was a combat exercise, after all. Four more figures materialized out of the darkness. "Seven!" Nolan hissed.

The reply came back at once. "Three!" In another second, Halstead, Morgan, Hochstader, and Panopolis had joined them, dropping into a defensive perimeter, weapons pointed outward.

"Where the hell is Ringold?" Morgan snapped. "Anybody seen him?"

There were several muttered negatives. "No, sir," Tangretti said. "We just got here."

They waited several minutes more, the silence growing increasingly uncomfortable. It was possible that Ringold had missed the DZ by a bigger margin than the others . . . but not likely. With each passing moment, the chances that he was injured out there in the desert somewhere, or worse, grew.

"I think we should call an abort," Nolan said quietly. "I think something's wrong."

"We still have a mission to perform, Lieutenant," Morgan said.

"With all due respect, *sir*," Halstead said, putting an unpleasant stress on the honorific, "we have a teammate out there, somewhere. We need to find him."

"He's right, Lieutenant," Nolan added. "We'd better find him."

Morgan waited a moment longer, staring into the night as though he could make the missing man materialize by sheer force of will. "*Shit!*" he said at last. Reaching up, he keyed the small Motorola radio strapped to his combat vest. "Maple Sugar, Maple Sugar," he called. "This is Romeo One at DZ Tango. Abort, abort, abort. We have a man down and missing. Over."

"Romeo One, Maple Sugar," the reply came back almost

at once. "We copy. Stay where you are. Help is on the way."

The Marine UH-1 helicopter clattered out of the sky from the south a few minutes later. The war games, and the Marines with their armored vehicles, could wait. Other helos were already circling the exercise area, listening for the electronic beep of Ringold's SAR radio, a compact emergency transmitter that would let the search-and-rescue teams home in on him at once if he was lying out in the desert somewhere, injured.

It took eight hours to find him.

Friday, 7 August 1970

Desert exercise range
Twentynine Palms
Marine Corps Base, California
0815 hours

It was full daylight when the Huey lightly touched down in a different part of the desert, and Halstead, Tangretti, Nolan, and Morgan jumped out. They'd returned to the main base during the night, where they'd been debriefed, then given a chance to catch some unexpected sleep. None of them had been able to, of course. *What happened? It could have been me!* The thoughts chased one another round and round in Greg's brain, until the word came down, just as he and the others were getting ready to go to morning chow, that Ringold had been found . . . and that he was dead.

They hadn't moved the body yet. The crew from the SAR chopper that had found him was waiting for a legal team to come out from headquarters. There would have to be an inquest, of course.

Not that an inquest could help Mark Ringold.

Greg walked up to the body, forcing himself to see. Mark was lying on his back, both his main and reserve chutes unopened. His goggles and mask had been ripped away, and his blue eyes were staring sightlessly into the zenith. His torso was . . . *twisted* was the only word for it and, like something out of a surrealist painting, both of his legs had been driven upward, right through his body, the bloody, bone-jagged end of his right leg emerging through his chest, the end of his left leg protruding out his back, the booted feet, in a black-comic effect, protruding from the blood-drenched and torn coveralls just below the groin. Blood had soaked the sand black all around, and a bloody splatter of viscera gleamed on the ground a few feet away. His rifle was still strapped to his back, the black plastic hand guard splintered by the impact, the barrel bent almost double.

Greg sank to his knees, staring at the body. He hadn't known Ringold well; hell, he'd only met the man when he'd arrived on TAD orders the week before. Still, they'd become friends once they'd learned of the connection between their families. It was like losing a relative you hadn't known you'd had. His dad's friend's son . . .

Another thought followed that one close on its heels. How was this going to affect his dad? David Halstead never talked much about it, but Greg knew that he worried about the more dangerous aspects of his son's chosen career. Greg had started off as an electronics technician, a "twidget," but he'd volunteered for BUD/S, choosing to move into one of the Navy's more dangerous careers. His father had never said anything, other than that he was proud. This was going to be hard on his dad . . . and on his mom, too.

The really shitty part of it was that Mark had died in a damned training exercise. It was one thing to get killed by an enemy, someone physical you could face and respect and pay back big-time. But an accident was so . . . so *pedestrian*. And useless. Team One had been plagued with that sort of thing lately. Last June, five Team One SEALs, two from Golf Platoon and three from Echo, had died in a single incident near Can Tho, in Vietnam, when their helicopter—call sign Vulture Two-seven—had crashed for unknown reasons. Those guys hadn't even been on a mission; their flight had been part of an administrative move, from one AO to another.

He wished he'd known Mark better. Or did he? Death was in the cards in everything the SEALs did, whether it was combat overseas or training under combat conditions. Hell, SEAL recruits had drowned in BUD/S or, in one case he'd heard about, succumbed to cold and shock and a failing heart. Greg had lost buddies. He thought of Vinh, and the funeral in Saigon. Maybe it was better when you didn't know the guy all that well.

He glanced at Nolan, who was kneeling on the black sand

next to the body, holding one gloved hand. There were tears on Nolan's face.

"Please, sir," a corpsman who'd been with the SAR team told the lieutenant. "Don't touch anything until the investigators get here, huh?"

"I'm not touching anything, Doc," Nolan replied, his voice strained. "But I'm going to sit with a friend for a while, okay? Just a little while. . . ."

Chapter 16

Saturday, 8 August 1970

**Chico's Bordertown Cantina
Coronado, California
2145 hours**

They'd returned to Coronado the same day, where they faced the usual round of questions from various investigators. SEAL training—and the constant practice sessions that SEALs endured regularly once they'd left BUD/S—could be dangerous, and accidents happened, though every effort was taken to minimize risks. A popular story making the rounds outside the SEAL community was that graduation from frogman training involved taking the student out to sea, dropping him overboard, and having him swim back to the beach. If he made it, he graduated. If not, the Navy was spared the expense of a burial at sea.

The story, of course, was not true . . . or, at least, not entirely. Students *were* expected to complete a five-and-a-half-mile ocean swim without fins, and, later, a two-mile ocean swim *with* fins in under seventy minutes. In both evolutions, though, instructors paced the students in an IBS or other small boat, ready to pull them out if they got into trouble. The Navy had a fair piece of taxpayer change tied up in each BUD/S student, and it was in everyone's best interest that he survive the training . . . even if he didn't ultimately make the grade.

Accidents did happen, though, and occasionally men died as a result. Training for the Teams was not confined to BUD/S but continued throughout a SEAL's career, and the training was as tough, as demanding, and as realistic as the SEALs themselves could make it.

And a SEAL's death was no less strongly felt by his buddies because it had happened during a training exercise, instead of in combat.

On the evening after the day of their return, Halstead, Tangretti, Nolan, Morgan, Panopolis, and Hochstader decided to go into town. It was time for Ringold's wake.

Chico's was one of several bars in the Coronado–Imperial Beach–San Diego area staked out by the Navy SEALs and claimed as their own. The place was located on a street that ran just a few feet from the water, across the bay from the city of San Diego. Coronado was a small town on the slender peninsula that separated San Diego Bay from the Pacific Ocean. Sandwiched in between North Island Naval Air Station to the north and the Coronado Naval Amphibious Base on the Silver Strand to the south, Coronado existed mostly as a bedroom and commercial community for the military, for military families, and for those people whose livelihoods depended on the military presence—the proprietors of the tailor shops, the stores specializing in civilian clothing, the tattoo parlors and tobacco shops, the bars and restaurants and adult bookstores and whorehouses and the like.

The dimly lit bar's sound system was throbbing to the driving beat of "I'll Be There" as they walked inside. It was relatively early, and there weren't a lot of people in the place, though the table usually favored by Greg and Bill, the big one by the front window overlooking the bay, was occupied by three Marines. The SEALs acquired the table for themselves through the simple expedient of trooping over to the table and standing above the Marines, crowding their personal space. "You know, that's a damned big table for just the three of you," Halstead growled.

"Yeah," Panopolis added, picking at his teeth with the nail

of his little finger. "I think you boys want something more *intimate.*"

One of the Marines, a six-footer with sergeant's stripes on his khakis, looked like he might want to argue the point, but the other two quietly, almost meekly, got up and, with a tug at the sergeant's arm, vacated the table without a word. It was, Greg thought as he watched them scoop up their drinks and move off, purely a tactical retreat, with no shame attached. The three at the table were the only Marines in the place, while there were six SEALs. Only Panopolis and Hochstader were wearing Navy uniforms—tropical white longs. The rest wore civvies and were more anonymous . . . and, therefore, threatening. Besides, if Tangretti and Nolan were both on the short side, Halstead, Panopolis, and Morgan more than made up for them in size and mass, and this was definitely a situation, so far as the Marines were concerned, where discretion was the better part of valor.

Greg was disappointed, though. He was feeling mean enough just then to have enjoyed a good brawl, even if it meant a visit from the Shore Patrol.

The SEALs took the vacated table, as Nolan signaled for a waitress. Only recently, Greg reflected, had civilian clothing become not only permitted but *encouraged* by the Navy's high-ranking powers-that-be for men venturing off-base on liberty, and a large part of the reason for that had to do with the country's current political climate. Men in uniform, those powers believed, were incidents waiting to happen, particularly when they attracted the attention of some of the more militant members of the activist peace movements. Greg remembered the reception at the San Diego airport the year before . . . the ugly faces spitting and calling him "Pig."

Funny. The uniform had always been something to be *proud* of. . . .

"What'll you boys have?" the waitress asked. She was pretty, brunette, and had the yeah-I've-heard-that-one-before tone of voice of a woman who worked at the gates of a military base.

Hochstader leaned forward. "I think I'll have you turn this place into one of those topless bars. Improve the . . . uh . . ."

"Ambiance," Panopolis said, supplying the missing word.

"Yeah, that's it. The ambulance."

"You boys want to take your shirts off, it's fine with me," the waitress told him with a could-care-less shrug. "But the manager'll chuck you out. No shirt, no shoes, no service, y'know? Now, what can I get you to *drink?*"

They went around the table, naming their drinks. Halstead ordered scotch on the rocks, Tangretti bourbon. "The drinks," Nolan said as he pulled a wad of money out of his wallet, "are on me and Goldie."

Greg had been reaching for his own wallet. "Sir?"

"Party fund's back at Little Creek," Nolan explained as the waitress sauntered off. "I can cover until I get back there."

Greg understood and replaced his wallet. Ringold, like most other SEALs, had left money toward his "will," to be used for a party in his honor if he died. The only trouble was, Ringold and Nolan were Team Two. All their buddies were with the East Coast SEALs, operating out of Little Creek, Virginia, and the money was probably in the Team CO's office back there. Greg wondered if Nolan would really reimburse himself when his TAD with Team One was over, or if they would throw another party with Ringold's money. Probably the latter, he thought. Nolan seemed like a good sort, a good teammate.

"Thanks, Lieutenant," Bill said.

"And shit-can the 'lieutenant' crap," Nolan added. "Tom and I are incognito tonight."

Which put things on a friendlier, more informal footing right off. Officers and enlisted men tended to fraternize a lot more in the SEALs than in any other branch of the service, but there was still that yawning gulf of authority and social distance represented by those little metal insignia on the guy's collar, and the training and discipline of the mainline Navy died hard. Greg thought that Nolan and Morgan had probably worn civvies tonight more to let them shed their personae as naval officers than to avoid confrontations with hippies.

At least, that was the case with David Nolan. Halstead wasn't sure what to think yet about Morgan. The man could be as cold as a fish, and damned hard to read.

"Here you go, boys," the waitress said, bringing their drinks on a tray. "You want anything else right now?"

"I want you to have my child," Greg told her with as much

earnestness as he could muster. "When can we get together and arrange things?"

"Why?" she asked. "Don't you want him any more?"

The others laughed, hooted, and oohed as she grinned and strolled away once more, buttocks twitching enticingly beneath her short skirt. "I think I'm in love," Greg told them.

"No bra," Morgan added. "I wouldn't mind a piece of that."

"Stop drooling, sir," Greg said. "I can hear your dick hardening from here."

"Enough of that," Nolan said. He carefully slid a glass of Johnny Walker Black Label, Ringold's favorite, across the tabletop to its place in front of an empty chair. Then he hoisted his own glass. "Here's to you, Mark!" he said, before downing the drink in one hard chug.

"Mark!" the others echoed. "Hooyah!"

And then the party got rolling.

They'd all stowed several drinks already when Nolan let fly with a particularly bitter and acid-edged curse.

"What bit you, Dave?" By this time, all of the enlisted men were calling Nolan by his first name. None had so far dared—or gotten drunk enough yet—to venture the same familiarity with Morgan, who was drinking hard and saying little.

Nolan seemed to consider the question, staring at his glass a moment as he moved it in small circles on the table. "It's just the idea of a damned *accident*," he said at last. He tossed back his drink and brought the empty glass down on the tabletop so hard that Greg thought he'd broken it. "You know, Goldie and me, we've done some damned cool stuff together. Paddled a sampan seventy-some miles across the open ocean, to get back to friendly lines. The guy was *good*."

Greg raised his eyebrows at this and exchanged a glance with Bill. That seventy-mile figure, if accurate, tended to confirm some of what the Team One SEALs had heard about Nolan and Ringold . . . especially the story about them raiding Sihanoukville. Seventy miles might be just about right.

"I know he was, sir," Greg said. "Maybe, though, you ought to watch what you're saying in public."

Nolan looked up sharply, the color draining from his face.

"Shit. You're right." He shook his head. "This thing's really getting to me, guys."

"Know what you mean, Dave," Bill said. "We lost a buddy on our last Nam tour. LDNN."

"Got to go to his funeral," Greg added. "It shook us, let me tell you."

"Some of those Viet SEALs are damned good," Nolan said.

"Vinh was one of the best," Greg said.

"So, is there any word yet on what went wrong on Ringold's HALO?" Bill asked Nolan. The lieutenant, they all knew, had spent a fair part of the day talking with inspectors and investigators going into the young SEAL's death.

"Well, nothing official yet," Nolan said. "There'll be a full inquest, of course. But it looks like they figured out what happened, and that'll probably close the door on it."

"What happened?" Hochstader asked, leaning closer over the table.

"Anoxia. He blacked out on the way down and never opened his chute."

"Yeah, but why?"

"Ice. It looks like Mark's oxygen hose wasn't draining the way it should have. Maybe it was picking up some extra condensation from his breath that wasn't getting shunted away. Maybe the valve itself was frozen. They're still looking into that. Anyway, the guess is that when we jumped, his air hose was partly blocked with ice. Not enough for him to notice, necessarily, especially if he was excited. But on the way down, he probably got more excited and started breathing harder. Maybe even hyperventilating."

"More ice could've built up, too," Hochstader pointed out.

"Maybe. But the guess is that when he needed more O_2, it just wasn't feeding fast enough with that blocked hose. And that's all she wrote."

Greg leaned back in his seat, scowling. Such a damned *little* thing, a chunk of ice the size of a guy's thumb, and a man was dead.

"Well, it wasn't a bad way to go," Panopolis said. "I mean, you pass out, it's like going to sleep, right? Only you never wake up."

"Hell of a way for a SEAL to check out," Morgan replied.

"SEALs oughta buy it in a firefight, know what I mean? Guns blazing. Death has to knock 'em down and drag 'em out kicking."

"Hooyah!" Tangretti, Panopolis, and Hochstader chorused, almost together.

Greg, though, sipped his drink and didn't add a *hooyah* of his own. Morgan's attitude, he thought, was too much like that of a Wild West cowboy to suit him. The idea in most SEAL work was to get in quietly, get the job done with a minimum of violence, then get out fast . . . without turning an encounter with the enemy into some kind of macho, *High Noon*–style shoot-out.

"Hey!" Panopolis said suddenly. "Get a load of this."

Panopolis was sitting closest to the bar's window, which overlooked the street outside and, beyond, the waters of San Diego Bay, adazzle with the lights of the city. He jerked a thumb at the vehicle parked closest to the window, a gaudily painted VW microbus covered with psychedelic designs, flowers, and the multihued words LOVE and PEACEMOBILE, which was just pulling into a streetlight-illuminated parking space outside. "Hey, Dave, everyone! Check out the hippie transport!"

Kids began spilling out of the vehicle, two girls and four young men, shaggy in long hair and somewhat threadbare beards. All were very much a part of the hippie scene, complete with love beads and peace symbols. One man wore a denim jacket with a crudely painted MAKE LOVE, NOT WAR displayed across the back. One of the girls, a pretty blonde, wore a shirt tied tight in front to give her a bare midriff, while the other, a brunette, wore a T-shirt with a silkscreened picture of Che Guevara on the back. As they walked into Chico's through the front door, Morgan watched them with the same intense stare that a rattlesnake might give a hamster.

"Hey, Mr. Morgan," Bill said. "What's going down?"

"Damned hippie freaks," Morgan muttered. He shook his head. "Probably came here straight from a peace march, someplace."

"More like a love-in," Hochstader observed as they found a table toward the back of the place. The blonde and the guy with the MAKE LOVE, NOT WAR jacket began dancing while the others watched. "I kind of like the chick with the bell-bottoms and the bare-belly look."

"Our people are dying," Morgan said. "And they're . . . *dancing.*"

"Yeah," Bill said. "Life goes on, Lieutenant. *They* didn't kill Ringold."

"I don't like peaceniks or traitors either," Greg added. "But, hey. It's a free country, right?"

"Right," Morgan agreed. "Which means I'm free to go over there and toss those bums the hell out of here."

"Low profile, Tom," Nolan said. "Let's not do anything that's going to put us or the Teams in tomorrow morning's papers."

"Right," Greg said, grinning. "Don't start a fight. Do it the SEAL way. Sneaky."

"Well, well!" Morgan said, looking up. A dark smile crossed his face. "That's an interesting thought!"

"What is?" Nolan demanded.

"Well, we were on our way to disable some armored vehicles the other day," Morgan said, the smile turning cold. He nodded at the VW bus outside. "How hard would it be to take out *that* hunk of junk? A quick snip-snip to the brake cables, and those commie lovers could end up taking a swim in the Pacific Ocean tonight."

"You just shit-can that talk, Lieutenant," Nolan said fiercely.

"What the hell are you thinking of, sir?" Bill asked him.

"Hell, I'll *tell* you what I'm thinking!" Morgan stabbed his finger at the kids. "We are in a civil war here. We keep hearing about how we're supposed to be winning hearts and minds over in Vietnam. Well, son of a bitch, but Hanoi and Moscow are doing their damnedest to win hearts and minds over here. Am I right? Eh? Am I?"

"You're drunk, Lieutenant," Hochstader told him.

"Not drunk enough." He held up his glass, turning it against the light in the bar. "Well, maybe I am. What's your point?"

Something about the passion that had resonated in Morgan's voice had Greg thinking. "Wait, wait, wait," he said. "The man's right. We're at war, and not all of the bad guys are in North Vietnam. Or the U.S.S. of R."

"Christ, Twidge," Bill said, scowling. "You two are cruisin' for a bruisin', I can tell you! You don't make war on civilians! On kids!"

"Why not?" Morgan said. "That's what we're doing over there. In Nam."

"Have you been in Nam yet, man?" Bill asked.

"Not yet. But I will be soon, and then Thomas Morgan'll show you boys how this war *ought* to be fought!"

"Maybe you should wait and see what it's like before you start comparing their kids with ours," Nolan said. "And you damned sure'd better watch that talk about going after American civilians. That's crazy talk."

"Damn straight!" Bill said, shaking his head. "SEALs already have a piss-poor rep as stone killers. Bad PR, man!"

"If we have the rep," Greg said, "maybe we should live up to it."

"For your information," Nolan said mildly, "we still have something over here called a Constitution. And for your information, the U.S. military doesn't go around making war on *anybody's* kids."

"Shit, we're not talking about shooting kids!" Morgan said. He rubbed his eyes, looking suddenly tired. The sound system was playing "Aquarius" now, as though to emphasize the growing gulf between culture and counterculture. "But damn it, if we don't do something, the commies're gonna win the war here in America before we have a chance to win it over there! All I'm sayin', see, is that it would be so easy to run some deep cover ops right here." He nodded toward the kids.

"You know," Greg said, grinning, "I think Mr. Morgan's right. Half the problem's not knowing what we're up against. Wouldn't be hard to penetrate their organizations, you know. Some of our guys dress like 'em. Let their hair grow long. Hang out with 'em. Get to know 'em. Work our way into their peace groups, y'know? Infiltrate their organizations."

Hochstader chuckled. "I think Twidge and Mr. Morgan here just want a chance at that cute blonde."

"Yeah," Panopolis added. "You guys volunteering? I know it's a tough job, but somebody's got to—"

"Cut the bullshit," Morgan said, interrupting. "The idea . . ." He paused, and then his fist slammed down suddenly, rattling glasses on the table and making a bang loud enough that several of the hippies turned and looked toward the SEALs, startled. "The idea is to get a fucking line on whoever is orchestrating this damned peace movement and sabotaging us, shooting us in the back!"

"I can sympathize with you, Tom," Nolan said quietly. "I really can. But the military is under civilian control. Got to be that way, or America stops being America. Hear what I'm saying?"

"I hear you. I don't have to like it."

"Nobody said you did," Nolan replied. He studied his half empty glass a moment. "Shit. We're supposed to be remembering Goldie, not planning to overthrow the U.S. government!" He signaled the waitress. "Miss! Let's get another round over here!"

"Let's make it tequila, this time," Hochstader said. "Some shooters for the shooters!"

"Yeah," Panopolis added. "The *real* stuff. Not the crap you save for the tourists."

Greg was starting to feel a bit bleary but was doggedly determined to see this celebration through to its end. He was surprised at having found some common ground with Morgan, a man he respected, certainly, but who he'd never expected to like. The guy's attitudes toward American traitors, though, echoed Halstead's own. If the guy would just lighten up a little. . . .

The waitress banged a bottle of Monte Albán on the table and added a bowl of lime slices.

" *'Con gusano,'* " Greg said, picking up the heavy, squared-off bottle and reading the label. "What the hell's *'con gusano?'* "

"Means it's got the worm in the bottle," Nolan told him, grinning. "See?"

Greg held the bottle higher, squinting. There, at the bottom, was a slender, two-inch, pallid-skinned insect, a grub or larva of some kind. "Hey!" he said, turning to the waitress. "There's a goddamn *bug* in there!"

"You wanted the real stuff," she told him with a smile.

"That's right, Twidge," Nolan said. "Haven't you ever heard of doing the worm?"

"The guy who gets the last shot from the bottle," Morgan

told him with an evil grin, "gets to eat the worm!"

The waitress pursed her lips, appraising the men at the table. "You boys are SEALs, right?"

"That's class . . ." Hochstader began. He stopped, frowned, and tried again, carefully. "That's class—classif—"

"Fuck it," Panopolis said. "What if we are?"

"Well, I figure you boys must be SEALs, the way you rousted those Marines earlier. I hear you eat worse than a little ol' worm when you're off on your survival training courses and stuff."

"She's right," Bill said, nudging Greg in the ribs. "Remember Panama?"

"How could I forget?" Greg replied, continuing to eye the worm. He and Bill had both attended, at different times, an Army Special Forces survival school in Panama. Part of their indoctrination had been learning how to eat *anything* that provided protein—snails, lizards, ants, and, especially, large, juicy beetle grubs dug from hollows in rotting tree trunks. The experience hadn't been pleasant, but Greg had learned that he could gulp down whatever he had to. Grubs, he'd learned, were best when lightly toasted, but when swallowed raw they were no worse than a cold, wet piece of vermicelli. The trick was not to think about it or, better yet by far, to assume a predator's mind-set, to *glory* in the act of eating insect, snail, or worm simply because that's what humans did to survive.

But this encounter with the worm in a bottle of tequila was so . . . *unexpected*. He'd never been much of a drinker, despite the hard-drinking, hard-partying SEAL mystique, and he'd never shot tequila, ever. In true SEAL fashion, he grinned at the waitress and decided to make the best of the situation.

"Okay," he told her. "What's your name?"

"Debbie," she said.

"Okay, Debbie. Tell you what. If I eat that worm . . . and if I promise to brush my teeth afterward . . . will you go to bed with me?"

He'd expected a brush-off or even a slap, but Debbie cocked her head to the side and looked him up and down. "I might. I *like* SEALs. A *lot*. . . ."

A chorus of "Whoa!" and "Hey!" and shrill whistles

greeted that announcement, and Greg knew he was committed now. A definite part of the SEAL mystique included the girls, the SEAL-groupies and SEALettes, as they were sometimes called, who hung out near Naval Special Warfare bases and dated only SEALs.

Such women were also, and only half-jokingly, called security risks.

"I think it's cute," Panopolis said, looking at the worm as Debbie walked away again. "I think his name is 'Norm.' "

"Norm the Worm," Nolan agreed.

"How could you eat someone named Norm?" Bill asked. Then his eyes widened. "No, wait a minute. Don't answer that. . . ."

The others showed Greg how to properly shoot tequila . . . shot glass with an ounce of the golden liquid in the right hand, lime in the left, lick the back of the right hand between thumb and forefinger and sprinkle on some salt, lick the salt, down the tequila, bite the lime . . . and feel the burn going down.

It took five or six shots before he thought he was beginning to actually *like* it. . . .

"Y'know, I do wonder what that bunch is doing in Coronado," Greg said thoughtfully after a time, watching the kids. The dawning of the Age of Aquarius had given way to "Let the Sun Shine In," and both women were up and dancing now. The Marines, Halstead noticed through a gathering haze, were gone. They must have paid for their drinks and slipped out while the SEALs were talking, leaving the place to the SEALs, the hippies, and a handful of other patrons. "You don't usually see hippies in a military town like Coronado."

"Yeah," Panopolis said with a snicker, banging an empty shot glass onto the table and leaning back in his chair. "If their daddies are in the Navy or Marines, they're gonna get skinned alive!"

"There've been some demonstrations at some of the military bases around here," Greg pointed out. "Maybe they're here scoping out the amphib base or North Island."

"*That* would make the evening news," Nolan agreed.

"You know, we don' gotta blame commies for the peace movement," Hochstader said, the words slurring. "Hell, we don' gotta look further than C-B-fuckin'-S."

"A-ffirmative," Panopolis said. "Wal—Walter Chi Minh."

"Hell, it's not *his* fault," Bill said. "He calls it like he sees it."

"Shit. Everybody knows his special report right after Tet yanked the rug out from under President Johnson," Morgan said. "He told the whole damned country we were in a stalemate over there."

"We *were*," Nolan pointed out agreeably. He licked his hand, downed the shot, and bit his lime. "About as stale a mate as they come."

"Bullshit," Greg replied. "We beat the sons of bitches silly in Tet. The VC got so badly chewed up, most of their cadres are NVA now. A few more grand offensives like Tet, and Hanoi won't have shit left to fight with."

"*That's* the spirit, man," Morgan said. "If the reporters would just get *that* story right, 'stead of being so goddamned preju . . . prejudging . . . so goddamned one-sided all the time!"

"Shit," Greg went on, warming to the subject like the liquor warming his gut. "The reporting over here is *all* screwed up. We hear all 'bout how Americans are killing civilians in Nam on the evening news. I don't think once I've heard anything about Phuthon."

"A-ffirmative, man," Morgan echoed. "That's what I mean. You *never* hear about that shit from the media."

The SEALs had heard it through their own grapevine and in official briefings. Just two months earlier, on 14 June, Viet Cong and their NVA allies had overrun a village called Phuthon, not far from Danang, driving the civilian population to take shelter in a number of large, underground bunkers. For several hours, the Communists had moved from one bunker to another, firing flamethrowers or dropping hand grenades down the air vents. Hundreds of civilians had been burned alive.

Phuthon had become a rallying cry for many Nam vets who were sick of the one-sided reporting of the war by the various news agencies and by the so-called atrocity mill that seemed dedicated to discrediting American servicemen by exposing every case of civilian death and suffering that could be laid at the military's doorstep.

"There you go, Lieutenant," Hochstader said. "Don' in-filtrate the hippies. Infiltrate the goddamn network news agencies."

"Fuck you, Hochstader," Morgan said pleasantly. "There's a link with Moscow. You guys know I'm right!"

"Well, even if you are, it's not our deployment," Nolan said. "The FBI handles domestic surveillance and counter-espionage work. I'm just as happy to leave the flower children to them."

"Speaking of flower children," Greg said, "watch this!"

They'd nearly reached the bottom of the tequila bottle. With some careful pouring, he sloshed the pickled grub into his shot glass, then picked it out with his fingers.

"Debbie!" he shouted, loud enough to turn heads throughout the bar. "Debbie! There's a worm named Norm in my drink!"

"Hey, keep it down, guys," Debbie said, approaching the table. "We've been getting complaints, okay?"

"Okay, listen! It's time to do the worm! You still holding to your promise?"

"I *always* keep my promises!"

Morgan slipped his arm around her hips. "So, what'd you say if *two* of us ate that thing?"

"Jeez! What kind of a girl do you think I am?"

"A girl who likes SEALs! You said so!"

"Well, let's see you eat the thing, first!"

Holding the grub high between thumb and forefinger, Greg twitched it into a semblance of life. "Help me! Help me!" he piped in a hoarse falsetto. "This big bad SEAL is going to eat meeee!"

The hippies across the way were all watching now. Good. Greg opened wide and chomped down. It was soft, but not as squishy as the raw grubs he'd eaten in Panama. The flavor, if any, was pretty well masked by the sharp bite of the tequila it was pickled in.

As he held the grub in his mouth, Morgan leaned forward as though he was going to kiss him, then caught the grub's tail in his own mouth. Their lips brushed lightly, and the other SEALs hooted and clapped.

"Ooh," Debbie said. "Just like *Lady and the Tramp*. I loved that movie."

"Which one's Lady, is what I want to know," Nolan said.

"True love," Bill said, grinning. "And to think that a worm named Norm brought them together!"

The hippies, Greg noted with a small twist of satisfaction, were beating a hasty retreat toward the door. He stood, a little unsteadily, and bowed to his audience.

Morgan, to his surprise, did the same. *So maybe the guy's one of us after all,* Greg said to himself, trying to focus his drifting thoughts.

It was damned good to know.

Sunday, 9 August 1970

Starlight Motel
La Mesa, California
1040 hours

Morgan blinked himself awake. Movement was difficult; he hurt across every square inch of his body, as though someone had taken a tire iron to him. His head, though—that was the worst. The pain behind his eyes was a tangible, blue-white flare riding on his optic nerves and pulsing with the beating of his heart. His mouth . . . the less said about that, the better. A definite case of the 'zactlies, where his mouth tasted *'zactly* like his asshole.

He hazarded a look around the room. A motel room, from the look of things, though he was a little hazy about how he'd gotten there. From the look of things, he'd spent the entire night on the floor; Halstead lay flat on his back on the bed, legs over the side, his body as naked as Morgan's.

Man, what had gone *on* here last night? He tried to think past the blue-white headache. The wake had broken up about two or so. The rest of the guys had elected to head back to the base. He and Halstead had waited for Debbie.

Riiiiight. Debbie had driven them to the motel after she'd gotten off work. By that time, he and Twidge had been tight in every sense of the word, both as buddies, and as in well on the way to being wasted. They'd had some more drinks—the empty bottles were still on the floor—and they'd all gotten comfortably naked and were getting into a real, three-way orgy scene.

The last thing Morgan remembered was trying to align an uncooperative erection with Debbie's sensuously rolling buttocks. Yeah . . . that was it. She'd been on her hands and knees on the floor, her face in Halstead's lap, head bobbing up and down with reckless enthusiasm. Damn, he couldn't even remember now if he'd finally managed to slip his dick into the rhythmically moving target. He remembered grabbing her ass and moving in, trying to get lined up right for the lunge, but everything seemed to blur out after that.

On the bed, Halstead stirred, groaning. "God. *What* is that taste?"

"Stop shouting. You don't want to know." He'd made it to his trousers, which were lying where he'd tossed them. His wallet was on top, open. *Figures* . . .

Halstead sat up, looking at least as bedraggled as Morgan felt right now. "Oh, shit. Did we both pass out before . . . uh . . . before . . . I can't remember."

"I've been ripped off," Morgan said, holding up his empty wallet. At least his ID and other cards were still there. She'd just taken the cash, a couple of hundred dollars or so.

Staggering to his feet, Halstead padded over to his own discarded clothing and mournfully checked his wallet as well. "Yeah," he said, "me too." He shook his head. "Well, it could be worse."

"How the fuck could it be worse?"

"Oh, hell. I've heard I don't know how many stories about guys passing out like this, either from the booze or something extra slipped into the booze . . . and when they wake up, the broad's gone with their money, their watches, their clothes, *everything*. At least we won't have to wear motel towels back to the base."

"We know where she works. . . ."

"Negative, sir. We know where she *worked*. Five gets you ten she handed in her notice last night. She probably hit the road ten minutes after we passed out. Christ, she could be in L.A. by now. Or Reno." His eyes widened as he sat back onto the bed. "Shit. I bet we owe for the room."

"Nah. I think I remember paying in advance. I *think* . . ." He rubbed his eyes, gently. "What I want to know is where we are, and how we're gonna get back to the base."

"We're in La Mesa," Halstead said. He held up a notepad

with the motel's logo stamped on the top. "Place called the Starlight Motel, it says here. I'll call Doc. He'll come get us. And . . . um . . . no questions asked."

Morgan turned to face Halstead, his forefinger raised. "When we get back, Twidge . . ." he began.

"Yeah?"

Morgan closed his eyes. "So help me, Twidge, if *one word* of this disaster gets out, just *one word* . . ."

Halstead spread his hands, looking down at himself. "Sir, if you think I'm eager to advertise this . . . incident . . ." He shook his head. "Tell you what, Lieutenant. As far as I'm concerned, we both had a wonderful time last night. Didn't we? We kept 'em up and kept on going, all night long."

"Fuckin' A, Twidge. A couple of sexual superstars, that's us."

"We wore the poor girl out."

"Roger that. Think Doc'll buy it?"

"Sure. Even if he doesn't, he'll back us."

"And if anybody ever finds out different . . ."

"You'll hunt me down and shoot me. I know."

Morgan showed his teeth. "Yup. Simple as that." Funny, but he was beginning to feel a little more comfortable now, a little more like a member of the Teams.

Chapter 17

Saturday, 12 September 1970

Fletcher Avenue
El Cajon, California
1930 hours

"Aw, man," Bill said, shaking his head as they walked up the cement flagstone walkway. "I *really* don't know if I want to do this!"

"Oh, c'mon, Bill," Pat told him, reaching up to the doorbell. "It'll be good for you! Besides, the Logans won't bite!"

"Maybe not Melissa. Jerry, though . . . I dunno . . ."

Then the door opened, and Melissa Logan smiled at them. "Well, praise the Lord! Welcome, neighbors! Come on in! Bill, thanks so much for coming!"

"Don't mention it." He was feeling acutely uncomfortable. "Uh . . . nice house."

The Logans, obviously, were still in the chaos of moving in. Their new house was small, and while the living room was nicely ordered and the furniture was in place, a stack of cardboard boxes was visible in the hallway leading toward what were presumably the bedrooms.

"Thank you! I'd give you the grand tour, but we might not find our way back. I think we're going to be unpacking for the next three years!"

Jerry Logan advanced from the kitchen. "Bill! Good to see you!"

"Hey, Jerry."

He felt, in fact, like a fish . . . no, like a *SEAL* out of water.

A number of other guests had already arrived. Lee Peterson and his wife were there; Lee was a second-class yeoman who worked in the personnel office at the Navy Amphibious Base. His wife, Suzy, was a pretty if somewhat overweight blond who worked as a civilian employee at the base exchange. Lieutenant Commander John Perry was one of the chaplains at the base; his wife, Anne, often played her guitar at Sunday services, and she had it out now, resting across her lap.

"Hey, Bill," Chaplain Perry said, a broad grin on his strikingly handsome face. "Good to see you."

"Good to be here, sir."

"Ah!" Perry warned, plucking at the shoulder of his sports shirt. "No uniforms tonight, and no ranks. I'm John."

"Okay . . . John."

The informality didn't bother Bill that much. SEALs were used to relaxed relations between officers and enlisted men, especially in off-duty situations like this one . . . as the tequila-shooting session at Chico's a few months ago had proven. But he was uncomfortable with the group. He'd met them all, at one point or another, but he really knew only Jerry Logan well, and that only because until his move a few weeks before, the man had lived in the apartment next door to his. None of them were SEALs, and none were people he would particularly have chosen as friends.

And that, he realized, was snobbery at its worst. These were all good people. John Perry, especially, was an easy-going and friendly man who always made a point of talking to enlisted men. He thought he could get to like Perry a lot, if he got to know him better.

But if Greg and Wendy didn't come through that front door, as advertised, in another ninety seconds or so, he was out of here.

"I, ah, didn't realize that you were into all . . . all this stuff," Bill told Perry as he dropped into a nearby chair. Pat was in the kitchen, talking with Melissa and Suzy, and the other two men were continuing an obviously interrupted conversation on the other side of the room.

Perry chuckled. "You mean the Charismatics?"

"I guess." He'd been hearing a lot about the Charismatic movement lately from Pat, who claimed it was sweeping through every traditional church denomination, from the Baptists to the Catholics. Its members tended to interpret the Bible more or less literally, and they believed in the idea that God was working miracles today, that miracles and the charisms, the so-called gifts of the Spirit, were just as much for modern believers as they'd been for the early Christians. Bill wasn't sure yet whether he believed a tenth of what he'd heard, but he did know that Pat took it all very seriously.

"Well, Anne and I aren't really into it ourselves, that much," Perry explained. "But I can tell you, it's great to see kids getting so excited about Christianity, about a dynamic Christianity. Prayer meetings. Reading the Bible. I may not partake, but I sure can't disapprove." He grinned and patted his wife's knee. "And we cover a lot of the same ground, don't we, Hon?"

She laughed and rolled her eyes. "They're *very* heavily into Christian folk songs, so I guess we fit right in." The Perrys were well known on base for their folk-oriented church services, especially the youth services, where guitar music replaced the traditional piano or organ.

Bill laughed. "So, is that why you came tonight?"

"Oh, Jerry's been trying to get us out here to one of his prayer meetings for a long time. I told him we'd come and see his new house, and, yeah, bring along the git-fiddle.''

The doorbell sounded, and Jerry answered the door. Greg and Wendy walked in, with Greg looking as misplaced as Bill felt.

'' 'Scuse me, John,'' Bill said. He rose and went to meet Greg, slapping him on the shoulder. "Hey, Twidge. You don't know how glad I am to see you.''

"Yeah? Wanna slip out for a cold one?''

"Man, do I ever. But I promised Pat . . .''

"Affirmative. But I'll tell you, Doc. Holy roller prayer meetings are *not* my style!''

Nor were they Bill's. Some of what he'd heard—the speaking in tongues and the prophesying—sounded downright weird to him, and he simply was not willing to accept that any book written by men could be an infallible recording of the word of God.

Pat, however, claimed to have found a new dimension in her life, as she'd gradually—as she put it—''come to know Jesus'' in the course of weekly Bible studies with Melissa.

After some initial casual conversation and catching-up, the service got started, right there in the Logans' living room. There wasn't much in the way of formal routine. Jerry opened with a short prayer that they all be open to the workings of the Holy Spirit, and then they moved on to some music, singing song after song from dog-eared, stapled-together, mimeographed sheets that Melissa produced from somewhere. Anne played the tunes, most of which were mind-numbingly repetitious. After a particularly raucous performance of something called ''Sons of God,'' Jerry announced that it was a good thing that the Psalms commanded them to make a joyful noise unto the Lord . . . because if He wanted beautiful harmonies, he sure wasn't going to find them here tonight.

Later, they prayed . . . not the formal, rigid prayer of a conventional service, but a quiet and relaxed litany of unrehearsed thoughts, voiced by whoever felt like speaking. They prayed for Jerry and Melissa's new home and for the couple's happiness there. They prayed for the American servicemen in Vietnam. They prayed for peace. They prayed for President Nixon, that he would find the wisdom to know what to do, to find the best course for peace, and for a divided country. Eventually, the prayer became a kind of free-form vocaliza-

tion, with everyone murmuring to himself—to God, rather,
Bill decided—in a low-voiced buzz where only a few words
and phrases here and there were audible, snatches of "thank
you, Jesus," and "praise you, Lord" voiced more often than
others.

And, somewhere along the line, Bill's perceptions of reality
began to shift in some indefinable but very real way. The ten
of them were sitting in a ragged circle about the living room,
some on chairs or the sofa, others cross-legged on the floor.
Melissa, Bill saw, when he snuck a peek through slitted eyelids, looked almost stunningly beautiful, on the floor with her
long skirt completely covering her legs, her hands upraised,
her head back as she looked up with closed eyes at the ceiling
. . . or at something unseen beyond. Her smile was radiant,
utterly trusting and peaceful. He could hear the mingled, vo-
calized prayers around him, all softly spoken, a murmur only.
Some were in English, while others, eerily, were in no language Bill had ever heard. *Speaking in tongues,* the Logans
called it, a prayer somehow made in an unknown language
through something Jerry called one of the gifts of the Holy
Spirit. Bill wondered if it was some kind of autohypnosis; the
Logans and the Petersons and Pat might almost be in some
kind of self-induced trance. When he glanced briefly at Greg
and Wendy, sitting rather stiffly side by side on the sofa, he
caught Greg looking back, one eyebrow arched in a what-the-
hell-is-this expression.

When he closed his eyes again, however, and let the murmured prayers sweep over and around him, Bill felt something different, something unusual. His physical senses were
finely tuned and quite sharp; it was possible for him to sense
the presence of other people nearby, though he'd never been
able to explain to himself or anyone else how that was possible. In combat, though, he was always aware of the presence
of the other SEALs on his team . . . and of hostiles as well,
in a kind of ill-defined sixth sense that let him mentally picture the living room and be aware of someone *there* . . . and
there . . . and *there* . . .

And, right now, right here, he could sense the nine other
people in the room with him . . . and one more.

Or rather, One more.

Chills tickled up his spine, chills not of fear or of cold, but of something strange and awesome and wonderful. There was Someone else in this room with the ten of them, and it was impossible to pin Him down to one location. He seemed to be everywhere . . .

Is this *what it's like to know God?* Bill had always believed in God, but he'd never put much thought into what God might want of him, or whether any supreme being could possibly interact with humans on a personal scale. Maybe God had created the universe, but after that, things had pretty much run on their own, hadn't they?

Was a personal God possible?

If He was, what did that mean for Bill and Pat?

Was this, this *experience* what he needed? Bill was achingly aware that he'd been searching for . . . for *something* for a very long time, that he'd been feeling empty, that his old confusion over being a SEAL or being a corpsman had left him searching.

What have I done with my life so far? he asked himself. *Maybe Jesus will know what I'm good for. I sure don't. He couldn't possibly make things worse. . . .*

The bitterness in his own thoughts surprised him, welling up from some deep and private darkness somewhere beneath his conscious mind. Bill Tangretti didn't usually get so deeply introspective, but he was looking at his life so far, now, and he was finding it wanting. He felt like he needed . . . something, a direction, a goal, a purpose. Yeah, he was a SEAL. He could sneak up on an NVA sentry without being seen or heard, and snap the man's neck with one swift, accurate twist from behind, and what did that get him?

Blood on his hands.

Bill had no particular compunction against killing the enemy. SEALs were trained for combat, and for a very direct and personal, down-and-dirty combat, lethal at face-to-face range, that Air Force jocks, say, pushing their bomb release buttons at 25,000 feet, could never know or understand.

Still, his own evolution as a warrior had followed a rather twisty career path. He'd joined the SEALs originally more because of his father and his half-brother than anything else; they were both SEALs, so he was going to be one, too. Later, after his first Nam tour had been cut short when he was wounded, he'd decided to go to Hospital Corps School. He'd wanted to be more than an elite and highly trained killer. As a corpsman, he could save lives; as a SEAL corpsman, he could both save lives and take them, and for a time, the two-headed nature of who and what he was had nearly destroyed him.

He felt tears running down his cheeks, felt Jerry and Pat and several others kneeling close beside him on the floor, their hands on his head and shoulders and back.

"Ask Him into your heart, buddy," Jerry was saying, leaning his head close beside Bill's ear. "Ask Jesus to come in and take your life. . . ."

He felt . . . something moving inside, though he wasn't sure what it was. The sound of the people praying over him blurred into an indistinguishable haze of sound.

"Jesus . . . whatever You want me to do . . ." He didn't know what he was asking, but he meant the words with all his heart.

He felt warm, and very peaceful. . . .

Sunday, 13 September 1970

Circle-O Donut Shoppe
Coronado
0145 hours

"So . . . what do you think happened tonight?" Greg asked.

The all-night doughnut shop was located just up the main drag from Chico's Bordertown Cantina. He and Wendy had driven here after saying good night to the others, gently refusing an invitation from Pat and Bill to come over to their apartment for some coffee and talk. Greg had been more interested in Wendy and what she had to say after the evening's unusual events.

"I really don't know," Wendy told him. She took a bite out of a coconut-covered chocolate doughnut and chewed thoughtfully. "Pat, well, she's been caught up in this Charismatic thing for a while, now. At least since Davy was born. I guess her conversion, if that's what it was, was pretty gradual. Bill seemed to just, I don't know, snap."

Greg gave her a hard look. "You don't think he—"

"No, I don't mean it that way. He did look pretty happy."

"I dunno. When I see a grown SEAL cry—"

"Just because a man cries, for Pete's sake, it doesn't mean he—"

"I didn't say it did."

"I don't know many people who have their heads screwed on tighter than Pat."

"Can't speak to that. She's my sister and that means I *always* thought she had a screw loose. But, well, Bill was always the steady one of the two of us, I guess."

"That's not saying much, is it?"

Greg laughed. Wendy never failed to delight him, with her quick wit and her wry sense of humor. The episode in the Starlight Motel was the only time since he'd known Wendy that he'd even tried to make it with another woman, and the less said about that incident the better. Besides, sex with Wendy was so good, he'd be a fool to look elsewhere.

It wasn't just sex, either. He felt so alive around Wendy. He could really relax around her, be himself. And lately he'd begun feeling . . . wistful, perhaps, especially whenever he looked at his young nephew Davy and at the joy Bill and Pat exhibited together. He wanted a piece of that joy, and he thought he knew where to find it.

"I saw you talking to Commander Perry after the, uh, service or whatever it was," Wendy said.

"Prayer meeting."

"So what does he think of all this?"

Greg shrugged. "He said he's not into the Charismatic stuff himself. The speaking in tongues. The laying on of hands, and all that. But he did say that the whole thing is certainly scriptural."

"Pat was telling me about that. How it's all there in the Bible, and stuff."

"Yeah. Anyway, he doesn't see any harm in it, and according to him, lots of people have been getting turned on to God and the Bible this way, lately." He shrugged. "I guess it's better than being turned on by LSD."

"The best highs are the ones that come from inside," Wendy told him. "The ones you make yourself, without having to add chemicals."

"Like all that chocolate you're packing away, there."

"Beast." She popped the last piece of doughnut into her mouth and made a face at him as she chewed. After a moment, though, she reached out and touched Greg's arm. "You're worried about him, aren't you? About Bill, I mean."

"Yeah, I guess I am."

"I don't think anything has changed."

"Hasn't it?"

"I can't see him becoming a pacifist or getting out of the Navy or anything like that."

"Well, he can't just drop out of the Navy. The Navy would have something to say about that. But I wonder if he might want to give up on being a SEAL. Or if this Christian thing is going to mess up his head when he has to *be* a SEAL."

"Oh, I don't—"

"I'm serious, Wendy. He went through a pretty rough time, a year or two back, trying to reconcile in his own mind being both a corpsman and a SEAL. I don't think it was easy for him, and sometimes I wonder if he isn't still struggling with the same problem, maybe way down inside. It's entirely possible that he could go out on an op sometime, do his best to kill some NVA or VC target, wound the guy, then have to do everything he could to save the guy's life. When you're a SEAL, you have to stay focused. If you're trying to kill someone, you have to be totally concentrated on that, on *him*, and if you stop to think about the morality of the thing, you could find yourself in deep shit. Hesitate even *that* much," he added, holding up his thumb and forefinger a fraction of an inch apart, "and you're dead. Maybe your whole team is dead."

"Is that why you're worried? That Bill might let you and the other guys on your team down?"

Greg sighed. "I don't know. I guess, yeah."

"Bill strikes me as a very thoroughgoing professional," Wendy said. "He also strikes me as someone who really, truly *loves* you and the other guys he works with. He's not going to let you down."

"Yeah, but this Jesus stuff—"

"Do you believe in God?" she asked him.

He blinked. The question was so unexpected, he had to stop and think for a moment. What did he believe? "Yeah, I guess so." His parents were regular churchgoers, though he hadn't bothered in a good many years, now. Still, some of the indoctrination from Sunday school, back home in Jenner's little Grace United Methodist Church, had certainly rubbed off.

"Well, can you trust God to take care of him?"

Greg blinked again. Just how far was he willing to trust God, anyway? He'd seen at least enough over the past few years to convince him that, if He existed at all, God either didn't care what happened to his creatures much, or else he had one hell of a sick sense of humor.

"I . . . don't know. That's kind of a tall order."

"Well, I think that either he'll grow out of this, like a phase, y'know? Or else he'll find something real enough and solid enough to give his life some meaning, in which case I think you can probably trust God to take care of him."

"I'm still not sure I'm following your logic. More doughnuts?"

She shook her head. "I like just sitting and talking. Thanks."

"Sure." He stared at her for a long moment. She was so beautiful. More, she was so . . . *comfortable*. He liked talking with her, liked being with her, liked everything about her. He'd been so worried about Bill, but talking it out with Wendy had helped more than he could even say.

She looked up, and her green eyes locked with his. "What?"

"I was just thinking. . . ."

"A healthy habit to get into."

"Not always. But I was just thinking that Bill said he'd been feeling empty, like he'd been needing something. I . . . I think I know what he means."

"You're feeling empty?"

"Yeah."

"You want to go back and have them pray over you?"

"No. What I was thinking was that, well, I guess I'm sort of finally figuring out just what it is I've been missing, what I've been *needing*." Reaching out, he took her hand on the tabletop. "You. . . ."

Her eyes widened. "Greg—"

"No, let me finish. I know I don't have any right to ask you. I mean, I've been stationed here at Special Warfare for over a year, and that means I could get orders any day now, orders back to Nam, or to the North Pole, or God knows where. Maybe Bill thinks he needs God in his life. I dunno about that, but I feel like I need some stability, some certainty in mine . . . and I think that what I need is you. Wendy, will you marry me?''

In another second, she'd slipped out of her seat and come around to his side of the table, sliding into his lap, molding her arms about his neck, and devouring him with a long, slow, warm, deep kiss.

When they broke at last for breath, he looked down into her tear-smeared face. "Does that mean yes?"

Wendy giggled. "You know, Pat and I would joke sometimes, about how she grabbed Bill the moment he got off that airplane. She wanted to get married with a decent chunk of time afterward to enjoy him in. With me, well, I've been wondering if I shouldn't grab you before your orders came through, just because, well, I want to have something of you, want to have you before . . . before . . ." The gathering of a fresh flow of tears glistened through her lashes.

"Before I go get myself killed?"

"Something like that. No, that's not what I mean. But—"

"You want to nail down some happiness. *Now*, before it slips away. Yeah, I know." *I know. . . .*

Her arms tightened around his neck. "How about we go back to my place," she whispered, "and celebrate?"

It was the best idea he'd heard in a long time.

Chapter 18

Saturday, 31 October 1970

Mission Hotel
San Diego, California
2045 hours

"Hey, everybody, c'mon!" Pat yelled. "It's time to cut the cake!"

Talking and laughing, the guests began drifting across the large, gaily decorated patio toward the three-tiered wedding cake that had just been wheeled out of the hotel. Greg Halstead swept his bride close with one arm, looking down into luminous green eyes. "Kiss me, woman!"

"Yes, *sir!*" Wendy replied with mock deference. "Whatever you say, *sir!*"

"This is the Navy," he said severely. "The proper response is aye, aye!"

"Aye, aye, ai, ai, ai, ai—"

He cut her off by smothering her mouth with his. The kiss lasted a long time.

"C'mon, you two!" Pat called again. "Or you won't get any cake!"

Together, arm in arm, they walked past the shimmering turquoise blue of the lighted outdoor pool and pressed past the small crowd gathering at the cake.

"Big cake," Greg said approvingly, eyeing it up and down. "When does the naked girl jump out?"

"I'll give you naked girl," Wendy told him, nudging him in the ribs.

"Hmm, yes. I suppose you will. But *later. . . .*"

The cake was a fairly conservative affair, three-tiered

and white-frosted. Next to the usual plastic bride on the top, though, some wag had replaced the six-inch, tuxedoed groom with a foot-tall plastic model of the Creature From the Black Lagoon, elegantly hand-painted in gruesome greens and malevolent browns, its clawed, webbed hands raised in mimicry of a scene from the fifties horror movie classic. Scale replicas of an M1 carbine, a knife in a plastic scabbard, diving mask, air tanks, and swim fins—all accessories for the popular twelve-inch G.I. Joe action figure—completed the display.

"Hey, Twidge," Bill said, grinning, "it looks just like you!"

"And it's just right for Halloween," Panopolis added.

"I always liked tall men," Wendy said, shaking her head, "but that's a little ridiculous, don't you think?" She touched the top of the bride's figure, then the top of the monster's. "I don't know if I can handle someone so . . . *big!*"

"Now there's an opening if I ever heard one," Lieutenant Nolan said, laughing as he came up behind her. "Can I kiss the bride?"

"Of course!" They embraced, and Nolan gave her an enthusiastic kiss on the lips.

"Okay, okay," Greg said in mock indignation as they held the clinch for several long seconds. "Just because you've got all that gold braid—"

"Oh, it's much more than that," Nolan said, winking at Wendy. "It's honor and tradition, training and breeding. Everything that distinguishes an officer and a gentleman from the enlisted lowlife. Isn't that right, Wendy?"

"Oh, I don't know about that, Lieutenant," Wendy said. "He may be a lowlife, but he's *my* lowlife."

"You should check your naval history, Lieutenant," Greg told him. "There was an old saying that was popular with sailors back in the days of sail. You know, wooden ships and iron men, and all of that."

"And what was that?"

"Well, in the old sailing ships, the officers lived aft, under the poop. The men, the ordinary sailors, lived crowded together on the gundecks amidships, or forward, in the forecastle."

"Yes . . ."

"The saying went, 'Aft, the honor, but forward, the better men!' "

"I'll try to remember that, Twidge," Nolan said, chuckling. He gave Wendy another kiss. "If this guy doesn't come up to spec, Wendy, you see me. Okay?"

"I don't think I'll have any problems in that regard, Lieutenant!"

"Come *on* and cut the damned cake, for cryin' out loud," Lieutenant Morgan called.

"An excellent idea," Greg said. "Who's got the implement?"

"The implement" was a SEAL Mark I diving knife, long, heavy, and with a serrated back edge for sawing through hawsers. Greg stood next to Wendy, pressed close up against her, the two together holding the knife.

"As I stand here by the cake, with knife and wife," Greg told the listening crowd grandly, "all I can say is, thanks for coming, and thanks for being family. When my sister got married last year, they opted for a civilian wedding back home, and, while it was nice, not all that many of our Navy family could come up and attend. I just wanted to say that you're all family to us, and, well, thanks." They started to cut the cake, and then Greg stopped for a final word. "Oh, and if the cake makes any of you sick, my so-called best man is a hospital corpsman, and he can fix you right up!"

"I just want to know if you washed that knife after the last time you used it, Twidge," Chief Whittaker called out.

"Bad taste, Chief," Bill said.

"Aw, you ain't tasted the cake, yet!"

As the crowd laughed—with a few groans mixed in—Greg and Wendy sliced into the cake. Flashbulbs popped, and the strobe held aloft by the wedding photographer flared briefly. Guests oohed, ahed, and applauded.

The ceremony had been conducted on base that afternoon by Chaplain Perry. With vows spoken and bride kissed, the wedding party had made its way by caravan down the Silver Strand Peninsula and back up into San Diego proper, where the dining room and pool patio of the old Mission Hotel had been reserved for the reception. Most of the guests were military, and most of those were SEALs, which made the gathering a bit rowdier than the one for Pat and Bill the year before. The enlisted men, most of them, wore either dress whites—it was still warm enough to be the uniform of the day, even this late in the season—or dress blues, which were considered correct for all formal occasions. A few were in civvies. Some, men and women both, had donned costumes in honor of the day. Lieutenant Morgan, for instance, had used black greasepaint to paint a mask around his eyes, giving him the air of a rather sinister bandit or, as Greg had commented earlier, a demented raccoon.

Both Greg, as groom, and Bill, as best man, were in dress whites, the idea having been to match Wendy's white gown. Since the ceremony, Wendy had changed into a dark green dress, but the SEALs, most of them, were still in uniform.

Greg and Wendy fed each other the traditional first bites of cake, with Wendy making sure that the piece she crammed into Greg's face was far larger than he could manage in one bite. Awkwardly wiping frosting off his nose and chin with one hand, he grinned. "You know, I think I just bit off more than I can chew."

"Wait'll you taste her cooking," Bill said.

"And just how do *you* know about her cooking?" Pat demanded, turning on her husband.

"I . . . ah . . . just assumed, you know, new brides in the kitchen—"

"I may just give you a piece of this cake myself!"

"Incoming!" Nolan cried.

"Better duck and cover, Doc," Morgan added.

Greg joined in with the laughter. Wendy had a bit of frosting on her nose as well, and impulsively, he leaned over and licked it off.

He still wondered if he was doing the right thing.

Greg Halstead had been envious of his sister and his best friend for a long time, at least since their wedding the year before. The problem was that he still wasn't sure what it was he envied . . . their obvious love for each other? The evident comfort they had in one another's presence? The security? He'd been missing something in his own life for quite a while.

Of course, for the past month, Bill had been telling him that what was missing was Christ . . . a "God-shaped hole in his life," as he'd said a couple of weeks before. Bill's and Pat's conversions, coming out of the empty sky as they had, still had the people close to them a little off-balance, and even uncomfortable at times. Pat hadn't seemed to change all that much, but Bill really did seem to be a different man, sometimes.

Greg hadn't decided yet whether the change was for the good or not.

He did know that what he was missing wasn't God, or even God-shaped. His emptiness, he thought, was for something different . . . a state of mind, perhaps, or a state of being. It wasn't that he was lonely, but he did sometimes feel like his life lacked a certain element of certainty, of solidity.

A ship without an anchor. . . .

Was Wendy an anchor, a weight, dragging him down? Strange metaphor, that, he thought, a double-edged and unpleasant one. SEALs, like Navy aviators, had the reputation for wild living and fun in bed, like sailors with a girl in every port, only much more so; there'd been plenty of raw jokes among the BUD/S instructor staff about him having to give up the carefree bachelor's life, about being weighed down by family responsibilities, about turning into an "old, married hand" like Nolan and Tangretti.

As a matter of fact, the week before he'd damned near called the whole thing off . . . then decided that he couldn't do that to Wendy. Like the man had said a few hours ago, for better or for worse, richer or poorer, sickness and in health, they were one, now. The funny thing was, Greg wasn't even that dedicated to the typical SEAL's wild life. He drank, but not often and not that much—that night at the Chico's Bordertown Cantina notwithstanding—and the one time in recent memory when he'd tried to pick up a girl, well, that was the same night as the shooting party at Chico's, and he didn't like even *thinking* about that abortive encounter. It wasn't as though he had a wild life to give up.

Maybe, he thought with a surge of relatively uncharacteristic introspection, he still wasn't entirely sure of who he was, or of why he was doing what he was doing. He loved being a SEAL, and everything that went with it—but he loved especially the camaraderie, the fellowship of professional warriors. Bill had seemed so much happier after he settled down with Pat—and that was long before his conversion experience. Maybe that, Greg thought, was what he'd been looking for all along.

Maybe Wendy, like an anchor, could give his life some stability. He loved her, and he knew she loved him. What he didn't know, though, was whether he was ready to embrace that kind of stability yet. *Stop worrying at it like an old, junkyard dog,* he told himself. *You love her, you're married to her now, and that is most emphatically that!*

Greg and Wendy took plates of cake and vanilla ice cream to an out-of-the-traffic-flow spot near the side of the pool. Bill and Pat joined them. "Quite a party, guy," Bill said. "We should do this again sometime."

"Yeah? You thinking of getting married again?"

"Hmm, that is a problem. Who else around here can we get set up with a wife?" Bill stared pointedly at Lieutenant Morgan, who was standing within earshot.

"Ohhhh, no," Morgan said, shaking his head. "Not *this* boy!"

"No, really," Bill said. "We've got to get you hitched up."

"Why, because misery loves company?" He held up both hands. "If the Navy wanted us to have wives—" he began.

"They would have issued them to us in our seabags," Greg and Bill chorused, completing the old saying in near-perfect unison.

Chaplain Perry approached them, a paper plate with a piece of wedding cake in one hand, a fork in the other. "Okay, boys," he said, smiling. "Maybe now you can clear something up for me."

"What's that, sir?" Bill replied.

"What, in God's holy name," the chaplain said, pointing at Greg's chest with his fork, "is *that?*"

"What . . . this?" Greg reached up and touched the large, gaudily massive gold device pinned to his dress whites, just above his four rows of colored ribbons. "Latest thing in SEAL-wear, sir. That's my Budweiser."

"Your Budweiser." The tone of the chaplain's voice suggested that he was pretty certain that Greg was pulling at least one of his legs.

"SEAL emblem, Commander," Bill said. "They just authorized them last week."

"I've been seeing some of the SEALs wearing them these past few days," Perry admitted, "but I was almost afraid to ask what they were. It's certainly . . . *large,* isn't it?"

"You'll never catch me wearing one of those fucking things," Morgan said bluntly. "Uh, 'scuse me, Chaplain."

"I noticed you were out of uniform, sir," Greg replied, nodding at Morgan's medal rack. The space on his officer's jacket above the ribbons was conspicuously empty.

"So," Perry said, pointedly ignoring Morgan's language, "why 'Budweiser'?"

"I'll show you!" Greg left the group, walking across the patio to the wet bar, returning a moment later with a brown beer bottle, which he held out for the chaplain's inspection. "Here. See?"

"Good heavens!" Perry said, his eyes widening. "What's the Budweiser company have to say about this?"

The beer company's corporate logo and the new SEAL badge were not identical by any means, but both were ornate, and both were centered about an eagle with wings spread and head ducked low.

Compared to the Budweiser logo, in fact, the SEAL insignia looked unpleasantly cluttered. Centered in front of the eagle and extending below its body was an upright anchor. Horizontally across the device, clutched in the eagle's right talons, was a trident, the prongs extending off to the eagle's left. And gripped by the eagle's left talons at an angle above the intersection of anchor and trident was an ancient flintlock pistol, like a relic out of a pirate movie or some Revolutionary War museum.

"Don't know, sir. You think their lawyers would want to take on a bunch of SEALs?"

Perry shook his head. "And you SEALs really feel it's necessary to advertise yourselves with this thing?"

"Oh, it's not themselves they're advertising," Pat said, laughing. "It's their strength. You know how strong you have to be to lug all that metal around? I tried lifting that thing once and nearly strained my arm!"

"That's why they put us through all of those exercises and conditioning in BUD/S, Chaplain," Bill admitted, solemnly nodding his head. " 'Tis a heavy burden we bear. . . ."

"Fact of the matter is, sir," Greg added, "most of us think

it's just that . . . advertising. And being a SEAL is not something you normally want to advertise to people, you know what I mean?''

"It does seem a bit bizarre," Perry agreed. "I mean, you SEALs have to operate in secret a lot, from what I've heard. Wearing one of those things would be like a CIA spy wearing a badge, wouldn't it?''

"That's exactly what it's like," Morgan said, "and it's damned stupid. Somebody in Washington doesn't have his head screwed on tight.''

"Actually," Bill said, "the story I heard almost makes sense, in a twisted kind of way. You see, SEALs have been getting some publicity lately. You know, articles in *Newsweek* and the *New York Times*.''

"I guess some people think SEALs are pretty sexy," Greg said.

"*I* happen to think so," Wendy said, putting both of her hands around her husband's arm.

"Well, anyway," Tangretti continued, laughing, "someone doing PR work at the Pentagon decided that the SEALs really needed an insignia of their own, sort of like pilot's wings, y'know? Or maybe it was some SEAL officer with more pride than sense. Anyway, the word came down the chain of command to come up with an emblem or badge. And the SEALs were asked to submit their own design.

"Well, the story goes that a couple of SEALs thought that the idea of an insignia for a Navy military unit that valued secrecy was so silly, they decided to do something about it. After having a good many beers—'' He stopped himself, looking thoughtful. "Huh. I wonder if they were Budweisers, by any chance?'' He shrugged. "Anyway, after having a good many beers, they drew up the biggest, loudest, clunkiest-looking, *dumbest*-looking excuse for a breast insignia imaginable. They made it so garish, so plain *stupid*-looking, that the Pentagon was certain to reject it and drop the whole idea.''

"Oh, no," Perry said, closing his eyes. "I think I can see it coming.''

"That's right." Bill tapped his own insignia. "They submitted this design, the idiots in Washington thought it was the neatest thing they'd ever seen, and the next thing you know, the rest of us have to wear them."

"That sounds about right for the Pentagon bureaucracy," Perry said. "Never underestimate their capacity for mediocrity."

"Or silliness," Morgan added. "But that's why I won't wear the thing. Especially with all of the antiwar stuff lately."

"Good point," Pat said. "I've been hearing stories about Nam vets getting hate mail and the like from protest groups."

Greg nodded. "Yeah, and elite combat personnel—airborne and Army Special Forces and SEALs—have been getting the worst of it. Advertisement is just what we didn't need."

"Nothing like maintaining a low profile, huh?" Bill said.

"They *meant* well," Pat said. "The symbolism is beautiful. The eagle's for the air, and . . . what was the rest of that you told me last week, Bill?"

"The anchor is for the U.S. Navy," he explained. "The trident is King Neptune's scepter and represents the sea. The eagle represents strength and courage and also the air. The flintlock represents land warfare. The fact that it's cocked means that the SEALs are always ready. Sea, air, land. Strength, courage, always ready. The SEALs."

"Hooyah," Greg said quietly.

"Well," Perry said, laughing, "at least you can always use it for an anchor if you find you need one!"

"There's an idea," Greg said. "Every SEAL should have his own anchor, just in case!"

Damn it, he had to stop thinking about anchors. He was *not* having second thoughts about this marriage . . . he was *not*.

"Say, Greg . . ." A deep, familiar voice said at his back. He turned. "Hey, Dad."

"Hi, son. Do I get to kiss the bride?"

"Of course!" Wendy cried.

David Halstead gently hugged her and gave her a solid buss on the cheek. "Welcome to the family, Wendy. If anyone can keep this young hooligan in line, it's you!"

"I still may need to call you up for advice from time to time," Wendy told him. "Sometimes I wonder how to make him sit still in one place long enough to get three words out of him."

"That," David Halstead admitted, "can take some doing sometimes. If you ever find the secret, let me in on it." He turned to Bill and Pat. "Hey, you two. How's my young namesake doing?"

"Growing," Bill said. He put his arm around Pat's waist. "Of course I had to use a charge of C4 to pry Mommy away from him for her own brother's wedding."

Pat punched him hard in the ribs. "And who was it who made us late giving Jeannie all sorts of emergency instructions?"

"Hey, we're raising a future SEAL here," Bill said. "Gotta be real careful how you handle 'em."

David chuckled. "Four months old and you have him on raw meat already?"

"Yeah, we start drownproofing him next Tuesday."

Pat hit her husband again, harder.

David's grin faded as he turned to face his son. "Listen, Greg, I never got a chance to tell you. I had a long talk with Tod Ringold, oh, must have been a month or two back. He said you sent him a really nice letter, right after, you know, after Mark . . ."

"Least I could do," Greg replied. "I didn't really know Mark all that well, but I liked him, and I knew you and his dad were close."

"We were shipmates during the war. That kind of thing can forge bonds . . . as I'm sure you already know. Anyway, Tod was really touched, and he appreciated what you said in your letter."

Greg nodded. He wasn't even sure now what he'd said at the time. He did know that the official letters and telegrams announcing the death of a son or a husband could be devastating with their cold formality, with their time-honed clichés and artificial empathies. *It is with deep regret that we must inform you . . .*

He'd wanted Tod Ringold to know that his son had been with friends when he died in the California high desert, that he'd been with people who'd *cared*.

He looked around the hotel's pool patio, at SEALs and other guests mingling by the pool or seated at the round, metal tables. He felt . . . stifled, somehow, and perhaps a little claustrophobic, a no-good feeling for a guy trained to lock in and out of a submerged submarine's coffin-sized escape trunk. Damn it, he was a *SEAL*; was he really ready for the home and hearth bit?

Impulsively, he swept Wendy into his arms, kissed her deeply, then threw his head back and gave a piercing howl. "Be right back," he said, and then he was sprinting for the wall of the hotel. Once there, Greg kicked off his shoes and socks, then shucked off his white jersey and square-knot tie, handing them to Hochstader. Then, in white trousers and a T-shirt, he spread his arms and leaned against the brick wall. Fingers and toes finding holds that seemed impossible, he began moving up the face of the building, alternating arms and legs in a fly-walk that might have made a gecko—a small lizard with suction cups on its feet—jealous.

He was going to climb that wall, for no better reason than that he *could*. . . .

2108 hours

Wendy watched her new husband run to the wall of the hotel overlooking the pool, then turned to Pat. "I'm a little new at this SEAL-wife stuff, Pat," she said. "Are they always like this?"

Pat sighed. "Well . . . SEALs can be a little crazy sometimes."

"A *little?* Greg's climbing up the outside of the damned hotel!"

"Sometimes . . . they need to blow off steam." Pat fixed her friend with a searching stare. "You know, Bill used to be just as crazy. He's settled down a lot now, since . . . well . . ."

"Since you two became Christians?"

Pat nodded, a little embarrassed. Neither she nor Bill cared much for proselytizing, and she didn't like being pushy.

"I don't think that's quite Greg's style," Wendy said.

"Well . . ." she started to say, then stopped. "No. You're probably right. My brother never was the spiritual type, I guess."

Greg was halfway up the building now and still climbing,

moving faster than Wendy could have imagined possible. More and more SEALs were gathering underneath, chanting "Go! Go! Go!"

"My husband, the human fly," Wendy said.

"Get used to it, Wendy. I think all SEALs are certifiable."

"You're married to one!"

"Well, maybe I'm a little crazy too. You know, you don't *have* to be crazy to marry a SEAL ..."

". . . but it helps. Right. I've heard that one before." Wendy found herself wondering just what she'd gotten herself in for.

"Bill's told me stories," Pat said. "Some SEALs, especially on the East Coast, I understand, make a point of never entering their hotels the usual way, through the lobby and elevator. They go in from the outside. Like that."

"Why?" Wendy asked. "For security reasons?"

"I think just because they *can,*" Pat said. "Don't expect it to make sense."

A small man in a tuxedo bustled out of the building, looking up at Greg and wringing his hands. "You people can't do that!" he said. "I'm sorry, but I'll have to ask any guest who does that to leave immediately!"

"Just one problem, sir," Nolan told him, grinning. "That's not a guest. That's the groom."

"This is terrible!" the manager said. "The Mission cannot possibly accept liability for anything that might happen! I'll . . . I'll call the police!"

"I wouldn't do that, sir," Bill said, planting himself in front of the man. "My friend knows what he's doing."

"But, but, suppose he should fall?"

"He won't."

"The hotel can't accept responsibility," the man insisted. "I must—"

Somehow, as he turned away, he connected with Bill's foot and went sailing through the air, arms outstretched, to land with a splash in the pool. Several SEALs applauded and cheered. The manager surfaced, spitting water and spluttering imprecations.

Bill waited a moment, then extended a hand, helping the dripping man clamber from the pool. "I'm terribly sorry, sir! How dreadfully clumsy of me! . . ."

"This . . . you . . . I'll . . ."

"Uh oh," Bill said, pointing up. "I don't think you'll want to miss this, sir."

"I don't want to see!" The manager beat a hasty retreat toward the hotel, leaving a trail of water on the patio pavement.

Greg had reached the top of the building, four floors up. He vanished for a moment over the top, then reappeared, standing tall for a moment, arms outstretched, transfixed by the spotlights from below as the reception's guests broke into loud and sustained applause.

"Tell me again, Bill," Wendy called to him. "This is that low-profile stuff you guys talk about, right?"

Bill was about to reply when Greg spread his arms, flexed his legs, then launched into a spectacular swan dive from a good fifty feet up above the patio. For a moment, he appeared to hang in space, a spread-eagled figure all in white, arcing over and then down . . . and down . . . and down . . . to a perfect landing smack in the middle of the pool's deep end. There was a climactic splash, and several female guests squealed as the spray fell on them or their tables. The SEALs present, though—which was to say the majority of the men at the party—whooped, cheered, and applauded. As Greg broke the surface, blowing hard and waving, a chorus of *hooyah*s echoed from the surrounding buildings.

Wendy leaned close to Pat. "So this is what it's like being married to a SEAL, huh?"

"Wendy, my girl," Pat said, shaking her head, "you ain't seen nothing yet!"

Chapter 19

Thursday, 19 November 1970

Danang, Republic of Vietnam
1015 hours

Military aircraft—big C-130 Hercules transports and C-140 Starlifters—screamed on the tarmac as a flight of helicopter gunships clattered past. Bill Tangretti and Greg Halstead walked across pavement that shimmered in the morning heat, crossing from the Quonset hut that had been dragooned as the SEAL barracks to the two-story cement-block structure designated as the "spook shack," the lair of the tactical branch of Navy Intelligence, and the SEAL detachment's Navy Intelligence Liaison Officer, or NILO.

They'd been in Danang for a week now, though with little to show for it beyond the various familiarization classes and hygiene lectures demanded of all incoming personnel. So far, they both felt a little at loose ends, like gear adrift. They'd not been assigned to a regular SEAL platoon, nor was there any indication as yet that they would be working with PRUs or other native Vietnamese units.

In fact, there was every possibility that this was going to turn out to be a pretty dull deployment. Officially, Bill and Greg belonged to a small detachment of SEALs stationed at Danang designated as Detachment Echo, a part of the U.S. Naval Advisory Group detachment on the base, though what advice they were supposed to give, and to whom, were still unanswered questions. The role of SEALs as active participants in combat in Vietnam, though, was obviously being downplayed damned near to the point of nonexistence.

Morale at the base was not good. When asked what they

did for fun, the other SEALs derisively talked about "chasing mortar tubes." It seemed that the VC had developed the trick of burying mortar tubes in the ground within range of the base and carefully concealing them. At night, the VC would sneak up to the tube positions, drop two or three rounds on the base, then slip back into the woods. The SEALs at Danang were being sent out on patrol after each attack in mostly vain attempts to find the weapons' hiding places. It was, all things considered, a sickening misuse of good and highly trained men at a task that could and should have been left to ARVN forces.

Lieutenant Rodger MacMillen, the SEAL officer who would be their CO for this tour, promised them that some real fun was in the works, but he refused to say much about it. "The SEAL mission is changin'," he said in his slow, Texas drawl. "And you boys are gonna get all the action you want, believe me."

This morning, though, Bill and Greg had been ordered to report to the Intelligence Center. The local SOG commander wanted a look at them, and the word was there was a possible op in the works.

Maybe the nothing routine was about to change.

"I tell you, Twidge," Bill said with a heady, galloping enthusiasm that he could scarcely contain, "that the Lord is working it all out!"

They were talking as they walked across to the Intelligence Center, both men in the camouflage utilities and T-shirts favored by SEALs between missions. Aircraft engines shrilled and whined at the nearby airstrip. A platoon of Marines marched past, wearing utilities and carrying seabags. From the expressions on their faces, everything from battle-seared indifference to pure glee, they looked like they might be marching to the airfield for a flight home.

"Yeah, yeah, right," Greg replied. "Look, Doc, we've been over this. . . ."

"Yeah, I know, but don't you see? C'mon, both of us were trying to get orders back here, right? Didn't want to get split up. Didn't want to spend the rest of our lives stuck at BUD/S. And we'd been hammering away at Personnel for, what was it? Fifteen months, trying to get transfers! And nothing! Then I just relaxed and leaned back, gave it all to Jesus, and, bam!

We've got our orders and our billets and we're on our way to Nam!''

"You make it sound like poetry, Doc. But did you ever stop to think that maybe that bit you pulled using Admiral Zumwalt's name might have been responsible? I mean, not to knock your faith, or anything, but I think in Navy circles, the name of Zumwalt pulls a lot more weight than the name of Jesus.''

"Man, I can do *all* things in the name of Jesus! They might not know it, but *He* rules the Navy and Admiral Zumwalt and even the personnel officer at Nav Amphib, Coronado!''

"If you say so, Doc,'' Greg replied wearily. They trotted up the cement steps to the spook shack, and Greg opened the door, holding it for him. "Just keep in mind, though, that our getting sent back here wasn't entirely an unalloyed blessing. Wendy and me, well, I think we'd have been just as happy if Jesus had left us in California!''

That hurt, Bill thought as he stepped through the door and into the air-conditioned comfort of the Intelligence Center. Greg had just stomped squarely on the one point that had been bothering Bill—that had been the focus of most of his prayer time, in fact—ever since he'd gotten his orders.

Pat, he knew, was bitterly unhappy that both her husband and her brother were back in Vietnam. He'd been so excited when his orders came through that he'd not even thought about how Pat would react when he told her. Her tears had been unexpected . . . and painful. They'd prayed together, of course, and after that she'd put a brave face over her emotions and told him she knew God would take care of both him and Greg, but Bill had felt the continuing hurt inside her, deep down and carefully walled off. Nor would she talk about it after that, and that had left him feeling like she was shutting him out of a part of her life.

What was worse, he'd lied to her in a way by carefully *not* telling her just how hard he'd fought for the assignment, or what he'd done to win it. He still felt bad about that, and he didn't know how to deal with it other than, as he was doing with so much else these days, giving it all back to God.

They checked in with the Marine guard at the front desk and were directed down a gleaming corridor to an office area filled with sailors and Marines working at their rows of gray steel government-issue desks. The air was filled with the on-going clatter of typewriters, punctuated by the frequent ringing of telephones. The place looked more like a typical military personnel office than an intelligence center.

"Petty Officers Halstead and Tangretti reporting to Commander Garvey, as ordered," Greg told the yeoman at the receiving desk.

"Have a seat, and I'll tell him you're here."

They took the indicated wooden church-pew bench in a waiting area fenced off from the rest of the office by low, plastic dividers, and Bill turned his thoughts to the growing battle inside. For a time at the beginning of his last tour, Bill Tangretti had felt divided—torn in two was a better description, actually—over the dual role he had to play as hospital corpsman and as SEAL, as healer and as warrior.

Well, that dilemma had resolved itself easily enough. You carried out your mission, followed orders, and fought like hell for your teammates, and that satisfied the warrior half of the soul . . . then you patched up the guys who'd been wounded, regardless of the color of their skin or which side they'd been fighting on, and that took care of the corpsman.

Now, though, Bill was being pulled in other directions, as a married man and as a born-again Christian. By not telling Pat how hard he'd fought for this billet, he felt like he was betraying her in a way. Even worse, in some ways, was the insistent tug he felt with his responsibilities as a husband. If he was killed, it was going to hurt Pat and hurt her badly.

And even more to the point—was Bill Tangretti going to be able to cut it as a Christian SEAL?

Oh, he had no problem at all, as some of his teammates had suggested back in California, with the sixth commandment. The original translation of the words in the Bible, after all, was "Thou shalt not commit murder" and had nothing to do with killing as it applied to war. After all, if God had really meant that his chosen people shouldn't kill anyone at all, he'd had a funny way of showing his resolve when he'd promptly commanded the children of Israel to slaughter the Canaanites and Amorites and Hittites and all those other *ites* inhabiting the Promised Land. . . .

But ever since he'd announced his conversion back at Coronado, some of his teammates had been, well, looking at him a little ... *differently*. Nothing had been said, really, but he had the feeling that some of them didn't know if they could trust him to hold up his end of the IBS.

That was a large part of what being a SEAL was all about. Back in BUD/S, each trainee boat crew had to work together, and the physical evolutions were designed to shape them all into a smoothly integrated and working unit, whether it was doing log PT or carrying a rubber boat around on their heads. A man who couldn't or wouldn't carry his share of the load was quickly cut out of the program. SEALs worked as a *team*, which was why both Tangretti and Halstead had wondered about whether Morgan had what it took to be a SEAL.

That, probably, more than anything else, was what had stiffened Bill's resolve to prove that it could be done. He would be a Christian and a SEAL, and he would be good at both. Jesus had already shown the way. *"Render unto Caesar the things that are Caesar's ..."*

He would do it and prove that he was still part of the Teams.

"So," Bill said carefully after the two SEALs had taken their seats. "Is this deployment going to be a problem for you guys? Are you really sorry we're back?"

Greg looked thoughtful. "No, not really. I mean ..." He waved his hand, taking in not only the office but, by implication, everything beyond the walls of the building. "... this is what the SEALs are all about, right? Any time they have us back in CONUS, whether it's training newbies or carrying out training evolutions ourselves, we're preparing for war. For *this* war, because we don't happen to have any other wars available, right now." He looked at Bill, almost as though he were measuring him. "SEALs are warriors, Doc. That's the name of the game. We're not like your average grunt who got drafted and is just putting in his three years, or whatever. We're professionals. And part of our profession is being very good at killing people. Right?"

"Hooyah," Bill replied. He said it quietly, though. There were, after all, quite a few people within earshot.

"I suppose I have to say you and I are damned lucky to have had this chance," Greg continued. "Or, as you would say, I guess, we're blessed. The available slots are drying up."

That was true enough. During the sixties, lots of SEALs had pulled three, four, even five tours in Vietnam, with each tour lasting six months and alternating with six months to a year spent Stateside, either training new SEAL recruits or undergoing advanced training themselves. Nowadays, however, the war was changing, and so were the SEALs. There were lots more SEALs, for one thing, than there'd been even two years ago, during Tet, the result of an aggressive recruitment program and the wholesale transfer of lots of men from the UDT.

At the same time, fewer SEALs were being stationed in Vietnam. The glory days when both SEAL One and SEAL Two maintained a couple of direct action platoons each were over. Now, small groups of SEALs worked alone or in twos or fours with Vietnamese LDNNs, and with a heavy administrative load that made venturing into the bush on ops with their counterparts hard to arrange.

The yeoman emerged from Commander Garvey's office. "You two want to go on in now," he told them.

Five men were waiting for them in the office. Two of them they'd already met—Lieutenant MacMillen . . . and a second Navy lieutenant as well, Lieutenant David Nolan.

The other three in the room included a Navy commander behind the utilitarian gray steel desk, another Navy lieutenant whom they'd not yet met, and an older man in camouflage utilities without any rank insignia or pins at all. He was wearing dark glasses, though the fluorescent lighting in the room didn't seem *that* bright.

Greg faced the man behind the desk. "Electronics Technician Third Class Halstead, Hospital Corpsman Third Class Tangretti," he said with precise formality, "SEAL Team One, reporting as ordered, sir."

"Good morning, men. Thanks for coming. I'm Commander Garvey, MACV Studies and Observations Group, and you'll be answering to me while you're stationed here. You know your CO, of course. And I gather you two know this gentleman." He nodded at Lieutenant Nolan.

"Lieutenant Nolan!" Greg exclaimed. "Good to see you again, sir."

"Good to see you two." Nolan extended a hand and they

both shook it. "Still hanging around in bars shooting te-quila?"

"Not lately, sir," Bill told him. "The worms were getting hostile."

Nolan chuckled.

"Over there," Garvey went on, "is Lieutenant Kelso, your team NILO, and, ah, Mr. Jones. Welcome to Danang, both of you."

"Thank you, sir," Bill said.

"It's good to be back in the Nam, sir," Greg added.

Kelso gave Greg a disbelieving look. "Vietnam is not ex-actly a good place to be, Petty Officer," he said.

"Oh, I don't know, sir," Greg replied. "If you're a SEAL, this can be a *very* good place to be."

Garvey opened one of the manila folders before him on the desk and began leafing through it. "Okay . . . Halstead? This is your second tour in-country, am I right?"

"Affirmative, sir."

"And Doc, this is your third."

"Two and a half, sir," Bill replied. "My first tour got cut kind of short."

"Just before Tet, '68. I see that. And both of you men volunteered for this?"

"We both volunteered for another tour, sir," Bill told him.

"Good God, why?" Kelso asked. It was more of a demand than a question.

Bill hesitated. What was this spook getting at, anyway?

"According to your records, both of you are married. . . ."

"Yes, sir," Greg said, a bit defensively. "Lots of SEALs are."

"Actually," Bill added, "the studies I've seen indicate that married men are steadier and less likely to take stupid chances. Is there a problem with that?" He was having to squeeze down pretty hard to keep his impatience, touched with anger, in check. "And if you don't mind my asking," he continued, "what's the point of all this?"

"Yeah," Greg added. "Why the third degree? Sir."

Garvey leaned back in his chair, fingers drumming a brief tattoo on the top of his desk. He seemed to reach a decision. "Men, I'll tell you what's on our minds. During the past year or so, the emphasis in the war over here has shifted, and the

SEAL mission is changing with it. There's less emphasis now on patrolling or killing VC, less emphasis even on gathering intel or maintaining nets of informers.'' He glanced at the unranked man in sunglasses. ''The Phoenix Program, as I'm sure you're aware, produced positive results . . . but has fallen into, um, controversy, let's say.''

''That's one word for it,'' Bill said. Phoenix had been the CIA's program to attack the Communists throughout South Vietnam by striking at their leadership. The original concept was to identify VC cadres, senior officers, tax collectors, political officials, and the like. Capturing them opened new avenues of intelligence, even active help as former VC cadres turned on their former comrades. In some cases, assassinations had been sanctioned, especially when high-ranking officers could be identified and targeted. The SEALs, the Army Green Berets, MACV-SOG, various CIA-sponsored militia groups, and the PRUs all had played a part in the program.

And Phoenix had damn near won the war.

But the downside had carried too heavy a political cost for the effort to be maintained. Too many South Vietnamese government and military officials found Phoenix to be a splendid way to pay back old scores, to settle family feuds, or to remove rivals. No one could say how many South Vietnamese had been killed or imprisoned by agents of their own government not because they were Communists but because they'd made it onto someone's shit list.

And word of Phoenix had spread back in the States, where peace groups claimed that U.S. forces were engaged in wholesale genocide, that they were participating in illegal assassinations and kidnappings. Somehow, the country's perception of a *just* war fought against Communism to uphold democracy was mutating into something else . . . an unjust war in support of a dictatorship for less than honorable reasons.

Bill still wasn't sure where he stood on the matter now. Most SEALs had been enthusiastic proponents of Phoenix, because the program had been getting results. The abuses of the program, though, were hard to stomach from any moral stance, and by now, the Saigon government was so corrupt and American goals so muddied that it was hard to know any more *what* was right and wrong.

''The new emphasis for special operations forces in-country," Garvey continued, "is going to be POW and downed-flier rescues. That's the hot button back home, the one that all the politicians are pushing just as fast and hard as they can."

"As America pulls out of Vietnam," Lieutenant Mac-Millen added, "there's going to be a real push to get as many of our POWs out of enemy hands as possible and to keep downed U.S. fliers from being captured. Everybody remembers how the North Koreans used American POWs as bargaining chips, back in 1953."

Bill and Greg both nodded their understanding. At the level of day-to-day SEAL operations, no one gave much of a damn for political considerations . . . but it was unthinkable to leave American boys in VC or NVA hands. A number of SEAL ops in the south had been mounted to rescue U.S. POWs. So far, at least, all had come up dry.

But the SEALs kept trying. Everyone recognized that they were particularly good at missions of that type, requiring good intel, excellent reconnaissance and covert infiltration techniques . . . and the firepower to pound the hell out of the enemy when they found him, making a rescue and fast E&E possible.

"We're putting together a new ongoing mission," Garvey told them, "under the code name Bright Light. SEALs, Army Special Forces, Long Range Recon units all over the country are being organized as quick-response teams with the specific mission of getting our people out of Communist hands. That means whenever a pilot is down in hostile territory, we'll have the men and the air assets to go in and get him out. And if intel brings in word that one of our boys has been captured, we have people to try to go in and winkle him out. This program, I should add, has the very highest priority level. It will be taking precedence over most of the other missions that the SEALs have been called upon to carry out in the past."

Mr. Jones, the unranked man sitting quietly by the wall, stirred. "What I am about to tell you men," he said, his voice deep and even, "is classified secret. It is not to be discussed outside of this room. Am I clear?"

"Clear, sir," Bill replied. SEALs knew how to keep secrets.

"Right now, as we speak, an operation is under way aimed smack at Hanoi itself, one that we are confident will liberate a number of our boys being held up there as POWs."

"Hoo*yah!*" Greg snapped, his face lighting up.

"All *right!*" Bill said. For some months now, the plight of American POWs being held in North Vietnamese prisons had been very much in the American public's consciousness. A raid to get some of those people back would do more to boost American morale than all of the bombing missions yet mounted against the north.

Garvey fixed the two SEALs with a hard look. "Interested?"

"Yes, sir!" Greg said.

"It sounds good, sir," Bill echoed. "Are we going up north, then?"

"Negative," Garvey said.

Bill blinked, confused. "But I thought you said—"

"Why were you telling us about POW rescue ops in Hanoi," Greg asked, echoing Bill's own thoughts, "if you didn't have a part in the thing for us?"

Mr. Jones stood up. "Normally, men," he told them, "that kind of information would be strictly need-to-know. I authorized bringing you in on that much, and no more, in order to impress upon you the importance of *another* mission that we are putting together from right here."

"Right," Garvey said. "Hanoi is a different department and won't concern you two. But we do have something else in mind for you, for *one* of you, actually, if you want to volunteer."

Bill felt a small shock. "One of us, sir? Which one?"

"That's up to you guys," Nolan said easily. He crossed his arms and sat on the corner of Garvey's desk. "We're putting together a special op. It's going to be me, one other SEAL, and a team of LDNNs and local tribesmen already on the ground."

"This *is* a volunteers-only mission," MacMillen added. "You can both refuse, and it will not reflect on your records. If you both volunteer, one of you will go, the other will be an alternate in case something happens to the first one. The one who stays behind will start training with one of the new pilot rescue teams."

"It's also secret," Jones told them. "More secret than what you just heard about Hanoi. If you do refuse it, you will not be permitted to discuss it, among yourselves or with anyone else."

"We understand the need for security, sir," Greg said.

"Good." Jones walked over to the back of the room, where a map cover had been pulled down over a large wall map, like a window shade. Raising the cover, he exposed a large-scale topographical map of the northern panhandle of South Vietnam, roughly from Qui Nho'n to Dông Hoi, up beyond the DMZ in North Vietnam. The western edge of the map took in all of southern Laos, from Muang Khammouan, just across the Mekong River from Thailand, south to the Cambodian border.

Red lines had been drawn in with Magic Marker, starting inside North Vietnam near Dông Hoi, crossing into Laos and running south. A major junction of trails was shown at Tchepone, where Route 9 branched off for Dông Ha, just south of the DMZ, and Quang Tri, capital of South Vietnam's Quang Tri Province. The main red line continued south, branching occasionally to send shoots off toward the east and southeast, before plunging south into Cambodia in the vicinity of Attapu.

Bill knew at once what the map represented, of course. The Ho Chi Minh Trail, or the northern half of it, anyway, running through the supposedly neutral country of Laos, a highway ferrying millions of tons of supplies, ammunition, and weapons, as well as tens or hundreds of thousands of troops from North Vietnam into the embattled south.

"What we need," Mr. Jones told them, "is a little sneak-and-peek for us across the border, into Laos."

The Trail, Bill thought, his heart hammering a bit harder. *They're sending a Team after the Trail!*

And here he'd been afraid that this was going to be a dull deployment. . . .

Chapter 20

Thursday, 19 November 1970

SOG Intelligence Center, Danang
1052 hours

Greg was stunned. He'd heard plenty of rumors, of course, about classified American ops in Laos, but this was the first time he'd had those rumors confirmed. "Laos?" he asked.

"I'm sure you can understand why this is classified," Garvey told him.

"Operations across the line are *extremely* sensitive politically," Kelso said.

Greg nodded. "They can be physically dangerous too, as I understand it, sir."

"I don't think you catch my drift, Petty Officer," Kelso said. "Since the U.S. invasion of Cambodia last March, our involvement in that country has created a firestorm of protest back home. Kent State. Weatherman bombings. Right now, Washington is pretty damned eager to avoid any further incidents that might spark off more protests."

"Since the middle of this year," Garvey said, "since June or July or so, every single proposal for a POW rescue effort in either Laos or Cambodia has been torpedoed by Washington. That territory is off-limits now, and God help the man who wanders over there and gets into trouble."

"The ARVNs are still in Cambodia," Bill pointed out. The last U.S. ground troops in Cambodia had been pulled out at the end of June. Saigon had announced, however, that its troops would stay in Cambodia for as long as necessary. On October 24 and 25, two new South Vietnamese drives had been launched across the Cambodian border, aimed at NVA supply caches and portions of the Ho Chi Minh Trail.

"Of course," Garvey said. "It's their war, now."

"Deniability," Mr. Jones added softly. "What they do in Cambodia, out of military necessity, is *their* business."

And I believe in the tooth fairy, too, Greg thought with a mental snort.

"I don't think I need to tell you," Garvey said with an irritated glance at Jones, "that the United States does still have assets on the ground in Cambodia, Laos, and in North Vietnam."

Greg nodded. Though very little was said about it, there were plenty of rumors throughout the Special Warfare community about SOG ops throughout Southeast Asia. Most of the "assets" Garvey had just mentioned would be locals—Vietnamese in North Vietnam; Laotians, Meo and Montagnard tribesmen, and Nung mercenaries in Laos; Cambodians, Khmers, Montagnards, and Nung in Cambodia. The CIA had been heavily involved in both Cambodia and Laos ever since the early sixties, and probably even before that, organizing natives into anti-Communist guerrilla forces. But Americans would have gone into all those regions, too, organizing supply lines and communications protocols, delivering orders, carrying out training programs, providing motivation. The CIA maintained listening posts and radar guidance beacons in Laos, guiding bombers in from Thailand on the way to targets in North Vietnam.

And, sometimes, they must carry out more specialized, more direct operations as well.

"Your mission, should you decide to accept it," Garvey went on, mimicking the spymaster's voice on *Mission Impossible,* "will be to cross the line into Laos, one of you with Lieutenant Nolan. You will meet with two Vietnamese SEALs and a team of CIA-trained Laotian mountain tribesmen. We are interested in a particular section of the Ho Chi Minh Trail."

"Right," MacMillen said in his easy drawl. "Y'all'll do some scouting for us, fill in some blank spots on the map, then skedaddle back across the line for pickup."

"I'm afraid," Garvey told them, "that, given the political climate at this time, we will not be able to extract you on site. If you run into trouble, you're going to be on your own."

"In other words," Greg said with a dry chuckle, and picking up on the commander's television spy program reference, "the Secretary will disavow all knowledge of our actions."

"You *could* say that," Garvey said, his mouth twisting in a reluctant smile. "You will not be more than twenty to thirty kilometers inside of Laos at any time, however. If things get too tough, you should be able to slip back across the border and radio for a pickup. That's at least as much because we don't want to call Charlie's attention to our interest in this region as it is because of the political climate back home. So, before we go any further, I should ask you. Are you two interested in volunteering for this op? I'll say again, it's dangerous, and you don't have to accept."

Greg exchanged glances with Bill, unsure what his swim buddy would say. The other SEAL winked at him, however, and grinned.

"A chance to cross the line, sir?" Bill said. "Hey, I wouldn't miss it!"

"Same here, sir," Greg replied. "Count me in!"

"I'm only taking one of you," Nolan said. "Who's it going to be?"

"Me," the two chorused.

They looked at each other. "Uh, how about if you take both of us?" Bill said. "I mean, we're a team. Swim buddies. We were together with Delta Platoon, under Lieutenant Casey and, well, we've been together ever since."

Nolan shook his head. "I don't think so. The idea is to keep a low profile."

Garvey laughed. "Nolan here has been in trouble with his superior officers more than once. He has this annoying tendency to charge off by himself or with just one other SEAL, instead of going in with a whole team."

"Well," Nolan said, his arms still crossed, "if I can do the job, carry out the mission more easily with one man than with six, why the hell not?"

Garvey shrugged. "He does have the record to back him up on that. And the old days of running seven-man SEAL squads on patrol and snatches is pretty much over, now. The emphasis is in training the locals to do it on their own."

Greg exchanged another glance with Bill. "Tell you what,

sir. Give us some time to settle this ourselves, which one's supposed to go.''

"Fair enough," Garvey said. "As I said, the other will be alternate and will begin working with the new pilot rescue and recovery team immediately. The code name of the Laos operation is Freedom Trail. Everything we say about it is, naturally, classified.''

"You will be operating in support of *future* Bright Light missions," Jones told them. "While many POWs—especially the men taken by the VC—are held in various temporary camps in the south, Hanoi has issued orders that as many American prisoners as possible are to be moved north. Especially now that the POW issue is becoming more prominent back home. North Vietnam's military leaders are beginning to realize that U.S. prisoners of war are valuable commodities. Obviously, the only way to get them north, unless they're airmen shot down over North Vietnam, of course, is to march them up the Ho Chi Minh Trail.''

Jones appeared to be taking center stage now as he laid out the operation. He walked over to the map and drew his forefinger along the red line running north through Laos. "Obviously, ever since we realized that the Communists were sending supplies into South Vietnam along the Ho Chi Minh Trail, we've been interested in mapping it out, finding out where things are, and identifying the choke points, the places where we can do the most good with an airstrike. To that end, we've been sending men in since the mid-sixties to map the trail. And the Air Force has taken the lead in dropping sensors and various types of detectors into this whole region. We've got devices out there, delivered by parachute and hanging up in the trees, or dropped like bombs so that they penetrate the forest floor and bury themselves, that can detect the movement of a four-wheeled vehicle, even the passage of a bicycle, and radio the information to electronic warfare aircraft.

"But the Ho Chi Minh Trail isn't just a single road through the jungle. It's more like a whole spaghetti tangle of paths. In places, the Ho Chi Minh Trail doesn't occupy one specific area but is spread all over an entire province. Bombing one stretch of trail doesn't do a damned thing. We bomb one out of existence, they just divert to another trail a few klicks away. We think we've got one set of roads identified, only to find out later they've been sending a hundred trucks a day down another stretch of road just over the next hill, or maybe along a whole different set of parallel trails forty klicks away. That might give you some idea, *some*, of just how hard it is to nail these bastards from the air.''

His finger traced its way to that part of southern Laos close alongside the DMZ, the place where Route 9 crossed the border from Dông Ha to Tchepone. ''There are, however, a few choke points where the Communists just don't have that much choice. One of the best ones is up here, right about where the Ho Chi Minh Trail leaves North Vietnam and starts going south. Tchepone, here, just twenty klicks in from the South Vietnamese border and right astride Highway 9, seems to be a major terminus for the whole northern section of the Trail. When the Communists take our boys north, most of them have to go through here.''

''So you're thinking that this would be a good intercept point,'' Greg said. ''For an ambush?''

''Exactly. The bastards tend to bunch our boys up when they take them north. More efficient to guard them that way, and to maintain security. When our ground assets report that a party with probable POWs is moving north up the trail, we can organize a strike, with helicopter deployment, somewhere along this stretch, between Muang Nong and Tchepone. LRRPs can track them until Army Special Forces and other Bright Light units can be brought into position and the ambush sprung.''

''And you want us to map out the area around Tchepone,'' Bill said.

''That's it,'' Jones said. ''You will be inserted at night, by HALO, at a prearranged DZ on the Laotian side of the border.''

''We're going to handle this the same way the Air Force handled the bombings in Cambodia, back before they were officially allowed to do it,'' Garvey said. ''You see, the orders would be cut to bomb some innocuous piece of jungle just this side of the border. The aircraft would go in, rendezvous at the target, and then an air controller would call them up and say their target had been changed. Give 'em a vector to a new target . . . only this one might be five or ten or even twenty miles on the other side of the line. The flyboys would go dump on the target and report a mission accomplished. Back at the airfield, the ACs would be busily shredding any evidence that U.S. forces had violated the border. Neat.''

Greg's eyebrow went up at that. He didn't like operations where one part of the military command structure didn't know what another part was doing. That was a great recipe for a screwup.

"You will be guided into your DZ by your VN opposite numbers,'' Jones continued, with an unpleasant glance at Garvey. Greg guessed there was some dirty laundry there that SOG didn't want aired . . . something about the shredded documents perhaps. "From there, you will proceed to the general vicinity of Tchepone, where you will pick up the Ho Chi Minh Trail. We'd like you to follow the trail as far south as is practicable, ideally all the way to Muang Nong, about here. That's a distance of about forty kilometers, but you'll be operating parallel to the border from about here . . . all the way to here, so if you have to abort for any reason, you'll only be about twenty klicks from Vietnam. We want you to map the main trails and the rest stops. Camps. Caches. Anything that might be of tactical or strategic interest in the entire region opposite Khe Sanh.''

Greg drew a long, slow breath, then let it out again. These people weren't looking for ambush sites. What the SEALs had just been asked to do was nothing less than a complete tactical survey . . . the sort of survey SEALs and UDT personnel were trained to carry out on enemy-held beaches just ahead of an invasion.

"You know, Commander,'' Greg said quietly, "if I didn't know better, I'd swear that someone was getting ready to launch another across-the-line invasion. Laos, this time, instead of Cambodia.''

Jones looked at him sharply. "We would really prefer that you not even speculate about that, Petty Officer,'' he said. "This mission, as we've already explained, is a preliminary ground investigation being carried out in conjunction with planned deployments for Operation Bright Light.''

"Yes, sir.''

"Naturally, if you see targets of opportunity, we will expect a full report. Intelligence knows the Communists are bringing a hell of a lot of stuff down Highway 9 and across the Laotian border near Khe Sanh,'' Kelso said. ''If you can pinpoint key targets, we can take them out with air strikes.''

''Right.'' Greg didn't let the laughter he felt touch his face. If air strikes could have knocked out the Ho Chi Minh Trail, the war would have been over a long time ago. He was convinced that his first guess was the correct one. This was a sneak-and-peek ahead of a ground strike of some sort, and probably a big one.

Well, it wouldn't be the first time that the men being sent in on reconnaissance hadn't been told what the real mission or objective was. No SEAL had yet been captured in combat, but there was always that first time . . . and it was never wise to give too much information to the people who were risking getting picked up by the enemy.

''We will be most interested in whatever you happen to see in there,'' Jones said. ''But understand that such reports will be secondary to your main mission, which is to identify key enemy encampments, emplacements, stops, and caches in the target region.''

Garvey looked at Bill. ''You were right a while ago, son, when you said that married men are steadier than bachelors. And that is precisely what we need here, steady men who can slip in quietly, nose around, make observations, and, at all costs, avoid any direct confrontation with the enemy.''

MacMillen smiled. ''Bachelor SEALs have this tendency to cowboy it on an op like this. I think it's in their blood.''

''Believe me when I tell you,'' Garvey went on, ''that if you have to leave any bodies behind, particularly if you get into a shoot-out that focuses NVA attention on this area, your mission will have failed.''

''It's just a little old sneak-and-peek, gentlemen,'' Lieutenant MacMillen told them. ''Not a hop-and-pop. Not a wham-and-scram.''

''Not even a loot-and-scoot,'' Greg said. ''We, ah, get the idea, sir.''

''When do we go, Mr. Nolan?'' Bill asked. Greg nudged him in the ribs with an elbow, and he added, ''Uh, I mean, whichever one of us is going with you—''

''We'd like to have the team on the way within the week, actually. The sooner we can drop you out there, the less chance there is of anything about the op leaking.'' Garvey gave a sour look. "Entirely too much high-level intel has been ending up in Hanoi, lately. Some of us are smelling a rat. A *burrowing* rat."

Greg nodded, catching the reference to a mole. Anyone with an ounce of sense who'd worked within the military structure in South Vietnam knew that the enemy had agents everywhere, even inside supposedly secure U.S. installations. Phones were tapped, radio calls intercepted and broken, and even high-ranking South Vietnamese officers might be in the pay of the north . . . or simply and stupidly saying the wrong things to staff personnel, assistants, secretaries, mistresses, or relatives who happened to be working for Charlie. There were times, Greg knew, when the enemy had known of South Vietnamese or American moves before the troops actually involved knew, so efficient was Hanoi's intelligence and communications network in the south.

"I'm curious, sir," Bill said. "Why the Navy for this op? Why SEALs? I'd have thought the Green Beanies would be all over that region by now."

"There *are* Army Special Forces recon units out there," Garvey agreed. "Strictly top secret and deniable, of course. All of them operate under SOG. There is some reason to suspect, however, that some Special Forces channels have been compromised. You SEALs seem to have a better record of keeping Charlie out of the loop."

"We're also asking for one of you to volunteer, frankly," MacMillen put in, "because both of you have exceptional records, and you both seem to be among the best sneakers and peekers we have. You also come highly recommended by a friend of mine, a certain Navy lieutenant who led a rather daring covert raid on the island of Ham Tam a year and a half ago."

"Lieutenant Casey!" Greg exclaimed. "How's he doing, anyway?"

"Oh, fine," MacMillen said with a half shrug. "Fine as can be expected, anyway, with a leg missing. You boys hear he's been put in for the Medal of Honor?"

"We did hear that, sir, yes."

"Well, it's going through channels, and I expect he's going to get it. That was a ballsy thing you guys did at Ham Tam, climbing a sheer rock cliff to come down on the enemy from his blind side.''

"Well, it didn't quite work the way it was supposed to, sir," Bill said. "Someone spotted us and we got into a fire-fight." He touched the ugly puckering at the side of his head. "That's where I picked up this, in fact."

"Nolan here actually made the pitch to try using one of you two," Garvey told them. He tapped the manila folders on his desk. "MacMillen agreed. And I've been through your records and know you won't let us down."

"We'll damn sure do our best for you, Commander," Greg told him.

"I know you will."

"I am wondering about the HALO drop idea," Bill said. "Jumping at night, into unknown territory . . . and that ground you're talking about is some of the worst in the world. I wonder if a helo insertion wouldn't be safer."

"That's just what we *don't* want, Petty Officer," Kelso said. "Helicopters clattering around the very area we're interested in? HALO insertions are quiet and they're secure. You'll have pathfinder elements on the ground to guide you in. Nothing can go wrong."

Greg burst out with a laugh. "Excuse me, sir," he said, recovering. "But it's when someone tells me that nothing can go wrong that I *know* the thing's screwed!"

"Do you want to reconsider volunteering, Halstead?" Garvey asked.

"No, sir. But I would like to know we're not just being pushed off into the dark, on a half-assed mission with no real thought behind it." He pointed at the map. "Doc is right, by the way. Some of that terrain is pretty rough . . . all jungle and mountain, both together, with hills that nine times out of ten are going *up* instead of down."

"Yeah," Bill put in. "It's the kind of ground where a man can struggle along all day and log five miles . . . *if* he's lucky and if he isn't worried about keeping the noise down to avoid waking the neighbors."

"Affirmative," Greg continued. "Twenty klicks is no big deal in training evolutions back in the States. Hell, SEALs have to qualify with a twenty-kilometer-plus *run* in under two hours, but that's on the Strand back at Coronado. Flat, sandy beaches. Girls in bikinis, working on their tans. Long, flat stretches of highway. That terrain in there, hell, twenty klicks is *forever* in the mountains.''

"I told you that the SEALs were wrong for this kind of op, sir," Kelso said. "Navy personnel have no business carrying out missions better suited to mountain troops."

"With all due respect, Mr. Kelso," Bill told him, "Mountains have nothing to do with it. I personally know a SEAL who wandered all over the Seven Mountains region, down near Chau Doc, right after Tet."

That would be Hank Richardson, Greg thought, Bill's half brother, a Team Two SEAL who'd operated in the Delta with the near-legendary Lieutenant Mariacher. "He's right, sir," Greg added. "SEALs can go anywhere, fight anywhere. But it doesn't make sense to take unnecessary risks."

"We've studied this carefully, Tangretti," Garvey said, "and we're convinced that HALO is the way to go, here. Your DZ is a relatively open, flat area on top of Ban Kôon Mountain. You should have no difficulty."

"If that's all, gentlemen," MacMillen told them, "we'll plan on having further briefings over the course of the next few days. Let me know by tomorrow morning, zero-nine hundred, which of you is going. Meanwhile, you two just keep on familiarizing yourselves with Echo and with the base. Be thinking of the sorts of weapons and equipment you'll want to draw, and any suggestions you might have for how to field this op. Plan on the one of you who goes flying out of here at twenty-one hundred on the twenty-sixth . . . unless there's too heavy an overcast. You'll have a new moon, which means no light over the DZ, so the only real question will be the weather. If the sky is overcast, Freedom Trail will be put off twenty-four hours. And unless there are any questions right now, you're dismissed."

The SEALs started to leave. At the door to the office, though, Bill turned and gave Jones a sidelong look. "So . . . how *did* the Cambodian incursion go, anyway?" Bill asked him. "If you don't mind my asking, that is."

"We've only heard the news Stateside, sir," Greg added. "And we're not sure just how much of what we hear is the straight skinny. We've been wondering if you guys thought that the invasion was successful."

"It would take too long to list everything we captured," Jones told them. "But I can give you a few isolated figures. In the Fish Hook, our people captured one strategic NVA center called The City, a two-square-mile complex completely camouflaged beneath the jungle canopy. They found four hundred huts, interconnected bunkers, bamboo walkways, bicycle paths, street signs, truck garages, mess halls, a pig farm, and a swimming pool. There were one hundred eighty-two separate caches in that area. One cache alone contained four hundred eighty rifles. The biggest cache contained six point five million antiaircraft rounds, half a million 7.62 millimeter AK rounds, several thousand rockets, several General Motors trucks, and a number of complete, working telephone switchboards. Our people called that one Rock Island East, after the Rock Island Arsenal in Illinois.

"Was the invasion successful? Yes. Absolutely. The stated purpose of the operation was to find the Central Office for South Vietnam and to clear the border region of enemy caches and materiel. There is, admittedly, some debate still over whether we destroyed COSVN, but by any objective reckoning, the mission to seize the enemy's supplies was a resounding success. As evidence, I can only say that it's been six months since the invasion of Cambodia, and we have not had a single major NVA offensive during that time. We hurt them, and we hurt them very badly indeed."

"Thank you, sir," Bill said. "We appreciate the rundown."

"Not at all."

Outside the Intelligence Center once more, in the hot, wet tropical air of Danang, beyond the reach of American air conditioners, Greg and Bill looked at one another for a long moment, then broke out laughing.

"Jones" had clearly been part of the planning behind the Cambodian invasion earlier that year. That he was now participating in this op, whatever its true nature might be, strongly suggested that the same sort of operation was going to take place again.

"Invasion," Bill said. "Definitely an invasion!"

"And one of us is going to be on point," Greg added. "Son of a bitch!"

"*Which* one?" Bill asked. "How do you want to do this?"

Greg considered the question. "Fight you for it," he grinned as he spoke. He was six inches taller than Bill, and brawnier as well.

"Uh uh." Bill shook his head. "Pat would kill me if I hurt you. Tell you what. We turn around, march back inside there, and tell them we're both going. Nolan can't squawk about having to take two SEALs instead of one. It's not like we're making him take a whole squad."

"I don't think that'll cut it," Greg replied. "Nolan strikes me as the kind of SEAL officer who knows exactly what he wants and how he's going to get it. Mark Ringold told me as much, last summer."

"I hate the idea of being split up, y'know?"

"Sure, I know," Greg replied. "But, well, you know the Navy. They don't exactly run things for the convenience of the inmates."

It was, in fact, a little startling that the two had been together for as long as they had, beginning with the Delta Platoon deployment, extending through their unusually long assignment at BUD/S, and ending with both of them being assigned to Danang. That last was at least partly Bill's doing, with the strings he'd been pulling back at Coronado, but the fact remained that the two couldn't expect to keep going from duty station to duty station like Siamese twins, joined at the hip.

"Besides," Greg added, "have you thought about Pat?"

"What do you mean?"

"Look, this op is dangerous—"

"*All* SEAL ops are dangerous."

"Yeah but this one is doubly so, or they wouldn't be asking us to volunteer, know what I mean?"

"All the more reason for both of us to go."

"Look, Doc, give it a rest, okay? It's not going to happen!" Bill looked hurt, but Greg pressed on. "And because it's so damned dangerous, think about Pat, okay? You want her to lose a brother *and* a husband on the same op?"

The expression on Bill's face changed to one of shock. Evidently, he'd not thought that one through. "Well, I didn't mean that—"

"Didn't you hear them in there?" Greg continued, relentlessly. "They didn't come out and say it, but they'd obviously been through our records. I think they know you married my sister, and they're looking at this like a kind of Sullivan brothers case.''

The Sullivan brothers had been five young men who'd joined the Navy early in World War II. All five had been assigned to the same ship, and all five had died when that ship had been sunk by the Japanese. As a result, Navy policy now forbade stationing family members together on the same ship or the same duty assignment. This case didn't exactly follow the same pattern, but it was close enough. Greg could imagine the firestorm in the press at home if they found out that a woman had lost both her husband and her brother on the same mission.

"I don't like you trying to use Pat to win this argument," Bill said. He sounded like he was starting to get mad.

"I'm not. One of us is going. Which one?''

Bill sighed. "I'll match you. Odds and evens, two out of three.''

Greg nodded. "Okay. But . . . if I can't use Pat in this argument . . .''

"Yeah?''

"Then no fair you calling on God to help you win. Fair?''

Bill laughed. "Fair!''

"Ready? Odd. One . . . two . . . three . . .''

Seconds later, they knew who was going, and who would stay behind.

Chapter 21

Friday, 27 November 1970

30,000 feet over Lao Bao
On the Laotian–South Vietnamese border
2217 hours

The C-130 Combat Talon droned through the moonless night, flying west. Halstead and Nolan were seated in the aircraft's cargo compartment, fully suited up for HALO and ready to jump.

Ready to jump. When Greg leaned back against the bulkhead and closed his eyes, the image came, unbidden, of Ringold's twisted body, lying in the desert, his legs literally rammed up through his torso by the force of his landing. His eyes snapped open; he could feel the sweat forming on the skin of his face beneath the squeeze of his oxygen mask and in the palms of his hands inside his black gloves. *Can I do this? . . .*

Nolan, at least, seemed calm. Nothing ever ruffled that man's placid exterior.

Greg didn't like the idea of a night HALO for this op, especially on a night when there would be no moon at all, no way to gauge the distance left to fall save the altimeter fixed to his reserve chute. Still, what he thought of as the training effect had kicked in . . . his body remembering and guiding him through the routines of his pre-jump checklist, with very little need for thought.

"So," the C-130's crew chief said conversationally, "what'dja think of the Son Tay Raid, huh?" He was a master sergeant with the Air Force 5th Special Operations Squadron, who was doubling this night as crew chief and jumpmaster.

Nolan shrugged. "It was a damned good try," he called back. "Too bad it was a dry hole."

"Yeah," Greg added. "They should have used SEALs." The Combat Talon was part of SOG's resources, based at Danang. The crew chief had worked with SEALs before and knew what they could do.

"Hell, that wouldn't have made a difference on whether or not there were POWs there," the chief said.

"Nah, he means on the ground, going in before the raid," Nolan replied.

"Yeah," Greg added. "Put one or two SEALs in before the raid, scope the place out. They could've warned the mission planners that the prisoners were gone."

"I still think that was some cool shit," the chief said. "I mean, our guys hitting a suburb of Hanoi! Crazy!"

"That about sums it up," Nolan said, and Greg laughed.

"The question now, of course," Nolan added, "is whether we keep this up. The North Vietnamese are going to be damned nervous about their POW camps now, and those may be harder to hit, but there're lots of other good targets that a small, well-trained commando team could hit. And, someday, we might be able to hit the camps again."

"How long you boys been with Detachment Echo?"

"Not long," Greg said. "Why?"

"Well, it's just that SOG has been carrying out a lot of ops up north, ever since the sixties. They're just not the sort of missions that get written up proper, with after action reports and shit like that, you dig?"

"I knew they were into a lot of spooky stuff," Greg told him. "But nobody's said much to us so far."

"And they won't. I been flyin' Talons for a year now, and I was assigned to Air America before that." It was an open and well-known secret that the civil airline known as Air America was a lightly painted front for a CIA transport and supply operation that extended across Southeast Asia. "Man, you wouldn't believe some of the shit that goes down! Sometimes I think SOG is running this whole damned war."

Actually, Greg had learned a fair amount about the Studies and Observations Group, both through his previous experience and in the briefings he'd received so far, in Vietnam and in the United States. Though completely distinct from the old

Phoenix Program, SOG shared a common purpose with that operation and, like Phoenix, was a child of the CIA.

SOG had been created in 1964 by the Military Assistance Command–Vietnam, its creative and free-form approach to combat and intelligence a direct response to the free-form tactics and approaches used by the Communist insurgents. Originally using only Army Special Forces to carry out its missions, it soon grew to include Army Rangers, Marines, ARVN special forces, Air Force Special Operations Forces, and the Navy SEALs. Ultimately, the group evolved four different departments, each tasked with a different aspect of containing the enemy's multipronged assaults.

The Psychological Studies Group, or PSG, was headquartered at Tay Ninh and was responsible for PsyWar ops. They were the guys who flew the C-47s that dropped leaflets over enemy infiltration routes and strongholds, and broadcast propaganda over airborne loudspeakers . . . the "Bullshit Bombers," as they were known to everyone else.

The Air Studies Group deployed and monitored the electronic surveillance equipment airdropped over infiltration routes from the north. When these seismic or sonic detectors reported a high concentration of movement in the area, the ASG could call in air strikes to hit that section of the trail.

The Maritime Studies Group, predictably, employed a lot of Navy SEALs and was responsible for covering the entire coastline and the inland waterways of both North and South Vietnam, and portions of the Cambodian coast as well. Both Halstead and Nolan had heard plenty of rumors within the SEAL community about raids and recon missions carried out by SEALs and UDT personnel, including stories of SEAL listening posts on islands in the mouth of Haiphong Harbor, and SEAL ops to mine ships both at Haiphong and Cambodia's Sihanoukville.

Finally, the Ground Studies Group ran ops out of Saigon, Ban Me Thuot, Kontum, and Danang, conducting Long Range Reconnaissance Patrols, or LRRPs, interdicting infiltration routes and trails, searching for allied prisoners, and carrying out sabotage of enemy equipment and facilities. The GSG carried out the majority of SOG operations, but its success depended on close coordination with the ASG, which provided much of its intel.

Detachment Echo's missions were primarily directed by the MSG, but lately, the GSG had been drawing on Echo SEALs more and more to carry out trail reconnaissance—especially across the border in Laos near the DMZ—and to conduct pilot rescues in I CTZ, the northern combat zone in South Vietnam.

Ever since the beginnings of their involvement in Vietnam, the SEALs had been operating with SOG, or under its umbrella, as often as they were working for MACV. Usually there were a number of bureaucratic layers between the mission originators and the people who carried those missions out . . . but sometimes, SEAL detachments such as Echo worked directly for the SOG commanders and analysts. Lately, according to what Halstead had heard in the Det Echo barracks at Danang, the biggest problem for people working under the aegis of SOG was the American military command's growing ambiguity over having Americans operate across the various lines that marked out legal operational areas. It was almost as though even the people responsible for the deep black ops—LRRPs into North Vietnam, say, or ambushes along the Ho Chi Minh Trail—were growing afraid of American reaction back home to operations not condoned by the Rules of Engagement.

That changing perception of the war, he thought, was responsible for the recent slack period in Detachment Echo operations, their use in hunting down mortar tubes, and their current low morale. Certainly, black ops were still being carried out but under a thicker cloak of secrecy than ever.

It was a little frightening, Greg realized, and created a very lonely feeling, to know that among the people giving the orders and planning the missions out here, the right hand quite literally didn't know what the left was doing. Lately, many of the men had even been thinking about the threat of betrayal, the possibility that someone higher up in the command authority would put them out in the field somewhere, then abandon them. Brother SEALs could always be trusted; some of the people running black ops across the lines could not.

Perhaps worst of all, most SEALs who'd served in Vietnam were used to developing their own sources of intelligence; hell, a few lucky units had bypassed the official SOG and MACV intel lines altogether, relying entirely on their own networks of informants, captured documents, and field intel analysis in order to put together their own ops. Working directly for SOG, however, the SEALs were completely reliant on intel developed and passed on by someone else, usually a someone else unknown to the SEALs, a someone else whose trustworthiness was untestable.

Such was the case with this mission in Laos. Halstead and Nolan both had been invited to participate in details of the planning . . . but the mission concept, its objective, and most aspects of its execution all had been worked out by others, with little or no input at all from the men whose lives depended on *everything* going right.

"Five minutes, gentlemen," the crew chief announced. "Check your gear!"

Carefully, the two SEALs stood up and checked one another's gear, paying particular attention to the oxygen bottles, hoses, and masks. Both men, clearly, were remembering Ringold, lying in the desert at Twentynine Palms.

This insertion was a good example of how much about the mission was out of the SEALs' control. Neither of them had liked the idea of a HALO insertion on a moonless night. Nolan, in fact, had been pushing going in on foot. The SEALs had been allowed their share of input during the past week, as they and the mission planners of Det Echo and the Danang SOG HQ had gone over the insertion from every possible angle, seeking a viable alternative, but in the end, the Freedom Trail insert was going down as originally planned, with a High Altitude Low Opening jump with full combat gear.

Besides HALO, they'd considered a low-altitude jump, relying on the C-130's pilot and his FLIR navigation to find the target, then jumping on a static line at an altitude of no more than 2,000 feet, and possibly as low as 500 feet . . . which was just barely enough altitude for a chute to fully deploy. That one had been rejected fast, with even more potential body bag tickets than the HALO, including the problem of not being able to see the DZ, the fact that they wouldn't have enough altitude to allow a controlled landing, and the danger that a low-flying C-130 would be heard and investigated, or even shot down, a very real danger so close to the heavily defended Ho Chi Minh Trail.

Other possibilities had included a helicopter insertion—rejected by Garvey and Jones on the grounds that it would be

too noisy and would attract too much unwanted attention—
and Nolan's suggestion, literally walking in from South Vietnam. Lots of SOG recons into Laos had been deployed in just
that fashion, with a small team of men setting out from one
of the firebases along the border and infiltrating Laos or Cambodia on foot. Garvey had turned thumbs-down on that one,
though, at last. Time was important, and too much would be
wasted by a team trying to cover twenty kilometers or more
on foot in rough terrain. Worse, the area around Highway 9,
the road coming in from Laos just south of the DMZ, was
heavily traveled by NVA regulars and VC, and an American
commando team ran a tremendous danger of being spotted
before they'd even reached the area they were supposed to
be checking out.

So in the end, HALO it was, and Nolan and Halstead could
only take Garvey's word for it that the Combat Talon's pilot
would put them in the right place, that the Vietnamese and
Hmong guerrillas waiting for them would not have been compromised or replaced by an NVA ambush, or that the situation
on the ground in Laos was not very much worse than the
mission planners were telling them it was.

"Two minutes," the crew chief warned. "The colonel says
he's got your LZ in sight to the north."

"Good job," Nolan told him. "Where you guys headed
after this, anyway?"

"Udorn, Thailand," the master sergeant replied. "And after that, ten days' I & I in the fleshpots of Bangkok."

I & I was an old reworking of the standard R&R, which
stood for "Rest and Recreation." I & I meant "Intercourse
and Intoxication."

"Ha!" Greg shook his helmeted head. "Some guys have
all the luck! Well, you can rest assured that we'll be remembering you real fondly while we're down there."

"Yeah, I just bet you will!" The sergeant listened to his
intercom link for a moment. "Thirty seconds."

Greg walked to the start of the ramp, peering down into
the darkness off to the aircraft's starboard side. Yes . . . he
could see it, a tiny rectangle of four green lights marking out
the DZ.

Assuming Charlie hadn't tortured the plan out of one of
the South Vietnamese commandos and was waiting patiently

near those lights for the SEALs' arrival. Every SEAL in Southeast Asia was keenly aware that the enemy had standing orders to kill or capture American SEALs at all costs, with considerable cash rewards as an inducement. The last price tag Greg had heard was the equivalent of seven thousand U.S. dollars, a hell of a lot for any peasant-soldier in this part of the world, and a fascinating statement about economic motivations in a Marxist society.

"Here's to Mark Ringold!" Nolan called out. "Hooyah!"

"Hooyah!" Greg replied. He laughed. "You know, I will never forget the look on those hippies' faces when I did the worm!"

"They probably still puke their guts out whenever they think about it."

"Ready, gentlemen!" the crew chief shouted. "Stand in the door!"

They stood side by side, above the Herky Bird's downsloping ramp, as wind and night howled outside.

"Altitude thirty thousand, two hundred," the chief told them. "Go!"

Linking arms, the two SEALs ran down the ramp and dove into darkness. For a moment or two after they released one another, they fell together, arching their backs to assume the classic starfish spread, and then Nolan drifted far enough off to his right that Greg could no longer see the other SEAL.

He thought again about Ringold. *Can that stuff,* he told himself savagely. His O_2 mask and gear were working perfectly, he'd checked all parts himself, and, besides, that was never going to happen to him. It was a fixed and unvarying law of nature that whatever killed the last guy, whatever you were now prepared to face, when it came to your turn to check out, it would be something *else* that flew up and smacked you between the eyes.

Greg didn't mind playing the odds at all. Bill Tangretti, he thought with a grin to himself, would probably put it all in God's hands, trusting Him to bring them through. *Well, I'll trust the god of statistics. Or maybe it's just plain luck....*

Luck or God, it didn't really matter. Fear was the killer out here, and Greg was in favor of anything that let you control that ancient enemy, from training to belief in miracles to rabbits' feet and Zen mantras, if it came to that. He thought about Wendy.

As he continued the descent, his thoughts turned to Pat . . . and suddenly he was very glad that Bill wasn't out here risking his ass on the same mission. Maybe, after all, it was best if the two of them split up, and *stayed* split up.

Just to be fair to Pat.

Long minutes later, when his luminous altimeter dial showed 4,000 feet, Greg yanked his rip cord, felt the chute unfolding from his back, then gasped as the ram air canopy grabbed hold and he felt the familiar jerk against his harness making him feel like he was headed back for the C-130. He'd already oriented himself so that he was facing the diamond of four soft, green lights marking the LZ; now he released his equipment pack, paying it out on the end of a fifteen-foot strap, and concentrated on adjusting his risers to steer himself in for a landing.

In the last handful of seconds, he could see the clearing by starlight; an instant later, his equipment pack hit the ground, he bent his legs gently . . . and then with the same shock he might have received from jumping off a chair, he hit the ground less than twenty feet from the lighted beacons and recovered at a walk.

He dropped flat at once, however, pulling at the Capwell locks that secured his parachute harness, then loosing the straps holding his AK-47 to his side. If this was an ambush, he was going to go down fighting. . . .

"End zone!" a voice called from the darkness, not far away.

"Drop kick!" Greg replied. A moment later, a Vietnamese in tiger-stripe camo, carrying an AK-47, appeared. Behind him was a tall, angular man in olive drab fatigues, with an impassive, paint-blacked face and an M1 carbine. "Four!" Greg challenged, keeping both men covered.

"Seven!"

Which made eleven, correct. Greg relaxed, though not much. He heard a thump in the darkness to his left, the sound of canvas dragging . . . and then Nolan swooped in to the LZ beneath the black canopy of his ram air chute.

"End zone," Nolan called softly.

"Drop kick! Nine!"

"Two."

It took moments only for them to gather up their chutes, harnesses, and HALO gear. The Viet commando led them to a shallow ditch already prepared nearby, where the gear was carefully buried.

"Well," a familiar, accented voice said as the big man in OD started shoveling dirt into the trench. "We work together again." Nghiep Van Dong moved into the clearing, touching the floppy brim of his boonie hat. "Is good to see you, Mr. Twidge."

"Dong!" Greg exclaimed softly. "What the hell are you doing way out here?"

"I could maybe ask you same, Mr. Twidge. Me, I fighting Communists. *Sat Cong!*"

"Sat Cong!" Greg replied. *Kill Communists.*

Nolan scanned the hilltop. The stars were very bright, lending a frosty if faint illumination to the landscape. "Better keep it down, people," he said.

"I have my Hmong on perimeter," Nghiep told him. "We have reconned the area. There are no Communists nearby."

"Good job."

Greg relaxed a little. "Man! It's been . . . what? A year and a half?"

"Something like that. Since you returned to your country last year. How is Doc?"

"He's doing fine."

"You guys know each other?" Nolan asked, surprised.

"Yeah, Nghiep was in Delta Platoon."

"And I also hear much about Doc and Twidge," the other Viet commando said.

"This," Nghiep said, "is Mai Xuan Dai. He LDNN. Like me." He spat something in a musical language, not Vietnamese, and another man approached, face blacked, in tiger-stripes, and carrying an M1. "And I would like to present also Dhu Mung."

"Pleased to meet you," Dhu said in startlingly precise English.

"The pleasure is ours," Greg said, surprised. "You speak excellent English."

"Thank you. I learned from . . ." He stopped, and smiled. "A friend, let us say. From the Company. He taught me first and later took me back to your country, where I attended school for a time. Then he brought me back to my own people.'' His head inclined a bit, showing pride. ''I am Blue Miao. You would say, *Hmong*.''

Greg nodded. The CIA had been working in Laos for a long time, and one of their principal tasks had been to organize local tribesmen, including the Hmong, also known variously as the Meo or Miao. Some of these remote tribes had reputations as terrifying warriors. Since the United States wasn't allowed to overtly help the Kingdom of Laos in its bitter civil war, the presence of men like Dhu was probably the only reason Laos hadn't fallen to the Communists already.

''Dhu has five of his people with him,'' Nghiep said. ''Only he speak English. Three of the others speak Vietnamese.''

''Kind of a mixed bag.''

Nghiep shrugged. ''In war, you take what you can and thank Buddha for blessing.''

''*Phai!*'' Greg replied. ''Absolutely right!''

He was enormously relieved that Nghiep was a member of the Freedom Trail team. He'd operated with the man before, and there was nothing like sharing a firefight with someone to learn that person's mettle. With Nghiep on the team, there were fewer questions about Mai or the Hmong soldiers. It didn't rule out the possibility of treachery and betrayal, but it made them a hell of a lot less likely.

Greg was intrigued by the social dynamics of the group. Ethnic Vietnamese, he knew, hated people from the various hill tribes—the Montagnards, or ''Mountain People,'' for instance, and the Chinese-descended Nung—so much that Saigon had nearly broken with the United States several times over the issue of arming the tribes to fight Communists. The feeling was that, once the war was won, the Vietnamese would go back to their old pastime of killing mountain tribespeople, and it would be a damned sight harder if the tribes were armed.

The real issue, though, seemed to be that the Vietnamese considered themselves civilized, with houses, farms, and modern cities like Saigon itself, while many of the tribespeople were still barely out of the stone age. Possibly the Vietnamese didn't want to be reminded of their own primitive forest origins.

They set out as soon as the equipment was buried and the light beacons were switched off and stowed away in a backpack that also held the team's radio. With their flight suits buried, the two SEALs were clad now in black jeans, shirts, and combat vests, which, from a distance, might be mistaken for Vietnamese peasant garb. Halstead wore a green headband to keep sweat-slicked hair out of his eyes; Nolan favored a black-dyed boonie hat. Both men carried sterile AK-47s—more for the fact that enemy troops wouldn't be able to distinguish the sound of the SEAL assault rifles from their own in a firefight than for any reason of security.

Traveling with one of the Hmong on point, they followed trails all but invisible in the close darkness of the forest, and soon, as the hill dropped away beneath their feet and they started a steep descent, Halstead and Nolan were completely blind, unable to see each next step in a long and perilous succession of uncertain steps. Soon, each man was walking with one arm outstretched, his hand on the pack or shoulder of the man ahead. Both SEALs might have reason to mistrust the motives or the skill of the SOG officers who'd put this op together, but within fifteen minutes, they were trusting their Hmong guides with very nearly the enthusiasm they normally reserved for other SEALs.

During the past week as they'd prepped for the mission, Greg had wondered aloud more than once whether it wouldn't be better to simply infiltrate an entire team of SEALs into Laos, despite Lieutenant Nolan's preferences. After all, SEALs trusted SEALs and could be depended on to watch one another's backs. They knew one another's working styles and moods and abilities and, most important, knew how to work as a *team*, a skill instilled in every BUD/S recruit from the moment he was assigned to a boat crew.

Doing things this way, however, clearly had advantages. A SEAL squad would still have needed local guides, and parachuting seven men into Laos would have been that much riskier than sending in two. Nghiep and the others knew the terrain; the two LDNN explained that they'd been in the region for almost three weeks now, tracking NVA supply columns as they came down the trail from the north and, at

Tchepone, either continued on south or split off on Highway 9. The Hmong knew the area and the people as well, and they brought to the partnership a hatred of the invading Communists that even the Vietnamese would be hard-pressed to match.

And the two SEALs knew their orders, which, for obvious reasons, SOG HQ hadn't wanted to transmit by radio. They would provide the brains for this union, while the others provided the hands and legs.

Freedom Trail was, in fact, an excellent example of the force multiplier effect of a small elite team. Two SEALs could extend their expertise to a larger native contingent as effectively as could seven . . . and could do it without being quite as obvious as a larger force.

All that was really necessary was mutual trust between the SEALs and the men they led.

And that was something that couldn't really be determined in full until the moment they encountered the enemy.

Chapter 22

Sunday, 29 November 1970

18 kilometers northeast of Tchepone
Laos
0535 hours

They'd spent their first day in Laos reaching the Hmong camp, a jungle-clad hideaway in the mountains northeast of Tchepone. There wasn't much in the way of amenities—a lean-to type tent, heavily camouflaged, with bamboo-lined, frond-covered pits to store food and ammunition, a nearby stream for water, a latrine pit dug in the jungle. From twenty feet away it was impossible to even see that a camp existed.

After grabbing some sleep during the day, the SOG team had set out just after dark, moving down the network of trails that crisscrossed the face of this valley wall. Their destination was a major north-south path ten kilometers to the west, which Nghiep had identified as a major branch of the Ho Chi Minh Trail in this region. By the time the sky was growing light the next morning, they'd reached a rocky overhang where the hillside dropped away to an open plain. A large road cut across the plain, unpaved and deeply rutted. It had rained heavily in the region during the previous week, Nghiep told them, the tail-end of Typhoon Patsy, and the red ground was muddy in patches, ideal for holding tracks.

As he lay on his belly on the limestone outcropping, Greg studied the tracks through a pair of binoculars, thinking that it looked as if a hell of a lot of people had been using the country of Laos as a throughway recently.

The history of tiny, landlocked Lane Xane—the Land of a Million Elephants, as the country had been known for centuries—was as tragic in its own way, if not quite as bloody, as that of Vietnam. Formerly a part of French Indochina, occupied by the Japanese during World War II, Laos received its independence as part of the Geneva Accords of July 1954, with Prince Souvana Phouma as its first ruler. The not-so-loyal opposition was the Communist Pathet Lao, which was led by Phouma's half brother, Prince Sauphanouvong, and which, with help from both Hanoi and Beijing, already controlled the northernmost districts of the country, near the Chinese border.

In 1957, Sauphanouvong had agreed to coalition rule, but the experiment ended when a wave of anti-Communist feeling—aided and abetted, no doubt, by the American CIA—swept the country and brought it to the brink of civil war. By 1960, a right-wing coup seized power under General Phoumi Nosavan; a neutralist counter-coup, led by Captain Kong Le and supported by the ousted Souvana Phouma, took power not long after that, and then the civil war was on in earnest. The Americans became even more deeply involved when they tried to prevent a possible alliance between the Communists and the neutralists by supporting a right-wing front under Nosavan and Prince Boun Oum. Hanoi, meanwhile, sent thousands of North Vietnamese troops into the country in the guise of native Pathet Lao rebels, and NVA troops clashed regularly with CIA-trained and -backed guerrillas. By 1962, most Laotians were so strongly in favor of complete neutrality for their country that the issue had taken on international proportions and the support of the peace commissioners in Geneva.

Laotian dreams of neutrality, however, had never really had a chance of fruition. The North Vietnamese, if they were to supply the insurgents in the south, had only three choices—to force their way across the heavily defended DMZ that sliced Vietnam in half across its narrowest point, to ship supplies by sea to Sihanoukville and risk interception by American sea and air units, or to bypass the DMZ by establishing the network of roads and paths through Laos and Cambodia that became known as the Ho Chi Minh Trail, thereby violating Laotian neutrality. And Washington, for its part, had been unwilling or unable to honor that neutrality. It was estimated that as many as 60,000 troops and 1,200 tons of military supplies were moving south along that path every year, which made the Ho Chi Minh Trail as important a logistical asset for the Communists as Cam Ranh Bay or Danang was for the Americans. U.S. aircraft had savagely bombed the trail throughout eastern and southern Laos, and CIA and SOG advisors had actively worked both with the Royal Laotian Army and with Nung and Meo tribesmen, turning them into respectable anti-Communist forces.

By all accounts, though, this sideshow war was going even more poorly than the much more public and visible war in Vietnam. Repeated onslaughts by American B-52s and tactical bombers had never more than slowed the steady flood of supplies moving south. Maintenance and defense units known as Binh Tram—a high percentage of the Ho Chi Minh Trail's original engineers and construction workers had come from the North Vietnamese village of Binh Tram—maintained way stations, rest areas, and repair depots at camps spaced every fourteen to twenty kilometers along the trail; bridges, pipelines, and whole sections of highway destroyed by the bombings were often repaired and fully operational again within twenty-four hours. Public pressure back home in the U.S. in the wake of the Cambodian invasion made further escalation in Laos politically suicidal. The only options seemed to be continued covert missions like Freedom Trail, or turning the whole show over to the Army of the Republic of Vietnam and claiming complete disinterest.

U.S. policy appeared to be embracing both options, but with little hope of positive results.

"I'd like a closer look at those tracks down there," Nolan said softly.

"Me, too," Greg replied. He looked north, up the road, then back the other way. "Seems clear. You think maybe they use it mainly at night?"

"Some parts of trail used a lot in daytime," Nghiep told them. "This part, in open, probably mostly at night."

"Yeah. They'd want to stay out of sight from our recon aircraft," Greg said. "Okay, let's find a way down there."

They left Mai and the six Hmong on top of the cliff as lookouts. Halstead, Nolan, and Nghiep found a way off the cliff by squeezing through a narrow crevice in the boulders, then chimney-walking down to the level of the road. After carefully checking for traffic once again, the three men walked out to the edge of the road.

Parts of the mud had dried recently, preserving a bewildering array of tracks, both of vehicles and of the characteristic footprints of men wearing *binh tri thien.*

They were more interested, though, in the long, accordion-pleated prints that looked as if they'd been made by heavy construction equipment . . . steel treads, in fact. Nolan pointed at one. "Check it out."

Greg nodded. "What do you think? PT-76?"

"Several of them, from the look of it. I'd guess four . . . maybe five, one following after the other."

"Could've been a whole battalion of the things," Greg replied. "Each tank in line is going to chew up the tracks of the one that went before."

He felt an icy chill as he examined the tracks deep-bitten in the rutted earth of the trail. The PT-76 was a Russian light amphibious tank, a vehicle widely used by Russian client states and trading partners around the globe, from China to Cuba to North Korea. In the Soviet Union and the various Warsaw Pact nations, it was employed strictly in the reconnaissance role; it weighed only fourteen tons, and its armor was so thin that it was vulnerable to fire from a .50-caliber machine gun, but it was good at swimming across deep rivers, and it could manage forty-four klicks per hour on open terrain.

But tanks weren't often encountered in Vietnam on either side. The terrain, a hellish mix of forest, mountain, rice paddy, and swamp, put together with an enemy who preferred guerrilla tactics to open battle, pretty much precluded the use of tanks in their massed-armor role, which was better suited to the rolling terrain of middle Europe or the plains of western Russia. The Americans had used the M-48 successfully in a mobile fire-support role, but the enemy had possessed no armor to speak of. Halstead had heard of one major armor battle in Vietnam, tank fighting tank at a place called Ben Het in 1969, but that was strictly the exception to the rule.

The tracks in that dried roadbed, though, suggested that the North Vietnamese were moving light tanks south, and in large numbers.

"I'd sort of like to know where those things are going," Greg said. "Wouldn't you?"

"Yeah," Nolan replied. "It'd be kind of interesting if the NVA were actually planning on coming out and duking it out with us, huh?"

A shrill, warbling whistle sounded from the clifftop. The SEALs looked up and saw Dhu hold up his hand, fist clenched, then point north up the road—*someone coming*. Immediately, the team slipped back into the foliage at the foot of the cliffs and froze, becoming one with the rocks and vegetation.

Minutes passed, and then Greg could hear voices calling to one another, voices speaking Vietnamese. A moment later, a bicycle appeared on the road, crossing from right to left. The bicycle was followed by another . . . then ten more, the soldiers riding them wearing khaki-brown North Vietnamese uniforms and cloth-covered sun hats. Each man carried a pack strapped to his back, a canvas satchel bulging with supplies. The road passed so close along the cliff's base that the two SEALs could have sent cyclists tumbling by jamming their AKs out into the bicycle's spokes as they passed; Mai and the Hmong could have bombed the column by dropping hand grenades over the edge of the cliff had they wished to.

They contented themselves with waiting and silently counting.

"What do you think, Twidge?" Nolan asked, his voice a soft whisper as the cyclists vanished out of sight toward the south.

"I doubt that they're riding all the way to South Vietnam on two wheels," Greg replied. "My guess is that they're headed for a base farther down the line."

"My guess, too. Dong?"

"I say same," Nghiep said, nodding. He pointed north. "We up that way last week, find nothing. Not been to south, yet. Could be base, maybe big one."

They decided to follow the trail south.

The Laotian countryside was gloriously beautiful in the early morning light, all steep hills and narrow valleys sheathed in verdant, startling green. Some of the hills were so steep that the upper reaches poked up above the greenery, gray and brown knobs capped with more green. Streams spilled over spectacular waterfalls into hollows worn away in soft stone over eons; much of the rock in this region was limestone, remnants of some ancient and long-vanished sea, and easily carved by running water. According to the geology surveys and reports the two SEALs had studied back in Danang, there were a large number of caves in the area, caves that could be expected to have been converted by the North Vietnamese into bunkers, storage facilities, and even entire underground cities. SOG reconnaissance of the region in 1967 and '68 had uncovered evidence of mammoth subterranean facilities in several regions, including whole munitions factories and army camps.

The ten men paralleled the trail at a safe distance, keeping a screen of trees between themselves and the road. Soon the cliffs fell away, and they found themselves on a low and gentle ridge overlooking that section of the trail. At close to midday, the Hmong signaled once again that something was coming. The Hmong tribesmen seemed to have an almost psychic knowledge of threats still well beyond the reach of the Americans' senses. The man on drag, watching their rear, whistled a warning, and the patrol melted to the forest floor, motionless and watching.

This was no twelve-man party on bicycles. Greg counted

fifteen Russian-manufactured Zil trucks, five of them loaded with men, the other ten piled high with supplies. The trucks, painted in blotchy green and brown, had small forests of green vegetation lashed to the roofs of their cabs and the tops of the truck beds, improvised but effective camouflage. Their cargo must have carried a pretty high priority for them to be risking this run in broad daylight . . . and Greg's mouth suddenly went dry at the thought that American planes, alerted by ASG sensors in the area, might decide to hit this column now, catching two Americans, two Vietnamese, and six Hmong tribesmen in a thundering barrage of so-called friendly fire.

Nolan caught Halstead's eye and signaled, pointing south, indicating that they should try to follow this group. Greg nodded, then passed the word to Nghiep and Mai. Very carefully, then, the ten SOG warriors rose from cover and began pacing the column, following as it ground slowly south.

The trucks were accompanied by lots of troops marching single file down the road, rifles slung over their shoulders, heavy satchels, packs, or A-frames on their backs. With the men on foot, the column was moving slowly, and the SEALs had no trouble keeping pace with them. If there was a base up ahead, it would be well hidden, and it would be a lot easier to find the place—and to spot its guards—if they could follow a convoy all the way in. Greg was wondering just how far over the ridge they would have to be to avoid getting barbecued by an American napalm strike when Dhu suddenly raised a fist, then pointed. *Flankers! Take cover!*

The SEAL went to ground, dropping behind a large and moss-covered log. NVA columns frequently put out flanking parties and even circled back the way they'd come, in attempts to shake off or find enemy units shadowing them. Greg had not actually seen the enemy troops leaving the main column, but he trusted Dhu's instincts. He lay in soft and moldy jungle soil, straining to hear. He thought . . .

Yes. He heard the snap of a twig . . . the crunch of sandal on loose stone. Men were approaching from the other side of the log, heading, from the sound of it, directly toward the hidden SEAL.

Greg began easing himself further beneath the overhang of the log. The wood was rotten and soft, the earth beneath it nearly as loose as sand, and he was able to partly bury himself as the *crunch-crunch* of approaching footsteps drew nearer.

"*Con co,*" a voice said almost directly above the spot where Halstead was hiding. "*Co la nguoi Hanoi, phai khong?*"

"*Da khong,*" another voice said, even closer. God, they were standing right on top of him! "*Toi languoi Haiphong. Thuoc?*"

"*Vang, xin.*"

Greg's language lessons had given him a fair grounding in Vietnamese, but he had trouble following the language when it was spoken quickly, or when he didn't know the context of the conversation to begin with. He thought one guy had asked the other if he was from Hanoi, and the response had been no, he was from Haiphong. A cigarette had been offered and accepted. The log creaked, rocking slightly above his head and back, and some loose moss dropped inches in front of his face. Halstead heard the strike of a match, the contented hiss of indrawn breath, smelled the bite of cigarette smoke. A moment later, there was a rustling sound, and then two pairs of legs slid down and dangled over the side of the log, just a foot from the hidden SEAL's head. The two North Vietnamese appeared to be sitting together almost directly above Greg's hiding place, sharing a smoke.

He couldn't look up to see them, but he could watch their feet dangling just above the ground, so close he could have touched them, so close the closer man might have kicked him in the face if he'd swung his legs back beneath the log. Greg heard a metallic clatter, and then the butt of an AK-47 dropped into view, butt plate on the ground, muzzle up, leaning against the side of the log. He heard a canteen being uncorked. "*Nuoc?*" Water.

"*Vang! Xin!*"

He listened to them drinking noisily, and a few drops of water pattered on the ground inches from his hand. His hand, he realized now, was dangerously exposed. The black and green greasepaint smeared on it kept it from standing out, but at this range it still looked terribly hand-like, and if one of the enemy soldiers happened to glance down . . .

Greg wanted to pull his hand in beneath the overhang but feared that any motion at all would catch their eyes. He was scarcely breathing, but each inhalation brought with it mingled scents—harsh cigarette smoke, tired feet, and the pungent taste of *nuoc mam* fish sauce on the soldiers' breaths.

If they spotted him, he would have to try to take them down unarmed. He might be able to bring his AK-47 into play, but the firefight would alert the whole column, and these woods would quickly be filled with angry North Vietnamese. Not only would they get him but they would almost certainly get every one of his companions as well.

It was not a pleasant thought. The North Vietnamese had a special hatred reserved for SOG operatives who were unlucky enough to fall into their hands. Halstead had heard stories—and he was pretty sure that they were more than the usual round of barracks bullshit—of SOG personnel found later, after they'd been captured, stripped, strung up by their ankles, their intestines pulled out, and their genitals cut off and stuffed into their mouths. He'd heard stories of SOG prisoners kept alive for several days before finally being allowed to die.

Neither SEAL was going to allow himself or his partner to be captured. Greg had discussed it at length with Bill already, and he knew that Nolan would feel the same. No SEAL ever left another SEAL behind, alive or dead; that was axiomatic, a kind of unwritten code within the Teams. Still, with only the two of them—while they respected the others in their team, they couldn't yet judge their reliability in this regard—it might prove impossible for one of them to carry out his wounded buddy. In such circumstances, a bullet to the brain would be an infinite kindness. . . .

Better if he went down fighting. If these two did spot him, he would try to take them both out quietly. If one of them shouted and alerted the others, he would try running . . . angling northwest in the general direction of the trail. That would guarantee his being spotted and shot, but at least he would be able to get well clear of Nolan and the others.

"Hoi thuc! Hoi thuc!" a new voice called from the distance, the tone angry and demanding, telling them to hurry it up. The two sets of legs slid the rest of the way off the log, and a sandaled foot landed squarely on Greg's hand, turned, then boosted up again. The log creaked alarmingly as the two

NVAs jumped off the other side and trotted off through the forest, headed back toward the trail.

Greg's heart didn't stop pounding for a long, long time.

The SOG unit continued shadowing the enemy force, still moving south. The Communists were sharp, and they were canny. Four more times in as many hours they sent out flanking parties, armed men circling out and around to either side of the column searching for just such a shadow as the SOG team, though they never again got quite as close as they had gotten to Greg. The SEALs, and their Vietnamese and Hmong allies, went to ground each time, becoming a part of the jungle landscape, unmoving and unseen as the NVA flanking parties passed them by.

It was midafternoon before shouts from the marching column and the sounds of the trucks being dropped to a lower gear alerted the SEALs that something was happening. The lead Hmong materialized out of the forest ahead at the same time, gesturing and speaking in low tones to Dhu.

Nolan dropped to a crouch beside Halstead. "Either it's a smoke stop," he whispered, "or they've gotten where they're going."

"I think it's the latter," Greg replied. He pointed. A side trail split off from the main road, the spur just visible through the trees perhaps fifty meters ahead, and the trucks were being chivvied into a hard left turn that would take them directly across the SOG force's path.

That seemed to be what the Hmong scout was talking about, too. Dhu crawled over to the spot where the SEALs were waiting. "Ha says that the side road there seems to lead up that hill to the left. He's not sure, but he thinks there may be a settlement of some kind."

"How can he tell?" Greg asked.

"He smells smoke," Dhu replied. "And livestock, and gunpowder."

"Good enough for me," Greg said. He looked at Nolan. "How do you want to play this, Lieutenant?"

"Very carefully. Nghiep!" The call was a whisper, projected just loudly enough to catch the LDNN's attention.

"Yes, Lieutenant?"

"You have an encampment here on any of your maps? One big enough to handle fifteen trucks?"

"No, Lieutenant. No camp like that. Not here. But, like I say before, we not be this way yet. . . ."

"It might be new," Nolan mused. "Maybe a replacement for one that got bombed out."

"Just one way to find out," Greg said. "Come on!"

"Belay that!" Nolan snapped, the whisper harsh.

"Huh? How come?"

"Only one of us goes in there at a time. And I'm first. I want you to stay with the radio."

Greg gave an instant's hesitation, then nodded. This was not the time or place to discuss who should go in, or similar macho idiocies. The first consideration any SEAL had was for the mission. The second, and so close behind the first as to be virtually tied for first place, was a professional attitude, one that put the mission and the safety of the other men in your team above everything else.

Besides . . . maybe what Bill had been saying about married men was true. He wasn't exactly anxious to go crawling around inside a heavily defended NVA army base. At least, not until after dark.

"Right," he said. "We should find a site for our OP first, though." He studied the loom of the cliff off to their left, then pointed. "Up there."

Nolan chuckled. "Maybe I'm the one getting ahead of myself. Okay. Let's go."

They found an ideal spot for an observation post. It was a cave—well, a pocket eaten into the rock, really—with a massive overhang that provided protection from being seen from every direction but directly ahead, and the opening itself was partly blocked by ferns and tangled vegetation.

Located almost at the top of the northern wall of a narrow, U-shaped valley opening toward the west, the sheltered spot gave them a near-perfect perch overlooking what seemed to be a North Vietnamese rest and supply complex nestled away in the box canyon below. Perhaps the best part of it was that it lay less than fifty feet from a telephone ground line, which gave the SEALs the chance to use some of their special gear to tap into the North Vietnamese telephone system. Each major base along the Ho Chi Minh Trail, it was believed, was connected to the adjacent bases by ground lines, giving them secure communications all the way from Cambodia back to

Hanoi—"secure," that is, from radio intercepts. SEALs and other SOG forces regularly tapped the line in order to try to pick up chance calls that carried important intelligence.

"Okay," Nolan said when they'd finished setting up their gear in the cave. "I'll take first recon. You take the second. Challenge and response will add up to twelve."

"You should take someone with you. Sir."

Nolan considered this. Maybe he was thinking the same things about cowboys that Greg was. He nodded. "Fine. Nghiep? You're with me."

"Yes, Lieutenant."

Together, the two crawled away through the forest, disturbing scarcely a single leaf or fern in their passing.

Two hours later, Greg was outside the cave on a bare cap of limestone, looking up at a sky rapidly dimming its way toward twilight. Mai was taking his turn on the telephone line tap, while four of the Hmong were on perimeter defense, and the other two were exploring the top of the mountain surrounding the valley, looking for North Vietnamese gun positions and bolt holes. This spot gave Greg a good view out and down into the enemy complex.

The more they studied the place, the bigger and more elaborate it appeared. Though it was hard to see, even from here, it was evident that the SOG team had followed the truck convoy straight to what amounted to a small city, partly constructed of thatched huts and partly dug into the face of the cliff itself.

The place was a guerrilla's dream. The only way American aircraft could hit the place at all—assuming they could even *see* it, which was not at all likely—would be if they came in from the west, along the valley's lie, and pulled up before they hit the bottom of the U. An attack from any other direction would be blocked by limestone cliffs eighty feet high. And such an attack along the valley's length would be suicidal. Greg could look across the valley to the southern side and see the muzzles of large machine guns and antiaircraft gun mounted on ledges high up on the cliffs, protruding from cave openings in the rock, or on the very top of the mountain, nestled into gun pits well dug in and barricaded with sandbags. Those guns would have nicely placed, overlapping fields of fire that would spell disaster for any strike aircraft save, possibly, a B-52 . . . and those giants simply couldn't release their bomb loads with accuracy enough to guarantee taking out what was in that narrow valley.

Hell, even if they did manage to thread the needle and deliver a bomb load on target, Greg suspected that most of the complex would remain safe. The thatched huts and camouflaged buildings outside the caves were probably rec centers, mess halls, perhaps political lecture rooms or even schools. The important stuff—supply caches, hospitals, munitions factories, barracks—those would all be deep inside the caves extending into the rock from the base and sides of the U.

The trucks, Greg saw, had been driven in beneath a massive limestone overhang at the base of the cliff all the way at the end of that box canyon. There didn't seem to be room enough to get them all under cover, but they were close enough to the cliff that hitting them at all would be a matter more of wild luck than of skill, and yard upon yard of olive-green camouflage netting had been strung up above those trucks that hadn't made it into the mountain. The place would be nearly impossible to see.

Even knowing the coordinates of this place wouldn't help the planners of an air strike. The only way Greg could see to even have a chance of taking this place out would be to attack it from the west, on the ground. The NVA troops would be bottled up inside and trapped . . . and even then they probably had bolt holes opening up on top of the mountain. They might lose their trucks and heavy equipment, but most of the troops would escape.

That assumed that they wanted to escape. The limestone complex was a formidable fortress, one that any ground commander would think twice about before tackling with anything less than a full brigade and massive artillery support.

A Hmong materialized suddenly, almost magically, out of the nearby vegetation, and silently pointed west. Greg brought up his AK . . . but a moment later, "Drop kick!" sounded from the gathering darkness.

"Five!" Greg called softly.

"Seven" was the reply. Nolan and Nghiep joined them a moment later. They held a quick and informal debriefing on the limestone outcropping, bringing Mai in from the tap so he could listen in, too.

"So, what'd you find?" Greg asked the SEAL lieutenant.

"Christ, it's an anthill," Nolan replied. "I couldn't get all the way up the valley. Too many bad guys, and I couldn't risk being spotted." He pulled a small notebook out of his combat vest, produced a pencil, and began sketching out the valley. "Truck park," he said, indicating the base of the U. "Fuel storage in the caves, here, here, and here." His pencil moved to the north side, almost directly beneath the OP. "Crates of empty shell casings here, outside some small cave openings. One-three-oh mike-mike, mostly."

"Shell casings. For a munitions factory," Greg said. The NVA favored 130mm artillery pieces, though they were by no means exclusively wedded to that caliber.

"Yeah," Nolan grinned. "And you put our OP right on top of the thing."

"Yeah, well, we'll put out no smoking signs."

Nolan indicated the drawing again. "Livestock over here on the south wall. Chickens. Geese. Goats. Pigs. I didn't get too close, because I didn't want the guard geese sounding the alarm. Up here, I saw two 130-millimeter field pieces. Towed guns. And something under a tarp that might have been a ZPU-4."

The ZPU-4 was a wheeled, quad battery of 14.5mm antiaircraft machine guns, designed to be towed by a truck. It had an effective antiaircraft range of 1,400 meters—over 4,000 feet—which made it deadly against low-flying strike aircraft.

Nolan went on. "Over here I found some milling scrap. Metal filings and lathe cuttings."

"So . . . a machine shop?"

"That's my guess. Probably for making repairs, maybe for adapting captured equipment. It would also be damned useful for salvage and make-do-with-what-you-got work. You know, scrounging empty shell casings or busted truck engines and turning them into laser death rays."

"Set phasers on annihilate," Greg replied, nodding. He sighed. "Okay, my turn for a look-see, Lieutenant. Any suggestions?"

Nolan indicated the center of the valley. "Well, there are

some light buildings here. I couldn't get in there because it was still pretty light, but the daylight's going fast now, and you might have a better shot at them. I'd like to know what's in there.''

"Yeah, so would I. Okay, you got it.''

"Let me show you their guard layout." For the next several minutes, Nolan marked out positions on the map, showing the guards he and Nghiep had spotted, marking trails, places where lots of people had gathered, even places where they'd noticed unusual numbers of footprints, indicating heavy traffic.

"And . . . Twidge?" Nolan said, at last.

"Sir?"

"No cowboy stuff. You come back here, you hear me?''

"Loud and clear, Lieutenant." He paused. "Uh, Lieutenant?''

"Yeah?''

"Are you married?''

Nolan grinned. "I sure am. Five years now. Met her in college.''

Greg grinned back. "Okay, sir. Just wanted to make sure. Mai?''

"I come.''

Together, Halstead and the LDNN crawled into the twilight.

Chapter 23

Sunday, 29 November 1970

Ban Kôon NVA complex
5 kilometers northeast of Tchepone, Laos
1815 hours

Greg and Mai crawled most of the way back down the hill to the mouth of the valley, taking their time, moving only when they were sure there was no one close by. The entrance to the box canyon base was well hidden behind a screen of almost impenetrable vegetation; the road itself that the trucks had followed to this place was almost invisible, covered over with dead vegetation. Greg suspected that the North Vietnamese came out and cleared the palm fronds and leaves off the road when a truck convoy came in, then immediately replaced them, breaking up the telltale tire tracks. The screen blocking the entrance was so good that Greg was forcibly reminded of the Batcave on the campy *Batman* TV show back home and wondered if Hanoi watched American shows for inspiration.

There were sentries, of course, in the spots Nolan had marked, and Greg and Mai found several more through the simple expedient of sitting absolutely still, watching, and listening, until men betrayed their presence with a movement, a sneeze, or a casual exchange of conversation. The North Vietnamese were good . . . but they were not expecting trouble, and human beings are not designed to sit absolutely motionless for an hour on end.

SEALs, on the other hand, did just that. Greg and Mai waited until a group of twelve NVA soldiers showed up at the camp's entrance, and then, when all of the hidden guards were watching the new arrivals, he and the LDNN slipped in along the north face of the cliff through a tangle of vines and mountain vegetation, passing at one point within fifteen feet of an NVA guard who was leaning against a tree trunk with his SKS carbine slung over his shoulder while he smoked a cigarette.

Nolan had called the place an anthill, and that, Greg decided, was as good a description as any. He could see dozens of people in every direction, a few armed and on guard, but most simply doing the things that people do. A number were seated about a cook fire near the south wall of the canyon, the fire screened from overhead view. The sounds of singing floated across the intervening space, haunting and melodious in its own five-toned way. There were women here, he saw, most in military fatigues, but a few wearing more traditional female Vietnamese dress, serving meals, tending fires, chatting with men. He wondered if these were regular soldiers—the Viet Cong, certainly, employed women in their ranks—or ''hostesses,'' as they were known, provided for the comfort of the fighting men.

There was a lot of random traffic inside the camp, and the two SEALs had to be careful in picking the times for their moves. Fortunately, the vegetation was thick here at the bottom of the canyon, with plenty of trees, ferns, even jungle growth like hanging vines and massive trees with ten-foot trunks interspersed among the buildings to provide cover. Greg thought that, had he been tasked with setting up this military village, he would have ordered all of the vegetation cleaned out, to prevent just such acts of infiltration and information gathering as he was attempting now.

But then, of course, the Vietnamese were above all concerned with camouflage. American reconnaissance aircraft must overfly this region nearly every day, and so far no one had any idea that this complex was here. Greg was certain that, had Intelligence known about even the possibility of this base, he and Nolan would have been ordered to check it out.

He and Mai agreed to split up. The Viet SEAL would check out the south wall and see how close he could get to some of the storage areas there. Greg would investigate the buildings in the center of the camp. Moving from cover to cover, he approached a group of three large buildings, one open, without walls, like a picnic pavilion back home, the others enclosed. The open building seemed to be the site of a large open-air gathering, men and women seated on mats, using their fingers to eat from bowls. At one point, Greg reached the road used by trucks and other vehicles moving through the camp toward the back of the valley. There was no cover here, and no way to cross except to sling his AK and casually stroll across in full view of that entire dinner party and God alone knew how many other sets of watching eyes high up in the surrounding cliffs. His black garb—and the sheer, brazen impossibility of an American being *here*— made him effectively invisible to the valley's inhabitants. It helped that the floor of the valley was now almost fully dark, with only a little light still visible in the sky directly overhead.

Eventually, he reached his first goal, a large, long structure as big as a barn, though not nearly as tall. There was one door and several windows; blackout curtains had been drawn, but bright light streamed out around the curtains, softened somewhat by the mosquito netting covering each window. He could hear a voice inside and had the impression—a kind of low, constant rustle and scrape—that there was a large audience in there. Crouched in the bushes outside one of the open windows, he listened long enough to gather that it was a political lecture of some kind, with exhortations to "stay true to the class struggle." The speaker was clear and precise enough for Greg to have little trouble following the words.

"The soldier's supreme duty," the voice said, rising to a near shout, "is to fight on the side of Revolution! We have freed one half of our homeland, but there remains yet the other half. How can we, in the north, enjoy the sweet taste of independence, when our brothers in the south remain in chains and slavery? . . ."

Pretty routine stuff.

"I want to pass these around to all of you," the voice went on. "Proof, for you to see with your own eyes, that the revolutionary struggle is not ours alone. Even in America, yes, even there, our brothers in the Revolution fight for justice, for right, for *freedom! . . .*"

Greg wondered what that proof was and made a mental note to check back here once the political rally had broken up. There was another building twenty yards further on that he wanted to check out. It was a typical hooch, a thatch and bamboo structure raised about three feet off the ground on massive log supports, the structure partly masked by a jumble of shrubs and thick vegetation. He heard voices from that direction and froze, spotting a moment later what looked like two Vietnamese officers walking toward it.

He couldn't quite catch what the soldiers were saying, but the conversation was certainly animated. They weren't wearing shoulder boards, so the only clue to rank he had was the collar tab that denoted that they were field officers—as opposed to generals or student officers. They didn't look very old, though, and he thought they were probably one- or two-star lieutenants, the equivalent of U.S. Navy ensigns or j.g.s.

More than once, Greg knew, SEALs had picked up important information in camps like this one by sneaking in close and actually listening in on briefings, discussions, and planning sessions. He watched as they approached the hooch, climbed the rickety steps, and went inside. Greg waited until the coast was clear, then slipped swiftly across the dark compound, dropping to his back and wriggling his way beneath the elevated building.

The floor was just above his face and made of bamboo crosspieces covered over with rattan mats. The floor covering was not perfect, however, and Greg found himself able to lie on his back near one corner of the hooch and peer up through the hand-wide openings between several of the crosspieces for a perfect view of nearly the whole of the building's interior.

It was brightly lit by an oil lamp on a table. Another table had fruit, a bottle of brandy, and several glasses, and there were a number chairs scattered about the room . . . an unusual luxury out here in the jungle.

He'd expected—hoped, really—that the officers were attending some sort of briefing or planning session, but it turned out to be a lot more mundane than that. Both of the men, it was clear now, were far along on the road to being falling-down drunk; one was holding a half-full bottle of brandy with a French label, a name he didn't recognize. There was also a woman present, a young and very pretty woman wearing black slacks and a bright red blouse. The officers had already divested themselves of their jackets and were now taking turns drinking brandy and talking . . . talking very loudly, and with what was obviously not a little boasting.

Greg couldn't catch everything that was being said, for the woman's voice was low and soft, almost inaudible, while the men were both so drunk that he could scarcely understand the words through the slurred vowels and tones. He was pretty sure, though, that both were boasting about how well they would satisfy her, how they would *fill* her. One rocked back on his heels as he held his forefingers apart, indicating a distance of about nine inches. The other officer guffawed and waved him to silence, then showed the woman a bigger size, perhaps twelve inches. At that, the woman lost her composure, laughing so hard that both men were taken aback. One shouted something angrily about *showing* her, stood up, and began taking off his pants. The other man, not to be undone, began stripping as well, and in a few moments, both men were nude.

They were also, clearly enough now, excited, though if the hand gestures they'd been making a moment before had anything to do with their erections it was obvious that there'd been a lot of wishful thinking involved.

The woman, still fully dressed, poured them both fresh drinks, talking louder now in a coy, almost bantering tone. "I don't know if I am strong enough to take on the two of you at once," she told them.

At that point, one of the men stood up and advanced on the woman, then took a liquor-tangled misstep that sent him crashing onto a wicker chair. Clumsily, he managed to right himself and sit heavily on the seat. The woman slid into his lap, one arm around his neck, while the other drew teasing designs against the hairless skin of his chest. The man began fumbling at the buttons on her blouse, making such a hash of it that she eventually undid the blouse herself, pulling it off easily and tossing it to the side.

The other man had been leaning against the table, downing brandy at an alarming rate. At this point in the proceedings, he seemed to realize that his partner was ahead of him in the game, and he lurched unsteadily across, dropped to his knees in front of the other two, and began roughly fondling the woman's naked breasts. For a time, it seemed like they were having a minor battle over her, each fighting for the privilege of rubbing her nipples.

Greg was not normally the voyeuristic type, but he didn't want to go far from the big lecture hall, and this was as good a place as any to wait until the Marxist pep rally ended. Besides, it was always possible that one of the drunken officers would say something both intelligible and useful from an intelligence standpoint.

In any case, he found himself fascinated by the woman's face. As the foreplay proceeded, both men's movements had become more and more mechanical. At the same time, her facial expression had assumed a look that Greg could only describe as utter and complete boredom.

He found himself remembering that expression on a Western face . . . on the face of that waitress in San Diego back in August.

And the rest of the scene played itself out with eerie familiarity as well. The soldier in the chair was contenting himself with her right breast now, while the one kneeling on the floor tried sucking her left. Their movements, though, were becoming slower still, and less animated. In a few moments more, Greg heard a rasping snore from one of the men—he couldn't tell which one—and both had stopped their possessive, roughly caressing movements. The woman, trapped between them, looked from one to another, the boredom on her face transforming into something more like sheer disgust. Both were sound asleep.

Carefully—though Greg suspected the woman could have kicked them both and failed to wake them—she slid out from between them, easing out from under the man sprawled across her legs and leaving him propped up against his buddy. With a half smile on her lips, she walked across the room, retrieved her blouse, and then, presentable once more, walked out of the hooch.

She left the two naked lieutenants in a rather awkward and decidedly compromising position, both naked, the one sitting in the chair with his head all the way back in a pose guaranteed to leave him with one hell of a crick in his neck, the other still kneeling on the floor with his head buried most suggestively in his comrade's lap.

In that moment, Greg felt an almost overpowering sense of

fellowship with those two poor officers. Hell, he'd *been* there, passed out drunk when he was supposed to be having sex with a beautiful woman.

Amusedly, he wondered how much those two would remember when they came to in the morning or, worse by far, when some of their friends discovered them. From what he'd heard, the North Vietnamese tended to be somewhat puritanical about such things.

From the direction of the lecture hall, a burst of noise, people talking and moving, caught his attention. Crawling to a better vantage point, he saw that the meeting was, indeed, letting out. A large number of soldiers were leaving the building, talking with one another as they made their way toward the back of the valley . . . and the caves where their sleeping quarters were hidden.

Greg waited for several minutes more, listening, every sense taut against the night. The big building, so far as he could tell, was empty now. The light he'd seen emerging from beneath the blackout shades was out. Quietly, he slipped up to the wall, then made his way to a back window. The window was covered with mosquito netting and a blackout curtain, nothing more. Releasing the netting at the bottom, he swung one leg up and over the sill, gave himself a boost, and stepped into the building.

It was pitch black inside, and he pulled out a pencil flash hooded with a red filter and switched on the beam. By the darkroom red of the light, he found himself in a kind of classroom, with hardwood floors, a large desk in the front, and perhaps sixty or seventy folding wooden chairs. There were stacks of papers and what appeared to be several photographs on the desk.

Stepping across to the desk, he took a quick look at the photos. They were black-and-white prints, five by sevens and eight by tens. He scooped up a number of them without looking at them—it was too dark to examine them closely here anyway—and stuffed them into his combat vest. There were also large numbers of documents, some newspapers, and what appeared to be photocopies. He couldn't take everything, but he took a sampling from various piles. If they were left in an unguarded room like this, chances were they weren't classified, and they probably weren't even that important. By the same token, if they weren't classified, the teachers in this classroom probably wouldn't notice that some were missing, or they would assume that they'd been taken by someone in the audience.

A large magazine with a black-and-white cover and Vietnamese writing caught his eye, and he added that to his booty. He was reaching for one of the newspapers when a voice sounded just outside the door. *"Chao! Co khoe khong?"*

"Khoe, cam on."

It was a friendly exchange of greetings, but it sounded like it was right on the front doorstep of this place. In three swift, silent steps, Greg was back at the window. He checked that there was no one hanging about outside, slipped out the window, and reattached the netting.

A check of the luminous dial of his watch showed that he was ten minutes late for an agreed-upon meeting with Mai. It was time to get back to the OP. There was plenty left to check out down here, but there would be time for other clandestine visits, possibly later, when not so many soldiers were about.

On the way out, though, he did stop beside the road to take a closer look at the tracks printed there in the dried mud. He'd seen no sign of North Vietnamese tanks during his visit, but the tread marks were clearly visible here by starlight. They left the big question unanswered. Had the tanks stopped here briefly on their way south? That could spell a real problem for ARVN and the U.S. forces still in-country. Or were they part of a local defense force, which would mean trouble for any future ARVN intervention in Laos. He was still pretty sure that he and Tangretti had been right, that Freedom Trail had more to do with paving the way for an invasion of Laos than it did with prisoner rescues or SOG ambushes.

No matter. They would gather what information they could. It wasn't his responsibility to sort out what was really going on in the headquarters of MACV and SOG.

Exfiltration from the camp was easier than the infiltration had been, for there were fewer sentries posted near the entrance to the valley. Greg and Mai slipped out into the forest beyond the valley, then retraced their steps—cautiously in the dark—back up to the top of the northern cliff face and the hidden SEAL OP.

They spent the next hour going over the combined results of both recons, drawing up a more detailed and complete map. Mai had found two small caves on the south wall that stored, he estimated, at least a ton of rice, and possibly more. He'd also located a radio room by spotting the antenna wire snaking out of a cavern mouth and up to the top of the southern cliff. By comparison, Greg's discoveries of a tryst with a camp hostess and a Marxist political indoctrination session didn't amount to much.

But it was all part of the overall picture that the team would try to piece together over the course of the next day or two.

Finally, Greg had the chance to examine some of the booty he'd liberated from that classroom. With a rain poncho hung over the mouth of their cave, he and Nolan huddled together in the back of their OP, examining each photo and document in turn under the dull, eye-straining dimness of a red-filtered flashlight.

The documents appeared to be routine stuff, political tracts and exhortations to fight for the Revolution. The newspaper was a Hanoi edition dated mid-October. The headline declared that Nixon had proposed a "standstill" cease-fire, but that this was totally unacceptable to the Party and to the people. Nixon, the article insisted, was grasping at any chance for peace and would soon abandon his corrupt partners and puppets in Saigon.

The photos were a lot rougher; the first one was a shocker. It showed a city street, a mob of people, some angry, some afraid, many simply staring. In the foreground, a man with long hair and a peace symbol necklace lay on the ground in fetal position, knees drawn up to his chest, arms protectively cradling his head. Above him stood a policeman; specifically, to judge by the well-known black-and-white checkered band around the uniform hat, it was a Chicago policeman, and he was holding the man's shoulder with his left hand, while the right had reached as high up over his head as he could, an instant before he brought a nightstick down on the citizen's body.

Another photo. Four policemen—Chicago cops, once again—walked down a street with an angry mob in the background. They wore body armor and carried clubs dangling from their belts. The four of them were holding a struggling girl; she couldn't have been more than eighteen and was probably younger. Her hands were cuffed behind her back, and they were carrying her stretched horizontally between them. Her thrashings in the policemen's grip had bared her midriff. Somehow, her exposed navel gave her an air of pathetic vulnerability. Blood smeared her head and shoulders.

And another. Soldiers, this time, in full battle gear, wearing gas masks that gave them an alien, monstrous appearance, and carrying rifles with naked bayonets, stood shoulder to shoulder, facing a mob of shouting teenagers. Tear gas billowed in the air. It might have been Kent State. It might have been any of a number of other confrontations between National Guard troops and civilians in the past three years.

He felt an angry double-mindedness about those photos. He didn't like to see civilians confronted by raw power. He'd heard stories, though, about how demonstrators sometimes carried cellophane bags filled with blood or food coloring, which they would smear over their faces for the benefit of the television cameras and news photographers. He'd heard that some of them taught their fellows techniques for *looking* like they were taking a beating, for becoming a dead weight and forcing several men to carry them off to the paddy wagon, which looked great in news photos. He'd heard that some activists deliberately provoked police—who must already be on the verge of either panic or unreasoning fury—hoping to rouse some newsworthy response from them with swinging billy clubs or masks of rage.

The blood in those photos . . . that *had* to be fake, didn't it?

Then he found another kind of photo.

This one seemed almost peaceful in comparison with the others. Seven people stood in an anonymous room. They looked like typical students except that they were armed, four men with long hair, three women, two in tight jeans, the third in a miniskirt. They stood together in an obviously staged, move-a-little-closer-so-I-can-get-you-all-in pose. Two of the men and one woman were flashing peace signs. One man carried a shotgun, while the others sported various types of pistols, like desperadoes out of one of those stilted daguerreotypes from the Wild West. All were laughing, as though revolution were little more than a fun and somewhat daring social encounter. Behind them, tacked up on the wall, was a large North Vietnamese flag. Cardboard letters beneath the flag spelled out CSAO.

He had no idea what the acronym was . . . and at the moment, he didn't really care.

He knew one of the women.

She was in the center of the group, wearing blue jeans and a University of Chicago Law School T-shirt and holding what looked like a .22 caliber High Standard automatic. It had been four years now, and the woman in the photograph was wearing more makeup than she'd usually worn back when he'd known her, but she was nonetheless recognizable.

Marci Cochran . . . his girlfriend at San Francisco State. They'd been getting pretty serious, thinking about getting married, in fact, until he announced his plans to join the Navy. She'd already been pretty deeply involved in the political activist scene, and she'd dropped him like a hot rock when he'd told her he was joining up. Hell, he'd thought she would understand. Maybe he hadn't realized how committed to her radical cause she was. It hardly mattered; if she hadn't dropped him, he never would have ended up marrying Wendy. Damn, he'd *loved* the bitch. Even now, even after Wendy, the memory was a wincing hurt, though by now he couldn't really tell if the pain was more closely related to having lost her or to the memory of the humiliation he'd felt.

The other items scarcely mattered after that. What the hell was Marci—if that *was* Marci—doing in a photograph found in a North Vietnamese army camp?

He remembered the lecturer's voice, back in the NVA camp. *I want to pass these around to all of you, proof, for you to see with your own eyes, that the revolutionary struggle is not ours alone. . . .*

Was this photo the proof the guy had been talking about? Proof to North Vietnamese soldiers that there were revolutionaries in the United States, as well?

It raised other questions, too. Had that photo been taken specifically to send to Hanoi for propaganda purposes? Or had it been something else entirely, stolen or somehow intercepted by North Vietnamese agents? That didn't seem likely

. . . but the idea that Marci or her friends had sent the photos to Hanoi was all too real a possibility.

The entire haul of documents and photos appeared to be propaganda pieces of one kind or another, the tools, no doubt, of the camp's political officer. Leafing through the rest of them, he was particularly struck by the North Vietnamese magazine he'd taken, a large edition about the size of *Life*. On the cover was a black-and-white photo of a Western woman surrounded by smiling Vietnamese. She was seated in the saddle of an antiaircraft gun—it looked like a ZPU-4 quad antiaircraft gun—and she was wearing sunglasses, a bush jacket, and a North Vietnamese helmet. She was pointing up into the sky with a vacant, dumb-blonde smile showing perfect teeth.

He recognized that woman, too. Hannah DuPlessey was a minor Hollywood actress who'd gone from soft porn to so-called serious pictures after she'd married a left-wing Italian film director. She was one of a small army of Hollywood personalities who'd jumped on the peace activism bandwagon; like a number of other celebrities, she'd actually gone to Hanoi against the wishes of her own government and let herself be used as a propaganda machine. The story inside had plenty of photos of Hannah and more smiling Vietnamese, as she visited hospitals, looked horrified at bombed-out bridges, and stood waist deep in crowds of hungry-looking Vietnamese children.

It unnerved Greg a bit to realize that he actually felt more in common with those two North Vietnamese soldiers he'd seen in the hooch than he did with Americans who could do something like this. Good men—Vietnamese and American— were dying over here in an effort to stop Communism and to save the South Vietnamese government, and people back home could pull stupid, treacherous, *treasonable* shit like this. It just didn't make any sense.

He remembered the people shouting "pig" and "baby killer" at the airport, and suddenly everything, the war, the separation from Wendy, *everything* seemed like it was for nothing. He loved the SEALs, loved what he was doing, but unless the people he was fighting for back home were behind him, hell, if the people back home were *traitors* . . .

What was the use of continuing the fight?

Chapter 24

Wednesday, 2 December 1970

65,000 feet over Dông Hoi
North Vietnam
0945 hours

Like a death-black arrowhead, long and lean and flat, the spy plane hurtled south across enemy territory with a speed and at an altitude that made it casually indifferent to notions like airspace violations or SAM threats. The SR-71, the high-tech successor to the old U-2, could fly higher and faster by far than any man-made vehicle not more properly classified as a spacecraft.

The Blackbird, as the SR-71 was popularly known, brushed the fringes of space itself, flying at altitudes that put it above ninety-seven percent of the planet's atmosphere. Lieutenant Colonel William Chisholm, swaddled in a pressure suit little different from that worn by an astronaut on his way to the Moon, sat in the Blackbird's cockpit, hand light on the stick as he first surveyed his console display, then looked out the canopy window to starboard. At an altitude of better than twelve miles, the sky overhead was a deep, infinite blue, shading by imperceptible increments to sky blue only at the horizon. A scattering of cumulus clouds at 15,000 feet looked like tiny cotton balls, each riding its own, distinct shadow, giving each a prominent three-dimensional feel. The color of the sky, the crystalline clarity of detail on the ground, the curve of the Earth's horizon itself, all contributed to a heart-pounding, throat-closing thrill that had all the elements of a profound religious experience. Chisholm was not a religious man, but at times like this he felt particularly close to God.

The shoulder patch on Chisholm's pressure suit identified him as a *Habu* pilot; the name, given to the Blackbird by the Japanese, referred to a deadly black pit viper native to Okinawa. There was a hill just outside the Kadena airbase known as "Habu Hill," from which the locals still watched the powerful black recon aircraft hammering into the sky.

They'd just gone feet dry, passing over the coastline of North Vietnam from the Gulf of Tonkin. Chisholm and his backseater had left Kadena Airbase on Okinawa a scant hour and a half before, rocketing southwest past Taiwan and slipping close enough to the People's Republic of China's island of Hainan to make them light up their radars and scramble aircraft. Not that a MiG ever had a prayer of catching a Blackbird. . . .

From there they'd turned south, streaking toward the North Vietnamese coast at three times the speed of sound. Entering North Vietnamese airspace was not a particularly momentous occasion. In the three years that Chisholm had been driving Blackbirds, he'd overflown North Vietnam dozens of times, not to mention North Korea, the People's Republic of China, and the Soviet Union itself. The flights were never publicized, of course, and the Communists were left with what must have been a teeth-grinding frustration, but the photographs the Blackbirds returned, Chisholm knew, contributed to the world's uneasy balance between peace and nuclear holocaust. In a way, Blackbird flights were a stabilizing factor in a world gone slightly mad.

He'd been shot at plenty of times over all of those countries . . . but not many SAMs could maneuver well enough to hold a lock and catch the aircraft, which was traveling far faster than any bullet. The SR-71's top speed was classified, of course; even Chisholm didn't know where the remarkable aircraft's speed envelope ended, but he'd passed Mach 3.6 on several occasions, and missions at Mach 3 were routine.

President Johnson had authorized the first Blackbird overflight of North Vietnam in May of 1967, specifically to check up on the rumor that Hanoi was receiving ballistic missiles from Beijing capable of reaching Saigon. The flights had proven that no ballistic missile launch sites existed anywhere in North Vietnam—the Blackbird could literally photograph the entire country from end to end in about an hour—and they'd been a vital part of the American war effort ever since. The reconnaissance aircraft's five-foot-tall high-resolution camera could peer down into open holds aboard ships in Haiphong Harbor or photograph license plates in the streets of Hanoi. During the past year or so, Blackbirds had been employed in an extensive search for POW camps; last spring, SR-71s had brought back the photos of rock piles and Morse-code laundry that had positively IDed the Son Tay camp and set things in motion for the raid there the week before. Chisholm had flown several of those missions and even been allowed to see a few of the photos afterward. He knew there'd been POWs at Son Tay up until at least early July. Where they'd been taken after that, though, was anybody's guess.

This morning's mission had been a real urgent, hurry-up affair. Chisholm didn't know the identity of the target but gathered from his preflight briefing that someone wanted confirmation of a large camp or base of some sort just discovered within the past couple of days on the Ho Chi Minh Trail. Such bases were usually so well hidden that it was almost impossible to pick them out from the air. Still, the SR-71's cameras were so good that if the photo interpreters knew exactly where to look, they would be able to pick out details like tire tracks in the mud, or litter dropped by careless troops, or even the troops themselves. Infrared cameras could pinpoint fires, even when the fires were under cover, or isolate hot truck engines or other heat sources. They were making a relatively low pass today specifically so that ground detail could be photographed clearly.

"One minute to target, Boss" sounded in his helmet headphones. Tucked into the SR-71's backseat was Major Mike Kelly, Chisholm's Reconnaissance Systems Officer, or RSO. It was Kelly's job, among many things, to keep track of the bewildering array of electronic signals constantly bombarding the aircraft . . . and to run those cameras and sensors that did not run themselves. "We're being lit."

Chisholm saw the warning lights on his own console. Tracking and SAM radar sites all over the North Vietnamese panhandle were hammering at the Blackbird now, and they could probably expect a launch any time now.

"Nyah, nyah, you can't catch me," Chisholm said laconically.

"Commencing camera run," Kelly reported. They would be across the narrow breadth of North Vietnam in mere seconds now and over the target area in southeastern Laos. "Throttling back." The slower the black aircraft was traveling, the better the pictures. They were still moving at better than twice the speed of sound.

A tone sounded in his ear.

"They're locked on," Kelly said. "Weapons radar. Looks like a Guideline."

Guideline was the NATO code name for the SA-2 surface-to-air missile, a two-stage antiaircraft missile fired from a rail launcher. With a range of 55,000 meters and a maximum altitude of 24,000 meters, the SA-2 was one of the few SAMs that actually had the oomph to bring down a Blackbird. "Oh, shit," Chisholm said, and then he chuckled, because there was a humorous twist to the use of those words in this situation.

"We got Oscar Sierra light," Kelly told him. "Active guidance."

"Rog, Oscar Sierra." The warning was emitted from an ECM box in the Blackbird's tail, designated Oscar Sierra— "O.S."—reputedly because a pilot's first words when the missile alert light switched on were generally "Oh, shit." The box helped scramble the radar pulses from the tracking missile, making it harder to maintain a lock.

"You got a launch?" Chisholm asked.

"Not sure, Colonel. But they're definitely tracking us."

"I'm opening her up," Chisholm said. "Hang on back there!"

The Blackbird's powerful Pratt & Whitney engines increased their thrust, the roar building to a waterfall of raw noise that the sleek black aircraft's faster-than-a-bullet speed would swiftly outpace.

"Visual!" Kelly called. "I've got a visual launch at five o'clock!"

Chisholm turned in his seat, peering back toward the starboard wing far aft of the cockpit. He could see the missile too, a tiny, goddamn telephone pole balancing into the sky on a slender white contrail.

No sweat. Any missile fired at a Blackbird literally had to be aimed sixteen miles ahead of the aircraft to give it any chance at all of connecting with a target twelve to sixteen miles high and traveling at three thousand feet per second.

"Let me know if we need to jink." He was gripping the joystick a little tighter now. No pilot, not even an iceman, could remain completely cool and unexcited when some character started lofting telephone poles at his aircraft. Still, at these altitudes and speeds, no missile could match a Blackbird's maneuverability, and a relatively easy turn would probably lose it.

A new alarm sounded, followed an instant later by a shrill *bang* that jolted the two Air Force officers against their harnesses. For a second or two, the aircraft oscillated wildly. "Shit!" Chisholm said, with a lot more feeling this time. "Unstart! We've got a malfunction!"

For a small eternity, Chisholm battled the SR-71's controls. An "unstart" meant that one of his engines had suddenly dropped to something like twenty percent efficiency. Unstarts had been a particularly wicked problem during the early design and test phases of the SR-71 development, especially when the pilot often couldn't tell which engine had died and turned off the wrong one, but they'd been solved by the addition of an electronic control that killed *both* engines in the event of an unstart in one, then relit both automatically. The pilot and RSO never even felt the jolt then, which was caused by one engine running at full blast while the other was practically idling.

Now, though, something was seriously wrong, and Chisholm suspected the unstart control. From the feel of it, as the aircraft gave a series of nasty shudders and lurches, it was the port engine. He compensated by cutting back on the power to his starboard engine, then trying to initiate a start sequence.

"Missile inbound!" Kelly warned him. "Sir, we've got a missile—"

"I hear! I'm trying to relight!" Damn it, start! *Start!*

This was getting hairy.

Once, Chisholm had been on a mission with a particularly high pucker factor over the port of Vladivostok, the eastern door into the Soviet Union. The bad guys had scrambled

fighters but had nothing that could catch the Mach 3–plus
Blackbird. Almost as if in foot-stomping frustration, some
button-happy commissar on the ground had ordered a mass
SA-2 launch. That was nothing new. They'd used a barrage
of fourteen SA-2s to bring down Francis Gary Powers's U-2
in 1960, a volley that had nailed one of their own fighters as
well. That day over Vladivostok, six missiles had detonated
in the Blackbird's slipstream, one after another, but the SR-
71 had been traveling so fast that each missile had exploded
far behind the point where the aircraft had been at that instant,
anywhere from two to five miles away. He'd completed the
photo recon run over eastern Siberia, swung south, and gone
on to photograph the whole of North Korea in a matter of
about ten minutes.

This time was lots worse. Only one missile . . . but the
Blackbird's port engine simply wasn't drawing the way it
should. Each time he tried to ease the throttle up, the thump-
ing and jolting grew worse. Suddenly, with a final, decisive
bang, both engines quit, and the sleek *Habu* began nosing
down. Someone had once said that the SR-71 had all of the
glide characteristics of a falling manhole cover and that, Chisholm thought as he wrestled the controls, was doing an in-
justice to the manhole cover.

He started going through the engine relight sequence again.
Already they were down to fifty-three thousand feet, and the
luminous white pointers of the altimeter were starting to
sweep around the dial counterclockwise like a small, whirling
propeller.

"Missile . . . detonation . . ." Kelly said from the backseat.
"Five miles . . . back."

In a moment or two, the bastards would probably be dancing in the streets, convinced they'd just downed one of the
hated Yankee *Habus*. But it hadn't been the missile. Probably
it was something *really* deadly, like the failure of a ninety-
eight-cent transistor.

Forty-seven thousand feet. Start, damn it, *start!*

They were beginning to spin now, a flat pancake spin,
slowly at first . . . but the centripetal force was building. The
Blackbird's center of spin was far aft of the cockpit, putting
them, in effect, at the end of a long string being spun at high
speed. The forces generated could plaster both men against

their consoles if their seat restraints weren't secure.

He remembered stories he'd heard, told by other veteran Blackbird pilots. There was the tale of the Blackbird that had flamed out over West Virginia. Its pilot had managed to restart at thirty thousand feet; the sonic boom had rattled the entire state and toppled an old brick chimney, which killed two workers. There was also the story, more humorous—at least in retrospect—of the Blackbird that had flamed out over Utah. The pilot had tried to relight almost all the way down to the deck ... succeeding, finally, by kicking in his afterburners directly above the Mormon Tabernacle.

There'd been a lot of complaints about Air Force testing and sonic booms over populated areas after *that* one.

Thirty-five thousand feet, and sky and ground were gyrating wildly past the cockpit windscreen, green alternating with blue in a bewildering flicker of color and texture. "This is Tango Hotel niner-two," Chisholm called over the emergency radio frequency. "Mayday, mayday. Engine failure, and we are going down. I say again, Tango Hotel niner-two, engine failure and going down . . ."

He kept trying to restart, but the instruments—when he could see them at all through the vibration—showed catastrophic pressure failure in both port and starboard engines. He waited until they were below twenty thousand feet before hitting the eject handle. . . .

10 km northeast of Tchepone
Laos
1115 hours

"Lazy Dog, this is Trailbreaker. Lazy Dog, Trailbreaker. Come in. Over."

Static hissed and crackled in Nolan's headset. He tried again.

"Lazy Dog, Trailbreaker. Lazy Dog, Trailbreaker. Come in. Over."

After three days of investigating the NVA complex at Ban Kôon, the SOG team had slipped away, moving north along the trail until they were far enough from the camp that they could risk stringing up an antenna wire and chancing a call back to Danang. They were still in the mountains, emerald green and verdant, in a heavily forested area some five kilometers east of the Ho Chi Minh Trail and perhaps twenty kilometers north of Highway 9.

Danang, strangely, had seemed almost disinterested in the information about the NVA rest camp, but they'd shown a keen interest when Nolan had told them about seeing track marks in the ground, suggesting tanks. They directed the team to stay put twenty-four hours and call back at eleven hundred the next morning, Wednesday, 2 December.

Nolan had been trying to raise Danang for fifteen minutes now, but it was beginning to look as though nobody was home.

"Trailbreaker, Trailbreaker, this is Lazy Dog," a voice said suddenly, crackling in his ears. It was faint, but he could make it out. "Do you copy? Over."

"Lazy Dog, Trailbreaker, we copy. You are very weak. Over."

"Trailbreaker, Lazy Dog," the voice said, a bit clearer this time. "How me? Over."

"Lazy Dog, that's better. Over."

"Trailbreaker, Lazy Dog. Be advised we have a new mission for you. This is an extreme Bright Light alert. Repeat, extreme Bright Light alert. We have a Fallen Sparrow very close to your position."

Fallen Sparrow . . . a downed American aviator. An extreme alert meant that someone had slapped one hell of a high priority on the operation. He wondered what the whole story was.

"Ah, Lazy Dog, we copy your extreme Bright Light. Go ahead."

Lazy Dog began feeding Nolan map coordinates, which he checked on a large-scale topo map of this part of Laos. His eyebrows arched up his forehead when he saw the area where the aircraft had gone down . . . in the Se Bang Hieng Valley, perhaps ten kilometers—just six miles—north of their current position.

He felt the hairs prickle at the back of his neck. His orders were simply to reach the crash site, secure the wreckage, and try to locate the aircraft's two-man crew, with no details about the plane or the mission; the chance, however, of an American plane coming down so close to the SOG team's position in the middle of so very much jungle seemed to be a coincidence beyond all reason or belief.

The aircraft must be in the area because Trailbreaker was in the area, which meant that it was almost certainly a reconnaissance aircraft of some kind.

The extreme urgency—and the unsettling fact that headquarters had first told him to secure the downed plane's wreckage, even before locating the crew—suggested that the plane was carrying classified equipment. It could be almost anything—a Martin B-57 with its classified laser targeting gear, an F-111 with its secret navigational equipment, even a U-2—but he had a feeling he knew what the secret aircraft must be. Only a downed Blackbird could have gotten SOG HQ in Danang in such an uproar.

"We have a regular Bright Light unit scrambling," Lazy Dog told him when he verified the coordinates. "It's going to take several hours for them to reach your position, however. We have reason to believe that heavy NVA patrol activity in that area could be a threat to Fallen Sparrow. It is most important that the competition not reach the sparrow first."

"I understand, Lazy Dog. We're moving now."

"Roger that. We'll have helicopters in your area for retrieval within two hours. Lazy Dog, out."

"Trailbreaker, out."

Dhu was squatting on the ground nearby, watching as he packed up the radio. "Looks like we have another march ahead of us," he told the Hmong.

"That's good. We've been in this one area too long. The NVA are going to be all over us if we're not careful."

Nolan decided not to tell the Hmong that they were probably going to be getting even closer to those patrols. The North Vietnamese would be looking for any downed American aircraft . . . and if they had reason to suspect that it was one of the fabled SR-71 Blackbirds, they'd throw their whole damned army into that valley if they could manage it.

He glanced at Halstead, who was crouching on the hillside nearby, watching the jungle on the valley floor. He'd been subdued since they'd infiltrated the Ban Kôon complex, maybe even depressed, and his mood seemed to have been triggered by the photographs that were now stored in a waterproof rucksack for delivery to SOG HQ.

Nolan had asked what the problem was, but he'd gotten an evasive answer.

Well, whatever it was, Halstead would snap out of it. He was a pro, the sort of man who usually had his brain in charge of his emotions, rather than the other way around.

"Hey, Twidge!" he called. "Time to *di-di.*"

"Whatcha got, Boss?"

"From the sound of it, a downed recon aircraft. Might be a Blackbird. Six miles north."

Halstead pursed his lips and gave a low whistle.

"Exactly," Nolan continued. "Round up the LDNNs, secure the area, and let's move out. I want to be humping inside of five minutes."

"Better break out the beeper ears," Halstead suggested. "If they're only six miles away and ejected, they could be anywhere around here."

Every pilot carried a combination radio and emergency beeper to aid the search and rescue people, and the information passed on from Danang had included the appropriate frequencies. The SOG team carried several small personal transceivers that could dial in to the emergency frequency, letting them home in on the downed aircrew even if they were stuck in a tree . . . or dead.

Usually. Nolan remembered Ringold's smashed radio, and how long it had taken to find his body . . . and that had been in the desert, wide-open terrain without a tree in sight. The jungle here was so thick that it could easily have swallowed up that whole damned airplane, and no one would find it for decades.

And, of course, the enemy had radios, too. It was a sure bet that they would have patrols out on the ground, looking for the wreckage and looking for the pilot.

"Do it."

Three minutes later, they were moving through the jungle, heading north.

Se Bang Hieng Valley
30 km northeast of Tchepone
Laos
1535 hours

They were lucky. They were the first to reach the wreckage.

Halstead crouched at the edge of the sudden and shockingly violent clearing, staring at their find. They'd seen the smoke boiling into the sky from four miles away, and that had spurred them on, knowing that the NVA would have seen that ominous black mushroom as well. And Nolan's guess had been right. That needle-slim prow could only have been an SR-71.

There wasn't a lot left. The Blackbird had come in at a steep angle, plowing through the jungle canopy and apparently breaking in half among the treetops. The aft section, with the engines and fuel, had exploded on impact, and debris was scattered across a broad oval of the forest floor over a hundred yards across. The nose of the Blackbird, from pointed tip to just aft of the cockpit, was almost intact, however, the largest single piece of wreckage at the crash site. It had slammed into the trees on the southwest edge of the oval, nose-high and crumpled, but still more or less in one piece.

That was not good. There were a large number of pieces of equipment still intact, avionics, radar, communications equipment, and the like, all highly classified, all of unimaginable intelligence value to the Russians or Chinese if they could just get their hands on them.

The Hmong spread out, forming a thinly stretched perimeter around the entire crash site, with orders to watch for approaching NVA troops. The SEALs, American and Vietnamese, did a careful search of the crash site itself, satisfying themselves that no one else had reached the area yet and that the wreck, which was still so hot that pieces of the hull were smoldering, had not been disturbed.

Now, while Nolan reestablished contact with Danang, Halstead mounted guard over the crash. He pulled out one of the handheld radios, already set to the pilot's emergency beacon frequency, and moved it back and forth, trying to get a signal. There was nothing . . . nothing . . . no, wait! There was something, so faint he'd almost missed it. He had to hold the radio's antenna just right to pick it up, but it sounded as if a chirp was coming from *that* direction, toward the northeast.

He followed the line with his eyes. Mountains loomed there, the Truong Song Mountains, the spine of green-clad ruggedness that divided Vietnam from Laos.

"Hey, Lieutenant?"

Nolan looked up from the big backpack radio. "Yeah?"

"I think I got a beep. It's pretty faint."

Nolan frowned. "Danang says they've got a sterilization team on the way, but it's going to be an hour or two, yet."

"Look," Halstead told him. "I know the airplane is what worries Danang the most, but we've got to get the pilot and RSO out, too." He nodded toward the northeast. "That's Vietnam over there. North Vietnam. I don't know what the range is, but they could be across the line. Even if they're not, they're going to be picked up pretty damned soon, this close to the trail."

"You have an idea, Twidge?"

"Yeah. Let me take Nghiep and two Hmong. We'll track the signal and try to get the people, while you take care of this shit here."

Nolan needed only a moment to arrive at a decision. It wasn't normally considered a good idea for a small command to divide itself into even smaller units, but Nolan had that reputation of his for preferring small-unit ops to big ones, and the smaller the better.

He nodded. "Sounds like a plan, Twidge. Take plenty of ammo, just in case. Keep in touch with your radio. We may need to dust off out of here in a hurry."

"Roger that." He rose from the ground.

"And Twidge?"

"Yes, sir?"

"Watch your ass out there. I don't want to have to come looking for you."

"You sound like my wife. Sir."

Nolan chuckled.

Halstead gathered Nghiep, Dhu, and another Hmong, and the four men started toward the mountains.

Crash site, Se Bang Hieng Valley
Laos
1720 hours

The sun was well down in the west as Nolan sat by the radio, listening for . . . something, a radio call from one of the Hmong on the perimeter, warning of an approaching NVA force, a call from Halstead, reporting that he'd found the downed Blackbird's crew, a request for smoke from an incoming Jolly Green, *anything* to indicate that he wasn't alone in this green hell.

If there was one thing Nolan didn't care for, it was sitting in one place, waiting for the bad guys to come to him. SEALs had plenty of experience doing just that and had raised the ambush to the level of an art form, but that didn't mean that he had to *like* it.

There was no sign of the North Vietnamese, but smoke was still curling into the early evening sky. They would come.

He heard something, a faint disturbance in the air.

Mai approached, his AK gripped tightly. "Lieutenant! I think . . ."

"Quiet. Yeah . . . I hear it too." The sound was growing rapidly louder, the familiar and ever-welcome clatter of approaching helicopters. Nolan reached for the radio, switching to the air control frequency.

"Trailbreaker, Trailbreaker," a voice said over the headset. "This is Red Hawk, inbound. Give us some LZ identification."

Nolan nodded at Mai, and the LDNN tossed a smoke grenade into the clearing. Immediately, green smoke poured from the canister, billowing into the evening sky.

"I see green smoke," the helo pilot called.

"Ah, roger that, green smoke," Nolan replied. "Come on in. The LZ is secure."

Moments later, an HH-53, one of the huge SAR helos known as a "Jolly Green," gentled its way toward the clearing in the forest opened by the crashing Blackbird, nose high, its rotor wash flattening the grass and sending the green smoke swirling wildly about in ragged tatters.

Nolan ducked his head and trotted beneath the still-turning rotors as a team of a half dozen heavily armed men vaulted from the cargo deck. He recognized an old acquaintance, Lieutenant Morgan, clad in tiger-stripe camo and wearing a green headband. "Tom!" he called, reaching out a hand. "Welcome to Laos!"

Morgan shook his hand. "Thanks, I think." Heads low, they started moving to clear the helicopter's rotor hazard area. "What's the status?"

"The crash site is secure," Nolan shouted back at him. He pointed toward the southwest end of the clearing. "One piece needs to be blown. I'm afraid my team didn't have the demolition gear to make sure of doing a good job."

"No sweat. We came loaded for bear, and we've been briefed on what not to leave for Ivan to get his mitts on."

"Good. As for the competition, there's no sign of them yet."

"Aircraft crew?"

"Our people are tracking down an emergency beeper signal northeast of here."

"Sir, would that happen to include Twidge Halstead?" another man said.

Nolan had to look at the man hard to recognize him through the thick green face paint. "Hey! Tangretti, isn't it?"

"Good to see you, sir. How's the grass over here on the other side of the fence?"

"Hides just as many damned snakes as it does back in Nam," Nolan told him. "Your buddy's out humping the boonies right now."

"Go make sure the crash site is secure, Doc," Morgan told him.

"Aye, aye, sir." Tangretti trotted off.

Two more helicopters, a pair of Cobra gunships, growled low overhead, like carnivores searching for the scent of their prey.

"You have new orders for me?" Nolan asked Morgan. He patted the rucksack slung from his hip, the one holding the photos and other intelligence documents taken from Ban Kôon. "If not, I've got some hot shit here I need the chopper to take back."

"Take it back yourself," Morgan told him. "My orders are to see you and the LDNNs on the chopper and out of here. I think they're going to want to talk to you guys about what you saw a couple of days ago.''

"And the Hmong?''

A shrug. "They stay here. They'll help my team, and we'll leave them here when we pull out. They'd never fit in with the Danang social set, you know.''

Morgan was being facetious, but in a way he was right. Most Vietnamese hated the Hmong tribespeople, and they wouldn't be made welcome. Nolan thought about Dhu, though, who was nothing at all like what he thought of as a member of a Southeast Asian mountain tribe.

This was a strange, damned war. "I'd better try to raise Halstead," he said.

"We have two more Jolly Greens inbound," Morgan told him, "with people to find the Blackbird's crew and take them out. If they can make contact with Twidge, they'll haul his tail out too.''

Nolan nodded. "And your people?''

"First priority is to deny what's left of the Blackbird to the enemy. Next, see that the Blackbird's crew, and you people, are safely out of here." Morgan gave him a slow and evil grin. "And after that, well, we're going to spring a little surprise on our northern friends.''

"I think," Nolan said with a grin, "that I'm sorry I won't get to see that.''

He meant it, too, even though he knew that what Morgan was talking about was another long bout of sitting and waiting for the enemy to come to him.

Chapter 25

Wednesday, 2 December 1970

Truong Song Mountains, east slope
35 km northeast of Tchepone
Laos
1735 hours

Halstead eased himself forward, peering through the densely clotted vegetation. He and the three other SOG commandos had managed the stiff climb toward the foothills of the Truong Song Mountains in a little more than an hour, covering, by Halstead's estimation, about four kilometers.

By now it was clear that the radio beacon was on the near side of the mountains, not too far. Halstead almost felt disappointed; the mountains were further than they'd looked from the crash site, and there'd been a real possibility that the pilot and RSO had come down on the other side, in North Vietnam. It would have provided him with some interesting tales to tell his fellow SEALs if he'd had to enter North Vietnam itself to rescue those guys.

Instead, it looked like they'd come down further up the Se Bang Hieng Valley, so deep down a fold in the western flank of the mountains that their signal had been blocked. Now that the SOG team was climbing down into the valley, however, the signal from the beeper was quite strong.

On the downside, though, was the fact that he was only getting one signal. That could mean many things . . . that the other crewman's transmitter was damaged, that he'd come down so far away that the transmitter was out of range . . . or that the NVA had already reached him.

He could hear the steady hiss of falling water just ahead.

As he started to push through the vegetation, though, Dhu held up one hand, clenched in a fist. Wait!

Halstead froze, gripping his AK-47. What had the Hmong seen or heard?

Then he heard it as well . . . voices, *shouts,* from somewhere just beyond that green wall. Carefully, the team moved forward again, sliding on their bellies. The shouting was in Vietnamese . . . and it sounded angry.

Vegetation gave way to a sharp drop into a stream-carved gully. A small waterfall spilling into a sluice of fast-moving white water was creating the hiss, while on the opposite shore, perhaps fifteen yards away, five North Vietnamese soldiers confronted two American aviators.

The Americans looked like astronauts, swaddled in bulky silver pressure suits, though they had removed their helmets. One was on the ground, his leg splinted with two thick, straight branches tied on with parachute cord. A parachute hung from one nearby tree, and Halstead guessed that the man on the ground had broken a leg when he'd landed in this less than ideal terrain for such activities, and the other man had found him.

And then, unfortunately, the NVA had found them both.

The Vietnamese seemed to be trying to get the standing American to pick up his buddy and carry him; both aviators appeared dazed and uncomprehending. Halstead watched in horror as the NVA soldier who appeared to be in charge of the party swung his AK in a flat, brief arc and slammed the buttstick into the standing American's stomach. The force of the blow doubled the man over and nearly drove him to his knees. The other Vietnamese closed in, jabbing the man with their gun barrels, shouting at him with disconcertingly musical words, and for one terrible moment, Halstead thought they were going to kill both Americans on the spot.

Halstead considered the tactical problem facing his team. Five Vietnamese . . . at least, five that could be seen. Four rescuers . . . but only two of them were SEALs, with SEAL-caliber training in small arms and close quarters combat.

And two friendlies inside the kill zone.

Halstead had talked about situations like this with other SEALs, the tactical need to bring down a large number of hostiles who were mingled with friendlies. It required perfect planning, perfect timing, perfect aim . . . and in the field, perfection is never possible.

But he had to do something, and fast. Chivvied along by prods from assault rifle muzzles, the one American was hoisting the other over his shoulders in a clumsy fireman's carry. The NVA unit fell into line then and began moving toward Halstead's left, following a trail that descended the hill along the side of the cascading stream.

And then, like the pieces of a puzzle coming together, Halstead saw his chance.

The NVA troops and their prisoners were in a line, two Vietnamese, the two Americans, and the last three Viets bringing up the rear. That meant only the three in the back were looking in the direction of their prisoners, and they would offer the greatest threat to the aviators once the shooting started. Not only that, but each man in the line blocked the fire of the man behind; the North Vietnamese soldier directly behind the Americans, the one with his rifle pointed at the small of the walking prisoner's back, was the biggest threat.

Quickly, silently, Halstead reached out, touched Nghiep on the arm, and pointed at the two NVAs in the lead. He waited until the LDNN nodded his understanding, then raised his own AK-47, drawing down on the third NVA soldier from the rear. There was no more time for thought; in another second or two, the column would pass out of sight, and the SOG team would have to follow them until another favorable opportunity arose.

Please, God, he thought, and he squeezed the trigger. His AK-47 barked on full auto, sending a stream of rounds slamming through the Vietnamese soldier, spinning him around and back and nearly dropping him in the lap of the man behind. Smoothly, Halstead released the trigger, tracked back to the next man in line, and squeezed again, sending a second burst into the tangle of two men, one alive, one dying or already dead.

The NVA soldier at the rear of the column dropped to his knees, rifle tracking, not the captives, thank God, but the trees where the fire had come from. Halstead was aware of a thousand tiny, crisp details as he loosed his third burst—the aviator carrying his buddy diving to the ground with the first shot; Nghiep's AK cracking to his left and the two lead enemy soldiers falling; the last man in line pitching forward, falling head-first into the stream; the two Hmong opening fire with their carbines, showing a decent sense of fire control and discipline.

Perhaps three seconds after the fusillade began, Halstead shouted, "Cease fire! Cease fire!" He shifted to Vietnamese. *"Ngung ban!"* The North Vietnamese were all down, four sprawled along the trail, the fifth half submerged and snagged on a tree limb in the water ten yards further downstream; the two Americans were just raising their heads and looking about, dazed at the suddenness of their rescue.

Halstead and Nghiep emerged from the screen of forest vegetation, while the Hmong remained under cover, guarding against the possibility of a counter-ambush. If anything, the aviators appeared more fearful of the apparitions with black-and-green-painted faces emerging from the tree line than they'd been of their captors. "I'm American," he called out, shouting above the rush of the water. "We're here to get you out."

"Thank God," the injured aviator said. The name on the cloth strip on the right breast of his suit read Chisholm. "Thank *God*. . . ."

By the time Halstead had picked his way across the stream, he'd already pulled out his radio and was calling for help. "Trailbreaker One, this is Trailbreaker Two. Do you read me, over?"

"Trailbreaker Two," a strange voice replied, startlingly loud. Halstead had expected to encounter problems with transmissions from this deep and narrow valley. "Trailbreaker Two, this is Comanche Three-one on SAR. What is your position, over?"

Halstead's eyes narrowed. This sort of situation was always hairy. The speaker sounded American—hell, Halstead thought he could detect a bit of Down East twang to the way he said the words—but there were North Vietnamese intelligence officers who spoke very good English indeed.

"Comanche Three-one, Trailbreaker Two. I need some ID here before I buy you a drink. Over." In his file back at Danang were several names and phrases that the enemy would not know and could not guess.

"Trailbreaker Two, Comanche. Who's buying? Over."

"Comanche, this is Twidge. Over."

"Okay, Trailbreaker. Wait one."

There was a pause, during which Halstead could hear the clatter of rotor blades someplace close by. He watched emotionlessly as Nghiep checked each of the downed NVA troops; one, he saw, was still moving, his intestines spilling from his belly in a glistening red and purple mass of loops and coils. The LDNN was drawing his knife. . . .

"Trailbreaker, it says here your mother's maiden name was Jackson. And I have a message from a friend of yours back at Fallen Sparrow who says that if you don't get aboard this damned helo, somebody named Pat is never going to speak to him again. Over?"

Halstead chuckled. "Okay, Comanche. Come on in. We have two packages for shipping." He looked around at the surrounding forest. This far up the flank of the mountain, there wasn't a helicopter-sized clearing closer than the Blackbird-scythed crash site several miles back down the slope. "Finding an LZ is going to be tough, though. I'm at the bottom of a V-shaped valley, and the trees in here are thicker than fleas on a hound dog's back. Over."

"Not to worry, Trailbreaker. We got it covered. By the strength of your signal, you're close. Pop us some smoke, okay?"

"Roger that," he said, reaching for an M18 canister attached to his combat harness. "I think I hear you, and it sounds like you're to the south or southwest." He pulled the ring and tossed the smoke grenade. In two seconds, violet smoke gushed into the air, swirling among the trees as it reached for the open sky.

"Trailbreaker Two, I see purple smoke."

"Roger, purple smoke. Come on in."

As they waited, the aviators both shook Halstead's hand. "I'm Will Chisholm," the injured man said.

"Mike Kelly," the other added. "Man, I don't mind telling you, we're glad to see you guys."

"All part of your friendly search-and-rescue service, gentlemen."

"Listen, our aircraft. It came down off that way, somewhere. . . ." Kelly pointed toward the southwest.

"Don't worry, sir," Halstead told them. "We already have it covered. I came from there, in fact."

"If any of the avionics survived . . ." Chisholm began.

"There won't be enough left to analyze, sir. Believe me."

"You guys are good," Kelly told him, shaking his head. "What are you, Army Special Forces?"

"Studies and Observations Group," Halstead replied. "Let's just leave it at that."

After checking on Chisholm's leg, broken when his chute hung on a tree and slammed him into the trunk, Halstead examined each of the NVA bodies on the trail. All were dead, including the eviscerated one. Nghiep stood thoughtfully nearby, quietly wiping his K-Bar knife on a frond. Stooping suddenly, Halstead reached up and took a finger's worth of thick, green paint from his own face and drew a single line down the center of the forehead of one of the dead soldiers, squarely between his eyes.

"What's that for?" Chisholm asked.

"Calling card," Halstead replied. When they found their people here, the NVA would know that it had been the SEALs, the Men With Green Faces.

Minutes later, the hammering thump of the helicopter's rotors sounded from directly overhead. Looking up, Halstead could see bits and pieces of the machine through the tree canopy above.

"Okay, Comanche," Halstead called. "You are directly over our position. We have one injured man, here. Better send down a basket. Over."

"Rog. Watch your heads."

Moments later, the branches in the trees above his head, already dancing in the smoky swirl of the chopper's rotor wash, were smashed aside in an avalanche of broken twigs and leaves by a descending Stokes stretcher, a flat board inside a mummy's case–shaped form of something like tough chicken wire dangling from a harness and cablehoist. With Nghiep's and Kelly's help, he got Chisholm into the basket and carefully strapped in, as the helicopter, a big HH-53 Jolly Green, hovered patiently overhead.

"Okay, Comanche!" Halstead radioed. "Take him away!"

Minutes passed as the Blackbird pilot was hauled up through the canopy to the Jolly Green. Then, with a radioed warning, a canvas bundle was lowered through the trees, attached to something like a three-armed, bright yellow anchor with the flukes folded.

The "anchor" was a forest penetrator, which could be dropped on the end of a cable through even the thickest interlacing branches; the flukes pulled out and down, forming three extremely narrow, hard, and uncomfortable seats arranged at 120-degree intervals around the penetrator's central shaft. The bundle contained three STABO harnesses, with which they could secure themselves to the penetrator for the ride up through the trees.

"Ah, Comanche," Halstead called. "There are five of us down here. Our package, two SEALs, and two Hmong."

"The Hmong stay here," the voice from overhead replied. "Tell them to rejoin the rest at the crash site."

Halstead didn't like that. This region was going to be swarming with NVA soon, and he felt like he was abandoning them. SEALs do *not* leave their own behind.

"It's okay, Twidge," Dhu told him. "*This* is where our war is."

"Okay," Halstead said, but still with a guilty twinge of uncertainty. "But you take care of yourself, okay?"

Dhu showed him his teeth, stark white in a black-painted face. "Don't worry about the Hmong," he said, grinning. "Worry about the NVA we capture!"

With the penetrator's seats unfolded and locked in place, Halstead, Kelly, and Nghiep fastened themselves securely around the central shaft, strapping themselves in and tightening the cinches on the D-rings of their STABO harnesses. "We're set down here!" Halstead called. "Haul away!"

The cable above their heads tightened, giving a loud *thrum,* and then they were rising from the ground, rising into the lower levels of the treetops. They locked their arms over their heads to protect themselves from the slash of branches; leaning forward slightly, Halstead looked down and caught a final glimpse of Dhu and the other Hmong standing among the NVA bodies, looking up.

He wondered if he would see them again. It seemed unlikely, and yet . . . who could say? He'd not expected to see Nghiep Van Dong again, or Lieutenant Nolan. It was a strange and often unlikely war. . . .

Minutes later, they were aboard the helicopter, their two prize ''packages'' safe as the big HH-53 throttled up and accelerated across the treetops, angling toward the South Vietnamese border . . . and Danang.

Thursday, 3 December 1970

Blackbird crash site
Se Bang Hieng Valley
30 km northeast of Tchepone
Laos
0834 hours

It was early morning, and the sunlight was falling in long, dusty shafts through the forest at Morgan's back. He was on his belly now, on the face of a low and tree-cluttered ridge overlooking the debris field where the Blackbird had come down. Like the other members of his team, he was armed with an AK-47, a ChiCom model that would not scream ''American'' when he opened fire. The Blackbird was completely destroyed now, the wreckage blown to bits just before nightfall yesterday. The destruction of the aircraft's avionics and camera gear came before all other considerations and could not be left to the chance that the SOG sterilization team would get itself into trouble before the night was over, something that would prevent them from destroying the plane.

Now there was nothing left of the wreck that was larger than a tabletop, and anything with circuits, wiring, or camera parts had been so badly fragmented, burned, and scattered that the best electronics experts in the world would never be able to piece it together in any meaningful way.

Once the wreck had been destroyed, they'd gathered up their equipment and, for the benefit of anyone else who might be watching, marched off, single-file, into the forest toward the southeast.

An hour later, however, they'd come back, circling around to the north after carefully making sure they weren't being followed. Slipping into positions scouted out earlier, they silently settled in for a long wait.

SOG had played this game before with the enemy. An American plane would come down, sometimes on one side of the border, sometimes on the other. An American rescue team was kept ready, just in case . . . but the trick lay in the fact that the North Vietnamese appeared to keep teams ready, too. Each time an American aircraft was shot down—and especially if that aircraft was a U-2 or an SR-71, spy planes that were not officially in the Southeast Asian theater at all—reaching the pilot and the top secret equipment became a race.

A race with potentially deadly consequences.

Special ASG units were kept on alert whenever one of these secret we-were-never-here aircraft was making a run out of Okinawa or Thailand. This time, it had simply happened that a SOG team—Operation Freedom Trail—had been in the area, close enough to reach the crash site before any of the ASG teams could make the flight from Danang. That bit of luck wasn't due entirely by chance, as it turned out, since the SR-71 *was* in the area specifically to check out some of the intelligence radioed back by Operation Freedom Trail. Still, in an op like this, time was very definitely of the essence, and sending in Nolan's team had let them get the jump on the bad guys by a considerable margin. So far, the operation was going perfectly.

Maybe a little *too* perfectly. Morgan now had less than complete faith in the system that had put him here, and that was a worrisome thought. He didn't think they would be written off and abandoned . . . but increasingly in this mad war, faceless men with gold-heavy shoulderboards in nice, secure rear areas in Danang or Saigon or Virginia made decisions that treated Morgan and the men he worked with like expendable plastic pieces on some titanic and ill-understood game board.

He was still seething privately over what he perceived as outright betrayal at Son Tay. As a special SOG operative, he'd been trained to take part in Operation Kingpin, a major effort to free American POWs being held at Son Tay, a few miles northwest of Hanoi. The idea had been for him to HALO into a deserted field ten miles west of his objective, then make his way by night overland to the POW camp area. There, he was to use a starlight scope to observe activity within the compound identified as the site where as many as seventy American POWs were being held. An extra set of eyes on the ground, it was thought, would be invaluable in confirming intelligence acquired by photo-recon flights. With a backpack radio, he could alert the incoming helicopters, loaded with U.S. Army Special Forces troops, about any last-minute changes in the defenses in the area and about the exact locations of the POWs.

Two days before he was to leave Danang for Udorn Air Force Base in Thailand, however, Morgan had been ordered to stand down. The reason he'd been given had made sense, he supposed; that extra pair of eyes on the ground might improve the quality of intelligence gathered prior to the raid ... but it also created one hell of a danger if the man on the ground was captured. If the NVA guessed ahead of time that the Americans were interested in Son Tay ...

Then he heard the full story of what had happened. Early in the predawn hours of 20 November, fifty-three elite Army troops under the command of Colonel Arthur "Bull" Simons had attacked the Son Tay camp in a daring helicopter raid, engaging not only NVA camp guards but also a number of Chinese and possibly Russian advisors barracked in a nearby school building. After a furious firefight, the camp was secure, the roads leading to it blocked ... but Son Tay, it turned out, had been a dry hole. There had been no POWs there to rescue.

By any standards, the raid had been a remarkable success; only one man had been slightly wounded in the entire op, and the only helo lost had been a deliberate sacrifice, crash-landed in the camp's courtyard to provide immediate access for the troops on board. But the POWs had been gone. There'd been no one there to rescue. As always seemed to be the case, the weak point of the op had proven to be intelligence.

Just two days earlier, an acquaintance of Morgan's at Udorn had sent him a brand-new patch, one of the popular "beer can insignia" that, increasingly, were worn by military personnel on special assignments and missions though the designs were not authorized. Some, like this one, weren't even supposed to be worn, but they made great souvenirs. This one was a beaut: a mushroom with vertical wavy lines rising above it, representing something odoriferous, and down below within the mushroom's black shadow, two small eyes looking out. Beneath the design were the letters KITD/FOHS. Some members of the Son Tay raiders had ordered a number

of the patches made up at a uniform shop in Thailand before
they'd returned to the United States.

The letters, according to the guy who'd given Morgan his
patch, stood for Kept In Total Darkness/ Fed Only Horse Shit.

It was now believed, according to some of Morgan's
sources, that the POWs had been moved as far back as July.
July! And members of the planning staff had been fully aware
that the POWs might have been moved. There was a story
circulating now about a North Vietnamese defector who'd
given Saigon the names of the active POW camps in the
north, omitting Son Tay from the list.

The Intel bastards at Danang, some of them, anyway, had
known, and they'd risked Simons and his team anyway. . . .

For Morgan, the cluster-fuck at Son Tay had finished
things, so far as he was concerned, between him and SOG.
After a rather noisy confrontation with his pseudonymous
handler at Monkey Mountain, the electronic eavesdropping
facility at Danang which had run Kingpin, he'd gotten them
to confirm his official transfer to the U.S. Navy SEALs, still
working under the SOG aegis, of course, but no longer directly responsible to the idiots who'd ham-fisted the Son Tay
op.

He preferred working with men who valued good intel as
much as he did, who didn't put covering their own asses
above good tradecraft, and who backed you up in a crunch.
Damn it, the SEALs were *tight.* They looked out for each
other, covered each other's backs . . . instead of protecting
their own backsides.

Morgan's legs were almost numb from sitting in the same
position, unmoving, all night. It was now full morning, and
still there'd been no sign of enemy activity. He'd made up
his mind that, if no one showed within the next three hours,
he would booby-trap the wreckage, then E&E back to the
South Vietnam border.

C'mon, he thought to himself fiercely. *C'mon! Show yourselves!*

There was a tremendous and very special opportunity here,
one Morgan had been carefully briefed on at Danang. Frequently, the NVA recovery teams would arrive on the scene
of a crash with foreign advisors of their own, the Communist
equivalents of the SEALs and Army Special Forces who "ad-

vised'' their South Vietnamese counterparts. The ''secondary school'' at Son Tay had been a barracks for such advisors, and both Chinese and Russians had been spotted on occasion with NVA patrols, especially in Laos and Cambodia. There were rumors, none confirmed, that Russians occasionally flew North Vietnamese MiGs and that Soviet and Chinese crews occasionally manned the antiaircraft guns and SAM batteries ringing Hanoi and other critical targets in the North. The SOG teams were always on the lookout for a chance to capture one of these advisors, and frequently the best opportunities presented themselves when the enemy was trying to reach a downed American spy plane. So far as Morgan knew, none of the recon planes shot down by the enemy so far had been captured by the other side . . . not since the 1960 shootdown of Gary Powers's U-2 over Sverdlovsk, at any rate.

But they would keep trying. Though it was not exactly a matter of public record—especially after the United States had been embarrassed by Powers's shootdown and the revelation that they'd been making reconnaissance overflights of the Soviet Union for years—U-2s and SR-71s had continued the overflight program and routinely entered Soviet, Chinese, and North Korean airspace, not to mention the skies over Vietnam, Cambodia, and Laos.

Each time SOG tried a stay-behind ambush, of course, they were running a risk. Generally, if only North Vietnamese troops showed up, the SOG team would kill them all. If the enemy patrol was too strong, the ambushers would let it go and withdraw without even engaging them. But if foreign advisors were spotted, the orders were to go to virtually any lengths to capture them. Morgan didn't know if any had been captured yet—that kind of information would, for obvious reasons, be very closely guarded—but every team hoped to be the one to bring a Russian or Chinese advisor back to Danang.

There! He'd heard something off toward the north, the crack of a twig, the rasp of fabric, and Morgan felt a quickening of his pulse. Someone was coming!

And if there were any foreign advisors with the group . . .

Blackbird crash site
Se Bang Hieng Valley
30 km northeast of Tchepone
Laos
0842 hours

Tangretti held his position, frozen in place, scarcely daring even to breathe as the enemy walked toward the ambush. He could see them now, soldiers in camouflage uniforms moving single file along the trail. There were nine men in all, and—his pulse quickened—the third man in line was much larger than the others, taller and brawnier than his Vietnamese comrades. He was wearing a fatigue cap, and the bit of hair showing at the back of his head, close-cropped almost to the skin, was blond.

Jackpot! . . .

The members of the stay-behind team kept silent, motionless, watching as the NVA patrol filed closer. The troops stopped just outside of the ambush zone, and Tangretti could almost imagine them reaching out with every sense, including the sixth, trying to read the terrain ahead, the forest, the possibility of ambush, trying to *smell* the existence of American or South Vietnamese commandos lying in wait for just such an opportunity as this.

The two sides held their respective positions for nearly ten minutes. Finally, the big foreigner in the Vietnamese column tapped one of the NVA troops on the shoulder and pointed. Nervously, Tangretti thought, the man moved forward into the ambush kill zone, his eyes very big and trying to look everywhere at once. As he took one gingerly step after another, Tangretti realized that he was expecting at any moment to trip a Claymore—the usual signal to commence fire in this sort of situation.

Morgan, the crank for the Claymores in his hand, let the Vietnamese soldier live for the moment, watching as the man made it all the way to the edge of the debris field. He poked around aimlessly for a few minutes, took a careful look around, and finally returned to the waiting patrol, moving with a lot more lightness in his step on the way out than he'd managed on the way in.

At last, the entire Vietnamese patrol started in.

Tangretti found himself praying under his breath, and the thought bothered him. Was he praying that they would be able to kill these men? He wasn't entirely certain, and the prayer itself was little more than an inaudible and almost unintelligible *"God help me God help me God help me"* that ran on and on as he eased his rifle a little higher, tucking the butt in a little tighter against his cheek. His assigned fire zone was clearly marked out between two specific trees on the path the Vietnamese troops were following. He watched the big foreigner enter his killing zone, watched the man move across it, his head twisting this way and that as though he could *feel* the threat of the AK's muzzle as he crossed its line of fire.

Morgan twisted the hand crank, and two Claymores set among the trees at the head of the path detonated, hurling super-shotgun blasts of lead balls in a deadly, bloody scythe that chopped down three of the Vietnamese in messily disintegrating tangles of flesh, uniform, and gore. Tangretti clamped his forefinger down on his weapon's trigger, opening up with a long burst on full-auto, sweeping the weapon from one side of his kill zone to the other three times . . . four . . . a fifth time before his receiver clicked empty. He hit the magazine release, dropping the empty, slapped home a heavy, fresh loaded mag, and brought the weapon back to his shoulder.

But the ambush was already very nearly over. Tangretti saw a last Vietnamese soldier, his AK-47 raised muzzle high, doing a slow pirouette as bullets from the ridgeside ambush tore through his body. The man collapsed, and then silence descended once again over the ambush zone. A moment later, a low, steady moaning began, the sound of a man in gutshot agony.

Morgan gave a signal, and Tangretti and three other SEALs from Echo slipped forward from their ambush positions. Tangretti approached the trail slowly, his AK at the ready. Several bodies lay in front of him, legs, arms, and torso twisted at impossible angles. One Vietnamese was leaning partly upright against a tree trunk, trying to hold his intestines inside. Another lay prone on the ground, still moving, slowly and with nightmare awareness trying to pick up pieces of skull and brain splattered from the top of his head. There was nothing to be done for either of them but a mercy shot. Tangretti took out the one with the head wound with a single shot to the base of the neck. *God forgive me. . . .*

He sensed movement and turned, assault rifle raised.

It was the blond foreigner, right arm squeezed hard against his bloody side. The ambush had been designed to kill everyone except the advisor, but, as the old maxim had it, no plan survives contact with the enemy. The advisor must have moved forward into the path of a burst from the ridge. With his free hand he was reaching for an AK-47 lying nearby.

"Stoy!" Tangretti snapped, holding the AK to his cheek and aiming it directly at the man. His Russian, from a language course back at Coronado, was adequate only for a few precise commands, but it was enough to get the message across. *"Stoy!* Stop!"

The man stopped, looked up, and stared at Tangretti with wide, ice-blue eyes.

"Slushaisya eelee ya budu strelyaht!" Tangretti commanded. *Do what I say or I'll fire!*

Understanding dawned in the Russian's eyes. At least, Tangretti hoped he was Russian. It was possible, of course, that he was East German or even Polish . . . but Russian seemed the likeliest possibility. *"Nee strelyaee. . . ."* the man said.

"Ruki v'vayrh! Smatri u minya beez shtook!"

The man nodded and held his free hand up, palm out. "I speak English," he said. "Treat me carefully, please. My name is Major Grigor Alekseivich Obinin. I am, what you might say, a prize."

The other SEALs were moving among the dead Vietnamese now, checking for documents, collecting rifles. Tangretti could hear Morgan on the radio, calling in the extraction helo.

The Russian's eyes narrowed. "And who are you? U.S. Special Forces?"

"Never mind, Ivan," Tangretti replied. His heart was hammering in his chest. They'd just captured a Russian!

Nearby, MM1 Jacowicz knelt beside a dead NVA soldier and carefully marked the man's forehead with a streak of green paint.

"Ah, *ya panimayu,"* the Russian said, understanding. He seemed almost satisfied. "You must be Navy SEALs. . . ."

Interlude

A year can be a long time in the life of men, or in the life of a country.

For Greg Halstead, Bill Tangretti, David Nolan, and Tom Morgan, the rest of the deployment with Det Echo proved relatively uneventful after that doubled-up mission across the line inside Laos. Congress banned the use of U.S. troops on the ground in Cambodia and Laos, effective on 1 January 1971; and, while there were plenty of rumors that American Special Forces were still over there, Det Echo's involvement in Laos seemed to be at an end.

Tangretti's guess, though, that the sneak-and-peek at Ban Kôon was in reality an advance recon for an invasion proved to be all too accurate. On 8 February, 12,000 South Vietnamese troops surged across the border near Khe Sanh into Laos, marking the beginning of Operation Lam Son 719. Named after the location of a Vietnamese victory over the Chinese in 1427, the operation had as its objective to drive a fifteen-mile-wide salient deep into Laos, straight down Highway 9 all the way to Tchepone, twenty-two miles from the border. The ARVN 1st Armored Brigade struck along Highway 9, while airborne troops and ARVN Rangers secured firebases to the west and north. The idea was to cut the Ho Chi Minh Trail at a vulnerable point, ending the steady stream of men and supplies headed south. The troops went in wearing jaunty white scarves, sporting broad grins for the television cameras.

Initially, the attack went well. By 22 February, however, just two weeks after the attack had begun, the ARVN advance slowed to a crawl. Unexpectedly heavy resistance from NVA strongholds in the forest-thick mountains threatened to bog down the invasion to a standstill.

And then the North Vietnamese counterattacks began, closing in on the gains made so far, relentlessly threatening to isolate the entire invasion force. The real shocker developed when North Vietnamese tanks appeared—PT-76s and the larger, heavier, deadlier T-54s, slashing through the ARVN firebases and descending on the 1st Armored Brigade like the locusts of Armageddon. The tanks, it appeared, had been hidden nearby all along. Once again, as happened so often, faulty intelligence was blamed. Surely *someone* must have seen those tanks, known they were there. . . .

If so, the word had never reached the people who needed to know.

In a desperate attempt to salvage a quickly deteriorating situation, General Xuan Lam, the ARVN commander of the invasion, airlifted his 1st Infantry Division all the way to Tchepone in a leapfrogging series of flights, accomplishing the longest heliborne assault of the war, but to no avail. By 10 March, Xuan ordered withdrawal . . . and before long, the retreat turned into a rout. By 24 March, the ARVN invasion force was back inside of South Vietnam, having suffered almost 10,000 casualties, half the total number of troops ultimately committed.

Throughout the entire invasion, U.S. forces had by law been limited to air support and logistics. At that, 107 American helicopters had been lost, along with 176 Americans among the aircrews.

By almost any standards, Lam Son 719 was one of the blackest disasters of the entire black history of the Vietnam War.

Halstead and Tangretti sat out the invasion in Danang, expecting to go in if they were needed to recover U.S. pilots from the battle zone . . . but the orders never came, and Halstead, at least, was left with the growing conviction that Washington had decided to cut and run, to abandon South Vietnam as quickly as possible, and to hell with the consequences. Greg's first enlistment was up in March, but he signed the papers and shipped for six. He'd actually considered—for all of ten minutes—the possibility of getting out of the Navy when his enlistment was up, but somehow the civilian world back home just wasn't very appealing right now, with its peace marches and demonstrations, and he and Bill were due for a deployment Stateside now, so they soon would be with their families.

Besides, he was a SEAL. He could imagine no other life for himself.

Back in the United States, meanwhile, Pat Tangretti and Wendy Halstead set about finding houses. Young Davy wasn't walking yet, but it wouldn't be long. And now Wendy was pregnant, too, with the baby due in August. The apartments were already cramped, and they would soon need more room still.

Unfortunately, housing at Coronado was at a premium, with waiting lists for enlisted housing that could go on for month after uncertain month. While the men were wrapping up their last deployment in Danang, Pat and Wendy had gone house-hunting off-base. Pat had found a place in Fletcher Hills, in the desert's-edge suburb of El Cajon, a ranch house built on a concrete slab, with a stone patio and a peach tree in back and rose bushes along the west side of the house. Wendy had found a two-bedroom house twelve miles down the parkway, not far from Balboa Park, just five minutes from the zoo, which, she claimed, would be perfect once the kid came along.

. Greg and Bill returned to the United States in May of 1971. After taking two weeks' leave, most of which was spent fixing up the new houses, they reported to their next duty stations. For Greg, that had been a training tour at the Amphib Base at Coronado, testing out the latest mod of SDV. This time it was Bill's turn to be assigned to the SEAL Training Command as a junior instructor. Not even his newfound Christianity, he declared, could stop him from thoroughly enjoying being on the giving end of Hell Week, just this once. Both men passed their tests for first class, and their promotions came through in September.

Meanwhile, the war in the United States continued, more viciously, more divisively than before. More and more ordinary Americans—as distinguished from the radicals, the student demonstrators, or the bomb-throwing Weathermen—felt that American involvement in Vietnam was wrong.

On 29 March, Army Lieutenant William Calley went before a court-martial board for his part in ordering the My Lai Massacre, all the way back in March of 1968, shortly after

Tet. The trial further divided a divided country, with Calley's detractors calling him a war criminal, his supporters insisting that he was being made a scapegoat. Whatever the truth, the disgrace of Company C, 11th Infantry Brigade, focused American attention as had nothing else on the concept of an *unjust* war, a war that Americans with their traditional sense of honor and fair play had no business fighting in the first place.

It also increased the savagery of the antiwar radicals. America was pulling out of Vietnam, but not fast enough— and, by their way of seeing things, all American servicemen were "pigs," "fascists," or "baby killers."

For the SEALs, the My Lai affair was one more piece of proof that poorly trained, poorly motivated soldiers were not soldiers at all. The press rarely reported the other side of the story. They never talked about how Company C, newly arrived in-country with an original complement of under 100, had lost 42 men in 32 days to mortarings and booby traps and had never so much as *seen* their attackers. The press certainly didn't report how one of Calley's men had been captured by the VC, and how the entire company had heard the man's shrieks throughout an entire, hell-horror night. They'd thought the VC were using amplifiers and a microphone to broadcast the man's torture from five miles away, but when they'd found the body they'd realized that no amplification had been necessary. The American soldier had been skinned alive—everything except his face—after which he'd been soaked in salt water, and his penis had been ripped off.

But that was the reality of the war in Southeast Asia. The crimes of units like Company C could not be excused, but they could, sometimes, be understood . . . as could the steadily free-falling morale of U.S. troops in Nam, the soaring incidence of drug use, the stories of shooting civilians from helicopters for sport, the stories of unpopular officers being "fragged" with a grenade tossed into their tent at night, or even of incidents of outright mutiny.

War is, above all else, an exercise of will between two peoples. America was winning the war in terms of battles won and enemy dead; it was losing in the hearts and minds of Americans who simply did not have the will to continue.

The SEALs, for their part, closed ranks and soldiered on. They knew they were a cut above the draftees and dopers, the grunts and REMFs and FNGs who'd carried the brunt of America's war in Vietnam for so long. To the Naval Special Warfare community, it was self-evident that the way to win a war was not to try smothering it with large quantities of money, rhetoric, and scared, undisciplined, badly trained teenagers.

At the same time, it was obvious that America was going to abandon Saigon as quickly and as expeditiously as possible, no matter what friends, allies, or enemies around the world might think. Vietnam had made the SEALs. They'd originally been created by Kennedy's belief that Communism could be contained by elite covert units like the SEALs and the Army Green Berets, and Vietnam had been both the forging and the tempering of the Teams.

But now the retreat had begun, as ignominiously as the rout of Lam Son 719. The SEALs were increasingly finding themselves the target of both unwanted publicity and of unwarranted attacks by a nation that found its veterans inconvenient reminders of a war it wanted to forget.

Chapter 26

Monday, 15 November 1971

University of Southern California
San Diego campus
2130 hours

For Greg and Bill, Stateside once again, their careers had become like the nine-to-five jobs in the civilian world that most SEALs claimed to detest. Most of the time, they were up at six and checking in on base by eight and, unless they had the duty, which they pulled about one night in five or one weekend in four, they were home with their wives for dinner by five-thirty or six.

While Vietnam could not be forgotten, its reality—the blood and terror and stink and nightmare memory—were all receding into the rarely examined past. Bill had nightmares, occasionally. Greg never admitted to bad dreams, even to himself, but he was becoming increasingly bitter about the people he considered to be traitors, the radicals of the Students for a Democratic Society who advocated the violent overthrow of the American government, and the high-profile, news-making celebrities like Joan Baez and Hannah Du-Plessey who openly sided with the enemy.

Greg still remembered with considerable bitterness that photograph he'd seen in Laos, the one with Haiphong Hannah seated behind the sights of a Russian-made antiaircraft gun, and her cheerful wish that she "had one of them in my sights right now."

And then there was that other photograph, the one with Marci . . .

Every once in a while, something happened to remind him of the war that was still underway, both back in Vietnam and in the streets and living rooms of Hometown, USA. The talk at the USC campus, one evening in mid-November, brought back a lot of the pain . . . and some of the pride in what he and the other SEALs had accomplished, as well.

Greg Halstead, resplendent in full dress whites—complete with his rack of medals from two tours hanging beneath the gaudy brass Budweiser on his chest—arrived at the campus at 9:30 with Wendy, Bill, and Pat, all in tow. He'd tried at first to warn Wendy and Pat off, but both women had insisted on hiring sitters to watch David and three-month-old Mark so they could come hear his talk. Frankly, he was damned glad of the support. As the appointed hour approached, he was getting more and more nervous. He could face VC and battle-hardened NVA regulars, but a classroom full of college students . . .

He wasn't entirely sure how he'd been talked into this dog-and-pony show. The Public Affairs Officer at Coronado had approached him, asking if he would like to participate in a program designed to increase understanding between returning servicemen and the civilian population. The question was one of those "have you stopped beating your wife?" jobs that could hardly be refused without coming off looking like Genghis Khan; he wasn't sure what one man could do or say to improve the antimilitary sentiments he'd been seeing so much of lately, but he was willing to give almost anything a try.

It seemed that a Professor Levinson at the University of Southern California was hosting a series of evening seminars, bringing in various speakers to discuss aspects of the war and the antiwar movement as a part of his sociology course. He'd already had a lieutenant from the college's ROTC staff address one session, as well as a woman known for her radical antiwar sentiments. Levinson, the PA officer explained, wanted to have someone who'd actually fought in Vietnam, preferably an enlisted man, address his group. Reluctantly, Greg had agreed.

"You don't think this is a little like moving into Indian country, do you?" Bill Tangretti asked as they walked into the lecture hall. The room was about half filled with students already, and Greg's uniform attracted angry glares and narrowed, suspicious eyes.

"Definitely hostile," Greg agreed. One tough-looking kid in ragged jeans and long, dirty hair caught up in a ponytail gave him a particularly challenging stare; he countered with a stare of his own, edging it with the cold and calculating expression of a man contemplating the fish he is about to gut and eat raw. The kid broke eye contact first, looking away with a nervous flutter to his eyelids.

"No worse than when you wear your uniform at the supermarket," Wendy told him.

"Don't sweat it, bro," Pat added. "You'll do fine."

"Well, I'm glad I have you guys in the tactical reserve. I just wish I could have brought along the *Iowa* for long-range firepower."

"Breathe on 'em, Twidge," Bill told him with a grin. "Your breath'd make a flamethrower wince."

"Thank you, Mr. Encouragement."

Professor Levinson, a small, earnest man in black goatee, horn-rimmed glasses, and elbow-patched sports coat, the very image of the serious Ivy League academic, advanced on the

SEALs and their wives as they stood uncertainly in the doorway. "Welcome, Mr. Halstead," he exclaimed. "Thank you so much for coming!"

"No problem, Professor." He'd met Levinson earlier in the week, when they'd set up the details for the seminar. "Good to be here."

That was a lie, he thought. He resolved not to tell any more this night. He did not plan to lead these people by the hand or tell them what they wanted to hear. Levinson had invited him to talk about what he believed about Vietnam, and by God he would talk about just that.

He honestly hadn't known whether to expect a large crowd tonight or not, nor had he been sure whether he would have been comfortable with a large crowd, or a smaller, more easily managed one. The place was fast becoming packed. Most of the crowd, he thought, were typical college students, more or less neatly dressed. There were some denim jackets, some sandals, some headbands, a few peace signs in jewelry or silk-screened T-shirts, a lot of long hair. Beyond the paraphernalia, though, there was little outward sign of radicalism or revolution.

But there was plenty of hostility here. The kid with the ponytail slouched in his seat, arms crossed, glaring at Greg with nothing less than hatred. A student who didn't look like he was old enough to drive filed in, stopped, turned grandly to display the Viet Cong flag crudely painted on the back of his leather jacket, then dropped into his chair with a sneer. As more and more students entered the room and found seats, Greg caught fragments of muttered conversation: "fucking fascists," "warmongers," "baby-killers."

He thought he knew, now, the meaning of the old Vaudeville term *tough house.*

Greg glanced toward the back of the room for reassurance. Pat and Wendy both smiled at him, and Bill threw him a jaunty thumbs-up. He was curious, though. Several seats down from his friends a man in a tweed sports jacket, thin, dark, obviously older than any of the students in the room, was making entries in a small notebook. Who the hell was he?

Professor Levinson gave the introduction. "Ladies, gentlemen," he began. "As part of its ongoing series of guest speakers exploring the social problems facing us today, the USC Humanities Department is pleased to present this forum for Electrician's Mate First Class Gregory Halstead, of the U.S. Navy. Greg is a member of something he calls 'Navy Special Warfare,' which, though I don't pretend to understand it all, does not involve serving on a ship.''

Greg had asked Levinson not to mention ''SEALs.'' Most Americans had never heard of the Teams, and those who had, through *Newsweek* and various newspaper articles over the past few years, tended to associate them with the Phoenix Program, as assassins, or with the CIA and their clandestine ops in Cambodia and Laos. More than anything else, though, he retained the old SEAL's reluctance to stick his head up in enemy territory. SPECWAR people survived by maintaining a low profile.

''Mr. Halstead has been in Vietnam for two, ah, tours, as he calls them,'' Levinson continued. ''He has seen combat, and I think we can all agree that it will be interesting to hear his side of the discussion, as to whether or not we should be in Vietnam in the first place. Greg?''

Surrounded by cold silence, Greg walked up to the front of the lecture hall. He'd been considering going up the steps to the podium but decided at the last minute to lean against the stage instead. If these people wanted a close-up look at a baby-killer from Nam, then, by God, he was going to give them one.

''I've been asked,'' he said slowly, ''to come here tonight and talk to you about Vietnam. I could stand up here, I suppose, and talk about honor, duty, and tradition . . . or I could talk about what I think we're accomplishing, or not accomplishing, in Vietnam. But . . . somehow I don't think that most of you are in the mood to hear a lot of propaganda or light-at-the-end-of-the-tunnel nonsense. I have a feeling that most of you are here because you have some pretty strong feelings about the war. I'd like to hear them. And, if you have any questions that you'd like to ask of someone who's been over there, I'll be glad to answer any that I can.

''So, let's just skip the propaganda and go straight to the questions. Anybody?''

For a long moment or two, the silence dragged on. The students had come here expecting to hear a lecture of some kind, possibly an apologetic for America's involvement in Southeast Asia. They'd obviously not expected to find the responsibility for saying something resting on them.

"Any questions?" Greg asked. "You *must* have *some* questions, or you wouldn't be here!"

He was hoping for one particular question, the question that seemed to be in every American civilian's thoughts lately. He'd given some thought to how he should reply. All he needed was the opening.

"Um . . . sir—" one long-haired girl in the second row began, her hand raised tentatively, as though she half expected Greg to bite it off.

Greg interrupted her with a grin. "Not 'sir,' miss. That's for officers. I *work* for a living." Surprisingly, there was a ripple of laughter through the room. "Call me Greg," he went on. "Or Petty Officer Halstead, if you'd rather. But I prefer Greg."

"Okay . . . uh . . . Greg. Uh, I just wanted to know, like, I mean . . ." She stopped, flustered. "I mean, did you ever *kill* anybody over there?"

There were a few titters from the audience, a handful of shocked gasps. Everyone in the room seemed to lean a little closer, waiting for his reply.

It was not the question he'd hoped for.

"Yes, miss," he said. "I am a Navy Special Warfare operative, and that's a five-dollar way of saying that, among other things, I am trained to engage the enemy in combat. I'm afraid the killing goes with the territory."

Her eyes grew very large. "How many? . . ."

His mouth hardened. "I really have no idea."

"Aw, come off it, man!" the student next to her, a man with a thin blond beard, broke in. "Don't you guys go in big for body counts, and all that?"

"Not necessarily. In Vietnam, you don't often even see the enemy, much less count him. The body count thing is mostly the Army, and in my opinion it's a damned stupid way of doing things. Battles are not won by just racking up numbers."

"What kind of things did *you* do over there?" someone else asked. "How did you know who to kill?"

"Yeah," someone else asked. It was the tough-looking guy

with the hair. "Did you take names out of a hat? Or just go in and kill everyone, like at My Lai?"

"As a Special Warfare operative, I was assigned various different types of missions. One op might involve finding a Communist 'tax collector' who was illegally extorting money from the people of South Vietnam in order to support his revolution. We would find him, capture him, and turn him over to the South Vietnamese authorities. If he and his men fought back, a firefight would develop, and the usual ending would be a dead tax collector. That was what was called 'direct action.'

"Lately, though, most of our missions have involved trying to rescue American pilots shot down in enemy-held territory, getting to them and getting them out before the enemy can capture them. That has resulted in a number of firefights, and a number of dead enemy soldiers."

A male student in glasses and a carefully tattered denim jacket rose in the back of the room. "Look, man, cut the shit! All we want to know is what the fuck we're doin' in Vietnam, right?" He looked around, as though searching for support from his side of the room. "I mean, right?" Several other voices chorused agreement.

"Yeah," the kid with the VC flag shouted out. "How come you people are in Vietnam in the first place, huh? Those people you murdered over there never did anything to us!"

Thank you! Greg thought fervently. It was the question he'd been hoping for. He turned to face the second speaker, leaning forward slightly, eyes cold. The silence in the room was startling, charged with an invisible but very tangible electricity.

"That," he said quietly, "is an excellent question. Why did you send us over there?"

The kid blinked, startled, looking as though he'd been slapped. "I . . . uh . . . *huh?*"

"*Why did you send us over there?*" Greg demanded, relentless. "How old are you?"

The kid blinked again. "Tw-twenty."

"As of July twenty-fifth of this year, you have the vote. You don't like the way the government is doing things? Change it. That is your Constitutional right. More than that, it's your Constitutional *duty.*"

"Yeah, but we weren't allowed to vote back in '68," a young woman called out. "You can't blame us—"

"Then why the hell do you blame *us?*" Greg shot back. "The military, I mean. Since I've come back home, I've had people spit on me, call me names, even assault me, right here in my own country. *I* didn't start the damned war. My friends in the service didn't start the war. My commanding officers didn't start the war. All things considered, all of us would have much preferred to stay here and go to school, get ordinary, well-paying, *safe* jobs, and enjoy being home with our families.

"Now I'm not here to go into the wheres and whens and whys, but the short version of the story is that the U.S. military went to Vietnam because the president said we had to, and Congress backed him up. We didn't want to go, but we did as we were ordered. And now I can ask you people something that has been on my mind for a long time.

"Why did you send us over there?"

"Yeah, man," a tall black student said. "Like, you was just followin' orders, right?"

"The *Nazis* were just following orders!" a white kid next to him called out. "Like with the SS and the death camps and everything!"

"The government of the United States of America," Greg rasped out, "is a democratically elected constitutional republic, a *representative democracy,* and as such has nothing in common with Hitler's Third Reich, beyond the obvious fact that both are governments. The citizens of Germany, thirty-forty years ago, let Hitler come to power through apathy and the effect of mob psychology, but once they had him, there was nothing they could do to get rid of him. You people are different. You have a say in how this country, and our government, are run.

"The people of the Soviet Union today . . . or of Red China, or of North Vietnam, for that matter, have little or no say in how *their* governments are run, who leads them, or what their government's foreign or domestic policies should be. The news is tightly controlled, so that people learn from the papers what they *should* believe, what the government *expects* them to believe, not what other people like themselves are thinking, saying, and doing."

"The people in Russia are freer than we are!" one woman cried out.

"*Are* they?" Greg asked her. "Are they really? Are they allowed to assemble, like this, and say what they genuinely think, the way we are now? Are there open forums for debate, like this one, where people with opposing views can meet and talk? Have you read *Pravda*? Do you have any idea how the 'news' printed in *Pravda* is formulated, assembled . . . then submitted for review by government censors, to make absolutely certain that there is no hint of criticism about the government?"

"We have censorship here," a student replied, angry. "The censors drove *The Smothers Brothers* off the air!"

That one stopped Greg cold. How do you compare the idiocies of network television censors with the cold-blooded malevolence of the KGB?

"To my way of thinking, censorship is when the authorities control your life so thoroughly, so completely, that they can even begin to try to control the way you think. That means suppressing all dissent. All expression of different ideas. That means that the only story you hear is the story the government wants you to hear. I'm afraid that I can't quite put the decisions of timid network executives who don't want controversy in the same class as the wholesale slaughter or exile of Christians, of Jews, of freethinkers, of people who dared to speak out, of people who dared to criticize their government.

"In the meantime, I still haven't heard an answer to my question. Why did you send us over there?"

"You pigs wanted the war!" one student wearing a big metal peace symbol on a chain around his neck shouted. "The military-industrial complex—"

"*Don't* give me that military-industrial complex shit!" Greg snapped back. "That's about as big a cop-out as there is! Look at me. I'm in military service. But like most servicemen, I'm married. I have a wife and a son. Do you for one moment imagine that I *wanted* to leave them?" He folded his arms, letting his gaze skim across the entire roomful of faces. "Before I joined the Navy, I was a college student, up at San Francisco State. I joined for various reasons, all personal, but I assure you that I did *not* join because I wanted to go to Vietnam!"

"But how can you blame *us* for sending you!" one mini-skirted girl said, leaning forward in her chair, her eyes glistening, on the verge of tears. "I didn't want you to go! None of us did! It's the *government* that—"

"The Congress of the United States," Greg said, paraphrasing slightly, "shall have power to provide for the common defense, to declare war, to raise and support armies, to provide and maintain a navy, to make rules for the government and regulation of the land and naval forces, to provide for calling out the militia in order to execute the laws of the Union, suppress insurrections, and repel invasions." He stopped and pursed his lips, a thoughtful expression. "That's from the Constitution of the United States of America. Article One, Section Eight. If you want to see who is responsible for Congress, check out Article One, Sections One through Five, right up there at the front of the document. In short, it says that you, the people, have the authority to choose who represents you in the government.

"So I'll ask you again, one last time. Why did you send me to Vietnam? I didn't want to go, I have no quarrel with the people over there. I don't like killing people, and I don't like the idea of them trying to kill me. Why did you send us?"

"The war is immoral!" the kid with glasses shouted. "And everyone who helps that war is immoral too! We should just get out, and let other countries settle their own problems! We shouldn't even have a military! Violence never settles anything!"

"Whoa," Greg replied. "Hold on there, Ace. 'Violence never settles anything'? If by 'violence' you mean 'war,' then I'd have to say that violence settled the fate of Nazi Germany rather pointedly, wouldn't you? Violence settled once and for all whether we were going to be a nation of slaveholders or free men. Violence settled whether or not we should be an independent nation, or a colony of Great Britain. Right or wrong, it determined whether we were going to populate this continent, or the Indians . . . whether the Normans would rule England, or the Anglo-Saxons." Greg had always loved history, and now he felt himself stretching out, getting on a roll. He loved this sort of debate. "Hell, violence has settled more issues than calm, rational discussion ever has! I'm not saying that the decisions were right, but the decisions *were* made.''

"That's not what I mean, and you know it!"

"You mean, I assume, that violence, or the *threat* of violence, doesn't settle moral issues. 'I'm right because I'm stronger than you' is not a valid logical argument.'' He shrugged. ''I could argue that a *lot* of moral issues have been decided by the winners of various wars. Slavery, for instance. Or the right of one people to herd people who look different or pray differently or act differently into gas chambers or slave camps." He glanced at Bill, sitting with arms folded at the back of the hall, between Pat and Wendy. "I could also argue about whether or not there is even such a thing as an absolute right or wrong. I'm not sure there is such a thing, though I know and respect people who believe that there is.

"You know, world peace is a wonderful idea. I, for one, would love to see the world disarm. I would love to see war be outlawed. Unfortunately, not everybody who shares this planet with us feels the same way we do. Maybe, someday, we'll outgrow this insanity and be able to beat our swords into plowshares, and all of that. But for now, the only way we can be sure our ideas about democracy and freely elected governments will survive in a world filled with, um, let's say, competing ideas about how governments ought to work is to maintain a strong national defense.'' He spread his hands. "Sure, I hear some of you wondering what a strong defense has to do with helping a government like South Vietnam. And, I have to admit, I don't know. That's not my job, figuring out the whys and how-comes of our foreign policy. And military professionals are not supposed to determine foreign policy. That's why MacArthur got fired in 1951. That's one reason why our form of government is better than the military juntas in South America, or the military-supported dictatorships in the Soviet Union or North Korea or North Vietnam. You civilians are my bosses. All of you. I work for you, follow your orders, do what you tell me, because that's my job.

"And I, for one, wouldn't have it any other goddamn way. . . .''

The hour, at last, was ended. The kid with the ponytail was sulking. The one with the VC flag looked uncertain, as though Greg hadn't quite fit his expected stereotype. The girl who'd asked if he'd ever killed anybody was arguing in hushed, angry tones with the guy who'd asked about body counts. Greg was pleased. It looked like some of the students were actually beginning to *think*.

"Great job!" Bill said, advancing down the aisle with a big grin. "And you didn't even need to kill any of them to make your point!"

"I think he did magnificently!" Wendy said.

"Mr. Halstead?" It was the sports-jacketed man that Greg had noticed earlier in the back of the lecture hall, extending his hand. "I enjoyed your talk. A lot."

"Thank you, sir. And you are?—"

"Ben Carmichael. I'm a reporter for the *New York Times.*"

"The *New York Times?*" Bill asked. "You're kind of a long way from your usual beat, aren't you?"

"Oh, the *Times* gets around. Actually, I'm helping to put together an article that's going to run in two weeks." He looked at the prominent Budweiser on Greg's chest. "You're a SEAL, right? Navy Sea, Air, and Land team?"

"That's right," Greg said guardedly.

He glanced at Bill, one eyebrow going up. Back in 1969, Bill had made some ill-considered comments to a reporter at Cam Ranh Bay. At issue had been the fact that Bill, a hospital corpsman—the Navy's equivalent of a medic—had been returning from an op carrying a Stoner light machine gun. He'd been rescued from certain embarrassment and possible outright trouble by no less a personage than Admiral Elmo Zumwalt. The admiral had unceremoniously ejected the reporter from what was supposed to be a secure area . . . but he'd given Bill a word of advice that both men had laughed about more than once since then: "Doc, *don't* talk to reporters!"

Bill, eyes twinkling, gave Greg a wink.

"I wonder," Carmichael continued, "if you would like to say anything about how the war is going."

"We're getting out," Greg replied with a shrug. "U.S. involvement is winding down. Most of our ground forces are out of there now. In fact, what was it, last August? The Secretary of Defense said that all ground operations in Vietnam would be conducted by South Vietnamese forces, from now on."

The reporter cocked his head and gave a half-grin. "Is that the way things really are over there?"

"What, you don't believe your own government?" Bill put in mischievously.

"Doc . . ." Greg began.

"I know, I know. Don't talk to reporters."

"And your name is?" Carmichael asked Bill.

"Bill Tangretti." He jerked a thumb at Greg. "I'm with him."

The reporter's eyes flicked down to Bill's civilian clothes, up to the scar on the side of his head, and back to meet his level gaze. "You're a SEAL?"

"I'm a *careful* SEAL. Which means I don't wear my medals in public, and I don't engage in public debates with college students."

"So, Mr. Halstead," Carmichael said, turning to Greg. "Mind if I ask you a few questions?"

"Not if you don't mind my not answering them."

"Fair enough. Are the SEALs still continuing operations over there?" Carmichael asked.

Greg considered how best to answer. Some information about NAVSPECWAR operations was necessarily secret. Other things, though, were a matter of public record. "There is one active SEAL platoon left in Vietnam now," he said. "That's Mike Platoon/Det Golf, SEAL Team One. They are due to rotate back to the United States in about three more weeks. There are no plans to replace them, so after 7 December, there will be no American SEAL direct action units left in-country."

That bland statement ignored the presence of special advisory detachments and the SEALs assigned to the ongoing Bright Light operations . . . but he couldn't talk about those.

"Pearl Harbor Day, huh?"

Greg smiled. "Hadn't thought about that. Yeah."

"So . . . what do you guys think? Did the United States make a difference over there?"

"I don't think South Vietnam would exist as an independent country today if we hadn't been there," Greg replied.

Carmichael made a note. "And with the United States pulling out, do you think South Vietnam will be able to defend itself?"

"That's up to Saigon and the South Vietnamese. Of course,

they've wanted to *win* their war a lot more than we have, it seems like."

"You don't think we've been allowed to win?"

"No, sir. I don't."

"You think we could've won if we'd . . . what? Been allowed to invade Cambodia and Laos? Invade North Vietnam?"

"I can't really comment on that, sir." He was already regretting the crack about not being allowed to win. While it was what he believed, it probably overstepped the bounds of what a man in uniform should say on the public record.

Carmichael paused, tapping the blunt end of his pen against the notebook. "You know, there's been a lot of criticism lately about how the war was managed, both by the high command and by Washington. You have any thoughts about that?"

Greg shook his head. "I don't really think I should comment on—"

"You mean like Johnson micromanaging things from the White House basement?" Bill asked, interrupting. "Or the stupid ROEs and the dumb regulations about what lines we couldn't cross and how we had to tell the bad guys in advance where we were going to be operating, and stuff like that?"

"Doc," Greg said, warning dripping from that single word.

"Well, hey! You're the one who was talking about freedom of the press, freedom of speech, and all of that just now!"

"Mr. Carmichael," Greg said quietly, "freedom of speech is all well and good, but for obvious reasons it's against the law for service personnel to make political statements while in uniform."

"Well, your friend here isn't in uniform, is he?" Carmichael said. "Tangretti, you said your name was?"

"I'd rather you not print my name," Bill said. "SEALs prefer to keep a low profile, you know?"

"No problem. I don't have to refer to you by name. But you said a moment ago that . . . what was it? You had to tell the bad guys where you were going to be? Now I'm not a military man, but that doesn't make sense."

Bill laughed. "Tell me about it! But it's true. For about the past year or so, all missions have had to be cleared in advance with both military and civil commands, and that means notifying the Vietnamese authorities. We have to tell them where we are going to operate and give them a general framework of when. Since both the Vietnamese government and their civil authority are . . . well, let's say, there are leaks in both of them. Lots of leaks, and they're all running north. There were times, and I'm not making this up, when Hanoi knew our plans before our own people had been briefed."

Carmichael's gaze shot to Greg. "Is that true?"

"No names?"

"No names."

"It's true."

"But . . . that means the enemy would know you were coming."

"That's *right!*" Bill said. He looked at Greg. "You know, this boy shows definite promise as a military tactician!"

Greg nodded. "You know, it was just amazing how, all of a sudden, the enemy either wasn't where he was supposed to be when we went in to catch him . . . or he was there with ten times our numbers, waiting in ambush. It was about that time that we decided there was no way we were going to win, no way we could even do our jobs. Our last month or so over there, we pretty much sat on our asses and watched the world go by."

"Went on patrols," Bill added. "Chasing mortar tubes."

"Chasing? . . ."

"Never mind. In-joke."

"But then . . . it's safe to say that you boys didn't like the way the war was being run?"

"We didn't like the way it *wasn't* being run," Greg replied. "If you're going to fight a war, then for God's sake, fight it. If you don't go in prepared to see the thing through to the end, then you might as well not bother going in at all."

The reporter was scribbling in his notebook. "Okay! Thanks a lot!"

"We have your name and know where to get you," Bill said, grinning, "if we don't like what you write!"

Greg wished that it could be that easy. He could mount a silent patrol deep in enemy territory, stage a deadly ambush, or rescue an American flier from certain death or capture.

Getting along with civilians, though, or the press, was going to take a whole new set of skills, and he frankly wasn't sure that he had what it took to succeed in this new and land mine–laden territory of public relations.

Chapter 27

Friday, 3 December 1971

Halstead residence, Balboa Park
0306 hours

The luminous dial of the bedside clock showed just past 3 A.M. when the phone rang, a harsh and raucous interruption to a warm and pleasant dream. Rolling onto his stomach, Greg Halstead picked up the receiver. "Hello?"

"Heyyy . . ." a voice on the other end said. "It's the baby-killer himself! You ain't so tough, tough guy. We just wanted you to know that we can get to that pretty little woman of yours any time we want. I think we're gonna wait until the next time you go overseas to kill more babies. We'll just come right up to your door and—"

Greg pursed his lips and gave a sharp, single whistle into the telephone mouthpiece, followed by two quick, mechanical-sounding clicks. The unusual sounds were enough to make the caller stop.

"This call is being monitored by agents of the FBI, working in cooperation with Bell Telephone," he said, putting a nasal edge to his voice and speaking in what he thought of as a federal-agent monotone. "Obscene and threatening phone calls are a violation of the law. Your number is now being traced and will be handed over to the proper authorities—"

There was a sharp click as the caller hung up.

Greg replaced the receiver and rolled over onto his back. In the next room Mark, wakened by the phone, started to cry.

Wendy stirred beside him, opening her eyes. "Oh, the
baby . . ." She started to sit up.

"Stay put, hon," Greg told her, lightly kissing her forehead. "You got him last time." She'd been up less than an
hour ago for Mark's semiregular 0200 feeding.

"Wha' time's'it?" she murmured.

"About three."

"What . . . was that *another* one?"

"Yeah. We'll see if the federal-agent gag slows them up
for a while."

"Jeez, you'd think even obscene phone callers had to get
some sleep sometime."

"Hm-hmm. I just wonder how they're getting our number.
It's not like we advertise in the Yellow Pages." Rising, he
padded into the baby's room, scooped up his son, and after
a dry-diaper check, he put the baby to his shoulder and started
softly singing.

> *When the Navy gets into a jam*
> *They always call on me*
> *To pack a case of dynamite*
> *And put right out to sea . . .*

This was . . . what? The tenth or twelfth night in a row,
now, that some jerk with a misplaced sense of humor had
called him or Wendy in the middle of the night. When Wendy
answered, the caller's comments had ranged from the frankly
obscene to the terrifyingly threatening. When Greg began answering, the caller usually called him "pig" or "baby-killer"
and threatened to hurt Wendy.

> *Like every honest sailor*
> *I like my whiskey clear.*
> *I'm a shootin', fightin', dynamitin'*
> *De-mo-li-tion-eer.*

And other SEALs at Coronado had been reporting the same
problem. More and more of them were getting similar threats
or just simple idiot nuisance calls. What he wanted to know
was how the hell civilians were getting hold of the home
phone numbers of Navy SEALs.

Lulled by the old "Song of the Demolitioneers"—a ballad first sung to the tune of the Georgia Tech anthem by the Navy SEALs' WWII frogmen predecessors—young Mark was soon asleep once more. Greg returned to bed, trying to slip in quietly to avoid waking Wendy again, but she reached out for him as soon as he was down and began moving her hands, slowly, restlessly caressing. He quickly forgot all about obscene phone calls . . . at least for the time being.

Tangretti residence, El Cajon
0536 hours

Bill Tangretti was up early—"zero-dark-thirty," as it was known in Navy circles. On days when he didn't have the duty at BUD/S, he was expected to be on the base at 0800 hours, which, with getting up, showering and shaving, and having breakfast, meant he had to get up at six.

Lately, though, he'd been trying to rise an hour earlier than that, slipping out of bed and coming out to the living room to pray, read the Bible, and . . . well, the people at El Cajon Four Square Gospel Church might call it "meditating on the Word of God," but he hadn't quite gotten to that point, yet. Meditating was something for hippies with a Zen guru, not for Christians—at least not the way Bill thought of the word.

He'd been having more and more trouble lately, though.

It was, he was finding, harder than ever to keep focused on Christianity, to hold onto that first, wild rush of joy and excitement he'd known when he'd first asked Jesus into his life. Somehow it had been easier in Vietnam, where just surviving a tour or a mission or a day was a problem. Now, with what amounted to a "normal" job, the sheer sameness of day-in, day-out routine seemed to be eating away at the foundations of his conversion.

He knew he could just go to church each Sunday, say the right words, put his tithes in the collection plate . . . but that was not what being born again was supposed to be about.

Bill wondered if he was just bored. It was possible, he supposed. Herding eighty or ninety-some tadpoles through the current BUD/S course wasn't nearly as exciting as being shot at.

Something heavy thumped against the front door, followed

a moment later by the tinkle of breaking glass and the sound of tires squealing on the pavement outside. Bill surged up from the couch; as he moved to the door, he could see the flicker of dancing firelight slipping through the curtains at the living room window, and his first thought was that the house was under attack.

He wasn't armed. All he was wearing was a pair of boxer shorts and a light robe, so he kept low as he pulled the door open, ready to go flat if the fire outside was a diversion aimed at getting him into someone's sights.

No gunfire greeted him. The front porch was covered with shards of brown glass, where someone had thrown a half-full bottle of whiskey against the door. Fire blazed on his front lawn; someone had spilled gasoline or some other accelerant there in the rough shape of a three-foot-wide swastika and set it ablaze. He pulled off his robe and used it to beat the flames down, smothering the fire before it had more than badly singed the grass.

Only then, with the fire out, standing there half-naked in the chilly, late-fall air, did the import of what had just happened strike home. Someone had just delivered a message, a *threat,* and one aimed very directly at him and his family.

In Vietnam, he would have returned fire. But here, in a quiet southern California suburb, safely tucked away in a secure corner of the United States, he didn't quite know how to respond.

Greg. He would see what Greg had to say. And the police, too, of course. Bill had been hearing stories lately about other SEALs getting hate mail, obscene phone calls, and other nuisance harassment.

Wadding up his scorched robe in one hand, he stalked back toward the house.

Mess hall
SEAL Training Center
U.S. Naval Amphibious Base
Coronado, California
1215 hours

Greg had never seen Bill this worked up. "Take it easy, Doc! You're gonna blow a gasket!"

Bill shook his head. "I don't get it, Twidge! You always used to be the hot-headed one, the one who thought these punks were traitors and ought to be shot. How come you're so cool and collected now?"

They were sitting at a table in the staff mess hall. Through the broad windows on one wall, the diners could look out over the BUD/S grinder, where a formation of newbie UDT/SEAL trainees in white T-shirts and green helmet liners were being put through their paces. The faint shouts of the instructors were just audible above the clatter of silverware, the buzz of conversation, and the bump and scrape of moving chairs.

Chow today was a choice of sliders or rollers—hot dogs or hamburgers, as they were known in the civilian world. The recruits outside, likely, would get a box lunch later, eaten in the comfort of a mud pit or while soaking at the edge of the surf.

Greg leaned back in his cafeteria chair, studying his friend. Bill had looked him up earlier that morning, telling him about the burning swastika incident, and suggesting that they have chow together. Greg had agreed.

"I'm *not* cool and collected, Doc," he replied after giving the question some thought. "It's the fact that we don't have a clear target. We don't know who these bastards are, so how are we supposed to take 'em down?"

"There's got to be a handle we can use. Look, I've been checking around with some of the other SEALs, the instructors, y'know?" Greg nodded, and Bill pushed ahead. "Some of them have been getting phone calls too."

"I'd heard some stories," Greg told him. "Any other criminal stuff?"

"Some. One chief said that some jerk threw a bag of garbage in his yard. Saunders said that someone pulled the old flaming dog shit gag on him. You know, doorbell rings, and when you open the door there's a paper bag burning on your porch? Stomp on it to put the flames out, and—"

"Yeah, but that's all nuisance stuff. Sounds to me like they're really out to nail you."

"Yeah. I'm trying not to be paranoid about it, but, yeah. . . ."

"Don't fight it, Doc. I always try to keep a good, healthy dose of paranoia available, for emergencies."

"You know," Bill said, "I can't help wondering if it's tied in with that damned newspaper story."

On 29 November, the story on SEALs and the war had appeared, as promised, in the *New York Times.* Neither Tangretti nor Halstead had been named, but their protest—that SEALs in Vietnam hadn't been allowed to win—had been broadcast loud and clear. Their specific complaint—that for the past year, SEALs had been required to clear their operations planning with the South Vietnamese civil authority and, therefore, with Hanoi as well—had struck an especially resonant chord. Numerous editorials and opinion pieces had been published in the week since, most of them calling into question the whole idea of America's reliance on a corrupt and incompetent ally.

The number of American deaths in Vietnam was pushing fifty thousand now. People were openly and repeatedly questioning whether even *one* American should die for the survival of a place like South Vietnam.

"You think that reporter is giving out our phone numbers?" Greg asked.

"I was wondering about it."

"Nah. How do you explain the other SEALs who've been harassed? I was wondering about that professor, Levinson, for a while. He had my number, got it from Public Affairs, but he didn't know yours. Anyway, that reporter seemed legit to me."

"Then what's the answer, Twidge?"

"Damned if I know. We're operating in an intel vacuum, though. We need more intelligence on the target."

Bill thought about this for a moment. "You know, if we could get that intel, what do you think we could do about it?"

"Let's take this just one step at a time, Doc. We need that intel. But we're going to need some high-powered help to get it."

"What'd you have in mind?"

"Not 'what.' 'Who.' An old buddy of ours, over in Personnel." When Bill looked puzzled, Greg grinned. "Didn't you hear? He's still Team Two, but they have him here on TAD while they put together a new Bright Light team. I hear he came in a couple of weeks ago. They put him in Personnel to keep him out of trouble.''

"Who the—'' Bill shook his head. "I mean, who are you talking about?''

"Our old swim buddy, Lieutenant Nolan. Let's trot over there and hear what he has to say. . . .''

Personnel Office
SEAL Training Center
U.S. Naval Amphibious Base
Coronado, California
1440 hours

The young woman at the desk in front of Lieutenant Nolan's office couldn't have been more than twenty years old, but she looked older with her long, flower-print skirt, her blond hair pulled back in a severe bun, and her wire-rimmed granny glasses. She was a civilian, one of the handful of government service workers in a room otherwise occupied by enlisted men in Navy whites. "You two can go in now," she told the two SEALs.

Bill nodded and stood, walking past her desk toward the lieutenant's office door. Greg stopped by her desk, a broad grin stretching his features. "Hey, what's a beautiful chick like you doing in a place like this?" he asked with cheerful directness.

The woman gave him a cold look. "God, can't you people think of a more original line than that?"

"Have dinner with me and I'll think of a better one."

She rolled her eyes, then swiveled her chair around to face her IBM Selectric. "Bug off, creep. I have work to do."

Bill was shocked, not at the woman's brush-off but at the fact that Greg had been handing her a line. "Twidge!" Bill said. "What the *hell* do you—"

Greg cut him off with a wave of his hand. "Later, Doc," he said. "The lieutenant's waiting."

Bill pushed open the door, thoughts whirling. Why in the name of Admiral Zumwalt would Twidge try to make a pass at Nolan's secretary? He'd thought everything was copacetic with him and Wendy.

Nolan looked up from his desk. "Hey, Twidge! Doc!

Christ, they'll let anybody walk into this place!''

"Afternoon, sir,'' Bill said. "Thanks a lot for seeing us.''

Greg grinned. "Howdy, Lieutenant. It's been a long time.''

"It has indeed. Sit down, sit down. What can I do for you two?''

"Partly a social call, sir,'' Bill told him. "Twidge here just told me today that you were in town.'' He looked around the tiny cubbyhole of an office, which was nearly filled by Nolan's desk and a couple of chairs. Books, most of them bound sets of Navy regulations, lined one wall. A gray plastic model of a guided missile frigate rested on a shelf. A framed photograph, showing Nolan in civilian clothes, cheek-to-cheek with a pretty, dark-haired woman, rested on his desk. "How do you like being a desk jockey?''

Nolan's face wrinkled with distaste. "God, don't remind me.'' He brightened. "Hey! You two interested in some action?''

"What kind of action, sir?'' Greg said. "Not another worm. . . .''

"No, not another worm. They have me here going through the service records of SEALs, looking for people to put on a Bright Light quick-response team.'' He picked up one manila folder from a stack of identical folders, then dropped it back again. "Shit, all SEALs are good. How do they expect me to decide which ones to choose? I'd rather go with guys that I've operated with.''

"What, is this another Nam deployment?'' Bill asked. Despite his more immediate worries, he couldn't help but feel a quickening of his pulse, a tingling excitement. *I am bored,* he thought wryly. *Pat would hate it if I went back, but . . . Lord, to get out of this place . . .*

"Not Nam,'' Nolan replied. "Okinawa. The Pentagon's getting real touchy about sending combat units *into* Vietnam when we're supposed to be drawing down. But the idea would be that we stand ready to go in whenever one of our flyboys is on the ground and in trouble.''

"Sounds cool,'' Greg said. "Is this a serious offer, sir?''

Bill looked at Greg with surprise. *Curiouser and curiouser,* he thought. *This is the guy that was telling those kids he didn't want to go over there.*

Nolan spread his hands. "As serious as it can be, under

the circumstances. My bosses are looking for a solid TO and
E by the end of the year. Deployment would be early next
year, sometime. He looked from one SEAL to the other, then
back again. "But somehow, I don't think you're here to volunteer for another overseas deployment."

"It'd be great if you'd keep us in mind, sir," Greg told
him. "We *are* interested. But you're right. We've got a problem, and we're thinking maybe you could help us."

"I will if I can. Somehow, I didn't quite buy the idea that
you guys were here on a courtesy call, flattering as that might
be. So, what's the word?"

"It seems that someone's declared open season on SEALs
and their families," Bill said. He began describing the phone
harassment and other incidents he and Greg had experienced.

And Nolan listened, his face creased by a deepening frown.

Tangretti residence, El Cajon
1453 hours

The phone rang, and Pat walked across the kitchen. *That'll
be him,* she thought. Bill had promised to call her that afternoon when he got a chance. She took the receiver down from
the wall. "Hello?"

"Heyyy, sweetheart," a muffled voice said "I keep wondering what you look like naked. I'm looking forward to finding out, y'know?"

Pat's breath caught in her throat. She felt a paralyzing fear
rising in her gut.

"We were watching you this morning when you went to
the A&P," the voice continued. "You look real good in those
tight jeans, baby. *Real* good!"

Involuntarily, her free hand dropped to her thigh, touching
the skin-tight fabric of her jeans. For a horrible, dizzying instant, she was afraid that she was going to fall. They were
toying with her, the bastards, telling her that they really did
know who she was, that they knew where she lived, that they
were *watching* her. . . .

"Damn it, who is this?" She was furious with herself as
soon as the words were out. As if this jerk was going to tell
her who he was!

"Heyyy, sweet cakes. I know you're hot for me. Don't fret,

baby. We'll be together soon enough. Maybe tonight, huh?''
The phone clicked sharply, and then she was listening to the
chilling buzz of a dial tone.

The doorbell rang.

She gasped . . . startled. Hanging up the phone, she stared
through the open door of the kitchen, through the large room
that served as both living room and dining room, at the front
door beyond, heart hammering. She didn't know whether to
answer, or . . .

She wished she had a gun. The laws for gun ownership in
California, however, were both strict and convoluted. Besides,
she'd never felt the need before this. She'd been taking Tae
Kwon Do lessons for a few months before she'd gotten too
pregnant with Davy, but that had been a long time ago, and
she hadn't even won her green belt.

Pat remembered, with a stark, crisp clarity born of rising
terror, the time three years back when she and Bill and Greg
had been jumped by a gang of toughs.

She felt safe when Greg or Bill was with her; she detested
the feeling of inadequate helplessness when they were gone.
It was the helplessness, more than anything else, she thought,
that left her feeling weak and sick, with a pounding in her
chest and a trembling in her knees that she simply couldn't
control.

Pat waited for a second ring of the doorbell, and when it
didn't come, she pulled a large carving knife from the wooden
knife block on her kitchen counter and advanced on the front
door as though it were an objective to be taken and held. As
she reached for the doorknob, conflicting thoughts assailed
her. What if it was a delivery man, and she opened the door
and he saw her standing there brandishing a kitchen knife?
Why hadn't she resumed her Tae Kwon Do classes after Davy
was born? God, he was just down the hall having his afternoon nap. How could she protect him? Wouldn't she be better
off not answering the door and taking the risk? What if there
were several of them, and they rushed her? . . .

Jerking the door open suddenly, she took a step back . . .
Then her gaze focused on what was there and she nearly
screamed. A dead cat, an orange-and-white tabby with a great
deal of blood matting its fur, was hanging by the neck from
the porch light fixture. A piece of paper had been safety-

pinned to the animal's side: BABY-KILLER had been crudely printed on the paper in red Magic Marker.

She took a step forward to cut the animal down, then stopped herself. She would call the police, let *them* deal with it, let *them* see what she was going through here, alone. Besides, she didn't want to disturb the . . . evidence.

At the same time, Pat was keenly aware of hostile eyes focused on her. She couldn't see anybody. Chatham Street was deserted except for a handful of parked cars, and there was nothing across the street but a small, open lot and, beyond that, some more tract housing. She didn't see anyone or anything out of the ordinary.

But they were watching her, gauging her reaction. She knew it, could *feel* it, and the very thought made her skin crawl.

She slammed the door, then slumped against it, eyes closed, breathing hard as she battled to bring her fear under control. Yes . . . she would call the police.

And then she would call Bill. She knew he couldn't stay home with her, but, well, right now she needed him, needed him more than she'd ever needed anyone in her life.

Personnel Office
SEAL Training Center
U.S. Naval Amphibious Base
Coronado, California
1503 hours

Bill was just wrapping up the telling of the swastika on his lawn when Nolan's phone buzzed. He picked it up. "Yes?" He listened for a moment, then said, "Very well. He's here. I'll put him on." He extended the receiver. "Doc? Your wife's calling for you."

Bill felt an unpleasant sense of disquiet as he accepted the phone. "Honey?" he said. "It's me. What's wrong?"

"Bill!" her voice sounded shaken, on the ragged edge of tears, fear, and fury. "Bill, there's . . . there's been another . . . another thing happen."

"Pat! Are you okay? What happened?"

Greg looked alarmed. "Bill! What—"

Bill held up a hand, commanding silence.

"There was another phone call," Pat's voice went on. "They . . . they've been watching me, Bill! Watching us! He told me what I was wearing, where I'd gone! I, oh, Lord Jesus! I feel so *dirty!* . . ."

"Pat! It's okay! It's okay, babe! Listen. Did you—"

"The doorbell rang right after I hung up. Bill, somebody hung a dead cat on the porch! And a sign saying 'baby-killer'! It was *awful.* . . ."

"Did you call the police? Pat? Did you—"

"Yes. Yes, I did." She wasn't crying, not quite. He could sense the struggle in her voice as she tried to hang on to what shreds of composure she had left. "I called the police, and they have someone coming out. But . . . but what can they do?" He heard the catch in her voice. *"Bill, what if they try to hurt Davy!"*

"You sit tight, Pat," Bill said. "Stay with Davy. Don't go outside. When the police come, you talk to them through the door. Make them show you their ID through the picture window. Got it?"

"Y-yes . . ."

"Make them show you their ID before you open the door. I'll be home in thirty minutes."

"Th-thank you, Bill. I, I'm sorry—"

"Nothing to be sorry about. Don't worry, it'll be all right. I love you."

"I love you."

He returned the phone to Nolan's hand. "I've got to get home. Now." In short, terse phrases, he told the two SEALs what had happened.

"You take off, Doc," Nolan said. "Your CO at the training center is Lieutenant Commander King, right?"

"Yes, sir."

"I'll call him and square it." He looked at Greg. "Twidge, you go with him. I'll give your CO a call too."

"I'd appreciate that, sir."

"Hey, SEALs stick together. Bill? You gonna be okay?"

Bill was hunched forward, his fists clenched, a black cloud swirling somewhere just behind his eyes. He could actually feel the rise of his blood pressure, a kind of hot, upward surge climbing his spine to his brain that set his ears to ringing. "I'm going to kill them," he said, in a voice so low and deadly that the others didn't catch the words at first.

"What was that, Doc?" Nolan asked.

"I said I'm going to *kill* the bastards," Bill said. He took a step forward, swaying a little bit. He had to reach out and catch hold of the corner of Nolan's desk to remain standing. *The unspeakable filthy shit-eating cock-sucking mother-humping bastards* . . .

Bill had battled to control his language ever since his conversion, but *this* . . . this was too much. Too much for him. Too much for God, if it came to that. He slammed his fist against the desktop, glorying in the nerve-steadying pain.

"Bill," Greg said, reaching out to hold Bill's shoulders. "Listen to me, buddy! These sons of bitches are pushing your buttons, okay? They're trying to make you crazy! Don't let 'em manipulate you that way!"

"They want manipulation?" Bill told him with a deadly fury in his voice. "I'll give 'em manipulation! I'm gonna track these bastards down and I'm gonna *kill* them! I'm going to take my K-Bar and carve them into bloody little pieces, one inch at a time!"

"Doc," Nolan said quietly. "Have you given any thought to the possibility that these people are trying to provoke an incident with the military?"

"I don't think he's giving any thought to anything, Lieutenant," Greg said. "Except possibly justifiable homicide."

"Nothing justifiable about it," Nolan snapped. "Doc, if you find these people and do something stupid, man, I can see the headlines now. 'Berserk SEAL attacks civilian.' Doc, you've got to think about your career, and you've got to think about the Teams.

"You kill somebody, Doc, or even just beat the shit out of them, and you could hurt a lot of shipmates. There are people in the media who'd just love to climb all over an elite military unit like the SEALs. And there are some who'd love a chance to make up some kind of My Lai incident."

Greg shot Nolan a sharp look. "You think maybe that's what's happening here? They're trying to make Doc start a riot?"

"I don't know anything," Nolan replied. "But, damn it, that's the problem. We're operating in the dark. We need intel."

"That's really why we came to see you, sir," Greg told him. "I've got kind of an idea on how we could get a lead on these bastards. But we're going to need some help. Some gold-braid help, I mean."

Nolan nodded. "You can count me in. What do you need?"

"Look, let me get Bill home, and make sure everything's all right there, okay? But I'll come back before you wrap up tonight. I'd like to talk to you about something."

"I'll be here. Or give me a call, if you can't come back in."

"Thank you, sir." He hesitated. "Ah, you won't tell anybody about this, will you?"

Nolan's eyes narrowed. "You thinking security?"

"Someone's giving out phone numbers, sir. We don't know who, but they must have access to this base, or someone on base. I think we ought to mount our own little intel op, and find out just where the leak is."

"I couldn't agree more, Twidge," Nolan said. "Go on. Get him out of here."

"Aye, aye, sir."

For Bill, it was a grim and fearful drive home.

Tangretti residence, El Cajon
2240 hours

He lay on his belly in the chill of the December evening, black clad and invisible in the shadow beneath the parked car. More times than he cared to remember, he'd waited on ambush somewhere, unmoving, waiting for the enemy to come to him.

Greg had never expected to have to pull a waiting op in California, though. Not one that wasn't a part of a training exercise.

There was, of course, no guarantee that the enemy would strike tonight. The anonymous voice on the phone call to Pat had suggested that they might do something tonight, but that could just as easily be a part of their mind-fuck routine, a way to keep their victims off-balance, confused, and fearful. The only way to counter this kind of assault was to mount a silent, invisible watch. He would stay here on the ground all night, if he had to . . . and if nobody showed, he would be back tomorrow night . . . and the night after that, for as long as it took to get the intel they needed.

He was used to long waits.

Greg was treating this exactly like an op in Nam. The enemy, he reasoned, wouldn't be as well trained, as alert, or as dangerous as North Vietnamese regulars, perhaps, but the chance for slipups and mistakes always increased whenever amateurs were involved, and he could counter the unpredictable nature of *this* enemy only by being thoroughly prepared and completely professional.

For the stakeout, then, he was clad completely in black, from the wool cap on his head to the black coral shoes on his feet. He hadn't blackened his face—he reasoned that if he should be spotted by a member of the El Cajon Police Department, he could talk his way out of trouble more easily if his face wasn't covered with black paint, but he could keep the shine off his face by keeping the cap pulled low, and by smearing a bit of grease on his cheeks beneath his eyes.

He was unarmed, except for a single tenpenny nail. Again, if he was picked up by the police, he didn't want to add a weapons violation to his dossier. Something like that would certainly result in a captain's mast and, possibly, being kicked out of the Teams . . . and that on top of whatever fines or jail time he racked up with the civil authorities.

He had a Motorola holstered in his combat vest. The channel was open. Pat and Wendy had another, inside the house, Bill carried one on his patrol in the back of the house, and Lieutenant Nolan had a fourth with him in his car, as he waited out the night in the parking lot of a church just up the street. Nolan had arranged for them to get the radios, as well as the combat vests and some of their other equipment. They were probably breaking half a dozen regs by borrowing the radio gear for this sort of op, and a dozen more by using it to carry out a covert surveillance of civilian suspects, but this was for a brother SEAL and his family, and there wasn't a whole lot that Greg wouldn't do for Bill or for his sister.

On the off chance that the bad guys had his Chevette IDed, he'd rented a car that afternoon, a Ford Mercury, and left it parked on the street almost directly across from Bill's mailbox. That car now provided cover for his stakeout. He was lying flat on the pavement beneath the chassis, watching the front of the Tangretti house.

Bill was watching the back, but, in Greg's opinion, the attack was more likely to come from the front. The bad guys would want to be able to make a fast getaway, and that meant a vehicle; Bill's yard backed up against someone else's yard on the other side of a six-foot-high redwood fence, and he didn't think it likely that the enemy would try coming over that.

Bill had felt the same way and argued that he should take the watch out front. Greg had refused, claiming that it was his idea. Privately, he still wasn't sure how Bill was going to react once he confronted these people. With Pat threatened, any semblance of Christian love and forgiveness had vanished, replaced by a cold and murderous fury Greg had never seen in his friend even in the middle of combat.

Especially in the middle of combat. Firefights were won by people who kept their cool, not by berserkers, not in this day and age.

He *felt* the approaching vehicle first, as a kind of prickling in that vague awareness of his surroundings that many SEALs attributed to a sixth sense. A moment later, he heard it, then saw the pickup truck drive by, cruising slowly. From his vantage point, flat on the pavement beneath the car, he couldn't see the driver or his passengers, but he was pretty sure that several people were riding on the truck's flatbed. The vehicle slowed, almost coming to a stop, then picked up speed again, driving west to east down Chatham Street.

"Night Owls, this is Night Owl One," Greg said into his radio. "Red candle. Over." They'd worked out a series of code phrases, against the slight possibility that the targets were using a shortwave radio scanner, or the much better chance that a local police cruiser might pick them up.

"Want me around front? Over." Bill's voice was tight and hard.

"Negative, Night Owl Two. Stick to the plan. Over."

"Rog."

A vehicle approached from the west again. Shifting position slightly, Greg managed to get a look at it as it approached, the same pickup, coming down Chatham Street with the headlights out. The driver must have looped around the block after making his first pass, and now he was coming in for the attack.

"Night Owls, Night Owl One. Red torch. Stand by."

The truck pulled up in front of the Tangretti house, and this time it stopped. Three sets of feet landed on the pavement a couple of yards away from Greg's hiding place as the people in the back of the truck vaulted onto the street. "C'mon! C'mon, man!" someone rasped. "Let's do it!"

A cat yowled.

Greg eased far enough out from beneath the rental car to see what was happening clearly. Two tough-looking men in their late teens or early twenties were on the sidewalk, huddled around Bill's metal mailbox, while a fourth sat in the pickup's cab behind the wheel. The people on the sidewalk seemed to be wrestling with a large cat. "Ow! Son of a bitch nailed me!" one cried.

"Shut up, Slicker! Just *do* it!"

The pickup looked like a Ford. The license plate read CS39B.

Like a shadow, Greg slipped belly-flat across the street, rising to a crouch just behind the pickup's left-rear fender. Positioned in the driver's blind spot, and hidden by the truck itself from the three on the sidewalk, he reached up quickly with the nail and punched the tip, hard, through the red plastic of the pickup's left taillight. When he pulled the nail out, it left a neat, small hole through which the light inside gleamed like a tiny, brilliant white star in the center of the much larger red glow.

Dropping to his belly again, he rolled back beneath the Mercury. The men on the sidewalk were stuffing something inside the mailbox. He heard the lid bang shut, the muffled screech of the cat. A match flared . . . and then the mailbox went up in a gush of gasoline-fed flames, lighting up the peaceful neighborhood. The cat shrieked and squalled and howled in hell-tortured agony, slamming itself against the inside of the box, then, mercifully, went silent as the fire continued to blaze. The truck was already rolling forward as the three kids ran after it, grabbed the tailgate, and leaped on board. He heard them laughing and hooting as the truck suddenly accelerated, racing down Chatham Street, the white star clearly marking the left taillight.

"Night Owl Three, Night Owl One!" Greg called. "Target is headed east on Chatham. We've got a clear mark, left rear. License Charlie Sierra Three Niner Bravo."

"Roger that, One," Lieutenant Nolan's voice replied. "I'm rolling." Seconds later, Nolan's white Impala flashed past at high speed, racing after the target.

Greg rolled out from under the car just as Pat and Wendy emerged from the house, Pat with a blanket, Wendy with a small CO_2 fire extinguisher. "You call the police?" he asked.

"Yes," Pat told him. "They said they'd have a car here right away."

"I'd better change, then." He stood guard a moment longer, though, as Wendy put the fire out with several bursts from the fire extinguisher. Then, with the fire out and no sign of watchers or further attack, he pulled off his wool hat and started for the house.

The fire trucks arrived ten minutes later, and the police a few minutes after that. By that time, there was little more to do except show the cops the horribly burned body of the now-dead cat inside the charred mailbox and give them the note Wendy had found thumbtacked to the fence nearby. It was a crudely spelled and worded document, melodramatically created by pasting letters painstakingly cut from newspapers and magazines to make a kind of psychedelic flyer.

HERE IS A DEAD BABY LIKE SEALS KILLED.
FUCK SEALS AND FUCK SEAL BICH WHORES!
TELL YOUR PIG WELL FUCK U & BURN YOUR HOUSE
AND YOULL LOOK LIKE WHAT WE LEFT U IN THE MAIL!
WE KNOW WERE YOU LIVE, BABY!

"Well, we'll look into it, sir," the police officer told Bill. "But I wouldn't hold out too much hope. I called in that license you got. It was reported stolen off a car in San Diego this afternoon. By now, the truck has its real plates back on, and the stolen ones have been ditched someplace."

"Officer," Bill said, "these bastards are threatening to kill my wife!"

"I know, I know . . . but until we have anything more concrete, I can't classify this as anything more than malicious mischief. I'll tell you what, though. I'll put a request through to have a black-and-white come by every hour or two, just to check up on you. And you just have to call, and we'll be here like that." The cop snapped his thumb and forefinger, by way of demonstration. Greg thought that a mild exaggeration. In the ten minutes it had taken the police to arrive this time, Bill and Pat could both have been dead, and their house half burned to the ground around their bodies.

The policeman started to turn away, then stopped, turning to face them again. "You guys are military, aren't you?"

"Navy," Bill told him.

"Nam?" There was something about the way he said it that suggested that he'd already guessed, somehow, from Halstead's or Tangretti's attitudes or voices or demeanors, that they'd spent time in-country. Often, you *could* tell, just by talking to a guy.

"That's right," Greg replied.

The cop shook his head. "Me too. Fourth Marines. I was in Danang, '67."

"We just got back from the Big D last spring," Bill said.

"Hey, no kidding? Arizona Territory still there?" The name referred to a large stretch of terrain west of the city, heavily infiltrated by the enemy.

"Still there. We did a fair amount of mortar-tube hunting out that way," Greg told him. "I guess we chewed some of the same dirt, huh?"

"Sounds like. Navy, huh? But not blackshoe."

"That's a roger."

The cop nodded, thumbs hooked into his gunbelt. "Look, guys, I wish I could help you. I really do, one vet to another, y'know? But unless we can catch the culprit doing the dirty deed, well, we're kind of hamstrung officially, y'know?"

"We understand," Greg told him.

"You know, we have a lot of service families out here. There's not been much trouble before now, but, well, for the last year or two, there've been a lot of incidents. Lots of people take it out on the homecoming vets. It's not right, but there's not much that can be done. Officially."

"Used to be, the homecoming vets got a parade, and maybe the keys to the city," Bill said. "Now it's firebombs and dead cats in the mailbox."

"Well, keep your eyes peeled, and give us a call if you

see anything suspicious. We'll catch these guys if we can."

"You'd better, Marine," Bill said. "These guys threatened my family. They come after them, I'm going to—"

Greg laid a hand on Bill's shoulder. "Easy there, Doc."

The cop looked at Bill, eyebrows going up. " 'Doc.' You a corpsman? A pecker-checker?"

"Yeah."

"A corpsman saved my ass during a rocket attack, in '67. Well, Doc, you do what you have to do. Just be careful, okay? Out here, from my vantage point, *you* guys are the civilians, and I don't want to have to call for a body bag for you."

"We hear you, officer," Greg told the man.

An hour later, the two SEALs and their wives were in the Tangrettis' living room.

"Look," Pat was saying. "I . . . I really don't know about this. I mean, you're breaking the law!" She looked from her husband to her brother. "How can you guys even *think* about this? Greg! You're the one who stood up in front of all of those college students last month and told them about the Constitution, about how the military was subordinate to the civil authority!"

Greg sighed. "I don't like it any more than you do, sis. But, well, you heard what the police said. They can't do anything, except send a squad car past every once in a while."

"Fat lot of good that'll do," Bill added. He was sitting on the sofa, leaning over the coffee table. He'd spread out a newspaper and was disassembling a .45 Colt automatic.

"If you ask me," Wendy said, "they don't *want* to help."

"Actually, hon," Greg replied, "I think that cop was kind of telling us he was going to look the other way."

"God, Greg, how can you say that?" Wendy wanted to know.

"Oh, just a feeling. Letting us know he was a Marine, and a Nam vet. Reminding Bill of the relationship between Navy corpsmen and the Fleet Marine Force, which is a damned special one. Emphasizing the word 'officially.' I think he was as much as telling us that if we could catch these bastards, we had his permission to beat the shit out of them."

The doorbell rang. After a frozen moment, Wendy went to answer it, with Greg standing just behind the door with a drawn Smith & Wesson 9mm automatic. It was Lieutenant

Nolan, wearing civvies and a light nylon jacket. "Success!" he said, walking into the living room with a broad grin on his face.

"You found where they live?" Bill asked, wiping down the Colt's receiver with a gun oil-soaked rag.

"Sure did." He looked at Greg. "Your idea with the tail-light worked like a charm, Twidge. I slipped in behind them just down the street here and had no trouble spotting them from half a block back. The back of their truck might as well've had a neon sign hung over the tailgate. I was able to stay way behind them all the way onto the Fletcher Parkway, and they never knew they were being followed." He pulled a slip of paper out of his jacket pocket. "I followed 'em straight to an apartment complex in La Mesa. Here's the address. I also watched while they pulled the license plates off their truck and put new ones on. The old plates went into a dumpster in the parking lot."

"You know which apartment they're in, sir?" Greg asked.

"Not yet, and we don't know that they all live in the same place. But now that we have their real license number, I'll be able to call in a favor from a buddy of mine who works down at the DMV. We should be able to have their address by Monday afternoon. *Then* we can go to work on these clowns."

"You know, sir," Bill said, "it might not be too good of an idea for you to be mixed up in this any more. I really appreciate your helping out tonight and getting the address and everything, but after that, maybe it would be better if you didn't—"

"Belay that, Doc," Nolan replied. "We're SEALs."

Pat stood up suddenly, her face rigid with the attempt to chain her emotions. "I don't *believe* this!" she said.

"Pat—" Bill said, but she brushed him aside.

"David Nolan, how can you even consider such a thing?" she demanded. "Greg, just think about what you guys are thinking about here! Beating these creeps up is one thing, but you guys are talking about kidnapping and assault, and I don't care what the cop was telling you, he wasn't giving you per-mission for *that!* You could all end up in jail for, I don't know, *years!*"

"That's only if we get caught, babe," Bill told her. He

punched in the slide stop on the .45, drew the slide to check the action, then released it with a loud *snick*. "And we're not going to get caught. We're SEALs, remember?"

"How the hell do you expect me to forget?" Pat turned away angrily and stalked from the room. Wendy hesitated, then followed her, leaving the three SEALs alone.

Bill started to go after them, but Greg caught his arm. "Let her go, Doc. She'll be okay."

"I do wish I knew we were doing the right thing, Twidge."

Greg looked at his friend in surprise. This was a startling change from Bill's earlier black fury. "Your initial blood lust worn off, Doc?"

Bill turned to face him, his expression unreadable. "I still want to kill the bastards," he said. "It's like, well, if they'd just come after me, I know I could've handled it, y'know? Like those punks we took down in San Francisco, a couple years back."

"I remember."

"But this cowardly shit, going after me by going after Pat. I didn't know how to deal with it. I still don't. At first, all I wanted to do was get my hands on them, and fuck the consequences. But when I see how torn up Pat is, I just, well, I don't know what's right, what's the right thing to do."

Greg shrugged. "I don't see much option, do you? We've got to neutralize the threat."

"He's right, Doc," Nolan added. "This is something the authorities just aren't equipped to handle, not until *after* a crime is committed."

"Right," Greg agreed. "We could ignore it, and run the risk of something very bad happening to Pat or Wendy or both of them. We could turn it all over to the cops and, if we're very, very lucky, the bad guys might get caught, and one or two of them might get handed, oh, say, a year in jail for making terroristic threats or committing malicious mischief. And a year later, they're back, and they're looking for revenge.

"Or we do it like we planned it. Are you still with me?"

"Yeah. I'm with you, Twidge. All the way."

"Your, ah, beliefs aren't going to get in the way?"

Bill looked as miserable as Greg had ever seen him, but he spread his hands. "The Bible says, 'Vengeance is mine, sayeth the Lord.' But, you know, there's nothing in the Bible at all that says God can't get a little help from time to time in the vengeance department. Like from the U.S. Navy SEALs. . . .''

Chapter 28

Tuesday, 7 December 1971

Brandenburg Apartments
La Mesa, California
0035 hours

Four days had passed since they'd traced the ''Happy Hippies,'' as the SEALs had taken to calling their harassers, to this apartment complex in La Mesa. Nolan's friend at the California Department of Motor Vehicles had come through with a name and an address by Monday afternoon, as promised, though by that time they were pretty sure that they'd identified the bad guys' apartment simply by keeping track of the traffic going in and out the building's doors. The information from the DMV confirmed their legwork.

Calmly, Greg sat in the front seat of Lieutenant Nolan's car and studied the building through his binoculars. It was a typical four-story apartment building, one of a complex of perhaps a dozen identical structures constructed of pale tan brick in two wings around a central lobby. The lobby had two entrances, front and back, which were always kept locked. Residents used a key to get in, while visitors could buzz the intercom to be admitted. There were also locked doors at the outer ends of each wing, while the ground-floor apartments had small patios off of sliding glass doors.

Each apartment had a big, sliding glass door, the ones above the ground floor opening onto railed balconies. There were also two regular windows for each apartment, which, according to a map acquired from the Brandenburg Apartment Office, were bedrooms.

The SEALs' survey of the objective located the right apartment—4-A—on the west wing, fourth floor, all the way at the end away from the lobby. It had been rented to one Barry Slidell, who also, according to the DMV, happened to be the registered owner of the Ford pickup Greg had tagged during his late-night stakeout. Watching from different cars parked at different times in the large lot behind the apartment, the SEALs decided that there were at least three men in 4-A. The men were code-named Moe, Larry, and Curly. Slidell, as it happened, was Moe.

A number of other men, and women as well, came and went on a semi-regular basis, so many over the course of the weekend, in fact, that the watchers were convinced that the apartment was being used as some sort of combination commune and crash pad for half of the turned-on generation of the San Diego area. They'd tried to get close enough to identify some of the visitors, but that hadn't been possible without the risk of giving away the fact that the apartment was under surveillance.

Lieutenant Nolan had gotten pretty close, though, by the simple expedient of dressing nicely and walking in on the coattails of someone who'd let himself in with a key. A cheerful "good morning," it turned out, was enough to gain admission to a building that was theoretically concerned with security. He'd gotten as far as the door to 4-A, listening from outside to the thump of rock music inside . . . and to verify that the central hallway of the wing was too heavily traveled to risk sending an assault team in by the front door.

There were other ways, however, for enterprising SEALs.

In a final planning session Monday evening, Halstead, Tangretti, and Nolan had decided to hit the place that night, after midnight. The two enlisted SEALs had made a final trip to the base to pick up some necessary equipment, then rendezvoused with Nolan in the parking lot immediately behind apartment 4-A.

"I've been watching all evening," Nolan told the two SEALs when they joined him. "Nobody's come in or out on this side, though visitors could have come in out front."

"Do we have a good idea how many are living there?" Greg wanted to know. "We're pretty sure about Moe, Larry, and Curly, but with the traffic we've seen, there could be an army up there."

"I considered talking to the apartment management," Nolan said. "But I didn't want to attract too much attention to apartment 4-A, if you know what I mean."

"Probably smart."

"Besides, the management might not know how many are sharing that pad," Tangretti added.

"True," Nolan said. "What I did do was get a name—Civiglietti—off the mailbox for apartment 3-A, right underneath. You remember I heard rock music playing real loud through the door when I checked out the passageway, the other day? I called the office, claimed I was Mr. Civiglietti, and asked who the hell lived upstairs, because they were making so much noise."

Tangretti gave a cold chuckle. "Nice dodge, sir. They tell you anything?"

"Not much, and I couldn't push very far. They said the apartment is rented in the name of Slidell, but then, we already knew that. The manager just said something like, 'Those kids playing their music at all hours again? I'll look into it.' Kind of suggests that all three must crash there, but it doesn't tell us how many there are in all."

"I wish we could keep them under observation a bit longer," Greg said, looking up at the corner apartment. "Maybe get a listening device up there so we could hear 'em talking, learn how many are there, maybe even hear what they're planning."

"That's a negative," Tangretti said sharply. "I am not cutting these people any slack. I am *not* giving them one more chance to threaten Pat. You hear me?"

"I hear you, buddy," Greg replied. He was worried, though. Yeah, the threat against his sister and his best friend had made him madder than hell, but for a while there, he'd thought Tangretti had lost it completely. He'd started off by just plain going ballistic. Then he'd wavered a bit, when Pat had questioned what they were doing. And now, during the past several days, Tangretti seemed to simply burn with a deep, dark, barely controlled fury that was more frightening than his initial blind rage. In his current state of mind, Doc seemed perfectly capable of taking a LAW out of the SEAL armory at Coronado and blasting that corner apartment to bits.

At least this way, with the stakeout and the promise of a raid, Greg felt he'd reined in Tangretti's wilder side. The op would make certain that no one—not innocent bystanders and not the Happy Hippies themselves—would be killed.

He was just damned glad that Nolan saw things the same way he did, and was willing to help. The lieutenant's help had been invaluable in their getting some time off these past few days, and for securing the equipment they needed from the SEAL armory on base. He'd also performed the soft recons of the target and done more than his share of OP duty here in the parking lot.

"So, you boys ready to rock 'n' roll?" Nolan asked.

"All tuned up," Greg replied.

"I still wish I was coming with you."

"Sir, with all due respect," Bill said from the backseat, "that is one dumb-ass stupid fucking idea. If the two of us get into trouble and get caught, well, it'll mean a mast for sure, and probably a general court, maybe even jail time, but the consequences would be a lot worse for an officer. Hell, you guys are supposed to know better!"

"That's a big affirmative, Lieutenant," Greg added. "You're already taking a hell of a chance with your career just being out here with us. We don't want you to go down with us if we get busted."

"Oh, I understand all of that," Nolan said. "And I agreed to it when we were planning this thing. I just wish I could help with the breaking-and-entering bit. Sounds like fun."

"You just pull lookout duty, like we worked it out, sir," Greg told him. "And give us a holler if things go wrong out here."

While Nolan was wearing civilian clothes, both enlisted SEALs were again clad in black, with combat harnesses and radios. They wore black woolen ski masks over their heads, arranged so that only their eyes and mouths showed . . . more for the sake of disguise than for camouflage. Greg didn't intend to kill anyone, but that meant that the victims of tonight's raid might be able to pass on a description of the raiders to the police, and while Tangretti seemed beyond caring now,

Greg wanted to at least try to preserve his career in the Navy and his clean slate with the local police.

Greg looked at Tangretti, questioning, and the other SEAL gave a short, hard nod. Tangretti drew his Hush Puppy, leaned against the side of the car, and braced the heavy muzzle over his jacket-clad forearm. He took careful aim, squeezing the trigger slowly . . . and then the weapon snapped off a harsh chuff, and at the same instant, the streetlight casting a revealing glare across this side of the apartment complex parking lot flared and died in a shower of broken glass.

"Nice shot," Greg commented, as they waited to see if there was any response from the surrounding buildings.

"I didn't think I was going to have to turn vandal, Twidge."

"Hell with it. Jesus and Con Ed'll both forgive you."

"Well, Jesus will, anyway," Tangretti said, holstering the weapon. "C'mon. Looks like everybody's asleep."

Together, they trotted across the narrow strip of grass between the building and the parking lot. With the streetlight gone, it was comfortably dark on this side of the building. Greg reached the wall first, explored it gently with one gloved hand, then crooked his knee, placed the right toe of his black canvas coral shoe into the groove between two layers of bricks, reached up with both hands for a ten-finger hold above, and hauled himself up.

It was a slightly easier climb than his scaling of the hotel wall at his wedding. The bricks didn't offer much of a purchase, but he was deliberately climbing between the stack of balcony porches and bedroom windows, which gave him sills and decorative woodwork and the cement slabs of the balconies themselves to work with. With carefully considered and tested climbs and reaches, he went up the wall like a large, black spider. Tangretti followed, preferring the less dramatic approach of chinning himself on the balcony slab, scrambling up to stand on top of the black iron railing so that he could reach the next balcony slab above, and repeating the process. With the streetlight out, the two black-clad men were nearly invisible as they moved up the wall, from balcony to balcony, all the way to the top.

In less than two minutes, both SEALs silently stepped over the railing on the fourth-floor balcony. It was just before

0100, and they could still hear the thump of a stereo bass blasting away at a rock tune coming from inside. Damn, Greg thought, how did the neighbors sleep with all of that racket going on? Nolan's trick with the phone call about the noise had been right on the money.

Their first move was to spill a length of black nylon line from a canvas pouch that Tangretti had carried strapped to his back. Greg secured a small pulley to the iron railing on the balcony, and Tangretti fed the end of the line through it, dropping one end over the rail to the ground.

The two black-clad intruders then stepped up to the sliding door. Tangretti tried the handle, and verified that it was locked. No problem. Greg pressed a large suction cup with a handhold against the glass next to the door's handle, while Tangretti pulled out a glass-cutter wheel and dragged it around the suction cup's outside rim. Though such equipment was not normally a part of the SEAL TO&E in Vietnam, the Teams also trained against the possibility of dealing with enemies in more civilized regions, like Europe, and there were buildings with glass doors in Vietnam, even if most hooches in the boonies didn't even have glass in the windows.

Tangretti finished the cut, and Greg lightly tapped on the glass; the circle popped free with a faint click, pulling free while still attached to the suction cup, and the sound of rock music from inside suddenly seemed louder.

The two SEALs drew their pistols and braced themselves. Tangretti did a silent countdown with his fingers: *three . . . two . . . one . . . now!*

Greg reached through the opening with one hand, unlocked the sliding door, then dragged it wide open, stepping through the doorway, brushing past the long green curtain hanging across the opening. Sound assaulted his ears, the hammering beat of heavy rock music. The room was dark except for the acrid purple glow of a black light on top of a stereo cabinet; the air was thick with the sweetish stink of marijuana.

The only lighting came from scented candles and the harsh, violet flicker of a UV apparatus illuminating a psychedelic, black-light poster on one wall. Two young men in blue jeans and sandals, with long dirty hair and scraggly beards, were sprawled in beanbag chairs on opposite sides of the room, Moe to the left, Curly to the right; a pretty teenaged girl,

stripped down to panties and bead necklaces, danced eroti-
cally to the pounding music on the carpet between them,
while a second young woman, still fully dressed, snuggled on
Moe's lap, her arms around his neck and her mouth locked
over his.

The inside of the apartment was a mess, with beer cans,
empty bottles, candy wrappers, and cast-off articles of clothing everywhere. Ashtrays scattered about the floor held still-
burning, hand-rolled joints, and a faint bluish haze of smoke
hung near the ceiling. Someone had spray-painted MAKE
LOVE, NOT WAR across the wall opposite the sliding door, and
Greg wondered what the apartment's management would
have to say about *that.*

As the SEALs stepped into the room, the dancer clapped
her hands to her mouth and vented a shrill, short scream. Moe
stumbled up to his feet, sending the girl in his lap sprawling
on the carpet; Curly, a beer clutched in his hand, just sat and
stared at them with a vacant, glassy expression that suggested
too many beers, too many tokes, or both.

"Down on the floor, face down!" Tangretti snapped, holding the pistol in a two-handed grip. "All four of you! Now!
Arms and legs spread out, far as you can reach! *Move!*"

Their attack was so sudden, so swift and unexpected, that
the civilians offered no resistance at all. Greg slapped the beer
from Curly's hand and propelled him bodily, facedown, onto
the floor. Tangretti slammed a coral shoe behind Moe's knees,
dropping him as well, and the two women scrambled to join
their boyfriends. "Please!" Curly burbled. "Please! Please!
Please! . . ."

While Tangretti kept the prisoners covered with his .45 and
watched both the front door and the hall leading to the apartment's bedrooms, Greg went to each civilian in turn, using
plastic ties from SEAL prisoner-handling kits to secure their
wrists behind their backs, then again to tie their ankles.

"Who are you?" the woman who'd been on Moe demanded. "What the fuck do you want?"

"Don't hurt us!" Moe said. He was actually crying as Greg
finished securing his feet. "*Please* don't hurt us! If this is a
rip-off, the stuff's—"

"Quiet," Greg rasped, taking a large wad of white cotton

and stuffing it in the kid's mouth, beneath eyes that were bulking out of his face in stark terror.

"I've got money!" Curly added. "You can have all of it! All of it! Please, please, please. . . ."

In another moment, all four were silent, their mouths lightly packed with cotton. Greg walked over to the stereo tape deck and casually drove his elbow into the face of the machine, chopping off the music with a satisfying crack of shattering plastic. "That'll make the neighbors happy," he said. It would also let them hear if anybody was coming up the hall outside.

Another teenaged kid, code-named Larry, chose that moment to come out of the hall leading to the bedrooms, wearing nothing but boxer shorts. "Hey, man, what's all the—"

He stopped dead at the sight of the two SEALs in the living room, both of them covering him with pistols. The kid's eyes grew wide, then wider, then rolled up in his head, as he took one swaying step and then crashed to the floor.

"Check the bedrooms, Twidge," Tangretti said, producing a squat metal can with a small screw cap from his combat harness.

The apartment, as they'd learned from the maps from the apartment complex office, had two bedrooms. The first was a rat's nest of sleeping bags and dirty mattresses, with no occupants. The second actually had a real bed, nearly lost in the clutter of newspapers, clothing, and trash on the floor. A naked girl with long, dirty blond hair whimpered from the bed's far corner as Greg entered the room, trying to curl herself up into an unnoticeable ball.

"C'mon out," Greg told her. He tried to keep his voice gentle. The targets for tonight's raid were the three males; the women were simply in the way. "Don't be afraid. Nobody's going to—"

She was up and running almost before he could react, bolting for the door. Swiftly, he reached out, grabbed a handful of hair, and brought her to a sobbing halt with one hard yank. Then he grabbed her left arm and marched her into the living room. "Here's another," he told Tangretti, dropping her to her knees.

Tangretti was sitting astride Moe, holding a cloth diaper moistened with liquid from the can over the man's mouth and nose. He looked up, as his prisoner's struggles grew weaker and weaker. "Well, well," he said. "Who do we have here?"

Something about the way Tangretti said the words made Greg take another, closer look at the naked woman's face. Her blond hair spilled down to her waist now, and the granny glasses and ankle-length skirt were gone, but she was, he was almost certain, the GS worker he'd seen outside of Nolan's office the week before.

That would go a long way to explaining how these creeps were getting their hands on the addresses and phone numbers of SEALs.

"You two are SEALs, aren't you?" the woman said, struggling against Greg's grip on her arms. "You've *got* to be SEALs! You won't get away with this!"

"You'll have a hard time proving that, sweetheart," Greg told her, roughening his voice to disguise it. "On the floor!"

He began using a prisoner-handling kit to tie her wrists and feet, cursing to himself as he finished the job. This put a new and unfortunate wrinkle in the op. The idea, of course, had been to invade the apartment and take down the occupants without them having any idea who the midnight raiders were. Moe, Curly, and Larry might assume that their attackers were SEALs, but it would be guesswork only. Nolan's secretary, however, might be able to attempt an ID simply on Greg's and Tangretti's build or voices, even if they were trying to mask them, and she would know more about SEALs and their capabilities simply from having worked on the base with them.

On the other hand, their impromptu mission had just scored a major jackpot, since it was now obvious how the harassment groups had been getting the names, family details, phone numbers, and addresses of SEALs. Greg doubted that she would be able to give a coherent enough description of them for any charges to be made . . . and, in any case, she was going to have legal problems of her own, shortly.

Tangretti finished putting the last of the other prisoners down with an ether-soaked rag. The room stank now of ether. Greg was glad to see that Tangretti had remembered to carefully snuff out all of the burning cigarettes. Ether was fiendishly flammable, especially in an enclosed room.

Greg accepted the rag from Tangretti and held it over the

secretary's mouth and nose as she gasped and struggled, taking her slowly down into an ether-sodden sleep. This, arguably, was the trickiest part of the whole operation. They were anesthetizing six people, always a touchy procedure, and if one of them should have a reaction, or a weak heart, or simply be unlucky enough to start choking on his or her own vomit, the two SEALs had to be ready to do something about it, even if that meant calling an ambulance and risking capture.

At last, though, all six were unconscious, but breathing easily. The SEALs loosened the gags to keep their airways clear, opened the sliding balcony door wide to air out the fumes, then proceeded with the next phase of the operation.

Greg touched the transmit key on his radio. "Gold Braid, this is White Hat."

"Gold Braid here," Nolan's voice came back. "Go."

"Target secured. Six packages."

"Copy, White Hat. It's clear out here. Whenever you're ready."

"Rog. Give us another couple of minutes."

"Roger that. I'll be waiting."

"Oh, and Gold Braid? You might be interested in hearing that you know one of the packages. The blonde who works outside your office."

There was a stunned silence, followed by a low-voiced "Son of a whore. . . ."

"Roger that. Give us five. White Hat, out."

They began going through the apartment carefully. In the kitchen, tucked away beneath the sink, they found a plastic garbage bag filled with brownish, dried marijuana leaves, while in the bathroom was a bewildering collection of pills, and plastic baggies each holding a single sugar cube—almost certainly LSD. There were plenty of revolutionary paraphernalia as well—Viet Cong and North Vietnamese flags, posters displaying the aged face of Ho Chi Minh, and various pamphlets and flyers put out by groups ranging from the Students for a Democratic Society to the Communist Party of the United States.

Greg cleared the bottles and dirty paper plates from the dining room table and dropped a collection of wallets and women's handbags on the tabletop. Tangretti found a small address and telephone number book in a kitchen drawer near the phone, and added that to the pile. In a few moments, they'd identified all six of the apartment's occupants. Moe was confirmed as Barry Slidell, in whose name the apartment was rented and the pickup truck was registered. The woman from Nolan's office was twenty-four-year-old Bonnie Mason; her base ID listed her as a GS-5, which suggested that she'd worked for the government for at least several years now.

They gathered up all of the driver's licenses and other ID they could find, then began bundling the three men for transport. Stooping, Tangretti scooped up the unconscious nude body of the secretary and carried her toward the sofa.

"Careful what you grab there, Doc," Greg told him. "We're already guilty of breaking and entering, criminal trespass, unlawful restraint, and in another minute or two, kidnapping. Let's not add sexual assault to the list."

"Not to worry," Tangretti said, unceremoniously dumping the unconscious woman onto the couch beside the other two. "Hell, I don't even want to *touch* it. We don't know where it's been!"

The women they left slumped together on the sofa side by side, still carefully tied, but with the gags removed from their mouths so that they wouldn't choke in their sleep. The men they wrapped up inside blankets taken from the bedrooms, folding and taping and tying until each made a relatively convenient, if somewhat bulky, package.

"Gold Braid, White Hat," Tangretti called on his radio. "We're ready to deliver."

"White Hat, wait one." There was a long pause, and then Nolan gave them the go-ahead. "White Hat, it's clear. Come ahead."

One after the other, they hauled the bundled and unconscious men out onto the balcony, secured them to the rope they'd left strung there, and lowered the captives down four flights to the ground, a much simpler and more direct means of getting them out than lugging them through the hallways and elevators. Nolan was at the bottom waiting for them, untying each bundle from the rope and lugging body and blanket back to Greg's car. In another ten minutes, all three prisoners were resting side by side in Greg's backseat, the blankets piled over their anonymous shapes.

The two SEALs took a last look around the apartment, then

descended the way they'd come up, bringing the rope and pulley with them so that they'd leave no trace behind of their trespass. They shook hands with Nolan. "Thanks again, Lieutenant," Greg told him.

"Yeah, sir. We really appreciate it."

"Just don't get caught with these bozos."

"Nah. Not a chance." Greg handed Nolan a canvas pouch. "Here's their ID and shit. There's also a little black book with lots of phone numbers and addresses. Navy Intelligence might be interested in a lot of this stuff."

"They look like a cell?"

"Hard to say," Greg replied. "They had the posters and the flags and the literature. My guess is that the CPUSA and maybe the SDS were funding them, probably on a freelance basis." He jerked his thumb over his shoulder. "Miss Mason, up there. How long was she working in personnel?"

Nolan's mouth hardened. "Two years, she told me."

"Time to dig up a lot of targeting intelligence. My guess is that the SDS or somebody was paying them to harass SEALs. Maybe it was just to hurt SEAL morale. Maybe they figured we were the extreme violent types, and they were figuring on jerking our chain until somebody popped . . . and maybe took some innocent civilians with them."

Nolan snorted. "In other words, the SDS might've been using these idiots as patsies. Tell 'em they're just going to hurt our morale, but in fact, they were expecting you guys to kill 'em." He looked up at Greg. "If that's true, you be careful with them up there tonight, okay? You kill one of them, and you'll play right into the bad guys' hands."

"Understood, sir," Greg replied. "We're going to scare the shit out of them, but they'll still be alive when we're done. You'll take care of the cops?"

"Yup. And Intelligence, and base security." He hefted the pouch of IDs. "I'll tell the cops there was a drug rip-off going down, and have 'em show up and untie the ones you left up there."

"Good. They'll find enough acid, weed, and speed to keep those young ladies answering questions for a long time. And by that time, maybe JAG or Security can start talking to Mason about what she did at Coronado."

"Right. Okay, then. Good luck!"

"Same to you, sir. We'll see you tomorrow morning."

"Yeah," Tangretti said darkly. "Unless we decide we're just having too damn much fun!"

Mission Trails Regional Park, California
0315 hours

Miramar Naval Air Station was one of the dozens of military facilities scattered around the San Diego area, north of the city proper, halfway between El Cajon and the oceanfront at La Jolla. Adjacent to Miramar, off the southeast corner of the base and south of Route 52 was the Mission Trails Regional Park, a small piece of near-wilderness tucked into a fold of steep, sere hills and near-desert on the very fringe of San Diego's urban sprawl.

Tangretti had been here more than once, usually with other SEALs on training excursions out of Miramar, but once he'd come up here with Pat for some horseback riding and a picnic. A dirt road led to a parking area well off the main highway, and far enough from civilization that they wouldn't be disturbed. They had to make two trips to carry the three men to the site they'd already picked out and prepared, along with the props they needed for their little play.

The men were starting to revive in the clean, crisp, fresh air. Maskless now, Tangretti and Greg prepared their prisoners, started a small fire, then waited for them to revive beneath a dazzle of crystal-sharp stars and a brilliant half-moon in the sky.

"Think they're awake now?" Tangretti asked, nudging Larry with the toe of his coral shoe.

"One way to find out," Greg replied cheerfully, crouching next to the fire.

All three of the prisoners began squirming at that, terrified of whatever it was that Greg was considering.

All three of the victims were stark naked and shivering violently, though Tangretti didn't think that the shivers were entirely from the chill of the desert night air. Two of them were still lying on the ground, resting a bit uncomfortably on top of the blankets they'd been brought here in. The SEALs had used a special prisoner control tie on both of them, hog-tying them with their ankles pulled all the way up to their buttocks, and with their arms cinched behind their backs so that each hand clasped the opposite elbow. A noose had been put around their necks and tied off to their feet, keeping them arched uncomfortably backward. They weren't in immediate danger of choking, unless they tried violently struggling to free themselves. If that happened, the nooses would tighten and they'd begin slowly strangling . . . and also making enough noise that one of the SEALs would be able to tend to him. Both men had been hooded, which left them not only unable to see but also with hearing and smell muffled enough to threaten them with partial sensory deprivation. Tangretti had no doubt that they were now straining to hear every sound, trying to anticipate what was about to happen.

Their condition was less an act of sadism than it was a part of a deliberate and calculated process. Some SEAL training routines ended with BUD/S trainees being captured in mock raids or ambushes, and their treatment at the hands of their SEAL captors was as humiliating as—and often physically rougher than—what had happened to these three.

They'd taken Slidell and tied him up apart from the others, roping him upright to a dead tree trunk just in front of the campfire, with his legs pulled apart and his ankles, like his wrists, tied behind the trunk. He was gagged, but the hood had been removed. On a flat rock positioned at the edge of the fire where he could see them, Tangretti had laid out several props smuggled out from work. There was his diving knife, of course, long and Parkerized black, with a nasty-looking saw-blade serration along the top, for cutting through fishing nets or line. There were several surgical scalpels and several hemostats—bright silver scissorslike devices with blunt tips, used for pinching severed blood vessels and stopping bleeding. And there was his favorite . . . a bacteriological wire loop.

The wire loop, which he'd borrowed from a friend at the base dispensary, was usually used in the bacti-lab to transfer bits of growing bacteria cultures from a sample to a petri dish, for incubation. As a hospital corpsman, though, Tangretti had more than once in the past used the wire loop for another, less well known purpose. Every once in a while, the emergency room doctor would ask that a patient with the typical symptoms of gonorrhea—a thick, milky or puslike discharge and intense burning during urination—be tested for gram-positive cocci. Tangretti or another duty corpsman would take the loop, which was a straight piece of wire perhaps five inches long extending from a wooden dowel handle, with a tiny loop in the end perhaps a quarter of an inch wide, and take a sample from inside the patient's urethra.

There was no gentle way to go about the collection process. The wire loop was heated in a Bunsen burner flame until it was literally glowing red-hot; the corpsman would wave the wire back and forth a moment or two to cool it, then, holding the man's penis in one hand, would push the loop inside the opening of the urethra, rotate the loop around inside to collect a sample of pus and the epithelial cells lining the tube, and pull it out.

Generally, Tangretti was kind to his victims. He would heat the wire red-hot, wave it in the air a moment, then press it against the skin of his own wrist to prove that the wire cooled very rapidly and was not as hot as the red glow of a moment before suggested. He would then resterilize the loop, cool it, and advance on his victim. At that point, more than once he'd had a patient faint on him just at the thought of a red-hot wire going up the inside of his penis.

This time, he wasn't being kind, and he wasn't going to demonstrate. Squatting by the fire, Tangretti held the wire loop in the flame, turning it back and forth, watching it grow hot. When it was bright, cherry red, he stood suddenly, turned, and held the glowing wire a few inches in front of Slidell's wide-open eyes.

The man started as if someone had stabbed him, struggling wildly against his bonds. Smiling coldly, Tangretti reached down and took the man's limp penis in his hand, and slowly brought the wire down . . . down . . .

Slidell screamed into his gag, shrieking, moaning, then shrieking again until it sounded as though his throat was going to tear. When Tangretti actually touched the wire, now quite cool, to the tip of the man's organ, Slidell surged against the ropes so hard that blood appeared where the lines bit across his upper arms, urine and feces dribbled down the inside of his thighs, and his muffled scream echoed from a nearby hill, dragging on and on and on . . . until suddenly, abruptly, he sagged against the tree, head lolling.

The two prisoners on the ground nearby, though hooded, had heard those screams and must have thought the SEALs were doing something hideous, something unimaginable to their friend to have left him in such searing agony. Curly was quietly strangling himself on the throat noose. Larry was pitching back and forth violently, screaming into his own gag. When Greg went to Curly and grabbed his shoulder, the man must have thought his own time had come, because he suddenly emptied both his bowels and his bladder in a violent, stinking gush of liquid, then shuddered and lay still.

"I think," Greg told Tangretti quietly, "that we can safely say we've just scared the shit out of these guys, don't you?"

Tangretti pointed at the hog-tied man at Greg's feet. "Let's start with him."

The one known as Curly was broken completely now, babbling almost incoherently as soon as Greg removed his gag. Within a few minutes, he was telling the SEALs about friends in the SDS, about plans to demoralize the SEALs and members of the U.S. Marine Corps, about secret payments, about SDS contacts and informers and even the codes they used to contact one another.

For the next few hours, until the stars faded out and the sky slowly grew lighter, they questioned the three men both together and separately, recording everything they had to say on a small, portable cassette recorder. There was enough information here, Tangretti thought, to put a serious crimp in at least a part of the SDS's antiwar activities . . . in particular, their campaign against U.S. servicemen.

Before they left, Tangretti picked up his diving knife, walked over to Slidell, still tied nude to the tree trunk, and placed the blade lightly beneath the trembling man's scrotum. "We know where you live," he said quietly, his lips inches from the man's ear.

"Please don't do it please don't do it please—"

"I was considering doing to your dick what you guys did to that cat," Tangretti continued. "A little gasoline, a match . . ."

Slidell's eyes were squeezed tightly shut, tears rolling down his cheeks. "*Pleasepleasepleaseplease—*"

"I'm going to let you keep the pathetic little thing, though," Tangretti continued. "*This* time. But if my wife is ever threatened again, if she tells me she so much as caught a whiff of your foul carcass floating down from somewhere upwind, then I *will* hunt you down, and I *will* finish the job. Do you read me, mister?''

The man nodded, a jerky, terrified jiggling of his head.

''This conversation, by the way, never took place. You three got ripped off by bad guys, right? You should know that even if something happens to the two of us, we have a lot of friends who also know where you live, and they will hunt you down, all three of you, and you won't like what happens.''

''Our advice to all of you,'' Greg added, ''is to tell the cops you got kidnapped by unpleasant people looking for your stash of marijuana at your apartment. If we hear a different story, well, we'll have to have another little get-together. Okay? See you.''

''W-wait!'' Larry was flopping on the ground, trying to brace himself up on an elbow. ''You can't just . . . just leave us out here in the middle of nowhere!''

''Oh, we'll tell the cops where you are,'' Tangretti told him. ''They ought to be able to find you eventually. Maybe in a couple-three days. You boys just sit tight, and think about how lucky you were this time.''

And with that, the SEALs walked off into the growing light of the dawn.

But Tangretti was unusually quiet during the drive back to El Cajon. He'd not realized, before this, that he was capable of such violent rage against anyone, even the enemy . . . and the knowledge of his own anger had left him shaken. Had Jesus really made any kind of a difference in him? Conversion experiences like his were supposed to make you a new man inside; if *this* was the new man, he doubted that God would want to have much to do with him. At the same time, Tangretti was newly aware of a different kind of support community than the church or a prayer group. Pat had been threatened, and the SEAL community had rallied.

It was a good feeling, knowing that you weren't alone.

I'm sorry, Lord, he thought, sending the prayer in a vaguely skyward direction. *Maybe I'm just not cut out for your army, after all. I'm a SEAL, and, right now, I guess that's where I'm supposed to be.*

Chapter 29

Easter Sunday, 2 April 1972

30,000 feet above Cam Lo
12 miles south of the DMZ
1630 hours

Lieutenant Colonel Franklin T. Halliwell reached into the breast pocket of his flight suit, pulling out the leather glasses case tucked inside and removing his glasses. Half magnifying lens and half plain glass, he only perched them on his nose for very close work . . . like now, as he studied the visual readout on his electronics warfare console, trying to make sense of the signals he was receiving aboard the high-flying EB-66. *Somebody* down there was painting the aircraft, and it looked suspiciously like a Fan Song, which was the NATO code designation for the weapons radar director system used by Russian-built SA-2 Guidelines. The trouble was, there weren't supposed to be any SAMs this far south. . . .

"Somebody down there sure is interested in us," he said, speaking over the aircraft's intercom.

"Well, it's nice to be wanted, isn't it?" Major Randolph Layton, seated in the pilot's seat just ahead of Halliwell in the aircraft and to his left, replied. "They just don't want an old codger like you getting bored, is all."

"Old codger's about what I feel like, Randy," Halliwell replied. "I tell you, I'm getting way too old for this shit."

"Ha! You're only as old as you feel, Frank. You're only as old as you feel."

"I dunno," Halliwell said, grinning. "Right now I feel about as old as this pig we're flying."

"Well, there you go. She's only, what . . . twenty? Twenty-two, maybe? What the hell are you complaining about, old man?''

In fact, Halliwell was fifty-six, a little on the high side for combat missions, but not by all that much. He'd been flying combat for seven months now, during which time he'd completed sixty-four missions, counting this one, but except for the crowding on board the old EW aircraft, it wasn't that uncomfortable a way to go to war. Hell, it was so routine he was usually in danger of being bored to death.

The EB-66 *was* old, ancient and all but obsolete; it had started out as a tactical bomber and reconnaissance aircraft known as the Destroyer, a product of lessons learned during the Korean War, but the only models flying now were the ones converted to electronic warfare use, the tailgun replaced by chaff dispensers, and a four-man electronics suite built into what once had been the bomb bay. Its aircrews called the big, two-engine plane the Souiee, as though it were a pig to be called to the feeding trough. Its primary mission was to fly ahead of flights of B-52 bombers, identifying and jamming enemy radar in order to clear a path for the big boys coming up in the rear. Today, the run consisted of two EB-66s on a mission to overfly the Ban Karai Pass, on the border between Laos and North Vietnam. They were on course, on time, about ten minutes from target. Somewhere far astern, a flight of six B-52s was following the Souiees as they rumbled toward the northwest. Beginning two days ago, on Good Friday, all hell had broken loose in the northern part of South Vietnam, and the U.S. Air Force was throwing everything it could into the effort to slow what was beginning to look like a major Communist invasion.

They were already calling it the Easter Offensive.

Just a year ago, the Army of the Republic of Vietnam had launched a major offensive going the other way, into Laos, in an attempt to take Tchepone and cut the Ho Chi Minh Trail. To put it kindly, Marvin ARVN had gotten his butt kicked. Operation Lam Son 719 had been an undiluted military disaster, right up there with First Bull Run and Kasserine Pass. The South Vietnamese had been licking their wounds ever since, and there was serious doubt throughout the American military that Saigon was going to be able to get its act together. As far as could be told from Lam Son 719, Vietnamization was a complete and utter failure.

And now, it looked like Hanoi had decided to give a good, hard shove and see if the ARVN was as flimsy and termite-riddled a shell as it seemed. So far, things did not look good. The NVA was swarming south across the Demilitarized Zone from the north, and down Highway 9 out of Laos from the west. All of Quang Tri Province was in danger, including the city of Quang Tri itself and, just fifty klicks down Highway One from Quang Tri, the ancient capital of Vietnam, Hue. The last intelligence reports put 40,000 crack NVA troops on the march. The only thing even inconveniencing them so far was American air power, which was being slammed into the enemy's southbound columns as fast and as hard as possible.

And, of course, the NVA was slamming back for all he was worth.

"SAM! SAM! SAM!" one of the EW officers in the rear of the aircraft called. "We have a launch!"

"I confirm," Halliwell replied, checking his screen. *Shit!* The NVA had upped the ante, moving SA-2s south of the DMZ. "We've got a telephone pole coming up at eight o'clock. Passive tracking."

"I see it!" Layton called over the intercom, twisting in his harness to look back over his left shoulder.

"It's gone active!" Halliwell said, shouting now. His heart was hammering in his chest. Shit! These guys were trying to *kill* him! "Break left! Break left!"

"Moving into a SAM break!" Layton warned. "Hang on, all!"

The aircraft canted suddenly to the left, and Halliwell's stomach tried to climb up inside his throat. Standard tactics: when a missile climbs after you from the rear quarter, turn into it, hard as you can. The SAM was traveling so fast that it wouldn't be able to compensate in time and would either miss or tear itself apart trying to follow its target's turn. At least, that was the theory. . . .

"C'mon . . . c'mon . . . c'mon" sounded in Halliwell's earphones, Layton muttering beneath his breath as he hauled the aircraft hard to the left. "*Move* your ass, you big, damned—"

The explosion tore through the rear portion of the plane, a violent crack of thunder, a flash of white light. The shock slammed Halliwell hard against his seat restraints and left his ears ringing. Smoke boiled up out of the electronics suite aft, and Halliwell heard someone screaming. The harsh rasp of the bailout warning sounded over his headset. Dazed by the blast, working almost entirely by training-honed instinct, Halliwell reached down, fumbling for the ejection seat firing mechanism. He could hear Layton calling over the radio. "This is Bravo One-niner, Bravo One-niner, mayday, mayday! We've been hit by a SAM and are going down! Mayday!"

"Punch out, Randy!" Halliwell yelled at the pilot. "Punch out!"

Layton waved with one hand. "Right behind you, Frank! Go! Go!"

Halliwell squeezed the firing trigger. A dorsal panel on the top of the aircraft blew away, spilling raw daylight into his eyes. A second later, the ejection seat fired, hurling him up and out of the stricken aircraft and into dazzling sunlight.

The first thing he noticed as he sailed up into space, his ejection seat dropping away beneath him, was the cold, icy and bitter, cutting through his flight suit like a knife as his body hit wind with a speed relative to his body of something like six hundred miles per hour. The second thing he noticed was that he was *spinning*, that blue sky above and white cloud deck far below were alternating with the speed of someone flipping pages past his eyes. Damn it, ejection wasn't supposed to be like this! Spinning this fast, he'd black out in seconds.

Ideal in a situation like this would be to simply let himself fall, dropping through the thin, cold atmosphere all the way down to fourteen thousand feet, where a pressure sensor would trigger his main chute automatically.

But something was terribly wrong. This spin suggested a problem when he'd exited the aircraft, and there was a chance that his chute had been damaged in the punch-out. He had two, and only two, choices—to let himself fall to the warmer, friendlier climes at fourteen thousand feet and see if his chute deployed by itself, or to open the chute manually now, exposing himself to the risks of frostbite and anoxia, but stopping the spin and proving that his chute did work.

And if it didn't, he would have thirty thousand feet to think of something, instead of only fourteen.

The hell with it, he thought, fumbling for the rip cord. *At least I can stop the damned spinning!*

He yanked the D-ring and felt the chute smoothly sliding from its pack, silently unfolding . . . deploying . . . and then the canopy opened and hung on the sky, yanking him against his harness with hammer-blow savagery. For several seconds, it felt like he was going back up, climbing his harness toward space . . . and then the shock was past, and he was swinging beneath a gloriously open canopy. Above, he saw white parachute and crystal blue sky; looking down between his dangling legs, he could see only clouds, a low, heavy overcast that had socked in all of Quang Tri Province since early that morning. Visibility above the cloud deck was unlimited, and he craned his head around, searching the surrounding sky, looking for Randy and Makowsky and Samuels and the rest. Damn . . . he should be able to see their chutes! Where were they?

Movement caught his eye, far back behind him, over his right shoulder. Working himself around in his harness, he managed to rotate slowly in that direction to get a better look.

What he glimpsed made his heart sink. It was the EB-66, spinning now at the end of a long, downward-arcing plume of white smoke. It looked like the entire tail section of the aircraft had been blown clean away, and the Souiee was tumbling now, like a flying toy airplane with its stabilizing tail broken off.

He saw no other chutes, no chutes at all . . . and when the EB-66 vanished into the cloud deck, Frank Halliwell was left achingly, horribly alone in the empty sky.

The suddenness of his change in circumstances left Halliwell reeling. Those five men had been his *friends,* poker buddies, drinking partners, confidants . . . and now they were all dead. It was impossible to take it all in.

It was starting to grow dark. Halliwell blinked. That couldn't be right. It was still afternoon, and the sky was bright and clear, but the crisp line that demarcated cloud deck from sky at the horizon was starting to ripple and swim, growing blurry. Damn, what was wrong with his eyes? It was as though his vision was fuzzing out, starting at the outside and working in. . . .

Oxygen! Somehow, training reasserted itself through the shock and pain of his loss. *Oxygen!* At twenty-something-thousand feet, people who weren't on O_2 quickly succumbed to anoxia and blacked out. He could *die* in the next few minutes . . . or end up brain-dead, which was worse. He fumbled at the side of his parachute pack for the small bailout bottle of oxygen strapped there, yanking out the rubber hose attached to one end, sticking it in his mouth, and tugging at the green knob that started the flow going. Greedily, he gulped down several deep breaths and knew an almost giddy sense of relief as his blurring vision cleared. He slowed his breathing, then; too much oxygen could be as deadly as too little.

His left hand was throbbing. When he looked at it, curious, he saw blood spilling out of the cuff all over his wrist, and a nasty tear that went through leather, skin, and muscle straight down the center of his index finger.

That, he thought, explains the spin. He must have snagged on the edge of the hatch coming out of the aircraft. The snag had set him tumbling, ripping open his hand in the bargain. Well, he had plenty of time . . . fifteen or twenty minutes before he finally reached the ground. Carefully, he peeled off his glove, tucked it into a pocket of his flight suit, then with clumsy, one-handed care, pulled out his first-aid kit and began dressing the wound as best as he could. He managed somehow to get the antibiotic powder in, and to wrap the finger up in a length of roller gauze, enough, he hoped, to stop the bleeding. As he was cleaning the tear, though, he thought he could see the shiny white gleam of bone through the fast-welling blood, and the thought made him a bit queasy.

He wondered where he was coming down. From what he remembered of the EB-66's location, course, and speed when they were hit, he was pretty sure he was still south of the DMZ, which was a good thing, all things considered. Then he remembered those intel reports about forty thousand enemy soldiers moving into Quang Tri Province, and a trembling, panicky fear rose up in his throat and almost made him lose his bailout bottle tube. If those reports were accurate, he would be coming down in a rather busy sector of South Vietnam, possibly smack dab in the middle of one of the biggest flat-out fights this war-weary country had seen so far. Quickly, he reached up and switched off the small radio beacon beeper attached to his survival vest. The device had begun sending out a homing signal as soon as he'd ejected in order to vector in SAR—Search And Rescue—aircraft, but it could also serve as a homing beacon for the enemy. Charlie had big ears, and he put a premium on American pilots captured as POWs, since they were turning out to be prime bargaining chips at the peace table.

He'd descended a long way, fifteen thousand feet, perhaps. The cloud deck was coming up fast, a broad, featureless plain of white that took on an eerie landscape quality as he dropped toward it. Instinctively, he pulled up his feet as he dropped into the mist, and then he was surrounded by clammy, dark shadow.

A moment later, he emerged from the bottom of the cloud layer, in a region that was clear but more dimly lit than the open skies at higher altitude. He was suspended between two flat surfaces—gray overcast above, and a layer of whitish ground fog hugging the surface below. It was hard to make out details, but he could see the shadows of rolling terrain just beneath the fog, and in the distance, tree-covered hills loomed up out of the fog-like islands in a soft, gray-white sea.

Motion caught his eye to the left. Twisting his head around, he could see . . . an aircraft! An American plane!

It wasn't much . . . an O-2 that looked about one step up from something that ought to be dusting crops. He was both thrilled and dismayed, thrilled because it was so good to see somebody else in that wide, empty sky . . . and dismayed because that O-2 was almost certainly an FAC, a Forward Air Controller, one of the small and certifiably insane fraternity of men who searched out enemy targets at treetop level and marked them with smoke rockets for the big, nasty boys that followed. If there was a FAC here, he must be coming down right on top of something pretty heavy.

No time to worry about that now. He pressed the transmit switch on his radio. "FAC Oh-two, FAC Oh-two, come in please!"

The voice of the FAC pilot came back almost immediately,

startling Halliwell. The guy must have been monitoring the frequency.

"This is FAC Oh-two, call-sign Birddog on Guard Channel. Identify yourself. Over."

"Birddog, this is Bravo One-niner. I've got a little problem here. Over."

"Bravo One-niner, Birddog, where are you? Over."

"Birddog, One-niner. Look up and to your right. I'm the parachute at about ten grand. Over."

There was a pause, and then the FAC pilot gave a startled "Son of a bitch!" There was another pause. The O-2 was in a gentle left-hand turn, apparently circling beneath Halliwell's position. "Ah . . . One-niner, I have you in sight. Let's can the chatter, though. I homed in on your beeper, and it's a good bet the gomers did too. Have a nice landing, and I will advise. Over."

"Roger that. Bravo One-niner, out."

He switched off the emergency survival radio and began preparing for his landing. He could hear gunfire now, cracks and snaps and stuttering pops that seemed to come from everywhere. At first, he was afraid they were firing at him, but he saw nothing, no tracers, no flashes, just shadowy ground and fog. He might be coming down smack in the middle of a firefight, but he had no idea where the combatants were.

The ground was coming up toward his feet awfully fast now, and the fact that the terrain was masked by fog made the descent that much more terrifying. He could be dropping into a swamp or a well or—

He hit with a shock that felt like it was driving his legs right up his ass, collapsed to the ground, and rolled. When he rose to his feet, scrabbling at the parachute harness, he found he was in a dry rice paddy, with a treeline about fifty meters away.

An explosion thumped in the fog to his left . . . and another one, and a third. A machine gun opened up with a long, crackling rattle, and Halliwell suddenly felt stark naked, as exposed in the paddy as a cockroach on a dinner plate. Unbuckling his chute, he ducked his head and ran as fast as he could, angling across the field toward the trees. Gunfire pursued him. Damn! Had he been seen? It was hard to imagine how anybody within three miles couldn't have seen him hanging from his chute like that.

He reached a three-foot-deep ditch running along the edge of the paddy just short of the trees and dove in, head first. He lay there for several moments, listening to the thump of explosions and the rattle of small-arms fire, before he finally convinced himself, and his hard-hammering heart, that none of the gunfire was actually aimed in his direction. Carefully, carefully, he raised his head above the edge of the ditch.

He couldn't see anyone. There was no indication at all that he'd been noticed.

Halliwell took a moment to collect himself and check himself out. Judging by the way he'd sprinted to the ditch, he was in pretty good shape . . . not bad for a fifty-six-year-old, anyway. Except for his cut finger, in fact, he was in fine shape. He reached up to rub a piece of grit from his eye, and found his finger blocked by something. His reading glasses! Somehow, despite the missile hit, the ejection, the five-hundred-mile-per-hour hurricane, the wild spin and the long descent, his prescription reading glasses had managed to stay on his face! It was one of those ridiculous bits of war story detail that no one would believe when he told it, once he got out of this.

Once he got out. They had to have the SAR chopper, the Jolly Green, already in the air and on the way.

At first, a minute or two later, he thought he heard the chopper inbound, and he started fumbling for a flare. Then the droning of an engine drew closer, and he realized that he was hearing the little pusher O-2 coming in at damn-near treetop level. He switched on the radio and heard the pilot's voice calling. ". . . niner, this is Birddog. Please switch to Channel Echo. Do you copy? Bravo One-niner, Bravo One-niner . . ."

Halliwell switched channels on his radio and pressed the transmit key. "Birddog, Birddog, this is Bravo One-niner on Echo, do you copy? Over!"

"Read you loud and clear, One-niner. How are you doing? Over."

"I seem to be in one piece, Birddog."

"Good job. What's the name of your dog? Over?"

Halliwell blinked, looking up at the overcast, trying to spot the O-2 by the sound of its engine. His dog? Then he remembered the personal information card he'd filled out when he'd been assigned to Southeast Asia, a listing of such vital statistics as his wife's maiden name, his favorite ballplayer, and his favorite color, just in case he found himself in a situation exactly like this one.

He told the O-2 pilot his dog's name—Oscar—and went on to repeat some of the other information from his file. The O-2 pilot was playing it by the book; the North Vietnamese had been known to try to lure rescue choppers in close enough to ambush them from the ground.

"Roger that, Bravo One-niner," Birddog said at last. "I have positive identification. You find a place to hole up and wait out the night. We'll have the Jolly Greens in after you at first light. Over."

"Hey, wait a minute! Birddog! You can't . . . I mean, you're not going to *leave* me here!"

"Sorry, One-niner. The weather's shitty and we can't get anyone in, not before dark, anyway. You just sit tight and think good thoughts. We'll be in first thing in the morning to dust you off. Over."

"Roger." Halliwell tried to sound cheerful and thought he'd probably failed. "I'll be here. Bravo One-niner, out."

"Birddog, out."

The lawn-mower-engine sound of the little O-2 dwindled then and was slowly lost. Halliwell took a look around and decided that the treeline, which appeared to be the near edge of a fair-sized patch of woods, would offer him his best bet of staying out of sight. First, though, he would have to go back and retrieve his parachute, which was still lying in the middle of the rice paddy. Retrieving the thing hadn't seemed all that important, somehow, when he'd first hit the ground and thought he was being shot at. Now, though, if he was going to be here all night . . .

He was just starting to emerge from the ditch when the descending whistle of an incoming mortar round changed his mind. He hit the dirt, and a second later the round struck the rice paddy not far from his chute, sending up an enormous geyser of dirt and gravel and smoke and assaulting his ears with a thunderclap of raw noise.

Someone had just decided to zero in on that rice paddy.

Maybe they'd seen the chute, and maybe it was just a lucky shot. Either way, Halliwell didn't feel like he wanted to tempt fate. He would go the other way, up into the trees, and find a place to hide for the night.

It didn't really matter. They would be coming to get him in the morning.

Tuesday, 4 April 1972

GRU Intelligence Center
The Citadel, Hanoi
People's Democratic Republic of Vietnam
1215 hours

Colonel Dimitri Pavlovich Kartashkin looked out his second-floor window from a vantage point on the north side of the Citadel, overlooking Hanoi's Phan Dinh Phung Street. *I hate this war,* he thought with something approaching despair. *It is just possible that I hate this war as much as do the Americans.*

His posting to this miserable country was threatening to become a full-time career. His requests to be posted back to Moscow, back to someplace where he could again see his beloved Tatiana, had repeatedly been ignored or point-blank denied. "You are too valuable where you are, Dimitri Pavlovich," his immediate supervisor, General Druzhinin, had told him. "Remember that sacrifice is necessary to advance the cause of revolution."

Druzhinin was an ass.

Kartashkin had cared little for the Vietnamese people's struggle against the imperialists and their Saigonese puppets since Grigor's disappearance just over a year before. It was still not known what had happened. Grigor Alekseivich had been assigned to a North Vietnamese recovery unit with orders to find the wreckage and pilot of an American reconnaissance aircraft downed by SAMs near the DMZ, just across the border into Laos. The crash site had been positively located by a Soviet Kosmos spy satellite, and Grigor's team had gone in.

They simply had never come out again. The bodies of his NVA team members had been found, apparently dead in an ambush at the crash site. Of Grigor, however, there had been no trace. It was as if the jungle had swallowed him up.

Kartashkin knew what had really happened, of course. This kind of thing had happened before, more than once. The strike teams of the American Studies and Observations Group specialized in snatching important-looking personnel, men who might provide the CIA with particularly valuable intelligence. The downed American aircraft was almost certainly one of the top secret SR-71 Blackbirds; the enemy would have expected a Russian advisor to show up and investigate.

Kidnapping one another's advisors was all part of the game in Southeast Asia, of course. Nothing personal, just business, as the Americans would say. A number of captured American fliers had been transferred from the custody of their North Vietnamese captors to that of KGB or GRU units in the Soviet Union. Kartashkin had participated in the interrogation of two American officers in Leforvo Prison, in Moscow, before he'd been assigned to Hanoi. How else does one gauge the strength and effectiveness of one's enemy?

But somehow, Kartashkin had never expected the game to strike this close to home. But for the workings of chance— Kartashkin had had an important meeting coming up with Giap's chief of staff—he would have been on that patrol into Laos, and he would have been the one to be languishing now, if he were alive at all, in some CIA prison facility in Danang or Virginia.

He stood at his office window, staring out across the northern fringes of Hanoi, and thought of what might have been.

There was a knock on his door. "Come," he said, in Vietnamese. Major Nguyen Tan Tram, his aide, entered the office. "A special courier has just arrived for you, sir."

"Good. I've been expecting him. Bring him in, please."

"Yes, sir."

Nguyen left the office, then returned a moment later with a Soviet Army major, who carried a briefcase handcuffed to his wrist. "Colonel Kartashkin," Nguyen said. "Major Mikhailin, GRU."

"Major," Kartashkin said. "Good to meet you."

"I have the file you requested from Moscow," Mikhailin said. He cast a meaningful look at Nguyen, as if to say, *This is not for him.*

"Major Nguyen?" Kartashkin said. "Would you excuse us for a few minutes?"

"Yes, Comrade Colonel." The Vietnamese officer left the room, closing the door behind him.

"So," Kartashkin said, "what news from Moscow?"

"The place is the same, I am sure, Comrade Colonel, as when you saw it last." Mikhailin placed the briefcase on the desk and unlocked the handcuff. "There is great official concern about the American boycott of the Paris talks. And there is considerable interest in the report that that American actress is expected to visit Hanoi this month. You will no doubt receive special instructions concerning her."

Kartashkin nodded, though he cared little about either bored and vacuous American actresses or the politics of the peace talks. Nixon had broken them off for an indefinite period, claiming that Hanoi had failed to negotiate seriously. Move and countermove. Bluff and counter bluff. An endless and boringly pointless game. As for Jane Fonda, who was expected to visit North Vietnam this coming July, she was better known than Hannah DuPlessey but would have no greater effect on the war effort. She was another propaganda tool, and nothing more.

Mikhailin thumbed the dial of the case's combination lock, opened it, and removed a manila envelope sealed with string and marked SECRET in prominent Cyrillic letters. Kartashkin accepted the envelope, then used an army knife lying on his desktop to cut the string and slit open the envelope.

Inside, also prominently marked SECRET, was a file folder thick with mimeographed sheets, forms, and records, and even a fuzzy photocopy of an original photograph. The entire file was nearly ten centimeters thick.

"A lot of material on this one," Kartashkin said, leafing through the folder. He picked up a bio sheet. "Lieutenant Colonel Franklin Teal Halliwell," he said, reading the English words. The document was a copy of an official Department of Defense/U.S. Air Force form and included a summary of Halliwell's career.

"This is the American shot down near Cam Lo?" Mikhailin asked.

"Apparently the only survivor of a six-man reconnaissance crew," Kartashkin replied. He picked up the copy of the photograph and studied the lined face. After a moment, he replaced the picture and began paging through another set of documents, each page stamped SECRET.

"*Bozemoy . . .*" Kartashkin said, shaking his head in wonder. "My God." The statement, a mild curse in atheist Russia, spoken quietly, was less one of surprise than of confirmation. He'd hoped for something like this.

"What is it, Comrade Colonel?"

"As we suspected from the notebooks and artifacts gathered at the crash site, our friend Halliwell was one of the aircraft's electronics warfare officers. He will have intimate knowledge of American EW systems, as well as of their radar and weapons guidance systems."

"The general told me to tell you specifically and emphatically that Halliwell must be captured, and he must be captured alive. I am to remain in Hanoi until he is brought here, after which you and I are both to return with him to Moscow."

Kartashkin looked up sharply from the document he was studying. "Indeed!" This was what for years now he'd been hoping for, yes, even *praying* for, though as a good Communist he would never admit to that—a release from this pathetic, Third World excuse for a country and from this unending war.

A return to Moscow. Perhaps his exile was about to end at last. . . .

He'd hoped as much, as soon as he'd seen the wreckage of a crashed American aircraft shot down just two days ago, near the DMZ. Kartashkin had flown down to the border personally to investigate the site and had wondered the entire time whether he was going to be the target of another abduction, as poor Grigor had been. The plane, an American EB-66 electronic warfare aircraft, had crashed in a region overrun by North Vietnamese troops and had been safe enough to approach. NVA soldiers nearby had recovered a single parachute, proof that one, at least, of the plane's crew had bailed out and survived the landing.

The wreckage at the crash site was intact enough to yield clues about the missing man. Five bodies confirmed that there was only one survivor. Name tags, dog tags, and personal effects had identified all five . . . and several recovered notebooks and a name in a flight log had given an identity to the sixth, one Lieutenant Colonel Frank T. Halliwell. Kartashkin, certain that the man was an EW expert, had transmitted the name and other information to Moscow for confirmation and to see what other information might be included in the man's file. The GRU tried to maintain comprehensive files on all senior American military officers.

Some files—and Halliwell's was one of them—were far thicker and more interesting than others.

Paging ahead through the file documents, Kartashkin at last found why Halliwell was so important to his superiors. "Well, well," he said, reading. "Assistant deputy commander of a SAC missile wing. . . ."

"Moscow believes that Halliwell carries in his head much that would be of extreme interest to the GRU," Mikhailin told him. "Missile arming codes. Targeting information. Possibly even key information on American fail-safe codes and procedures. The man may be the most important prisoner ever taken."

"I can see that. Unfortunately, he is not a prisoner *yet.*" Kartashkin closed the file and walked across the office to his door. "Comrade Major Nguyen? Step back in here a moment, if you please."

"Yes, sir!"

"Major Mikhailin has confirmed much of what we guessed from the EB-66 wreckage," he told the Vietnamese officer. "The man is an expert in electronic warfare."

He did not add that Halliwell had recently been with an American ICBM wing. That information was classified at a level above that which could be shared even with Moscow's closest allies. It also guaranteed that Halliwell, once he was captured, would be sent at once to Moscow for a full interrogation, and Hanoi would not like that. If they were going to expend men and material on Halliwell's capture, they would want some of the benefits for themselves. It could be a touchy situation, one that Kartashkin would address when it arose, and not before.

"Then he will be an extremely important captive!" Nguyen exclaimed.

"He must be retrieved," Kartashkin told his aide. "Tell your people to expend every resource available on his capture.

And . . . if he is killed by some trigger-happy peasant, I will have the people responsible executed on the spot. Make that perfectly clear to all concerned.''

"I will, Comrade Colonel.''

"Halliwell is to be taken alive at all costs. Do you understand?''

"Yes, sir!''

"And when he is taken, he is to be brought here, to the Citadel, by the swiftest and most secure means available. I am to be notified at once.''

"Yes, sir! I will inform my people immediately.''

"Good. Dismissed.''

"What is Halliwell's situation, Colonel?'' Mikhailin wanted to know.

"His position is known down to within about three square kilometers,'' Kartashkin replied, pulling a map out of its case on a table near the widow and unrolling it for Mikhailin's inspection. "He landed quite close to this intersection here . . . Highway 561 and Route 8.'' He swept his finger around the map in a broad oval. "There are currently in this general area some forty thousand North Vietnamese troops, including an extremely heavy concentration of armor and antiaircraft assets. The nearest South Vietnamese forces are almost five kilometers away. The offensive has utterly shattered the enemy's defenses, and he is in full retreat.

"So far, American search-and-rescue attempts to recover Halliwell have failed. An HH-53 helicopter was dispatched to pick him up yesterday, but it was damaged by heavy antiaircraft fire and forced to turn back.

"That evening, a flight of American A-1s dropped large numbers of small antipersonnel mines around Halliwell's position. That has confirmed for us his approximate location but has also made it difficult for our allies to go in and pick him up. A number of Vietnamese have already been killed or wounded attempting to cross the minefields.''

"Our allies should not be held up by a few mines.''

"Have you ever walked into a minefield, Comrade Major? Knowing that each step could be the one to rip the leg from your body, shred your foot, or sever your genitals? Ah, I thought not. The problem is bigger than you can imagine, and we do not have unlimited control over these people.'' He smiled. "We can *advise* them to enter the minefield, but they are not compelled to follow that advice. Still, this will be only a temporary obstacle. We will capture Halliwell, and soon."

"Can our people reach him before the American rescue helicopters do?"

"The weather in Quang Tri Province has been bad lately," Kartashkin replied. "Heavy fog. Some rain. And, worse from their point of view, the area is saturated with antiaircraft artillery of all calibers, including weapons emplaced in several of the villages nearby, where the American rules of engagement will keep them safe."

Mikhailin's eyebrows climbed higher on his face. "The Americans will not bomb villages?"

Kartashkin smiled. "The political efforts within the United States have born unexpected fruit, Comrade Major. Washington has found it . . . shall we say, politically expedient to forbid their field commanders to bomb or shell villages where innocent civilians may be put at risk. Our allies, of course, have taken advantage of this, to extremely good effect. The Americans will not be able to approach Halliwell's refuge without being shot down."

"If American search-and-rescue aircraft cannot get through to Halliwell's sanctuary, then . . ." Mikhailin said.

"Then his capture is assured," Kartashkin said, completing the thought. "I am more concerned about his being beaten to death by some angry farmer than I am about his being rescued by his own people. And the minefield will help us almost as much as it helps him, by keeping him in place and forcing the Americans to rely on vulnerable aircraft for their rescue efforts, rather than one of their SOG units or SEAL Teams.

"Halliwell's capture by our allies is truly only a matter of time. . . ."

Chapter 30

Orange Beach 2
Okinawa
1455 hours

Tangretti propelled himself along the fast-shoaling, sandy bottom with gentle strokes of his swim fins. The water was clear but chilly, with a temperature of sixty-five degrees, bearable, but a bit on the cool side. He was beginning to wish he'd taken Lieutenant Nolan's advice and worn a wet suit.

But that wouldn't have been right, somehow. The men who'd been here before, twenty-seven years ago, hadn't worn wet suits. Of course, for that matter, they hadn't worn SCUBA gear, either. Members of the original Teams, the Navy's Underwater Demolition Teams, had gone into combat on this beach and countless others throughout the western Pacific wearing nothing but swim trunks, fins, and mask, and, in the cold northern waters off Iwo Jima or here at Okinawa, a layer of grease to protect them from the cold. The Naked Warriors, they'd been called, by one who'd written a book about their exploits a few years after Korea.

His own father had been one of their number.

He checked his watch and his depth gauge. Thirty feet, twelve minutes. He was doing fine, so far as bottom time was concerned. To his left, Twidge Halstead was passing him with a gentle, steady scissors kick, exhaust bubbles tinkling in the water as they spilled from his SCUBA rig.

They were well inside the reef line here, and the waters of the lagoon were calm. The bottom, here where it grew shallow just off the beach, was white sand thickly scattered with

the prickly shapes of tarball-black sea urchins. It continued
to shoal as he kicked toward the shore. Tangretti increased
his pace a bit, rising slowly toward the sun dazzle on the
watery ceiling.

A moment later, his head broke water and he pulled his
legs under him, touching down on the sandy bottom and bracing himself against the surge of the ocean. Lifting his face
mask, he saw rows of low, rolling sand dunes on the beach
fifty yards ahead. Surf broke in white rollers at the mouth of
the Bishi River to the left; beyond, looming up from the top
of the limestone cliffs flanking the river, the bluff, tan facades
of apartment buildings overlooked the azure sea and white
beaches below. Directly ahead, more buildings rose from terrain that, not all that long ago, had been empty swampland
and salt marsh.

Halstead surfaced a few feet away, lifting his mask and
surveying the beach. "So, what do you think, Doc? Is this
the spot?"

"I think it is, Twidge." Tangretti pointed to the left.
"Bishi River, there." He pointed directly ahead, beyond the
dunes. "Kadena is back behind those dunes. Yeah, I think
this is the spot, or pretty damned close. Let's go!"

They swam side by side until the bottom shoaled to the
point where it was too shallow to swim. Then they removed
their fins, stood up, and waded the last dozen yards to the
beach. There, they unfastened their SCUBA tank harnesses,
leaving their gear in a pile above the high water line.

It was quiet here, almost eerily peaceful. A handful of other
people were on the shore further to the south, sunbathers and
swimmers, but the two SEALs had this part of the beach to
themselves.

What's the date, anyway? Tangretti thought. *8 April, yeah.
We're only a week or so off.*

On the first day of April 1945, Operation Iceberg, one of
the largest and most complex amphibious operations yet un-
dertaken in the Second World War, commenced off this six-
mile stretch of beaches on the southwestern end of the long,
skinny island called Okinawa. Ruled by Japan since 1879,
Okinawa, largest of the Ryukyu Islands, was widely considered to be a part of Japan proper, rather than one of her recent
Pacific conquests. Everyone connected with the invasion ex-

pected one hell of a fight. The long, white, sandy beach, called Hagushi, was sheltered by the offshore reefs, which were broken only where the Bishi River flowed into the sea. The coastline here was just fifteen miles from the southern tip of Okinawa and ten from the island's capital at Naha. Two vital airfields, Kadena and Yontan, were located beyond the dunes; indeed, the whole island was only about five or six miles wide at this point, and a successful landing here would make the seizure of several important objectives possible early in the invasion.

This particular strip of beach had been designated Orange 2, just south of the mouth of the Bishi River. And two days before the landings had begun, this beach had been the target of the Navy's Underwater Demolition Teams. UDT-21 was the unit assigned to survey Orange 2 and eliminate obstacles.

Tangretti had always wanted to come here, to this spot. His father, Steve Tangretti, had told him about the place, and about what had happened here, many times. Now, at long last, he was able to fulfill a promise he'd made to himself some time ago, and visit this place himself.

He'd arrived in Okinawa two weeks earlier, together with Halstead, Lieutenant Nolan, and several other SEALs who had volunteered for what was being somewhat ambiguously known as the Strategic Technical Directorate Assistance Team 158. MACV-SOG was officially being disbanded this month, and the STDATs were designed to take the place of the Studies and Observations Group . . . without anyone knowing that its place *had* been taken. The STDATs were theoretically supposed to continue advising South Vietnamese units in SEAL training and tactics, but the focus would almost certainly be limited to Bright Light–type operations. Hell, they weren't even stationed in Vietnam anymore but would respond to deployment orders from temporary basing here, at the Kadena airbase in Okinawa.

They'd been working pretty hard since they'd arrived on Okinawa, and this was the first weekend day when Tangretti and Halstead were able to take liberty and go on an excursion to the beaches near the base. They'd ''borrowed'' the SCUBA gear by employing a mild scam, convincing Lieutenant Nolan that a SCUBA survey of this part of the reef and the beach behind it fit nicely into a set of planned training exercises involving STDAT 158, and that they could carry out a preliminary survey on their day off if they could check out the requisite gear.

They knew that Nolan saw right through the excuse; Bright Light units weren't expected to have to perform beach surveys or anything else requiring SCUBA. Nolan was a good sort, though, who cut them plenty of slack. And it wasn't like there was a heavy schedule at Kadena. The handful of SEALs stationed there trained regularly and were expected to keep their gear cleaned, properly inventoried, and ready to go, but it wasn't like they were in hostile country, with daily military briefings and operations to carry out.

It hadn't been hard, then, to get permission to use SEAL equipment for their "reef survey." They'd picked up SCUBA gear at Kadena, then requisitioned a boat tied up down in Naha to take them up to the reef. With their launch anchored at the reef, they'd swum in, wading ashore at the same place, as near as Tangretti could figure it, that his father and other members of UDT-21 had investigated twenty-seven years ago.

Steve Tangretti was a legend in the Teams. He'd started off as a Seabee in World War II and been recruited to serve with the Navy Combat Demolition Units that had helped clear Omaha Beach on D day. After that, he'd transferred to the newly formed Underwater Demolition Teams operating in the Pacific. Ten years ago, in 1962, he'd helped to create the Navy SEALs, drawing volunteers from the UDTs and helping to design the training program and mission profile parameters. He was still in the Teams today, though he was rapidly approaching mandatory retirement age.

UDT-21 had gone ashore at Orange 2 on 29 March 1945— twenty-seven years earlier almost to the day. Tangretti's father had been carrying out beach reconnaissance and, when several of his teammates had been pinned down on the beach by an enemy machine gun, he'd swum out to a waiting LCP(R) to get help. The landing craft couldn't make it across the reef at low tide and couldn't risk drawing enemy fire from shore, but Tangretti and a UDT officer named Waverly had swum back to the beach with a rubber raft and a couple of M1 carbines, engaging enemy troops on *this* beach until the wounded men could make it to the safety of the sea.

The elder Tangretti had later said that he was pretty sure he'd killed his first man here, a Japanese soldier glimpsed as a toppling khaki blur over the sights of his carbine. He'd also helped take out a small flotilla of Japanese suicide boats, motorboats packed with explosives, that had been hidden in a small, inland lagoon just beyond the dune line, beneath the cliffs rising near the Bishi River. He and Waverly had raced down the beach and leaped into the water just ahead of a massive bombardment launched from a battleship offshore.

It was a bit sobering to know, Tangretti thought, that his father had been *that* close to being a casualty of both hostile and friendly fire . . . and that if he'd been caught in that bombardment, Bill Tangretti wouldn't be here on this beach today.

"So," Halstead said, interrupting Tangretti's thoughts. "Where to now?"

"I'm not really sure," Tangretti replied. "Now that I finally got here, it's like I don't really know where to go, or what to do."

"Doesn't much matter, does it? For me, it's good to be getting out from under all the brass hassles lately."

Tangretti looked at his friend. "ROEs got you dragging?"

"Well, not here, anyway. But if I hear another lecture about what I can and cannot do in Nam, I may start carrying protest signs myself."

Tangretti chuckled. "That I've *got* to see!"

"They send us to Nam to kick ass and take names . . . then they tell us we can't hurt anyone when we do it. What's next, social worker sessions with the NVA, to see why they're feeling hostile? Sitting down in a circle to hold hands and express our innermost feelings?"

"You know, Twidge, I heard a story from an airman over at Kadena yesterday. Enough to curdle the milk in your corn flakes."

"I'm not entirely sure I'm ready for this, Doc."

"It seems there was this Thud driver . . . you know, F-105s?"

"Yeah."

"He was on a routine assigned patrol a few days ago, over Quang Tri. That province is red-hot now, you know, with the Easter Offensive and everything."

"Go on."

"Okay, he's diddy-boppin' along, doing his thing, when he spots a couple of enemy tanks on the highway a couple miles north of his position."

"Not beyond the DMZ. . . ."

"Oh, no. He knew he wasn't allowed across the line. These tanks were definitely inside South Vietnam. So he calls 'em in, then peels off and zooms on down to pay the bad guys a visit. Hits 'em both with whatever ordnance he was carrying, and leaves behind two brightly burning North Vietnamese tanks."

"Good for him. What's the punch line?"

"This guy heads on back to base at Danang. Figures he's good for a medal or a commendation or at least a pat on the back. Instead, he gets slapped with a one-hundred-fifty-dollar fine by the FAA—did you know the FAA was running air traffic control over all of South Vietnam?"

"Yeah."

"I didn't. Never occurred to me. Anyway, it seems he'd left his assigned flight corridor without proper authorization, so he gets tagged for a hundred and fifty bucks. Man, there ain't no justice!"

"You got that right. What a stupid fucking way to run a war!"

"That's just it. We're *not* running it. Not anymore. We're just trying to stay afloat while we get the hell out, and not caring a lot who gets hurt in the meantime." Tangretti took a long, slow look at the surrounding dunes and blue water. "Things've sure changed since the big war, thirty years ago, huh?"

"They're calling the Second World War the last *good* war," Halstead said. "Never knew there was such a thing as a 'good war,' but the way we fight 'em sure has changed."

"My dad and UDT-21 came ashore here," Tangretti said, "right *here,* on this spot, and they knew what they were fighting for. They had to stop the Japanese Empire from gobbling up most of Asia and the Pacific, and they did. I can just imagine what those guys would say to fighting according to the rules."

"Your dad's still in, isn't he?"

"Yeah."

"You told me once he was in Nam a few years back? What does he think of all this?"

"Nothing you can share in mixed company, that's for sure. You know, it's really crazy. We fought the Japanese to an unconditional surrender. Now they're our friends. Look at those apartment buildings over there! That's prosperity, man . . . and Okinawa isn't exactly the most prosperous part of Japan right now."

"That's just because so many Americans are based here. Spending money. Unemployment's still a bitch here."

"Well, yeah. The point is, the Japanese are our good buddies now, after we damned near clobbered them into the stone age, like Curtis LeMay likes to put it. Can you imagine, after fighting this half-assed, on-again, off-again, pull-your-punches war with Hanoi, that the North Vietnamese'll ever be our friends?"

"They're Communists, Doc. Can't be friends with *Communists*. That'd be hypocritical."

"Oh. Nixon can go to China and talk about recognizing them and everything, but—"

"Aw, screw it, Doc. You know none of this makes any sense! It gives me a headache thinking about it!"

"Well, I guess times change."

"Well, things've changed *here* a lot in twenty-some years, I'll tell you. Those buildings weren't there back then." Halstead turned around, then shaded his eyes, staring south along the beach. "Wow. Something tells me those babes in bikinis over there weren't here either."

"They didn't *have* bikinis back then."

"I think some of those chicks only have half a bikini now. Let's wander on down that way. What d'ya say?"

"Twidge! Damn it, I thought you were happily married!"

"Hey, doesn't stop a guy from looking and admiring."

"Looking and drooling, you mean. It ought to!"

Halstead looked at Tangretti, head cocked to one side, a mischievous twinkle in his eyes. "Thus sayeth the Gospel of St. Doc."

Tangretti opened his mouth for a sharp retort, then snapped it shut again. Since the experience with the hippies in California, he'd solidly put his conversion experience behind him. He was careful to tell himself that he hadn't actually *rejected*

Christ or Christianity—those were too important to him to be simply or casually abandoned—but he'd been forced to put the whole idea of salvation on hold for a time while he attended to being a SEAL. Being a Christian was a full-time job, something that ought to fill and remake him completely. But being a SEAL was a full-time job, too, and he was still having a little trouble figuring out how to make the two overlap.

The worst part of it was the feeling that he'd turned his back on Pat, somehow, leaving her to continue the Christian part of their life, while he focused on the SEAL stuff. That could be a sign of rough weather ahead, if he let things go too far.

Maybe as soon as the national agony of Vietnam was at last, truly, and completely ended, he could worry about getting his own life back in order.

He wondered what was planned for the SEAL Teams once the war was over. There were already rumors—unpleasant ones—of SEALs being called into their COs' offices and unceremoniously told that they were out of the Teams, that they could transfer to Explosive Ordnance Disposal or salvage work or even get out of the Navy, but that the Teams didn't need them anymore. Tangretti didn't believe those rumors for a second; the Teams would not abandon their people, any more than a SEAL would leave a teammate behind during an op.

But it was true that the Navy SEAL Teams had been built up quite a bit during the Vietnam War, and, in peacetime, the Navy wouldn't need as many SEALs as were probably already on the roster.

Well, that was a problem to be dealt with some other time. Halstead had started walking on down the beach, moving in the general direction of the sunbathers . . . who most likely were the American wives and kids of U.S. servicemen stationed on Okinawa. Much of the island, especially the interior, was given over to various U.S. military bases, of which the Air Force base at Kadena was by far the largest; many dependent families had come to live here with husbands or, in a few cases, wives who were in the service and stationed on Okinawa. Tangretti decided to strike out inland, clambering up a steep dune to see what lay beyond.

He had seriously considered talking Pat into moving to Okinawa, as long as he was going to be stationed at Kadena for the next year or so, but the time or two he'd raised the subject, she'd insisted that she and Davy were going to stay where they were, in El Cajon. He worried about her; those damned hippies still knew where she lived, and he wasn't around to keep an eye on things, but she'd told him in no uncertain terms that she could look out for herself.

But there were problems with upping stakes and moving to Okinawa, too. The island was, just this year, being officially returned to Japan after twenty-seven years of U.S. occupation. There was the possibility of anti-American demonstrations. Perhaps even worse, the island was already crowded, and living quarters for dependent families were at an absolute premium. Hell, Pat could be on a waiting list until damned near the time when he was due to rotate back to CONUS.

And, fortunately, the incident with the hippies back in California appeared to have ended with a lack of official fireworks . . . fewer fireworks, at any rate, than the people involved had had any right to expect. Nolan had later told Tangretti and Halstead that he'd been privately warned by his commanding officer that military operations aimed at American civilians were so far beyond the pale that anyone, officer or enlisted man, who tried such a thing would end up buried so deep beneath the Naval prison at Portsmouth that he would never see daylight again.

On the other hand, though, the intelligence gained by Naval Intelligence and the FBI on SDS subversion efforts had been invaluable, and the official word was that harassment calls and threats against members of the Special Warfare community had now all but ended. Simply identifying Bonnie Mason as the SDS's agent in the personnel office at Coronado had probably turned the tide on that front. Mason had been arrested on various charges—most of them having to do with either the misuse of classified or private information or with drugs—and received a jail sentence that was later commuted to time served. She'd left the San Diego area then, and nobody seemed to know where she'd gone. The three men Tangretti and Halstead had detained in the desert had all been arrested as well, though charges had later been dropped. Since that night, however, neither Pat nor Wendy had received a single obscene or threatening telephone call. They'd promised to tell other members of the SEAL community if anything happened while their husbands were overseas. If Moe, Larry, or Curly were still in Southern California, they were keeping a damned low profile.

And they were keeping the hell out of the way of the SEALs. It looked like that crisis, at least, was over.

Tangretti just wished he could put the whole unsavory episode out of his mind. He felt like he'd been tested . . . and that he'd failed, that he'd been forced to throw down his helmet liner and ring the damned bell. Instead of trusting God, he'd damned near exploded, and if it hadn't been for Twidge, he knew that he could well have killed those creeps and wrecked his own life, and Pat's as well.

He reached the top of the dune. Below him, inland, were more dunes and a small, neatly manicured lagoon fronting a pricey-looking apartment complex, complete with marina and small boats, with a channel leading toward the river. He couldn't be sure, but he thought this must have been the inland lagoon where his father had encountered the Japanese suicide boats and where he'd exchanged fire with enemy soldiers. Where he'd killed for the first time.

By now, Bill Tangretti had killed many men, so many that he wasn't sure of the number. He didn't like the fact, but it came with the territory.

He was a SEAL, after all. . . .

A big part of the problem with Vietnam, he knew, was America's current squeamishness about war and killing. He didn't *like* killing people; most·SEALs didn't, whatever the antiwar creeps said. But killing and death and destruction were inescapable parts of war. It could not be cleaned up or sanitized, not without making the entire situation a hundred times worse.

In World War II, the United States had fought a pitched battle here on Okinawa. This sliver of land in the East China Sea covered just 922 square miles, but the battle had taken two months to win. The battle had killed three thousand Americans . . . and total U.S. casualties had been closer to fifty thousand, as many in those two months as had died so far in Vietnam. One hundred twenty thousand Japanese soldiers had died; one hundred forty thousand Okinawan civilians had died as well, many of them suicides after the Japanese had told them they would be raped and butchered by the barbarian invaders.

Tangretti caught himself as he juggled those numbers, and he gave a wry smile. It was almost as though he were saying, *Now that was a war.* . . .

But, damn it, which was worse . . . to commit to all-out war, as hurtful and as distasteful as that might be, to fight the war and fight it to the end, to victory? Or to play this endless game of escalation and negotiation, of ROEs and legitimate targets, dribbling American boys home in body bags a few tens or a few hundreds at a time, watching the total casualty figures mount, and all for no decent or honorable or *fitting* reason that he could see? . . .

Scary thought. What kind of a world was young Davy going to inherit?

Turning south, he started walking along the line of dunes. Before too long, he caught up with Halstead, who was sitting on the sand, talking to a pair of pretty, teenaged, American-looking girls who were lying facedown on their beach towels, their bikini tops unhooked as they baked out the tan lines on their backs. One was blond, the other brunette. "Blondes" and "brunettes," Tangretti's father had told him more than once, were the code words the Teams used at Okinawa and elsewhere to refer to swimmers unrecovered and to swimmers already picked up.

He wondered if Halstead was trying a pickup on these two.

"Yeah," Halstead was saying as Tangretti approached, "we're what they call Frogmen. You know, like Richard Widmark, in the movie?"

"Richard who?" one of the girls, the blonde, asked.

"You're showing your age, Twidge," Tangretti said.

"Hey, Doc!" Halstead said. "Meet Kathy and Sarah. Their dads are Air Force officers, over at Kadena."

"Nice to meet you, ladies," Tangretti said. "Twidge? We ought to be getting back."

"Well, you know, Kathy and Sarah offered to drive us back to town."

"Sure," the brunette said. She raised herself off her towel and pointed inland, affording a not-quite accidental glimpse of a pertly erect nipple. ''Our car's parked on the road, right over there. We could give you guys a lift, if you wanted.''

''That's very kind of you, miss,'' Tangretti said. ''Unfortunately, we have a boat to return to Naha. *Don't* we, Twidge.''

''Hell, we could come out for that later. There's no hurry.''

''If you like,'' the blonde said, ''Greg, here, can go back with you, Kathy. I could swim out with this one. He's kind of cute, and I'd enjoy the swim, and stuff.''

''I don't think so,'' Tangretti said, a little more coldly than he'd intended. ''Thank you, but I'm married, and happily so. Besides, we have a pile of SCUBA gear to get back to Kadena. Nice meeting you, ladies.'' Turning on his heel, he strode off north, up the beach.

Halstead caught up with him a few minutes later. ''What the hell, Doc?'' he demanded, angrily. ''Why are you being such a prick?''

''*I'm* being a prick?''

''I think I liked it better when you were playing the holy roller. At least I knew where I stood with you!''

''Twidge,'' Tangretti said, his voice dangerously quiet, ''what the *fuck* do you think you were doing back there? What about Wendy?''

''I don't know what business it is of yours, Doc,'' Halstead replied.

''Wendy is a good friend, for your information. She's Pat's best friend. I don't want to see her hurt. And I want to know what the problem is with you. You never used to chase girls like that. You're starting to act like Hank.''

Hank Richardson, a SEAL with Team Two on the East Coast, was Bill's half brother—his mother's son by an earlier marriage to an NCDU man killed at Omaha—and a notorious skirt-chaser. Tangretti's father, for that matter, still had a reputation as a womanizer, complete with rumors that he'd bedded female Viet Cong in Saigon to get information. Bill had always been something of a straight arrow when it came to women and sex.

Maybe that was why Halstead's behavior bothered him so much.

Halstead was silent for the next dozen yards or so. At last, though, he shook his head. ''I'm sorry, Doc. I didn't mean to jump down your throat. I . . . I don't really know what the deal is. Maybe I'm just not quite ready for this married stuff, y'know? And, well, I think Wendy understands. We've talked about it, and all, and when we're separated for so damned long, it's, well, it's not like I'm really *betraying* her or anything. . . ."

"It isn't, huh? Last I heard, it was 'forsaking all others,' man. Anything else is a cop-out. You keep talking about Americans betraying their country and everything. Maybe you should take a look at a husband betraying his wife."

"I didn't *do* anything!"

"No, but you damned sure were thinking about it." He remembered a phrase of Halstead's, at the restaurant, long ago, and smiled. "I could hear your dick hardening from here."

Halstead blinked, then chuckled. "Well, maybe you did at that."

"Seriously, buddy," Tangretti said, "I think you'd better watch yourself. My dad played fast and loose with the marriage vows, and I know things got pretty unhappy at home." They reached the spot where they'd left their SCUBA gear. "Wait," he said. "What's that?"

He could just hear the grumble of an engine, coming from the direction of the dunes inland. Suddenly, the great, gray bulk of a Navy HH-53 helicopter heaved itself up from behind the limestone cliffs in the direction of Kadena, hesitated a moment, then descended down the dune line, heading straight for the two SEALs.

"I think," Halstead said, "that our liberty has just been revoked."

"Looks that way," Tangretti replied. "Wonder what's up?"

The helo settled onto the beach fifty yards away, and Tangretti could see the crew chief leaning from the side hatch, waving them on. Retrieving their SCUBA tanks, fins, and masks, the two SEALs trotted across the beach, ducking their heads and squinting their eyes as they entered the swirl of windblown sand stirred up by the still-turning rotors.

"You Halstead and Tangretti?" the crew chief yelled at them as they approached the chopper.

"That's us," Tangretti shouted back. The rotor noise made gentle conversation impossible.

"Get aboard! You guys are wanted back at Kadena!"

"We've got a boat out on the reef," Tangretti said.

The chief shook his head. "Fuck it. We'll send somebody to get it later and tow it back. My orders are to bring you in *now*."

"What?" Halstead replied. "We in trouble or something?"

"That's your guilty conscience speaking, Twidge," Tangretti told him as he boosted himself aboard.

"Beats me," the crew chief said, answering Halstead's question. "But a Lieutenant Nolan said to find you guys out here and drag you back by the stacking swivels if we had to. Said to tell you it was a Bright Light alert!"

Tangretti and Halstead exchanged knowing glances as they strapped themselves into a couple of seats in the back of the HH-53, and the big machine lifted off the beach in a scream of rotors and a small hurricane of sand whirled about by the rotor wash. In the distance, Tangretti could see the two girls they'd talked to, delightfully topless, their mouths open with astonishment as the helo lifted into the sky, canted sharply to port, and headed back across the dunes toward Kadena.

Their vacation was over. They were headed back to Vietnam.

Chapter 31

**Intelligence Center
Danang, Republic of Vietnam
0912 hours**

The rules, Greg decided, were starting to hedge him in, to tie him down. He was feeling suffocated, like taking a drag at your mouthpiece at eighty feet and realizing nothing was coming through.

And he couldn't even tell which way was up, which way to swim in order to snatch that next, desperately needed, life-giving breath.

Tangretti was right, he'd admitted to himself during the long C-130 flight from Kadena to Danang. He was married now, had spoken an oath that bound him to Wendy, and there was no longer room in his life for the popular girl-in-every-port image cultivated by many sailors and most SEALs. Wendy was more than enough woman for him; her memory kept him company when he was overseas, and the promise of being in her arms again kept him going. Those girls on the beach in Okinawa had been convenient targets of opportunity . . . but nothing even remotely approaching a replacement for Wendy.

So why had he started slick-talking those two? He knew damned well that they'd both been willing, fascinated by the little he'd told them about his being a frogman, and excited by the promise of a quick, strings-free fling with a genu-wine war hero, as Morgan would have said. He knew where things would have gone if Doc hadn't been there with his moralistic preachments and stick-in-the-mud disapproval.

Not that he blamed Tangretti. Doc had been *right*. . . .

It was the rules. Day by day, it seemed, the SEALs and other units like them were being given longer and longer lists of Thou-shalt-nots, and they'd been given a long list indeed during their initial briefing at Kadena, yesterday afternoon. They could not call in fire on an enemy target without getting full and proper clearance first . . . just to make certain that there were no civilians in the line of fire. Individual enemy commanders or political officers or agents could no longer be targeted; nothing whatsoever that smelled in the least like the dread word assassination was to be allowed in this new, cleaned-up version of the Vietnam War. The Rules of Engagement, or ROEs, were to be carefully worked out before any planned engagement, and strictly adhered to.

Greg thought again about the story Tangretti had told him yesterday, the one about the F-105 pilot fined for leaving his flight corridor. He thought about the rules laid down during their last tour in Nam, the ones requiring them to notify civilian and military authorities that they were going to be operating in a given area on a given date. The colossal, hopeless insanity of a war fenced in by bureaucratic hedgings, feel-good weasel-words, and political panderings was becoming too damned much to bear. Sometimes Greg thought that if he couldn't break free of the artificial and deadly restrictions, he was going to go stark, shrieking nuts.

It had taken a while for things to click, but Greg had begun to appreciate that a lot of his unrest lately had less to do with Wendy or their marriage than with the fast-rising walls of rules and regulations, the ROEs and Thou-shalt-nots that put his life and the life of his teammates at risk solely to pick up a few votes for some politician Stateside, or to make sure that the newspapers and television anchormen couldn't say unpleasant things about the generals and admirals who were prosecuting this war.

Was that why he was kicking against the traces of his marriage? Seemed like damned thin pop psychology when he thought about it that way, but the more he did think about it, the more Greg thought that that was what was going on.

He'd have to think about it some more, once this op was over.

In the meantime, there *was* another op. After an initial briefing at Kadena yesterday, Bill and Greg boarded a Danang-bound C-130 with Lieutenant Nolan and fellow STDAT 158 SEALs MM2 John Kilroy, GMC Randy Calahan, and an old buddy of theirs, DM1 Robert "Boomer" Cain, from their days with Delta Platoon at Nha Trang. In Danang, they'd met another old friend from earlier deployments, Nghiep Van Dong, still with the LDNN, and with him a number of other South Vietnamese SEALs. Arriving at the base, they'd settled down in their old SOG barracks, not far from the Intelligence Center where their second briefing was scheduled for this morning.

The American SEALs entered a room already filled with brass. The briefing was supposed to bring the Technical Directorate Team up to speed on what was turning out to be an unexpectedly important recovery operation, but it looked like quite a few senior men had decided to work their way into the meeting, for reasons that Greg could only guess at. Present in the Intelligence Center meeting room were a handful of Army and Air Force officers, including Lieutenant Commander Kelso, their NILO during their tour at Danang with SOG, who'd since picked up a promotion and returned for another tour.

Their briefing officer this morning was an Air Force colonel named Myers, who seemed moderately distressed to be discussing the situation with a bunch of Navy men. It was as though he found the fact that the Air Force had managed to misplace one of its light colonels somewhat embarrassing. Also present was a clutch of other senior officers, including Air Force General Ellison, an Army general named Mattingly, and a Marine colonel. In fact, it appeared that the five SEALs—not counting Nolan, of course—were the only enlisted men in the room.

It was not exactly a comfortable environment, and the fact that the tension inside that briefing room was tight enough to play like a drum didn't help things one bit.

"One week ago," Myers was saying as he pointed to one particular part of a large-scale topographical map hanging on the wall, "one of our people bailed out of his electronic warfare aircraft after it was hit by a SAM in this general area, near the town of Cam Lo. The others aboard the downed aircraft are presumed dead. Lieutenant Colonel Frank Halliwell, however, landed safely. Using his call sign, Bravo One-niner, he was able to make contact with an O-2 pilot, call sign Birddog, almost at once and managed to hide in a small patch of woods about . . . here, roughly bounded by several villages and their associated rice paddies and gardens, and the Song Mieu Giang River, which flows west to east, here. Unfortunately, he came down almost on top of this intersection of Highway 561, coming down from the north, and Route 8, running east and west. Since the beginning of the enemy's Easter Offensive, this area has seen extraordinarily heavy NVA traffic. Not long after he was down, Halliwell used his emergency radio to call in targets for a strike by A1s and F-4s. Damage assessment after the strikes confirmed six tank kills—PT-76 recon tanks—and a large number of trucks. That'll give you an idea.''

It did indeed. Greg remembered the tanks he and Tangretti and their team had tracked in Laos . . . the tanks that had helped defeat the South Vietnamese invasion of Laos last year.

It sounded like Hanoi had decided to push those tanks into South Vietnam now, in a go-for-broke attempt to win the war here and now.

''Birddog called for help and vectored in a rescue force, two Slicks and two Cobra gunships. They ran into a hail of small arms and antiaircraft fire. One Slick was shot down, and one of the Cobras was damaged, forcing the rest to retire.

''With the failure of that rescue, we decided to try to isolate Halliwell, to keep the Charlies away from his position. We sent in flights of A1 Sandys loaded with gravel. Saturated a wide band around the patch of woods where he was hiding.''

''Excuse me,'' the Army general said. '' 'Gravel'?''

''Yes, sir. It's what we call the things. Small mines, each about the size of your fist. A Sandy can come in low and drop hundreds of them in a precise pattern.''

''They're frozen when they're dropped,'' Kelso added. ''They arm when they thaw out. Some of the stuff is downright diabolical, made up to look like dog shit or rocks. Powerful enough to blow a man's foot off if he even steps close to the thing. They came up with the gimmick so they could mine the Ho Chi Minh Trail from the air.''

Greg grimaced. America might be on the way out of Vietnam, but the horror of this war would remain for the Vietnamese people for a long, long time to come, no matter who won ultimately. Kids playing, farmers plowing their fields, lovers going for an evening's stroll . . .

A second unpleasant thought followed close on the heels of the first. Surrounding Halliwell with mines might keep the North Vietnamese away from him for a time, but it wouldn't for long.

It was also a great way of telling the enemy *exactly* where the downed flier was hiding.

"Over the next few days, the SAR boys kept trying to go back and pull Halliwell out," Myers said, continuing the briefing. "They ran into the heaviest concentration of antiaircraft fire ever encountered in this damned war . . . a lot of it from guns hidden in these surrounding villages. One of the helos was hit but managed to get back to base. An F-4 Phantom out of Nakhon, Thailand, call sign Nail-38, was hit by a SAM-2. The crew ejected safely. The pilot was captured on the ground. The observer landed a couple of miles from Halliwell's position and, so far, has managed to evade capture."

"So . . . that means you have two men on the ground behind enemy lines?" Nolan asked.

"That is affirmative. We've been keeping FAC aircraft on top of both men and using heavy air strikes to break up enemy attempts to get at them. But the effort has turned into a Mexican standoff. The black hats can't get at our men, but we can't get in to pick our boys up. On Thursday, after a heavy bombardment of the area, we tried to sneak a Jolly Green in to Halliwell. It was shot down by an antiaircraft cannon hidden inside a village. Five men were killed."

Ouch. Greg wondered when the mounting casualty toll reached the point where the high command decided that no more lives or aircraft would be sacrificed for one man.

"Yesterday," Colonel Myers went on, "Friday, we tried a different tactic. Called in multiple strikes by B-52s all around our people's positions. General Abrams himself had to push the order through. It's probably the first time in history that a B-52 strike was used as a diversion or in support of a rescue effort. It cooled the region down a bit, but subsequent efforts to get helos in were forced off by hidden antiaircraft guns."

Lieutenant Nolan shifted in his seat. "Colonel, I certainly

applaud the fact that you don't want to abandon any of your men to the enemy. But, if you don't mind my saying so, isn't this an unusual effort for one man?''

''Damn it, Lieutenant—'' the Air Force general said, his face reddening.

Myers held up his hand. ''No, no, General Ellison. He's right.'' He seemed to sag, his shoulders slumping a bit. ''Yes, Lieutenant. I hate to admit it, but it is. These men, both of them, but especially Halliwell, are special. We would have tried to get them out in any case, but the situation *demands* that both men be extracted, and as quickly as possible. We cannot risk having them fall into enemy hands.

''It turns out that the observer in the F-4, a Lieutenant Clark, is the son of a well-known World War II general—''

''Wait a minute,'' Greg said, his fascination with history tweaked. ''Mark Clark?''

''That's the one. You can imagine how the media would play this back home if the son of a prominent World War II general was paraded through Hanoi . . . or used as a bargaining chip at Paris. The peace talks are broken off now, at Nixon's orders. Clark could give Hanoi the leverage they would need to force us back to the table, on *their* terms.''

''Alternatively,'' Kelso put in, ''there is the chance that they would be able to break him through torture. Antiwar statements from the son of General Clark, put together with whatever Jane Fonda or Hannah DuPlessey decided to say on Hanoi's behalf, well, it wouldn't be good.''

''But you said that Halliwell is even more important,'' Nolan said.

''Colonel Halliwell,'' Myers explained quietly, ''is privy to certain information which must not be allowed to fall into enemy hands. Specifically, we're afraid that if the North Vietnamese get him, they will pass him on to their Russian friends. If that happens, Halliwell will never be returned. He would be too valuable to the Russians for intelligence purposes. They would keep him and wring him dry.''

''What does he know, Colonel?'' Boomer asked, bantering. ''Nixon's unlisted number in California?''

''Actually,'' Myers replied coldly, ''Colonel Halliwell used to work for SAC, as the assistant DCO of a missile wing in South Dakota.''

Greg pursed his lips as he heard the muffled exclamations from the other men in the room. *That* explained Myers's embarrassment at losing Halliwell . . . and it damned sure explained the incredible commitment the Air Force was showing to his rescue.

"If the KGB or GRU got hold of Halliwell," Kelso said, "they could learn a great deal about our missile procedures that we'd really rather they not know."

Greg had heard scuttlebutt, both back at Coronado and in Okinawa, that the wreck of a Soviet submarine had recently been found in the North Pacific, where it had foundered and sunk due to some malfunction. The rumors held that the CIA was engaged in an all-out attempt to recover that sub, using a civilian research vessel, the *Glomar Challenger,* to lift it from the seabed. The main reason such an operation would be carried out would be to inspect the Soviet's warheads in order to determine their firing codes and targeting data, and, to get it, the CIA was willing to spend tens of millions of dollars.

The Russians would want to interrogate Halliwell for precisely the same reason.

"Do we have reason to believe that the enemy knows Halliwell's importance?" Nolan asked. "Might they suspect he's important to us from the lengths you've gone to to recover him?"

"They know who he is," Kelso replied. "On Tuesday, we intercepted radio traffic from Hanoi to NVA battalion commanders around Cam Lo. They mentioned Halliwell's name and rank and gave very specific orders that he was to be captured alive by any means possible and at any cost."

"Since he's SAC," Myers added, "the Russians probably have a file on him this thick." He held up his thumb and forefinger, four inches apart.

"What the hell was a guy like that doing on a combat mission in the first place?" Greg demanded. "I thought they tried to keep people with highly classified information out of the line of fire!"

"Normally that's true," Myers replied. "In this case, his expertise at the EW console of an EB-66 was deemed . . . of great importance. His mission profiles kept him clear of the SAM batteries in the far north and well above the range of conventional antiaircraft artillery. Damn it, no one expected the North Vietnamese to have SAMs so far south!''

"Yeah," Tangretti murmured, almost beneath his breath. "We're gonna have to talk to those gomers about that."

"Sure," Greg added. "They could spoil this whole war for the rest of us with irresponsible garbage like putting missiles where they're not supposed to."

"They break the rules," Boomer said, "they gotta pay!"

"All right, all right," Nolan said. "Can the comedy, people. Let's hear what the man has to tell us."

"Yes, well," Myers continued, "in any case, the decision was made not to try further conventional helicopter rescues. Even though our F-4s hammered the known gun positions pretty well, it is more than likely that a large number of guns remained undetected, or that others were moved in once the F-4s completed their run.

"We cannot, obviously, abandon our man, however. We need to come up with an alternate means of getting him out. To that end, we brought your team down from Okinawa. We have also put into operation a plan of our own designed to get Halliwell out of this heavy concentration of enemy firepower, here, and down to a quieter sector where we can extract him."

"That sounds pretty damned risky, sir," Tangretti said.

"We had no choice. Our FAC spotter planes confirmed that Vietnamese troops were using mine detectors to work their way through Halliwell's Maginot Line, as we called it. The Sandys kept going in, strafing the enemy troops and sowing more mines. We kept hitting 'em with F-4s and F-105s, too, dropping cluster bombs and generally raising hell all over that part of the province. But the gomers kept working at it, bringing in more men and more mine detectors. It was a standoff for several days, but they finally began making progress, especially when fog interrupted our strikes. The only alternative is a ground retrieval. We looked at many plans, but, well, the only one that shows any hope at all of success would involve special units, like your advisory team."

The reluctant way Myers said those last words sounded to Greg like something torn from a man under threat of torture.

"The SEALs have plenty of experience sneaking into areas of heavy enemy concentration," Nolan pointed out, "carrying out an op and slipping out again without anyone being the wiser.''

And you'd have been a hell of a lot better off using us from the get-go, Greg thought, a little bitterly. From the very beginning, this war had been mismanaged by people convinced that bigger and better and more expensive was the way to go, despite plenty of evidence to the clear contrary. Using B-52s to isolate a downed flyer and prevent enemy recovery efforts was on a par with doing retinal surgery with a cavalry saber . . . or going after a mosquito with a tank. A B-52 raid was not exactly discriminating enough to perform well as a *tactical* weapon. . . .

But trust the military mentality of any service to blunder around for a while with sabers or tanks before finally admitting that another branch of the military might be able to pull off the job.

''That's why we brought you people in,'' Myers said, though it must have been like pulling teeth for the Air Force officer to admit to a reliance on the Navy. ''We're also working with several Marine Recon teams in the area.''

''I still don't like this,'' the Air Force general put in. ''There's got to be another way than relying . . .'' He broke off, giving the SEALs an unreadable look. ''Relying on a bunch of John Wayne cowboys.''

''We've been over this, General,'' Kelso said. ''If there were another way that offered any hope at all of Halliwell's rescue, we would employ it.''

Myers cleared his throat, then indicated the mined-in region with a finger. ''As I, ah, said earlier, the idea was to get Halliwell out of this pocket, through this enemy-held territory to the east, then south to this portion of the Song Mieu Giang River. Up here, where he was trapped, the river is too open and too narrow to afford much cover. Down here, another couple of miles or so, the banks are heavily forested, most places, and the river's wide enough for a swimmer to stay hidden if he has to. We're guiding Halliwell by radio overland to this spot, where we hope you people can make physical contact.''

''Guiding him, sir?'' Nolan asked. ''I assume you've taken precautions along the way. Charlie has damned big ears.''

''That's damned near the best part of this whole frapping

mess," Myers said. "Somebody came up with one hell of an idea on that." Myers picked up a transparent mylar sheet and carefully hung it in place so that it lay squarely over the map. Drawn on the clear plastic in green Magic Marker were a number of elongated blobs . . . some as straight as cigars, others hooked to left or right. It looked for all the world like aerial views of golf courses laid end to end across the Vietnamese countryside.

"It happens that Halliwell is an avid golfer," Myers said. "He's played on courses at Air Force bases all over the world. We've learned from officers who played with him that he knows many of the holes on those courses better than most of you know your own backyards." He pointed at the first cigar-shaped blob, which started right where Halliwell had been holed up. Realization hit Greg. It *was* a golf fairway, with the tee positioned at the starting point. "We began directing him like so, feeding him course and direction by telling him to play such and such a hole. The first one, for example, is the first hole at Tucson National . . . 450 yards, heading southeast. That way we could guide him precisely, keep track of his position on the ground, and be fairly sure that the Charlies, even if they're listening in on our frequencies, don't have an idea in hell what we're talking about. Not many Vietnamese, it happens, go in for golf, and those who do won't have all of these holes memorized, the way Halliwell does.

"Early this morning, we got Halliwell out of his hole and on his way. We're vectoring him toward the river, right here. It's worked out to eighteen holes, the front nine getting him to the river, the back nine getting him down the river from here . . . to here. We call this Point Clubhouse. You boys will meet him at Point Clubhouse . . . which is still about two miles inside some very hostile territory. If you can reach him any earlier on his line of march, great . . . but he's definitely going to need help from Point Clubhouse on. This area here," he swung his hand over a broad swath, "is what amounts to the NVA front lines right now, and it's crawling with troops, tanks, SAM-2s, you name it."

"How the hell did you get him through that minefield?" Nolan asked. Greg had been wondering the same thing. He was damned glad they wouldn't have to sneak into the field, then out again once they picked him up.

"During our last air strike yesterday," Kelso explained, "our F-4s dropped a few in the minefield southeast of Halliwell's position. We were taking a risk, of course—there was a chance that the F-4s wouldn't get all of the mines in the corridor—but apparently they did well enough for Halliwell to sneak through. Once he was in the clear, he's been moving pretty fast."

"Is he? How's his health?" Greg asked.

"Not bad, considering that he's been lying in a hole for a solid week. He went for several days without water, before it rained and he was able to catch some. He's been foraging for raw corn and berries in a nearby field. He also reports that he injured his hand in the ejection, though that doesn't seem to be too serious. By the time you reach him, he will be exhausted, though, and weak from exposure and hunger."

"Perhaps more important," Nolan said, "how are his spirits holding up? A week behind enemy lines . . . that's damned tough. And being on the receiving end of a B-52 strike would be enough to ruin anyone's day."

Nolan, Greg thought, had just put his finger on a key point of this op, more critical, possibly, even than the large number of enemy troops in the area. If Halliwell's mental attitude wasn't in good shape, the SEALs would be facing a much tougher mission. The man couldn't be real happy after a week in the field . . . and at the receiving end of friendly fire, no less.

"The FAC controllers said that he nearly lost it after the B-52s went through. He pulled together, though, and has been playing golf. They say he seems upbeat enough now, if a little worn out." Myers shook his head. "This has to be pretty hard on a guy fifty-six years old."

"This would be hard on a twenty-six-year-old, Colonel," Nolan said. "Have you been able to airdrop supplies to him? Food? Water?"

"Not so far. One attempt when he was in the hole failed when the canister landed on the wrong side of the Maginot Line. We can't do it now, because the drop would alert the North Vietnamese to his location. We were able to get him out of the minefield okay, but we expect the enemy to get through the mines sometime later today. When they do, they'll find out he's gone, and begin searching the entire region. We can't do anything to risk giving away his position.

"Now, let's start working out the details of the operation." Myers paused and looked at the five other SEALs seated in the room. "Only the six of you? We'll need to augment that, possibly with Marine Recon. I think we can—"

"Sir, the six of us will be all that is needed," Nolan said, interrupting. "We'll need some of the local LDNNs as guides, but this will actually work better if we pare it down to bare essentials. Three teams of two men each, each team with two LDNNs—"

"That's a negative, Lieutenant," Ellison said. He gave the SEAL officer a hard look, then frowned at Myers. "Colonel, I agreed to this approach because General Caldwell and General Mattingly both felt that an interservice operation would be in the best interests of all. I must tell you, though, that I am not pleased about the way this operation is shaping up, not pleased at all. Using these, these trained *assassins* to infiltrate the enemy's lines does not strike me as a viable means of accomplishing our objective."

"General," Myers said, "this plan gives us our best chance of success. We've all agreed to that. I needn't remind you, sir, that this plan has been discussed and approved by the Joint Chiefs. The president himself is following this operation closely." Myers looked at Nolan. "Please understand, Mr. Nolan, that this operation is a team effort. There will be no grandstanding, and there will be no unnecessary risks taken in recovering Colonel Halliwell and Lieutenant Clark. We will give you your orders, and you and your men will carry them out. To the letter. Do you understand?"

"Aye, sir," Nolan said. "Perfectly."

"Good. Now, here's the way we see the mission going down . . ."

Two wearing hours later, the briefing session broke for lunch, and Greg and Tangretti walked across to one of the enlisted men's mess halls. "Idiots," Greg said disgustedly. "It's a wonder South Vietnam has held out as long as it has."

"It'll be okay, Twidge. The lieutenant had a funny look on his face when he signed off on that stuff."

"Nolan always looks like that."

"I don't think so," Tangretti said. "My guess is that he's going to do it his own way. No matter what."

"Well, it damned sure wouldn't be the first time, would it?"

Greg wondered, though, what a handful of SEALs were going to be able to do in what had to be one of the largest and most involved military rescue operations ever mounted.

And one where some of the brass, at least, weren't at all keen on Navy participation.

Chapter 32

Monday, 10 April 1972

North of the Song Mieu Giang River
Near Dông Ha
12 miles south of the DMZ
0410 hours

Lieutenant Colonel Frank Halliwell crouched in the darkness, measuring his chances. He would only get one shot, and the kill would have to be clean and swift. He took another step forward ... then another, tensing, ready to spring. He was almost close enough now. ...

He lunged forward, hands outstretched, fingers closing on the neck of the scrawny chicken that he'd been stalking for the past five minutes. Just as he landed on knees and elbows, something else, large, massive, struck him from the left, knocking him over and rolling him into the dust.

The chicken fled, unharmed, with a raucous squawk and a flutter of scattered tailfeathers. A knife flashed in the moonlight, descending; Halliwell threw up one arm, blocking the stab ... then grunted as the blade, deflected by his move, flicked past his head and buried its point in his left shoulder.

He nearly screamed with the shock and the pain of it, but he held onto his assailant, rolling with him, batting the knife aside as he reached for his own survival knife inside its vest sheath.

The moment, the horror, seemed frozen in time. He could see nothing of his assailant except his eyes—slanted, Asian eyes—inches from his own. The smell of the man's breath, heavy with the fermented fish sauce with which Vietnamese laced their meals, was overpowering. For seconds that dragged on for an eternity, Halliwell gripped the other man's knife hand, while his own knife hand was held in the sweaty grip of his enemy. Then Halliwell managed to lash out with his foot, rolling the man off his chest, following through with the roll, landing on top of the Vietnamese and dropping all of his weight onto the handle of his knife.

He felt the point of his knife slice through the other man's flesh, sliding neatly between two ribs. He saw the other man's eyes widen with shock and realization and pain, felt a gushing, sticky warmth as blood geysered from the man's punctured chest and soaked Halliwell's hand and arm and flight suit. The enemy soldier's eyes took on a puzzled, almost wondering expression . . . and then there was no expression at all. Halliwell let the body slump back onto the ground.

After a trembling moment, he was able to pull the knife out and wipe it on the grass.

Oh, God, what have I done?

Killed a man, obviously. It was self-defense.

I couldn't help it.

He's the enemy. Look at that uniform!

What was he doing hunting chickens in the middle of the night, armed with nothing but a knife? He might have been a deserter. He might have been—

He tried to kill you. . . .

The chicken was long gone.

Halliwell sheathed his knife, took an apprehensive look around, then turned and started moving back toward the forest at an easy jog. They would find the body—there was no way he could hide or bury it—and then they would know he had come this way. His heart was hammering so hard the NVA wouldn't have to track him. All they would need to do was follow the sound of his heartbeat, like in that Edgar Allan

Poe short story. Damn, damn, *damn* it all to hell!

This was only the second night since one of the FAC pilots who'd been playing the role of guardian angel for him had passed on the idea that they could guide him to the river by having him play a game of golf. He was currently on his fifth hole, with thirteen more to go, but only four more before he reached the river . . . "the Swanee," as the FAC pilots called it, to avoid telling Charlie that the river was their destination.

This hole, they'd told him, was the fourth at Abilene . . . due east, 195 yards long. He'd shot a hole in one there, once, and thought that was a damned good omen.

Now, his shoulder throbbing like a son of a bitch, his jumper covered with blood, both his own and the blood of the man he'd just killed, he was terribly afraid that this would be the *last* hole he ever played. Who did they think they were kidding, chivvying him through the Vietnamese countryside like this? He was hurting, *hurting,* damn it, and physically he was just about shot. With nothing to eat but some berries and raw corn, with precious little even to drink, his reserves were just about gone.

Even if he could reach the river, what then? The enemy would have that route covered; NVA troops were swarming through this whole area, and most of them seemed to be looking for him. He didn't have a chance in hell, and he might as well just sit down and wait for it all to end.

He'd never known war could be like this. War had always been a remote, clean affair . . . fought from behind an electronic warfare console, as he captured the enemy's radar signatures and tagged them neatly with their proper code group IDs. War had been a cup of coffee or a candy bar gulped down between bantering exchanges with the pilot or the other EW officers, and possibly the cold shiver of excitement he'd always received when he overheard the bombardier of one of the big, swept-wing Buffs calling "Bombs away" over the radio.

His jog, dragged to a weary stagger by exhaustion and shock, slowed further as he took a bearing on a shadowy clump of trees ahead, checking his survival compass to make sure he was staying on a course of zero-nine-zero.

It wouldn't be so bad if he didn't think this whole exercise was just some sort of colossal game in the minds of the head-shed people working on getting him out. That B-52 raid . . . when had it been? Three days ago, he thought. That one had taken the cake, man. He'd been absolutely, one hundred percent certain as the bombs came down, and the great, fast-rippling shock waves had flattened forest and paddy alike, and the ground itself had risen up to smack him in the chest time after time after mind-numbing time, that the people back at Danang had finally decided that they couldn't get him out and they couldn't let him fall into Communist hands . . . so the only solution was to see to it that he died with his secrets before the North Vietnamese could get him.

Hell, he still wasn't sure that some of them didn't have some kind of idea like that, maybe as a reserve plan, in case his golf game got mired in a sand trap. As long as he kept moving, as long as he stayed out of enemy hands . . .

He wondered how long he would live if he *did* get captured? Did they have a squadron of F-105s or F-4s waiting at Danang right now, with orders to go in and tear a particular enemy patrol to shreds if he was taken? Man, with friends like that . . .

No. *No.* He didn't mean that. His buddies, his fellow officers and aviators flying those missions, they were in this to cover his ass and get him back home. He *knew* that.

Still, he wouldn't put it past some REMF of a general or chief of staff, somewhere, to have that squadron on the tarmac, ready to roll. Just in case. It only made sense.

Sense? Yeah. Where the hell was the sense of this damned, fucking excuse for a war?

He remembered a story he'd heard, an incident from much earlier in the Vietnam conflict . . . back in 1965, or maybe 1966, when the war was still an "engagement" or an "action," and the long lines of body bags and coffins hadn't yet made the evening news. An American military plane, an F-105, as he recalled, had been downed over South Vietnam by an enemy SA-2, the same missile that had nailed his EB-66. The story had kicked up one hell of a row. A North Vietnamese SAM site, in South Vietnam? Unthinkable! As he recalled the incident, that F-105 had been the first, or one of the very first, American aircraft downed in the war.

The decision had been made at a very high level in the Pentagon to take out that missile battery, partly as retaliation, partly to pass a strong warning on to Hanoi that America would not allow such blatant escalation or outright violation of South Vietnamese sovereignty. Sixty F-105 Thunderchiefs, the slow and somewhat clumsy flying targets wryly known by their pilots and ground crews as "Thuds," would make the assault.

One week before the strike, however, no less a personage than the secretary of defense had gone on television, announcing that a raid was being organized to take out that SAM site. Talk about flare-lit tip-offs! The whole world now knew exactly where the Air Force was going to attack, and what their target was. Several officers further down the chain of command tried to get the mission canceled on the grounds that it had been compromised by McNamara's statement, but they were chewed out for rocking the boat . . . or threatened with official action for what was perceived as cowardice. The mission *would* go in, because the secretary of defense had said it would.

On the day before the raid was scheduled to go, reconnaissance aircraft had photographed the SAM site. The missiles were gone. In their place, quite recognizable in the high-definition SR-71 photos, were telephone poles, *literal* telephone poles painted up to look like SA-2s and propped up on wooden sawhorses to look as though they were on their launch rails. Nearby were hundreds of camouflaged gun positions, antiaircraft machine guns and light artillery of all calibers and descriptions.

It was a trap, with dummy SAMs as the bait.

Again, the mission commanders submitted a request that the mission be canceled, on the grounds that reconnaissance showed that the target had been moved and that the attackers would be flying into a trap.

The request was denied. The attack would be carried out, because the goddamned secretary of defense had said it *would* be carried out, and the Air Force would not be allowed to make a liar out of him.

The next day, sixty F-105s had gone in and gone in hot, dropping their force packages, dodging flak, and reducing several large and hostile telephone poles to smoldering splinters. Six of the aircraft were shot down in the hail of triple-

A that rose from the hidden gun positions around the so-called SAM site.

Six brave men killed. For telephone poles . . . and so that a big-mouthed politician wouldn't be embarrassed. The miracle was that losses had been *only* ten percent, in a raid that never should have been allowed to happen. If there was a bright side to the debacle, it was that the North Vietnamese decided to play coy and pulled back their SAMs, reserving them for air defense around cities in the north. In fact, there'd been no SA-2s at all in the south . . . until the one that had knocked Halliwell's EW aircraft out of the sky.

The asinine stupidity of the command staff and the planners back in the Pentagon never failed to amaze Halliwell. He'd had more than enough of that kind of bureaucratic stupidity when he'd worked at SAC . . . though at least there the idea was that the slower the bureaucracy, the less likely someone was to push the button that would end the war. Out here, though, that kind of second-guessing and half-assed paper shuffling just got good men killed.

Yes, Halliwell held considerable contempt for the political side of the war. He was fast developing an appreciation for a side of war that he'd never seen, down here in the filth and mud and blood . . . a part of the war that had never touched him in his nice, safe, *dry* seat cruising along at 30,000 feet with the war spread out below like some kind of fancy, full-color mapboard in a complicated war game.

He looked at the blood covering his hands, then tried once again to wipe it off on the grass, on some palm fronds nearby, on the bark of a tree. Damn it . . . the stuff wouldn't come off, not all of it. He was starting to think that he knew what poor Lady Macbeth had gone through. *Out, out damned spot!* . . .

God, I'm tired.

Why don't you just give it up? You know you're not going to make it.

I'm not going to just quit. I'm going to keep going. I'm going to make it to the clubhouse or die trying.

Then you're going to die. . . .

I'm going to die trying. . . .

How the hell were they going to get anyone in to meet him? He couldn't make it through enemy lines on his own, not in his condition, and the enemy forces here were just too damned thick.

It all seemed so useless . . . as fucking useless as an air raid on a bunch of fucking white-painted telephone poles.

Somehow, though, he kept moving, putting one foot in front of the other as he staggered on along the fourth hole at Abilene. . . .

Wednesday, 12 April 1972

Near the Song Mieu Giang River
Near Dông Ha
12 miles south of the DMZ
0350 hours

Lieutenant Nolan crouched in the moon-shadow, unmoving, as invisible in that black forest as any other tree or shrub or natural growth, a part of the forest, rather than an intruder. He heard another burst of singsong Vietnamese from just ahead and slowly, slowly, moved his hand, clenching his fist, signaling. *At least two NVA, just ahead. Moving this way. . . .*

Shadows, almost without form or substance, the SEALs in the column melted to left and right of the trail, with scarcely a movement among the fronds and leaves to mark their passage.

Seconds passed as Nolan lay beneath a dripping canopy of flat, waxy leaves. He heard the clink of metal on metal, and then a line of men was filing past, walking east along the trail.

Silently he counted them off, eight North Vietnamese soldiers with AK-47s and full field gear. Nolan took note of several interesting details: there was no mud on the sides of their boots or their trouser legs, and the men's faces and shirts weren't wet with sweat. They walked past in a silent, businesslike manner, their eyes scanning both sides of the trail as they passed.

They did not see the hidden SEALs.

After waiting several minutes—the first patrol might have a tail-end-Charlie team bringing up the rear—Nolan signaled, and the SEALs materialized once again out of the shadows.

There were eight of them, the five Americans, plus Nghiep Van Dong and two other LDNNs. All had their faces heavily coated with green and black greasepaint; all were heavily armed, with weapons ranging from the M-16s of the LDNNs to Twidge Halstead's Stoner and Boomer's M60. Nolan was carrying an AK-47, a weapon he'd come to prefer during his sojourn with SOG along the Ho Chi Minh Trail. The weapon was damned near indestructible and more rugged and forgiving than anything else in the SEAL arsenal.

Silently, the lieutenant signaled the SEALs on his team. *Careful. Enemy ahead.* They would continue their advance off the trail to the left, which would make for slower going but less chance of blundering into the enemy. Those soldiers who'd just walked past were fresh. They'd not been blundering about on muddy trails for an hour or sweating under the strain of humping ten-pound AKs, as much weight again in ammo, plus backpacks and field gear across uneven ground at night. The inescapable conclusion was that there was a camp nearby, probably *very* nearby, and Nolan wanted to know where it was.

Gunfire crackled in the distance, punctuated by the thump of mortars and light rockets. The North Vietnamese Easter Offensive was still going full-blast and showing no signs whatsoever of running out of steam. At least four NVA divisions had swarmed across all of Quang Tri Province, isolating South Vietnamese forces and their few American advisors inside Quang Tri City itself, and the city of Dông Ha, on the Song Mieu Giang River. Enemy units were reported approaching Hue, thirty miles down the coast from Quang Tri.

And it wasn't just Quang Tri Province that was hot. Six days ago, North Vietnamese and Viet Cong forces had exploded out of Vinh Long Province, cutting communications within twenty-five miles of Saigon itself. They'd also come storming across the border out of Cambodia along Highway 13, which ran directly south toward Saigon. They'd booted the 5th ARVN Division clean out of Loc Ninh, near the border, but were so far holding at An Loc, a few miles further to the south. According to the news reports back home, South Vietnam was reeling back from what was almost certainly a fatal blow. Comparisons of the ARVN's poor showing a year ago during Lam Son 719 and the overwhelming force displayed now by the North Vietnamese Easter Offensive were inevitable, as were the pointed criticisms of Washington's Vietnamization policy. Most reporters were giving the Saigon government a few more weeks or months of survival at best.

America had responded by stepping up their air support. Yesterday, a series of B-52 air strikes had begun pounding enemy concentrations as far as 145 miles across the DMZ into North Vietnam. So far, though, there was no indication that the withdrawal of American troops was to be halted or even slowed, and not even a whisper that Nixon might actually start building up U.S. ground forces in Nam once more. The American public seemed solidly focused on the idea that if South Vietnam was going to go to hell, it could go to hell alone.

None of this larger aspect of the war reached down to the tiny band of camouflaged, heavily armed men slipping through the forest north of the Song Mieu Giang River, however. The gunfire was far off, toward the southeast and Quang Tri. Their immediate surroundings were quiet, almost preternaturally so, as though the night birds and insects, normally present in cacophonous array, were holding their symphony in check.

That, too, Nolan thought, suggested that a lot of people were gathered nearby, moving about just enough to disturb the normal patterns of nocturnal wildlife activity.

Ahead, just visible in the shadow-edged patterns of moonlight and trees, Nghiep held up his hand, fist clenched. *Enemy in sight!*

Stealthily, the SEALs crept closer, with Boomer, Liet, and Kilroy staying back to watch the team's flanks and rear. A dozen men sat in a circle in a clearing up ahead, talking with one another in low tones. Parked behind them, so thickly planted with tree limbs and fronds that it resembled a forested island mounted on tracks, was the boat-shaped hull of a PT-76 tank.

Nolan took his time scanning the encampment. Elsewhere along the edges of the clearing were the shapes, just visible beneath banana leaves and camouflage netting, of other vehicles—BTR-50P armored personnel carriers. It looked like a whole armored infantry platoon, at least, with one light tank in support, had drawn up in a laager just off a nearby branch of Highway 9. The fact that they were just sitting there, instead of pushing in closer to Quang Tri, Dông Ha, or Hue, suggested that they were here as part of the search net thrown out to snare Lieutenant Colonel Halliwell. The patrol that had walked past a few minutes ago must have come from this encampment.

The team's options were limited. North was Route 9, the main road from Cam Lo to Quang Tri, and it would be crawling with traffic, everything from NVA soldiers on foot and on bicycle to columns of PT-76 tanks. Nolan could hear the rumble of heavy traffic from here. South lay the river, and since the Song Mieu Giang also ran from the vicinity of Cam Lo to Quang Tri, it would be heavily trafficked as well.

But the river would give the SEALs their best cover. Silently, he signaled the others, then pulled back. Using hand gestures only, Nolan assembled the team, then got them moving toward the left, slipping through dense, rain-dripping foliage toward the river.

At the riverbank, he split the team. Halstead, Tangretti, and Nghiep would go on ahead with him. The rest, under Calahan's command, would wait here for their return . . . and act as a force-in-reserve in case the lead element ran into trouble. If they heard gunfire, they were to come on the double, lay down suppressing fire, and open a corridor through which the four could withdraw.

There was no discussion, only nods and silent hand clasps, before Nolan and the others slid down a muddy bank and into the black water. Half wading, half swimming, they began moving west once more, passing the armored column in the safety of the river.

Nolan had given considerable thought to the men he would bring with him. Nghiep had as much experience as any LDNN Nolan knew and was familiar with every riverbank, hollow, stream, and paddy in this region. Tangretti and Halstead impressed him as good men under pressure, experienced and unflappable operators.

Their contrasting personalities were complimentary. Tangretti seemed to be the easier and more laid-back of the two, but when he decided to dive into something, he plunged. Witness his conversion to Christianity . . . and the way he'd gone after the people threatening his wife. When he decided to act, it was with a swift, sudden, single-mindedness of purpose that could be deadly to anyone in his way.

Halstead, on the other hand, was slower to make decisions and more thoughtful about what he did. He had to believe in what he was doing, and he took his time gathering the information he felt he needed. At the same time, he was . . . *intense* was the word Nolan could think of that best characterized the guy. What he believed, he believed deeply and with a focus as keen in its way as Tangretti's single-mindedness could be.

They were both damned good men to have on your side, which was why he'd asked them to volunteer for this deployment. Neither man, he knew, had particularly wanted to leave his family . . . and God knew they'd both served deployments enough in this green hell never to *have* to return to Vietnam again. . . .

They'd volunteered anyway. Part of that, he was pretty sure, was the simple mystique of being a SEAL. SEALs did *not* turn down missions. They went where they were needed and did what needed to be done . . . the ultimate mark of the professional warrior.

But part, too, had to do with what they believed. Halstead was a patriot, convinced that the war in Vietnam was part of a larger war, a *civil* war within American society. Tangretti was no less a patriot, but he seemed to genuinely love the Vietnamese people, wanting to help them escape what he perceived as the genuine horror of a Communist dictatorship.

Both believed in what they were doing. That, too, was the mark of the professional.

Ahead, Nghiep held up his fist, then pointed. Crouching so low in the water that only his nose, eyes, and the green bandanna stretched over his scalp were above the surface of the water, Nolan studied the riverbank ahead. It took a moment for his brain to assemble the picture—a bit of shadow that didn't quite fit here, a bit of pale light reflected from a patch of bare skin, the long, black deadliness of an automatic weapon's muzzle—but when the picture came together, the North Vietnamese soldier squatting on the river's edge twenty yards upstream seemed to leap out of the shadows at him. The man was sitting very still—he might well have been asleep—with his AK braced butt-down in the mud, his hands clasped over the banana magazine, and his head lolling forward.

Nolan passed on Nghiep's warning to Tangretti and Halstead, then signaled the LDNN to keep moving. It looked like the man was dozing; Nolan unholstered his Hush Puppy and kept the heavy, sound-suppressed muzzle pointed at the man as the four of them slowly filed past, scarcely causing a ripple in the running surface of the river.

Five minutes later, they were all past, moving slowly against the current, sticking to the shadows beneath the riverbank. They continued upstream to a point about fifty yards above the snoozing sentry before clambering out of the water and onto the shore. Nolan made a note of the sentry's position. Coming back downstream, they would have to take him out, rather than risking having him woken by the clumsy movements of the aviator.

As they resumed their westward overland march, he wondered if, perhaps, the river wouldn't offer the best route in and out of this area. A sampan, maybe, and clothing that looked like NVA uniforms or Viet Cong peasant garb.

A twig snapped in the night, as loud and as singular as a rifle shot.

The SEALs went to ground, waiting and watching. Nolan could hear the scuffling footsteps now of someone approaching . . . someone who didn't care at all whether anyone heard him or not. Nghiep looked back at Nolan, dark eyes wide as he signaled warning. Nolan nodded, then signaled to Nghiep to stay put. He would check this out himself.

Easing forward through the underbrush, he tried to position himself in front of the oncoming noisemaker. A moment later, he could see the man, a dark shadow in the gloom of the forest.

He was on a trail, which was a bad idea to start with, and appeared to be headed straight for the NVA camp.

Nolan kept crawling forward, trying to get closer. The man wasn't walking like a Vietnamese. In fact, he seemed a lot bigger, in a gangly, rawboned way, and he *ambled* rather than moving with the catlike grace of combat-experienced Vietnamese on either side. The man's walk almost screamed "American."

But Nolan had to be sure. He edged forward a bit more,

keeping to the shadows of logs and tree trunks. Damn, the guy was noisy, too, his footsteps echoing through the darkness. Worse, he was too far away to risk a dive-and-tackle. If Nolan didn't stop him, though, he was going to blunder on down the trail straight into the arms of the encamped NVA.

"Ssst!" Nolan hissed. "Bravo One-niner!"

"Wha?—" The figure spun, staring not at Nolan but *past* him, mouth gaping with surprise, eyes wide and white in a mud-smeared face. Nolan could recognize the man's flight suit now, though it was torn and coated with mud. The guy had been through a lot and looked like he could hardly stand.

"We're friends," Nolan whispered. "What's your dog's name?"

"Uh . . . Monty. Like in Montgomery."

That gave Nolan a moment's pause. "Monty" was the name of Lieutenant Clark's terrier . . . not Halliwell's poodle. Nolan had been so focused on reaching Halliwell, he'd nearly forgotten that there were *two* U.S. Air Force aviators out here.

He'd just found the *other* one, Nail-38, General Mark Clark's son. . . .

"Lieutenant Clark? Good to see you. We're here to get you out."

"Thank God! . . ."

"Quietly, please. There is a large enemy camp less than one hundred yards away, that way, down the trail. Come with me, and keep down."

This, he thought, would make General Ellison a bit happier, with one of his lost sheep, at least, safely restored to the fold.

But the enemy troops in this direction were just too damned thick to risk pushing on, especially since he had Clark on his hands now. For a moment, he considered sending Tangretti and Halstead back with Clark, with orders to rejoin the others and return to base, while he and Nghiep pushed on to try to reach Halliwell, but that, he knew, was less than bright by several hundred kilowatts. It was nearly dawn, and to continue on ahead would be to risk discovery and capture for them all. At last report, Halliwell was still at least two kilometers further on up the river.

They would have to back out, get Clark back to the Forward Observation Base, and try again tomorrow.

Chapter 33

Song Mieu Giang River
12 miles south of the DMZ
2214 hours

Halliwell had reached the river sometime last night, completing the ninth hole and, urged on by one of the FAC pilots orbiting overhead, half-wading, half-swimming the black Song Mieu Giang. He'd just made it; as he'd laid there in the mud of the river's south bank, he'd watched the flickers and firefly glimmers of dozens of flashlights probing among the trees on the other side, as his pursuers searched the edge of the water.

This is it. This is as far as I go. I can't make it any farther.

He'd practically begged the FAC pilot overhead to leave him alone, to let him rest, but the bastard had kept at him, chivvying him, urging him to tee off on the back nine. There were a lot of impatient foursomes, the man told him, coming up the fairway behind him, and they were carrying very large clubs.

Frankly, Halliwell didn't know why the North Vietnamese hadn't picked him up right then and there. The river was only ten or twelve yards across at that point, and he'd clearly seen the silhouettes of the enemy soldiers behind the dazzle of their flashlights as they'd swept them across the water and probed the opposite bank. He'd been lying in plain sight, half in the water, half out; somehow, *somehow,* they'd missed him, mistaking his ragged, mud-coated frame for just another clot of refuse washed ashore from upstream.

If they found him, the insistent, relentless little voice in his

416

head cajoled, he would get food and water and medical attention. They didn't want him to die, after all. At the moment, the enemy troops searching for him probably wanted him alive more than he wanted to live.

Fortunately, the North Vietnamese had not appeared eager to try crossing the river. Halliwell was a lanky six-two . . . and the river had been up to his chin most of the way across. The water would have been well above the heads of his pursuers, which meant they would have had to swim—not easy with pack, rifle, and field gear. If they'd spotted him, of course, they would have been across the river like a shot; as it was, though, they'd been reluctant to commit themselves to a late-night swim.

Considering the mud, the polluted water, and the leeches, Halliwell knew just how they felt.

Eventually, enough strength had returned to his limbs that he'd been able to begin wading downstream, only his head above the water, fearful with each step that the next would plunge him, splashing, into a hole in the bottom and that his struggles would bring the enemy across the river.

When daylight came, he'd dragged himself ashore, covered himself with palm fronds and sheets of cast-off bark, and fallen into an exhausted sleep.

Now it was dark once more, and he was traveling downriver. By chance, he'd literally stumbled across a partially charred railway tie at the water's edge, and now he was using the four-foot log as a kind of lifejacket, letting it carry him downstream.

His tired mind continued clicking off the yards. He no longer had to keep track of the lay of the fairways in his bizarre mental game of golf; from now on, he would follow the river as it wound its way gently east toward Dông Ha. He still needed to keep track of yardage, though, so that the FAC pilots could keep track of where he was. To that end, he was now playing the back nine at Tucson National, using his emergency radio to tell his guardian angels overhead each time he reached a hole, each time he was teeing off once more.

His radio batteries weren't going to last much longer. When they were gone, he knew, he might as well pack it in. They would never be able to track him, never find him if the radio died.

Hell, when the radio gave out, so would he. There would simply be nothing more to keep him going . . . not the hope of escape, not the hope of rescue, not even the hope of a thick steak at the officers' club . . . or a long, hot, cleansing shower, followed by a soft bed with clean sheets and the loving embrace of his wife. . . .

Got to stop thinking about that. . . .

Damn, he could see her now, slim and beautiful and sexy and *clean* . . . no mud at all. Her smile, so dazzling, so welcoming, so warm. He reached out for her. . . .

It's a hallucination, Hal. You're seeing things. Put it out of your head.

Christ.

What was Ginny doing now? They would have gone to visit her the day after he'd been shot down, to let her know what had happened. By Tuesday or Wednesday, a week ago now, she would have received the usual telegram from the base personnel office at Davis-Monthan, something warm and caring—in a coldly officious way—about how efforts to recover him had failed, that they would keep trying, that they shared with her her worry and grief and anxiety in this trying time.

Oh, God. Poor Ginny. What she must be going through. . . .

It had been eleven days now since his aircraft had been shot down. With little to eat or drink in all that time, he was fast reaching the ragged end of his endurance. His legs simply wouldn't carry him any more.

He was pretty sure the knife wound in his shoulder was infected, and probably the wound in his hand as well. He'd felt feverish for several days now, though it was hard to tell through the overall abuse he'd been suffering. His body ached as much from sleeping on the hard ground as it might from a high fever. He knew he was dehydrated; he'd not had much to drink until he'd reached the river . . . and now that he had enough to drink, he'd developed one hell of a case of diarrhea, enough to wring the last few drops of moisture from already desiccated tissues and leave him miserably dry and cotton-wool scratchy inside, even while he was floating in the water. The diarrhea, he thought, was probably from the contaminated water. Good thing he was already in a filthy river, because it didn't much matter *what* he did while he was in it.

Worse was the cough he was developing, a raspy, chest-ripping hack that carried with it the deep, liquid gurgle that suggested developing pneumonia. He didn't know which threat was worse . . . the possibility of dying of pneumonia out here in the mud and stinking water . . . or coughing at the wrong time and calling down the dogs who were chasing him down.

Twelfth hole . . . six more to go before he reached the clubhouse.

He didn't know if he was going to make it.

Something was moving up ahead.

He was having trouble focusing his eyes . . . but the long, lean, black shape slowly edging up the river could not be natural. Tree trunks did not move against the current.

A sampan, twenty feet long, with a gunwale barely above the surface of the water, with an upturned wicker basket amidships for a deck house, and the grim, black shapes of at least five armed men crouching on board.

Halliwell froze, then slowly allowed himself to slide off the log, keeping its comforting, wet bulk between him and the oncoming sampan. He could hear the purr of its outboard motor now, throttled back to the point where it only just kept the sampan edging forward. An insane, almost overpowering urge to cough crawled up the inside of his throat, but he fought it down, clamping his jaws shut and forcing himself to breathe slowly and carefully through his nose.

He was close to the south bank of the river here, but the water was quite deep, at least five feet. Keeping one hand on his log-lifeboat, he let himself slip deeper, until only his nose and eyes were still above the surface.

Light burst from the darkness, a powerful spotlight stabbing against the southern shore, moving from one tree trunk to another, darting into the bushes, then flicking down to paint the edge of the water with a white illumination seemingly as bright as a flare. He could hear the soldiers aboard the sampan talking, see them pointing.

They were coming, and closer still . . . within easy rock-throwing distance . . . hell, almost within touching dis-

tance. He couldn't understand their high-pitched chatter, but
it sounded like they'd just spotted something that interested
them a lot. Slowly, he let his head sink below the surface of
the river, letting the black water close over his head. For a
moment, he was enveloped in cool blackness; then light exploded around him, illuminating myriad specks of grit, mud,
and organic matter drifting in the water and backlighting the
railway tie beside his head. Blinking in the dirty water, he
could see now the log as a huge, black shadow against the
light and, inches away now, the longer black shadow of the
sampan's bottom.

The light shifted and turned, sending dazzling shafts
sweeping through the drifting muck. The Vietnamese on the
sampan had obviously spotted the railway tie and were examining it closely. Suddenly, the tie bobbed down in the water, striking the side of his head. The bastards were pushing
at it, trying to see if it was floating free or hung up on the
shore.

Then, miraculously, the light switched off, and he was left
in wet darkness once again. He heard the sampan's outboard,
a water-muffled clatter, as it motored slowly past just a few
feet away.

He stayed under for as long as he could . . . but at last he
rose from the water, gasping and choking, trying his best to
keep the sound down to a strangled rasp as he groped for the
support of his log. The sampan was cruising slowly upstream,
the powerful little hand-held spotlight probing the riverbank
and surface.

They didn't hear him.

And no wonder. Gunfire was erupting in the night, floating
up the river from the east. Halliwell couldn't see anything in
that direction, but it sounded like a short, sharp, violent firefight, with at least one heavy machine gun *slam-slam-
slamming* its deadly tattoo somewhere out there in the
darkness. The gaggings and wheezings of an old Air Force
light colonel half drowned in the river had been covered by
the sharper and more insistent sounds of a firefight.

The firing was coming from the direction the river was
taking him, and he wondered if that was good or bad. Gunfire
meant there must be friendlies just a short way downstream.
Or did it? He'd heard a lot of random, heavy firing going

on around him during the past week and a half. Some of it had been skirmishing, far off in the distance. But some was probably NVA troops spooked by shadows or each other, blazing away in the darkness. It suggested that there had been attempts to get people up the river, though Halliwell knew that any such attempt wasn't going to get very far. There were just too damned many NVA around.

In any case, drifting into the middle of a firefight wasn't conducive to long life and good health. He wondered if he should find someplace to hide on the riverbank, a place to lay low and simply wait until either he was found or the war decided to move someplace else.

Nah. Too much trouble. It was easier to cling to his log and keep bumping and drifting his way downstream, counting off the yards as each dragged past.

The gunfire sounded louder, more urgent. Damn, who was shooting whom out there? He thought he could hear the roar of aircraft now and the concussion of exploding ordnance.

Halliwell decided that he really didn't care anymore.

He let the river carry him on.

Near the Song Mieu Giang River
Four kilometers from Point Clubhouse
2214 hours

The North Vietnamese soldier stepped out of the shadows of the treeline ahead, one hand gripping his AK-47, the other tugging his trousers back into place. His head came up, he saw Bill Tangretti standing less than ten feet away, and his eyes opened wide as he snapped his weapon down into line with the SEAL's green-painted head.

Bill had only a fraction of a second to react, dropping to the ground, taking the impact with the ground on his shoulder as he rolled left, dragging his M-16's muzzle toward the target. The NVA soldier fired first, but Bill's sudden drop had caught him by surprise; the bullets snapped and cracked inches above Bill's head as he squeezed the M-16's trigger, sending a short, sharp burst slamming into the enemy soldier's chest.

The AK-47's muzzle climbed as the Vietnamese continued to fire, and that small application of weapons physics saved

Bill's life. The Vietnamese pitched backward, still spraying full-auto rounds into the branches overhead before he slammed against a tree trunk, his chest exploded in blood and chips of shattered rib cage, and he crumpled to the ground.

Automatic gunfire barked and chattered from the darkness beyond the treeline as Bill hugged the ground, with dozens of flickering points of light marking the muzzle flashes of enemy weapons. Bill took aim at one of the closest flashes and returned fire, sending a stream of 5.56mm tumblers slashing into the night. Behind him and to his right, Boomer Cain elevated his M203 and squeezed the trigger; with a hollow-sounding thump, the grenade launcher lobbed a 30mm packet of high explosives into the woods, where it detonated a long second later with a flash and a savage crack of thunder. To his left, Nghiep rose to his knees and began loosing quick, lightning bursts from his M-16, as though trying to mark and bring down every target at once.

"Back!" Nolan cried from behind, somewhere. "Fall back! We'll cover!"

Bill fired another burst into the woods, then began slithering backward. Gunfire crackled all around; he could feel the snap of bullets burning through the air above his head as Nolan and Twidge and the rest lay down an all-out, go-for-broke blanket of covering fire.

They'd come ashore off a PBR less than an hour ago. The patrol boat had managed to fight its way past the NVA forces encircling Dông Ha and had rendezvoused with the SEALs at a Forward Observation Base several miles west of the town. The idea had been for the SEALs to board the craft and make their way upriver as far as possible, before slipping ashore within a kilometer or two of Halliwell's last reported position.

They'd made it ashore and were just two klicks shy of Point Clubhouse, but the area had been thick with enemy patrols. Three times in the past hour, they'd narrowly avoided North Vietnamese units moving along the trails south of the river. Finally, plain bad luck—in the shape of a North Vietnamese soldier who'd strayed away from the main NVA force to take a leak—had caught up with them. Their covert approach was blown, and there was nothing to do now but fall back to the river for pickup.

The hell of it was, this was the second time today they'd

tried to break through the NVA lines to reach Halliwell's position. That morning, before dawn, they'd tried to run all the way up the river in the PBR. At a bend in the river code-named Point Florida, however, they'd come under heavy fire from both shores. Rocket-propelled grenades had hissed across from the shorelines and detonated in the water with shrill bangs and towering geysers of white spray, as the mixed SEAL/LDNN team aboard had returned fire in a savage, brief battle.

Clearly, the brute-force approach simply could not work, not this time, not here.

Bill rolled across the top of a moss-covered log, landing next to Greg, who had his Stoner propped across the fallen tree trunk and was hosing the dark woods.

"You okay?" Greg yelled the question above the chatter of his weapon.

"Hooyah!" Bill yelled back, the SEAL battle cry. He took aim with his M-16 and fired until the magazine ran dry. Dropping the empty, he slapped in a fresh mag, then opened fire again. "Okay!"

"Fuck it," Greg yelled. "Time to get out of Dodge!"

"I'm with you!"

Nghiep and Boomer were behind the firing line now, taking up their positions. Like a well-oiled piece of machinery, the SEALs providing cover fire rose and moved back, while Bill and the others covered them. Greg walked slowly backward, firing his Stoner from the hip in precise, aimed bursts, then turned and sprinted for the next line of cover twenty yards to the rear. Bill spotted movement . . . a rush of khaki uniforms emerging from the treeline, just visible in the pale moonlight. Swinging his rifle, he opened up with a long, chattering burst of full-auto fire, watching the NVA troops topple left and right. Whether they were dead, wounded, or simply evading his fire, he couldn't tell, but he kept on firing until Nolan yelled "Covering!" and Greg's Stoner opened up once more from the rear.

More NVA troops were emerging. "Grenade!" Bill yelled, tossing the M-33 and dropping for cover. The baseball-sized device had a fifteen-meter burst radius and could be as deadly to the man throwing it as to the target. Four seconds after arming, the grenade exploded with a ringing bang that clipped the leaves from nearby trees and left one Vietnamese lying in the clearing, clutching his belly as he shrieked in gut-tortured pain.

The North Vietnamese seemed to lose interest in the SEALs after that. The team fell back, continuing to withdraw in leapfrogging pairs, one man covering while another retreated. In far less time than it had taken them to get this far, they reached the river, splashing out into the water and scrambling aboard the waiting PBR.

"No joy?" one of the boat crew asked Bill as he reached down and gave him a hand aboard.

"No joy at all," Bill replied. "I'm beginning to think this op is jinxed."

"Back to the FOB," Nolan said, coming over the rail. He looked angry.

"What now, sir?" Greg asked him as the last SEAL came aboard and the PBR began motoring downriver. Gunfire continued to crackle in the brush ashore, but none of it seemed directed at them.

"We've tried it by water and by land," Bill pointed out. "And the SAR boys tried it by air. What are we going to try next . . . tunneling?"

"Don't laugh," Nolan told him. "I heard the generals were kicking around ideas that included dropping Halliwell a helium tank and a weather balloon to float him out . . . or bringing in engineers to dig a four-klick tunnel."

"Right," Boomer said, nodding. "Like they could do that in the time Halliwell has left."

"If they meant dropping him a skyhook, the balloon might work," Kilroy pointed out. He was referring to the Fulton Surface-To-Air-Recovery, or STAR system, developed by the Army and Air Force in the early 1960s under the code name Project Skyhook. With STAR, a deflated twenty-three-foot balloon, an insulated nylon suit with an attached harness, line, helium tanks, and associated equipment were airdropped to the man who needed extraction. He donned the suit, attached the cables, inflated and released the balloon, and waited for an MC-130H Combat Talon to come along at low altitude and snag the balloon, yanking him into the sky before winching him aboard.

"Shit," Nolan told him. "Halliwell's been out there how

long? Injured. Probably sick. Half starved. Dehydrated. If the shock of snatching him off the ground didn't give the poor guy a heart attack, he'd probably be dead of exposure and cold by the time they hauled him aboard.''

"What about multiple boats, Lieutenant?" Greg asked. "Force our way past the NVA strongpoints on the river."

"No, no, *no*," Nolan replied, shaking his head. "We've tried bigger. Now we're going to play it my way. We're going to pull one like at Sihanoukville."

Bill cocked his head to the side. "Sihanoukville. You went in by boat there, didn't you? Look, you guys, I don't want to sound defeatist, but we're *not* getting a boat up this river.''

"Oh, yes we are," Nolan replied. "We're just going to stop playing by the rules.''

Bill admired the determination in Nolan's voice, but he had no idea as to what the man planned to do.

Chapter 34

Thursday, 13 April 1972

Forward Observation Base
On the Song Mieu Giang River
Near Dông Ha
0035 hours

The Forward Observation Base, or FOB, had been established in an old French blockhouse built on a hilltop just above the Song Mieu Giang. Dông Ha was out of sight downriver, toward the east, where the steady crackle of small arms fire and the occasional thump of mortar or rocket detonations proved that the Communist forces were still pushing against the ARVN perimeter around the town.

The FOB had been secured by a company of ARVN Rangers, some of the best-trained and best-equipped troops in South Vietnam's army. Several Huey helicopters with U.S. markings rested in the moonlight-painted darkness nearby, under heavy guard.

The old blockhouse had started as an FOB and Observation Post for ARVN troops defending Dông Ha and Quang Tri City; as the Communist advance had continued, sweeping past this hill from the west and lapping around the towns to the east and southeast, it had become an island of relative peace lost within the much larger sea of a fast-deepening war. The ARVN troops holding that island weren't strong enough to push far beyond its shores, but they were strong enough to discourage any casual North Vietnamese thrust in their direction.

At first, there'd been no major testings of the perimeter, nothing at all, in fact, except for some sporadic mortaring and sniper fire. There'd been one serious attack on Wednesday afternoon—about ten hours ago—but the ARVN Rangers, aided by the ever-present umbrella of Sandys and Phantoms circling overhead, had broken it up.

Since then, everything had been almost hauntingly quiet, and there was at last the possibility that the NVA would bypass the FOB for now. From the enemy's point of view, the base was unimportant, no more than a distraction from the real goals of the offensive. Once Dông Ha fell, and especially when the provincial capital at Quang Tri fell, the FOB would be completely untenable, and the troops holding it would be trapped . . . save for those few who might make it out by air.

The ARVN forces had already planned to abandon the FOB, in fact, until some very senior members of the U.S. advisory staff in Danang and Saigon had intervened. It happened that right now this crumbling French outpost was the closest thing to a secure helicopter LZ on the river, and it was the allied defensive position closest to Halliwell. All of the SEAL attempts to reach Halliwell and Clark had been deployed from here; the ARVN Rangers had orders to hold the FOB at all costs until the operation to rescue Halliwell was completed or shut down.

Nolan paused outside the bunker's door for a moment, eyes scanning the night to the west and the north. The view from the hilltop was excellent, which was why the French soldiers who'd built the blockhouse had chosen the site. A partial moon low in the east provided light enough to reveal rolling fields, rice paddies, and patches of woods. On the north side of the river was a small village, now deserted. Some of the hooches and thatch-roofed huts extended out onto the water on spindly stilt-legs; a number of sampans were still moored beneath the riverfront buildings, which showed evidence of having been abandoned in a frenzied haste.

Something like heat lightning flared to the east, briefly reflected by the black river, and, a moment later, Nolan heard the rumble of explosions. It sounded like the Communists were really pounding Dông Ha. It wouldn't be long before the FOB was completely cut off; once that happened, rescuing Halliwell was going to become so difficult logistically that further attempts would likely be impossible.

Nolan was damned if he was going to let this thing beat him.

Shaking his head, he stepped past the camouflage-garbed ARVN Ranger standing guard at the doorway and ducked through into the bunker's cool interior.

The bunker's main room, cement-walled and gloomy despite the naked electric bulbs hanging from the ceiling, was filled with men. A Vietnamese radio operator sat hunched over the console of a big set in one corner. A U.S. Marine officer and an ARVN major stood at a large map unfolded over a table in the center of the room. Also present were Lieutenant Commander Kelso, an Air Force colonel, and a surprise—none other than Lieutenant Tom Morgan.

"God, look what the cat dragged in!" Nolan exclaimed. "Morgan! Where the hell did you come from?"

"Hey, Nolan," the other SEAL said. "Should have expected to see your ugly mug out here."

Kelso cleared his throat. "Ah, yes," he said. He indicated the Air Force officer. "Lieutenant Nolan? Thank you for coming. This is Colonel Virgil Bellows. We were heloed in just a few minutes ago to assess the situation." He pointed to the Marine officer. "That is Major Clarence C. Donahue, Marine Recon. And Lieutenant Morgan you obviously know."

"Is this the officer?" Bellows asked.

"Lieutenant Nolan has personally led all three of the SEAL

attempts to get through to Halliwell," Kelso said. "His first effort succeeded in picking up Lieutenant Clark."

"Well done," Bellows said, squinting at Nolan.

"How is Clark, sir?" Nolan wanted to know.

"He's safely back in Danang," Kelso replied. "In the hospital, of course, recovering from exposure and dehydration. But he's going to be fine. They'll be air-evacking him back to the States in another few days."

"Our problem, Lieutenant," the Marine major added, "is getting Halliwell out. Clark wasn't on the ground as long as Halliwell, and he wasn't wounded, so Halliwell is probably in much worse shape by now."

"Roger that." Nolan walked over to examine the map. "What is Bravo One-niner's current position?"

"The last report from the FAC boys had him within half a kilometer of the clubhouse. Somewhere right about here. Still on the river, hugging the south bank," Donahue said. "He's on the sixteenth hole now, with two to go . . . only about eight or nine hundred yards."

"But the FAC pilots also report heavy enemy activity all around him." Kelso didn't sound hopeful.

"The gomers are pulling out all the stops," Morgan observed, "almost like they're willing to risk anything to get the guy."

Kelso looked at Nolan almost reproachfully. "When you said you'd run into a tank and some APCs out there, some of the brass back at Danang didn't believe you . . . but that's been confirmed by air, now. For the North Vietnamese to actually hold back armored assets that they need right now at Dông Ha and Quang Tri is really an astonishing piece of information. It means they're willing to risk losing the initiative in their offensive just to nail Halliwell."

"Almost like Halliwell's becoming an asset for our side," Morgan said. "Maybe we should leave him there and really screw the black hats up."

"Not funny, Lieutenant," Colonel Bellows said.

"Sorry, sir."

Nolan studied the map. "Do they have a good idea of where he is now?"

"If they did," Bellows said, "they would have him by now."

"No, I mean in general." He swept his forefinger along the stretch of river where Halliwell was moving at that moment. "Do they know he's somewhere here, on the river? Or are they still searching throughout this whole area?"

"An excellent question," the Vietnamese Ranger major said in precise, lightly accented English. "While they appear to be concentrating their search forces east of Cam Lo, they do not seem to know his exact position."

"Not yet, anyway," Donahue added. He looked at Nolan. "For a while there, it looked like they were concentrating on the river, that they knew he'd gotten there. But Major Ky, here, has had his Rangers patrolling throughout this region, and he's reported apparent enemy search activity all over the area."

"They don't want to leave any open doors," Nolan suggested.

"Damned straight," Morgan added. "If they're not absolutely certain where he is, they don't want to risk getting suckered or going off after red herrings."

"Exactly," Bellows said.

Nolan continued studying the map. "But you still can't get a helo in?"

"Every attempt so far has been driven back by ground fire or antiaircraft," Donahue replied. "And the FAC pilots have been taking a lot of hits. Especially the OV-10s, the hedge-hoppers. Hell, just by watching our FAC flights, they know he must be somewhere around here, despite dummy flights and diversions."

"How's he holding up, anyway?"

"He's a game old son of a bitch," Morgan replied. "Sick. Exhausted. But he keeps pushing. I'm beginning to think that if we don't get him out of there soon, he's going to walk all the way to Quang Tri and embarrass the hell out of all of us."

"He must be having trouble getting food, though."

"Yesterday at dusk," Bellows said, "we tried an airdrop. Food. Water. First aid supplies."

"How'd you manage that without tipping off the hostiles?"

Donahue grinned. "They dropped lots of supplies. Twelve different packages, scattered all over the landscape."

"A dozen parachutes coming down in twelve different

places,'' Morgan added. "Must've had the gomers running in circles.''

"Yes. Unfortunately, the one aimed at Halliwell fell on top of a hill with steep sides and a lot of loose dirt and gravel on the way up. Apparently, he was too weak to reach it.''

"Not good.''

Donahue nodded. "Roger that.''

"Colonel Bellows, sir?'' the Vietnamese soldier at the radio called. "General Ellison. For you.''

"Excuse me, gentlemen.''

When Bellows left the table, Nolan looked at Donahue. "What's your part in all of this, Major?''

"They brought us in a couple of days ago,'' the Marine replied. "Probably about the time they snagged you and your SEALs. Marine Long Range Recon.''

Nolan nodded. "I know 'em well. Good people.'' He meant it, too. Marine LRRPs performed many of the same types of hairy sneak-and-peak ops that SEALs were famous for, and they had the rep for being damned good at what they did. "Morgan? What are you doing here?''

"They've had me here at Danang for four months now, doing liaison work with the Marines. Enough to drive a man to drink.''

"Well, if you squids can't hack it,'' Donahue said, grinning.

"Semper fuck.'' Morgan looked at Nolan. "They're talking back in Danang about making this a real combined forces op, which is why I'm here. Your SEALs. Donahue's LRRPs. And Major Ky's Rangers.''

"Affirmative,'' Major Ky said, pointing at the map. "If we send in a number of patrols—''

"Lieutenant Nolan?'' Bellows called from the radio. "General Ellison wants to talk to you.''

Nolan walked over to the radio and accepted the headset from Bellows. "Nolan here.''

"Nolan?'' Ellison's rough voice demanded. "This is Hotel One-one. I hear your op tonight was aborted.''

"That's affirmative, sir. We ran into, I would estimate, a company-sized element, got into a firefight, and had to back off. The enemy was just too thick for us to manage an overland approach.''

"Damn it! Couldn't you have fought your way through?"

Nolan silently counted to five before answering. SEALs were not cannon fodder to be thrown into frontal attacks on powerful enemy positions. The ideal SEAL op was one that never even made contact with the enemy except for what was called for in the mission planning.

"Sir, that was simply not an option, not unless I wanted to lose my entire team and put the mission at risk."

"I needn't remind you, Lieutenant," Ellison's dry voice said, "that we are all expendable, when it comes to recovering Halliwell."

Easy for you to say, Nolan thought. *You're in Danang in that nice, air-conditioned office of yours.*

"I understand, General. We're getting ready to try again."

"That's the spirit!" Ellison's voice said. "And here's how it's going to go down."

"Sir, I—"

"Listen up, now. You've met Major Donahue, I'm sure. We're sending in a Marine Recon platoon. They should reach your FOB sometime tomorrow morning. I want your SEALs to provide pathfinders for these boys. Split 'em up, one or two SEALs and a native guide to each Marine LRRP. Lieutenant Morgan can give you the specs on combined ops, call signs, and so forth. At the same time, we're going to do some major carpet bombing ahead of your position, really clean out the enemy between the FOB and Point Clubhouse. You and the Marines ought to be able to just walk right in. A walk in the park."

Nolan always got a distinctly bad feeling in his gut when any superior officer told him that a particular mission was going to be easy. It was almost as though some jealous and officious god of battles was eavesdropping . . . ready to jinx any op that was supposed to be "a walk in the park."

"Sir, I—"

"And listen, Nolan," Ellison continued. "This op is being watched very closely, all the way to the top, know what I mean? Pull this off, and there're gonna be medals in it all around. Play this right and I think you can be pretty damned sure of picking up a Silver Star."

Nolan's temper, already frayed, snapped. "*Fuck* the med-

als, General. Save your Silver Star for that poor bastard stuck
out there in the boonies!''

"Ah, well . . . I can understand, you're tired and you're under a lot of pressure. Now, listen up. Here's what I want you
to do. Let your people stand down tonight. When the Marines
arrive at first light, you—''

Nolan pressed the transmit key and blew hard into the microphone. When he ran out of breath, he clicked the key several times, then called, ''Hotel One-one, Hotel One-one, this
is Fox Oscar Bravo One-four. You are breaking up, repeat,
you are breaking up. Do you copy?''

''Nolan! Damn it, what's the matter with this thing? Nolan!
Are you there?''

He blew into the mike again. ''Hotel One-one, I do not
copy. Over.'' He met the astonished eyes of the Vietnamese
radio operator, grinned, and shrugged. Then he reached over
and pulled the power cable.

''Sir!'' the Vietnamese said. ''You—''

Nolan glanced at Bellows, who seemed absorbed in the
map with Donahue, Morgan, and Ky. ''I think the set's over-
heating,'' he said. ''I suggest you leave it unplugged for, oh,
thirty minutes or so. Then see if you can raise Hotel One-one
again.'' It wouldn't hurt to be out of communication for that
long. And he didn't want to be operating in violation of a
direct order.

The Vietnamese soldier looked unsure, then responded to
the twinkle in Nolan's eye. ''Ah. I understand. Yes, sir. Unit
too hot.''

''Yeah. Nothing worse than a hot unit.'' He walked back
over to the map table.

''Problem?'' Donahue asked.

''Nothing serious. I told him I have a plan for one more
try tonight. I gather your Marines are coming in tomorrow?''

''Affirmative.''

''Okay.'' He looked at Bellows. ''Colonel, we've been trying to play this with big numbers, lots of men, lots of equipment, and we haven't even made it to first base. I want to try
once more . . . but this time we're going to try it *my* way.''

''Uh-oh,'' Morgan said, chuckling. ''Colonel, you want to
watch this man. Give him his head and he'll swim all the

damned way to Hanoi. Alone. And probably capture the whole damned politburo.''

"Indeed?'' Bellows looked at Nolan curiously. "And just what is your way, Lieutenant?''

"Two men. Me, and one of the LDNN.'' He would ask Nghiep Van Dong, whom he knew and trusted. "We go right up the river . . . but in a sampan, wearing black pajamas. I think we can slip in, pick up Halliwell, and slip out, and the black hats'll never even know we were there.''

Donahue grinned. "I like it.''

"A typical Nolan op,'' Morgan added, nodding.

"I don't,'' Bellows said. "I've read your file, Lieutenant. You have a history of going into tight places solo, or with just one or two others.''

"Yes, sir. I also get the job done that way.'' He was thinking now of the sneak-and-peak turned wham-and-scram at Sihanoukville. Two men had made it where a dozen would have failed.

"You've been reprimanded for that kind of cowboying. With only one man, you won't have anybody to cover you if you're spotted. And you won't be able to carry enough firepower to cover your asses if things blow up.''

"Sir, with all due respect, if things blow up on us, my ass is grass anyway. A whole platoon, hell, a whole *company* wouldn't be able to bull their way through, not if they were humping M60s and a couple of light cruisers for good measure. But two men, me and an LDNN, will have a damned good chance of getting in without even being spotted.''

"Hmm. You tell the general this idea of yours just now? You discuss it with him?''

"Not in detail, sir, no. But he did make it clear that I was to do everything in my power to get Halliwell out, that I was expendable, in fact, while Halliwell was not. When I said I was going to try again, he told me that that was the spirit. Oh, and he said I could have the rest of my people stand down while I went in.''

"I see. Well, if the general approves it, I guess it sounds like it's worth a shot. You're taking a hell of a chance, Lieutenant.''

"I don't think so, sir. It would be worse going in with a lot of people. You attract attention that way.''

"Wouldn't be surprised if there was a medal in it for you, son."

What was it with the Air Force and medals? "The general said something about a Silver Star. Shit, I really don't care about the ironmongery, though, sir. I just want to get Halliwell safely out of there."

"Good man," Bellows sighed. "I don't know if you gentlemen realize it, but this thing has become the largest single operation ever attempted in order to rescue one man. A lot of people are watching what we do out here."

"That was what the general said, sir."

"The whole POW issue has become the central focus of the war at home. I'm sure you realize that. If Halliwell is captured, not only are the secrets he carries at risk . . . but it could put one hell of a hole in the president's war policy."

Here it was. Politics again.

"I got a report this morning. Do you realize that Halliwell's wife has been receiving hate mail?"

That rocked Nolan. He felt as though he'd been punched in the gut. "Sir?"

"Hate mail. From antiwar groups and people. Not that they have the balls to sign their names, of course. Stupid stuff . . . like 'your husband doesn't belong over there, and I hope he dies. I hope the North Vietnamese kill him.' Shit like that."

"Christ," Morgan said, shaking his head in disgust. "Some people . . ."

"Halliwell is becoming the focus of quite a bit of media attention back home," Bellows went on. "If the NVA gets him, well, it's going to be a major setback for the president. A setback for his policy, and that could mean a setback for our withdrawal from Nam. If we can save Halliwell, though, it's going to play big back in the States. It could be a big boost for morale."

Nolan had the feeling that Bellows was giving him a pep talk, something he really couldn't stomach right at the moment. "Sir, if you'll excuse me, I want to go check out our equipment and see about snagging one of those sampans I saw across the river."

"Go ahead, then, son. You're dismissed."

"Sir!"

He headed for the bunker door as quickly as he could.

Nghiep would be with the rest of the team, probably down by the river.

Bellows's comment about Mrs. Halliwell's getting hate mail bothered him. It was the same sort of thing that had happened to Tangretti and to a number of people in the SEAL community, the harassment, the demoralizing attacks, the sheer stupid viciousness by people who claimed to be on the side of peace, love, and enlightenment.

It was enough to make even a combat-hardened SEAL sick to his stomach.

Maybe, though, there would be an evening of the score, of sorts, if Halliwell was safely returned.

Chapter 35

Thursday, 13 April 1972

On the Song Mieu Giang River
0415 hours

Fifty more yards . . . half of a football field. Piece o' cake . . . nothing to it . . . except that Halliwell could no longer make his battered and tormented body obey his commands. Commands? Hell, his brain was so fuzzy now, all he wanted to do was drop off his floating log and go to sleep . . . and sleep . . . and sleep . . .

Last hole. Four hundred fifteen yards.

It had taken him . . . what? Three hours to cover the seventeenth? Four? And then he'd lain in the mud, exhausted, unable to move, for hours more, despite the increasingly frantic buzzes on his survival radio as the current FAC pilot tried to rouse him.

Those Forward Air Controllers. He'd developed a lot of respect for them in the past eleven or twelve days, however

long it had been since he'd been shot down. There were a
bunch of them who'd been playing guardian angel, some in
F-4 Phantoms out of Danang or Nakhon Phanom, Thailand,
others flying OV-10 Broncos or pusher-prop OV-2s. They
were always there, circling above him day or night, and he'd
lost track of the number of times they'd saved his ass. He'd
watched one OV-10 hedgehop fields and villages, actually
trying to draw enemy fire, getting enemy gun crews to reveal
their positions, and once one of those spindly-looking puddle-
jumpers had attacked a formation of NVA soldiers with nothing more than the smoke rockets slung beneath its wings,
devices used for marking targets for what Air Force guys
thought of as *real* airplanes. Except for a few stark and lonely
stretches, in bad weather or during a heavy air strike, those
FAC guys had always been there, and their presence had been
a steady comfort, even when he'd been staying off the radio
to avoid giving away his position to enemy triangulators or
to conserve his batteries.

Lately, though, these guys had become a steady, almost
intolerable annoyance. There was one in particular, one whose
voice he could recognize now, who had a peculiarly vicious
talent at nagging him along, challenging him, demanding that
he finish another ten yards . . . or five . . . or two . . . and calling him everything from pussy to coward when he wasn't
demanding that Halliwell *prove* himself again and again and
again.

He was starting to hate those voices on his radio, and that
one voice in particular. Damn it, hadn't he proved enough
already?

Twenty yards to go. Sixty feet. Um . . . seven hundred and
. . . something inches. Seven hundred inches wasn't so bad.

This was the hardest part of the whole trek. His reserves
were gone, down to the bare-scraped bottom of the old barrel.
The river had gotten much wider, which meant he didn't have
to worry as much about being seen by NVA troops on the
north bank, but it also meant that the current was much
slower, much more sluggish, especially near the shore. He
was getting almost no help from the current at all, with every
yard dragged from the river bottom by mud-laden boots.

God, his shoulder hurt. The wound wasn't deep, but despite
his one-handed attempts to clean it, it was definitely infected.

That's what comes of soaking it in sewer water, he thought.

Five more yards. Almost there. He managed to lift his head high enough to survey the riverbank on his right. Most of it was steep, bare earth and clay sliced away by the river's flow, far beyond his present ability to climb. Up ahead, though, the bank flattened out where the current had deposited a broad crescent of black mud. Above the bank were scattered trees, not thick enough to be called a forest but too thick to allow a helicopter to land.

Three more yards. Hell . . . that mud flat was close enough to the mark, unless his brain had been so fogged for this past few hundred yards that he'd lost count along the way. It certainly felt like he'd come a lot farther than four hundred fifteen yards. Still pushing his log like a huge and awkward paddleboard, he angled toward the shore, his boots sinking into the muddy bottom with each kick, threatening to hold him, to drag him back, and down. The railway tie that had brought him so far wedged itself into the mud shoal. He started to climb ashore, and found that his legs were failing him, weighed down by heavy, clinging mud.

He was not going to make it even one more yard.

Only gradually did it dawn on him. Four hundred fifteen yards, close enough, and on the eighteenth green. This was what he'd been struggling to reach now for so long . . . four days, was it? He couldn't remember. It seemed like forever. Rolling off the log and into the mud, he looked around hopefully. This was *it,* the clubhouse. . . .

Only there was no clubhouse. No building. No waiting drink. No soldiers or Marines here to pick him up and take him somewhere dry and clean. Nothing but mud and water, and the dead certainty that he could not make it any further, no matter how his FAC angels goaded, insulted, pleaded, or threatened.

Nothing, no one here.

The disappointment was crushing, almost too much to bear. Feeling a death-cold numbness of both body and spirit, he thumbed the transmit switch on his radio. "FAC, this . . . this is Bravo One-niner." His lips were so leaden he could barely speak. "FAC, Bravo One-niner. C'min. Over."

"Bravo One-niner, this is FAC, call sign Nail Two-seven. Go ahead. Over."

Nail. That would be one of the F-4s out of Nakhon Phanom. He rolled over onto his back, searching the deep, ultramarine blue of the predawn sky, searching for the orbiting Phantom, but he saw nothing.

"Nail, Bravo One-niner. Reached the clubhouse." He hesitated, trying to gain control of his uncertain voice. Then his emotions, bottled for so long and through so much terror and frustration and disappointment, foamed up in sudden, almost explosive release. "There's nobody here." His voice cracked, and tears streamed down his face. "Damn it, *there's fuckin' nobody here!* . . ."

He started coughing, a deep, wrenching, pneumonia cough that felt like it was tearing his lungs out.

Damn. They'd never told him anything specific, of course, not with the likelihood that Friend Charlie was listening in, but the implication had been clear that once he reached the clubhouse, he would be back among friends. There was nothing here . . . no helicopter, no American troops, no ARVNs, nothing, not even an open space big enough for a helicopter to use as an LZ.

"Ah, roger that, One-niner. Don't sweat it. You'll have white-hats for company anytime now."

"R-roger that. White hats." Did he mean white hats, as in good guys? Or was there a double meaning intended, white hats, as in Navy sailors? Damn this elusive, slippery jargon of slang and circumlocutions they had to employ in order to avoid telling the listening enemy anything important. He wasn't sure what the FAC pilot was saying . . . except that his arrival was acknowledged and help was on the way.

Halliwell slumped onto the mud flat. He was too tired to move, almost too tired to care, once that first, eye-burning burst of emotion had welled out of him, leaving him limp and trembling.

After a long time, he managed to crawl a bit further up onto the bank and thoroughly coat himself with black mud. That would help to hide him from enemy passersby, perhaps. Hell, it might also hide him from his rescuers, but he was too weak to do anything else.

One way or another, this was the end of the line. . . .

On the Song Mieu Giang River
0520 hours

Nolan raised his head cautiously, peering out from behind the layer of banana leaves covering him. He was lying prone in the bottom of a sampan taken from the village across the river from the FOB, with Nghiep Van Dong kneeling in the bow of the slender, shallow-draft vessel, paddling. They had no outboard, and there'd been no time to have one flown in. That suited Nolan fine. Loud engines and fast sampans attracted the ear and the eye, which was exactly what he wanted to avoid just now.

It was nearly dawn, the sky fully light and only the tree-scattered shorelines of the river still deep in shadow. Visibility was clear now for hundreds of yards, with a faint, steaming mist coming off the water.

Nghiep had been paddling them upstream now for nearly four hours. Both men wore the black garb of Vietnamese peasants and carried AK-47s hidden in the bottom of the sampan. In addition, a SEAL PRC-77 backpack radio was concealed beneath the pile of banana leaves in the bottom of the boat, as was Nolan himself. Though Nolan was not a big man—he could pass as a Vietnamese from a distance—it was a fair guess that any traffic on the river was going to be carefully examined from the shore by alert men with powerful binoculars. One Asian man alone in a small sampan wasn't worthy of note . . . but if they got a look at Nolan's face the proverbial game would be up.

"How much farther?" he asked, keeping his voice low.

"Not far," Nghiep replied, also quietly. Voices carried all too well across still water in the early morning. "Next bend in the river, maybe."

Nolan eased himself a little higher, resting on his elbows and pulling his AK a little closer to hand. There was a distinct possibility that the NVA knew exactly where Halliwell was, and that they were using him as bait for a trap. They'd certainly been doing something similar when he'd been walled off behind his minefield barricade, setting up their triple-A and waiting for the American SAR helos to blunder into the killing zone.

He doubted that they were trying anything like that now, though. The North Vietnamese effort to reach Halliwell—not to mention the intercepted radio traffic proving that they knew who he was—suggested that they were desperate to capture the Air Force officer at almost any cost. Using him as bait now—and risking having him killed or rescued—would be decidedly counterproductive.

In the bow, Nghiep Van Dong remained calm, his paddle dipping into the water on one side of the craft, then on the other. The small Vietnamese had volunteered for this op almost before Nolan had finished telling him what was involved. "I come with you, Lieutenant" was all that he'd said.

"Hey, Dong?"

"Yes, Lieutenant?"

"Where are you from, anyway? I don't think you ever told us."

"Small ville, Lieutenant. You not hear of it."

"Try me."

"Bao Loc."

"You're right. I don't know it."

"Central Highlands, on road between Saigon and Dalat." He was silent for a few moments, before adding, "Is FULRO stronghold. My people, my family all FULRO."

Nolan had to think for a moment before he remembered what FULRO stood for. Then he had it. The Front Unifié de Lutte des Races Opprimées was a guerrilla organization of sorts, one organized only recently with funds and supplies provided largely by the French. The name meant United Front for the Struggle of the Oppressed Races. He didn't know much about the group, save that it had its roots in the local Montagnards' resistance to Saigon's policy of enforcing second-class citizenship on nonethnic Vietnamese.

Most Vietnamese hated the 'Yards. What was Nghiep and his family doing mixed up with a Montagnard resistance force? "I wouldn't have expected Vietnamese and the Mountain People working together."

"Some of us look to the time when you Americans leave Vietnam," Nghiep said. "When that happens, perhaps differences between South Vietnamese and Montagnards will not be so great as they seem now."

Nolan digested that for a moment. If he was reading Nghiep's understatement aright, some of his people were anticipating the fall of Saigon once American ground forces abandoned the country and were already organizing guerrilla groups to resist the new Communist masters. The thought of a Communist government in Saigon harassed by a pro-Western guerrilla group in just the way that the South Vietnamese government had been hounded by the Viet Cong insurrection was so ironic that Nolan had to bite down hard to avoid laughing out loud.

"What does Saigon think of this?" he asked. "Or your LDNN officers?"

"Saigon does not need to know," Nghiep replied. "And my CO, he FULRO too. Many LDNN are. When you go, we still here, still fighting."

"Maybe that won't be necessary, Dong. The idea is to get Hanoi to accept a negotiated peace."

"How long, Lieutenant, would such a peace last, if American troops not here to defend it? If American ships not offshore? If American SEALs not here to help LDNN?"

Nolan decided not to press the South Vietnamese SEAL further. Obviously, not all Vietnamese had the same high hopes for America's policy of Vietnamization that some American politicians and high-ranking military officers did.

"We coming to bend now. Watch good."

Gently, the sampan edged around the point of a sharp bend in the river. Beyond, the steep and mud-crumbly bank gave way to a mud flat, where silt carried downstream by the river had been deposited by water redirected by the curve.

This was the site identified as Point Clubhouse, but there was no sign of Halliwell. Nolan lay motionless in the sampan as Nghiep guided them closer with slow, even strokes of the oar. There was a fair amount of debris washed up on the flat shoal by the last river flood.

Including a railroad tie. Nolan felt a quickening of his pulse, a rising excitement. The FAC pilots had reported that Halliwell had found a log or railroad tie and was using it as a makeshift raft. If that was the log . . .

A small, inner shiver pricked the back of Nolan's neck. He was being *watched,* he knew it. He looked more carefully at the mud bank and noticed an oddly man-shaped lump of mud.

Two eyes stared at him from one end of the lump, less than four feet away. Blue eyes. Western eyes. *It's him!* ...

"What's the name of your dog?" Nolan asked quietly.

The eyes widened. The form stirred, and Nolan could see now that a survival knife was clutched in one mud-coated hand. "Oscar," the shape said, the word barely audible through the thick mud coating. That matched with the information in Halliwell's record.

"Congratulations, Colonel," Nolan whispered, grinning. "Game's over. Ready for the nineteenth hole? A nice, thick steak? Maybe a double scotch?"

"Right ... now," the man said, "I'd settle for a hot shower and about fifty hours' sleep." He shook his head. "I thought I'd had it. Thought you two were bad guys."

Nolan handed the man his canteen. "We just act like it, sometimes."

Halliwell was so weak that Nolan and Nghiep both had to clamber out of the sampan and work together to lift him up and put him in the bottom of the narrow craft, laying him on his back and covering him over completely with banana leaves. Nghiep resumed his kneeling position in the bow with a paddle, while Nolan sat in the stern, hunched over to look as small as possible, with his AK-47 by his side.

As Nghiep poled them back from the bank and nudged the sampan around to face downstream, Halliwell extended a muddy hand. "I'm Frank Halliwell," he said. "Sure glad to meet you."

"Lieutenant Nolan," the SEAL replied, grasping the hand. "I feel like I know you already, sir."

Halliwell didn't let go. It was as though he desperately needed the feel of human skin against his own. To *know* that he was among friends.

"Please. I'm Frank."

Nolan smiled. "And I'm David." Nolan wasn't usually so casual with non-SEALs, especially when they were senior officers. But Halliwell needed social contact, social affirmation as much as he needed the physical contact.

Finally, Halliwell released him. "You a Marine? Army Ranger?"

"Actually, I'm Navy. You've had a lot of people working long, hard hours to pull you out."

"I know." The words were slurred, almost mumbled. It was as if Halliwell wanted to talk, *needed* to talk, but his mind and body both were failing him. "I'm . . . I'm grateful."

"Don't even mention it, Frank. I'm damned glad to have been able to help." He studied the shoreline to the right, watching for anything out of place, any sign of hidden watchers, or ambush. If they were going to strike, if this was a trap, they would have to spring it *now*. . . .

"I . . . I really thought I'd had it."

"Well, not to worry you, but we're not quite out of the woods yet. We're about three kilometers from our forward base. They've got helos there to fly you out to Danang, but we've got to get there, first."

"Lots of competition?"

"Lots of competition. And they're not going to be happy at seeing you go. You just lie there as still as you can and make like a bunch of bananas. We'll get you out."

"I know you will."

Overhead, a pair of A1s howled past, Sandys on close-air support, wings heavy with bombs and other assorted ordnance. Higher up, so small they were nothing but specks drawing thin, white contrails across the deep, early-morning blue of the sky, a couple of F-4 Phantoms mounted high guard. North, across the river, an OV-10 banked as it hedge-hopped over the trees . . . a diversion to convince NVA searchers that the *real* activity was over there.

Leaving the paddling momentarily to Nghiep, Nolan reached down and picked up the handset on the radio. "Post Office, this is Mailman," he said, using call signs agreed to just before he'd left the FOB. "Post Office, Mailman."

"Mailman, Post Office" came back. It sounded like Colonel Bellows himself on the other end. "Go ahead."

"Post Office, we have your package. We're beginning the route now, special delivery. Over."

"Outstanding, Mailman! Watch where you step. Nail reports a lot of bad, junkyard dogs in the neighborhood. Over."

"Roger that. Keep us posted. Mailman out."

For the next two hours, they paddled slowly down the river, hugging the south bank, once pulling into overhanging tangles of vegetation to wait as another sampan passed slowly upriver on the opposite shore. Twice, they stopped when they spotted large numbers of troops ahead, apparently deploying to attack; both times, they slipped into the shelter of an over-hanging, overgrown riverbank while Nolan got on his radio and called in air strikes by the guardian Sandys and Phantoms who were flying shotgun for the tiny party on the river below. Both times, the low-flying aircraft screamed in at treetop level, scattering ordnance across the landscape, which erupted seconds later in billowing clouds of black smoke shot through with orange flame. The napalm erupted in a broad swath across the landscape, the bloody light reflected in the river, the fireballs boiling into the early morning sky.

Nolan watched the air strikes with tight-lipped silence, oc-casionally using a pair of binoculars he'd brought along to watch the results. Back in the States, and among troops in Vietnam who hadn't seen the results up close, napalm strikes evoked the black-joking term "crispy critters," taken from a popular breakfast cereal.

No one who'd actually seen the results of such a strike made such jokes, save, possibly, as a release during those times when the horror closed in with its suffocating embrace, and then only with others who'd seen and felt and tasted the same horror. Through the binoculars, Nolan could see several North Vietnamese troops, their clothing burned away, hurling themselves into the river, desperate to stop the pain.

And when the rumble of the jets faded away, they could hear the screams.

"It always seemed so much . . . cleaner," Halliwell said quietly, "when I was in an aircraft at thirty thousand feet. You never see this part of the war from up there. I guess you guys are used to it, though, huh?"

"You never get *used* to it, Colonel."

They continued their journey. Another hour would do it . . . if they didn't run into any more major problems along the way.

On the Song Mieu Giang River
0802 hours

Colonel Dimitri Pavlovich Kartashkin leaned over the map spread out on the folding table. A Russian-built PT-76 grumbled nearby, filling the air with blue smoke and the bite of diesel fumes.

"You are sure of this?" he asked Colonel Thuan in thickly accented Vietnamese. As long as he'd been in this country, he still had trouble with the damned tones.

"Yes, Comrade Colonel," Thuan replied in excellent Russian. "One air attack here ... the next ... right here, both breaking up concentrations of my men as they moved toward the river."

"It suggests that they're moving him out. By boat, you think? Down the river, while covering him by air?"

"It almost has to be so," Thuan said. "Unless they are moving underwater. The American frogmen could attempt something of the sort."

American frogmen? Yes, the SEALs might try something that daring. "I doubt that they are swimming underwater. The American aviator will be too weak for such exertion. He would drown."

"Then it must be by boat."

"And not by *military* boat. They tried that yesterday. We should be watching for a sampan." Even as he said the words, realization warmed him like a detonating bomb. "Stop every sampan on the river between Cam Lo and Dông Ha! The man we seek will be on one of them."

He looked up at the fume-belching tank. "I suggest that you deploy this vehicle closer to the river." He pointed at a spot on the map. "Here. This should do it. Where you have a commanding view of the entire river."

"But the American air. Sir, they used *napalm!* ..."

"You have antiaircraft assets. *Use* them. I will not let Halliwell slip through my fingers!"

"It will be done, Comrade Colonel!"

"It had better be, Comrade Thuan. More rides on this than you could possibly know!"

Folding the map, he returned it to its case, then trotted over to the rumbling steel monster. The tank commander, sitting in the hatch, saluted him.

"That way!" he yelled above the tank's roar. "To the river!"

They would have Halliwell this morning. He could *feel* it.

Chapter 36

Thursday, 13 April 1972

West of Point Wisconsin
On the Song Mieu Giang River
0805 hours

"One more kilometer," Nolan told the man lying in the bottom of the sampan. "Think you can hold out that long before we turn you over to all those beautiful nurses?"

"I'll manage," Halliwell said. With plenty to drink, and some candy bars inside him for fast energy, he was sounding a little stronger now. "It's not the nurses I'm looking forward to, understand. It's the shower and the clean sheets."

Nolan chuckled. "Roger that."

A small geyser of water erupted from the surface of the river a few feet ahead of the sampan, followed a second later by the distant crack of a gunshot. "Sniper!" Nghiep called. "Somewhere on the north bank!"

Four more geysers stitched across the water, falling short.

Halliwell peered over the sampan's gunwale from beneath his banana leaf blanket. "Okay. Now I know how a duck in a shooting gallery feels."

"Keep down, Colonel. They have no way of knowing that we're not the real McCoy."

"I see some waving at us from the shore," Nghiep said. "They're signaling for us to go over there."

"Play dumb," Nolan replied. "Make like we don't understand." He picked up his AK and held it high above his head, waving it back and forth. Nghiep did the same, the unmistakable curve of its banana magazine sticking straight up.

Faintly, he could hear the North Vietnamese troops calling

446

to them across the water . . . and a moment later, two more splashes nearby marked the fall of warning shots. "I wonder just how badly they want you alive, Colonel," Nolan said.

"They will be calling others on this side of river," Nghiep pointed out. "Someone be here soon."

"Keep paddling."

More gunfire reached for the sampan, and Nolan was pretty sure that they were no longer warning shots. One round snapped through the gunwale between Nghiep and Halliwell's feet, and another buried itself in the sternpost inches from Nolan's back. They kept paddling, working harder now, trying to make better speed. There was nothing else to do.

Nolan's big worry was that NVA troops on the south bank of the river were being deployed to cut them off. The only way to avoid them would be to move further out into the middle of the stream, and that would make them a far easier target for marksmen on *both* sides of the river. At least here they were hard to see, their shape difficult to pick out from the backdrop of riverbank and foliage.

Perhaps hardest of all was enduring that scattered small arms fire without shooting back . . . but to return fire would simply confirm for the NVA troops that they were closing on a SAR team.

Nghiep held up his hand suddenly. "Lieutenant."

"What?"

"Trouble, I think. Look ahead, on the south bank at the bend in the river."

Nolan looked where Nghiep had indicated, leaning forward and shading his eyes against the morning light and the sundance coming off the water to the east. The river curved slightly south there, with thick forest reaching almost all the way down to the water. He couldn't see anything that might be—

No, there *was* something, a great, dark shadow squatting on the riverbank beneath a crisscrossing mass of camouflage nets and tree cuttings. Recognition chilled him. He glanced back upriver, then checked the small, plastic-covered topo map he'd brought with him. Yes . . . this was about a kilometer east of the spot he and his team had run into the NVA armored column yesterday. What he was looking at was a tank, probably the same PT-76 amphibious recon tank they'd seen in that NVA laager during their attempt to reach Halliwell overland. The tank's crew had repositioned their vehicle to serve as a squat, monstrous blockhouse squarely between the sampan and the FOB; the gunfire from the north bank must have been intended to push them even closer to the southern bank . . . and into the deadly arms of this waiting ambush.

It put the SEALs in a hell of a bad spot, too. If they called in an air strike, they would have to get well clear of this shore to avoid being cooked by friendly fire. If they tried moving out into the middle of the river, they would be immediately seen and attacked. If they tried to go back the way they'd come, or strike out overland, well . . . Nolan was enough of a tactician that he was willing to bet any money that more NVA troops were coming down the river from behind them right now with the express purpose of scooping up anyone and everyone they found along the way.

For the first time, Nolan wondered if his smaller-is-better philosophy worked. He was in the bottom of a bag already, and the bad guys were about to tie the neck of the sack closed. If he'd had a SEAL team with him, they might have been able to employ a sudden and decisive burst of superior firepower to break free of the trap.

But at the moment, it didn't look like they had a chance.

He reached for his radio. "Post Office, Post Office," he called, speaking quietly. There might be enemy sentries on the shore nearby, just yards away. "Post Office, this is Mailman! Come in, please!"

"Mailman, Post Office. Go ahead."

"Post Office, we got problems. Biggest damned Doberman I've ever seen, and it's smack dab in the middle of the sidewalk. Don't think we can make it to the front door. Over."

"Do you have coordinates? Over."

"Bad guy is smack on Point Wisconsin." Nolan read the coordinates off the map, then added, "But we're going to need some time to get clear, or the dogcatcher's going to bag us as well."

"We copy that, Mailman. Help is on the way, but give us a yell when you're in the clear. Over."

"Roger that. Mailman out." He checked upriver again. No

sign of pursuit . . . not yet. "Let's back out of here, Dong. Before—"

Gunfire erupted from the mass of vegetation on the bank just ahead, sending a burst of water spouts splashing and popping across the surface of the river just yards away.

"That's it!" Nghiep called. "They've seen us!"

The gun continued to hammer at them from less than a hundred yards ahead. Plying their paddles, Nolan and Nghiep pulled the sampan into the lee of an outthrust arm of mud and clay embankment, as the automatic fire continued to search and probe. From the sound of it, Nolan thought it was a heavy machine gun, probably a PKM, the Russian-made equivalent of the American M60. Bullets, 7.62mm rounds, geysered in the water and plowed heavily into the embankment. They couldn't withdraw without taking direct fire, and if they stayed put, it was only a matter of time before the bad guys showed up to take them in.

In fact, they were trapped, with no way out.

South of the Song Mieu Giang River
Near Point Wisconsin
0817 hours

Bill Tangretti heard the gunfire sounding from just ahead and dropped to cover behind a fallen log, signaling the rest of his team with an upraised hand.

Morgan moved up to join him, taking cover behind the log. "Sounds close."

"Yeah." Judging distances by sound alone could be deceiving, but that machine gun couldn't be more than a couple of hundred yards away. "What do you think, sir? By the river?"

"Sounds like it. They might have spotted our people."

"That's what I was thinking."

Morgan took a quick look around, checking the positions of the rest of the team—Boomer Cain, Twidge Halstead, and three Vietnamese Rangers. "Let's move," he said, signaling the others. Stealthily, slipping through open forest and black shadow, they started forward.

They'd set off overland from the FOB two hours earlier. Morgan had approached Tangretti, Cain, and Halstead while the three enlisted SEALs were in the process of deciding that they should put together an ad hoc patrol to go out and meet Nolan . . . and be on hand to cover his ass if he and Nghiep ran into something they couldn't handle. ''You're not figuring on going out there by yourselves, are you?'' Morgan had demanded.

''Hell, no,'' Greg had replied. ''We figured some of the ARVN Rangers would want to come with us.''

''I thought you'd all stood down for the morning.''

''We did,'' Bill had told him. ''That means we can do what we want, right?''

''Only if you plan on letting me come,'' Morgan had said.

They'd left a few minutes later, stopping only long enough to draw full weapons and load-outs, including smoke grenades and one canvas pack full of C4 plastic explosives, and a second with detonators. The explosives had been brought out so that the Rangers could blow the FOB when they abandoned it, and SEALs were not known for letting good explosives go to waste. They'd been hoping for LAW rockets, but unfortunately none had been flown out on the helos. The ARVNs were still trying to adjust to the shock of having so many NVA tanks thrown at them, and antitank weapons were hard to come by.

Traveling south for the benefit of any NVA observers, they'd looped around to the east, then north, traveling quickly until they reached the southern shore of the Song Mieu Giang. Turning west then, they'd proceeded slowly upstream, searching for anything that might pose a threat to Nolan, Nghiep, and Halliwell. Twice they'd faded into the underbrush and waited as NVA troops had hurried past, but both times the enemy troops were moving east, away from Nolan's position, and posed no immediate threat.

Bill had been thinking a lot about Morgan as they hiked. The man had changed; no longer was he the cynical and somewhat supercilious loner they'd known at BUD/S or, later, in Laos. Operating, presumably, had knocked some of the rough edges off the man; often, that was all that it took. You could teach a man all about team operations in BUD/S, but none of the lessons became real until you actually had a chance to apply them in the field, to experience them for yourself.

Morgan, he thought, was turning out to be all right.

Things had been smoother with Twidge lately, too. Maybe they'd both needed to say what had been said on the beach at Okinawa, or afterward. It was still clear that Greg was fighting some inner demon and that Wendy might well be in the line of fire, but their relationship with each other, SEAL to SEAL, was as close and as tight as it had ever been.

They'd been nearing the bend in the river identified as Point Wisconsin on their maps when a sudden burst of machine-gun fire from somewhere up ahead sent them all diving for cover. Sure now that the fire wasn't aimed at them, Morgan urged his team forward, sending Xuan Dan Nghan ahead to scout the way.

Xuan materialized out of the undergrowth ahead. "Many NVA," he said, voice low. "Machine guns. Trucks. APCs. And one NVA tank."

A tank. The North Vietnamese had arrived loaded for bear. Or SEAL.

West of Point Wisconsin
On the Song Mieu Giang River
0818 hours

The machine gun continued to chatter, stitching lines of water spouts up the river past the hidden sampan.

"Cowboy Two-five, this is Mailman!" Nolan was calling into the radio. "We're in a world of shit down here! Can't your friends take care of these bad guys?"

The OV-2 spotter plane roared overhead, the sun flashing from its wings. Moments later, a pair of F-4 Phantoms boomed in from the south, hurtling past as antiaircraft guns erupted all around, hurling long and sparkling lines of tracers after the low-flying aircraft.

"Ah, Mailman, Cowboy Two-five," the voice of the FAC pilot came back. "Sorry, but no can do. We can't see the target."

Damn! Both tank and the machine-gun position seemed almost blatantly obvious down here, but Nolan had ridden in enough helicopters to know that what was obvious on the ground was frequently far from obvious from the air . . . especially when the opposition had gone to a lot of trouble to hide their vehicles and emplacements from reconnaissance aircraft.

And the sampan was something like one hundred yards away from ground zero . . . a gnat's whisker when you started dropping cluster bombs and similar deadly toys.

"Wait one, Mailman," Cowboy called. "I've got someone on the other line. . . ."

Southeast of Point Wisconsin
On the Song Mieu Giang River
0819 hours

"I said, wait one," Morgan said into the PRC-25's handset. "We'll see if we can get in and mark it for you! Sierra One, out!"

"So what's the score?" Bill asked him. Machine-gun fire continued to chatter in the distance.

"Nolan's pinned down somewhere west of that tank position . . . we're not sure where, or how close he is. And the air can't see the tank."

"Tank heavy covered," Xuan told them, nodding. "Nets. Banana leaves. All cover."

"So we're going to go in and mark the bastard," Morgan finished. "Kill it if we can, but mark it for sure so the zoomies know where to shoot."

It was a fact of modern combat that tanks weren't necessarily the killers suggested by their reputation. It was tough tackling one when it was supported by infantry, but not impossible.

"Wish we could've brought along a LAW or two," Greg said.

"Trust in the Lord with all your might," Bill said, reaching into the pouch slung over his left hip and extracting two oblong gray blocks of clay. "And a little plastique doesn't hurt either."

"Be prepared, huh?"

"Always. Never know when you're going to need your plastic."

"Give me one of those, boy scout."

They prepared two sapper charges by inserting a couple of detonators into each block of plastique, then crimping pull-ring fuse igniters to each. Repacking their makeshift bomb, they crawled forward, approaching the edge of the clearing occupied by the enemy tank.

The vehicle had been positioned at the very edge of the river, inside the bend, where it commanded an excellent view both up and down stream. Four North Vietnamese troops were visible, one in the open commander's hatch on the tank's turret, the other three crouched next to the metal monster, peering out across the river. As Xuan had reported, the area was covered over by camouflage netting, which painted tank and soldiers in deep shadow, with scattered dapplings of early morning light.

The APCs and trucks, Xuan explained, weren't here. He pointed off toward the south, indicating that they were hidden back in the woods.

No problem. The tank was the main target.

The SEALs and Vietnamese Rangers were executing what was known as a hasty ambush, without time to carefully prepare positions. Quickly, they spread out along the edge of the clearing. "Let's have some cover in there," Bill told Cain. "A couple rounds of HE, and then some smoke."

The other SEAL nodded, pulling an M406 40mm grenade from a bandolier and snapping it home in the breech of his M203. Raising the weapon to his shoulder, he waited until Morgan raised his own weapon, an AK-47; the team CO would signal the beginning of the attack by opening fire.

"Now!"

Gunfire thundered and cracked as the SEALs and ARVN Rangers poured a devastating volley of full-auto gunfire into the clearing, sending the three NVA troops on the ground tumbling, and exploding the tank commander's head in a bloody splash of gore. Boomer's first grenade exploded against the PT-76, shredding nearby vegetation and bringing down a piece of the camouflage netting overhead; his second struck in the tangle of vegetation just beyond, eliciting screams.

The reconnaissance tank's armor was thin but still too strong to be penetrated by a 40mm grenade. Someone inside shoved the body of the tank's commander up through the hatch and then, as the body bounced like a rag doll on the ground, an arm reached up, grabbed the large hatch, and banged it shut. The tank's diesel engine gave a piercing roar, and then the vehicle was moving backward. Two NVA soldiers burst out of the foliage, running past the tank, and Bill cut them both down with a long burst from his Stoner.

"Smoke!" Morgan yelled. "We need smoke!"

Boomer snapped an M680 smoke grenade into the breech of his 203, shouldered the weapon, and let fly. Thick white smoke boiled from the ground beside the tank, quickly swirling into a thick mist that blanketed the vehicle, the vegetation, and the bodies sprawled on the earth.

Greg clapped Bill on the arm. "Let's rock and roll, pardner!" The two SEALs rose from cover, sprinting into the smoke. They could scarcely see the tank at all now, save as a great, gray shadow lurching through an almost impenetrable fog, but they could track it by the roar of its engine. Bill reached the tank's side and vaulted up onto the engine cover aft, careful to keep his feet clear of wheels and tracks. The stubby, truncated cone of a turret was slewing right, the 76mm main gun and the 7.62mm coaxial machine gun seeking targets.

Balancing himself as the tank continued to rumble slowly backward, Bill smacked the block of plastic explosives down squarely on the center of the hatch, which was so large it took up most of the top of the turret. Greg didn't mount the tank, but jammed his plastique into the right-side track well just above the tread and the number-one road wheel.

"Ready!" Greg yelled.

"Go!" Bill shouted, yanking first one pull-ring igniter and then the other. Turning, he leaped off the back of the tank as Greg set his fuses burning and started to run.

The tank's driver suddenly threw the left track into forward gear, while continuing to back with the other, slewing the vehicle suddenly and violently right. The PT-76 was now squarely facing the two running SEALs and the rest of the SEAL and Ranger team hidden in the forest beyond. The coaxial machine gun opened fire, and Bill and Greg both dove for the ground; for an insane second or two, Bill felt like he was trying to dig himself an instant foxhole with his fingernails . . . and then with a piercing, shrill bang, the plastic explosives on the top of the turret detonated with a flash and a fresh cloud of smoke. A half second later, Greg's charge fired, this one sounding deeper and more hollow as it erupted deep within the steel-shrouded confines of the track well. The blast ripped apart the tank's right track, and with an ear-splitting whine and clatter, the PT-76 threw the track in a snaking whiplash of undulating and disconnecting tread segments.

The driver started scrambling up out of his hatch, and Morgan shot the man down, firing over Greg's and Bill's heads. "Move it, you two!"

Bill rose to his feet, helping Greg up, and the two sprinted the rest of the way back to the impromptu SEAL ambush line.

"Nice work, you two!" Morgan said.

"You're both hired," Cain added. "Next time I have a tank I want killed, you guys're it!"

"It still would've been easier with a LAW," Greg replied. "I'm getting too old for this stuff at knife-fighting range."

"Watch it!" Morgan yelled. "Here they come!"

More North Vietnamese troops spilled out of the far treeline, their shapes just visible in the fast-dissolving smoke. Bill picked up his Stoner once more, worked the action, and opened fire, as the rest of the SEALs and Rangers hosed the oncoming troops with full-auto mayhem.

"Hit the tank with smoke again," Morgan told Cain.

The SEAL loaded another smoke round, took aim, and let fly. Fresh white smoke boiled into the sky past the tattered camo netting. It was impossible to tell if the tank was dead or simply damaged; its commander and driver were both dead, but there was a gunner unaccounted for, and the vehicle's weapons might still be very much alive if a fresh crew reached them.

At this point, however, the SEALs were happy to leave the tank to their aerial allies. Morgan was already on the radio.

"That's affirmative!" he yelled into the handset. "We marked the target with white smoke! Take it out!"

"Ah, roger that, Sierra One. What is your position, over?"

"On the target, but don't worry about that. We're just leaving! Sierra One out!" Morgan signaled the other SEALs. "C'mon, people! Hustle!"

"Time to get out of Dodge!" Bill added, laying down a savage, covering blanket of fire as the others passed him.

Then, turning, he ran after them, sprinting deeper into the forest.

A few miles to the north, the first Phantoms started peeling off. . . .

West of Point Wisconsin
On the Song Mieu Giang River
0821 hours

They'd waited out the sharp, fierce battle in the sampan, keeping low and keeping out of sight behind the sheltering embankment. When white smoke started showing through the trees, Nolan was pretty sure what to expect.

"Stay down, everyone," he said. Moving forward, he lowered himself full length across Halliwell's body.

"Damn it, Lieutenant," the Air Force officer said. "We haven't been properly introduced!"

"Quiet, sir," Nolan shot back. "You don't think I came all this way to see you take a piece of . . . uh-oh. Here they come!"

The first Phantom was coming in from the north, little more than a gull shape against a faint, dark gray haze as its pilot throttled forward. Then it was flashing low across the river as the antiaircraft guns opened up. Nolan could hear the guns all around and realized that hundreds of NVA regulars must be inhabiting this patch of woods beyond the riverbank . . . along with a small army of antiaircraft. The tracers flickering overhead seemed to coalesce into a wall of drifting dots of green light, a wall so thick that no aircraft could possibly fly through that green hellfire and survive . . . and still the Phantom kept coming.

The F-4 reached the south side of the river at almost the same time as its roar, booming overhead a hundred yards in front of the sampan's hiding place, a fistful of deadly black objects spilling from its belly as it howled low over the trees.

The explosions thundered an instant later, causing the water to shiver and the treeline along the river's edge to dance and jerk convulsively. Flame and oily smoke roiled into the sky, replacing the white fog with a death-black pall, and fragments—bits of metal, rock, splintered bits of tree—fell in a

pattering rain that splashed in the river and bounced off Nolan's back.

Seconds later, the second Phantom followed the tracks of
the first, howling in low across the water, chasing its own
shadow, then pulling up at the last moment as it scattered
another cloud of bomblets across the NVA-infested forest.

Nolan could hear the screams. . . .

After that, it was the Sandys' turn, as a pair of ancient prop-
driven A1s banked in and, with an approach speed that was
damned near sedate compared to the scram-bam of the Phantoms, droned overhead, bombs tumbling from their wings.
Fresh explosions and new fires erupted from further to the
south.

The machine gun was silent now.

"Dong!" Nolan called, resuming his place in the sampan's
stern. "Let's get the hell out of here!"

They started paddling, sticking to the shadows close along
the embankment.

Nolan could still hear the screams of the wounded.

On the Song Mieu Giang River
0825 hours

The shrieks and screams of dying men filled the air. Colonel Kartashkin staggered into the clearing, his uniform in
tatters, his left arm bloody and hanging limp at his side.

He'd been supervising a machine-gun team in the forest
when the commando strike had taken out the tank; seconds
later, the American Phantoms had struck, followed moments
later by their A-1s. The concussion had hurled him to the
ground; shrapnel had savaged his arm. By the time he'd re-
gained his senses and his feet and made it back to the clearing,
the attackers had vanished, leaving bodies and a dense plume
of smoke. Ears ringing, he emerged once more into a world
of light, of choking, swirling smoke, and of screaming
wounded.

Colonel Thuan—the upper half of him, anyway—lay in the
water. The PT-76, one tread gone, was tipped at a precarious
angle on the embankment nearby.

A cold chill, as cold as the winter wind in Moscow, shivered its way up his spine. He'd been right *there*, standing

next to the tank as he'd talked with Thuan. Had he delayed another few minutes . . .

Something caught his eye, something metallic lying on the ground. Stooping, he picked it up.

He recognized it . . . a single link from the 5.56mm ammo of a belt-fed Stoner light machine gun, and the recognition sent a fresh chill down his back. Kartashkin knew something about the Stoner—a good weapon, though it was prone to jams and needed meticulous field maintenance, unlike Soviet designs. He'd read about the weapon in the SEAL dossier he'd read in Moscow before his deployment to Vietnam; the only people who used Stoners extensively in Vietnam were the U.S. Navy SEALs.

SEALs . . .

West of Point Wisconsin
On the Song Mieu Giang River
0829 hours

Nolan and Nghiep kept paddling, stroking hard to carry them past Point Wisconsin. At the top of the embankment, the boat-shaped hull of the PT-76 rested at a forty-five-degree angle, the turret blasted away, orange flame still licking from the shattered engine compartment. Bodies were strewn along the riverbank, and some were still feebly moving. One man—Nolan knew that he would never forget that face—watched the passing sampan through a mask of scarlet, one eye gone, the other wide and wild and staring. The screams of burning men haunted Nolan; half a body, the man's chest bare and unmarked but everything from the waist down torn away, floated in a soup of bloody gore and drifting intestines.

Movement caught his attention. A man was standing close beside the tank, his form just emerging from the dense fog of smoke hanging above the embankment. Nolan started to reach for his AK, but the figure on the shore was unarmed and evidently badly wounded, sagging against the burned-out tank.

For a moment, the two looked into each others' eyes, close enough that Nolan knew the other man could see that he was a Westerner. For that matter, the wounded man was no Vietnamese, though he wore an NVA uniform without rank tabs.

The eyes staring into Nolan's were ice blue, and the shock of hair was blond.

Again, Nolan nearly reached for his weapon, but when the figure ashore moved again, it was to straighten, slightly, and raise his right hand to his brow . . . a salute. Nolan touched the brim of his Vietnamese hat in reply and kept paddling.

In another moment or two, they were past Point Wisconsin and on their way downstream. Behind them, in the forest, secondary explosions continued to cook off.

Half an hour later, Nolan pulled his oar against the water, using it like a rudder to turn the slender prow in toward the shore. On the hill above the water, the familiar gray-stone shape of the FOB brooded in the morning light.

"Wha . . . what now?" Halliwell asked. He sounded weaker again, as though he might be going into shock.

"We're here," he told the downed flier. "Or damned near. Think you can walk?"

"Son, I'll walk to Arizona if you want me to." Clumsily, he got to his feet, then overbalanced and nearly fell. Nolan helped him out of the sampan. A dozen Vietnamese Rangers, all in tiger-stripe camo, descended on them.

"Are these? . . ."

"Don't worry, they're on our side," Nolan told him. "And a damned good thing, too."

Halliwell took several hesitant steps, then nearly fell again. Nolan gave a signal, and one of the Rangers, a short, tough, wiry man, stooped, then plucked Halliwell from the ground, draping the Air Force lieutenant colonel across his back like a large and unwieldy bag of rice. He then began trotting up the hill toward the blockhouse.

"Lieutenant!"

Turning, Nolan saw Tangretti, Halstead, and Morgan jogging toward the beach. Their faces were green-painted, as though they were just in from an op. "Well," Nolan said, grinning. "What've *you* guys been up to?"

"Covering your ass, Lieutenant," Halstead told him. "What . . . you think the zoomies were able to find that tank all by themselves?"

"I should've known," Nolan said, laughing. He clapped Halstead on the shoulder. "Next time, Twidge, the tequila's on me!"

A mortar round exploded a few hundred yards way, sending up a poplar-shaped burst of dust and smoke.

"Starting to rain, guys," Morgan said. "Let's get indoors."

"Can we get Halliwell to the helos?" Tangretti wanted to know.

"Not at the moment. Seems the helos pulled out a while ago, along with Colonel Bellows. Right now, every North Vietnamese soldier in the province is coming our way."

"Shit," Nolan said. "I think you guys pissed them off."

They actually saw very little of the battle that followed. Crouching inside the FOB blockhouse, they rode out a savage mortar and rocket barrage followed by at least two assaults by ground infantry.

They still had their air cover, however, and the Air Force Phantoms and Sandys roared in time after time, spilling high-explosive ordnance all around the barren hilltop, breaking up enemy formations, seeking out and destroying NVA armored personnel carriers, and leaving enemy dead strewn everywhere.

"Seems like you're an awful popular fellow," Tangretti told Halliwell.

"Oh, yeah," Halliwell replied, puffing contentedly on his first cigarette in almost two weeks. "I'm thinking I should sell tickets."

A thunderous cacophony of explosions sounded close outside, and gravel rained on the blockhouse roof.

"Man," Nolan said. "I'm glad those guys are on our side."

"And I'm sure glad you SEALs are on mine," Halliwell replied. "I owe you one, Lieutenant."

"Not at all, sir. Just doing our job. Service with a smile, and we deliver."

Thunder pealed again, crack upon unholy crack, as concrete dust rained down from the bunker's ceiling.

"You sure delivered my ass," Halliwell told him. "And I'm grateful."

The battle dwindled away after that, after the last enemy attack was broken up by air strikes. They bundled Halliwell, stretcher and all, into the back of an ARVN M113 personnel carrier, which clattered up a few minutes later with several friends. Tangretti, Nolan, Halstead, and the other SEALs rode shotgun up top, bouncing and breathing dust as the line of personnel carriers raced further east, trying to outdistance the swirling remnants of the NVA forces around them. Ten minutes later, they reached a clearing at the bottom of the hill, just as the first HH-53 Jolly Green touched down.

A few minutes later, Halliwell was on his way back to Danang aboard the lead helo, while the SEALs crowded into a slick to follow. Nolan leaned back in the hard, upright seat of the UH-1 and watched the FOB blockhouse dwindle away, until it was lost in the mist that was hanging now above the Song Mieu Giang River.

Sometimes Nolan wondered just what it was that made him love the Teams.

The expression on Halliwell's face had said it all.

Chapter 37

Thursday, 31 October 1972

Aboard the South Vietnamese naval junk
Minh Hoa
Off the Cua Viet River
South of the DMZ
0300 hours

Lieutenant Nolan traced his finger along the shoreline on the chart. "You're sure?"

The Vietnamese skipper nodded, pointing for emphasis. "Very sure! This spot!" Quan Ngoc Thanh, the captain of the tiny junk, seemed certain of his navigational skills.

Well, there was no way Nolan was going to try second-guessing the man. The tubby little South Vietnamese naval junk wallowed uncomfortably in the offshore swell some two

thousand yards off the beach, which was a featureless strip
of black almost lost against the paler, star-strewn black of the
sky and the deeper black of the sea. There were no landmarks
to be seen.

Twidge Halstead was with him on the junk's cramped and
primitive bridge, staring at the coastline through a pair of
binoculars. "Damned if I can see the river mouth, Boss," he
said. "I've got some lights that might be campfires."

"*Very* sure," the Vietnamese skipper repeated. He stabbed
a forefinger onto the chart, indicating the coastline perhaps
five kilometers south of the mouth of the Cua Viet. "*This*
spot!"

A second Vietnamese officer on the bridge stepped forward. Lieutenant Huang Long Dzu looked worried, despite
the heavy smear of green and black paint on his face. "We
very close to DMZ here, Mr. Nolan," he said. "We in much
trouble if Captain Quan wrong."

"Then we'll just have to be careful when we get ashore,"
Nolan replied curtly. He continued studying the chart, unwilling to be drawn into yet another debate with the inexpe-
rienced LDNN officer.

The chart, unfortunately, was not particularly informative.
Except for the mouths of several rivers, the coastline was
largely featureless, an expanse of sand dunes and salt marsh.
They were utterly reliant on Captain Quan and his interpre-
tation of the navigational information passed on by the USS
Newport News, an American cruiser operating off this part of
the coast.

The Cua Viet River was a broad, coastal estuary fed by
several smaller rivers—among them the Song Mieu Giang,
where Nolan had participated in the rescue of Lieutenant Colonel Halliwell six months earlier. Just six kilometers north of
the Cua Viet was the southern edge of the DMZ, itself an
eight-kilometer-wide strip of land centered on the Ben Hai
River.

The DMZ, just five miles across at the point where it met
the South China Sea, was supposedly neutral, though it was
well known that the North Vietnamese had regular infiltration
routes across and even *under* it . . . as well as artillery positions and army bases thickly strewn along the Ben Hai's
northern bank.

At the mouth of the Cua Viet was a small naval base . . . little more than a few docks, storehouses, and barracks. Originally built by the South Vietnamese, with American help, of course, the base had fallen to the North Vietnamese during the Easter Offensive and never been recaptured.

This night's mission called for five men—Nolan, Halstead, and three LDNNs—to be put ashore in a rubber boat south of the Cua Viet. They would hide the boat, move inland four or five kilometers, then move north until they reached the river. At that point, they would move downstream until they were close enough to observe the Cua Viet naval base. There were unsettling reports that the North Vietnamese Navy had brought in some new Russian-made patrol boats, moving them south from Haiphong.

What really had both Vietnamese and American admirals' hair standing on end was the possibility that those patrol boats might include a couple of Komars. Komar missile boats were old technology with wooden hulls first launched by the Soviets in 1959, but each carried two SS-N-2 Styx missiles. No one in any Western navy could forget that identical boats, serving in the Egyptian Navy and operating within the safety of Alexandria Harbor on 21 October 1967, had scored three hits against the Israeli destroyer *Elath* and sunk her.

Aerial reconnaissance of Cua Viet had been inconclusive, even with overflights by all-seeing SR-71s. If there were Komars at the old South Vietnamese base, they were well hidden beneath camouflage netting or inside harbor-front shelters.

And so, this night's SEAL sneak-and-peek had been approved at the highest levels in both the South Vietnamese and American naval forces. The last U.S. ground combat battalion, the 3/21, had withdrawn from Vietnam last August, but the U.S. Navy still cruised constantly just off the coast. America's full-time involvement in Indochina had begun with an unsuccessful North Vietnamese torpedo boat attack against American destroyers in the Gulf of Tonkin . . . at least, so official sources insisted. It would be ironic—and politically devastating—if America's involvement in South Vietnam ended with a successful patrol boat missile attack on U.S. ships.

The SEAL/LDNN team would not take direct action if they did identify Komars. They would note the enemy boats' numbers and positions and deliver the information to the Navy, which would then handle the matter themselves, by air strike, by off-shore bombardment, or by deploying South Vietnamese SEALs or Rangers to take the base down. All of the SEALs and LDNNs carried AK-47s, but contact with the enemy was to be avoided at all costs.

Such missions were fairly routine now, the last vestige of SEAL activity in Vietnam. At this point—since late summer, in fact—there were only three SEAL officers and nine enlisted men in the whole country, operating as part of the STDAT that had replaced MACV-SOG the previous April. Before too many more months were past, even those SEALs would be withdrawn. Nolan smiled. Lieutenant Tom Morgan had a bet going with the other remaining SEALs to the effect that he was going to be the last SEAL in-country.

Nolan hadn't accepted the bet. If he knew the SOG-commando-turned-SEAL, Morgan would probably find a way to pull it off.

For now, though, a tiny SEAL contingent was preparing, once again, to slip silently and unseen into enemy territory, a scenario that had already been played out countless times throughout the course of the war in Vietnam. Nolan and the others had carried off several successful sneak-and-peeks during the past few months, as well as several prisoner snatches. Before much longer, though, all such ops would be totally in the hands of their LDNN protégés.

Tonight, the LDNNs were under the direct command of Lieutenant Huang, a brand-new LDNN officer who'd just arrived from Saigon. The enlisted South Vietnamese frogmen were the stocky, muscular Duong Van Lam and the wiry Le Duc Vien, both experienced men who'd worked with American SEALs before.

Nolan considered Huang for a moment, trying to control his own misgivings. The man was brand new to the South Vietnamese SEALs, and tonight would be his first op outside of training. The man had completed the LDNN training program, of course, which, designed by U.S. Navy SEALs, was damned near as tough as BUD/S, and designed to weed out the unfit and the weak sisters. So far as the SEALs were concerned, the LDNN frogmen were among the best, toughest, and bravest men in the South Vietnamese armed forces.

He had considerable doubts about Huang, though. Oh, the man was politically reliable enough; in fact, Nolan was pretty sure that the man had won his appointment to the LDNN officer's program by being well-connected to someone on President Nguyen Van Thieu's staff. But Huang tended to fret over the petty details of an op and showed a serious tendency to micromanage.

And now, tonight, his eyes showed his fear through his mask of green grease-paint.

Nolan had tried to get Huang replaced, but his request had been firmly denied. That, too, suggested that the man had political ties. Damn it, everything about this war was tied up in politics. It was a damned good thing, he thought, that America was finally getting out. So far as Nolan was concerned, the war had been mismanaged at nearly every level; if Washington wasn't going to allow the people it sent over here to do their jobs and win the damned war, then the only other choice ought to be to get the hell out and leave the war to the people directly involved.

"Very well, Captain," Nolan told the junk's skipper. "Hold your position here. I'll get my team together and we'll take off."

"I wait here, Lieutenant," Quan told him. "I wait right here, no matter what."

He left the tiny wheelhouse, followed by Halstead and Huang.

Duong and Le were waiting in the junk's well deck with the rubber CRRC. Like the others, they wore tiger-stripe camouflage and black combat vests, and their faces were already done up in war paint, the green-and-black fright masks favored by Navy SEALs.

Tangretti was with the Vietnamese frogmen, helping them check out the CRRC. Unlike the men going ashore, he was looking most unSEAL-like, clad in green utilities. "Wish I was going with you guys," he said.

"No, you don't," Halstead told him, grinning through his face paint. "You don't ever want to go on an op with a real live, genu-wine hero. There's something about that 'conspicuous gallantry' bit that tends to draw fire."

"True," Tangretti said, giving Nolan a quick up-and-down. "You know, I always thought SEALs did their best

not to be conspicuous! Sir, I do believe you are not setting a
very good example for your men."

Nolan gave a good-natured chuckle. "Fuck you, Doc," he
said cheerfully. The other SEALs had been ragging him un-
mercifully for several months now. His exploits on the Song
Mieu Giang had attracted a lot of attention at high levels—
all the way up to the White House, it seemed—and the word
was that Nolan was now being considered for the Medal of
Honor.

So far as Nolan was concerned, it was no big deal one way
or the other. The little blue button was an honor, sure, but
who got it and who didn't was largely a matter of chance and
politics—chance because the men who won it had to be in
the right place at the right time and be noticed by the right
people, and politics because anything involving the presidential award of such a medal would be steeped in the politics
of America's involvement in Vietnam. It happened that
America needed heroes right now, to help counter the bitterness of the withdrawal from Nam and the almost daily rev-
elations about low morale and drug use and mutiny and racial
bigotry polluting every branch of the U.S. military. Nolan had
the feeling that if they decided to give him the MOH, it would
be less because he'd rescued Halliwell than because the president needed a Rose Garden photo op with some positive
news for a change.

The rest of the SEAL community, needless to say, seemed
to have a higher regard for the rumors. So far, only one SEAL
had won the Medal of Honor in Vietnam, and that was Lieutenant Frank Casey, for his raid on Ham Tam Island off of
Nha Trang back in 1969. If any more SEALs were going to
get the blue button in this conflict, they would have to win it
now or not at all.

"Well, you take care of yourself, sir," Tangretti told him.
He looked at Halstead. "Twidge, you keep your eye on him.
It wouldn't look good if a proposed recipient of the Medal
of Honor was to get himself killed before the president even
has a chance of hanging the damned thing around his neck."

"Roger that, Doc," Halstead replied. "Of course, if he
starts making himself too conspicuous, I think I'll just head
back out to sea. No point in sharing the glory, you know . . .
or the incoming."

The junk's engines were cut far back now, and the stubby craft was wallowing heavily in the swell. Working together, the SEALs and LDNNs managed to get the rubber boat up and over the side without capsizing it; as the others clambered aboard, Tangretti shook both Halstead's and Nolan's hands. "You two come back, hear?"

"Just make sure we have someplace to come back to!" Halstead told him. "I'm still not sure whose side the skipper's on!"

"Oh, he's on our side, all right," Nolan told them. "It's his mail-order degree in navigation that worries me. That man could get lost in a bathtub."

"Well, then," Tangretti told him, "you're in luck, because this sure ain't no bathtub." He pointed. "That's Vietnam." He pointed in the opposite direction. "That's the ocean." Finally he pointed at the deck. "And we're right here. Got it? What could be simpler?"

"Remind me to have a long talk with you when I get back about the fine points of navigation," Nolan replied. Checking to make sure his AK-47 was securely strapped to his back, he lowered himself down a rope the few feet to the bobbing raft, where the LDNNs helped him aboard. Tangretti and two of the junk's crewmen handed down the rest of their equipment—three LAW rocket tubes, an AN/PRC-25 radio, and a Starlight scope.

A few moments later, they were steadily paddling clear of the junk and making for the dark and distant shore.

It was quiet, with no sign of the enemy forces that regularly patrolled this stretch of coastline. The deadly Easter Offensive was long over now, and, at long last, most of Quang Tri Province was back in South Vietnamese hands.

It had been touch and go for a while there, though. After the rescue of Lieutenant Colonel Halliwell last April, the Communist forces had resumed their eastward and southward march. Dông Ha had fallen as predicted. Quang Tri City had been abandoned by the South Vietnamese on 1 May, in a rout that had seen the ARVN 3rd Division simply ceasing to exist, dissolving in chaotic panic.

Elsewhere in South Vietnam, the NVA had laid siege to Kontum in the Central Highlands, threatening to drive to the sea and cut Saigon off from the northern provinces. Other

Communist forces swarmed down Highway 13 to An Loc, threatening to burst through like a flood and descend upon Saigon.

But, after the initial rout, the ARVN had held.

Everyone, in fact, was astonished at how well the South Vietnamese Army had performed. Everyone, from President Nixon on down, was talking about how Saigon's showing proved once and for all that Vietnamization was a success, that America was leaving the war firmly in the hands of an able and willing ally, that the Army of the Republic of Vietnam could meet the Communists, even meet them at a significant disadvantage, and stand their ground. The day Quang Tri fell, Thieu had sacked his I Corps commander and replaced him with General Ngo Quang Truong, the best general he had. On every front, the ARVN, after initial confusion and rout, had dug in its heels and stood firm.

The ARVN had taken everything Hanoi could throw at them.

And then they'd fought their way back. True, they'd done so with the literally awesome support of massed American airpower; "You hold 'em and I'll kill 'em" was how Major General James Hollingsworth, the senior advisor to III Corps, had expressed it to his ARVN counterparts just before launching no fewer than thirty massed B-52 strikes against the NVA troops encircling An Loc. On 8 May, Nixon had touched off a political firestorm by announcing Operation Linebacker, which included heavy conventional bombing as well as the mining of Haiphong and other North Vietnamese ports. The idea, as always, was to strike hard at the NVA's supply routes, to cripple their efforts in the south.

By the end of May, all of the steam was long gone from the North Vietnamese assault. By June the ARVNs were starting to move back into lost territory. On 16 September, Quang Tri was retaken, and by October, the situation across the entire, war-weary nation had been stabilized.

Only gradually, though, was the magnitude of the victory becoming apparent. Nolan had contacts within the SEAL Intelligence community who'd told him that of the 200,000 North Vietnamese troops who'd taken part in the Eastertide invasion, over 100,000 had been killed or wounded. In addition, North Vietnam had lost over half its armor and heavy artillery. Any plans they'd had of overrunning South Vietnam in order to disgrace America now, on the eve of another presidential election, would have to be indefinitely postponed.

One intelligence report was particularly encouraging. Nolan had been told that no less a figure than General Vo Nguyen Giap, the head of North Vietnam's entire military establishment, the revered architect of Dien Bien Phu, was being gently eased from power, his duties assumed by his deputy, General Van Tien Dung.

The disaster of Lam Son 719 in 1971 had been avenged and South Vietnam's confidence in itself restored. In early October, Hanoi dropped its demands for a political solution to the war to accompany a military one—a major concession by the North Vietnamese.

Possibly, possibly, it was true that peace, finally, was at hand.

Nolan listened to the crash of surf ahead and thought to himself that South Vietnam wasn't out of the proverbial woods yet, however, not by several thousand rows of palm trees. South Vietnamese politicians had a nasty habit of shooting themselves in the foot; President Thieu himself had rejected the latest U.S.–North Vietnamese peace proposal, claiming that he mistrusted American promises . . . and, to tell the truth, Nolan wasn't sure he blamed the guy. The American government had been showing an almost indecent haste to get out of Vietnam, whatever the cost to Saigon.

Not long ago, Nolan had interviewed a former Viet Cong soldier who'd deserted and turned on his former comrades, a Kit Carson Scout now working for the south. "You Americans take too much upon yourselves," the man had said. "The South Vietnamese have not learned how to fight the Communists. They have learned how to lean on the American crutch."

That was what it all came down to now. Could the South Vietnamese trained by American advisors like Nolan stand on their own? Could they give up their addiction to American troops and firepower? At this point, it was the only hope they had for survival. With the last combat troops gone from South Vietnam, there were now something like sixteen thousand Americans left in-country, all of them in administrative, logistical, or advisory roles.

Maybe that was why he hadn't been able to get Huang replaced by a more experienced officer on this mission. The Vietnamese would have to learn for themselves that political expediency and military expertise could rarely be successfully combined.

They were drawing close to the beach now. Nolan crouched low in the prow of the little CRRC, his AK-47 at the ready, with Halstead on guard behind him; the three LDNNs paddled to left and right, guiding the craft in toward the beach. Fifty yards out, he signaled Huang with a tap to the arm and rolled out of the boat and into the warm water. His feet hit bottom and he waded forward, dropping to hands and knees for the final few yards, letting the waves carry him ashore as he skimmed though a tumbling, four-foot surf.

There was no sound but the gentle crash of waves rolling in on the beach. Nolan lay at the edge of the surf for a long moment, watching and listening, before turning and signaling the others with a small, hooded flashlight, the beam carefully directed away from the shore. A few moments later, he heard the scrape of the CRRC's bottom on the sand close by, and the other SEALs splashed ashore.

In training-honed silence, they dragged the rubber boat up the shelf of the beach, concealing it beneath the loose sand at the base of a dune. No words were spoken. They were two to five kilometers south of the Cua Viet River. They would move inland through the dunes to reach the open country beyond the beach area, then start making their way north. Nolan checked the luminous dial of his watch. It was 0330 hours, with sunrise scheduled for 0619. They would have to move fast if they wanted to work their way close enough to the naval base for a decent look around before dawn.

Nolan took point. He was a small, compact man, and in the dark he could easily be taken for a Vietnamese. Halstead was too big and lanky to be anything but an American, so he brought up the rear, humping his AK, one of the LAWs, and the bulky Starlight scope. They kept the three Vietnamese positioned between them, with Duong carrying the backpack radio and the other two carrying the remaining two LAW rockets; Huang's nervousness, Nolan thought, was beginning to affect the other two men, and he didn't want one of them slipping off by himself to be "accidentally" lost.

It wouldn't have been a good idea for any of them to become separated from the others. Once they were west of the dune region above the beach, they could see the campfires and lights of several encampments widely scattered across the landscape. When they crept close enough to one camp to peer inside with the Starlight scope, they could see that it was an armored company, twelve armored personnel carriers drawn up in a laager, with sentries posted and men sleeping on the ground. There was no clue as to what they might be doing out here; possibly they simply represented a local security force, positioned here to prevent incursions by South Vietnamese naval commandos, for instance, or teams of American SEALs.

The SEALs and LDNNs passed the laager by and kept moving.

More and more, though, Nolan was beginning to worry. They should not have been more than four kilometers south of the Cua Viet River, and by now they'd walked twice that north. There were no clear landmarks to help pinpoint their position, but Nolan was now certain that Quan's navigation had been considerably less than precise.

At last, though, they climbed a low ridge and, by the light coming from a slowly brightening predawn sky, could just make out the form of a river to the north. Halstead went down on his belly, bracing the Starlight scope on his arm as he scanned the area.

"Well?" Nolan asked him. "You see the base?"

Halstead pulled his head back from the eyepiece, the green glow showing against his cheek. He gave Nolan an odd look. "Um . . . I think we got us a major problem, Boss," he said. "It's not there."

"What do you mean, it's not there?"

"There's no base. Worse than that, that river isn't wide enough by half. Doesn't look like the Cua Viet estuary at all. More like a damned stream."

"Oh, God . . ."

"Yeah. Boss, I think we just marched all the way north to the Ben Hai."

Nolan sat back, thunderstruck. Damn it to hell! They'd just walked six klicks into the DMZ; that was fucking North Vietnam right over there on the other side of the river!

And Cua Viet lay twelve whole kilometers behind them.

The DMZ
South of the Ben Hai River
0458 hours

Halstead sat quietly, listening as Nolan explained their predicament to the three LDNNs, his AK-47 unobtrusively at the ready. It wasn't that either SEAL mistrusted the men . . . but panic can make a man do crazy things, and this was a situation where calm heads and cool reactions were absolutely essential if any of them were to get out of this alive.

There was no thought for the mission now, of course. The mission had been aborted the moment they'd come ashore north of the Cua Viet River instead of south. What they had to do now was get as far south as possible in the remaining hour or so before sunrise, make contact with the *Minh Hoa,* and get themselves picked up.

"We're going to get out of this, men," Nolan told the Vietnamese. "All we have to do is keep our heads."

Duong and Le were nodding agreement. Huang, Halstead thought, looked more nervous than ever, his knuckles white on the foregrip of his AK-47. He would bear watching.

"Okay?" Nolan asked. "Let's hump it!"

They fairly raced through the remaining darkness, jogging easily on hard-packed sand. The dune region behind the beach gave them an excellent path. To their left was the first dune line above the shelf of the beach, consisting of soft and shifting sand. To their right was a line of old dunes, long ago anchored by beach grass and other vegetation, transformed into low, undulating, grassy hills with sand embankments.

Between the two dune lines, new and old, was a middle ground of very large but firmly packed dunes, all running in parallel with the others along the coast, but split by numerous pathways and saddles in a network of mazelike complexity. The SEALs stayed between the middle dunes and the old dune line. They would move for ten minutes at a time, then stop, while Nolan and Halstead used the Starlight scope to scan the area ahead. In less than an hour they covered perhaps six kilometers, which should have gotten them out of the DMZ and back into South Vietnam.

But not South Vietnamese–controlled territory. The NVA held this entire area at least as far south as the Cua Viet and would have foot security patrols everywhere. There was a terrible danger that they would accidentally bump into an NVA patrol, stumbling into them in the near darkness.

They were still at least two kilometers north of the spot where they'd come ashore—over a mile—but it was now just before 0600 hours, with the sun due to come up in less than half an hour. Already it was light enough that when they moved between a pair of huge, overlapping dunes, they could see all the way down the shingle of the beach to the surf line, several hundred yards away.

Around them, sand dunes rose like gray, sleeping giants.

"Okay, men," Nolan said. "Quick breather while I call the *Minh Hoa*. Perimeter defense!"

Duong dropped off the radio, and then the three LDNNs spread out, Le and Duong moving inland to watch inland, beyond the dune area, and Huang to watch the beach itself.

"Seaview, this is Maverick," Nolan called, speaking softly into the microphone. "Seaview, Maverick. Do you copy?"

After a moment's hesitation, Halstead decided to follow Huang. There was something wrong with the guy, something more than simple nervousness, and Halstead didn't like it one bit.

He was crawling belly-down through the sand when he saw Huang lying just ahead, almost in plain view of the beach. Ten yards away, a North Vietnamese soldier was walking south along the dune line.

A beachcomber patrol. Sometimes, the North Vietnamese dropped off bundles of supplies, which drifted south along the coast with the prevailing current so that their comrades in the south could find them washed ashore. Or perhaps this one was searching for footprints or other signs that South Vietnamese commandos had come ashore.

Whatever he was doing, he was within a few steps of spotting Huang. The LDNN lieutenant had frozen in place and was staring at the oncoming NVA soldier with all of the intensity of a mouse paralyzed by the relentless approach of a snake.

Halstead gripped his AK, wondering what to do. Damn, there was nothing he could do except hold his position and hope the enemy soldier missed seeing Huang in the poor light. It was possible. The North Vietnamese was looking at the beach and the water to his left more than he was the dunes to his right, and it was still dark enough that he might well pass the LDNN lieutenant by.

Halstead held his breath, keeping his gaze off the NVA soldier, watching the man by peripheral vision only so he wouldn't feel Greg's eyes.

And then Huang stood up.

"Lai dai!" the LDNN officer cried. "Come here!" He started toward the soldier, weapon raised.

The NVA soldier whirled, eyes wide—he'd been on the point of walking right past, unseeing, when Huang had called him. He started to bring his own weapon around; Huang faltered, as though aware that things were on the point of going terribly wrong.

Halstead sprang forward. If either man fired, every NVA soldier within a kilometer would hear and be on the way. The North Vietnamese hesitated at the sight of Halstead's advance, unable to decide which weirdly green-painted face posed the greater threat. Halstead showed him by viciously sweeping up and around with the butt of his AK, smashing the soldier squarely in the jaw and knocking him to the sand.

A sudden *crack-crack-crack* of autofire shattered the morning quiet, as bullets snapped into the sand nearby. A second NVA soldier, following behind the first, had seen Halstead's attack and opened fire. When his first shots missed, however, his eyes went wide, and he suddenly dropped his rifle, turned and bolted up the beach, running as fast as he possibly could. Le rushed past Halstead and started after the soldier.

Halstead considered joining the chase but whirled instead on Huang. Nolan was already there, drawn by the shots.

"What the *fuck* were you thinking of?" Nolan said, descending on the LDNN officer like an incoming storm cloud.

"I think . . . I thought . . ." Huang was trembling. "If we take prisoner . . ."

"I don't think you *thought* very much at all," Halstead snapped.

Le reappeared, breathing hard.

"Catch him?" Halstead asked.

The LDNN shook his head. "Negative. He lose me in dunes up there. But I see NVA patrol. We have company soon."

"Just frigging great," Halstead looked at Nolan. "What do we do now, Boss?"

"I got in touch with Doc on the *Minh Hoa.* They're on the way, but it'll take time to reach us. They're still way south of us, down the coast. And Doc's passing our sitrep on to the *Newport News.*"

Fresh gunfire broke out from behind the dunes. "Firepower," Halstead said, nodding. "Good. Sounds like we're gonna need it!"

The SEALs and LDNNs dropped into a defensive perimeter, holding a position in the maze of small dunes perhaps a hundred yards behind the big dune line above the beach. The line of older, partly overgrown sand dunes blocked their view fifty yards to the west . . . but they could see several North Vietnamese moving down the sand-floored valley from the north, firing as they came.

Halstead looked at Huang. Of all the *stupid,* idiotic stunts! Had the man simply been rattled? Had he genuinely been trying to capture that NVA soldier? Or was he a traitor?

There was no time to think about that, however. The North Vietnamese came down the valley between the two dune lines at a run until the SEALs opened fire, knocking two of them down and driving the rest back behind the sheltering dunes.

A moment later, five NVA troops broke from cover, rushing up the valley. The SEALs opened fire, chopping down the charge before it had covered more than half of the distance between the dune lines. A machine gun opened up from the grass-topped dune hill to the west; Huang pulled out his LAW, extended the tube, and sent a rocket searing across to the other dune. There was a flash and a muffled bang and a splattering of loose sand beneath a cloud of smoke . . . and the enemy machine gun fell silent.

"Good shot," Nolan told Huang; Halstead held his peace. He was still too damned mad at the idiot to be willing to say anything nice, and he was still privately wondering if the man was a traitor who'd deliberately given their position away to the enemy.

For the moment, things were clear. The enemy patrol had been wiped out, though there might have been survivors who'd fled. They would have to assume that the enemy would be back, though, and in considerable numbers.

It was time to get the hell out of Dodge.

Nolan crouched for a time by the radio, occasionally consulting with a plastic-covered map. "Okay," he said after several minutes, replacing the radio handset. "If I have us positioned right now, Doc says he thinks the *Minh Hoa* is thirty, maybe forty minutes away. I also talked to the fire control officer aboard the *Newport News*. He said they're already in range with their main battery and can give us fire support at our word."

"Then all we have to do is hold out until the *Minh Hoa* is within swimming range," Halstead replied. He looked at the sand dune to his right, measuring it. It was a good forty feet to the top, with sheer, loose slopes, but he would have a much better view of the area from up there.

"What you thinking, Twidge?" Nolan asked.

"That we need to see what the hell is going on. Hang on a sec. I'll be right back. Let me have those binoculars." He accepted the binoculars from Huang and started climbing.

It took several desperately scrambling moments to make it without sliding back in a loose avalanche of sand, but the dune was hard-packed enough beneath the loose surface sand that he was able to get a purchase and make it to the top. Dawn was breaking, the eastern sky fully light now. West, the shadows of the dunes stretched for hundreds of yards off the beach and into the farmland beyond.

He saw movement there, coming down from the northwest.

Bringing the binoculars to his eyes, he studied the trickle of distant, antlike shapes.

"What you got?" Nolan called to him from below.

"Trouble," he called back. "Looks like forty . . . maybe fifty troops. They're on foot and they're headed this way." Turning, he looked south.

There were twenty more soldiers there, even closer, and they were coming on the double.

"I don't think we have thirty minutes," he called down.

Moments later, the first enemy troops spilled through the inland dune line, firing wildly as they came.

Chapter 38

The dunes
North of the Cua Viet River
0615 hours

"Fire!" Nolan yelled, and the SEALs and LDNNs cut loose with a withering, devastating volley of full-auto fire. NVA troops toppled as the survivors scattered, taking cover behind the surrounding dunes.

Halstead leaned into the butt of his AK and loosed short, precisely targeted bursts. As soon as easy targets vanished, he flipped the selector switch on the side of his weapon to single shot. Each SEAL and LDNN in the patrol carried five spare magazines, and extra rounds in their packs, but they didn't have enough ammo to get into a protracted firefight, and they damned sure didn't have enough bullets to go spraying them around the landscape on full-automatic rock 'n' roll.

For some reason, he found himself thinking about Orange Beach 2 on Okinawa. It seemed damned ironic that he should find himself in much the same position now, here on this beach, as Tangretti's father had been in on Okinawa twenty-seven years ago. Doc would get a kick out of it.

Shit, Doc would just be pissed that he wasn't here. It wasn't that SEALs necessarily craved bloodlust and combat— though he knew a few who did—but that they identified so strongly with their teammates that they didn't want them facing this sort of situation alone. That, after all, was what had led him and Tangretti and Lieutenant Morgan out to cover Nolan's tail, six months ago on the Song Mieu Giang.

An explosion, flat and partly muffled by the sand, banged

loudly off to the left. A second blast echoed across the beach farther off, to the north. The NVAs were tossing grenades blindly among the dunes.

The SEALs and LDNNs had scattered widely among the dunes, staying close enough to support one another but far enough apart that one grenade or automatic weapon's burst wouldn't catch more than one of them. It also made their numbers more uncertain, and their positions. Anything that confused the enemy or kept him guessing was good.

Flat on his belly, Halstead began crawling toward a better position that he could see just ahead, at the low saddle where two large dunes butted against one another, creating a kind of gateway through to the overgrown dunes to the west. From there, Halstead thought he might get a better view of the NVA positions. Nolan was firing from behind a dune about twenty yards to his left; Huang was on his right, exchanging fire with a light machine gun somewhere further to the north. Duong and Le were on the flanks, watching out for attempts by the enemy to circle around the SEAL unit to the north or south.

He reached the saddle and, AK at the ready, peeked over the top. His heart gave a sudden thump in his chest as he came literally face to face with a small, dark-eyed Asian in a green uniform and a canvas-covered sun hat.

The NVA soldier's eyes locked on Halstead's face, growing very, very wide; it was a reaction he'd encountered before when a VC or NVA soldier took in the startlingly dark, green warpaint favored by SEALs on patrol. Even as Halstead squeezed the trigger of his AK and sent a single round slashing messily through the man's throat and lower jaw, the man was backing away, shaking his head in nightmare terror, the AK-47 in his own hands momentarily forgotten.

"Trick or treat," Halstead told the soldier as he flopped backward onto the sand in a bloody spray of teeth, bone fragments, and torn flesh. Then he remembered what the date was, and his offhand comment seemed suddenly funnier.

Like a snake sliding through the sand, Halstead squirmed over the top of the saddle and down to the NVA body below. Gunfire snapped and crackled from the grassy sand hills to the west, but he managed to grab both the man's weapon and a canvas pouch with three more loaded magazines. Returning to his own side of the sheltering dunes, he spread the wealth around, tossing one fresh mag to Nolan, and a second to Huang.

He was just starting to move back to the saddle when Nolan shouted warning. He looked up in time to see a grenade coming through the notch between the sand dunes . . . a stretched-out steel sphere with a long fuse extension at one end, the body painted a bright apple green in color. There was no mistaking the Russian-issue RGD-5 as it landed with a dull thud in the sand almost at Halstead's feet.

With reactions already keyed to their highest pitch by the firefight, the SEAL scooped it up and hurled it back. A second later the same grenade flew back over the sand dune, tumbling in the air, bouncing on the sand, and once again Halstead grabbed it and flung it back in a deadly game of catch. Panic clawed at the back of his mind. RGDs had a time delay of about four seconds, and the fuse must have burned far down by now.

A third time, the grenade flew toward him, passing this time well above his head and landing in the sand at his back. *Shit!* he thought, trying to turn for yet another scoop-and-throw. *Should have tossed it somewhere el—"*

The grenade exploded with a flat bang, the force of the blast catching Halstead low in the back and in the backs of his legs, kicking him forward. As he hit the ground, he felt several spots burning like fire low on his back. At first he thought it *was* fire, that his clothing had been ignited by a thermite grenade, but then he realized that he'd just been sprayed by bits of hot shrapnel, that while damned painful, none of his wounds was serious.

Halstead rolled onto his back, readying his AK, snapping the selector switch to full-auto.

"Twidge!" Nolan yelled from the cover of the nearby dune. "Twidge! You all right?"

Halstead held up one hand, nodding, but said nothing. The pain was receding; he didn't think he was badly hurt . . . but the NVA soldier he'd just been playing catch with would assume that the blast had put him down hard. The guy would be coming around the dune any moment . . . *now!*

The man charged over the top of the saddle between the dunes, AK-47 held high and tight as he leaped down onto the beach a few yards from Halstead's feet. The SEAL was waiting for him, already tracking him with his own weapon, caressing the trigger and sending a burst slamming into the Vietnamese as he went airborne, tearing him open from belly to throat.

The man collapsed on the sand a few feet away, bloody and very dead.

Nolan crouched over him. "Twidge? You sure you're not hurt?"

Halstead tried to move, and pain seared at his back and thighs. "Fuck!" Then he swallowed, steadied himself, and nodded. "I'm . . . okay."

"Roll over."

He felt Nolan probing his back and legs. "You took some frags, but you're not bleeding that I can see."

"Damned, cheap Commie manufacturing," Halstead told him. "They really ought to work on their munitions quality control."

"I think you ought to work on your pitching arm. But forget the sandlot baseball, okay?"

"You're telling me!" He'd been damned lucky; the grenade had exploded perhaps ten feet away, and the worst of the shrapnel had missed him. It could have been a hell of a lot worse.

He spotted an enemy soldier working his way across from the western dune line and knocked him down with a single shot through the center of mass. He could hear Nolan now behind him, talking on the AN/PRC-25.

"Pinch Hitter, Pinch Hitter, this is Maverick," Nolan called. "Map coordinates Sierra one-three-niner-five by Kilo two-two-seven-eight. Request fire north, south, and west of my position, over!"

Halstead couldn't hear the reply, of course, but knew that "Pinch Hitter" was the big cruiser *Newport News*, patrolling offshore just over the horizon. During their briefing for this mission, the SEALs had been warned not to expect helicopter or air support, not with as much triple-A and SAMs as the bad guys had planted throughout this region. The *Newport News*, CA-148, would be their only support element.

But she was one hell of an element. One of the very last of the world's heavy cruisers, she'd been out of date when she'd been launched back in the late forties. She possessed no antisubmarine warfare assets, no missiles, no EW weapons, not even sonar . . . but she did have nine Mark 16 eight-inch guns in three turrets, two forward, one aft, as well as twelve Mark 32 five-inch guns in six turrets, three to a side. Her eight-inchers possessed one modern innovation, at least. They fired metal cartridges instead of the bagged charges employed in other cruisers of her era, which gave her main batteries a high rate of fire with considerable accuracy.

More NVA troops were trying to work their way across the valley between the grass-covered dunes and the maze above the beach, a sandy stretch already littered with bodies. Halstead was firing at this new threat when the first eight-inch shells rumbled in.

It sounded exactly like a freight train, a kind of deep-throated chugging that dopplered down in pitch as it passed overhead . . . and then slammed into the salt marsh and farmland behind the dunes with a cacophonous thunderclap of raw noise. The ground beneath Halstead's body bucked at the impact; a pillar of black smoke and earth crawled skyward in a slender poplar-tree shape, then collapsed in a black rain of debris.

"Where'd it hit?" Nolan yelled at Halstead.

"Five hundred over!" he replied. "Two hundred north!"

Nolan passed the information on to the *Newport News*. A minute later, a second freight train rumbled overhead, and the explosion erupted just beyond the far line of dunes, hurling white sand and several bodies into the sky.

"Two hundred over! One hundred north!"

The bombardment continued, soon without input from the SEALs sheltering behind the slender wall of dunes. The cruiser's fire was highly accurate; unfortunately, the rounds were so powerful that the ship's fire control officer was taking extra care to keep the rounds well clear of the SEALs' position.

One of the first rules of combat is that friendly fire isn't. The SEALs could be killed just as dead by an incoming eight-inch shell from the *Newport News* as they could by a North Vietnamese grenade, so the cruiser concentrated on laying down a heavy blanket of fire all around the SEAL position, trying to block off that stretch of beach from NVA reinforcements or flanking columns.

The trouble was that the North Vietnamese learned quickly, and they learned well. Long ago they'd noted how closely American air, artillery, and ships offshore supported U.S. ground combat units, and they knew that the closer they could get to the Americans, the safer they would be, because the American support units would not want to risk hitting their own people. Perhaps fresh troops couldn't make it through that rain of blast, hot steel fragments, and flame, but there were still an estimated thirty or forty enemy soldiers nearby, some of them as close as twenty-five yards away and all of them trying to work their way closer.

It was a slow and drawn-out business. The North Vietnamese could afford to move in slowly, taking their time, knowing that they had the Americans and their allies trapped in a tiny pocket among the dunes, unable to move unless they wanted to expose themselves to devastating fire from positions north or south along the beach. Occasionally, a small group would rush forward, trying to get among the SEALs, and then there would be a sharp, violent firefight among the dunes.

Halstead heard a burst of automatic fire and a scream. Turning right, he saw that Huang was down, with three NVA soldiers scrambling over the embankment he'd been hiding behind. Twisting in the sand, Halstead killed one with a single shot, then flipped his selector to full-auto and killed a second, just as Le emerged from a nearby dune and gunned down the third. Halstead sprinted to Huang's side as Le gathered fresh ammunition.

"You okay? Where you hit?"

"Leg . . . here. . . ."

A round had smashed into Lieutenant Huang's right thigh, missing the bone, it looked like, but causing a lot of bleeding. Halstead used the torn ends of Huang's trousers as a crude tourniquet, stuffed gauze from his first aid kit into both ends of the wound, and wrapped the leg with a roller bandage. Huang was in a lot of pain but indicated that he was able to keep fighting.

By this time, Halstead had forgotten his earlier anger. Huang was no traitor. He'd made a damned stupid call earlier, but that sort of thing was all too common in the fear and confusion of combat. Whatever his failings as a leader or a frogman, Lieutenant Huang Long Dzu was a teammate, and they would take care of him.

Eight-inch shells continued to descend on the beach and beyond, walling off an island surrounded on three sides by a storm of whirling death, thunder, and hot metal, and, on the fourth, by the sea.

Halstead checked his watch. It was just past 0700 hours, and the fight had been raging for over forty minutes. He joined Nolan by the radio as incoming shells continued to crash in a vast, sprawling semicircle around their position.

"I'm down to one mag, plus what's in here," he told Nolan, slapping his weapon. "What're we gonna do, Boss?"

"We sure as hell can't stay here," Nolan replied. "I can't raise the *Minh Hoa*. She ought to be offshore by now."

Halstead shaded his eyes against the sun, staring past the beach dunes to the sea and beyond to the horizon. He could just make out a smudge of black smoke above a long, lean shape—the *Newport News* wreathed in her own gunsmoke.

But there was no sign of the *Minh Hoa*.

"Maybe the skipper got lost again," Halstead suggested, a little bitterly.

"Could be. I wouldn't put it past him. But at this point, all we can do is swim for it."

Halstead nodded. He remembered the drownproofing sessions at BUD/S . . . both the sessions in which he'd been the instructor, and others where he'd been on the receiving end of things. *The water is your friend. When you've got your backs to the sea, head for the water where the enemy can't follow you. . . .*

"I could use a swim," Halstead said. "It's getting too damned hot."

A stuttering line of explosions ripped through the dunes to the north, causing both SEALs to involuntarily duck. "Get the others in here," Nolan told him. "Have 'em get rid of all excess gear. I have another call to make."

A few moments later, as Halstead, Le, Duong, and the wounded Huang gathered around, Nolan was shouting into his handset, trying to make himself heard above the bombardment.

"Pinch Hitter, this is Maverick," he called. "I say again, map coordinates Sierra one-three-niner-five by Kilo two-two-seven-eight. Request fire mission on my position, repeat, on my position in five, repeat, five minutes. Over!''

Halstead felt a chill at that. The situation was desperate, he knew, but he doubted that he would have had the guts to call in a delayed-fire mission on his own coordinates.

Nolan continued listening for a moment, then said, "Roger, I copy! Give us five minutes to pack up and move out! Maverick, out!''

Dropping the handset, he proceeded to use the butt of his rifle to smash the backpack radio, wrecking it so thoroughly that the North Vietnamese who found it wouldn't be able to make use of what was left. He looked at the others with a grim expression. Halstead did the same with the Starlight scope. They had one LAW rocket remaining, which Nolan set aside.

"Okay," he said, looking at the others each in turn. "Here's how we're gonna play this. We can't stay here 'cause we're almost out of ammo, and we'll get chewed to bits next time they try a hard push. Le and I will stay here and cover you three. We'll pull a leapfrog. Fallback line is those small dunes over there, right above the beach. Once you're there, lay down covering fire, and Le and me'll come running.''

As Halstead listened, he felt his stomach churning. It was a desperate plan, with way too many things that could go wrong.

There wasn't much else to be done, though. If the SEALs and LDNNs simply bolted for the sea, the enemy would close in and cut them down as they ran. Instead, they would pull a leapfrog maneuver to break contact. Two men would stay behind covering the other three as they made it to the final line of dunes at the top of the beach, an undulating white wall about one hundred yards to the east. Those three would then cover the first two from their new position, laying down a blanket of fire while the two sprinted back to join them.

By that time, the five-minute grace period would be nearly up. All five men would race for the beach, then, two of them carrying the wounded Huang. The NVA would move into their original position cautiously, expecting a trap . . . and be caught in the blast of incoming eight-inch rounds when the *Newport News* shifted targeting coordinates.

At least, that was the plan. Halstead reminded himself of

an old military adage, though. *No plan ever survives contact with the enemy.*

"Okay, everybody clear on what we're doing? We won't have time for second guesses."

"I don't like this, Lieutenant," Halstead told him. "I think we should stick together."

"Fuck that. You're wounded. Get the hell to the top of the beach and do as you're told. When we get together again, we'll leapfrog down the beach, covering each other as we go. And move like hell, because in four and a half minutes, this stretch of beach is going to be ground zero for a heavy cruiser. Okay, everybody ready?"

The others nodded, Halstead reluctantly. His wound wasn't more than a few painful scratches, and he didn't like leaving Nolan to face that mob of NVAs that would be coming over those dunes any moment now.

There was nothing more to be done, and the clock was running. Nolan was already unlimbering the team's last LAW rocket. "Okay! Go! Go!"

It was about a hundred or a hundred twenty-five yards from the spot where they were hiding to the final line of dunes. Duong put his arm around Huang's shoulder, and the two hobbled toward the last dune line in a clumsy kind of three-legged race. Halstead jogged with them, moving backward, facing inland, his AK-47 pivoting back and forth to cover their retreat. Behind them, Le and Nolan were firing as hard and as fast as they could, burning up their remaining AK magazines to give the NVA troops something other to think about than the three retreating men. Eight-inch shells continued to fall inland, crashing and rumbling in a weird and deadly symphony of destruction.

But the fire control officers aboard the cruiser must even now be relaying new target coordinates to the gunners. There would be no room for error in this at all.

The three men reached the last line of dunes without incident and dropped to their bellies behind a sand embankment, facing inland. At their backs, the tide was out, and the beach reached for better than two hundred more empty yards out to the line of crashing surf.

"In position!" Halstead yelled, alerting Nolan that they were ready. "C'mon, Nolan! Move your ass!"

Shells from the cruiser continued to shriek, fall, and thunder.

The dunes
North of the Cua Viet River
0705 hours

As Le Duc Vien blasted away at the oncoming enemy troops, Nolan shouldered the LAW rocket, taking aim at the thickest cluster of running men visible beyond the dunes. The Light Armor Weapon was designed to take out light tanks or APCs and was not that efficient a weapon against troops . . . except that in Nolan's experience, soldiers who thought someone was firing rockets at them tended to get nervous and usually tried to find someplace to hide. He raised himself up just a little, his finger tightening. . . .

Funny. He couldn't see anything. Stranger still, it felt as though he was lying on his back, when, just a moment before, he'd been kneeling in the sand, preparing to fire the LAW. Blinking, he managed to regain his sight in one eye, at least, his right. The left side of his head felt . . . strange, numb and tingling and very, very cold. For a moment, he wondered if the LAW had blown up in his face . . . but he'd had the weapon on his right shoulder, and something was definitely wrong with the left side of his head.

Nolan tried to reach up and touch it and found he was having trouble moving. ''What? . . .'' He tried to speak but couldn't hear his own voice. He couldn't hear much of anything, in fact, and his one-eyed vision seemed channeled down to a narrow circle of sky, as though he were peering through a cardboard tube.

Dimly, he was aware of Le bending over him, moving his head back and forth with one hand as he peered down into Nolan's face. Nolan tried to speak again but doubted that any words had emerged.

And suddenly, the LDNN frogman was gone, and Nolan was left lying alone on the bloody sand.

The darkness around him was growing thicker with each passing moment, as David Nolan slipped away into unconsciousness. . . .

Chapter 39

The dunes
North of the Cua Viet River
0706 hours

Halstead felt a growing sense of dread, of things-going-wrong as one man raced toward the beach from the original SEAL position. It was Le Duc Vien, and Lieutenant Nolan was nowhere to be seen.

"Damn it, where's the Boss?" Halstead demanded, confronting the man.

"Dead!" The LDNN was nearly crying, his face screwed up with fear and shock and pain. "He dead!" He stabbed one forefinger at the side of his head. "Shot here!"

Shit! . . .

It wasn't fucking right for the lieutenant to buy it now, just a few minutes from the water. Halstead thumbed his AK's magazine release, dropping a near-empty banana clip, then snapped home his last fully loaded magazine and racked the charging lever. "Wait here," he said.

"Wait!" Duong cried. "You no leave us!"

"A SEAL never leaves a buddy," Halstead told them. "*Never.* Not even when he's dead!" He glanced at his watch. "We have three minutes before hell breaks loose. Wait two . . . then head down the beach. Get into the water and swim for it. The black hats won't follow you out there."

He ran back into hell.

Gunfire cracked and snapped all around him. Pounding through loose sand, Halstead reached the spot where he'd last seen Nolan just as two NVA soldiers rounded a dune up ahead, their rifles fixed on the SEAL lieutenant who lay full-length on the ground.

Halstead charged, AK at his shoulder, firing short bursts as he ran. It was the sort of stunt that he would have been gigged hard for in training; all of the books and experts insisted it simply wasn't possible to hit anything if you tried moving and shooting at the same time.

Experts notwithstanding, he caught one Vietnamese with a three-round burst that spun the man back and away. Coming to a halt, he shifted aim as the second soldier turned to meet this unexpected threat, then fired again, catching the second soldier in the head and chest in a spray of blood and shredded flesh.

Dropping to his knees and skidding the last couple of feet, he reached Nolan, probing for a pulse at the throat. Nolan's head lolled to the right, exposing . . . oh, *God!* A piece of the lieutenant's skull the size of Halstead's palm had been shot away just above Nolan's left ear. Part of the scalp hung loose in a bloody flap of skin and hair; blood welled up inside the wound, but Halstead could queasily see arteries pulsing on the red-seeping surface of Nolan's nakedly exposed brain.

And the horror was that Nolan *wasn't* dead. As Halstead held his head, the SEAL officer's eyes fluttered open, and he actually tried to manage a smile. "Greg," he said, the croaking voice barely audible. "Buddy . . ."

Christ, how do you give first aid to a guy whose brain was exposed? There were rules about how to treat open head wounds, rules involving not trying to stuff anything back and applying sterile compresses and keeping the patient immobilized, but in a situation like this, the answer was, you *don't* . . . not with hostiles all around and closing in, not when the U.S. Navy was scheduled to drop several thousand pounds of high explosives right where you were sitting in another handful of seconds.

Scooping Nolan up in a fireman's carry, Halstead draped the SEAL over his shoulders, staggered to his feet, and started running.

It was damned lucky, he thought, that he was big while Nolan was little. If it had been the other way around, or if Halstead had been the one to get hit . . .

The pain in his back and legs was a cluster of small, searing agonies, but Halstead kept running. He thought again about Tangretti's stories about his dad. Was this what it was like, he thought, a little wildly, back on Okinawa, with Doc's father? Shells whistled in overhead, and he remembered Tangretti telling about his dad narrowly escaping a shore bombardment, that day twenty-seven years ago on Okinawa's Orange Beach 2.

A bullet plucked at his left sleeve, passing harmlessly through the cloth. Geysers of sand spat to left and right; he kept running, zigzagging where he could to throw the enemy's aim off but throwing most of his effort into reaching the last line of dunes . . . and staying on his feet.

The LDNNs were still where he'd left them, firing away at targets unseen at his back. "Hurry, Twidge!" Huang shouted at him. "Where we go?"

"What we do now?" Duong added. "NVA, he come! . . ."

"We swim," Halstead told them. "C'mon! Down the beach!"

It was well over two hundred yards down the shallowly sloping beach, and they couldn't make it fast because Halstead was burdened by Nolan's limp body, while Le and Duong helped the wounded Huang. Halfway down the shelf, they dropped flat. NVA troops were pouring through the last dune line now, and Halstead and the LDNNs had to pause to turn back the assault with a final volley from their AKs.

Too weak now even to get up again, Halstead crawled, clinging to his AK with one hand, and with his other dragging Nolan down the beach with a grip on the collar of his life vest. Gunfire continued to probe and snap past and around them, but after that final sting, the NVA troops didn't seem all that eager to pursue them. Minutes later, the team reached the in-rolling surf.

Halstead took another look at Nolan. He was still alive . . . but only just, and he appeared to have lost consciousness again. Halstead wanted to bandage the wound, but didn't dare take the time. With its freight-train rumble, a shell howled low overhead from somewhere beyond the horizon, smashing into the dunes close by the spot they'd just left, hurling up the characteristic giant black poplar shape of an ear-wracking explosion.

More shells followed, detonation upon detonation, shred-

ding the dunes in blast after blast after blast. "Come on!"
Halstead yelled, still dragging Nolan by the collar. Tossing
his AK aside, he plunged through the four-foot surf, letting
the incoming surge of water lift him up and sweep beneath
his feet. He swam several clumsy, one-armed strokes, then
paused to inflate Nolan's UDT life vest with a sharp tug to
its CO_2 bottle. The black rubber puffed up with a hiss, cradling his head and giving him some buoyancy. Halstead inflated his own vest, then started swimming again.

"Help me!" Something tugged at his left foot. "Help!"

Looking back, he saw Huang, floundering in the surf. The
other two LDNNs were further out, swimming hard. Reaching
back, he grasped Huang's outstretched hand and then, rolling
onto his back, Halstead began kicking hard, towing the unconscious Nolan with one hand, and Huang with the other.

Bullets chopped into the water nearby. As explosions continued to savage the landscape behind and beyond the top of
the beach, a handful of North Vietnamese soldiers raced down
the shelf, firing wildly at the swimming men.

God, Halstead thought, as exhaustion dragged at his body.
*We've come all this way, and the bastards are going to shoot
us now in the water. . . .*

He kept swimming, and, after a few more shots, the NVA
soldiers started bobbing about. At first, Halstead couldn't see
what they were doing, but then it dawned on him. They were
leaping about in knee-deep surf, waving their arms, cheering
. . . and punctuating their cheers with full-auto bursts into the
sky.

Well, Halstead was willing to concede to them a victory
dance. From their point of view, they'd just driven the invading force into the sea . . . probably to certain death. Even
over the continuing crash of explosions, Halstead could hear
their cheers and laughter now.

Then a black pillar of smoke and dirt erupted from high
up on the beach shelf, two hundred yards behind the cele-
brants. A second followed, closer to the water . . . and a third
. . . and a fourth. Suddenly, Halstead couldn't see any of the
enemy troops, could see nothing at all but erupting columns
of thundering smoke and debris as the beach tried hard to
turn itself inside out.

"Trick or treat," Halstead muttered, continuing to swim.

Several rounds exploded short of the beach, hurling spray and water high into the sky, but by that time the Team was well clear of the shore, swimming hard for the open ocean.

The water is your ally. . . .

And then, a long time later, it seemed, there was silence, save for the lapping of surface waves breaking over his body and the splashings of the other swimmers in the sea.

The sky was very blue, a beautiful day.

And the sea around the five swimmers was achingly, hauntingly, terribly empty. . . .

South Vietnamese naval junk *Minh Hoa*
5 kilometers offshore
0944 hours

Tangretti stormed into the junk's tiny pilot house, his face a mask of fury. "Damn it, Captain!" he yelled, startling the pilot at the wheel. "We've got to get in *closer!*"

Quan shook his head, stubborn. "No, Petty Officer Tangretti," he said, using the rate to emphasize that he was an officer in the South Vietnamese Navy, while Tangretti was a mere enlisted man. "No closer. We wait here."

Tangretti seethed with frustration. Since that last call from Nolan over two hours ago, ordering naval gunfire down on his own position, there'd been no word from Nolan or the others, no signal, nothing. The *Minh Hoa* had come within sight of the shore bombardment shortly after 0700, in time to hear Nolan order the *Newport News* to hit his position with everything they had in another five minutes. Tangretti had gone up onto the roof of the junk's pilot house, wedging himself in among the radio aerials and using a pair of 7x50 binoculars to study the shore.

At that range, perhaps as much as ten miles, there hadn't been very much to see. It had *looked* like there was a firefight on the beach, though he hadn't been able to tell for sure. There was smoke, but a lot of smoke was hanging thick behind the dune line, where the *Newport News* had been pounding enemy positions all morning. He'd tried to listen for small arms fire, but all he'd heard was the rumble of explosions.

Moments later, he thought he saw movement on the beach and allowed himself to think that maybe Nolan and Twidge

had made it to the water, that he was witnessing their escape
. . . and then the beach had erupted in black smoke and the
flash and thump of high explosives.

And after that, there'd not been much of anything to see.

For the next two hours, Captain Quan had circled his
stubby little naval junk about offshore, while Tangretti and
the junk's XO, Lieutenant Ba, had searched the surface of the
sea with binoculars and naked eye, searching for swimmers.
The odds were strong against the shore party's survival.
They'd had to reach the water through a deadly hail of gunfire, avoid being blown to bits by friendly incoming, and finally survive in the water as NVA shooters practiced their
marksmanship on five bobbing heads out in the water. The
final part of the bombardment had been so vicious, so final,
it seemed impossible that anyone or anything could have lived
through those last few minutes.

"Captain," Tangretti said after several minutes more.
"We're not doing them any good out here. Let's move in
closer. Hell, we dropped them off at three kilometers offshore.
You can at least go in that far!"

"Not in day," Quan said, shaking his head hard. "Not in
day! NVA guns all along coast there. There. And there. We
go in, they fire." He made a dramatic motion with his hand,
pantomiming a ship going down. "We sink!"

Tangretti stood in the wheelhouse, hands clenching and un-
clenching. Damn it to hell! There wasn't anyone else to talk
to, no one else to help. The *Newport News* was still circling
offshore, but a 17,000-ton heavy cruiser simply did not venture close inshore. That's what shallow draft vessels like the
Minh Hoa were for. There would be no air cover, no helos,
no SAR rescue.

There was nothing but the *Minh Hoa,* and Captain Quan
seemed less than eager to go in harm's way.

God, don't let them die, he thought, praying now, praying
harder than he had for a good many months now. *Jesus, keep
them alive, keep them safe, I know they're still alive, keep
them safe . . . and show me what I have to do to reach them!*

A solution came to him, but it didn't seem to be the sort
of solution that Jesus might suggest. It was much more of a
SEAL solution, in fact, but Tangretti didn't let that bother
him. Wheeling suddenly, he stalked out of the pilothouse,

clattering down a metal ladder outside. He trotted forward to the forecastle deckhouse, where the SEAL and LDNNs had racked out for the trip up the coast.

The compartment was small, narrow, and stank of fish and wet cable. He found his sea bag, carefully padlocked, and dialed his combination. Deep inside, hidden under dry utilities and camo garb, he found his gunbelt, holster, and .45.

Pulling it out, he buckled the Sam Browne belt around his waist, letting the holster hang low on his right hip. He drew the pistol and checked it, took a loaded magazine from a small belt pouch, fitted it in place, and slapped it home. Releasing the slide, he chambered a round, then flicked the safety up. He was now cocked and locked. Reholstering the weapon, he walked back to the pilothouse.

As he entered the small compartment once more, Quan folded his arms. "I sorry," he said, "but we can look no more. We go, back to Danang, yes?"

Tangretti walked over to the wheel and leaned against the pilothouse window, positioning himself so that both the helmsman and Captain Quan could see him clearly. He let his right hand rest lightly on top of his holstered weapon . . . and he could tell by the way their eyes were riveted to that bit of black leather that they were very much aware that he'd just armed himself.

"No," he said, keeping his voice low and under control. "We do *not* go back to Danang."

"Petty Officer Tangretti! I very sorry, but your friends dead! . . ."

"Maybe they are," Tangretti said. "But *if* they are, we're going to go recover their bodies. We're going to bring them back if you have to beach this tub on the shore, there. SEALs do not leave their own behind."

He did not draw his weapon. He did not threaten . . . at least, not overtly. Quan blustered and grumbled for some minutes more, but the order to put about was never given, and, slowly, the *Minh Hoa* began working her way closer inshore, zigzagging back and forth to cover as much area as possible. Tangretti took lookout duty again . . . but he was careful to keep his back always against a solid bulkhead.

Right now, he felt about as alone as Nolan and Twidge must be feeling right now, and he didn't like it one bit.

Three kilometers offshore
North of the Cua Viet River
1120 hours

It felt like they'd been adrift for days.

Early on, Halstead had ordered the three LDNNs to clip themselves together using the snap-and-swivels on their inflated life jackets and combat vests. The five of them drifted together now, moving slowly with the southbound current.

"Don't worry," he told them. "At this rate, we'll float clear to Danang in a couple of days."

He didn't tell them he was joking, any more than he mentioned his other worries . . . the danger of sunstroke at midday, the danger of dehydration, or of men going crazy from swallowing too much salt water, or of sharks, or of the poisonous sea snakes that were so common in these parts. All of them were suffering now from shock and exposure; Halstead was shivering despite the relative warmth of the water, and he imagined the LDNNs were doing the same.

He'd fastened Nolan to his own harness in such a way that Nolan's head was on Halstead's chest. He tried to keep the lieutenant's head out of the water, especially that horrible, fist-sized gap in the side of his skull, but there was no way to raise him clear of every wave, and the best Halstead could hope for was that the seawater would act as a kind of saline solution, irrigating the wound, and cleansing it. He found his thoughts drifting back, not to first-aid classes in BUD/S and later, but to high school, and a movie, part animation and part live actors, that he and his fellow students had been forced to endure time after time, in biology class, and at periodic school assembly programs. The movie, as he recalled, had been titled *Hemo the Magnificent* and was all about blood and the human circulatory system. A key revelation, at one point, he remembered, was the discovery that the one word that could best describe blood was . . . *seawater.* Blood, it seemed, was the body's way of capturing a little bit of the ocean that life had originally evolved in; the circulatory system used it to transport food and oxygen and to keep the cells moist and alive just as more primitive organisms had once used the sea. The salt content of blood and of seawater was still quite close.

At this point, Halstead didn't know how accurate a statement that was, but he found himself clinging to it now, praying that this long immersion in the sea wasn't hurting Nolan's exposed brain. He did know that corpsmen used saline solution—salt water—to wash out wounds and clean them.

Nolan was still alive. He was unconscious most of the time, and when Halstead pried open his eyelids to look at the pupils, he saw that the left eye was dilated wide open, while the right was narrowed down to a pinpoint . . . a sure sign of a skull fracture.

But he'd already known that, hadn't he.

Once, though, Nolan had come to, raising his head a little and looking around. "Did we get everybody out?" he asked, his voice strong and distinct.

"We sure did, Lieutenant," Halstead replied. "We got 'em all."

"Good. That's good." Then he lapsed into unconsciousness again.

They were no longer swimming but simply allowing the current to carry them. Each time the five of them bobbed to the top of a large, passing wave, Halstead tried to crane his neck around, searching the east horizon. He was pretty sure that more than once he'd glimpsed ships out there . . . once the lean, gray, greyhound warship shape of the *Newport News*, and several times the boxy lines of what could well have been the *Minh Hoa*.

But he was never able to tell for sure and wasn't even certain that he wasn't hallucinating.

"Twidge?" Duong called after a time.

"Yeah?"

"We're not going to make it, are we?"

"The hell with that noise! I don't know about you, but I'm just resting up for the swim to Danang." The others chuckled. *Good. If they can keep their sense of humor, we have a chance of pulling through.* "Mostly what I'm doing now is trying to decide whether to swim to Danang or to California. My wife's waiting for me, back there, and I haven't seen her in a long time."

God, how I miss you, Wendy . . . you and Mark. . . .

He thought about them for a long time.

Lying back in the water, his ears slipped beneath the surface. They were already starting to burn in the late-morning sun, and letting them go underwater cooled them nicely.

He could hear a far-off throb, like the beating of a heart.

My heartbeat, he thought. *I wish I could see Wendy again. . . .*

"Twidge?" The voice was muffled. He raised his head.

"Hmmm. . . ."

"I . . . I see . . ."

He kept his eyes closed. "What do you see?"

"I see *Minh Hoa.* . . . "

"Well, my friend, if you're going to hallucinate, you might as well hallucinate the very best things you can." He tried to call Wendy to mind, her freckled face, her auburn hair. . . .

"Is not hallucination! Is *Minh Hoa!*" He felt the LDNN tug on the linked harness straps. "Here! Here! Over here!"

Annoyed now, Halstead opened his eyes. "C'mon, Le. Not so—"

And then he saw the naval junk as well, wallowing straight toward them from the north, engine pounding against the heavy sea.

And Bill Tangretti, a pistol strapped to his hip like some modern-day pirate, was standing in the prow, wearing a grin that slashed his face from ear to ear. . . .

Sick bay, USS *Newport News*
South China Sea
2230 hours

Tom Morgan sat beside the sick bay bed, clutching Nolan's hand in his own. "And then I say to Twidge, I say, 'So help me, Twidge, if *one word* of this disaster gets out, just *one word . . .* ' "

"Lieutenant Morgan?" Halstead's voice said from close by. "What in the *hell* do you think you're doing?"

Morgan looked up. Halstead was leaning against the frame of the sick bay's watertight door, eyes wide. He was wearing a light blue Navy hospital robe and institutional pajamas. Behind him, still clad in OD utilities but minus his gunbelt, was Bill Tangretti.

"Sounds like a damned interesting story," Tangretti said. "I think I may want you to tell it again, sir."

"Mr. Morgan?" Halstead said. "I thought you were in Danang!"

"I, ah, they heloed me in this evening," Morgan explained. "I heard you guys were hit and wanted to check in on you." He nodded toward Nolan. "The, ah, the doctors want him to stay alert—"

"They want me to stay awake," Nolan said, his speech heavily slurred. His head and left eye were muffled in yard upon snowy yard of white roller bandages, and his visible eye was dull and lusterless. "They say if I go to sleep I'll die."

"They never told you any such thing," Morgan said.

"It's true, isn't it?"

"Nah. I just couldn't sleep. If I can't sleep, nobody sleeps! I just want you to stay awake and keep me company."

But it *was* true. The cruiser's chief medical officer had told Morgan an hour ago that Nolan wouldn't live through the night if he fell asleep. To tell the truth, Morgan had never seen anyone this side of death look quite this bad. Nolan seemed . . . *shrunken,* somehow, as though the wound and the long immersion in salt water had conspired to shrivel him up, like the husk of a dead insect.

"We appreciate your being here," Halstead told him.

"Hey, not a problem." He looked the other SEAL up and down. "I heard you got dinged up a bit, too. How you doing?"

"Shit, I barely got scratched."

"Twenty-two separate shrapnel wounds," Tangretti put in. "None serious, but he's going to have a hell of a time sitting down for the next week or two."

"And the rest of your team?"

"All intact," Halstead said. "Lieutenant Huang took a round in the leg. He's next door, doing fine, they tell me. The other two got out without a scratch."

"Well, from what I've heard, you were damned lucky."

"Lady Luck tends to favor the SEALs, sir. She wouldn't dare do otherwise, because she knows what would happen to her if she didn't."

"Hooyah!" Tangretti said.

Motivation. That had been what BUD/S was all about. That was what the Teams were all about, and the mutual support each SEAL gave his buddies.

Morgan knew he was a SEAL now, if only because he felt like Nolan and Halstead and Tangretti and the rest were somehow part of him, that he couldn't leave them or forget them or watch them die without having a piece of himself die as well.

He wondered what the future held. The war was almost over, that much was certain. Just a few days ago, Henry Kissinger had completed a round of secret talks with the chief North Vietnamese negotiator and reported that "peace is at hand" in Southeast Asia.

What was going to happen to the SEALs with the war's end? Hell, Vietnam had made the SEALs, had been their crucible and their tempering. They'd come a long way since their creation in 1962, from being specialized UDT commandos and naval advisors, to direct action platoons and Phoenix hunter-killer teams, then back to the role of advisors again.

If half of the rumors he'd heard were true, the Navy wasn't going to be needing SEALs much longer.

Fuck that. The SEALs were a team. They were *the* Teams, forged in fire and death and the brotherhood of warriors . . . and nothing the North Vietnamese or the bureaucrat REMFs or the politicians or the pencil-dicked desk jockey pussies in Danang or Saigon or the Pentagon thought or said or did could ever take that away from them.

"Hooyah!" he said, quietly, but firmly, echoing Tangretti's war cry.

And David Nolan squeezed his hand in reply.

Epilogue

Sunday, 28 January 1973

**Tangretti residence
El Cajon, California
1930 hours**

"Hooyah!"

The cork popped with a report like a gunshot. Champagne foamed down the green neck as Halstead poured.

Greg and Wendy Halstead, Bill and Pat Tangretti sat together in the Tangrettis' living room. Their champagne glasses full, Bill raised his high. "To Twidge Halstead! My buddy . . . and the third U.S. Navy SEAL to win the Medal of Honor!"

"To Twidge!"

"Twidge!"

The four drank together, toasting the SEAL and the news. The word had just come down the chain of command that afternoon.

Bill picked up the letter that Halstead had received from the skipper of SEAL Team One. *"For conspicuous gallantry and intrepidity,"* he read, "at the risk of his life above and beyond the call of duty while participating in a daring operation against enemy forces! . . ."

"Aw, knock it off, Doc," Greg said.

"My God!" Pat cried. "You've got the poor dear *blushing!*"

"Not a bad job there, old son," Bill told him, grinning. "Third Medal of Honor winner in the Teams . . . and the *only* enlisted SEAL to win the little blue button."

"And the further distinction," Wendy said, taking his arm in both of hers, "of being the first man to win the Medal of Honor while saving the life of another Medal of Honor winner! Not bad at all!"

"Will you guys knock it off?" Greg asked, laughing. "I didn't do anything—"

"Yeah!" Bill cried, interrupting. "Right! Just ran back into a firestorm to carry your CO out on your back!"

"I didn't do anything that any other SEAL wouldn't have done."

"You don't leave your buddies behind," Pat said.

"Speaking of which . . ." Wendy set down her glass, leaned across the coffee table, and kissed Bill on the lips.

"Whoa," Bill said, shaking his head. "What's that for?"

"Yeah?" Greg added, with a generous dose of mock indignation. "What was *that* for?"

"For not leaving your buddy behind," Wendy said. "Greg told me you forced that Vietnamese captain to keep on looking for them. If you hadn't . . ."

"If he hadn't, I'd be in Australia by now," Greg said.

Bill shrugged. "They would've done the same for me."

"How is Lieutenant Nolan, by the way?" Pat wanted to know. "Is there any word yet?"

"Well, he'll be in the hospital at Bethesda for a while, yet. I gather he still has to have an operation to get a metal plate put into his head. You know, where he lost a piece of skull. The, ah, the doctors say they probably can't save his left eye." Bill's hand went up to the ugly, puckered scar behind his own left eye, as though he was remembering something.

"If we could've gotten him some decent first aid faster . . ." Halstead began.

"Belay that talk, Twidge," Bill said sharply. "You saved the man's life. What else do you want?"

"I . . . don't know."

Perhaps, Greg thought, it was enough that the war was over for the two of them. They would not be returning to the hell-hole of Vietnam . . . not unless some new crisis broke out over there.

And if it did, the SEALs would be ready.

Bill looked at his watch. "Ah! Sorry, folks. Let me check

in on the news real quick, okay? Then we'll go out and do some serious bar-crawling to celebrate.''

"You!" Pat hit him with a small couch pillow.

Laughing, Bill walked across to the TV and clicked it on. The network evening news had already begun.

". . . in Paris today, and the cease-fire has officially begun,'' the anchorman was saying. "In Washington, President Nixon said that 'we have agreed to end the war and bring peace with honor.' At the Pentagon, Secretary of Defense Melvin Laird announced both that the draft has now been officially ended in the United States and, that in Vietnam, yesterday, Lieutenant Colonel William B. Nolde became the last American serviceman to die in this war that has claimed so many young American lives. . . .''

Halstead walked up behind Tangretti, looking over his shoulder at the screen. "So you think it's really over, Doc?"

"Sounds like it.'' He didn't sound happy.

"What are you thinking, buddy?''

"That it shouldn't have ended this way.'' He paused. "I was thinking about Nghiep Van Dong.''

"You hear he's getting the Navy Cross for that rescue op?''

"No! Since when?''

Halstead shrugged. "I dunno. But there's talk of a double ceremony, him and Nolan, as soon as the lieutenant's up and around and can shake the president's hand. That would make him the only Vietnamese to get the Navy Cross.''

"He deserves it.''

"A lot of 'em do.''

"The trouble is,'' Tangretti said, nodding at the television, "medals aren't going to be a hell of a lot of help to the Vietnamese now. Dong and all the other LDNNs really got the shit-end of the stick. Did you hear what the final agreement was for the peace settlement? All foreign troops to withdraw from Vietnam. That means all Americans . . . but the North Vietnamese can stay in the south . . . something like 160,000 troops, I heard. In fact, the NVA gets to hold onto everything they've captured in the south, a 'cease-fire in place,' including cities like Nha Trang and damned near all of the Central Highlands and about half of the Mekong Delta, and the South Vietnamese aren't allowed to try to take their land back, because that would be violating the truce. I heard President Thieu cried when he heard the terms. He said that America wouldn't lose anything if South Vietnam fell, but that he was fighting for the survival of his country, and his people.''

"So what's the answer?" Greg asked him. "Do we keep fighting?"

"Yeah, I can see Congress going along with that!"

"The idea is that if Hanoi violates the cease-fire, we go storming back in, big time, and really clean their clocks.''

Bill nodded. "Yes, I can see Congress agreeing to that, too. C'mon, Greg! You know as well as I do that the NVA will bide their time for a year, or two, or three, building up their forces. Then—" He smacked his right fist into his left palm. "Bam! And we'll stand by and not do a fucking thing to help them." Bill looked at Greg. "Maybe the traitors won after all.''

"Ben Franklin once said that treason is an excuse invented by the winners for hanging the losers. We didn't win, Bill, so I guess we can't use that particular word, huh?''

"We didn't lose. We won the battles.''

"Doesn't matter." Greg tapped his chest. "America lost the fight here. At least, I don't feel like we won.''

Bill shrugged. "Hey, peace with honor. Sounds like a victory to me. Maybe the best victory we could manage in a war we never should've been involved in in the first place. No, the ones who lost are the guys like Nghiep Van Dong and Le Duc Vien and Tien Pham Vinh and all of the other South Vietnamese we've known. Some of them are real jerks, Marvin ARVNs, like Quan, yeah . . . but a lot of them are brave, brave men who put everything they had, everything they were on the line for their homes and their families and their country.

"And then the United States Congress and the U.S. government and Henry Goddamn Kissinger and Jane Fonda and Hannah Fucking DuPlessey and a lot of other Americans went and sold them out. *That's* losing. . . .''

"They're our brothers, man," Greg said. He reached out and put his arm around Bill's neck, hugging him close. "We won't forget them.''

"We can't. . . .''

The doorbell rang. "That'll be the baby-sitter," Pat said, getting up and going to the door. "You old warhorses ready to go out?"

"We're ready, babe," Bill said.

"Always," Greg added. "Hooyah!"